EMPTY EVER AFTER

[EMPTY EVER AFTER]

A MOE PRAGER MYSTERY

REED FARREL COLEMAN

BLEAK HOUSE BOOKS

MADISON | WISCONSIN

Published by Bleak House Books
a division of Big Earth Publishing
923 Williamson St.
Madison, WI 53703
www.bleakhousebooks.com

ISBN 13: 978-1-932557-64-0 (Trade Cloth)
ISBN 13: 978-1-932557-68-8 (Evidence Collection)

Library of Congress Cataloging-in-Publication Data has been applied for.

Printed in the United States of America

11 10 09 08 07   1 2 3 4 5 6 7 8 9 10

Set in Warnock Pro

To the survivors

ACKNOWLEDGMENTS

I would like to thank Ben and Alison for keeping Moe in print. I would also like to thank Peter, Megan, Ken, and Ellen for being my first readers and listeners. And for their help with Chinese, a nod to Alice Wang and Dr. Fuh-Lin Wang. None of this would have been possible or worth it without Rosanne, Kaitlin, and Dylan.

"I'm trying to escape. Escape to anywhere, but I'm not. I'm not going anywhere. There isn't any anywhere, is there?"
—Daniel Woodrell from *Tomato Red*

[PROLOGUE]
1984

[THE MOURNER'S PRAYER]

We walked through the cemetery, Mr. Roth's arm looped through mine. The cane in his left hand tapped out a mournful meter on the ice-slicked gravel paths that wound their way through endless rows of gravestones. The crunch and scrape of our footfalls were swallowed up and forgotten as easily as the heartbeats and breaths of all the dead, ever. The swirling wind demanded we move along, biting hard at our skin, blowing yesterday's fallen snow in our faces.

"Bernstein!" Mr. Roth defied the wind, pointing with his cane at a nearby hunk of polished granite. "You know what it means in English, Bernstein?"

"No. I know stein means stone."

"Amber."

"Amber, like the resin with the insects in it?"

"Amber, yes. Bernstein, like burned stone. German, such an ugly language," he said, shrugging his shoulders. "But at least the words sound like what they mean."

We walked on.

"Alotta dead Jews in this place, Mr. Moe."

"I think that's the point."

"When I die, I don't want this ... this nonsense."

"Why tell me, Mr. Roth?"

"And who else should I tell, my dead wife? Wait, we're almost at Hannah's grave. I'll say Kaddish for her and then I'll tell her, but I don't think she'll listen. I wasn't a very good husband, so it's only right she shouldn't pay attention."

"What about your son?"

He stopped in his tracks, turning to face me, taking a firm hold on my arm. There were very few moments like this between Israel Roth and me. He'd suffered through the unimaginable, but he very rarely let the pain show through.

"I'm serious here, Moses." He almost never called me that. "This is not for me, to be cold in the ground. Kaddish and ashes, that's for me."

"Okay, Izzy, Kaddish and ashes."

"Good, good," he said. "Come already, we're almost there."

I stood away from the grave as Mr. Roth mumbled the prayer. "*Yis-ga-dal v'yis-ka-dash sh'may ra-bo, B'ol-mo dee-v'ro ...*"

"Amen," I said when he finished.

As was tradition, we both placed little stones atop Hannah Roth's tombstone.

I never said Kaddish for my parents. Israel Roth had tried to re-kindle whatever small embers of my Jewish soul still burned. Even so, they didn't burn brightly. I wondered if they'd burn at all when he was no longer there to stoke them.

"Would she forgive me, do you think?" he asked, again twining his arm back through mine.

"Would you forgive her?"

His face brightened. "See, there's the Jew in you, Mr. Moe. You answer my question with a question."

"*I* would forgive you, Izzy."

The brightness vanished as suddenly as it appeared. "You do not know my sins."

That wasn't quite true, but I didn't press.

As we got close to my car, I slipped on the ice and landed square on my ass. Mr. Roth took great joy in my fall. His joy seemed to dis-sipate as we rode out of the cemetery and back to Brooklyn.

"Poland had miserable winters," he said, staring out at the filthy slush and snow-covered reeds along the Belt Parkway. "The camps were muddy always, then frozen. Rain and snow all the time. The ground was very slippery."

"I'd think that would be the last thing people in Auschwitz would worry about. Slippery ground, I mean."

"Really? Part of self-preservation was to busy myself with the little things. Did you ever wonder what became of the ashes?"

"What ashes?"

"The ashes of the dead, of the ones the Nazis gassed then burned. They didn't all turn to smoke."

"I never thought about it."

He cupped his hands and spread them a few inches apart. "One body is only a little pile of ashes, but burn a few hundred thousand, a million, and you got piles and piles. Mountains. In the winter, the Germans made some of us spread the ashes on the paths so they shouldn't slip. Everyday I spread the ashes. At first, I thought, 'Whose ashes are these I am throwing like sawdust on the butchershop floor. Is this a handful of my mother, of the pale boy who stood beside me in the cattle car?' Then I stopped thinking about it. Thinking about the big things was a dangerous activity in such a place. Guilt too."

"But you survived."

"I survived, yes, by not thinking, by not feeling. But I've never stopped spreading the ashes."

We fell silent. Then, as I pulled off the exit for my house, Mr. Roth turned to me.

"Remember what I said in the cemetery, no burial for me."

"I know, Izzy, Kaddish and ashes. But where should they be spread?"

"You already know the answer to that," he said. "And we will never speak of these things again, Mr. Moe."

We never did, but never is a funny word. Time makes everyone's never a little different.

[EMPTY EVER AFTER]
2000

[CHAPTER ONE]

Some thoughts are traceable, but I don't know why I was thinking of Israel Roth and that winter's day in the cemetery. He was long dead now and I was all cried out. I was all cried out for the both of us. In death he was beyond the reach of my love and scorn. Even now, I am amazed at how he feared losing my affection. "You don't know my sins," he'd said. Hell, he didn't know mine. It's funny how that works. We were men of sins and secrets, Israel Roth and me. We could share love, but not sins. Too bad he died before mine were out in the open, before he could witness the bill come due.

You would think I'd be good at grief by now, having mourn- ed a mother, a father, a marriage, and a miscarriage before him. Miscarriage, what an asinine term. *Oh dear, I seem to have miscarried that baby. How clumsy of me!* That child had been a part of Katy and me, not a tray of dirty dishes. As I recall, no one shouted, "Oops!" But experience had taught me that God doesn't say oops. You have to have faith in God's big plan, so I'm told, and that misery is all just part of it. For Mr. Roth, misery had been a big part of the big plan. No more misery for him. He had gotten his wish. Kaddish and ashes, ashes and Kaddish. *Yis-ga-dal v'yis-ka-dash sh'may ra-bo, B'ol-mo dee-v'ro ...* I hadn't been quite so lucky.

Sure, there was some sense of relief in the secret being out, with Patrick dead and buried and buried again. Just lately, I find re- lief is overrated and secrets, no matter how potentially corrosive, can often sustain a man much the better than truth. I would know. Patrick's vanishing act had changed the course of my life. Without his disappearance in December '77, I would never have met his sister, Katy Maloney, my future and now ex-wife. With Katy and me, as with all things, the seeds of destruction were sown at birth. Even if we hadn't made Sarah, the most glorious child ever, I would not regret my time with Katy. She had taught me love and comfort and how not to be only an observer to my own life. So no matter what Patrick had or had not done, I could never hate him.

The same could not be said of my late father-in-law, Francis Maloney. I knew exactly how I felt about that cruel and callous fuck. My father-in-law chilled the earth when they laid him in it, not the other way around. He too had known the secret of his son's disappearance, that I had found Patrick all those years ago and let him slip away. For twenty years, neither of us had managed the courage to confess our sin to Katy. We held the secret between us like a jug of acid, both of us scared to let it drop for fear of being maimed by the backsplash. We were right to fear it. For when, in death, Francis let go of the jug, the splash scarred us all.

Foolishly, he had assumed it would burn me worst. But the anticipation of the burn, the years of his taunting about ghosts and payback had hardened me. Secrets do that. If the secret's big enough, you build a wall around it until there's only wall and very little left of yourself. And Patrick's secret was only one of many. As a PI, I had become a collector of secrets, a gatekeeper of orphaned truths. I kept the secrets of the murdered and murderers alike.

Since the divorce, secrets and loss were my only companions. I suppose, then, that it wasn't such a mystery, my thinking about Israel Roth on a rainy Sunday in July. Katy and I had tried briefly to reconcile, but there are some wounds from which recovery is neither possible nor truly desirable. We had sold the house even before the divorce was finalized. Katy moved back upstate to Janus and I bought a condo in one of the new buildings across from the water in Sheepshead Bay. Sarah stayed in Ann Arbor over the summer instead of coming home to work at one of the stores. The wine business wasn't for her. Like father like daughter. *Christ, I hoped not.*

The phone rang and there was someone at the door. Amazing! I had sat alone for hours staring out at the rain making shiny little ripples out of the petroleum film floating atop the bay. Now I was pulled in two directions at once.

"One second!" I shouted at the door.

I picked up the phone, "Hello."

"Dad!"

"Sarah! What's wrong? Where are you?"

"At school still. It's Mom."

"What's Mom?"

"Call her."

"Sarah, what's going on?"

"Somebody disturbed Uncle Patrick's grave."

I would never get used to her calling him Uncle Patrick. It was weird, like me thinking of him as my brother-in-law. As it happened, Patrick had been murdered before Sarah was born. She was now older than he ever was.

"What do you mean, someone disturbed his grave?"

"I don't know, Dad. Mommy was hysterical crying when she called me. You better call her."

"Okay, I'll take care of it." There was that banging again. "One second!"

"Dad, did you say something?"

"No, kiddo, there's somebody at the door."

"So you'll call Mom?"

"As soon as I get the door, yeah. I promise."

"Call me later and let me know what's going on."

"I will. Thanks for calling me about this."

"I love you, Dad."

"You too, kiddo."

The banging at the door was more insistent, but I wasn't in the mood for anyone else's crap. Divorce, no matter how amicable, isn't easy, and Katy, Sarah, and I were still in the midst of realigning our hearts to deal with the new tilt of our worlds. That's why Katy had moved back upstate, why Sarah had made work for herself in Michigan, and why I was watching raindrops in Sheepshead Bay. The last thing I wanted was to be dragged back into the thing that had blown us all apart. I must've looked pretty fucking fierce to Mrs. DeJesus, the maintenance man's wife.

"For chrissakes!" She didn't quite jump back at the sight of me. "I'm sorry, Mrs. DeJesus. I was on the phone with my daughter and …"

"Look!" she said, pointing down at my threshold and along the blue flecked terazzo floor of the hallway. "Mud everywhere, Mr. Prager, to your door. And this!"

I knelt down to try and compose myself. There, on my welcome mat, was a withered red rose and, beneath it, drawn in the mud, was the Chinese character for eternity.

[CHAPTER TWO]

Boneyards were about the only places yellow crime scene tape seemed not to attract a crowd. The bold black *CRIME SCENE DO NOT CROSS* was rather beside the point. There wasn't much of a crowd inside the tape either. Even that number was shinking. With the one deputy sheriff gone to pick up his boss and Katy headed back to her car to dry off, only the younger deputy and myself remained inside the perimeter. The longer I stood out there, the easier it was to see why Katy was distraught. Her father's headstone was toppled and smashed to bits, while eleven rain-soaked red roses had been neatly arranged in a circle on her mother's grave.

Then there was Patrick's resting place. Although Patrick Michael Maloney's grave wasn't quite empty, *he*, or what was left of him, was gone. The lidless coffin box was still at the bottom of the hole, buried now not by dirt but under several feet of rainwater and murky runoff. Splinters, jagged shards, and larger chunks of the muddy coffin lid were strewn about the family plot. Even in death, the most damage was done to Patrick.

"Fooking kids, vandalous little gobshites," the caretaker said.

"Watch your mouth, Mr. Fallon," said Father Blaney.

"Sorry, father, but it had to be them kids."

I didn't agree. "Kids? I wouldn't bet on it. This was a lot of work, not just random vandalism."

"And kids don't leave roses," added the priest.

"A sin writ large, no matter," said Fallon. "In Ireland tis not how you treat the living by which yer judged, but by yer care for the dead."

"Amen to that, Mr. Fallon." The priest crossed himself.

Both men stood under the priest's umbrella just beyond the yellow tape, neither seeming much bothered by the rain. The same could not be said for either the young deputy sheriff or myself. Father Blaney took notice.

"Come lads, get out of the wet."

The deputy, feeling he had to prove himself, politely refused. I was too old to worry about proving anything to anyone, even if it meant sharing an umbrella with Father Blaney.

I'd known the man for more than two decades. He was an old world priest, as avuncular as a meat hook and as politically correct as a minstrel show. He didn't exactly get touchy-feely with his parishioners. So it was no wonder that he and Francis Maloney had been thick as thieves and equally disdainful of me.

"How have you been getting on, Moses? I mean, since Katy's seen the light and ridded herself of you."

"I'm good," I lied.

"A pity." He showed me a crooked grin of gray teeth and chapped lips.

I almost laughed. One thing about Blaney, you always knew where you stood with the man.

"Do you suppose Katy will return to the church now that she's returned to her senses?"

"I was born a Jew, Father. Katy chose to be one. What do you think the implications of that are for you?"

Fallon smiled. I'd never met the caretaker before that day, but I liked him for his smile. Blaney saw it too and scowled. When Blaney scowled, clouds darkened.

"Such a lovely place, even in the rain," said the priest, changing subjects.

"'Tis that," Fallon agreed.

The Maloney family plot was in a secluded corner of an old Catholic cemetery up in Dutchess County. This section of the graveyard, a grouping of low hills overlooking a stream and woods beyond, was reserved for the families of the local movers and shakers. My late father-in-law had certainly been one of those. Back when our paths first crossed in the winter of '78, Francis Maloney Sr. was a big time politico, a major fundraiser for the state Democratic party. Francis was an old school power broker in that he kept a low profile but wielded influence from the Bronx to Buffalo. A valedictorian at the Jimmy Hoffa Charm School, Francis Maloney Sr. traded in nepotism, patronage, kickbacks, and threats as easily as most men breathed. He'd have rather paid for your vote than make his candidate earn it. "Cleaner that way, less risk involved," he would have said.

Blaney, who'd baptized all the Maloney children and had performed Katy's first wedding ceremony, took inventory. "A shame," he said.

Fallon took the bait. "A shame?"

"Such a big plot of land and it will never hold the family but for Francis Sr. and Angela. With Francis Jr. in Arlington and Katy … Well, never mind about Katy." He crossed himself again.

"What about Patrick?" I asked.

"The boy, please God, will never rest for his sins. His spirit is destined to roam."

"Resurrection, Father?"

"Don't be an ass, Fallon. Pushed out like a splinter more likely. His kind are a blight on holy ground."

I was far away from laughing now and stepped out from under his umbrella to stand in the rain with the young deputy. At that point the rain was preferable to inhaling the fumes that malicious old bastard breathed out. It was more a matter of principle than kinship with Patrick. The truth was that Patrick and I spoke only once, very briefly. That was on February 15th, 1978. I stood on one side of his boyfriend's bedroom door and Patrick on the other.

"Do I have your word?" I asked.

"Yes."

That was it, the entire conversation, and for twenty years I thought his one word was a lie. The irony is that his lie became my lie and my lie became my secret. He had promised to turn himself in that coming Saturday, to stop hiding, and to finally face his family. God, I was so full of myself that day. I found Patrick. *I* found him! Not the NYPD, not the daily busloads of volunteers, not the newspapers, not the fortune hunters, not the passel of PIs his family had hired before me, but me. That day I proved I was worthy of the gold detective's shield I was never to get. Whether I deserved it or not was moot. I'd already been off the job for months by then.

But that Saturday came and went. Nearly twenty years of Saturdays came and went without word of Patrick. Oh, there were a thousand false leads and sightings that amounted to nothing. Offer a reward for anything and the roaches will crawl out from under the floorboards, the hyenas will come out of the bush. Only once, in 1989, when I was looking into the suicide of my old pal and NYPD Chief of Detectives Larry "Mac" McDonald, did I ever truly believe I was close to getting a handle on what had become of Patrick. But that lead was crushed beneath the wheels of a city bus when the Queens District Attorney Robert Fishbein was run down on a Forest Hills' street. None of it mattered now, not any of it.

The rain was letting up some. Katy had just gotten out of her car. She seemed composed, but it was hard to disguise the distress deepening the lines around her eyes. There was a time when I believed it could never hurt me to look at her. Even after the miscarriage, when she took her guilt, fury, and indignation out on me, it was grace to look upon her. And when we hit that inevitable dead spot in our marriage, when the sameness of our days made me feel light years away from her, the sight of her face was always reassuring. Now it stung. What we had was gone. I broke it. Francis broke it. There was far more breakage out here than a headstone and a coffin.

I looked away.

Over Katy's right shoulder, I could see a Janus Village sheriff's car pulling into the cemetery followed by a dark blue and yellow State Police SUV. My cell phone buzzed in my pocket.

"Excuse me," I said to no one in particular, pulling the phone out of my soaked jacket. I ducked under the tape and hurried along the path toward the stream below the Maloney family plot. "Hello."

"Mr. Prager?" It was an older woman's voice, but a familiar one somehow.

"Yes, this is Moe Prager."

"I don't know if you'll remember me, it's been a few years. I'm Mary White, Jack's—"

"—sister. Of course. How are you, Mary?"

There was silence at the other end of the phone, an unsettling silence.

Jack White had been an actor, a painter, and a bartender at Pooty's in Tribeca. Pooty's was the bar Patrick Maloney disappeared from in December of '77. Beside Jack's other interests, he was Patrick's lover. It was behind Jack's bedroom door that Patrick stood and uttered the only word he ever spoke to me. Jack was the man who sat across from me, hand clamped around my wrist, promising me Patrick would return to his family. When Patrick broke that promise and vanished again, Jack went back home to Ohio. He taught drama to troubled teens until he died of AIDS in 1986. After we discovered the truth about Patrick, I'd flown Mary in for Patrick's funeral.

"Mary, what is it? What's the matter?"

"It's Jack's grave."

My heart stopped.

"What about Jack's grave?"

"I've visited him there every Sunday since the week I buried him. No one but me and a few of his old students has ever left flowers at the grave. Then last Sunday ..." she trailed off. I could hear her fighting back tears.

"What about last Sunday?"

"Roses."

"Roses?"

"Almost six dozen red roses were laid on Jack's grave."

"Maybe one of his students hit the lottery," I said without an ounce of conviction.

"No, I checked. We keep in touch. They are very loyal to Jack even after all these years."

"Wait, Mary, let's back up a second. What did you mean there were *almost* six dozen roses?"

"There were seventy-one roses. Five bouquets of twelve were propped up against his headstone," she said. "But on his grave itself, there were eleven individual roses—"

"—arranged in a circle, the tips of the stems meeting in the middle."

There was that ominous silence again.

"There's more, isn't there?" I asked.

"My God, Mr. Prager, how did you know?"

"In a minute, Mary. First tell me the rest."

"This afternoon, when I went to his grave ..." Now she could no longer fight back the tears. I waited. "I'm sorry."

"No, that's fine. I know this is hard for you."

"On the back of Jack's headstone someone had painted that Chinese symbol with the rose, the one Jack had tattooed on his forearm. Do you remember it?"

"I do." I'd seen something just like it on my welcome mat a few hours ago.

"And at the corner of the painting were the block letters PMM. Why would somebody be so cruel, Mr. Prager? Jack never hurt anyone in his life."

Now the silence belonged to me.

"Mr. Prager ..."

"Sorry. I'm here. It's just that someone's disturbed Patrick's grave as well."

"Oh my God!"

"Mary, would it be all right if I called you later. It's too complicated to talk about now."

"That's fine. You have my number. Please know that my prayers are with you and your family."

"Thank you, Mary."

When I wheeled around, Katy was coming down the path toward me. The sight of her stung a little less this time. Maybe it was repeated exposure. Or maybe it was that the thickest clouds moved east and what was left of the sun shone like an orange halo behind her head.

[CHAPTER THREE]

Mr. Fallon's quarters were small and tidy, not unlike the man himself. His house—a bungalow, really—was way on the other side of the cemetery, close to the tool shed and equipment barn. All three—shed, house, and barn—were of similar rustic construction and painted a thoroughly depressing shade of brown, but everything looked neat and well-maintained. Fallon himself was less than thrilled at the prospect of our company, but the sheriff thought the bungalow was the best available option given that the station house was on the opposite side of the hamlet. So we formed an odd cortege, my car behind Katy's behind the priest's behind the sheriff's behind the caretaker's backhoe, and snailed across the fields of stone in the dying light. The youngest, wettest deputy and the crime scene investigator from the state troopers stayed behind.

Sheriff Vandervoort was a gruff, cinder block of a man who, in the space of a very few minutes, had twice boasted that his ancestors had lived in these parts since New York was New Amsterdam. He wore his insecurities like a rainbow. He was well aware of who the Maloneys were, everyone around here was. They knew about the hero son shot down over 'Nam and his big wheel father. Although nearly three years dead, the mention of Francis Sr.'s name still turned heads in Janus. Vandervoort knew, all right, and if he'd forgotten, there was little doubt Father Blaney would take the time to refresh his memory.

Vandervoort was just the sort to do things his way, like interviewing us as a group. It was a dumb move, but I wasn't going to moan about it. In the end, it would probably save me some leg work. Small town policing, even in the new millenium, was different than any policing I understood. I'd gotten my first taste of that when I saw how the deputies mishandled the crime scene. As far as I could tell, they'd done nothing to preserve the scene beyond stringing the yellow tape. For a while there, I thought they might invite any passersby to add their footprints to the increasingly muddy mess that was the Maloney family plot.

The deputy who'd accompanied Vandervoort sat at Fallon's small kitchen table taking notes as the sheriff asked his questions. Katy sat at the table too, as did the priest. Fallon had dried off a spot on the counter near the sink where the two of us sat. Most of the early questions were for Fallon and they were pro forma, the kinds of things you'd expect to be asked.

Did you hear anything? "Not me own self, no."

Did you notice anything suspicious last night or this morning? "No."

When did you first notice the damage? "Near noon. Was a slow day with the wet. Not one visitor I can recall. A disgrace to be sure. It took me that long to work me way over to that part of the cemetery."

Has anything like this happened before? "Like this? Jesus and his blessed mother, no! In thirty years as caretaker, I've had but two incidents and then only a few stones were toppled."

When? "Years ago."

Who did you call first? "The father there."

Other than revealing that he had been the one to alert Katy to the desecrations, Blaney's answers shed less light on the matter than Fallon's. I could tell by the tone of the old priest's answers that he held the sheriff in even lower esteem than me. That was really saying something. I didn't know whether to feel sorry for Vandervoort or relieved for myself. The first part of Katy's interview was about the same. She had asked Blaney to meet her at the family plot. Afterwards she called the sheriff and Sarah. And no, she couldn't think of anyone who might want to do this sort of thing. I was glad he hadn't asked me that question in front of Katy. Then things turned ugly.

"Your brother Patrick was murdered. Is that correct?" Vandervoort asked.

"Yes, but what does that have to—"

"Can you describe the circumstances surrounding his death?"

Katy went white. She bowed her head and stared at the linoleum floor.

"I can answer that," I said, jumping off the counter.

"I'll get to you in a minute, Mr. Prager. Right now I'm asking your wife—"

"Ex-wife," Blaney corrected.

"I'm asking your ex-wife what happened to—"

"Okay, that's it! Interview's over." I grabbed Katy by the elbow and we started for the door. "You want to ask her anything else, you go through her lawyer. My *wife*," I said, glaring at Blaney, "is going home. She's had a terrible day. I'll be back in a few minutes to answer any questions you have for me."

I could see Sheriff Vandervoort doing the calculations. He might've been a bit of a bully, but he wasn't a total schmuck. There was little for him to gain by jumping ugly with the sole surviving Maloney. Town Sheriff was an elective office and although the late Francis Sr. wasn't exactly a beloved figure, a lot of people around this town owed their livelihoods to him. Ill will has lost a lot of elections over the years and my guess was Vandervoort understood as much.

"All right." The sheriff stood aside. "I'm very sorry, Miss Maloney."

"Prager!" she snapped.

"I was just trying to do my job. If I need anything from you, I'll call. Rest up. I'm sure we'll get to the bottom of this."

Outside, I saw Katy to her car and told her to go back to her house and get some rest, that I'd call on my way home to Brooklyn to let her know how things turned out. She asked me to stop back at the house. I told her no. We had twice suffered the fallout from horizontal despair. Divorce creates new history, but it doesn't blot out the past. It was just too easy for people who'd once loved each other as much as we had to succumb. Yet, the thing that drove us apart was never far away and fresh regret makes the next time that much harder. Neither of us needed to compound the hurt, especially not after the grief of the day. I had skillfully avoided mentioning the rose on my doormat and my talk with Mary White. But I could see in her face what she must've seen in mine: it was happening all over again. I didn't watch her leave. I'd already seen that once too often.

"Sheriff," I said, stepping back into the kitchen, "I believe there's some things you want to know about Patrick's death."

"That's right."

"Short or long version?"

"Short," he said. "If I need any details, I'll ask."

"Patrick was a student at Hofstra University on Long Island in December of seventy-seven. He'd gone into Manhattan for a college fundraiser at a bar in Tribeca called Pooty's. Sometime during the night, he vanished. Eventually his parents got worried and contacted the cops. After the investigation turned up nothing, his folks started organizing twice daily bus trips of volunteers to go down into the city to put up posters and look for the kid."

"I remember that. My folks went a couple of times. I think they just wanted the free ride to Chinatown." The sheriff amused himself.

Father Blaney gave Vandervoort a category five scowl. Christ, with this guy around I might rise to sainthood in the old priest's eyes. The sheriff got the message.

"Sorry, that was a bad joke. Continue."

"When that didn't work, the Maloneys hired PIs."

"That's where you came in," he said to me.

"I was just retired from the cops and I wasn't licensed then, but yeah. I tracked the kid down to an apartment in the West Village where he was staying with his lover."

"So the kid was a fag, huh?"

I ignored that. "When I tracked him down, he asked me to give him a few more days and that he'd come back to his family on his own and on his own terms. I agreed.

"But he never turned back up. For twenty years, I assumed he'd run again."

"Such hubris, Moses," said the priest, "to play God like that. You should have grabbed the boy by the scruff of his neck and dragged him back home."

So much for my beatification. Blaney was right, of course. Not bringing Patrick home was the single biggest mistake of my life. Not confessing the truth to Katy was a close second.

"So what *did* happen?" Vandervoort was curious.

"I'm surprised you don't know, sheriff."

"There were rumors," he said. "There was something about it in the local paper, but no details. Sometimes I think the people up here are still scared of the old man even though he's dead."

I was right, the sheriff was shrewder than he looked.

"A pissed off dealer who worked the Village wanted to whack somebody as an example to his crew. It was Patrick Maloney's unlucky day. They took him back to Brooklyn, tortured him, killed him, and wrapped him in a plastic shower curtain. They buried the body in an empty lot out by a Cypress Hills cemetery. A couple of years ago, I got a call from a hospice in Connecticut. One of the members of that old drug crew was dying and he wanted to confess about witnessing Patrick's murder. How he located me is irrelevant. He died the next day. The cops found Patrick's body right where the guy said it would be and Katy re-interred his remains here."

"A Cypress Hills cemetery, did you say?" Fallon asked.

"I did."

"Is that not near where Houdini is buried, Mr. Prager?"

"That's right, Fallon."

A somber smile washed over the caretaker's face. "That being the case, it would seem the Maloney lad has perfected an escape Houdini never mastered."

All of us understood and let the line hang there for a moment.

"What about the dealer?" Vandervoort broke the silence.

"Dead."

"The lover?"

"Dead."

I withheld the information about Jack's grave and the muddy visit to my front door. Whatever was going on was beyond the capacity of a small town cop to manage and, more importantly, it was personal.

"Anybody else you can think of who'd want to do this?"

"Like you implied, sheriff, my father-in-law was more feared than loved. So if it was only *his* headstone that had been fucked—destroyed, I could understand it. But what was done to Patrick's grave was pretty extreme. I don't know who would do something like that."

That was no lie. This just seemed to come out of the blue. There was no significance to the date or season that I could tell, no precipitating event. There hadn't been any mention in the media of the Maloneys or me or my cases in years. My brother Aaron and I hadn't even opened a new wine shop in quite some time. With the exception of the phone call from Mary White, neither Katy nor I had had contact with anyone connected to Patrick or the events surrounding his disappearance since 1998. Even Rico Tripoli, the man who got me involved with the Maloneys in the first place, was dead.

"I'll be taking my leave then," the old priest said. He wasn't asking permission. "I've nothing to add. Fallon ... Sheriff ... Deputy ... Moses ..."

But as Blaney stepped to the door, there was a knock. The other deputy and state crime scene investigator came in without waiting for an invitation.

"Well ..." Vandervoort prompted.

"The scene's a mess," said the crime scene guy, frowning at the sheriff, "but you knew that already. Took lots of pictures, foot impressions, dusted the coffin lid, the headstones, bagged the roses. I've got some samples to take back to the lab. I'll need elimination prints and shoe impressions from anyone who stepped on or near the site. Frankly, I'm not hopeful."

That made two of us.

I called Sarah on my way back to Brooklyn and minimized the situation. There was no need to worry her about this stuff and I didn't want her flying home. Although my secret about her Uncle Patrick had caused her parents to split, she really wasn't a party to it. I couldn't see a reason for making her one now. As promised, I rang Katy, but only after I got home. If we had chatted while I was close to Janus, it would have been too easy for her to talk me into coming over. Katy didn't pick up, so I left a message. I prefer thinking she was asleep.

[CHAPTER FOUR]

Carmella Melendez was in a foul mood, not like that was headline news or anything. The first time we met, she was cursing at her partner in the lobby of my old precinct house, the Six-O in Coney Island. The first words she ever said to me were, "Yo! You got a problem?" *Nice, huh?* The thing was, I *had* been staring at her. Her looks, in spite of the tough-bitch demeanor and foul mouth, invited staring. Carmella had coffee-and-cream skin, plush and pouty lips, and straight, jet black hair. She had a pleasantly curved and athletic body, but it was her paradoxical brown eyes from which I could not look away. They were fiery and cold all at once. It was easy for a man to lose his way in those eyes.

That was more than ten years ago, when she was maybe twenty-four and one of the youngest detectives on the NYPD. She took a lot of shit for getting the bump to detective at that age. Women take a lot of shit on the job no matter what. You can set your watch by it. If a guy had gotten the bump at that age, he would have taken a lot of crap too. But not all crap's the same. For Carmella, no matter how it was couched, it always came down to her looks. Every day was a struggle for her to prove to the world she was more than just pussy on the hoof and that struggle put quite a sizeable chip on her shoulder. After I got to know her a little bit, I realized that chip had been there for quite a long time and for a very different reason. In any case, that chip got shot off her shoulder in '89 during a gun battle at Crispo's Bar in Red Hook.

Things had changed between us in the last eleven years. She was by no means less pleasing to look at. If anything, Carmella had blossomed from simply stunning to beautiful. The years had softened her harder edges and she had learned to dress and makeup to her strengths. If it sounds like I'm a little in love with her, maybe I am. We even shared a kiss once that resonates to this day, but there are reasons we can never be together, reasons as solid as the wall of secrets I built over the years between Katy and me. We were also partners now. Prager & Melendez Investigations, Inc., established 1998. As Ferguson May, the late great philosopher of the 60th precinct was wont to say: "Don't shit where you eat. Don't fuck where you work." Too bad Bill Shakespeare and Fergie May were born centuries apart.

"What the fuck's eating you?" I asked Carmella, who had just slammed down the phone.

"Brian."

"Brian what?"

"I told him the lawyer wanted both digital and Polaroids of the accident scene and that brain dead asshole only took digitals. Now he's gotta go all the way back to the Bronx again today. Remind me why we hired him again."

"The knucklehead's trying," I said, regretting the words even as they left my mouth.

"Trying! What the fuck do you get for trying in this fucking world?"

She had a point, but there was something else going on. I knew better than making a frontal assault. Carmella would just clam up completely if I kept questioning her.

"I got us a new client."

But instead of leaning forward as she normally would, she found something quite a bit more fascinating about her Starbucks cup.

"Hey, Carmella, did you hear me? Earth to Melendez, please come in."

She forced herself to look my way. "A new client, yeah. Who is it?"

"Me."

That got her attention and I explained about what had happened the day before. She did what a good detective does: she listened. When she was young, she'd been too much of a shark, too aggressive. Listening was a skill that had come to her over the years.

"Describe the tattoo again," she said. As I spoke, she pulled something out of a brown shipping envelope on her desk. "Did it look something like this?"

"Holy shit!"

Wrapped in clear plastic, it was a perfect likeness of a small illustration Patrick Maloney had done of the Chinese character and rose. He had given it to Jack when they were together. Jack left it to Mary. Mary had sent it to me in 1986 after her brother's death. I'd given it to Katy during our first try at reconciliation. As far as I knew, she still had it.

"When did you get this?" I asked.

"Friday, in the mail."

"Fuck."

"Hey, Moe, if you spent more time here instead of at those stupid wine stores ..." she didn't finish the sentence.

"Yeah, yeah, yeah, I know. Let me have a look at that envelope."

She handed it over. "No return address."

"Mailed from ... Dayton, Ohio." I got that sick feeling in my belly.

I flipped it over a few times, not sure what else I expected to find. There are few things in the world more generic than brown shipping envelopes.

"Bag it just in case," I said, handing it back.

"In case of what?"

"I don't know yet. Someone's fucking with me and I don't like it. Here, take this too." I handed Carmella a list of names. Next to the names were addresses, phone numbers, descriptions. "Some of them are probably dead and a lot of the other info is old. Put Devo on it now. I want as much info as I can get on these folks by the time I get back."

"Back from where?"

"Dayton."

"What's in Dayton."

"Not what, who. Mary White, for one. And the person who mailed that package."

"Whatever."

Normally, I would have expected to get shit from Carmella for acting like the boss and telling her who to assign to what. And she would have been justified in giving it to me. Although I had put up seventy-five percent of the money to start the business, she was the one who did the heavy lifting. Carmella hired the staff and managed the office. She also worked the tough cases. For the most part, I worked cases here and there and collected my share of the profits. While I split my time between the wine stores and the office, Carmella was fully committed to Prager & Melendez Investigations, Inc.

"Are you sure you're okay?" I asked.

"So long, Moe. Bring me back some cheese."

"That's Wisconsin."

"What's Ohio got?"

"Buckeyes."

"I'm not even goin' there."

[CHAPTER FIVE]

Mary White smelled of sweet perfume and mixed feelings when she greeted me at the door of her house. I think she was glad to see me as I was one of the few living connections to the best months of her brother's life, but unhappy about why I'd come. I wasn't too thrilled about that part myself.

"Come on in the kitchen. I'll make us some tea."

Jews are comfortable in the kitchen. As a people, we find vast comfort in food. We aren't great cooks, but we are great eaters. I sat at the Formica table and watched Mary fuss with her pot and cups. She seemed out of sorts. But what did I know about her, really? We'd only met once before—at Patrick's funeral—and spoken a couple of times on the phone. I did think having me there made her a little nervous. As heavy as Jack had been skinny, Mary wasn't the type of woman to have had droves of gentlemen callers. She kind of reminded me of my Great Aunt Florence. Nice, but a bit socially awkward. A spinster, my mother called her. What an odd word, spinster.

The little brick house on the outskirts of Dayton was a 1950s museum piece; neat and clean and with all the original equipment. Mary caught me staring.

"This was our folks' house and I inherited it. I suppose if Jack had lived longer, we might have sold it eventually. When you're done with your tea, I'll show you Jack's old room."

Walking around Jack's perfectly preserved boyhood room was more than a bit spooky and only reinforced that museum feel. It was also reminiscent of my first visit to the Maloneys' house. It was the second time Katy and I were together. The first time, we'd stood over a floater that had surfaced in the Gowanus Canal in Brooklyn. The cops thought it might've been Patrick. I couldn't help thinking things might've been easier if the body *had* been Patrick's. Anyway, Katy showed me Patrick's room that day much as Mary was showing me Jack's.

But in the Maloneys' living room, there'd been a shrine to the family's real pride and joy, Francis Jr. There were glass display cases that held all of the dead pilot's high school trophies, his game balls, ribbons, loving cups, and assorted memorabilia. The cases also held photos of him in his dress Navy blues, his wings, and posthumously awarded medals. Katy had since given the game balls and other sports memorabilia to the high school and packed most of the other stuff away. There were no such displays here. Jack told me once that when he came out to his parents, they thought the solution was for him to go to more Reds games with his dad. They weren't the kind of people to build shrines to their gay son.

I offered to take us over to the cemetery, but Mary insisted on driving. We made small talk on the way, Mary chatting about the nearby air force base, indicating local points of interest. Given the circumstances surrounding my visit, I wasn't terribly interested. As we neared the cemetery, her conversation took a more serious turn.

"I don't know what you hope to find, Mr. Prager. Like I said on the phone this morning when you called, I got rid of all the roses and I scrubbed the painting off the stone myself."

"Why'd you do that, scrub the paint off, I mean?"

"I don't know. I was angry, I guess. I want Jack to rest in peace, not to be part of ..." She collected herself. "I just want peace is all, for Jack and myself."

That was easy enough to understand. I had been pretty vague with her that morning about what had been done to Patrick's grave, but I thought the time had come to tell her all the details.

"My lord!" Mary slammed on the brakes. And to her credit, it wasn't lip service. She seemed utterly horrified by what I described. "I'm so sorry, so very sorry." She repeated it several times as we made our way slowly to the gravesite.

"It's okay, Mary, it wasn't your doing."

"This is it."

We'd stopped along the way to buy some flowers—not roses— to lay on Jack's headstone. When Mary turned off the car, we both reached into the backseat to collect our bouquets. I asked Mary for a minute by the grave alone. She hesitated, her earlier discomfort once again showing through.

"Go on," she said, if not happily.

I wasn't a grave talker. I took no solace in speaking to bones, grass, and granite. Besides, it's not like Jack and I were old buddies. I liked what little I knew of him and he had seemed really in love with Patrick. No small accomplishment. Although I didn't know Patrick, I'd learned a lot about him during the course of my search for him. Much of what I learned, I didn't like. I didn't care that he was gay; not then, not now. I even felt sorry that he suffered from paralyzing OCD, but he could be a bully like his father. He'd even gotten physical with a girl he dated while working through his sexual identity. No, I hadn't requested the time alone to chew the fat with Jack about his old boyfriend.

Like Mary said, the roses were gone, but I could see where she'd scrubbed the paint off the back of the small headstone. It wasn't a grand thing, Jack's tombstone. It was a low chunk of bevelled granite; tasteful, modest, Midwestern. I liked that. I liked that a lot. I laid my flowers down and extended my hand to Mary.

While not exactly Father Blaney, Mary wasn't much for touchy feely either. She sort of winced when I held out my hand. I remembered her being warmer when we had her to New York, but this was her home turf and this was her brother's grave. Patrick had been an abstraction to her, someone who only existed in her brother's phone calls and letters. So his burial, twenty years after the fact, was almost surreal. Jack, on the other hand, had been very real to her.

"Hi, Jack," she said, laying down her flowers, "Mr. Prager, Patrick's brother-in-law, has come all the way out from New York to see you ..."

I sort of tuned out to the rest of her chat. Mary was right, there wasn't much to see. But sometimes, you have to see for yourself that there's nothing to see. It was like when I looked at the envelope in the office. I didn't figure there'd be anything on it, but I had to look for myself. Suddenly, I was feeling pretty beat. There'd be time to rest that night. I was going to stay over in Cincinnati and fly out early in the morning.

When Mary was done, I picked up a pebble and placed it on Jack's headstone. I did it without thinking. I noticed Mary staring at me and not with a glad expression.

"Why did you do that?"

"Habit. It's a Jewish tradition."

"But what is it for?"

"You know, Mary, I think it serves a lot of purposes. It shows other mourners that the person buried by that headstone isn't forgotten. I guess it also lets the spirit of the person buried there know too, though I don't think that's in the Talmud. But a wise man I loved very much once told me it was symbolic of adding to the mound, to show that a memorial was an ongoing thing and would never truly be finished."

"Oh."

"I meant no disrespect. Would you like me to remove it?"

Her mouth said no, but her body language said yes. I chose to take her at her word. That's what Israel Roth would have done. For the second time in two days I remembered our visit to the cemetery all those years ago. I was smiling as we pulled away, remembering Mr. Roth. I also saw that Mary could not take her eyes off that pebble.

I asked Mary if she'd like to go to dinner, on me, of course. She said no. I tried to contain my disappointment. It meant I'd have time to get a lot of rest and maybe call one or two of Jack's old students.

Not that I thought talking to them would get me anywhere, but again, I just wanted to hear it for myself. At first, Mary was reluctant to share any of the names or numbers with me, though she eventually relented. Again, I understood. Mary just wanted this over with so she could get back to the way things were. She liked her routines. The older you get, the less you like change. And the disturbance of her brother's grave was a little more serious a change of routine than her dry cleaners moving to a new location.

I thanked her for her putting up with my visit. And when she said she was sorry for what had been done at the Maloney family plot, Mary got that sick face again. If I didn't know better, I'd swear that bothered her more than having Jack's resting place messed with. She was tired and we kept our goodbyes brief. Tired as she might have been, I was willing to bet that the second I turned the corner, Mary would be heading back to the cemetery. That pebble I left on Jack's headstone would have to go.

I returned the rental and caught a shuttle bus to my hotel. I got back early enough to have ventured into Kentucky or Cincinnati, if I was so inclined. I was not. I felt the allure of a quick meal and a long stretch in bed more than the need to feel blue grass between my toes or … What was Cincinnati famous for, anyway? Chili, right? I could get some of that from room service. But first I ordered a double Dewar's on the rocks at the hotel bar and found a quiet table away from the TV. I took out the list of names and numbers Mary White had given me and punched the first number into my cell.

I left three messages before I got a live human being on the phone. Too bad, in a way. I was just perfecting my message.

Hi, my name is Moe Prager. I knew Jack White a long time ago in New York, and his sister Mary tells me you and Jack were close. I was just wondering if you wouldn't mind spending a few minutes of your time talking to me about Jack. It would mean a lot to me if you could. My numbers are …

But like I said, someone picked up on my fourth call.

"Yo."

"Hello, is this Marlon Rhodes?"

"Who da fuck wanna know?"

"My name's Moe Prager."

"Dat name s'posed ta mean sumptin ta me?"

"How about the name Jack White?"

That got Mr. Rhodes' attention. "Say watchu gotta say."

"I knew Jack White a long time ago in New York. He was close with my brother-in-law Patrick. I was thinking about Jack this week and I asked his sister Mary if she could put me onto any of Jack's old students because I knew he meant a lot to you guys."

"Don't be lyin to me, man. Dis about dat graveyard shit, right?"

"Right."

"You Five-O?"

"A cop? I used to be."

"Fuck y'all."

So ended our conversation. I waited a few minutes and called back. He didn't answer, so I left my finely honed message on his machine. I got two more of Jack's former students on the phone and though the conversations were longer and more polite than the one I had with Marlon Rhodes, they were equally unproductive. Both liked and admired Jack and both had, on occasion visited his grave, but neither had made a habit of it and neither had been there for months.

I drank another scotch, ate a bowl of awful chili, and went to bed. I had a long dreamless sleep without insight, vision or revelation. It was just exactly the kind of sleep I needed.

[CHAPTER SIX]

During the plane ride home I realized I was doing it again. I was keeping secrets under the guise of protecting someone else. That's crap. Secrets protect their keepers. I hadn't told Katy about what had happened to Jack's grave or that I was going to Dayton. When I spoke to Sarah, I severely minimized the extent to which the Maloney gravesite had been desecrated. If it hadn't suited my purposes, I probably wouldn't have shared all the details with Mary White. Had I shared them all? It gets hard to know. But if there is any justice, it's that the protection of the secret keepers doesn't last forever. For when any two people share knowledge, their secret is a shared illusion.

Looking back twenty-two years, it seems like madness to have not confessed to Katy what I knew about her father and brother. I was afraid to tell her I had found her brother and that I had let him go. Afraid to tell her that her father had been thrown off the NYPD in the early 60s for a brutal assault and that it had been covered up. Afraid to tell her that her father and brother had been locked in a perverse game of chicken. Afraid to tell her that her father had ordered two of his underlings to beat the piss out of me on a SoHo street. The truth would have hurt her, sure, but it might've hurt me much worse. There's a reason people say, "Don't shoot the messenger." I wasn't willing to risk losing the only woman I had ever loved by being the bearer of bad news. And my original mistake was compounded by the day, by the week, by the year, by the decade. Even now there were things I hadn't told her, things she had a right to know.

It's strange how they say you can't teach instinct. Learned behavior is learned behavior. Instinct is inborn. Yet it's become nearly impossible for me to distinguish between the two. Once you replace reason with self-preservation, secret keeping becomes reflexive. For me there was little difference between a secret and the blink of my eye. Only in retrospect can I distinguish between the two. So there on the plane home, in seat 24C, I decided for the second time since 1978 to come clean.

My resolve lasted the time it took to get to New York and have the wheels of the 737 hit the LaGuardia tarmac. When we touched down, I turned on my cell phone and found a long queue of messages. The first was a hangup from Katy. The other four were from my brother Aaron, Sarah, Carmella Melendez, and Sheriff Vandervoort. All of them were looking for me on behalf of Katy and their tone ranged from desperate to angry. Something was wrong, but no one would say what exactly. When I tried Katy's house and cell numbers, I got recordings. Now I was getting panicky. As a keeper of secrets, I was uncomfortable on the opposite side of the fence.

Although the Boeing was half empty, it took an eternity to deplane. When I finally managed to free myself, I did something I hadn't done for quite some time; I flashed tin.

"Listen," I said to a woman at the desk of the adjoining gate. "I need a quiet place to make some important calls."

"Follow me."

I was glad she took a closer look at my badge than at me. I was getting a little long in the tooth to be flashing a regular cop's badge at anyone. Like an aging comedian taking stock of his act, I realized the time had come to retire that joke. The gag was on its last legs.

"You can use this lounge, officer," she said, fiddling with a keypad lock. "No one will bother you in here and if you want to use the phone, just hit nine for an outside line."

I thanked her and waited for her to close the door behind her before getting back to my cell phone.

My first thought was to call Aaron, but it wasn't my second. Just the judgmental tone of his voice was enough to set my teeth on edge and I'd heard hints of it in his message. I was an enigma and a bit of a disappointment to my big brother. He didn't understand my being a cop in the first place and when I was forced to retire, he couldn't comprehend my missing the job so much. There was a lot he didn't understand about me. We were wired differently, Aaron and me. But the flash point between us for the last two decades was my stubborn refusal to leave my PI license in the sock drawer with the dust bunnies and the rest of my unrealized ambitions and accept my life as a wine merchant. That was always enough for him. It never was and would never be enough for me.

I tried Katy's numbers again to the same frustrating end. Again, I left messages. I hesitated to call Sarah before I knew anything. Trouble sucks, but it sucks worse when you're seven hundred miles away from it and you feel helpless. I didn't want to add to her frustration. Carmella was out of the office and not answering her cell, so that left Sheriff Vandervoort. At least he'd left me his cell number.

"Vandervoort."

"Sheriff, it's Moe Prager. What's going on?"

"Where've you been, Mr. Prager?"

"What the fuck does that matter? What's going on with Katy?"

"You better get up here."

"One more time, Sheriff, what's going—"

"Your ex-wife's had a little trouble. She's over at Mary Immaculate."

"Trouble! Is she hurt? What happened?"

"No, she's not hurt, not physically, anyway. We just had a little excitement and the doctors wanted to take a look at her."

"Sheriff, I'm an ex-cop and I respect other cops, but if you don't start speaking English to me, I'm gonna—"

"Mrs. Prager called us to her house and when we got there she was … unhinged and talking a little crazy. Maybe it was all the heartache from yesterday or—"

"Crazy how?"

"She said she got a call."

"A call. A call from who?"

There was silence on the other end of the phone.

"Sheriff!"

"She said she got a call from her brother Patrick."

I'd been to the Mary Immaculate Medical Center only once, back in 1981. I was up in the Catskills looking into an old fire in which some of my high school classmates had perished. One of the dead was my fiercest teenage crush, Andrea Cotter. That's when I first met Mr. Roth. During the investigation, Francis Maloney suffered a stroke and I rushed to be with Katy. Now as I drove, I remembered that last time, how I prayed for the cold-hearted prick to die. He knew it too. Even with a partially paralyzed face and mild aphasia, he warned me to be careful what I wished for. He was right. Eventually all death wishes come to pass and the fallout with them.

Vandervoort met me in the lobby. I wouldn't say he looked worried. Concerned was more like it. Oddly, I found his concern reassuring. As cynical a bastard as I could be, I had never been completely cured of hope. We shook hands.

"What happened, exactly?"

"I got a call at home from dispatch around seven this morning … Hey, you want to grab a cup of coffee? My treat." He was avoiding the subject.

"Sure. We'll talk as we go. You were saying …"

"They said your wife—ex-wife, sorry, called in hysterical, begging for us to get a car to her house. The dispatcher couldn't get anything out of her about what was wrong, if there's been a break in or what. So they sent a car out, but thought maybe I should know too.

Like we were talking about yesterday, people up here still know the Maloneys."

"I'm glad they called you."

"I got there a little after Robby, that's the younger deputy who was out at the cemetery with you yesterday. He's green, but he's good with people and he'd gotten your wife—ex-wife—"

"Just call her Katy, Sheriff. It'll make our lives easier."

"Okay. Well, he'd gotten Katy calmed down, but he couldn't get anything out of her except that she'd gotten a call. She wouldn't put the phone down no matter what Robby did. How do you take yours?" he asked as we stepped into the hospital cafeteria.

"Milk, no sugar."

"Wait here."

He was back in a minute with our coffees. "Let's sit before we go up to the Psych Ward."

"We?"

"Sorry, Mr. Prager. You're not family anymore. They won't let you up there without me."

I didn't like it, but it wasn't his doing. It was mine. Divorce impacts couples in different ways. It's an equation of losses and gains. The gains, however large or small, are usually apparent early on. The losses, as I was discovering, reveal themselves slowly, in painful, unexpected ways. We sat at the closest table.

"When you got there, what happened?"

"I told Robby to wait outside and your—Katy broke down. She said she knew what she was going to say would sound crazy, but it was true. Her brother Patrick had called. She recognized his voice."

"Christ!"

"Exactly. What was I going to say to that?"

"What *did* you say?"

"I'm no shrink, Mr. Prager. I said maybe she was just stressed out by what had happened yesterday and how it can get rough sometimes with people you love when they're gone. But that set her off again. 'I'm not crazy. It was my little brother," she started screaming. Then she started talking about little star or something."

"Little Star is a pet name she had for Patrick," I said. I hadn't heard those two words uttered in two decades.

"Oh, okay. Well, I told her I believed her, but that I needed her to come with me to the hospital. I gotta tell you, I expected that to flip her out, but she came along pretty calmly."

"Thanks for taking care of her, Sheriff Vandervoort."

He held his hand out to me. "Pete. Call me Pete."

"Moe."

We shook hands again and started for the elevator.

"So what do you make of it, Moe? You know Katy. I don't, so I'm just asking."

"Pete, my wife is the least crazy person I ever met. If she says she got a call, I believe her."

"From her dead brother?"

"I didn't say that. Someone's going to a lot of trouble to fuck with my family."

We stepped onto the elevator and had the car to ourselves. He pressed 6.

"Look, Moe, I gotta say this, so hear me out. This is a police matter and this is my jurisdiction. I'd hate for us to be at odds after making nice. You have to stay out of it."

I didn't say anything to that. He seemed relieved by my silence. I think he was even less anxious to hear me tell him lies than I was to tell them.

The days of involuntary institutionalization have long since gone. It wasn't even that easy to keep people for observation anymore unless a crime had been committed, so it was no shock to me that the shrink at Mary Immaculate was sending Katy home. A big man with soulful eyes and a calm manner, the doctor's name was Rauch. He possessed the ability to make you feel you were the most important person in the room and what you had to say was absolutely crucial.

"I've given her a Xanax to calm her down and a prescription for more if need be," he said. "From what I understand, she's had a lot to deal with in the last thirty-six hours, gentlemen. I am not familiar enough with her to make a formal assessment, but I can say that there are always unresolved feelings when it comes to the death of a loved one. It is no great leap to see how the desecration of her father's and brother's graves might stir up those feelings and set her off."

"So you think she was hallucinating, Doc?" I was glad Vandervoort asked and not me.

"Well, Sheriff, how many confirmed cases of resurrection can you point to? If I had to guess, and this is off the record, I'd say someone called and Katy heard what she wanted or needed to hear. Guilt and wish fulfillment make a powerful and, oft times, toxic elixir."

"Thanks, Dr. Rauch." I shook his hand.

"Mr. Prager, I don't think Katy is a threat to herself or others, but there is something troubling going on. I would strongly advise you try to get her to seek treatment. When that point comes, I can recommend some good people in the area. Now if you'll excuse me, I'll go sign the necessary papers."

Vandervoort and I had already agreed that I would take Katy home.

"You know, Moe, I am gonna get the LUDs for Katy's phone, just to make sure. Like the shrink, I believe in guilt, but I'm not keen on coincidences."

"Me either. Thanks. Can you excuse me a second, I've got to call my daughter."

Our ride back to the Maloney house on Hanover Street consisted of silence bookended around a burst of anger. Early on, Katy wasn't talking and kept her head turned away from me.

"I'm not crazy, Moe," she said calmly, head still turned.

"No one says you are."

"It *was* him."

"Patrick? Katy, come on." I didn't want to argue with her, but I wasn't going to placate her either. "Patrick's dead. You know it. We saw him buried."

"Did we?" There, she said it. Someone was bound to. "We saw bones and rags and sneakers buried, not my brother."

"Yeah, Katy, *his* bones, *his* rags, *his* sneakers. The cops confirmed it with dental records. That was Patrick."

"Then how do you explain the call?"

"Someone's fucking with you, with us. That's what all this stuff with the graves was about. That's why someone screwed around with Jack White's grave and—"

Now she turned to face me. "What happened to Jack's grave?"

I told her about the package at the office, about the Sunday call from Mary, and my trip to Dayton.

"Fuck you, Moe. You're doing it all over again," she said, a tear in the corner of her eye. "You and your god damned secrets. Just take me home."

When we got there, I expected her to run out of the car and flip me the bird, but she was full of surprises.

"Come in."

It was an order not an option. When I stepped through the front door, she called me into the bedroom. *Shit!* I hesitated to go in. There was already enough going on. But when I entered, Katy was standing by her night table, her face serene.

"When I called you, when I called the police, I used my cell."

"I know," I said. "That's the hangup number I got."

"Do you know why?"

"Umm ... Look, Vandervoort told me. When the deputy got here, you wouldn't let go of the phone."

"That's right. I wouldn't."

"So."

"It was early when the phone rang and I was still asleep."

"And ..."

"You call here sometimes, right?"

"You know I do, Katy. Just look at the red light on the phone machine. At least two of those flashes are my messages, but what's that—"

"Ssshhhh! How many rings before my machine picks up?"

"Four."

"Very good," she said. "You always were observant."

"Thanks, but—"

Before I could get the question out, she pressed the PLAY button on the machine.

You have seven new messages. You have one saved message. Playing new messages.

First message. Without hesitating, Katy hit ERASE.

Message erased.

Second message. Again.

Message erased.

Third message. And again.

Message erased.

Fourth message. And again and again and again until all the new messages were gone.

To play saved messages, press three. She flicked her right index finger.

First saved message. Six-forty-three AM. From outside caller: "Hi."

"Hello ... Hello, who's there?" Katy's voice was full of sleep.

"I miss you, sis."

"Patrick! Patrick!"

"Gotta go now. I love you."

"Oh my God! Patrick don't hang—"

Click.

End of saved messages.

[43]

We both stood there across the bedroom from each other, as far apart as we had ever been. Even at the few low points of our marriage, even in the depths of her anger when the truth of Patrick's disappearance first surfaced, she had never looked at me so coldly. We were strangers.

"Now," she said, "I'm tired, please get out of my parents' house."

I turned and left without a word.

How, I wondered, had Katy and I grown this far apart? We had once loved each other beyond all reason. From the first, our bodies had fit together as if carved to do just so. Did we fight? Of course we fought, all couples fight, but we could always see the love behind the anger. Now, and over the course of the last few years, there was only anger. Even during the inevitable dead spots in our marriage, when every day was like a long drive through Nebraska, we had rediscovered the passion. We had come through everything. I think for the very first time, when I walked out of her bedroom, I accepted that we would not come through this. That cold look on her face, not a judge's signature on a piece of paper, was our divorce decree.

Still a little stunned, I drove around aimlessly for a while. It was pretty country up here, though not as pretty as it once had been. Farms that I used to pass on my way up had been sold and turned into gated communities of McMansions with nine hole golf courses and artificial lakes. Some of the farms had been cut up into bigger lots. Those parcels were for super-sized homes, ones with garages the size of aircraft hangars. Sarah had a friend who called them Garage Mahals. To me, no matter how lavish the homes might be, no matter how tasteful, they were ugly. They just didn't belong.

I loved New York City, but it could be cruel to its neighbors. I once heard it said that being in close proximity to New York was like sleeping in bed next to an elephant. Everything was great until the elephant rolled over. It was what ruined Long Island and what was slowly happening here. To its neighbors, the city was a contrary beast. As its influence spread to surrounding areas, it sucked the local flavor out of the landscape. It's funny how people try to get away from the city, but never quite escape its gravity.

As the light faded, I rode back into Janus. The sheriff's office was at the end of Main Street. Robby, the young deputy, was at the desk. I hoped he got paid a lot of money given the hours Vandervoort was working him. He recognized me and flashed a smile that still had a lot of little kid in it. It was nice to see. I wasn't sure there was a lot of that left in me.

"Robby, right?"

"That's right, Mr. Prager."

I thanked him for helping with Katy.

"Sheriff Vandervoort's not around. I'm sorry. You want to leave him a note or something."

"No, thanks, that's okay. Any results from the crime scene?" I asked just to make small talk.

He hesitated. "No."

He smiled like a kid and lied like a kid. The job would beat that out of him soon enough.

"Look, deputy, you saw my ex-wife this morning. You saw for yourself what this is doing to her. Just let me know so I can be prepared when the shit hits the fan. And it's our secret. Sheriff Vandervoort will never know we even spoke about it."

"I shouldn't. I'm on probation and this is the only job I've ever—"

I put my hand on his shoulder. "Listen, kid, it's up to you."

That did the trick.

"There were some shoe impressions that didn't match any of the elimination impressions," he whispered as if Vandervoort was lurking. "They were a men's size nine running shoes that led away from the Maloney plot, across three adjoining plots, down into the stream."

"No big deal in that, right? Shit, in Janus alone, how many guys are out there with size nine running shoes?"

"You don't understand, Mr. Prager. These weren't just any men's size nine running shoes."

"What's that supposed to mean?"

"These were Shinjo Olympians."

"Shinjos? I've never heard of—"

"—Shinjos. That's right," he cut me off. "No one has. Not no one, very few people have. That's because they stopped making the Olympians model in nineteen seventy-six and the company went out of business is nineteen eighty-seven."

"Thank you, deputy."

I about-faced. Robby said something to me, but the blood pounding in my ears was too loud for me to hear him. I sat in my front seat for what seemed like hours. The next thing I was fully conscious of was unlocking the door to my condo.

[CHAPTER SEVEN]

The sun filled my rearview as I drove along the Belt Parkway to the Gowanus. This part of the Belt could be beautiful, especially in early morning. From Bay Parkway west, the roadway swooped along the shoreline and you could race with container or cruise ships sailing beneath the Verrazano and into the hungry mouth of New York Harbor. The deep blue of the water could seem almost structural and not a trick of light. In the orange of the sun the patches of rust on the skin of the gray bridge came alive. Not today. Today I was blind to beauty, to nearly everything, but I had made this drive so often I could do it in a coma.

Aaron and I owned four stores. City on the Vine near the American Museum of Natural History was our first. Two years ago we ventured into the wilds of New Jersey and opened Que Shiraz in Marlboro. Red, White, and You was our big volume location on Long Island. But our second store, Bordeaux in Brooklyn on Montague Street in the Heights, was closest to my house and to my heart. I'd run the store for years and even after I turned it over to a new manager, it was my base of operations. It was also less than three blocks away from the offices of Prager & Melendez Investigations, Inc. That was no accident. I had to go into the store, but I had other business first.

When I got off the elevator at 40 Court, I found Devo doing yoga in the hallway outside our office door. Carmella and I picked 40 Court Street for practical reasons. Besides its proximity to the State Supreme Court Building and the Brooklyn Tombs, it was filled to the brim with law firms. Funny how cops have no use for lawyers until they're off the job and looking for work. Then it's no longer about them having use for lawyers, but lawyers having use for them. And if you are going to feed off their scraps, you better have a good seat at the trough. 40 Court was front row, ringside, orchestra. Well over half the jobs we worked were farmed to us by lawyers or other investigative firms that shared our address.

Devereaux Okum—Devo—was a thin black blade of grass with a shaved head, soft voice, vaguely feminine features, and a shaman's eyes. He was in his early thirties and claimed he came from down South somewhere, but would never say exactly where. Frankly, he was more off-worldly than out-of-state. He had that 70s David Bowie mojo working. It was probably foolish, but Carmella and I never pressed him too hard on his background.

What we knew about him was that he was a vegan with a sweet disposition and formal manners who was great at what he did and worked harder at it than anyone else in the firm. Devo did gadgets. Gadgets, that's what modern investigations were all about. From tracking devices to cameras to computers, he had it covered. We paid him a big salary and had several times offered to get him licensed, even to give him a piece of the business. He had so far resisted our offers. He seemed content. I had known what that was like once, being content.

"Hey, Devo."

He didn't say anything, slowly letting out a deep breath, prayerfully pressing his palms together in front of him, a few inches from his chest. He turned to me, removing a sleek, white metallic box from his shirt pocket.

"Good morning, Moe."

"What's that?"

"This," he said, removing the earphones, "is the coming revolution."

"Looks like a cigarette case, not a revolution."

"It's an Apple product that won't be out for another few months yet."

I didn't bother asking where or how he'd gotten hold of it. He was always getting things logic and the law dictated he shouldn't have.

"What does it do, tune your circadian rhythms and access the internet?"

"It stores and plays music."

"It plays music, that's it?"

"That's it."

"How much did it cost?"

That elicited a sheepish smile.

"Okay, I'll bite. How much will it cost regular shmos like me?"

"Around four hundred bucks," he said.

"Just to play music."

"Just to play music," he repeated.

"Some revolution. They won't be able to give those things away."

"We'll see."

I had called Devo before hitting the Dewar's the night before. I wanted him to come in early specifically to discuss my dead brother-in-law's voice mail message from the great beyond. Until I could get a copy of it—and I meant to get a copy—I wanted to have some idea of what I was dealing with. When we sat down in my office, I described as closely as I could what I had heard on Katy's machine. I tried to mimic the intonation of the voice, the timing involved in the dialogue, etc. Devo didn't hesitate to ask the million dollar question.

"Was it Patrick's voice?"

"He's dead."

"Moe, I did not ask if it was actually him calling. I asked if it was his voice. Those are two very different things."

"I don't know," I said. "We spoke only once, very briefly, but Katy seemed pretty convinced. Katy would know her brother's voice."

Devo was unpersuaded. "She has not heard his voice in twenty years."

"Twenty-two plus, but who's counting? I don't think that matters. I haven't heard my mom's voice in longer than that and I'd recognize it."

"Possibly. I think it is situationally dependent, Moe, but let us come back to that in a moment. First, tell me if there was anything obviously mechanical about the voice. Was it robotic? Did it sound spliced? Were there inappropriate pauses? Was it scratchy like an old vinyl recording? Was there any background noise?"

"No, there was nothing like that. It sounded pretty much like I did it for you before. Why? Does that mean it wasn't doctored?"

"No, not at all. With a reasonable laptop and software you can download from the internet, you can make sound sit up and beg or fetch the newspaper. There would be no limit to what a person or persons with more formidable resources could do. I simply wanted to make certain that we are not dealing with pranksters or rank amateurs."

"Okay, rank amateurs and pranksters eliminated."

"Did the voice sound conversational?"

"See, Devo, that's harder to answer. There were so few words exchanged and Katy was so emotional ... And not for nothing, but what were you talking about before when you said recognition was situationally dependent?"

"Simply that the events of Sunday sensitized Katy for the call on Monday. The caller might just as easily have phoned late Saturday night before the desecrations were spotted, but he didn't. Why do you suppose that is?"

"Because Katy had to be primed to recognize the voice. The stuff at the gravesite played with her head. It got to those last shreds of hope and denial we hide deep inside."

Devo smiled a smile at me that made me feel like an apt pupil. Maybe he'd put a gold star next to my name.

"Do you have enough to make an educated guess about whether it was someone imitating Patrick's voice or some digital wizardry?" I asked.

"We are certain he is dead, are we not?"

"Everybody but Katy."

"Well, until I have a copy of the message, I cannot say. Even then, I may not be able to render a definitive opinion, but it is almost beside the point."

"How's that?"

"For someone to imitate a voice they have to hear it. And if Patrick is dead ..."

"... they either had to have known him or have a recording of him. Even if the mimic knew Patrick, it would be hard to do his voice flawlessly simply from memory."

"Imitation is a matter of trial and error, of feedback and fine tuning," he said. "Hard to get accurate feedback from old memories."

"So," I said, "either way, if it's some digitally enhanced trick or a clever mimic, there's a recording of Patrick's voice out there somewhere."

"Find that recording and—"

"—I'll find my ghost."

I shook Devo's hand. "How are you coming with that list of names I gave Carmella?"

"I should be finished this afternoon," he said.

Had he been any other employee, I would have slipped him a few c-notes in an envelope or sent over a bottle of Opus One. But gestures like that were just wasted on Devo. He was old school in that he found the job itself reward enough. He wasn't interested in the perks. I guess I liked him for that.

I can't say that I hate the wine business, although I have, at times, hated it. I've often thought that if I really despised the life, I'd be out of it. I've always had strength enough to walk away. The thing was, the business bored me. Like I once said, there's only so many times you can parse the difference between champagne and *methode champenoise* without completely losing your mind. For over twenty years the wine business had kept my bank account full and left my soul empty. It afforded me a few luxuries. I'd owned a house. I had a condo. I got to drive new cars every few years. My kid could go to whatever college she was smart enough to get into.

The wine business was never my dream. I wasn't a dreamer by nature. Even the profession I loved was the result of a drunken dare. I mean, how many college students in the late 60s were signing up to take the NYPD entrance exam? One year I'm tossing bottles at the cops, the next year I'm a cop getting bottles tossed at me. The wine business was Aaron's thing. The initial plan was for me to be an investor and then to come on board after I retired from the job with my twenty years in and a detective first's pension. Didn't work out that way and all because I fell prey to a conspiracy of fate. In a way, I was actually Son of Sam's last victim.

In August of '77, when Sam was finally captured, New York City was as close to defeat as it ever was or is ever likely to be. Beaten down by years of near bankruptcy, brutal winters, blackouts, and Mr. Berkowitz, the city was a madhouse. Any street cop would know. I knew. Rage was boiling just beneath everybody's skin, beneath the city's streets. We were always a pin prick away from explosion. And none of us was immune to the Vietnam hangover; our national headlong rush into pot, punk, polyester, and Plato's Retreat. I think sometimes if Gerald Ford had wanted to be a more effective president, he should have moved from the White House to Studio 54.

Anyway, when Son of Sam was arraigned, the brass wanted to make sure there were plenty of cops around for crowd control. So they bussed in uniforms from precincts all over the city. I was one of those uniforms. If you catch any of the old video from that day, you can see me standing just behind Detective Ed Zigo and to Son of Sam's left. Although I couldn't have known it then, it was my first appearance on television and my final shift in uniform. While I was gone, the precinct's linoleum had been waxed for the first time in months and some careless schmuck had thrown a piece of carbon paper onto the floor. When I returned, my foot found that piece of carbon paper. Cops who were there say the sound my knee made when all the ligaments snapped was enough to make you puke. Apparently, a few people did. I don't remember, because my head smacked the floor pretty hard. I woke up in Coney Island Hospital having taken my first misstep into the wine business.

Five months and two surgeries later, I was put out to pasture with pain pills and a patrolman's pension. Aaron had found the perfect store, but we were still a little short on funds and worried about getting our liquor license. That's when Rico Tripoli, my closest buddy from the Six-O, told me about some missing kid and how maybe, just maybe, if I found the kid, his influential father could get us our financing and license and how we'd be set for life. *Yeah, sure!* What Rico neglected to mention was that he didn't give a rat's ass about the missing kid or my future. I was to be his short cut to a gold shield and the means to the end of Francis Maloney's political career.

Rico was right in a way. We all got what we wanted. Rico got his gold shield. His handlers got Francis Maloney to retire from politics. Aaron and I got our financing and our license and we *were* set for life. I got a wife and love and a family as well. Yes, we all got what we wanted, everyone but Francis Maloney. I hated my father-in-law, but I never blamed him for his hating me for my part in his demise. We all got what we wanted and the only happy one of us was Aaron.

My big brother was tinkering with the register as I walked through the creaky wooden doors of Bordeaux in Brooklyn. Aaron had aged well. His hair was thinner and all gray, but his shoulders were still broad and unbowed. Other than my chronic disinterest in the business, he had everything he ever wanted. Our success had washed away the sting of our dad's smalltime thinking and bigtime failures. He had a wife he probably loved more now than the day they married, great kids, a big house on Long Island, and good health. Aaron didn't think so, but I envied him. It was a blessing to be born knowing what you want and how to get it. With few exceptions, my wants shifted with my cases.

"Hey, big brother."

"Christ, will you help me with this thing," he barked.

"Here, shithead." I banged the side of my fist into the till and it slid open. "You should come to this store more often. The drawer's been sticking like that for years."

"You should come to any store more often."

"Touché."

"So what's this *mishegas* with your wife?"

"Ex-wife, as everyone keeps reminding me."

"All right, your ex-wife."

"What *mishegas*? What's wrong with thinking your dead brother dug his way out of his grave, smashed his dad's headstone to bits, and is making phone calls?"

"*Oy gevalt!*"

"Yeah, big brother, *oy gevalt* indeed."

"What are you doing about it?"

"I was just about to call Ghostbusters."

"Very funny, Moses."

"I'm doing the only thing I can do. I'm gonna look into it. First, I have to pick your niece up at the airport."

He grinned. My brother and Sarah had a special affinity for one another. "When does she get in?"

"I'm leaving for LaGuardia in about an hour."

"Does she know what's going on?"

"Some of it. Look, Aaron, I just want you to know, I'm going to take as long as it takes to find out what's going on."

"We've prospered for two decades without your full attention. We should be able to survive another few weeks."

"Fuck you!"

"Fuck you, he says to me," he stage whispered to an invisible audience. "Let's face it, the best thing you ever did for us was getting us started. That shit with Katy's dad, look, you never wanted to tell me much about it, okay. It was your business, but enough already."

I wanted to explode. He was right, but he was wrong too. I put in my time. I got us some of our biggest accounts, hired our best people.

Even Aaron would have to admit that much. Klaus and Kosta were integral parts of our success and had been with us from year one. Both now owned small percentages of the business. Kosta was our head buyer and Klaus, besides running the day to day operations of the New Jersey store was, along with our lawyers and accountants, looking into the possibility of our franchising.

"Without me, there'd be no business," I said.

"Yeah, I heard that refrain before. It used to mean something, too, when you said it last century. That was then. Four stores and twenty years later, it's enough already."

"Did Abraham Lincoln write that for you?"

"What?"

"Never mind."

"Go play cops and robbers with your Spanish hotty." Aaron was very much of my parent's generation. I'm surprised he didn't call our African-American employees colored. He wasn't a bigot. Far from it. He was just old. He was born old.

"Puerto Rican."

"What?"

"Carmella is Puerto Rican and she's not my hotty. Where do you come up with these terms anyway, *Reader's Digest*?"

"What's wrong with *Reader's Digest*?"

No matter what our arguments started over, they always ended in the same place.

"You want coffee?" I asked.

"Sounds good."

"The usual?"

"Always. Hey, little brother ..."

"Yeah."

"I love ya."

"I know. Me too."

The Northwest terminal was bustling. The area airports were always busy, but there was just something about LaGuardia that brought out the closet claustrophic in even the most hardened New Yorker. I found myself wishing *I'd* made the travel arrangements instead of leaving them up to Sarah. All this foot traffic was going to make things that much more difficult. No doubt a late afternoon or evening flight would have been a better option, but there was no use giving myself *shpilkes* over it now. For the moment, I only wanted to think about the best thing in my life, Sarah.

I loved the kid so much it hurt. Maybe it was her only child status or that we were baseball buddies, but I had never gotten used to her being away from home. The sting was particularly sharp today with LaGuardia being just a stone's throw away from Shea Stadium. Sarah had a double-major as a kid, learning about baseball and aircraft as we sat and watched the big jets roar over Shea on their final approaches to the airport. I remembered the first game I took her to, a weekday matinee against the Padres. She lasted only a couple of innings in the baking sun and passed out on my shoulder. When she woke up, she said she was *firsty*. I remembered that day for other reasons too.

It was the summer of 1983 and I had been hired to look into the disappearance of a political intern named Moira Heaton. Moira was a plain looking girl, a cop's daughter, who had gone missing from State Senator Steven Brightman's neighborhood office on Thanksgiving Eve 1981. For two years Brightman had proclaimed his innocence. He'd done everything he could, cooperated completely with the police, posted a big reward, jumped through fiery hoops, but it was all to no avail. He had been tried and convicted in the press and in the court of public opinion. Trouble was, Brightman was the fair-haired boy, the next Jack Kennedy and he was too ambitious to just live out his days as a has-been that never was.

That's where I came in. Thomas Geary, one of Brightman's wealthy backers and the father of one of our former wine store employees, got the idea that I could magically clear the state senator's name. My reputation was for luck, not skill. As my early clients had too often said, "We tried good, now we're going to give luck a chance." I guess, if I want to be honest, they were right. I *was* lucky. My luck extended as far back as 1972. On Easter Sunday of that year, a little girl named Marina Conseco was kidnapped off a Coney Island street. And once seventy-two hours passed, the search for Marina silently morphed into a search for her remains. I found Marina severely injured but alive at the bottom of an old wooden water tank. She had been molested, then tossed in the tank and left to die. To this day, I'm not sure what made me look up and notice the tanks and think to search them. I was lucky then. I was lucky with Brightman too.

We were on the 7 train heading back home from Shea. Sarah was sleeping with her head of damp red curls resting on my leg. I was hot and tired too, but my eyes kept drifting to the front page of the *Post* that the man across the car from me was reading. On it was a picture of evil personified, a serial rapist the papers had dubbed Ivan the Terrible. He had scragly hair, a cruel condescending smile, and black eyes. They were the blackest eyes I'd ever seen; opaque as the ocean on a moonless night. With a little bit of digging, I found a connection between Moira and Ivan. He eventually confessed to her murder. I was a little *too* lucky with that one. It all came just a bit too easily. In spite of it, I found the real facts behind the fabricated truths that had been sprinkled on the ground before me like so many bread crumbs.

I could never go to a game or drive past Shea Stadium without thinking of Sarah's first Mets game. Every year I renewed my Mets season tickets, but it wasn't the same without her and it was never going to be the same. These days I usually gave my tickets away to Aaron's kids or Carmella's little cousins or clients. I checked the Arrivals screen for the hundreth time in the last ten minutes and noticed Sarah's flight number was flashing. So far, I had been able to filter Ivan the Terrible's kind of evil out of my kid's life and I meant to keep it that way. I dialed Carmella's cell number.

"What?" she barked. "It's so fucking noisy in here."

"Her flight's landed."

"No shit! There's like a screen two feet from my face."

"You remember what Sarah looks—"

"For chrissakes, Moe! I know your daughter for ten years. I know what the fuck she looks like. I could spot that red hair from halfway across the state."

"What the fuck's eating you lately?"

"My stomach's been bothering me for weeks. I'm sorry, Moe, I know I been cranky."

"Okay, she should be getting down here in a few minutes."

"Don't worry. Anybody comes near her, I got it covered."

"Anything suspicious?"

"I got my eye on a few mutts, but you know these town car drivers try to scam rides. We'll see soon?"

Not everything I got right was about luck. I was a good cop before my accident. I still possesed the ability to anticipate, to see what might be coming around the next corner, and what I saw coming was trouble for Sarah. Whoever had done this stuff with Patrick had gone through a lot of trouble. So far the only direct targets had been Katy and me, but if you really want to hurt, frighten or generally fuck with people, you go after their kids. That's why I had arranged for Carmella to come to the airport before me and stake out the baggage claim area. She was less certain about the set up than me.

"What about that lady in Ohio? They fucked with her brother's grave, no?"

"Collateral damage," I said. "It enhanced the effect of what was going on here, a bit of sleight-of-hand to distract me. It worked, too. I was out in Dayton looking at a grave when I should have been home keeping my eye on the ball. I'm not gonna let them catch me off guard again."

She was right about one thing. We'd see soon enough.

My least favorite part of the airport was baggage claim. Baggage claim was like the final insult after the long ordeal, just another opportunity to hurry up and wait. Folks looked defeated waiting for their bags. And no matter how they spruced up the area, the machinery always seemed positively medieval.

My phone buzzed, then stopped. That was Carmella's signal that people were spilling into the baggage claim area. Sarah appeared. I couldn't help hoping that I was being foolish and over protective, that Carmella was right. She wasn't. Everything seemed to happen at once. Even before I was fully conscious of Sarah's presence, the pocket of space closed around her. Carmella came out of nowhere and tackled someone, Sarah screamed, a crowd surged in their directions. I put my head down and charged through the sea of bodies.

"Get the fuck off me, bitch! You breakin' my finger."

A chubby black kid of maybe seventeen was face down on the floor, Carmella twisting his thumb and wrist behind his back. Sarah's expression was more surprised than anything else. Then I noticed a brown shipping envelope in her hands that I hadn't seen her holding when she first came into view.

"Give that to me, kiddo." I held my hand out to Sarah and she placed the envelope in my palm. "Let him up, Carm, so we can talk privately."

Carmella pulled the kid to his feet as I assured everyone that it was all right.

"Just a misunderstanding," I lied, sounding authoritative as hell. I didn't flash my badge. When the cops showed up—which they would—I didn't need to try and explain away a potential felony charge. "Show's over folks. Go get your bags and have a safe trip back home."

By nature, New Yorkers are disobedient bastards. On the other hand they take an inordinate amount of pride in their unshockability. This time unshockability won out and they went back to reclaiming their luggage while we hustled the kid into a corner. As we walked, I tore open the envelope. It was another wilted rose and a "self-portrait" of Patrick done on an eight by eleven piece of Masonite. The familiar initials PMM were in the lower right hand corner. This wasn't funny anymore.

"Okay, asshole, what's this about?" I said, pressing my face into the kid's. His wide, frightened eyes told me he knew I wasn't fucking around.

"Guy gimme a twenty ta give dat package to da red-headed girl come out dat door."

"What guy?" I asked, pressing my face even closer to his.

"Dat one," he said, pointing.

"Which one?" I stepped back to see where he was pointing.

"Him."

He was pointing at the portrait.

"Bullshit!" Carmella hissed in the kid's ear, tightening the thumb lock.

He winced. "I ain't fuckin wich y'all."

Carmella yanked and twisted. The breath went out of the kid and I thought he might pass out from the pain.

"Carmella, stop it!" Sarah said. "Dad, tell her to stop it."

"Look! Der he at." The kid's voice was barely a whisper, but he pointed toward the exit doors with his free hand.

I turned and my heart jumped into my throat. There he was, tattoo and all. The world around me crawled. There was a muted roar in my ears. I could hear individual noises—the squeaky wheel of a baggage cart, the smack of a suitcase as it hit the metal railing, a limo driver screaming "Mr. Child. Mr. Child. Mr. Child ..." the whoosh of the doors—but none of it made any sense. I told my legs to run, but they wouldn't move. I tried to shout, but I could form no words. Something was tugging my arm.

"Dad! Dad!" Sarah was shouting, pulling my sleeve.

"Moe, what's up?" It was Carmella.

"Let the kid go," I heard myself say. "Let him go."

"What?"

"Let him go."

My legs finally started moving, but not fast enough. Strong arms grabbed me.

"Where the fuck you think you're going, buddy?"

"Huh?"

"C'mon, pal," the Port Authority cop said. "And the three of youse too, let's go. Now!"

I didn't argue, but kept watching the door as I moved.

I didn't know ghosts used doors.

It didn't take long to straighten things out with the Port Authority cops, especially once we showed them our old badges and shields. You should never underestimate the power of the us against them mentality. Once cops, always cops. Raheem—that was the kid's name—was no fool either. He understood that he wasn't going to get a whole lot of sympathy once the policemen's love fest began. So for a hundred bucks and a sincere apology, he was willing to forget all about Carmella's tackle and death grip. For an extra fifty, he agreed to have coffee with Carmella so she could debrief him about how he'd been approached to deliver the package to Sarah.

I had to get Sarah back to my condo so we could talk about the full extent of what was going on with Katy and so she could decide if she wanted to stay with me or her mom. Having Sarah in the car to talk to was helping me not to obsess over who I thought I saw at the airport. The distraction of driving had also let me regain some measure of equilibrium. It wasn't Patrick—that's what I kept telling myself—but I was meant to think so. My new mantra was, "Don't fall for it. Don't fall for it. Don't fall ..." But Christ, that guy in the airport terminal looked an awful lot like him.

"So talk to me, kiddo." I wasn't quite pleading.

"I didn't like that back there."

I didn't like it either, at least not the part where I saw a ghost. I didn't think Sarah had seen him, so I played dumb. "You wanna give me a hint here?"

"How you guys treated Raheem."

"We were only being cautious. Don't hold it against Carmella. She was trying to protect you. Blame me. More has been going on at home than I've let on."

"Not that part," she said, staring out the window as we passed Shea and smiling wistfully.

"Then I'm a little confused."

"How the cops blew him off because he was a black kid and you guys were cops. If the roles were reversed and he had tackled you or Carmella, the cops would have beat the shit out of him. They wouldn't have been slapping him on the back and inviting him out for drinks like they did with you and Carmella."

"You're right. I'd like to tell you it's not true, but it is. That's a cop's world sometimes."

"Well, it sucks."

"There's a lot of injustice in the world, Sarah. Some of it's big. Some of it's small. In the scheme of things, today's events were a small injustice."

"You don't have to talk to me like I'm a little kid, Dad. Besides, there's no such thing as a small injustice."

"I didn't say it was right. I just said it's the way it is."

"Is that how you rationalized yourself to sleep when you were a cop?"

"When I was a cop, I slept like a baby. Being a cop isn't about the big questions. It's about doing the job."

"Did doing the job include mistreating innocent people?"

"Sometimes yeah, I guess it did."

"Then that sucks too."

"I'm glad I'm sending you to the University of Michigan so you can learn to use the word 'sucks' in every other sentence. You gonna try for the debate team next term?"

"Don't change the subject."

"Okay. Look, Carmella and me, we were just looking out for you. Raheem got the shit end of the stick today, but he also got a hundred and fifty bucks for getting his thumb twisted a little bit. You seem a lot more worried about his dignity than he did."

"That's not the point."

"Then I'm lost," I said.

"It wasn't necessarily what happened back there, but what it represented that bothers me. You guys got a free pass because you were once cops, not because of what you did or didn't do."

"Oh, kinda like how you got out of those speeding tickets last year because you were a cop's kid and had the PBA and Detectives Endowment Association cards in your bag that Carmella and I gave you."

Sarah had no snappy reply for that one, but sank into her seat and sulked for a few minutes.

"So what is it with you and Carmella anyway?" she said as we got off the Van Wyck and onto the Belt Parkway.

"We're partners."

"That all? Just business partners like you and Uncle Aaron?"

"Not exactly. I get along better with Carmella. I'm not a disappointment to her like I am to your uncle."

"Come on, Dad, Carmella is beautiful and you have that cop thing between you and—"

"Look, kiddo, if this is about me and your mother, forget it. What went wrong with us has nothing to do with Carmella."

"Not even a little bit, not even about you and Mom not getting back together?"

"I love your mom, but it just doesn't work between us anymore."

"But—"

"No buts. I hurt your mom and she can't get past it. Until this stuff with Patrick, we were both okay with that."

Patrick. Shit! I got a little queasy just saying his name. What had happened at the air terminal came rushing back to me. I worried Sarah might notice. Then, of all people, I thought of Francis Maloney and smiled. A reaction I had never before had nor was ever likely to have again. The strange thing about my late father-in-law and me was that in spite of our mutual loathing, we never fought, not really. We were engaged in a long cold war. And just like in the real Cold War, both of us kept a finger close to the button that would bring our worlds crashing down around our heads.

We barely spoke, but there was one question Francis Maloney Sr. never missed the opportunity to ask me, "Do you believe in ghosts?" He never explained the question, never once discussed it. He didn't want or expect an answer. After a few years, he didn't even have to say the words. The question would come in the guise of a sideways glance or a churlish smile. His favorite form of silent sparring was to raise his glass of Irish to me, a toast to his sworn enemy.

Only in death did he explain. The mechanics of his revenge from the grave were particularly cruel. Included in Katy's inheritance was a cold storage receipt. She thought it might be for her mom's wedding dress. When we retrieved the item from cold storage, it wasn't a wedding dress at all, but a man's blue winter parka, the blue parka her brother Patrick had been wearing the night he disappeared. Katy recognized it immediately. So did I. In the pocket of the coat was a twenty year old handwritten note from Francis:

"Your boyfriend gave this to me on February 17th, 1978. Ask him where he got it and why he swore me to secrecy. Did he never tell you he found Patrick?"

And so I came to understand the question he had asked me hundreds of times in a hundred different ways over the years. The coat proved I had found Patrick, that I had let him go, and that I had conspired to keep the secret from Katy forever. Patrick's ghost had essentially ended our marriage. Francis, thinking that his death would protect him from the fallout, had miscalculated. For as angry as Katy was with me, the extent of it was nothing compared to the animus with which she regarded her late father. Katy and I might never reconcile and she would likely not forgive me, but we would always share Sarah.

Sarah was the best of both of us. On the other hand, Katy would hate her father for eternity.

So I sat there in the driver's seat, smiling, thinking of the late Francis Maloney Sr. and wondering whether he would have appreciated today's delicious irony. I closed my eyes just for a second and saw him raise his glass of Irish. In my head I heard him ask, "Do you believe in ghosts?" And this time I answered, "Maybe."

"Dad, what are you smiling at?"

"I was just thinking about your grandfather."

"Your dad?"

"No, Grandpa Francis."

"But you hated him, didn't you?"

"Yeah. That's why I'm smiling."

"You're so weird, Dad."

"I suppose I am, sometimes. At least you didn't say I suck."

[CHAPTER EIGHT]

For the second time that day I drove into Brooklyn Heights, but the road ahead hadn't gotten any clearer. Now I was facing down the sun sliding slowly behind the curve of the Earth and the blue of the water was less assertive. The green spaces and bike paths that ran along the Belt Parkway were crowded with couples, joggers pushing strollers, tanned skater girls, dogs on long leashes, dogs on no leashes at all. Kites bathed in dying orange light flirted with the Verrazano Bridge and dreamed of untethered flight. These were not the cheap, diamond-shaped kites I flew as a kid, kites made of splintered balsa wood and paper, trailing tails of my mother's old house frocks or whatever other *schmattes* were laying around. No, these were proper kites, fierce and sturdy things that loved the wind and did not fear it. I wondered if I were a kite, would I love the wind or fear it? It's odd what you think about sometimes.

By the time I turned off the BQE at the base of the Brooklyn Bridge and into Cadman Plaza, the sun and the kites were gone. There may be no silence in Brooklyn, ever, but there are lulls when its symphony quiets down just enough to hear individual instruments: a tugboat horn, the squeal and rumble of a lone subway, the *thwack, thwack, thwack* of a low flying helicopter. I used to love this time of night. I would sit on the steps outside Bordeaux in Brooklyn and listen to the reassuring buzz of tires along the metal grate deck of the Brooklyn Bridge. The buzz was gone now that they had paved over the deck. I knew it was silly to miss it and that the bridge was far safer this way, especially in the rain. Still, I listened for the buzz as I walked from my car to the lobby of 40 Court Street.

Working nights never bothered me much nor did staying late at any of the wine stores. I did hate coming to 40 Court at night. Office buildings are depressing places, lonely and desperate places after dark. Bored square badges read the papers, slept in the shadows, spoke broken Spanish to the cleaning girls. As I walked from the elevator, I checked for light leaking through the bottoms of other office doors. I thought about the men and women behind those doors. *Was it always about the work? Was it about avoiding a loveless marriage? An empty apartment? Or worse, an emptier bed?*

Carmella didn't greet me when I came through the front door, so I went into my office and collected my bottle of Dewar's and two glasses before heading in to see her. Just lately, it seemed like she needed more than a few drinks and I'd been scotch jonesing since the airport. I hadn't wanted to drink in front of Sarah. Crazy, right? It's not like she'd never seen me drink before. I mean, she was twenty and I owned four fucking wine stores, for chrissakes. But she'd never seen me drink at home and never alone. She had never seen me drunk and I wanted to keep it that way.

I knocked on Carmella's office door and walked in. Her chair was turned toward the window, but not completely so that I couldn't see her profile. She was crying. I had seen her cry only once before, when the NYPD finally did to her what they had done to me. They had wanted to show her the door almost immediately after she was wounded at Crispo's Bar in Red Hook in '89, but the only thing Carmella Melendez ever wanted to be was a cop and she wasn't going to give up as easily as I had. Amazingly, she hung on for seven more years and made it to detective first before getting the boot. She'd taken a lot of shit to make it that far, but that last year had been particularly hard on her. And after her last shift, she broke down.

"Here," I said, as I poured. "You look like you could use this."

Carmella still did not face me. "I'm not drinking these days."

"No wonder you've been such a bitch." I was laughing. She wasn't. "Come on, you know I hate to drink alone."

"No!"

"What the fuck is the matter with—"

"I'm pregnant."

I drank my scotch, quickly, then drank the glass I poured for Carmella. After that, I said nothing. Sometimes, the two of us would talk about my divorce and what had gone wrong between Katy and me. We almost never talked about Carmella's social life. That was mostly my doing, I suppose. Her taste in men sucked and I wasn't shy about voicing that opinion. I also tended to pile on when the latest asshole would inevitably disappoint her. It didn't take her long to tire of hearing me say, "I told you so." She thought she could read my mind.

"Go ahead, say it. I know you're thinking it."

"No I'm not. What I'm thinking is are you gonna be okay?"

"I'm always okay. You know what I been through. I can take anything."

She was right. She had been through a lot. Her whole life seemed to be one long drawn out test of her will to survive. Outside her family, only I knew just how cruel that test had been. I walked over and knelt down in front of her chair.

"Just because you always survive doesn't mean you're always okay," I said, stroking her hair. I wiped her tears away with my thumb.

"What am I gonna do, Moe?"

"I don't know. What do you want?"

"I want not to have gotten knocked up is what I want." The anger shut off her tears. She looked up at the ceiling. "I pray to God, always. Since I was a little girl, I pray to God, but he don't answer my prayers."

She crossed herself, then flipped up the middle finger of her right hand. I went back around the desk and poured myself another scotch.

"You remember Israel Roth?"

"The *viejo*, your friend? Sure, I remember. Nice man."

"You know he survived two years in Auschwitz, right?"

"Yeah."

"What Mr. Roth used to say was that the problem with God wasn't that he didn't answer prayers. The problem was his answer was usually no."

"Smart man, but that don't help me."

"Have you told the father?"

"Fuck him!"

I didn't touch that line. "Who is he?"

"Doesn't matter, just another jerk in a long line of jerks." She stood up and came to stand close by me. "It's your fault, you know."

"How's it my—"

"You know," she said, threading herself through my arms and wrapping hers around me. "Why don't you love me?"

"Carmella, we've been through this bef—"

She pushed the end of the word back into my mouth with her tongue. At first, I just took it, but I was returning her kiss soon enough. When I had allowed myself to fantasize about being with her, I told myself that a second kiss would never match the first. I was right. The second kiss was better. The first kiss had been rather chaste, more a tender brush of the lips, heavy with possibility and light on passion. This kiss would not be mistaken for a chaste brush of the lips. Her slight sigh broke the spell and I pushed myself away.

"I'm not doing this," I said.

"Not that again. That was forever ago. You can't keep punishing me for what someone else did to me."

"It's never been about that."

"Then what's wrong?"

"You mean other than your being pregnant?"

That quieted her. There was chemistry between us. There always had been, but this kiss had been about distraction, not chemistry. It had done a fairly good job of distracting me as well.

"Oh, Christ, Moe, what am I gonna do?" She pulled herself close again and rested her head on my chest.

"Do you want the baby?"

"Me? I'm a thirty-five year old, unmarried woman. What am I gonna do with a baby?"

"That's not an answer. Do you want it?"

"Yes and no."

"Now that's an answer," I said, once again stroking her hair. "How far along are you?"

"Not so far."

"Whatever you choose, you know, it's good with me."

"I know."

I reached under her chin and tilted her head so that she was looking up directly into my eyes. "Just one thing, Carm, don't think that because you're not far along that you have a lot of time. The longer you wait, the harder it will get. Whatever decision you make will be a permanent one and you'll have to live with it forever."

She smiled sadly. "Maybe not forever, but just as long as I live."

"Yeah, I guess everybody's forever is a little bit different."

Now she pushed herself away, wiping off what was left of the tears with the backs of her hands. "Come on, we got work to do. Go put that bottle away and then get your ass back in here."

By the time I returned to her office, she had completely regained her composure. I hadn't invested in this partnership because of her looks. Of the two of us, she was the professional detective. I'd only ever been in uniform. When Carmella needed to, she could be all business. You couldn't've worked homicide the way she had without the ability to check your emotions. There were times when her knack for emotional distance verged on antiseptic and, given what was going on with my family at the moment, that was probably a good thing. I was too close to it, way too close.

She slid a thick file across her desk. "That's what you asked for. You've got current addresses—home and business—phone numbers, email adresses ... everything. There's only one guy, this ... Judas Wannsee, that we're having a little trouble locating."

In 1981, Judas Wannsee was the leader of the Yellow Stars, a Jewish anti-assimilationist cult headquartered in the Catskill Mountains. His group had provided cover for the woman who had started the fire that killed my high school crush. The group had attracted some national media attention in the early part of the decade, but by 1990 had fallen into the creases of history the way pocket change disappears into the furniture.

"Okay, have Devo keep looking."

"So, where do we start?"

"*We* don't. I'm flying solo. There are some people I need to talk to by myself."

"Okay, but—"

"You still have that package in the office?"

Carmella knew what I was asking for and pulled a large plastic bag out of her drawer.

"Good. Patrick and his boyfriend Jack had that tattooed on their forearms."

"So you told me, but that had to have been at least—"

"—twenty-three years ago. I know, but I want you to send some people out to tattoo parlors to see if anyone's had a tat like this done within the last few months."

"Moe, these days aren't exactly like when my dad was young and the only people who got tattoos were sailors and bikers. There are probably more than a hundred tattoo and piercing joints in Manhattan alone. Maybe double that. Never mind the boroughs."

I suppose I hadn't given it a lot of thought. "You really think there's that many?"

"Shit, everybody's got ink these days."

"I don't."

"I do."

"You do! What of? Where?"

"You should've asked me that about twenty minutes ago. There's a good chance you would have seen for yourself. But we'll talk about that some other time. I bet you Sarah got one."

"I don't think so."

Carmella just shook her head and smiled at me. "Okay, so we're going tattoo hunting. Anything else?"

"Casting calls," I said.

"Casting calls! Tattoos and casting calls, what's this about exactly?"

"At the airport ..." I hesitated.

"At the airport what?"

"Remember when Raheem pointed and said that the guy that paid him to deliver the—"

"—package looked like the guy in the painting. I remember. He fed me that same line of crap when we had our little debriefing. The kid was trying to get over is all. He was full of shit."

"No he wasn't, Carm."

"What?"

"I saw him."

"You saw who?"

"Patrick."

"You outta your fucking mind?"

"I think maybe I am, but I know what I saw and I saw him."

"So maybe he really isn't dead," she said.

"No, he's dead."

"Wait a—"

"I didn't see an older, not a forty year old Patrick. I saw Patrick from when he was in college. And there's only two explanations for that. He was a ghost or a—"

"—look-a-like," she finished my sentence.

"If he wasn't a ghost, then somebody was shopping around for a replica and the best way to find one in this city is to hold auditions for a very special part."

"Okay, Moe, I can see how this would work, but I don't understand the why. Who could hate you guys this much?"

"When we find out who," I said, "the why will be self-evident."

"*If* we do."

"When we do. When!"

We discussed a few more details and I got ready to head back home. Carmella was still in her office. I stuck my head through the door.

"You gonna be all right?"

She didn't answer immediately. "Me? I guess I will be, but this isn't only about me anymore, is it?"

"I guess not."

"About before ... I ... I—"

"I won't pretend I'll be able to forget it, but don't worry about it."

"Safe home," she said, turning her chair back toward the window.

Safe home yourself, I thought, although I knew she'd be spending the night here. Would anyone walk past our offices and wonder about the light leaking through the bottom of the door?

When I got back to Sheepshead Bay, Sarah had gone. Her note said she had decided to spend a few days with her mom. It was the right choice for all of us, especially for Katy. Folded into the note were my Patrolmen's Benevolent Association card and Carmella's Detective's Endowment Association card. The post script read, "You were right, Dad. I was being a hypocrite. Thanks for the card and thank Carmella for hers, but I won't be needing them anymore."

Sarah really was the best of both Katy and me.

[CHAPTER NINE]

Although Aaron lived there and our biggest money maker was on Long Island, the place still gave me the chills. When I was growing up and kids from the neighborhood would vanish over summer vacation, there would be whispers about their families having fled to far off places with idyllic names like Valley Stream, Stony Brook, and Amityville or to places with unpronounceable names like Ronkonkoma, Massapequa, and Patchogue. It was all Siberia to me. I lived in secret dread that one of my dad's business ventures would finally succeed and that he'd move Mom, Aaron, Miriam, and me to one of those awful places where people lived in big houses on quiet streets. My fears might have been allayed had I bothered looking at a map to see that Brooklyn and Queens were actually part of Long Island. I needn't have worried in any case. My dad's bad fortune would tie me to Brooklyn forever.

Elmont was a faceless town that was close enough to the cityline to blow kisses at New York across the Queens border. It was the home of Belmont Park Racetrack where the third leg of the Triple Crown, the Belmont Stakes, was held every June. If not for the track, Elmont would be notable for being on the glide path to Kennedy Airport and for its cemeteries. My parents were buried in Elmont. In the end, I guess, they had moved to Long Island, but, as yet, without Aaron, Miriam, and me. I had come to see a man in Elmont about an empty grave.

I have heard it said that concentration camp survivors sometimes pass on their torments to their children, that the victims become the victimizers. I don't know if it's true or not. People say a lot of things. What I do know is that Mr. Roth had been my friend, a second father to me, and a surrogate grandfather to Sarah. He was affectionate, warm, funny, and philosophical in spite of what he had endured, maybe because of it. Yet he, by his own admission, had been an unfaithful husband and a negligent father. I knew about some of his failings, but had come by the knowledge indirectly.

Steven Roth, on the other hand, was so utterly familiar with his dad's failings that escaping their reach seemed beyond his ability or desire. Steven was a bitter, angry man, so full of rage there wasn't room in him for anything else but alcohol. That toxic mix of bitterness, rage, and alcohol had caused his father and himself nothing but grief. He had done a long bid in prison for manslaughter—a bar fight, of course—and a second stretch for DWI. He had been in and out of marriage, jail, and rehab so frequently by the time his father passed away, it was difficult to keep count.

We'd met a few times over the years and it was never pleasant. My relationship with his dad was a constant source of irritation, an allergen from which he could not find relief. Once, a few months before he died, Mr. Roth hired me to get his son out of some trouble, big trouble. But when that trouble went away, Steven Roth treated me not with respect or gratitude, but with contempt. It all came to a very ugly head at the memorial service for his dad. Steven was lit like a roman candle and in a particularly foul mood, spouting off about how his dad should have been buried, not cremated and how *he* should have been the one to see to his dad's remains. When he shouted at Sarah that he would see to burying *her* father, I punched his lights out. Aaron tells me, I was still swinging when they pulled me off him. All I remember was that he was smiling at me. Even though I'd broken his nose and split both his lips, he was smiling.

Walking up the few steps to the front door of the neat little saltbox Cape, I had second thoughts about not bringing Carmella along. If things got ugly this time, there might not be anyone around to pull me off. I held my finger a few inches away from the bell and rechecked

the address. Well kept houses on twisty quiet streets were not usually Steven Roth's style. Not unlike my late friend Rico Tripoli, Steven
Roth's taste ran to the darker edges of town, to places where the black-
ness of their souls blended in with the scenery. I couldn't speak to his
resources or to his abilities as a schemer, but there was no doubt he
hated me enough to hurt my family anyway he could. I pressed the bell
and listened to the muted chimes ring inside the house.

When the door pulled back, I stood facing a very attractive woman in her mid-forties. Beyond her broad smile and positively sparkling
blue-gray eyes, it was difficult to say what was so attractive about her.
Her face, in fact, was rather plain and round and her hair was a mousy
brown. She was thin, I guess, but her generic jeans and sweatshirt did
nothing to highlight her shape. Yet there was something undeniably
appealing about her.

"Good morning," she said without a hint of guile or wariness.

"Hi, my name's Moe Prager. I was wondering if Steven—"

"Moe Prager! Moe Prager. Steven will be thrilled you're here." She
beamed and shouted over her shoulder, "Honey, come here, there's
someone to see you."

I was sure I wasn't dreaming it, but not of much else. I was having
a full out *Twilight Zone* moment. Then, when Steven Roth appeared
with his right hand extended and a wide peaceful smile on his face, I
thought to look for the hidden camera. When he took my hand, shook
it, embraced me, I was still in shock.

"Praise Jesus, my prayers have been answered."

"Praise Jesus," the woman repeated.

"Moe, this is my wife Evelyn. Evelyn … Moe Prager."

We shook hands.

"Come on in, Moses. That is what Steven's father called you,
right?" she asked, folding her arm in the crook of my elbow. "Come
have some coffee with us."

"Yes, he called me that and Mr. Moe most of the time."

"Steven has told me a lot about you and his father. I want to hear it from you."

The three of us sat around the kitchen table and shared coffee in a sort of stunned silence. Then Steven, who still bore the bend in his nose from when I broke it, spoke up.

"I'm sorry, Moe, for treating you the way I did in the past. I was such an angry and empty man until I accepted the Lord Jesus Christ as my savior. When Evelyn and I found each other and God in AA, I just knew this day would come. I should've sought you out, but I was weak and afraid. Even with the Lord, I have my weaknesses and my bad days. Jesus has forgiven me, but I have prayed for the strength to come speak to you and ask your forgiveness. I can only pray for my father's forgiveness, but I can ask for yours."

"Sure, Steven, I forgive you." Then I put his alleged faith to the test. "It's what your dad would want me to do." If anything would set him off and cut through his "The New Me" veneer, it was those words.

He smiled. "You always were a clever man, Moe, but you can't rattle my cage. The pain and rage are gone. I don't blame you for not believing me. I was a pretty awful human being for a very long time. I think my dad loved how sharp you were. You were clever and quick like him. I am glad he had you to comfort him in his later years. Lord knows, I was no comfort."

"No," I said, "you weren't, but he always loved you. Your dad told me he wasn't a very good father or husband. In some ways, I think Izzy felt he deserved what you put him through."

"No one deserves what I put him through or what happened to him in the camps, but growing up, it was so hard for me to have perspective. My life was one long terrible journey of understanding, a long lonely time with a cold heart in a barren desert. Then I was saved."

Tears were pouring down Steven Roth's face. Evelyn reached across the table and clutched her husband's hand. They bowed their heads in silent prayer. After a few seconds and almost simultaneously, they looked up and said, "Amen."

I stayed for about another half hour. Steven showed Evelyn and me some old family pictures. It was good to see Israel Roth's face again. In some of the photos, he was a young man. I had never before seen him as a young man. The emotional scars from the camps were more evident, the pain much closer to the surface in those days. I told some stories about Mr. Roth and me and how well he treated us over the years. Still, Steven showed no signs of resentment whatsoever.

"I'm glad that my dad could open his heart to someone and that all the love he had to give did not die locked up inside him."

Evelyn and I said our goodbyes in the kitchen. I thanked her for her hospitality and wished her well. She assured me that as long as she followed the path that the Lord Jesus Christ had laid out for her and Steven, they would be well. Steven Roth walked me to the door.

"Thank you, Moses," he said before once again embracing me. "You've helped lift a terrible weight off my shoulders."

"Steven, I can't explain it, but seeing you and Evelyn like this ... Well, it's done the same for me."

"I know you don't believe, but I also know that the Lord Jesus Christ has a place in his heart for you and can show you the way if you just look."

"I've always been good at finding things by myself," I said.

"Sometimes, it's not the finding so much as being prepared to accept what you find."

I drove around the corner and parked. My car was still, but my mind was all over the place. Hypocritical, intolerant, money-grubbing TV preachers made it kind of easy for the rest of us to turn devout Christians into cartoonish caricatures, but there was nothing remotely cartoonish about the time I'd just spent with Steven Roth and his wife. I hadn't known Evelyn before she found God. I had, however, known Steven and he truly was a changed man. He was right, I didn't believe and I was unlikely to ever believe, yet who was I to argue that Jesus Christ hadn't saved him?

Sitting there, I realized that neither Steven nor Evelyn had once asked me why I'd come. When God answers your prayers with something other than a resounding no, you don't question it. For them, my appearance on their doorstep was as much an act of God as the sun showing through the clouds or a landslide or hurricane. The appeal of turning yourself over to that kind of faith was not lost on me nor was the danger of it. The dangers of it certainly weren't lost on Israel Roth.

I thought a lot about Mr. Roth that day. I knew he would have been pleased that his son had found peace, however he'd come to it, and a woman to love who loved him back. He would also have been very pleased over his son's forgiveness. Of all the pain he took to his grave, the rift with his son troubled him most. I thought back to that long ago day in the cemetery and his talk of spreading the ashes of the dead on the walkways at Auschwitz so the Nazis wouldn't slip on the snow and ice.

"But I've never stopped spreading the ashes," he had said.

Maybe now he could stop.

"Rest in peace, Mr. Roth," I said, the shadow of a passing 747 darkening the sky overhead. I waited for the sun to return before putting my car in drive.

When I first met Nancy Lustig, I didn't know or like Old Brookville or the surrounding towns very well, but for the past decade Aaron and I owned a store right on the cusp of Long Island's legendary Gold Coast. Now that I knew the area, I liked it even less than I had all those years ago. People with money, especially newfound money, have a bizarre sense of entitlement that was hard for me to take. So in spite of the fact that Red, White and You was our most profitable location, it was my least favorite. During its inaugural year, when I managed the store, I used to imagine Nancy Lustig wandering into the shop some-day. I would imagine the surprise on her face and the conversations we might have. She never appeared, not while I was there.

Nancy Lustig had dated Patrick Maloney when they were at Hofstra together. She was from a rich family that owned a house—a mansion, really—less than a mile from our store. Nancy was a squatty girl back then and to have called her plain looking would've been giving her way more than the benefit of the doubt. She was an ugly girl, but so brutally honest with herself that I was awed by it. I think that's why she had always stayed with me. There's all kinds of brave. Sometimes, honesty is the hardest kind.

Frankly, I'd gotten so caught up in finding Patrick and with falling in love with his sister, that I completely lost track of Nancy. The last I recall, she had moved out west—Northern California, I think—shortly after the debacle with Patrick, but I can't even remember if that was something I actually heard or some invention of my own that I had simply come to accept as fact. It's a funny thing about getting older. You lose a sense of how much of your past is real and how much of it is self-fabrication and filler your mind spins out in order to let you sleep nights. I'm not certain if the ratio of real to imagined was knowable, that I'd want to know it. How many of us would, I wonder?

It took me a few seconds to be certain that the woman who answered the door was Nancy Lustig. Obviously, she was older now, but that wasn't what threw me. While I wouldn't have called her a knockout, the woman in the doorway was ... I don't know ... Attractive, I guess. Not from the inside out, the way that Evelyn Roth was attractive. It was more in the way the woman before me was put together. The thick, unflattering glasses were gone in favor of blue contacts. Her hair fell a few inches over her shoulders and was now a sort of dark blond with expertly blended highlights. The longish, lighter hair was a nice compliment to the new shape of her face. Nancy had lost at least thirty pounds, but more than diet had gone into resculpting her face. There were cheekbones, high ones, an angular jawline, fuller lips and a pert, provocative nose. Her makeup was flawless and her tennis outfit showed off a tanned, well-muscled body. The tight red polo shirt accented the shape of her new, gravity-defying breasts. Nancy crossed one leg in front of the other, tapping the floor impatiently with the tip her court shoe.

"Can I help you?"

"Moe Prager. We met back in the late Seventies."

She squinted, as if she hoped squeezing her eyes together might help her see into the past. Apparently, squinting was no help with time travel.

"Sorry," she said, "I got nothing."

"Patrick Maloney."

That did the trick. She screwed up her new face as if she'd just caught a whiff of steaming hot dog shit. I didn't blame her. It hadn't exactly been a storybook romance between Patrick and Nancy. In a desperate attempt to deny his homosexuality and cope with his burgeoning OCD, Patrick engaged in a series of doomed relationships with women. With Nancy Lustig, the inevitable bad ending was particularly ugly. There was a visit to a sex club, an aborted pregnancy, and violence. He dislocated her shoulder and might've done much worse had other students not pulled him off her.

"The detective. Yes, I remember." She didn't ask me in.

"That's right. How have you been?"

"Look, what's this about, Mr. Prager?"

"Moe, please."

"Let's stay on point. What's this about?"

"Patrick."

"Sorry, not interested," she said. "What, he woke up from a coma and wants to apologize or something? He develop a conscience after twenty years?"

"Nothing like that. Patrick's dead."

"Did he remember me in his will?"

"It happens that he was murdered shortly after he disappeared."

If I thought that would shake her up, I thought wrong. She yawned. I might have told her I stepped on an ant.

"You'll have to excuse me, Mr. Prager, but I'm leaving to play tennis in a little while, so if there's nothing—"

"You sure have changed," I said, trying a new tack.

She wasn't sure how to take that. "Thank you ... I think."

"Oh no, I meant it as a compliment," I lied. "You're quite lovely."

"Thank you," she said, flashing a satisfied smile. "It was a lot of hard work to bury dumpy old Nancy."

"I don't know, there were parts of her I kinda admired."

Nancy scowled at me like Father Blaney. I looked for clouds to move in overhead.

"Admired! What did you admire, my desperation? My willingness to take crumbs and castoffs? My—"

"Your honesty."

"Oh, that. Honesty's easy when it's all you have."

"I'm not sure it's ever easy."

"Why admire someone for something when they have nothing else? It's like admiring an amputee for still having the other leg. These," she said, running her hands over her now exquisite breasts, "are something to admire. On the whole, Mr. Prager, you can keep honesty. I'll take these. No one desires you for your honesty." She dropped her hands back to her sides.

"Why is it one or the other?"

Just then, as if on cue, a Land Rover pulled into the long driveway and beeped its horn.

"I prefer tennis to questions of metaphysics. Now, if you'll excuse me ..."

"Sorry to have bothered you," I said, and walked back to my car. I rolled out of the driveway onto Route 107 and parked. A few minutes later, the green Land Rover pulled onto the road and disappeared, heading north. I had to go north too, but I needed some time to mourn the old Nancy Lustig.

So I went from money to more money, from new money to old.

In the early 80s, Constance Geary worked for Aaron and me at City On The Vine for about six months while she finished up at Juilliard. She was pleasant enough, a hard worker, good with the clientele, but we never fooled ourselves she would stay on. I had the impression she got her hands dirty with the common folk as if she were fulfilling a missionary obligation. You know, like teaching Third World children how to read. Or maybe it was just so she could say, "Hey, I had a job once." It wasn't Constance I was interested in, but her father.

It was Thomas Geary who'd hired me in 1983 to find out what had happened to Moira Heaton and to resuscitate State Senator Steven Brightman's political career. I'm not certain to this day if Geary cared for Brightman in the least or if he simply fancied himself a kingmaker. After all, what else was there for him to do besides being wealthy and playing golf? Geary was one of those men who saw golf as universal allegory. If you understood the intricacies of the game, you'd see that life and golf were just the same. *Yeah, right!* Maybe Steven Roth should have taken up golf instead of God. I mean, who needs the New Testament when you've got a copy of the USGA Rule Book.

Crocus Valley was at the WASPy heart of the Gold Coast, a place where plaid pants and Episcopal priests never went out of fashion. Don't get me wrong, the residents of Crocus Valley had made concessions to the new millenium. Some even painted the faces of their lawn jockeys white! Behind the artiface of taste and restraint, the residents of CV were as screwed up as any other bunch of rich fuckers. I would know. I was privy to their liquor bills. If they ever considered changing the town's name, Single Maltville would have been perfectly appropriate.

The Geary place was on a bluff overlooking Long Island Sound and bordered on the east by The Lonesome Piper Country Club. It was at the Lonesome Piper, during Connie's wedding reception, that I first met Thomas Geary. He took me for a stroll along the driving range. During our short walk, he managed to lecture, threaten, and bribe me. All of it done with a calm voice and unwavering smile. He was a reflection of the town in which he lived. On the outside he was all class: well-bred, well-mannered, a perfect gentleman. But beneath his well-tanned skin, Geary was as much a thug and bully as Francis Maloney ever was, only less honest about it.

The corral-type fencing that once surrounded the white country manor had been replaced by a contiguous stone wall. There was an ominous black steel gate now as well. No longer could you simply turn off the road and into the estate. Anchored by massive stone pillars, the gate was a good twelve feet high, double the height of the wall. On one pillar was a security camera, on the other a call button and speaker. Childishly, I waved hello at the camera, then pressed the call button.

"Yes, who is it?" A woman's voice asked.

"My name's Moe Prager. I was wondering if—"

"Moe! This is Connie. Come on, drive up to the house. I'll meet you out front."

The gate swung open even before I made it back to my car. Connie met me under the front portico just as her father had seventeen years before on my first and only visit to the ten acre estate. She was very much the same as I remembered; more handsome than pretty. Looking at her now, I realized Constance was naturally what Nancy Lustig had had tried to make herself into.

"Moe, my God, look at you!" Connie grabbed both my hands and kissed me on the cheek. "You look great. How are you? Come inside."

I followed her into the house. It too was as I remembered it, at least the décor hadn't much changed. There was, however, an unmistakable medicinal tang in the air and a metal walker in the foyer next to an incongruous pair of hockey skates. Connie noticed me notice.

"The walker's Dad's. The skates are Craig Jr.'s."

"A son, *mazel tov*. Any other kids?"

"No. Craig's my pride and joy," she said.

"How's Craig's dad?"

"Fine. We're divorced almost ten years now."

"Sorry."

"Don't be. It was all very amicable. We're all better off this way. You were at the wedding, weren't you? I remember you being there. You and Katy, Aaron and Cindy, right?"

Just ask your dad. "We were indeed."

"How is Aaron? I always had a kind of crush on him, you know?"

Of course I didn't. I loved my big brother and he was a good look-ing man, but it was hard for me to imagine Connie falling for him.

"He'll be quite honored to hear it."

"Oh, God, please don't tell him." She turned bright red. "I'm so embarrassed."

"Don't worry, your secret's safe with me." I'm certain she had no idea how safe. "Aaron's great. You know, we own a store not too far from here?"

"Red, White and You. Yes, I've been there a few times, but no one I remember was around."

"Klaus and Kosta are still with us. They even own a part of the business now."

"Are they both still crazy?"

"As crazy as ever." I changed subjects. "The walker, you said it was for your dad."

"Used to be. He's pretty much bedridden these days. Alzheimer's," she said, as if that explained everything. I guess maybe it did. I watched Alzheimer's rob my friend and Pulitzer Prize winning journalist, Yancy Whittle Fenn of everything he ever had. First it erased his memory, then it erased him.

"Sorry."

"That sorry I'll accept."

"Your mom?"

"She's summering out West with some friends."

"You take care of your dad?"

"We have round the clock nursing, but I see him a lot. We can afford to keep him close to the things he loved. I'm not sure how much of him is left. We take him down to the stables when we can. He seems to still enjoy that."

"I remember he liked horses. Do you ride anymore?"

"Some."

"The piano?"

"The great love of my life, Moe. Yes, I still play. Come on, I'll get us a drink and I'll play for you."

"I could use a drink and I'd love to hear you play."

"Scotch with ice, right?"

"Good memory," I said. "Do you think I could go see your dad while you get the drinks?"

"Sure, but I don't think he'll remember you."

"That's okay, I'll remember for the both of us."

"Is that why you came, to see my dad?"

"It was, but no biggie. It wasn't that important," I lied. There was no need to add to anyone's pain. I had my answer. If he was in as bad a shape as Connie said, Thomas Geary wasn't involved in Patrick's resurrection. "Listen, Connie, does your dad ever hear from Steven Brightman?"

"Steven Brightman, now there's a name I haven't heard for a long time."

"That's a no then?"

"Absolutely. Once Steven resigned, I think my dad lost interest. Until then, he was one of Dad's pet projects. He is—was a very project oriented man, my dad. But if it's really important for you to know, I can ask Mom."

"No need. I'll just run up and see your dad and then I'll be down so I can listen to you play."

The medicinal smell was strong in Thomas Geary's room. His TV was on. He paid it as little heed as it paid him. Geary may once have been a bastard, but I could feel only pity for him now. His eyes were vacant, his mouth was twisted up into a confused smile. It was a clown smile absent the makeup and the humor. He looked so very lost, seeming to have forgotten not only who he was but what he was. I recognized the expression. Wit—Y.W. Fenn—wore it for the last year of his life.

I opened my mouth to speak to Thomas Geary, but closed it before any words came out. I might just as well have spoken to the TV. I left him as I found him.

Back downstairs, Connie handed me a glass of single malt—what a surprise—and had one herself. I expected her to play something dark and moody, but got Gershwin and show tunes instead. This way we could talk a little while she played. I told her about Sarah, about my own divorce. I didn't go into details. Connie said all the right things, cooed and sighed in the proper places in my stories, but I could tell she had built some walls of her own. The divorce, her dad's Alzheimer's were tough on her. I remembered something Mr. Roth had once said to me, "Money is a retreat not a fortress." Looking at the pain behind Connie's eyes and listening to it behind her pleasant chatter, I knew Israel Roth was right.

When I said my goodbyes, Connie held onto my hand a little longer than I would have expected and asked me if we might not go to dinner sometime. To talk about old times ... As friends, of course ... *Of course!* I thought about what had become of Nancy Lustig, how the brutal honesty had remained, but her humanity seemed to have vanished. I told Connie that I'd love to go to dinner. Who was I not to throw her a rope?

Time travel, I thought as I rode through the center of Crocus Valley, was not for the faint of heart. I had supposed, foolishly perhaps, that after my father-in-law's passing and the fallout from our shared secrets had taken its toll, that I could put the past behind me. However, the past, it seemed, was not set in granite, but rather as fluid as the future. I was as incapable of shaping one as the other. The past, *my* past, sang a siren's song to me that was beyond my ability to resist and I was forced to reach deeper and deeper into my pockets to pay the price each time I succumbed. By any measure, it had been a weird fucking day and I was off balance, way off.

Driving did nothing to restore my equilibrium. I just kept rehashing the events of the day. No one was who they used to be. They had all changed, some for better, some for worse, with no regard for my expectations. Steven Roth, Nancy Lustig, Connie and Thomas Geary, had had time to evolve, time to ease into their new skins, but for me it was disorienting. From where I stood—*Presto change-o!*—they had morphed almost before my eyes. That was wrong, of course. It had happened during the long overnight between last meetings.

I flipped the visor down, not only to block out the sun. I pulled open the lighted mirror on the back of the visor and stared at myself. How much, I wondered, peering at my tired-looking reflection, had I changed without noticing? I thought back to philosophy class at Brooklyn College.

Essay #1

If you own a car for a number of years and over the course of those many years you replace part after part, at what point does that car cease being the original car? Does that car ever cease being what it once was? If you were to replace every part, would it cease being the old car?

I can't remember what I wrote exactly. Probably something about the essence of the car remaining unchanged. I think I argued that proximity of time and of old parts to new kept the original essence of the car intact in spite of all other factors. In conclusion, I think I wrote, unless you were to change all parts all at once, the original car remains. I wasn't so sure I believed that anymore. I wasn't sure I believed it then. What did I know in college, anyway?

If I thought today's disorientation or looking in the mirror would lead me to any brilliant new insights or deeper truths, the blare of horns, the rapid *tha-dump tha-dump tha-dump tha-dump* of my tires against the grooves at the road's edge and the pinging of gravel in my car's wheel wells, dissuaded me from that notion. I jerked the wheel left and got the car back on the road. I flipped up the visor and tried as hard as I could not to use my rearview mirror. I had enough looking back for one day, thank you very much.

My cell phone buzzed. It was Sarah. Yes, it had been a weird fucking day and it was about to get weirder.

[CHAPTER TEN]

The dull green house at 22 Hanover Street was essentially unchanged from the first time I saw it in the winter of 1978. Neat, unadorned, perfectly maintained, the house had been a reflection of its owner, Francis Maloney Sr. I thought my ex-wife, a graphic designer by trade, might brighten the exterior when she moved in. Slap on a fresh coat of white paint, at the very least. Now as it was more a memorial to than a reflection of my father-in-law, I suppose Katy felt the need to keep up appearances. She claimed to hate her father and everything about him. But who knows, really? It was nearly impossible for me to figure out what she felt about anything anymore? At least she didn't feel the need to let the memorial extend past the front door. Katy had pretty much redone the interior of the house. It was more comfortable, more about her and what she'd become than preserving where she'd come from.

The first time I came, it was winter. Snowmen tipsy from the thaw had stood guard as I rolled down the street. A noisy oil truck was making a delivery at the house next door. But on a hot July night, with ice cream truck serenades in the background and the green flashes of lightening bugs filling the air, that first time seemed forever ago. Except for the sheriff's car parked in Katy's driveway, it might have been a perfect summer evening.

The TV was tuned to CNN. Larry King was breathless over the minutiae of this week's scandalous cotton candy or trial of the century. His panel of talking heads was, each in turn, louder and more hysterical than the next. Given the rapt attention of Sarah and Sheriff

Vandervoort, I might have thought they were witness to the second coming.

"Hey, I hate to interrupt Larry King, but—"

"Sorry, Dad." Sarah clicked off the tube.

Pete Vandervoort stood up and came over to me, shook my hand. I didn't like the look in his eyes. "Something's up," he whispered.

"No shit?" I turned to Sarah. "Where's your mom?"

"In bed."

"In bed. It's only—"

"Sarah, maybe you better give me and your dad a few minutes."

"Sure, Sheriff Vandervoort. Thanks for coming and staying with us. Dad, I'll be in the kitchen. You want something?"

"No, kiddo, that's okay."

"Sheriff?"

"No thanks." Vandervoort was careful to wait until Sarah was out of earshot. "We got a situation here that I don't understand. You sure you told me everything about the details concerning your brother-in-law's death?"

Of course not! "Yeah, why do you ask?"

"Come on outside a minute."

Vandervoort and I stepped out onto the little concrete stoop in front of the house. Two moths prayed at the altar of the porch light, unable to break free from the bonds of their devotion. The sheriff took a lazy swat at the faithful and refocused.

"It's not just about hearing voices anymore," he said. "She's seeing ghosts now too. That's why Katy's in bed. Took two of those pills the shrink at the hospital gave her."

"She called you?"

"No. Your kid did. Sarah's a beautiful girl … and smart. You should be proud of her."

"I am."

"Me and the wife don't have kids. Can't. We've been to every doctor in the county. Even went to see a few in the city. My family name dies with me."

"Siblings?"

"Two big sisters."

"How about adopting?"

"We've thought about it, but it's not for us, I don't think."

"I'm sorry, but—"

"No, I'm sorry, Moe. I got sidetracked there. So your daughter phoned me a few hours ago. She said that they were in town shopping, having lunch and your wife started acting funny."

"Funny?"

"Looking over her shoulder at odd times. Apparently, while they were at Molly's having lunch, Katy practically jumped out of her seat and ran out of the diner. When she came back, she was white," he said. "Your kid asked her what was the matter and she—"

"—wouldn't say. That's Katy. In most ways, she's nothing like her dad, but she couldn't escape him totally. She can hold stuff back sometimes. So what happened?"

"They stopped at the PrimeOil Station on the way back here. When Sarah was pumping the gas, your wife ran out of the car and darted across Stuyvesant Street. FedEx truck nearly cleaned her clock. She was pretty lucky, Moe. Took quite a spill. I guess when Sarah got her back here, Katy finally confided to her that she'd been seeing Patrick here and there all day long."

"Jesus Christ!" My jaw clenched.

"There's more to it."

"More how?"

"Come over to my car a second," he said, walking toward the Crown Vic. I followed. He reached into the front seat and came out holding a video tape. "The PrimeOil's been robbed a few times since they expanded it from just a gas station to a convenience mart. They got surveillance cameras all over the place now, so I figured I'd stop by on my way over here." He handed it to me. "Get it back to me when you're done with it."

"Is there something on it?"

"Wouldn't've told you about it if there wasn't."

Without thinking, I started for the house. Vandervoort grabbed my arm.

"Not so fast. You better wait till they're both asleep," he said. "Maybe we should talk in the morning."

The first part was a suggestion, the second part wasn't.

"Okay, Pete, I'll see you in the morning."

"Until tomorrow then." Vandervoort shook my hand and, like Connie before him, was slow in letting go. "Look, Moe, I like you and your family, but I'm going to need more from you than what I've gotten so far. Your wife isn't the only one holding back. Somebody's got to have it in for you and your family to go to this much trouble. That tape in your hand is a gesture of good faith on my part, so when you come by in the morning I hope you're in a generous and sharing mood. Do we understand one another?"

"We do."

He let go of my hand and said goodnight. I watched him pull away. Then I stashed the tape in the front seat of my car.

I made sure both Katy and Sarah were asleep before retrieving the cassette from my car. I watched the black and white surveillance tape over and over again. Apparently, the gas station had recorded and re-recorded over it a number of times. To say the images were muddy would be insulting to mud. Nonetheless, there was no mistaking Patrick. He knew he was on camera the whole time, giving a somber nod and salute when he came into the frame. He mouthed something that was beyond my abilities as a lip reader to decipher. The ghost wasn't taking any chances if someone thought, as Pete Vandervoort had, to retrieve the video. He arranged energy bars on the counter to spell out:

SO ALONE

The people behind this were good, very thorough. They had done their prep work, but the prep work was a blade that cut two ways. Yes, it meant they could pull off this haunting crap with great aplomb. It also meant they had done their research, the kind of research you can't do online or in libraries. That might be an opportunity for me. I rewound the tape and watched it again.

"There's something wrong."

I nearly had a heart attack. It was Sarah, standing in the dark of the hallway.

"How long have you been there?"

"Long enough. There's something about that guy that's just not right."

"Like what?"

"I'm not sure," she said, stepping into the living room. "I can't put my finger on it, but give me time."

"I don't think it's a ghost either, but it looks a lot like him."

"I guess."

"You're not the best judge, Sarah. You've only ever seen pictures of him and those are mostly ones of him before he changed."

"Changed?"

"Before he redid his hair, got the tattoo and the earring ... Just before. There aren't very many pictures of him like that."

"Yeah, Dad, but you also only know him through pictures." She knelt down by the screen and placed her right index finger on his face. "I'm telling you, something's just not kosher with this guy."

Sarah was right about one thing; I didn't actually know Patrick any better than she did. We'd never met, not face to face. It was just that Patrick, a man who was never really there, had consumed such an unnatural amount of my life that I felt as if I did know him. I shut off the VCR.

"Go back to bed, kiddo."

"I can't sleep."

"Me neither. Hey, you wanna go grab something at Molly's."

"Sure, Dad. Just let me throw some jeans on."

"I'll check on your mom."

Katy, still fully dressed, didn't stir when I came into the room. She seemed utterly zonked. We had shared the same bed for twenty years, but I wasn't sure I recognized the woman before me. It can take a lifetime to become familiar and only seconds to become strangers again. I made to leave, but stopped. I removed the message tape from her answering machine, took one more look at Katy, then left.

I think I knew something was wrong even before I turned the car back onto Hanover Street. Sarah sensed it too. I could see it in her expression.

"Dad, what did you do with the security tape?"

"Oh, shit!"

Our worst fears were confirmed when we saw the flickering light through the otherwise opaque living room window. It was a bit of a blur from then on. I couldn't remember putting the car in park or closing the car door behind me or putting the key in the front door lock. The first thing that stuck was the image of Katy laying face down in a sea of broken glass, blood oozing out of the gash on her forehead, the VCR remote clenched in her right fist.

"Dad! Dad!" Sarah was screaming. It didn't register as screaming. Her panic reached me as a tiny voice at the end of a kid's string and soup can telephone. "Dad, Mom took pills, lotsa pills."

I think I said for her to grab the bottles. I was already carrying Katy to the car.

[CHAPTER ELEVEN]

When Vandervoort came in, I jumped at him.

"This isn't funny anymore, Pete," I growled, pinning him to the wall. "This is attempted fuckin' murder."

If anyone in the emergency room waiting area hadn't heard the first part of my rant, that second part surely got their attention. I must've been pretty scary, not because Vandervoort looked frightened—frankly, I was rage blind and couldn't've described the sheriff's expression—but because a steel hand clamped down on my right shoulder.

"You okay, Sheriff?" a deep voice wanted to know.

"I'm fine. Thanks for asking. He's just a little upset is all."

Deep Voice was unconvinced. "You sure?"

"Why don't you go and sit back down," Vandervoort said. "You look like you could use some help yourself. What the hell happened to you?"

"Had to lay my hog down when some asshole in a SUV ran the light at Blyden and Van Camp."

The steel clamp eased off my shoulder and I turned. I regained the use of my right arm and my vision. Deep Voice was a big man, barrel-chested with a beer keg belly to match. He had a thick neck and thicker arms that were covered in blood and tattoos. He had a young doughy face, but was no kid. His gray beard was braided like a pirate's. It too was soaked with blood and the gash on his forehead was nastier than Katy's.

"Don't go anywhere. When I'm done with this gentleman," Vandervoort said, nodding at me, "I want to talk about your accident. Maybe we can discuss why you weren't wearing your helmet."

"Okay, Sheriff." Deep Voice was sheepish, touching his hand to the cut on his head. He went and found his seat.

I backed off Vandervoort and gave him the details as we walked outside.

"She was totally asleep when we went to Molly's. I didn't think—"

"Stop beating yourself up over it. You couldn't know what she was going to do. Where's your kid?"

"She's in the treatment area with her mom."

"So that guy on the videotape with the candy bar message, he—"

"—looks an awful lot like Patrick, but the tape's so fuzzy. It would be impossible to make a positive ID from it."

"Look, Moe, don't take this the wrong way, but your ex-wife did try to ... Well, she seems pretty convinced."

"So you believe in ghosts now too?"

"Nope, I'm just saying ..."

"I wasn't kidding in there, Pete. This isn't funny. If I catch that motherfucker, I'll—"

"Watch what you say and do," Vandervoort cut me off. "Maybe that's what these folks want, the ones behind all this. Your ex-wife goes off the deep end, you end up killing somebody and get shitcanned for life. Your daughter, for all intents and purposes, winds up an orphan. I'd say that's playing into their hands, wouldn't you?"

"You're right. You're right. I know you're right, but you shoulda seen Katy laying there on the broken coffee table glass. I thought she was dead, for chrissakes. Sarah was freaked."

"How is she now?"

"Sarah? She seems all right, but it's hard to know."

"And Katy, what do the doctors—"

"She'll be okay. They pumped her stomach. It's a good thing we got back when we did or more of that crap might've gotten into her system. They're keeping her here for observation."

"Maybe that's a good thing," he said. "I'll keep a man posted outside her door for the duration."

"Thanks, but I doubt they'll try anything here. Too many people around."

"Let's hope so. Listen, I better go talk to that biker in there, but don't forget our appointment later this morning."

"It's a date."

We shook hands. This time he gave my hand back promptly.

Sarah was waiting for me outside the treatment cubicle when I went back inside. She'd been strong through all of this, but now that the adrenaline was wearing off, the fear and exhaustion were showing through. She was white, her eyes shot red with blood. For the first time in her life, Sarah looked old. *Welcome to adulthood.*

"Dad, you're bleeding. Your shoulder."

"Oh, that," I said, pulling my shirt around to look. "No, that's sombody else's blood. A guy who had a motorcycle accident, put his hand on my shoulder."

For some reason, that was the last straw. Sarah broke down. She fell into my arms and began sobbing.

"Shhhhh, kiddo. It's okay. Everything will be okay. Shhhhh …"

When she was a little girl and would come crying about scraping her knee or some kid in her class making fun of her red hair, those words were magic. Now when I said them, she simply cried harder. Had she finally outgrown the magic, I wondered, or was it that the magic wouldn't work if the magician no longer believed in his powers?

Later that morning, I was quite amazed at how easily I rattled off the littany of secrets and sins to Sheriff Vandervoort. Yet, rattle them off I did. No hedging, no holding back, no compromising, no spin, just the raw, unvarnished facts. I suppose most of the people in my life knew some of the details of my involvement with the Maloneys, but drips and drabs of reality, no matter how sordid or saintly, never amount to the whole truth. And regardless of what people say, there is only ever one truth of things. There are different versions of reality, not of the truth.

Vandervoort now knew more about what had gone on between the Maloneys and me than anyone on the planet besides myself. By the look on his face, I wasn't so sure he was happy to hold the honor. It was a tossup as to whether Pete seemed more horrified by the revelation that Francis had once raped and beaten a transvestite prostitute or that he had once encouraged Patrick to commit suicide.

"Christ ... I'm not sure which I want to do more, throw up or take a shower," he said. "Do Katy and Sarah know any of this?"

"Not the real details, no. I've carried this shit around with me for twenty-two years. It ruined my marriage and that's where the damage has to stop."

"I'll do what I can. The thing is, I can see why someone might hate the father. And lord knows there's plenty of people who hate fags—sorry, gays, but that doesn't explain why this is going on. This has got to be about you," he said.

"That's the assumption I've been working under since it all started."

"Any ideas?"

"Too many, unfortunately."

"Anyone from around these parts?"

"Only the longest of longshots," I said.

"Yeah, like who?"

I hemmed and hawed a little.

"Look, Moe, I've cut you way more slack than—"

"You're right. I'm sorry. Secret keeping becomes second nature."

"Names."

"There's Katy's first husband, Joey Hogan, for one. I'm going to see him right now. Unofficially, of course."

"Of course. Who else?"

"Woman used to cut hair at the Head Shop, Theresa Hickey."

"Hot blond, married to a city cop, right?" Vandervoort asked, already knowing the answer.

"That's the one."

"Forget her. My big sister Mary knew Theresa Hickey. She dumped the cop years ago and moved down to Jupiter, Florida with some rich guy owns race horses. She hasn't been back here since."

"Tina Martell?"

Vandervoort smiled sadly at the mention of her name. "Sure I know Tina. She owns Henry's Hog over—"

"I know the place. Outside of town, over the tracks, right?"

"That's the one."

"She owns it?" I asked.

"Her old man left it to her. What's old Tina got to do with this?"

"Probably nothing," I said, "but remember when I was telling you about how Patrick had gotten a few girls pregnant?"

"Tina?"

"Yeah, Tina."

"Well, fuck me. I can't quite picture old Tina and Patrick. You know, Moe, for a—for a gay guy, this kid got a lot of—"

"It's testament to how hard it was for him to come to terms with who and what he was."

"I guess."

"I gotta get to the hospital. They've moved Katy into a room and I want to make sure all the bases are covered."

"Room 402," he said. "You'll find a deputy outside her door."

"Thanks, Pete."

"Remember, Moe, keep me posted."

Just as Vandervoort had promised, there was a deputy outside Katy's door. It was Robby, the young deputy who had stood out in the rain with me at the Maloney family gravesite. He smiled at noticing me and, I suppose, at the chance of conversation. There are aspects of policework that can be mind-numbingly dull. None duller than guard duty. The deputy assured me that everything had been quiet, that the only people to enter the room were nurses and doctors and not too many of them. As a matter of courtesy, I asked the deputy if I might not take a look myself. He liked that I asked.

Katy was asleep, but unnaturally still. I don't know, maybe that was my brain talking and not my eyes. Her attempted suicide had changed everything. For all our years together, I had assumed Katy was a rock, that she could bear anything. Only once, when she miscarried, did she break down. Even then, I thought she recovered well and had gotten back to the business of life quicker than most. But now I wasn't so sure I knew who my ex-wife had been all those years. Had she misled me or had I misled myself? Did I see who she wanted me to see or did I see who *I* wanted to see? Had she hidden the pain from me or had I blinded myself to it?

I thought about lifting the sheets to see if her wrists were restrained, considered consulting the attending psychiatrist to find out if Katy was sedated or if her sleep was a natural reaction to the trauma. I did neither. It was all I could do to swallow up the guilt I was already feeling. I knew I couldn't handle anymore revelations about the myths of our marriage, not now, not yet. When I walked back past Robby, he called out to me. Something about last night's Mets score, I think. For some reason it just made me angry, really angry, but not at him.

I started toward Joey Hogan's house. *Joey, what kind of name is that for a grown man, for chrissakes?* Joey was Katy's ex. Now I suppose, first ex is more accurate. Not that I had anything against him. On the few occasions fate had thrown us together, he had been more than cordial, friendly really. He was a stand up guy who cared so deeply for Katy that if another man made her happy, well then, that was okay with him. They had been high school sweethearts. Katy grew out of it, but Joey never did. As Katy said, she agreed to marry him for all the wrong reasons. He was loving. He was handsome. He was a good provider. It was time.

"You don't marry a man because he scores well on some stupid test," Katy had said many times. "Marriage isn't about a checklist. It's about passion."

I wondered if she would still feel that way when she got out of the hospital and took stock of the last twenty years of her life. In any case, there wasn't any passion left between Katy and Joey by the time they took their vows before Father Blaney. And moving into his parents' house right after the wedding hadn't exactly enhanced the chances of their rekindling any dormant high school sparks. Their divorce had been relatively painless, at least for Katy, and had come as a relief for the both of them.

Francis Maloney loved to use Joey to get under my skin.

"He still loves my daughter, you know," my father-in-law jabbed at a family barbeque, Katy and Joey chatting happily at the opposite end of the backyard. "All she'd have to do is say the word and that boy would take her back, no questions asked."

"Except she's never going to say the word."

Then Francis would smile that smile at me, raising his glass of Irish. "Ah, don't be so sure, lad. Do you believe in ghosts?"

He'd always find some excuse to ask me that fucking question. I never quite understood what he meant by it. I did now, of course. Back then, when I didn't answer, Francis would have a private little laugh at my expense. It was a laugh with red fangs and talons.

"Are you laughing now, you prick?" I shouted out the window.

Joey Hogan's impeccably restored Victorian put a lie to the adage about the contractor owning the worst house on the block. Man, with the spindle work, wrap around porch, clapboards, rows and rows of fish scale and diamond siding, a lot of trees had given their lives to let that house live again. Between the turrets and gables, between the asymmetry and compound angles, there was enough visual noise to keep my eyes busy for a week. And forget about the color scheme. Only on a Victorian could you use twelve different colors—including lavender or purple—without getting arrested. But I guess maybe that's why I liked Victorians. They could break all the modern rules and still look beautiful.

I halfway pulled into the driveway and stopped, the ass end of my car sticking out into the street. Around here you could get away with that without getting the rear of your car sheared off. Truthfully, I didn't think Joey had a thing to do with what had happened at the gravesite or with torturing Katy. Even if he wasn't as comfortable with another man having his ex-wife as he let on, I knew as surely as I knew anything that he could never hurt Katy. I guess it was possible that he might hurt me, but he wouldn't use Katy to do it. Nor did I think he had much in the way of information that could shed light on who might actually be hurting my family, but based on proximity alone— his home was less than a quarter mile from the entrance to the cemetery—I had to talk to the man. Yet, for some reason, I couldn't quite bring myself to pull all the way down the driveway.

I was afraid. I was afraid that Joey Hogan might accuse me of fucking up Katy's life. I was afraid that he was right. But it wasn't Joey Hogan who accused me. Christ, I wasn't even fully into the man's driveway. My own guilt accused. Guilt and me were usually strangers. Like jealousy, guilt was a cancerous waste of time. The world was only too happy to beat you up, so why do it to yourself? Anyway, I was suspicious of the eagerly guilty. They stank of martyrdom.

"Responsibility and guilt are not the same things, Mr. Moe," Israel Roth used to say. "We all do wrong things for all kinds of reasons, mostly they're not worth losing sleep over. Besides, what does guilt change? A real man, a *mensch*, he knows when to feel guilt. When you've done what I had to do to survive, you know guilt. I can see in your eyes, Moses, that you too know guilt. For this you have my pity and my respect."

Because guilt and I were usually estranged, because it was not my first instinct, I knew when I felt it, that it was right. I felt it now and it was right. It was to laugh, no? One lie, a lie that wasn't even mine to begin with, still impacted lives in ways I could never have anticipated. I thought of Katy laying in the blood and broken glass. I thought of her lying so still in bed and imagined Joey Hogan's face as I tried explaining myself to him. I backed out of his driveway and drove away as quickly as I could.

Located several miles outside Janus in sort of a municipal no man's land, Henry's Hog was on the wrongest side of the tracks. When my tires crossed the pair of tracks on Industry Avenue, I could swear that the sun's light became more diffuse and the air got thicker and smelled of burning oil. The dust and decay, however, were not products of my imagination. Industry Avenue, once a meaningful designation, had long since given way to irony. Even before my first and only visit here, the area factories had already been abandoned. Now the only industry around here was of the cottage variety: meth labs and warehouse marijuana farms.

Henry's Hog, an old wood frame house that had been converted into a bar, hadn't much changed. The joint was as welcoming as a stuffed toilet and its windows were as yellow as a smoker's fingers. The desolate paint factory and auto body shop that had once bookended the place were now masquerading as empty lots. There weren't any bikes parked outside, but I tried the doors anyway. Pessimistic about success, I nearly fell inside when the door swung open.

Age hadn't much improved the interior of Henry's Hog either. The aroma was a vintage blend of black lung and beer piss. I wondered if the lazy fly that buzzed me as I stepped in wore a nicotine patch. A broad-shouldered woman in a Harley tee and black leather vest leaned over the bar, reading the *New York Post*. Her body jiggled as if she were laughing, but I can't say she made any sounds that I recognized as laughter. And because she had her head down, I couldn't see much of anything but the top of her short gray hair.

"Excuse me, I'm looking for Tina Martell."

When she raised up to face me, I knew I had found who I was looking for, but not all of her. Tina Martell had once been the girl most likely to fuck you because she felt like it. She liked sex and didn't dose it out like saffron or gold dust the way the other girls in town had. That hadn't won her a lot of close girlfriends back in high school, but it made her pretty popular with the boys. When I met her, she was thick-bodied and big-breasted, but she had a cute face with a friendly mouth. She was tattooed and pierced a good two decades before every suburban kid came with a nose ring and ink as standard equipment.

Now part of her neck and throat were missing and ugly scars obscured her tattoos. A flap of white material covered the front of her throat above her collar bone. She sort of resembled a Salvador Dali painting, the entire left side of her face drooping down toward the scarring. Although her shoulders were still broad, Tina's breasts were much smaller. Seeing her this way, I understood Vandervoort's sad smile and his confusion over Patrick and Tina. She raised a clenched right hand to her throat.

"Who is ... looking?" she asked in a robot voice, pressing her other hand to the white flap of cloth.

"Throat cancer?"

"Breast cancer ... too," she said, with an unexpected smile. "I'm thinking of getting ... skin cancer and going ... for ... the trifecta. Wait, you look ... familiar."

I explained that we had met once, many years before. She remembered.

"You bought me a ... beer."

"That's right. You told me to go fuck myself."

She liked that, giving herself the thumbs up.

I explained about what I was doing there. The last time we'd spoken, Tina Martell hadn't been particularly sympathetic to Patrick's plight or mine. Not that I blamed her. Patrick had gotten her pregnant and asked her to marry him just as he had later done with Nancy Lustig. For all I knew, there were other women with whom Patrick had danced that dance.

She shook her head a little bit, eyes looking into the past. "I don't know what to ... tell you. I never wished no harm to ... come to him. Wished harm on some, but not ... him. Lotta tragedy in that family ... lotta tragedy. Too bad about Frank Jr., he was ... hot."

"So you don't know anything about the desecration of the graves or about—"

"I got my own ... problems, mister. Don't need to cause none for ... others."

"You know anyone else who might have it in for the Maloneys?"

"The old man ... maybe. Someone might've had it in ... for him. He was a bona fide ... cocksucker."

"Amen to that."

"But I can't think of no one who'd want to hurt ... the daughter. Hey, you want a ... beer?"

"It's kinda early."

"Early's a matter of ... interpretation."

"Sure. Fuck it!"

She put a Bud up on the bar and went back to her paper. I tried searching for some follow up questions, but came up empty. When the bottle was likewise empty, I said my goodbyes and headed for the door. Before I got halfway there, a familiar figure came strolling on in. It was Deep Voice, the biker who'd been in the ER. The doctors had patched up his head, bandaged the nasty road burns and scrapes on his arms, washed the blood off his face and beard, but he was still wearing the shreds of the clothing he'd worn last night. He stared at me without recognition. I realized I still had trace amounts of cop vibe and that didn't work for him.

I put my hands up in submission. "Haven't been a cop for a long time," I said. "Besides, I'm kinda hurt you don't recognize me."

The light went on behind his eyes. "Last night in the hospital. You were all up in the sheriff's face. What was that about?"

I should have told him it was none of his business and walked out, but I didn't. For reasons I was only vaguley conscious of, I wanted to talk to this guy. I wasn't at all sure why. I suppose I figured the why would come to me eventually.

"Let me buy you a beer." He was thinking about it when I made the decision for him. "Tina, two Buds over here, please."

We sat down at a nearby table and waited for Tina.

"How you know Tina?" he asked in that low rumble of a voice.

"We're old acquaintances is all. So," I asked, "how are you feeling?"

"Sore as shit, but they sewed me together okay. I'll live. It's not the first time I've had to lay a bike down."

"I don't doubt it. You got a name?"

"Crank."

Great, I was buying beer for a meth cooker, but I didn't react other than to reach my hand across the table to him. "Moe."

Tina brought the beers over and I paid her. "Hey, Crank."

"Hey yourself, Tina."

She walked away shaking her head at the odd pair of us.

"So what about last night?"

"My ex-wife tried to kill herself." He stopped mid-sip, eyes wide. "That's why I was so agitated. It's a long story."

"Always is. Your old lady okay now?"

"She'll live, but she isn't okay."

"Here's to her," he said.

We clinked bottles. A question was wiggling around in the back of my head. I thought it might be about something Crank had said last night. I tried recalling what he had said to Vandervoort about his accident. Just as words started to come out of my mouth, my cell phone vibrated. The question vanished.

"Hey, I gotta take this," I said waving the phone at him. "Feel better. Enjoy the brew."

I walked outside in a near panic. "Hello."

"Moe, where are you at?" It was Carmella.

"You wouldn't believe me if I told you."

"Try me."

"Sharing a beer with a meth cooker named Crank."

"You're right, I think you're fulla shit."

"I'm up in Janus. Katy tried to kill herself last night."

"Oh my God! Is she—"

"She'll live. We can talk about it later. What's up?"

"Can you get into the office? We got something."

"I got something too," I said. "Let me check in with Sarah and then I'll be down. Make sure Devo's around."

"Okay."

"How are you and ... I mean—"

"I'm still pregnant, if that's what you're asking."

"It is."

"Don't let's start that now. I need to keep things together when I'm here."

"Fair enough."

I got in my car, crossed back over the tracks and out of un-Wonderland, but fragments of that question I had for Crank were still scratching around the back of my head. By the time I hit the interstate, they were gone.

It seemed to me that this was one case being played out in two worlds; one up here and one back in the city. The weird thing was that in spite of it all playing out with my family and me at center stage, I felt more like a spectator than a participant. I sensed Katy slipping completely out of my life and I was helpless to prevent it. Maybe that was best for both of us, but I couldn't let her slip out of my life and straight into hell. No, I owed her to make this right.

[CHAPTER TWELVE]

Carmella was out of the office when I got back into Brooklyn.

"Is she taking a late lunch or what?" I asked Brian.

"She don't report to me, boss. She just ran outta here ..." he checked his watch, "like forty minutes ago."

Brian Doyle was a project of ours. He was NYPD for about fifteen years. That he lasted so long was proof of God. Rough around the edges and a bit too quick with his fists, he was an old school cop three generations of cops too late. But Brian was perfect for us or would be, once he learned to listen. He knew the street and had a knack for getting information out of the most reluctant people. Brian had never had to rough anyone up while in our employ, at least not that we knew of. People could see the potential for violence in his eyes and that was enough. The whiff of violence usually is.

"How did she seem to you?"

"She seemed like the hottest fuckin' detective I ever seen."

"That's not what I meant."

"How the hell should I know how she seemed?"

"*Oy vey iz mir.* Forget it," I said, rubbing my eyes in frustration. "Carmella said she had something for me."

"She did?"

"Oh, for chrissakes! Doesn't anybody in this fucking place—"

Doyle was laughing so hard, he started gasping for air. Even Devo came out of his office with a wide grin on his face.

"Okay, gentlemen, you got me. Now can someone around here tell me what the fuck is going on?"

Brian and Devo looked at each other.

"You first, Devo," Brian said, still wiping tears from his eyes.

Devo's office looked like a cross between a recording studio and the cockpit of a B2 bomber. I had been wise enough never to ask who paid for all the equipment.

"Before we get started, take these." I handed him the surveillance tape from the PrimeOil station and the little cassette from Katy's answering machine. "Once you've had a look and a listen, you'll know what I want from you."

He took the tapes, laid them down on a shelf, and asked me to take a seat in front of a computer monitor.

"Here," he said, a newspaper ad flashing up on the screen, "is a notice for an audition that appeared in the *New York Minute* six months ago."

CASTING CALL

Male caucasians between the ages of 18-22, 150-160 lbs., 5'8" to 5'10". For leading role in an indie docu-drama. Experience a plus, but not required. Must be willing to travel. February 16th, 11:00 AM. LaGuardia Runway Inn, Ballroom B. Tilliston Casting.

"The *New York Minute*? Never heard of it."

"It is one of those free weeklies you can pick up in newspaper boxes on corners around the city. Very popular for advertising bands, selling cars, subletting apartments, promoting clubs and such."

"Yeah, okay, but what's the big deal about this ad? I don't know shit about casting calls, but there's got to be notices like this all the time."

"Look at the screen." He clicked the mouse. "This is that same notice in the *LA Freeway*. He clicked again. "In the *Second City Loop*. I found this notice in about twenty places in publications of this type dating back six to eight months. Only the location of the auditions is different."

"Someone was casting a wide net, so what?"

"Yes, a wide net, but a shallow one. One notice in *Variety* would get more turnout than one hundred of these type ads in smaller free presses. My supposition is that they were looking for a non-union, inexperienced actor. In fact, they weren't necessarily even looking for an actor. If one reads carefully between the lines, one might conclude they were looking for someone they might be able to manipulate."

"One might. Good points."

He bowed slightly. "Also, I did some checking. I found someone who went for the audition at LaGuardia."

"How'd you manage that?"

Devo smiled slyly. "Come now, Moe, need you ask?"

"I know, I know, that's why we pay you the big money. So what did this guy you found have to say?"

"He said it was the oddest audition he ever attended. They didn't ask him to run lines, to do a scene or to discuss his training or experience. Apparently, it truly was like a cattle call. Appearance ... everything was about appearance. They had a very specific set of parameters even beyond what was listed in the ad. You had to have a certain type of complexion and visible tattoos were strictly verboten."

"That's odd," I said. "I thought movie makeup could cover anything."

"It can ... on film, but what if the role required—"

"—live appearances?"

"Precisely."

"Moe, pick up line two. It's your daughter," Brian's voice came loud over the intercom.

"Excuse me a second, Devo." I picked up. "Is everything okay with—"

"Mom's fine, Dad. I mean, as fine as can be expected. I just saw her and I think she's more embarrassed than anything else."

"Good. I'll be coming back up there tonight to check on you guys. Is the deputy still outside the door?"

"The cute one, Robby? Yeah, he's still there."

"Too much information, kiddo. Way too much."

"Oh, Dad, grow up. Besides, I have something I want to tell you."

"What?"

"Remember when we were watching that video of Uncle Pat—I mean, of the guy posing as Uncle Patrick?"

"I remember."

"I said something wasn't right about him even though he looked just like the pictures of Uncle Patrick."

"Yeah."

"I know what it is," she said. "He was too comfortable on camera, too much at ease."

"I'm not sure I'm getting you."

"Look, Dad, think about those old pictures of your family from Russia. You know how they're all so stiff and unsmiling and their eyes have that deer in the headlights thing going on. Then think about your folks' generation and then yours. People got more and more comfortable with having their pictures taken, but not necessarily with being videotaped. My generation is really the first generation that's grown up on video. Births, our first steps, first baths, birthday parties, bat mitzvahs, weddings, sweet sixteens, baseball games, dance recitals, almost everything my generation has done our parents taped. We're really used to being in front of the camera. We like it. Being on tape is ... For us, it's affirmation. All the people I go to college with have cameras on their computers. And Uncle Patrick was killed in what, nineteen seventy-sev—"

"—seventy-eight," I corrected.

"But you get my point. That was way before the ever present, all-seeing eye. That guy on the tape is no ghost, he's my age."

"Funny you should say that. I think Devo's arrived at the same conclusion. Thanks for the assist. I'll see you later." That was met with a very loud silence from the other end of the phone. "Okay, Sarah, what is it?"

"I think you should leave Mom alone for a little while. Like I said, she's pretty embarrassed and feeling kinda stupid about this. If she feels you're there to judge her or … I just think you should give her some time. I can look after her for now."

It bugged me that Sarah twice mentioned Katy being embarrassed, but I couldn't say why exactly. There seemed to be a lot of things I didn't have answers for just lately. In any case, I didn't pursue it.

"I'm very proud of you, Sarah. I think I'll take your advice, at least for a day or two. But I want to know if anything happens with your mother. I mean anything. Deal?"

"Deal."

"Love ya."

"Love you too, Dad."

I put down the phone and recounted Sarah's theory to Devo, after first explaining what was on the videotape I had given him.

"My guess," I said, "is that the guy you'll see on that tape is the guy who got the part."

"Yes, personal appearances and all. Why don't you go talk to Brian while I get started with the tapes?"

I hesitated. "Just one more thing. This Tilliston Casting, they legit?"

"I am afraid not. They were a post office box and a phone number. The phone number has been disconnected and the PO box closed."

I made a move for the door. Devo called after me.

"One last thing, Moe. Judas Wannsee."

"What about him?"

"Here." Devo handed me a folder. "I have tracked him down. He was a difficult man to find."

"He would be."

"He has changed his name several times in the past decade, but you should be able to contact him there."

"Thanks."

When I stepped back out into the main office, Brian nodded at Carmella's office.

"She's back, in case you're interested."

"Okay, but first, show me what you got."

Brian slid a Polaroid across the desk to me. It was of a freshly done tattoo. The tattoo was of a rose threaded through the Chinese character for eternity. 4/7/00 was written neatly across the bottom in black marker.

"By the way, boss, that ain't one Chinese character, but two that have been superimposed on each other. My bud tells me that even that's a sorta shorthand and that this one here means," he said, pointing at the back of one of his business cards, "long or no change. This one here means never eroding." He showed me the back of two more business cards. "The proper way to write it is like this or this here. These four mean forever and those four there stand for eternity."

"Thanks for the Chinese lesson. I don't know, Doyle, maybe we should can your ass and hire your friend."

"Maybe, but he ain't half as charmin' as me."

"I'd like to meet him. I've never met anyone completely devoid of charm before."

"Huh?"

"Forget it. Who'd you get the Polaroid from?"

"Mira Mira," he said, as if that were explanation enough.

It wasn't. "I'm listening."

"She's a tattoo artist. Works by appointment only and charges an arm and a fuckin' leg."

"Nice pun."

"Pun?"

"Never mind."

"Anyways, an old snitch of mine turned me onto her. When I showed this Mira Mira what I was lookin' for, she pulled that Polaroid right out of her ... whachumacallit ... her—"

"—portfolio."

"Yeah, her portfolio. She does Polaroids of every one of her creations. She even has photo portraits done of some of her work. She says those photos sell in galleries for thousands of bucks. Me myself, I don't see it, paying for a picture of a fuckin' tattoo."

"I don't think you're her target audience, Doyle. She tell you anything about the client?"

"White kid, twenty, maybe younger. Came in with a heavyset guy in his late sixties."

"Did she think they were lovers?" I asked.

Doyle cringed. "I didn't ask. She did say that the old guy had an eye patch over his left eye. Here's her contact info. I told her you might wanna talk to her."

I slid the Polaroid and the contact info into my jacket pocket. "I'm curious. Why'd she give you the Polaroid?"

"Because she said she was embarrassed that she had even done the job and ..." he hemmed and hawed.

"And ... I'm waiting."

"I paid her for it."

"Don't tell me how much. I don't want to know, not now, not when I'm thinking of telling you you did good. Just put in your reimbursement request to Carmella."

"Thanks, boss."

"And Brian ..."

"Yeah?"

"Don't pad the request because I'm going to ask this woman how much she charged you."

He opened his mouth to say something and thought better of it.

Carmella was once again sitting and staring out the office window. Only this time there was fire in her eyes and no tears to contain the flames.

"What an asshole!" she growled.

"Which one?"

"Me. The father. Take your pick."

"The father?"

"The baby's father. I told him that I was pregnant. That's where I was, meeting him for a drink. He didn't even ask me why I wasn't drinking. When I explained it to him anyway, you know what he asked me?" She didn't wait for my answer. "He asked if I was sure it was his. Like I'm out there soliciting sperm donations. What an idiot!"

"Him?"

"No, me. I sure as hell can pick 'em, can't I, Moe? What am I gonna do?"

"Just tell me who he is and I'll show him the error of his—"

"No. I wouldn't let him within fifty yards of this baby, the selfish, self-centered prick. Not now."

"Isn't there anybody you can talk to?"

"I'm talkin' to him."

"I mean a girlfriend, someone in your family."

"Someone in my family! Are you nuts? You know what they would tell me? Go talk to the priest. Yeah, like a priest's gonna help me make a decision about an abortion. After … You know, after what happened to me as a girl, my mother took me to a priest to have him bathe me in holy water, to wash away the stink and shame. You know what the priest said? He said that my mother should pray for God to forgive me. Forgive *me*, a little girl! What did *I* do wrong, Moe?"

"Nothing. Your mother was a foolish woman. And priests … What can I say? But I'm sure your brothers and sisters would—"

"No they wouldn't. I hate this fuckin' baby," she hissed, her face belying her words.

"Sure you do, that's why you're so torn up about it. That's why you said you wouldn't let the father get near it."

"Who asked you?"

"You did."

"I shouldn't've."

"Would you think about giving the baby up?"

That stunned Carmella, the air going out of her as if I had caught her solid in the solar plexus. I don't think the notion of giving the baby up was a possibility she had ever wanted to consider. It was the hardest option for a reluctant mother. Though I believe the concept of closure is complete bullshit, I have to think that carrying a baby to term and delivering it only to hand it over to strangers has got to be a vicious form of living hell. I'm not sure I could handle the uncertainty of it or the second guessing.

"I couldn't do that, Moe. How could I do that?"

Now the tears came. The fire was out. I took a step toward her.

"Leave me alone. Just leave me alone to think, okay?"

"Sure."

In contrast to her name, Mira Mira was as exotic as whole wheat toast. Oh, she was pretty enough—Italian, early thirties, svelte and dark—but with a Brooklyn accent that made mine seem minted on the Thames. And if her loft in SoHo was indicative of how lucrative tattoo artistry was, I was going to tell Sarah—a gifted painter—to lose the brush and oils in favor of the ink and needle. You could have played full court basketball in the place and have had room for bleachers and concession stands. The exposed brick walls were covered in enormous photographs of body art. Some were rather stunning and done in colors you were more apt to find in a Klimt than on a teenager's bicep.

"So, you wanna to tawk about an original Mira Mira creation."

"Not original, really," I said, sliding my business card and the Polaroid across the table to her. "I believe you already spoke to my employee about it."

"That Brian Doyle works for you, huh? A real freakin' charma, that guy."

"Charm is a funny thing. Depends on taste."

"Yeah, well, just because some assholes who are drownin' think they're just slow swimmers, don't make it so. You know what I mean?"

I didn't, but I wasn't here to argue with her. "Exactly. So what can you tell me about that tattoo?"

"Nothin'. I mean, nothin' I didn't already tell Prince Charmin'."

"Amuse me, okay?"

"Sure. Whaddya wanna know?"

"Everything. Anything. How were you contacted? Who did you deal with? Did they leave a contact number or address? What was the kid like and the guy with him?"

"Nothin' unusual in how he got in touch. Got a call from a guy sayin' he's seen my work and that he's got a friend that he wants to get inked. I asked him if him or his friend wanna come in to tawk about what kinda design they're lookin' for, but he says they already got somethin' specific in mind. I told him I didn't do crap. No Christheads or hearts or dragons, you know, that kinda crap and that I don't negotiate price. He says that ain't no problem and when can he come in."

"So you spoke to the older man, the one with the eye patch."

"Yeah, it was Cyclops I tawked to."

"Do you have names, addresses, phone numbers?"

"Sure do, for what it's worth. I mean, I don't like check references or nothin', but I make people sign all kinda fuckin' releases before I put ink to skin. You have buyer's remorse with a house, you can sell it. Body art, the way I do it, it's kinda hard to give back."

"Could I see the paperwork?"

"Nope."

"Why not?"

"My studio got busted into in May. All the files got trashed."

"Any other damage?" I asked.

"Some. Nothin' that couldn't get fixed."

"You remember any names?"

"Nah. I don't remember what they wrote on the release forms and when they tawked to each other, I don't even think they used names. Cyclops called the kid Kid. I don't remember the kid callin' Cyclops anything, but his expression called him Asshole. I don't guess that's what your lookin' for."

It wasn't, but I didn't want to lose the momentum. "So they make an appointment and ..."

"Yeah, at first when I see 'em I'm thinkin' it's the man boy love thing and that sugar daddy is buyin' his boy toy a little art as a token of his appreciation. It wouldn't be the first time. But as things went on, I changed my mind. It was more like boss and employee kinda situation. In fact, the kid didn't seem very into the whole tattoo thing at all. Kept whinin' about not likin' needles and shit like that. Cyclops told him to shut up and take it like a man."

"Nice guy, huh?"

"A typical cop."

I nearly swallowed my tongue. "What?"

"I'm pretty sure he was a cop. My dad, my uncles, my little brothers are all on the job. Just like you and Prince Charmin'."

"Well, Mira, you wouldn't have to be Kreskin to figure out that Brian and I were once cops."

"I guess not, but Cyclops was once a cop. I'm tellin' ya. And then when he pulls out that picture and shows me what he wants me to put on the kid, I almost threw them both out on their freakin' asses."

"The rose and Chinese characters?"

"Yeah," she said, tapping her finger on the Polaroid. "It was an enlargement of an old photo, all grainy and shit, but clear enough so's I could copy it."

"The person in the photo, was he a—"

"Tell you the truth, I just looked at the tat. It was a man's arm. That much I could tell."

"Why'd you want to throw them out?"

"Cause it was a bullshit job. Any hack coulda done the work and I didn't wanna waste my time."

"If it was a bullshit job, why come to you?"

"You're askin' the wrong party here," she said. "I don't know. Some people they think like expense equals quality. So for what I charged 'em, they got lotsa quality."

"You mind me asking how much quality they received?"

"Three large cash."

"He paid you three grand for—"

"That's where my prices start, not where they finish. And he tipped me an extra few c-notes on top."

"Nice work if you can get it."

She pointed at an eight foot by ten foot photo on the wall behind me. It was a tattoo of a peacock, its tail feathers fanned across a woman's upper thigh and right cheek. The colors were incredibly vivid, the iridescent blues and greens fairly jumped off the subject's flesh, but it was the subtle shadings, the gold and beige, the darker browns and black that were the real trick of her art.

"You do that, you can charge what I charge," she said. "Until then ..."

"I see your point. You're good."

"Good. *Pfffffff*. Fuck that!" She made a face like she'd bitten into a bad nut. "I'm the best."

"So what about the kid?" I asked. "I mean beside the fact that he was whining."

"He was handsome enough if you like the type. Kinda a young Travolta without the charisma."

Bingo! I thought back to when I first got involved with Patrick. The Maloney family had plastered the kid's high school prom picture all over the city. I remembered thinking that he reminded me of Travolta. But that was before Patrick had colored his hair and gotten his ears pierced, before he had gotten his tattoo.

I stood to go. "Thanks for your time. Here's my card if you think of anything else."

"So what neighborhood you from?"

"Sheepshead Bay via Coney Island."

"I went to Lafayette. You went to Lincoln, huh?"

"I did."

"Well, screw that, I like you anyway," she said.

"Oh yeah, why's that?"

"Cause most people walk in here or my studio and within thirty seconds say 'Mira Mira on the wall,' or some stupid shit like that. Not you."

I wished she hadn't said that last part, because now I couldn't get it out of my head. *Mira Mira on the wall, who's the fairest of them all? Mira Mira on the wall, who's the fairest of them all? Mira Mira on the ...* At least when a song gets stuck in your head, there's a melody to mitigate the annoyance. Like I didn't already have enough crap to drive me nuts.

[CHAPTER THIRTEEN]

I had surely disappointed Sarah a thousand times over the years in ways both large and small. Nothing hurt more than seeing disappointment in my kid's eyes, but letting your kid down is an inevitable and likely beneficial part of parenting. You can't pick kids up everytime they fall, you can't and shouldn't give them everything they want, nor is it in your power to come close to living up to their image of you. Yet, in spite of my myriad foibles, missteps, and mistakes with Sarah, there was one way in which I couldn't recall letting her down. I had always kept my word to her. It was in my nature to keep my word even when it worked to my detriment. You need only survey the shambles I'd made of my marriage to know the truth of that.

Had I walked out of Jack's apartment in the West Village twenty-two Februaries ago and called Katy to tell her that I had found Patrick ... Sometimes in my blackest moments, I think about what might have been had I, just that once, broken my word. I mean who the fuck was Jack White to me? And Patrick, what had he done to earn my trust? If anything, his behavior had earned my scorn. All those times my father-in-law asked me about ghosts, he was off target. He should have asked me about being haunted. For while I still didn't believe in ghosts, I did believe in hauntings. Who needs ghosts when questions will suffice? Ghosts, one in particular, were the reason I was heading back upstate and why I was about to break my word to Sarah.

Pete Vandervoort had taken up the post outside Katy's door. When he saw me approaching, a series of expressions washed over his face in rapid succession. He smiled, squinted, frowned, and snarled before settling on the world weary cop smirk. Instead of shaking his extended hand, I placed the Polaroid in it.

"What's this?"

"A ghost with a freshly inked tattoo," I said.

"Nice trick, a ghost with a new tattoo. Where'd you get this?"

"My people tracked the tattoo artist down and she gave that to us. I'll give you all her info after I talk with Katy. I think she needs to see that Polaroid."

"Good timing. She's up. Her shrink was in there checking on her about fifteen minutes ago. He said she seemed more stable. Whatever that's supposed to mean. More stable than what?"

"It's cover-your-ass-speak. Have you seen Sarah? I tried to get her on my way up, but kept getting her voice mail."

"Nope. Haven't seen her today. Why, is something wrong?" he asked.

"I promised her that I would back off for a few days, so Katy could catch her breath."

"I see, but they'll understand when they get a look at this. I mean, Christ, you can't sit on this. It proves that this has all been a set up," He handed the Polaroid back. "Go on in and show her."

I knocked before stepping in. My ex's expression was less ambiguous than the sheriff's had been. Disappointment was writ large in every fold of her face and her first words didn't leave much room for interpretation.

"What the hell are you doing here?"

"I—"

"Sarah told me you promised to—"

"I *did* promise and I meant to keep my word, but something came up that I couldn't keep a lid on."

"You're full of shit, Moe! Do you even believe half the things you say? You kept a lid on things for twenty years."

Her anger, it was like a separate entity. There were times I fooled myself that it was at an end, that Katy had gotten past it. No, it was metastatic, laying dormant for months at a time and then ... *Bang*! Like today, something I would say or do would set her off. That's why our early attempts at reconciliation were short-lived. Our mutual despair or old hungers could keep it at bay or out of the bedroom for a few hours at a time. Then it would flare up. The odd thing was that I knew at least a part of the anger wasn't even meant for me, but rather for my father-in-law. When Francis died, I was left the only available target.

"Look, I didn't come here to fight, but to show you this," I said, holding out the Polaroid. She took it. "Brian Doyle tracked down the tattoo artist who did that back in April and Devo found more than twenty casting calls for young men who would meet Patrick's physical description."

I felt myself wince, waiting for that second wave anger. It didn't come.

"Who is he?" she whispered.

"I don't know. Some kid desperate for an acting job, I guess."

"You don't know his name or anything?"

"Give us a little time."

"I want to see him again."

"What?"

"I want to see my brother again."

"He's not your brother."

"I don't ... care. I ... I ..." Katy tried choking back the tears, but it was no good. She was sobbing now so that her whole body shook. "I want ... I want to see ... him. I want to know ... why he—"

"He's not your brother, for chrissakes."

She crumpled up the Polaroid and threw the pieces at me. "I hate you! I hate you! I hate you! You've taken everything away from me."

"But Katy I—"

"Get out of here! Get the fuck out of here." She was squeezing the life out of the call button. Even before the staff could respond,

Vandervoort and Sarah came rushing into the room. "Get him out of here. I want him to leave. Get him out of here. Get him out—"

With little effort, Pete Vandervoort ferried me out of the room, but I could still hear Katy screaming and Sarah trying to calm her down. A roly-poly Filipino nurse and a psychiatric aide flew past us and almost immediately some coded message went out over the loudspeaker.

"What happened in there?" the sheriff asked.

"I'm not really sure. I showed Katy the Polaroid and she went batshit on me. When did Sarah get here?"

"Just after you walked in there. She was none too pleased."

"Figures. I seem to be having that effect on the Prager women today."

Just then, Dr. Rauch, the shrink who had seen Katy on her initial visit, came charging down the hall. He looked less pleased to see me than Katy and Sarah, but didn't stop to elaborate.

"Shit," Vandervoort said, "you're just making everybody's day."

"Yeah, you noticed that look too, huh?"

"Hard to miss."

A few seconds after Dr. Rauch went into the room, Sarah came out glaring.

"Dad, I thought you said you were going to give Mom some time. Now look at her."

"But we found proof that there is no ghost and that it's just some actor parading around out there like—"

"And you thought, what, that Mommy was going to be thrilled about that? You know, for the world's smartest dad, I think you're just totally lost sometimes."

"Look, kiddo, I know I broke my word to you about coming up, but I had to show Mommy what I found. What was I supposed to do, sit on it? What if she found out that I was keeping it from her? Can you imagine how she would've reacted to that? Either way, I was screwed."

"I guess you have a point, but still, you should've warned me, us. Her doctor's pissed."

"Your mother is my concern, not her doctor. Besides, I tried, to call ahead, but I kept getting your voice mail. Where were you anyway?"

"The movies. I needed a break."

The door to Katy's room opened again. Dr. Rauch held it open for the nurse and the aide. He told them he'd be up at the desk in just a moment. When they were out of earshot, he pointed his finger at me.

"Listen very carefully, Mr. Prager, I—"

"Doc, you want me to listen, I suggest you get that finger out of my face."

He looked at his finger like it didn't belong to him, shrugged his shoulders, and put his hand in his pants pocket.

"Very well, Mr. Prager. Why don't you and your daughter meet me in my office in ..." he checked his watch, "... ten minutes?"

"That'll be fine, Dr. Rauch," Sarah answered. "I know where it is."

He didn't wait for my response before heading to the nurses' station.

Rauch's office was like a movie set of a doctor's office. The carpeting was high end industrial in a sort of speckled sage green, a few shades darker than the matte finished walls. The shrink's desk was large but non-descript and cluttered with patient files, pharmaceutical company doo-dads and note pads, a phone, an engraved pen and pencil set and a plastic model of a human brain. His chair was the standard issue high back, black leather swivel. One wall was dedicated to enlargements of family vacation photos and a goofy *My Brother the Psychiatrist* needlepoint, one to overstuffed bookcases, and one to degrees and decrees of board certifications. It seemed that Rauch was certified to perform neurosurgery and sell real estate.

It took Dr. Rauch quite a bit longer than ten minutes to make his way to his office. Good thing he got there when he did. Sarah and I had already exhausted sports talk and small talk and were about to move on to thumb wrestling.

"I'm sorry for taking so long," he said. "But I stopped to have a conversation with Sheriff Vandervoort. He briefly explained to me what the two of you have been up to."

"Look, doc, I didn't mean to upset Katy, but I had proof positive that what's been going on has been a total set up. And given our history, I didn't feel like I could keep it from her."

He made a show of rubbing his chin and sighing. "I'm certain you had only the best intentions, Mr. Prager, and that you were acting in what you considered to be a reasonable manner. It may well be that under most circumstances, your actions today would have been completely within the realm of acceptable behavior. However, I feel duty bound to remind you that Katy just made a serious attempt to take her own life and that she is in a fragile state of mind. Your presence here today may have caused a serious setback."

"I'm sorry, doc, but like I said, I had proof that I needed to show my wife."

"Nonetheless, Mr. Prager, I am alarmed at how you simply disregarded my prohibition against your visiting Katy without my prior consent."

"Prohibition?"

"Yes, your daughter assured me that she discussed it with—"

What the fuck are you talking about? "Oh, that! Yeah, we discussed it. Like I said, I'm sorry. It won't happen again."

Dr. Rauch looked from me to Sarah and back again. "Yes, I see. Make sure that it doesn't. Sarah, could you please give me a minute alone with your father. He'll be right out."

When Sarah closed the door behind her, I nodded across the desk. "You first, doc."

"So I assume your daughter didn't discuss it with you."

"Not in so many words. She asked me to give her and her mom a few days. I guess she didn't think I'd react well to being ordered not to visit."

"Was she correct?"

"Probably."

"Look, Mr. Prager, Katy is my patient and therefore necessarily the focus of my efforts. That doesn't mean, however, that I am unconcerned about you. So I am going to give you some free advice that I have come by honestly. We can't escape our pasts. We can neither undo them nor make up for them, but ultimately they must be dealt with. Not everyone pays the same prices for their perceived transgressions. In a very real sense, the prices we each pay are dependant upon *how* we choose to pay them. Take a long hard look at the price Katy is paying. Know this, that regardless of how you may have contributed to her difficulties, the bill is hers to deal with, Mr. Prager, not yours. And no grand or sweeping gesture on your part can change that."

"Thanks, doc. I know Katy's your patient and you can't really discuss too much with me, but why did she freak out like that before. I would've thought she'd be relieved to know she wasn't seeing things."

"Part of her was relieved, but part of her was also disappointed. Can you understand that?"

"Yeah, I guess I can."

"You must also understand that logic and reason will not just make Katy's issues vanish. You can't argue her out of her depression. You can't just say, 'Snap out of it.' So no matter what proof or evidence or whatever you and the sheriff come across, you mustn't ever repeat today's episode. Please, if you want to see Katy, you must clear it with me beforehand."

"I give you my word." I stood. We shook hands on it. "One more thing, Dr. Rauch, if you don't mind."

"Yes."

"Is there anything else my daughter conveniently neglected to mention to me in her attempt to manage the situation?"

"It would be difficult for me to know what she didn't tell you as I don't know what she *did* tell you."

"Well, on the phone earlier, she kept saying Katy was embarrassed. I'm a pretty smart guy and I can understand why a person who survives a suicide attempt might be ashamed, but Sarah didn't say ashamed. She said embarrassed and my kid chooses her words pretty carefully."

"I'm not sure. I suppose it could be a reference to what she says drove her to overdose."

"The videotape?"

"That, and seeing her brother looking through the front window."

"What?"

"I thought you knew. While she was watching the videotape, she saw who she thought was her brother staring at her through the window. Given Katy's fragile state of mind and her serendipitous viewing of the security tape, it's easily understandable how his appearance, imagined or otherwise, might have been the precipitating event ..."

But I had stopped listening. "Fuck me! Now I gotcha."

I ran out of the office without saying goodbye. Sarah was pacing circles in the hall outside the office. She called after me, but I didn't hear a word.

[CHAPTER FOURTEEN]

Dramatic as the image might be, it wasn't like Day-Glo puzzle pieces assembling themselves on a black felt backdrop in the void. Things are apart. Things come together. It's not there, then it is. You can only see pieces come together in retrospect. As Dr. Rauch spoke, it wasn't his words I heard. I was transported back to the ER the night of Katy's attempted suicide.

"Had to lay my hog down when some asshole in a SUV ran the light at Blyden and Van Camp."

That was Crank's exact quote to Sheriff Vandervoort in the ER waiting area. What he said registered with me, but not in anyway my brain was prepared to handle at the time. I was too agitated about Katy to grasp the implications of what a bloody-faced biker said about some minor motorcycle accident. When I saw Crank the following day, something about the time and place of the accident made more of an impact. Still, I couldn't quite pull it all together. But now that I knew the kid in the videotape had been snooping around the Hanover Street house, I had the questions to ask and, more importantly, some of the answers. To access Hanover Street, you needed to turn off Van Camp. To get out of Janus and head toward New York City, you had to go through the intersection of Blyden and Van Camp.

"That biker, the one we saw in the ER."

"What about him?" Vandervoort asked, his eyes skeptical.

"Did he come in the next day to talk about the accident like you asked?"

"Hell, with all the excitement, I forgot about him."

"Shit!"

"Why, is he important?"

"Could be. I gotta go find him. In the meantime, do us both a favor."

"What?"

"Go back to the PrimeOil station and look over *all* their security tapes, inside and out, for the day that Katy tried—for the day Katy saw her brother in town. Look for any SUVs and try and get their tag numbers. Also, go back over the station's credit card receipts for that day and try to match it to the SUVs."

"Why?"

"Because I think our ghost drives a SUV."

Dusk had just passed the *baton noir* to the night when I pulled up outside Henry's Hog. I'll tell you what, the joint wasn't a damned thing like red wine. It didn't grow on you with repeated exposure and it sure as shit didn't improve with age. Jesus, maybe I had been in the fucking wine business too long.

Unlike my two previous visits, when horse flies outnumbered patrons, the place was buzzing with more than beating wings. There were a good fifty motorcycles parked out in front of the roadhouse, but the machines were all of a type. Ducatis, Moto Guzzis, BMWs, and Suzuki dirt bikes need not apply. These were Harleys, Indians, and custom choppers. There was the occasional Japanese faux hog mixed in with the odd classic Norton and Triumph as well.

I could almost smell the sweat, black leather and cigarette smoke as I got out of my car. That "Born to be Wild" wasn't blaring on the juke was the only missing part of the cliché. I felt for the familiar bulge at the small of my back. My snub-nosed .38 was now as old and as much a classic as a Norton or Triumph; a musuem piece, just like me. Currently, Glocks and Sigs were the rage. It was all about rates of fire and walls of lead, but sometimes it came down to a single bullet. My hopes were to never find out and for my revolver to stay holstered until the next time I cleaned it.

I had worn it nearly every day for the last thirty-three years. First it was my off-duty piece. Then it was my insurance when I worked my cases as a PI. Eventually, although I was loath to admit it to myself, the little .38 had morphed into a shopkeeper's gun, something to keep me safe when I made bank drops or closed one of our stores late at night. *A shopkeeper!* I mean, who says I wanna be a shopkeeper when I grow up? But that's what I was, a goddamned shopkeeper.

Some old Lynyrd Skynyrd was blasting when I walked into the noisy bar, my entrance seeming to cramp everybody's style. Except for the dead man singing on the juke, most all the patrons stopped what they were doing. If my cop vibe revealed itself a bit on my first two visits here, it was fairly screaming this time. I blended in like Neil Diamond at a hip hop show. I might just as well have yelled *Fore!* and asked to play through. Actually, if not for all the hostile facial expressions, I would have gotten a kick out of it. But I walked through the crowd as my namesake through the Red Sea and straight up to Tina at the corner of the bar. As I passed, the sea filled in behind me and the noise started back up.

"You again," she said, pressing her hand to the flap on her throat.

"Is there someplace we can talk?"

"Sure. Come … on. Butchie, keep an eye … on things."

I followed Tina into the backroom and down the stairs into her office. It might have been a biker bar on the upper level, but down here it looked like any other basement office. It was a business. There were bills to pay, a payroll to meet, and taxes to evade.

"So," she said.

"Crank."

"What about … him?"

"I need to find him."

I didn't wait for her to ask why or to do the Bribe-me-first Cha-Cha. I took out a roll of money and explained to her why I needed to find him.

"He's that important ... to you ... to find, huh?"

I shook my head yes.

"Put your money ... away," she said, closing the door behind her, "and ... fuck me."

I didn't have to say what. My face said it for me.

"You heard ... me." Tina unbuckled her belt, unhitched her leather pants, and made a show of slowly undoing her zipper. She reached up with her free hand. "You don't even have to ... look at ... me. I'll bend over or ... you can shut the ... lights."

I didn't flinch. My father-in-law and I had played a game of chicken that lasted two decades. If I hadn't flinched for him, I wasn't going to for Tina Martell. I'd also learned that chicken was a two team sport and that it worked both ways.

"You know, Tina, I didn't think you were ugly till right now," I said, starting for the office door. "I can find out what I need to know without Crank. But remember this, anything happens to my family because it took longer than it had to, I'll come back and burn this shithole down."

She stopped tugging on her zipper. "Once, I coulda had any man ... I wanted. I did and ... women too ... sometimes. Now look at ... me. I can't even suck—"

I kissed her hard on the mouth, running my hand through her short cut hair. She didn't exactly resist, but she didn't quite melt either. She stepped back after a moment.

"You must really ... need Crank," she said, looking anywhere but at me.

"Yeah, I do."

"A cabin back in the woods ... off Dunbar Road and ... Limehouse Creek Way in Craterskill."

"By the lake?"

She nodded. "Be careful … out there."

Before I left, I stuck my head back into the office. "No one's ever accused me of doing things I didn't want to."

Strolling into Henry's Hog was one thing. Driving up on a meth lab out in the woods in the middle of the night was something else. The cop vibe at the roadhouse earned me a few nasty stares. Here, nasty stares would be the very least of my worries. Meth was big business and these guys didn't fuck around. Shooting first and asking questions later was what they did with their friends. In my case, the questions would come after they had chopped me up and fed me to the local porcine population. As I rolled down Dunbar to the gravel road that was Limestone Creek Way, I thought that I might have asked Tina's advice on how to approach Crank without getting a shotgun stuck up my ass. It was a wee bit late for that now.

I had three options, none of them any good, but some more dangerous than others. I could have left my car where it was and tried to work my way through the woods to the cabin on foot. That was my 'if' option: If I was twenty pounds lighter … If I was twenty years younger … If my knees worked … Even then, I'm not sure I would have tried it. The woods around the cabin were probably full of eyes and ears and booby traps. Call me a worrier, but I didn't much feel like stepping into an steel trap or wire snare. I could have tried to sneak up on one of the lookouts and have my .38 convince him to take me to Crank. Again, I wasn't sure I could pull it off nor did I want to create any more ill will than my unexpected visit was apt to generate. I needed Crank's help, not his animosity. I went with option three. I restarted my car, put on the brights, rolled down my windows, blasted the radio, and headed straight for the cabin. I might be accused of stupidity, but nobody was going to accuse me of trying to sneak up on anyone.

That was all well and good until the front end of my car plowed into a log placed across Limestone. I didn't hit it hard enough to have the air bag deploy, but the seat belt tightened up and gave me a pretty good jolt. Before my head had fully cleared, someone reached out of the darkness and stuck a cold hunk of metal into my neck just under my jaw.

"Shut the car off, asshole. Put your hands on the back of your head, and get out easy," the man said, slowly pulling back the car door and guiding me with the end of his sawed-off. I still couldn't quite make him out, but the rifle caught enough light for me to see. "Walk. That way. Slow." He indicated which way with the gun barrel and moved it from my neck to my back.

If I had ever been more frightened, I couldn't remember when. I'd been involved in a few shootings, but they had just sort of happened. One minute there wasn't shooting and the next minute there was. The first time happened up in the Catskills. I was in the room when a crooked town cop blew the head off his fellow blackmailer. The next time was a set up. I'd been lured to a meeting at a shuttered Miami Beach hotel during the Moira Heaton/Steven Brightman investigation. When I showed, an ex-US marshal named Barto tried to kill me. I fired back. I think I hit him, but didn't stick around to make sure. Then there was the shooting at Crispo's bar in Red Hook when Carmella's partner was killed and she took that bullet in her shoulder. At Frankie Motta's house in Mill Basin, there were a few minutes of calm before the old mob capo and his former henchmen shot each other.

Being marched to your own execution was more than a little bit different. The string was going out of my legs and I didn't think I had the strength to walk much further. A thousand things to say went through my head, but my mouth just didn't seem capable of forming any words. On the other hand, the little voice, the one that never leaves me, had no trouble with words. "Be a man. Don't beg. Don't shit your pants. Be a man."

I was so angry at myself for worrying not about my family, but about how I would look to strangers when they blew the back of my head off, that I nearly turned around and charged the guy holding the shotgun on me. Given another few seconds, I think that's just what I would have done. Luckily, I didn't get a chance to find out.

"Pull his car off the road. I'll take it from here," someone said, stepping out of the darkness in front of me.

"Crank, is that you?" I said, my voice cracking.

"That was awfully fucking stupid, coming up here like that. Good thing Tina called ahead."

"Good thing," I agreed.

"Come on inside."

The cabin in the woods was just that, a cabin in the woods. There was a stone fireplace, a futon, a TV, a stereo, a small kitchen with a table and chairs, a bathroom and not much else. There wasn't any lab equipment that I could see and I hadn't spotted any chemical drums on the walk up. Crank followed my eyes and smiled.

"We don't cook the shit here, man. Biker don't equate to moron, you know."

"Glad to hear it."

"Tina says you wanna talk, so talk. You wanna beer?"

"Sure."

He handed me a Coors. Panic makes your pants wet and your throat dry. I hadn't realized how dry until the first sip of beer went down smooth as silk and cold as ice. From now on, Coors would definitely be my post-shotgun beer of choice. I wondered if they could work up an advertising campaign around that slogan.

"How you feeling?" I asked.

"Okay. You risked getting your ass shot off to check on my health?"

"That night at the ER, you said you had to lay your bike down when an SUV ran the light at Blyden and Van Camp, right?"

"Asshole blew right through the intersection without hesitating and didn't even tap his brakes after I went down. Good thing I was paying attention."

"Can you remember anything about the SUV? Color? What state the tags were from, how many people were in—"

"Pretty sure it was a pewter Yukon. New, I think. At least two people, men up front. New York plates. Sorry, but I was a little too busy to get the number."

"That's good, but how do you know there were two men up front?"

"Dome light was on. I can't tell you anything about them. Everything happened so fucking fast, you know? Does that help?"

"More than you can know. Thanks a lot, Crank."

I shook his hand. When I did, he pulled me close and whispered in my ear, "Don't come back here no more, bud. Makes the boys nervous to have cop types around and that don't do me no kinda good. We understand one another?"

"We do."

I turned to go and then the world shook. *Baboom!* The explosion wasn't in the cabin, but it was close enough to shake the place and blow out the windows. I bounced off the wall and saw the fireball rising up out of the woods about a hundred yards away. I thought I could feel the heat on my face, but I was probably imagining that. I ran over and helped Crank up off the floor.

"You gotta get outta here," he barked. "The timing don't look so good for you."

"I didn't—"

"I know you didn't, but they're not gonna believe that. Keep your head down by the door and listen. You'll know what to do."

Crank waited till I crouched down and then ran out the front door screaming, "He jumped out the window and headed toward the lake. Hammer, you get Blade and Cutter and get to the lake. Skank, you go check on the kitchen to see if anything's left of Skinny and the equipment. I'll check the woods to make sure he don't double back."

"Shit, Crank, ain't nothin' gonna be left a Skinny, not after—"

"Listen, Skank, get the fuck over there and check on Skinny or—"

"Okay, Crank. Jesus, fuckin' Christ, who the fuck died and left you God?"

I listened to all the footseps heading away from the cabin and the road where my car was parked.

Crank kicked the door with his heel. "Go now. Fire your gun when you get to your car."

I didn't hesitate. Taking off, I kept low as I could and close to the trees. My car wasn't too far from where I left it. I didn't bother checking the damage to the front end. As Crank asked, I fired off a few rounds. He didn't have to explain. I was giving him cover for when his crew got curious about how I had escaped.

As I drove back into Janus, I thought about what Crank had said about the timing of the explosion. It was one hell of a coincidence that his meth lab just happened to blow up during my visit. I didn't like it, not even a little. I called Pete Vandervoort. He was asleep, but when I told him about Crank's lab being launched into low Earth orbit, he agreed to meet me in his office.

Given the sheriff's looks, I was glad I'd avoided mirrors. And he was just tired. I'd crashed a car, had a shotgun stuck in my throat, and witnessed a recreation of the Trinity test. I had just about used up my yearly allowance of adrenaline and was now paying the price. I could literally feel myself crashing and unless he was hiding a fifty-five gallon drum of coffee somewhere, I wasn't going to last much longer.

I described the SUV to him that Crank described it to me.

"We've got a winner!" I think I remember him saying.

I recall his mouth moving some more after that, but I had already retreated behind a wall of sleep.

You reach a certain age in life and you've woken up in a few strange beds. Even so, it can be a pretty jarring experience. Waking up in a jail cell kicked that jarring thing up to a whole different level. The bed wasn't too terribly uncomfortable and the bleach and pine disinfectant aroma wasn't quite as pleasant as my dad's Old Spice aftershave, but I guess it had its charms. On the other hand, I didn't find the cold metal toilet hanging off the wall very welcoming. I kind of felt like Otis the town drunk on the old *Andy Griffith Show*. I think I half expected Barney Fife or Aunt Bea to show up with my breakfast.

My watch said it was 8:22 AM, but the florescent lighting and lack of windows kept the place in a kind of perpetual dusk. I threw some cold water on my face. I might have dunked my head into the water had the sink been larger than the ones in aircraft rest rooms. I was about to try the door to make sure the sheriff didn't have a frat house sense of humor. Just then he walked in and swung the door back open.

"Where's Opie?" I said.

"Huh?"

"Forget it, Pete. Thanks for putting me up. I was pretty zonked."

"I'd say. I've been checking on you every hour," he said, pointing at the security camera mounted on the ceiling outside the cell, "and you've been in one position for most of the night. Come on, I got some coffee for you out here."

We stepped into the offices. Here, the sun streaming through the windows confirmed that my watch was telling the truth. Vandervoort handed me a cup of coffee and motioned for me to sit down in front of his desk. Although his expression was neutral, I could tell that the news he had for me wasn't good.

"It's a dead end, Moe. We got your Yukon on one of the tapes and we got the kid walking into the convenience store at the station, but it's impossible to read the tags. The driver never got out of the vehicle to buy gas or anything and he drove off right after dropping the kid."

"Shit!"

"I know it's not what you wanted to hear, but it totally confirms that this is a set up. You got that much, anyway."

"Tape show anything about the driver?" I asked.

"Well, the good thing is that this tape was brand new, so it's much cleaner than the other one I gave you. No murky images on this one."

"But ..."

"But you can't tell anything about the driver. The windows are slightly tinted and there's some sun glare."

"Can I have the tape?"

"I knew you'd ask that." He shoved a plastic evidence bag across the desk. "Here you go."

"Any news on the lab?"

He started laughing. "The damned explosion registered on earthquake sensors. That was no small operation there, my friend. Somebody's not going to be happy about it going boom."

"I don't suppose they're going to file any insurance claims."

"I suspect not."

I got up. "Thanks for the tape and for the accommodations, Pete. I better get back down to the city and see if I can figure out how to come at this from another angle."

"Sorry the SUV thing didn't work out for you."

"Me too. Later."

[CHAPTER FIFTEEN]

There are times when Brooklyn feels more like home than others. This was one of those times. I considered stopping at the office, but decided against it. I'd stop by later and drop off the new videotape and see if Devo had made anything of the answering machine tape and the original security video. Without tag numbers, it was a waste of time to put people on tracking down the Yukon. There were probably hundreds, if not thousands, of Yukons registered in New York State. Crank and the SUV had been worth a shot, but the sheriff was right, it was a dead end. Dead ends, unlike closing doors, are not very zen. When one door closes, it's said, another opens. When you hit a dead end, you make a U-turn. I needed to clear my head and think. I used to do my best thinking in Coney Island.

I strolled down the boardwalk toward the looming monster that was the Parachute Jump; its orange-painted girders rising like dinosaur bones two hundred and fifty feet off the grounds of Steeplechase Park. What a silly beast it was, after all, serving no purpose but to remind the world of its impotence. It might just as well have been a severed limb. Besides the salt air, the boardwalk smelled of Nathan's Famous hot dogs, Italian sausages frying with sweet peppers and onions; the fat from the sausages hissing and spitting on the grill. It smelled of sun block too. The beaches were crowded, but not so crowded as when I was a kid. The beaches weren't as much of a magnet for city kids as they once had been.

With Sarah fully grown and nearly all my old precinct brothers moved or dead, I didn't find much cause to come back here as I used to. I still loved the wretched place. How could I not, but it had never been the same after Larry McDonald's suicide. This is where I saw him alive that last time in '89, the ambitious prick. He had been a murderer too, though I didn't know it then. I guess it broke my heart a little to find that out about Larry. That day back in '89, Larry and I stood on the boardwalk directly over where his victim had been found. Larry threatened me and my family. He said he was desperate. Maybe he was. Somehow his words and deeds had tainted the place a little. It was the divorce too. Divorce does more than split things apart. It taints things, all things, especially the good ones.

As I walked I thought back to my chat with Mira Mira and how she said the older guy with the eyepatch was a cop. Maybe there was an angle in that, but intuition didn't usually stand up under scrutiny. It had been my experience that people who insisted they knew things for sure didn't necessarily know shit. I don't care if everyone of the tattoo artist's relatives was a cop. Just because a man is a chef doesn't mean his kid can cook.

I thought about how much money was involved in arranging for the audition ads, for paying the kid and fixing him up to look just like Patrick. I thought about what it had cost to fly around the country for the auditions and to have arranged for the roses and the dramatics at Jack's grave. I estimated it had cost between ten and thirty grand, maybe a little bit more, to stage this little charade. A nice chunk of change, yes, but not big money. Any regular schmo, if he was motivated enough, could come up with that kind of scratch, so the money was another dead end. It all led back to the motivation. In the end, it was the only way I could figure to come at this. There was someone out there who wanted to hurt me and wanted to use my family to do it. For now, I had to go back to stumbling around in the dark, to interviewing everyone I could think of who might have a reason to want to hurt me.

It was no wonder that Devo'd had trouble tracking down Judas Wannsee. First off, the name was an obvious alias, a construct of the most hated Jew in history, Judas Iscariot, and of the Wannsee Conference at which the Nazis worked out the details for the Final Solution. Headquartered in the Catskill Mountains, his cult, the Yellow Stars, rejected the concept of assimilation and believed that the only way to avoid Jewish self-hatred was to announce your Jewishness to the world, to brand yourself a Jew, and to avoid the false comforts of fitting in. Most of the members did this by wearing the eponymous yellow star on their clothing to mark themselves as the Nazis had marked the Jews of Europe. Some went so far as to shave their heads and don the striped pajamas of those herded into concentration camps. In a few extreme cases, they had numbers tattooed on their forearms and ate a meager diet of stale black bread and potato soup.

If Karen Rosen had sought refuge from any other group, cult, or religion, Judas Wannsee and I might never have crossed paths. Karen was one of the three girls from my high school who had allegedly perished in a Catskill Mountain hotel fire in the summer of 1965, so you can imagine my response when her lunatic older brother Arthur came to me in 1981 claiming not only that the fire was no accident, but intimating that one of the dead girls wasn't dead at all. As it happened, he was right on both counts. Not only had his sister survived the fire, she started it. Exhausted from guilt and years of hiding, she found her way back to the Catskills and joined the Yellow Stars. Why she joined them is hard to say. Maybe she thought she could fashion her own murderous self-loathing into something that could be exorcised by slapping on the yellow *Juden* star. Maybe it was proximity to the scene of the original crime. By the time I found Karen Rosen at the Yellow Star compound and got to discuss it with her, liver cancer had since rendered her more dead than alive. When we spoke, she wanted from me something not in my heart to deliver: forgiveness.

Years later, I read an interview with Wannsee in a magazine. Although he gave no specifics, he discussed the issue of giving refuge and how the sins of those he had harbored over the years had come to weigh heavily upon him. *Yeah, tell me about it.* Shortly after the interview appeared, buzz over the group faded. Then the Yellow

Stars went the way of their buzz. It was a stretch, I know, but I wondered even then if he blamed me for pulling the first stone from the foundation upon which his little semi-secular temple had rested. Back then, it hadn't interested me enough to bother tracking him down. It did now.

Given his fanatical rantings against assimilation, there was a kind of perverse symmetry in his latest incarnation. Judas Wannsee had gone from the ultimate outsider and gadfly to faceless bureaucrat, from messianic to mundane, from bright yellow stars to grays and inspection stickers. The Department of Motor Vehicles office on Rte 112 in Medford on Long Island was the perfect physical manifestion of the anonymous new life Wannsee had chosen for himself. It was tucked neatly into the corner of one of the gazillion strip malls and shopping centers that scarred the island. Long Island had been transformed from a place of endless trees and beaches to a land of ugly, mind-numbing repitition. Deli. Chinese take-out. Dojo. Pizzeria. Card store. Phone store. Deli. Chinese take-out. Dojo. Card store. Phone store. Deli. Chinese take-out …

As I stood on the information line and listened to the beige woman at the desk endlessly repeat *How can I help you?* I had to snicker. There were several layers of irony in Judas Wannsee's transformation.

"Yes," I said, "I'd like to speak to your supervisor, please."

"What's this in reference to?"

"Just tell him it's about Bungalow number eight. He'll understand."

She hesitated and shook her head. Apparently, this situation had not been covered in *Information Desk 101*, so she handled it as she would if I'd come in to surrender some old license plates. She hit a button that generated a white numbered chit—A 322—and handed it to me.

"Take a seat. *Next!*"

I did as she asked, taking a seat on a long pew. The pews faced numbered stations where bored looking clerks did what clerks do. The pews also faced big electronic boards that posted chit numbers and stations in red lights:

F121 12

D453 10

A320 08

And whenever new numbers were posted, a bell would ring. The place seemed to have been designed by a Bingo playing priest heavily influenced by Pavlov. A322 12 flashed up on the screen quickly enough. The woman at window 12 directed me to walk over to a door. When I reached it, she buzzed me in.

"Down the hall," she yelled to me as I closed the door behind me.

The man I had known as Judas Wannsee sat behind a metal desk, shuffling and scribbling on papers. The walls were white and blank except for the mandatory notices about sexual harrassment, emergency procedures, and handwashing when leaving the rest rooms. They were devoid of pictures, posters, of anything that might have given a visitor insight into the man who occupied the office. He was twenty years older and it showed. He had thinned as had his hair. He was stooped somewhat and gravity had taken its toll on his face, but the eyes still burned bright.

"Mr. Prager," he said without looking up. "Bungalow number eight, indeed."

I knew he would remember. Bungalow 8 was where Karen Rosen had spent her last days, where we spoke that final time.

"I figured it was better than asking for Judas Wannsee or throwing a felt star on the counter."

"I suppose," he said, rubbing his chin. "Or you might simply have asked for Howard Bland. But no, as I recall, the simple way was not your way. You have a weakness for the dramatic turn. Please sit."

I sat.

"How did you find me?" he asked.

"I'm a detective."

"Lost is what you are, Mr. Prager. You always have been and I sense you will always be so."

That stung some. I didn't try to hide it. "And you're a hypocrite. What happened to all your speeches about not fitting in and showing yourself to the world as a Jew as a black man shows the world he is black? Look where you are now. You're a glorified clerk; faceless, pointless, invisible. Polonius too was full of high sentence, but at least he moved the plot along."

"The lost detective … Who quotes from Prufrock, no less."

The less I liked his attitude, the more I liked him for what had happened to Katy.

"I was paraphrasing, not quoting."

"Polonius? I think not. My speeches are like the soft tissue of dinosaurs, lost to history."

"Talk about a flare for the dramatic. Besides, that's no answer."

"And why should I be obliged to answer your questions at all?"

I suppose I could have grabbed him by the collar and twisted. It might have given me some short term satisfaction, but would've ultimately proven counterproductive.

"You're not obliged, but I might tell you how I tracked you down if you cooperate."

"You know, Mr. Prager, upon brief reflection, I find I'm not really so interested in how you found me. In fact, maybe how is beside the point. Let me ask, why?"

Again, I had a choice. I chose the non-violent option and explained. He never took his eyes off me as I spoke. He still had that ability to make you feel as if he could see right into you, into the darkest places, places where you stored your most shameful thoughts and unshared secrets. I was convinced he could detect the slightest hint of pose or artifice. When I finished, he considered what I had said before speaking. He still had it, the charisma. A lot of people want it. Some think they have it and don't. He had it in abundance.

"I can understand why you might have suspected me," he said, "but I'm sorry to disappoint you. I have nothing to do with the crimes perpetrated against your family."

I didn't want to believe him, yet I did, instantly. "Fair enough."

"I was quite piqued at you there for a time, I must confess. Your stumbling onto Karen did disrupt things for me. The group went on, even grew larger. I still believed in what I preached, but your presence caused me to have to look beyond my own belief system and motivations and to examine more carefully those who would follow my lead or, like Karen, seek refuge with us. You'd planted the seed. You see, I began the group because I believed in a set of values, not because I had a need to lead or a lust for power. Leadership and power are onerous, heavy yokes, not pleasures. Yet they were burdens I was glad to take on if it helped the misguided Jews of this great country.

"What I discovered, Mr. Prager, was that you could worship watermelon pits or sacks of gray pebbles or anything else for that matter and people would follow. Sadly, the world is populated by a lot of lonely, hungry, and lost souls. They all want to belong, to be loved, to be fed, to be anchored. Beliefs, unfortunately, are cold cold things. They give no comfort, no acceptance, no sustanance. Only other people can minister to those needs. Beliefs may inspire the founding of a group, but yearnings are the fuel that drives its growth engine. After years of self-exploration, of denial, and of rationalization, I knew what I had to do.

"I had already made my initial journey and come out the other side. I was a proud Jew by the time you and I had met that first time. I realized that if the group had true strength, it would survive and prosper without me at its center. If, however, I left and it collapsed, then my cause was folly. In the end, my decision to leave was set in motion by Karen's impending death and your arrival, Mr. Prager. It took me years to build a new identity into which Judas Wannsee might vanish. Even then, it wasn't as easy to let go as you might expect. No man wants to feel that what he's lived for has all be an illusion, a heat mirage on the asphalt in summer. Yet, eventually, Judas Wannsee faded slowly into the backdrop. So you see, I owe you not antipathy, but thanks. Just as my brother soldiers had inspired my first journey of self-exploration, you sparked my second."

"But this ..." I said, gesturing at the generic office. "Why the anonimity?"

"My first journey required the participation of others. I needed the rest of the world to react to my declarations of proud Judaism. The star, the tattoo, the pajamas, the name were all props meant to elicit responses. My growth, my self-discovery was a function of my reactions to those responses. And by confronting that daily friction, I was conditioning myself out of the shame and self-hatred of the assimilated Jew.

"This second journey has been a purely internal and personal struggle: Could I sustain my transformation without the participation of another soul? Could I be a proud Jew even if the rest of the world didn't know I existed? Could I remain unassimilated in the midst of utter assimilation? We have all heard the cliché, 'What a man believes in his heart, is what matters.' That was what I needed to discover, what I believed in my heart. For this question to be answered, I needed to remove all external things from my life that might serve to give me reinforcement, that might elicit response. Until the moment you walked through my office door, I had been remarkably successful."

"Hasn't it been long enough for you to get your answer?"

"Yes and no, Mr. Prager. What I have come to realize is that the answer requires one last journey. At the instant of my death, I will know for sure."

"A little late in the game, don't you think?"

"It's always late in the game for everyone. We're all of us on several journeys at once, different journeys, yes, but we all get the answer to the same question at the same time. I am ready for that answer whenever it may come."

"Goodbye, Mr. Bland." I nodded, standing. "Be well."

"And you, Mr. Prager. Although there is great value in being lost, try and find something in the meantime. There is no shame in comfort."

As I walked back down the hallway toward the bingo parlor, his words rang in my head. Just as his words had stayed with me for the last twenty years, these would stay with me until the day I died. But unlike Mr. Bland nee Wannsee, I was not ready for that answer, whatever it was and whomever its deliverer might be.

Right now I had to focus on closing chapters in my life. And with the exception of Judas Wannsee, all the significant people connected to my time in the Catskills were dead. Karen Rosen and Andrea Cotter, my high school crush were gone. Everyone from R.B. Carter—Andrea Cotter's billionaire brother—to Anton Harder—the leader of the white supremacists—was gone.

Closing chapters, that's what I was trying to do now, at least until I could think of a more inspired approach. When I was done reconciling the books, I'd take a look at the landscape and see who remained standing. One of them would be the man or woman behind the grave desecrations and the appearance of Patrick Michael Maloney's ghost. And since I was already on Long Island, I decided to make one more stop. It would no doubt be an unpleasant one.

A middle class hamlet with pretentions, Great River was tucked neatly between East Islip and Oakdale on Long Island's south shore. For many years Great River had resisted the Gaudy-is-Great infection spreading wildly across the rest of the island, but just lately its ability to fend off the disease had weakened. Acre lots that had once sported comfortable colonials and solid split ranches had begun sprouting giant "statement" houses, beasts that featured design elements from styles as disparate as Bauhaus and French Provincial. But the house that had to have won the Good Housekeeping's seal of disapproval boasted minarets, a faux moat, and scale model marble mailbox sculpted like the *Pieta*. In place of Michaelangelo's name, it read—in gold leaf, I might add—Mr. Michael Angelos and Family. Visitors to the home were probably confused as to whether they should purchase a theme park pass or prayer cards.

A little further on, I turned right before the gates of Timber Point Country Club and parked across from the expanded L-shaped ranch that I'd visited once, eleven years earlier. The Martello house looked much the same now as it had then, but things had changed. Currently, the house belonged to Raymond Martello Jr., a Suffolk County Police sergeant. The house had once belonged to his dad. The father had been a cop too, NYPD, the captain in command of the 60th precinct; my old house in Coney Island. I was ten years off the job by the time he was posted to the Six-O. Ray Sr. and me might not have known each other as cops, but we made up for lost time and got real well acquainted back in the late 80s.

I strolled across the street to talk to the tanned, shirtless man kneeling to adjust an inground sprinkler head on his front lawn.

"You Ray Jr.?" I asked.

"Why? Who wants to know?"

"No fair. You asked two questions. I only asked one."

He stopped what he was doing, gazed up at me, and got to his feet. Whereas Ray Martello Sr. had been a small, compact man, this guy was eye to eye with me. He was square-shouldered and ripped. He did the cop thing of getting in close to me—his nose nearly touching mine—and staring through me. He was checking me out and trying to intimidate me all at once. A sly, arrogant smile worked its way onto his face. I figured him for Martello's kid. Had to be. Had the father's looks and the same impudent style. I was feeling guilty about trying to get a rise out of him until I saw that fucking smile.

I noticed some rather intricate and unusually colored tattoos on his forearms, biceps, and delts. There were a series of Chinese characters on his left forearm done in bright red, not the usual dull blue. Both biceps were encirceld by bands of blue-green barbed wire highlighted with that same bright red, but the tat that caught my attention was on his right delt. It was the head of a Peregrine falcon done in vibrant shades of black, dark and light brown, off-white, and hints of blue. The yellow around the beak and eyes was so real, I could almost imagine pricking my finger on the tip of its hooked bill. I shifted position slightly and observed that the falcon's body and talons continued down his back. Here the work was even more skillfully executed, as the dappling on the birds belly, the texture of its feathers and the blending of shades was like nothing I'd ever seen. Well ... that wasn't true. I had recently seen something very much like it.

"Cop?" he asked, confident of my answer.

"Used to be. In the city. Nice ink work. Where'd you get it done?"

"Thanks." He pointed to his forearm, then his bicep. "These here I got in A.C."

"How about the bird? You get that done in Atlantic City too?"

"What are you, some kinda queer or something?"

"Or something," I said. "I knew your dad a little."

That wiped the arrogant smirk off his face and put a dent in his smart guy attitude. A city cop my age would know about what a corrupt piece of shit his father had been. In 1972, Raymond Sr., along with Larry McDonald and another thuggish cop I knew named Kenny Burton, had tortured and murdered drug kingpin Dexter "D Rex" Mayweather. Mayweather was king of the Soul Patch, the African-American section of Coney Island. But his execution wasn't some nobel act of misguided vigilantism done to rid the Coney Island streets of drugs. Rather it was done at the behest of Anello Family capo Frankie Motta in order to cover up an ill-conceived partnership between his crew and D Rex.

"Yeah, so you knew my pops, so what?"

"I was in Frankie Motta's house the night he got shot."

Martello Jr. blanched, then burned hot. His face did summersaults. It was as if a colony of beetles were under his skin, pulling his face this way and that. He knew who I was without asking.

"You got some set of balls showing up here, Prager."

"You think?"

"I do. In fact, I think if you don't get off my property pretty soon, I'm gonna have to shoot you for trespassing."

"Your father tried to shoot me once and look where that got him."

Mayweather's murder remained unsolved until, seventeen years later, a low level dealer named Malik Jabbar was arrested by a very young and very ambitious detective named Carmella Melendez. During his interrogation, Jabbar claimed to know who had killed D Rex. That was all it took for things to unravel. Within weeks, Larry McDonald committed suicide, Malik Jabbar and his girlfriend were executed, and Carmella's partner and another 60th precinct cop, a Detective Bento, were gunned down in a Brooklyn bar.

When I figured it out, I went to confront the terminally ill Frankie Motta. While I was there, Ray Martello and Kenny Burton showed up intending to do to Motta and me what they had done to D Rex. Things didn't work out quite the way they hoped. When the gunsmoke cleared, there were two men dead, one wounded, and one, me, still upright. Martello survived his wounds, but his heart crapped out on him on the operating table. He remained in a coma for a long time before they pulled the plug on him. The family might have better dealt with the tragedy and disgrace if, in the aftermath, the Brooklyn and Queens DAs hadn't held a televised press conference during which they made Martello the heavy in their little dog and pony show.

"Yeah, but I won't miss from this range," he said. "You'd look good bleeding from the eyes."

"Your dad thought the same thing."

"Smart man, my pops."

"That's not the words that come to mind when I think about your dad. Corrupt assassin is more like it."

The red of his face deepened and he coiled as if getting ready to strike. He didn't. Instead he shook his head at me.

"You want me to smack you," he said. "Well, fuck you, Prager. You'll get yours soon enough and you won't see it coming."

"You willing to risk everything on that?" I goaded him.

"To get rid of you, it'd be worth it. Any price to make you feel what we went through would be worth paying."

"Glad to hear you say it." I smiled.

"You're a sick fuck, Prager. Now I'm not going to warn you again. Hit the road, asshole."

"Don't worry, I'm going."

I left. There was nothing more to be gained by my further antagonizing him. I had a good feeling about Martello. He was the best looking suspect I'd stumbled across. Ray Jr. knew good tattoo work. One look at that falcon on his back told me as much and I wasn't discouraged just because Martello didn't fit the description of the older man who had arranged for the kid's ink work. Whoever was doing this thing wasn't doing it alone. Maybe Cyclops was a relative or an old cop friend of the family's. Suffolk cops are the best paid in the country, so he had the means. Martello had just made it crystal clear he had the motive. And, as I was about to discover, Ray Jr. had something else that got my attention. I drove up the block a little ways to find a spot to turn around. Coming back past the Martello house, I looked down his driveway and saw that one of his garage doors was open. Parked in the garage was a new pewter Yukon.

[CHAPTER SIXTEEN]

I aged a few years on the ride into Brooklyn, but no one sang *Happy Birthday* to me when I called into the office. At least everyone was now up to speed and, for the first time since this whole affair began, we were working the case like a case should be worked. Carmella gave Brian Doyle the shit end of the stick. His job was, for the time being, to be Martello's round the clock shadow. We'd get him some help as soon as we could. Not because we felt sorry for his ass, but because twenty-four hour surveillance is hard enough to do with a full team. It's nearly impossible for one person to maintain. The need for food and bathroom breaks gives the mark too many opportunites to slip away. And doing surveillance in the burbs is more difficult than in the city. Blending in isn't easy. Neighbors notice strange cars and unfamiliar faces.

Carmella said she would make calls to some friends in the Suffolk PD and the Suffolk County DA's office to check on Martello. Devo was getting credit reports and any other financial documents he could lay his hands on. When I walked into the office, both of them had promising news for me.

"I like him for it," Carmella said. "A captain I know out there says Martello's a prick."

"Brian Doyle's a prick too, but we hired him and he's not haunting my wife."

"There's more. This captain says—"

"This captain, how do you guys know each other?"

Silence.

"The mystery captain got a name?"

"Kirsten Rafferty. Why, you want her number?

"I don't date women who outrank me."

"I'm not even going there," she said. "So you wanna hear this or what?"

"Go ahead."

"Seems Martello got divorced ten years back and the ex started dating a guy assigned to Highway Patrol named Cruz."

"Yeah, so ..."

"A year later, Cruz was off the job and the ex was out of state."

"There's a punchline here, right?" I asked.

"The story goes that Ray Martello was like out of his mind over his ex dating another cop ... Men and their macho bullshit. Anyways, he didn't confront either Cruz or the ex-wife. Instead, he hooks up with Cruz's barely legal little sister. Martello asks the sister to keep their romance quiet because he doesn't want to cause trouble with her big brother and she's only too happy to oblige. Problem is, she's also happy to oblige when Martello suggests they start videotaping themselves ... You know what I'm saying? Do I have to draw fucking pictures for you, Moe?"

"So Martello lets Cruz know not only that he's been boning his sister, but that he's got the tapes to prove it. Cruz goes ballistic and assaults Martello, in front of several witnesses, no doubt."

"No doubt."

"Cruz gets kicked to the curb, the wife figures she needs to get far away from her crazy ex if she's ever going to date again, and Martello has his revenge."

"Gets better," Carmella said. "Because the story of why Cruz assaulted Martello gets leaked, the brass don't really want to bring criminal or disciplinary charges against Cruz. Cop vs. cop shit doesn't look good in the press, especially with what those guys get paid. Problem is, they need Martello's cooperation to keep it quiet."

"Nice way to make sergeant, huh? He gets everything he wanted and more, the vengeful dick."

"Vengeful is right. You gotta be a twisted fuck to go after a man's family like that. Sound familiar?"

"Unfortuantely, it does," I said.

"Listen to this. Martello's movements over the past year fit the time frame we've established. He went out with a bad hip about eleven months ago and didn't return to active duty till June. That gave him all the time he needed to set this thing up. Devo's got more coincidences for you."

"Listen, Carmella, after I talk to Devo, let's get outta here for an hour, okay?"

"Sure. I could use a break."

I rapped my knuckles on Devo's door and walked in without waiting.

"What's that?" Devo asked, pointing at my left hand.

"Huh? Oh this. Another videotape."

"I can see that, Moe."

"Right. It's from the gas station. It's got the kid and the guy who was driving him around on it, but you can't make much out. I figured it wouldn't hurt to let you have a try at it. Now I guess it's sort of beside the point."

"Maybe."

"Carmella tells me you—"

"Yes. Here, look at these." He slid some papers across the desk to me. "As you can see, Sergeant Martello was twice in cities—Los Angeles and Las Vegas—during the same time as the auditions were held in those cities. If we count New York, that is three cities. Of course, he may have been in many more of the cities, but Los Angeles and Las Vegas are the only two for which I have been so far able to obtain proof."

"Good work, Devo." I patted his shoulder. "Thanks."

"Moe ..."

"Yeah."

"It had nearly slipped my mind, but I did some analysis of the tapes you left with me previously. There is nothing much to be done, I am afraid, with the first security videotape. As you saw for yourself, it was terribly degraded and recorded over many many times. However, the phone machine tape did reveal something of interest. While I cannot say whether the voice is authentic or not, I can say it displays no obvious splices or edits, no abrupt clicks on or off. On the other hand, there is some very faint background noise."

"You mean like scratches and pops from a vinyl record, that kinda thing?"

"Nothing so obvious as that, no. I believe what I hear is the rumble of a cassette motor."

"Are you sure it isn't from the phone machine?"

Devo smiled at me like a proud father with his little leaguer. "A very astute question. I cannot be certain, but if that is in fact Patrick's voice, I would venture to say it was dubbed off a cassette tape and then filtered to suppress the other noise you would expect to find on an old tape. Find the person in possession of the original tape and you will be very close to having your answer."

The Sidebar Grille was near empty when Carmella and I walked in. During ten months of the year, the bar would be four deep with ADAs, defense lawyers, judges, cops, court officers, and even the occasional investigator, but July and August were quieter times around the courts as judges and lawyers heeded the call of the Hamptons. Only cops and skells don't do summer hours. The Sidebar Grille was famous for its food and convivial atmosphere. More plea bargains and monetary settlements had been sealed in here with steaks and handshakes than in any number of courthouses.

Maybe it was the emptiness of the place or the humidity. Whatever the cause, it didn't seem that the Sidebar's renowned aura was having much of an effect on Carmella. While she may not have been exhibiting any obvious physical signs of the pregnancy, my partner was showing nonetheless. She sat across from me, squirming in her chair, unable to look me in the eye. Carmella was uncomfortable in her own skin and that just wasn't her. She was learning the hard lesson, that children change your life whether you carry them to term or not. Soon she would learn that it was a change from which there is no retreat.

Marco the maitre d' was about a hundred years old, but never forgot a face or a name or how to put one to the other. He took Carmella's hand in his, placing his other hand atop hers.

"*La bella* Carmella, what may I get for you this evening?"

"A Virgin Mary."

Marco screwed up his face like he'd been stabbed in the heart.

"She's been under the weather," I said, hoping to head off Marco's interrogation.

"So sorry, *bella*. You get better, soon, you understand?"

"And for you, Moses ... Dewar's rocks?"

"How'd you guess?"

Marco winked, disappeared.

"You're still not drinking," I said. "Good."

"Good! Why good?"

"Because you're thinking of keeping the baby."

"I'm also thinking of not keeping it." She placed her right hand on her lower abdomen. She tilted her head down. "You hear me, you inconvenient little brat?"

"They're all inconvenient, Carmella. Every single one, always."

"I guess."

Marco brought our drinks over and chatted with me a bit, but I couldn't help but peer at Carmella out of the corner of my eye. She was in love and, inconvenient or not, that baby was to be born. Now the trick was getting her to know it.

[CHAPTER SEVENTEEN]

Brian Doyle got relief, all right ... Me.

I was certain Martello had taken notice of my car after our confrontation in front of his house the previous day. With the man's attention to detail and lust for revenge, he no doubt already knew my car and tag numbers. He probably knew my total mileage and how much longer I had before my next oil change. To guard against being easily spotted, I switched cars with Carmella Melendez. While she may have been a great detective and meticulous about her looks, the woman's car was a disaster area. There were enough old newspapers, gas receipts, and food wrappers in there to start a toasty bonfire and enough half full coffee cups to put the fire out. Still, the car smelled of her grassy perfume and that more than compensated for the mess.

I parked across Great River Road from the turn onto Martello's block. I nestled the car into a dark, cozy corner on the lot of a half-completed neo-Victorian just down the street from the theme park house. Night had long since settled in and the construction crews were well gone. My position afforded me a clear view of Martello's house, but it would be impossible for him to spot me without night vision equipment. I could also see the nose of Brian Doyle's Sentra. He was parked on Martello's block in amongst several cars that lined both sides of the street. Apparently, one of the neighborhood kids was having a pool party. I punched up Brian's number.

"Yeah."

"Okay, Brian, I'm in position. You can get going."

"You sure you don't wanna wait till my fuckin' bladder explodes?"

"Piss in a coffee cup, shithead. That's like on page one of your guide to surviving surveillance."

"Whadayu, nuts? I got like ten people on the porch over here. I'm not gonna provide entertainment for the evening."

"Anything happening?"

"Nah. He got home from his shift around four forty-five and he's been in there jerkin' off ever since."

"Okay, go home and get some rest. I got him now."

It didn't take Brian long to split. He must not have been kidding about his bladder.

About three hours later, the pool party was breaking up. As the departing cars took turns passing me by, the blast and thump of hip hop fractured the silence of the suburban night before fading away in the distance. I was sort of glad for the action. My wrists were aching from holding up the binoculars. And when I checked the sun visor mirror, I noticed funky circles on my face from the binocular eyepieces. I looked like the oculist's billboard in *The Great Gatsby*. T.J. Eckleburg, I think that was the guy's name. It's weird what you remember sometimes, but stakeouts'll do that to you. The boredom fucks with your head.

Just when the last car headed past me, my cell buzzed. It was Sarah.

"Hey, kiddo. What's up?"

"The doctor says Mom can go home in a day or two. She's doing much better."

"No unexpected sightings? The sheriff's still got someone watching?"

"Twenty-four hours a day, Dad. And no, no ghosts or anything."

"And you've been keeping busy?"

"I go to the hospital twice a day and then I just hang, but I am kinda anxious to get back to school."

"Good. I'm pretty sure we know who's been behind this whole thing. I'm staking out his house right now."

"Really?"

"Really. He's the son of a dirty cop. I guess he blames me for his father's death."

"Were you, Dad ... to blame, I mean?"

"No, but that doesn't matter if he thinks I am."

"Be careful."

"You too, Sarah. We'll talk in the morning, okay."

I occupied myself with the concept of blame for a little while, a very little while. Then I hopped off that slippery slope, picked up the binoculars, and tried getting back to work. The deathly quiet of the place gave me the creeps. How did Aaron ever adjust to living out here? Brooklyn at its most quiet is noisy and that noise had been my lullaby nearly every day of my life.

Things were changing in the Martello house. The strobe and colored flicker of his TV stopped, the front window going pitch black. A lamp snapped on and there was a brief show of Ray Martello's dancing shadow. About five minutes later, the porch and outside garage lights popped on. The electric garage opener whined, the door crawling up and out of sight. An engine rumbled. Puffs of exhaust fumes showed themselves like reluctant specters in the cooling night air. First brake, then backup lights flashed as the big SUV lumbered backwards down the driveway.

I supposed I was far enough away that he wouldn't hear Carmella's ignition catch, but I didn't trust the way sound traveled out here and decided instead to wait until he either passed me moving north or drove in the opposite direction along the border of the golf course. The Yukon's headlights rushed at me, sweeping from my left to right as the truck turned north toward Montauk Highway. I twisted Carmella's key, the engine perked right up. Still, I waited a beat or two to let Ray Martello get a block ahead.

Then, just as I put the car in drive, a cold chill made me twitch. I noticed movement in the shadows across the way; a slender figure emerging through the country club gates and turning onto Martello's street. I can't say why exactly, but I couldn't force myself to look away. I shouldn't have cared at all. It was probably some kid who'd met his girlfriend for late night putting practice on the 9th green.

"Keep your eye on the ball," I whispered to myself. "Keep your eye on the ball."

But as I rolled off the lot, my headlamps caught the slender figure, briefly bathing him in a harsh circle of light. Turning back, he squinted, shielding his eyes with raised hands. And in that brief second, all that I knew to be solid and real flew away, because standing there in that circle of light was Patrick Michael Maloney's ghost. Yes, this was the second time I'd seen him, but seeing him in the light that way ... Christ, it scared the shit out of me. My heart thumped so that I felt it pushing my chest against my sweat-soaked shirt. Suddenly, all the tattoos and videotapes were rendered irrelevant. What you think you know doesn't stand a chance against what you think you see.

I couldn't afford to scare him off, not this time. *Scaring off a ghost! Go figure.* Although only twenty yards ahead of me, I'd never catch him if he took off toward the golf course. So I forced myself to move, to not hesistate, pulling quickly off the lot and driving up the block in the opposite direction. I had the steering wheel in a death grip to insure that my hands wouldn't shake. Of course I knew how I should play it, but I wasn't at all sure I could pull it off. Having made a U-turn at the first intersection and doubled back, I eased the car along side him and let the servo suck the window fully down into the door before I spoke.

"Hey, buddy," I said in as steady a voice as I could manage, "I'm kinda lost here. Could you tell me how to get to Brightwaters?"

The ghost kept walking, neither turning toward me nor away from me. All I could do was stare at his profile, at that too-familiar tattoo on his bare forearm, and the Shinjo Olympians on his feet.

"Listen, man, I—"

He stopped in his tracks. I stopped the car, clicked it into park. Slowly, I slid my right arm across my lap to the door handle and began tugging on it ever so gently. There was a frozen second there when it felt as if I could've watched an entire baseball game between breaths or counted the beats of a hummingbird's wings. Then ...

Bang!

He took off back the way he came, toward the golf course. The car was useless to me now, so I was out the door after him. He was agile and pretty damned swift, making it through the country club gates in only a few seconds. While I had some moves on the basket-ball court, speed—even before my knee went snap, crackle, pop—was never my forte. An additional twenty years, three knee surgeries, and fifteen extra pounds weren't exactly helping the cause, but with my heart rate already up and adrenaline flowing, I actually gained some early ground on him.

It was an anomaly, not a trend. Once we both hit the grass and open ground of the golf course, I fell back. My deck shoes were no match for his track shoes. Although darker out here away from the street and porch lights, there was enough natural light to keep him from being completely swallowed up by the night. He kept looking over his shoulder to see how far he'd extended his lead over me or if I'd given up. If he thought I was going to quit, he really didn't know me. I'd have to cough out my lungs and liver before my legs would stop moving.

Bulldog or not, the reality was that my persistence would only count for so much. Eventually, he would get far enough ahead to duck out of sight, while I chased my own dick around out there in the dark. I didn't have long to wait. Since we'd hit the grass—which couldn't have been more than a minute earlier, but felt like an eternity—the ghost had been heading due south toward the ocean holes, but now he decided to cut sharply east toward where the sun would be coming up in only a very few hours.

Shit! I lost sight of him for a second behind a raised green, but caught a glimpse when I made it around the other side. He was gain-ing confidence as he went, getting a better sense of my physical limi-tations. Hugging the first cut of rough as he went, he would dart in and out of the small outcroppings of trees that dotted this part of the course. Then, he darted in, but didn't come out. I was about to go in after him when something four-legged and low to the ground shot out of the woods and skittered directly across my path. Two luminescent eyes stared back at me while I got my heart out of my throat. Free of the tree shadows and in the middle of the fairway, I could see it was a red fox. I hadn't run across many red foxes in Coney Island. Stray dogs, water rats, and horseshoe crabs, yes. Red foxes, no.

Before I could reorient myself, the woods coughed up the ghost fifty yards ahead of me and, like the fox before him, he ran directly across the fairway into a much larger stand of trees on the opposite side. Running as hard as I could, I took a diagonal line right to where he entered the far trees. I kept my eyes focused on that point, trying desperately to ignore my aching knee and the stitch in my side that felt more like a gash. As I approached the woods, an uneasy feeling came over me. I didn't sense danger necessarily. It was a feeling that there were more than foxes, owls, and fireflies in here. But whatever my concerns, it was too late to start worrying about them now.

In the woods, I knelt down behind a clump of thin-trunked trees. I could hear the ghost's footfalls—ghosts didn't have footfalls, did they?—on the dried undergrowth and fallen leaves that had accumulated over the years. Then I spotted him, but the irregular spacing of the trees made it difficult for me to follow his course. His silhouette flashed in and out of view. There it was again, that weird feeling. I tried to ignore it, to keep my eyes on the next clearing between the trees where I thought he would come back into view.

There he is! I'd gotten lucky. By keeping my place, I had confused him and he was now heading back my way. In a few seconds he would be passing about as close to me as he had been when he was caught in my headlamps. I eased myself up from the kneeling position and braced my back against the trees. Then I thought I was hearing things. The ghost's footsteps were now lost in an avalanche of crunching leaves. The woods were suddenly alive with a low thumping that had nothing to do with my heart. It didn't matter. I was committed.

I sprang. My timing was perfect. The sudden activity confused him too and it took him a second to realize I was almost on him. I was ten yards away, five, two, one … I was just stretching out my arms when something brushed my leg, knocking me off balance, but not down. Then, at the last second before I grabbed the ghost, I saw a blur hurtling at me. *Bang!* The wind went out of me even before my kidneys connected with the big tree behind me. When I got to my hands and knees, I got kicked in the head, hard. Unconsciousness took awhile to take hold. In the meantime, I let the thumping rock me to sleep.

It wasn't quite light out when I opened my eyes, but there was light enough to see Patrick's ghost was gone. The thumping was now exclusively in my head. I felt the knot above my left temple. It was tender and the hair over it was stiff from dried blood. The bleeding seemed to have stopped. I stood up slowly, in pieces, making sure I didn't revisit any of my most recent meals. I had a pretty good headache, but was walking okay. I knew what day it was, where I was, and had a notion of what time it was. I took a leisurely pace as I headed back to Carmella's car.

Stepping out of the woods with the first rays of sun over my back, I tripped over something in the deep rough. It was the half eaten carcass of a fawn; no doubt the handiwork of the red fox. Across the fairway, in the smaller woods, a herd of about twenty deer tried to look inconspicuous, standing perfectly still, trying to blend in with the trees. One of them probably had my blood on its hoof. I wasn't interested in finding out which one.

As I walked through the golf course's front gate, an older gentleman out walking his chocolate lab stopped me.

"You don't look so good, son. What happened?"

"I got mugged," I said.

"Mugged! By who?"

"Bambi."

That ended the conversation right there.

Carmella's car was where I left it, about two feet away from the curb, parked facing the wrong way, and the driver's side door ajar. At least I hadn't left it running. I seriously considered finding another cozy spot and keeping up the stakeout. That notion lasted until I spied myself in the mirror. I was never going to look in a car mirror again. I looked like shit, smelled like shit, and felt like shit. I was nothing if not consistent.

I closed the car door, started her up, and limped back to Brooklyn. It was the smart thing to do. The way I saw it, I had no idea if Martello had returned home. If he was home, he was probably sleeping and I could get someone from the office out here by the time he headed in for his shift. If he was still out, not knowing where wasn't as big a deal as it would seem. I had time to get coverage on him either here or at his precinct. Either way, there was little doubt that his young accomplice or stooge or whatever Patrick's ghost was to him, had already told Martello about our running with the deer.

Although I was far worse for wear and had failed to get my hands on the kid, my concerns about Ray Martello were confirmed: the asshole was behind it. You'd have to be from Pluto to think the kid's appearance at Martello's house was a coincidence. Now I had some choices to make. I could go to Vandervoort or the local cops with what I had, but, truthfully, I had *bupkis.* I had suspicions, a series of unlikely coincidences, and Ray Martello's palpable hatred for me. Unfortunately, none of it would stand up in court. That's why my screwing up with the kid really hurt. If I just had him, he could make the case for me. On the other hand, I didn't have to go the legal route. Judge and jury Moe had all the evidence they needed. There were ways to get back at people without taking them to court. If anyone could understand that concept, it would be Ray Martello Jr.

Driving back up Great River Road to Montauk Highway, I passed by a roadkill mother possum and two babies. I squeezed my eyes shut as I went, but all I could see in my head were the skittering red fox and the wrecked body of the dead fawn. I had had quite enough of the suburbs, thank you very much. It was time to get back to a place where I better understood the relationship between predator and prey.

[CHAPTER EIGHTEEN]

The ringing in my head woke me up.

First, I felt for the lump on my head, then I reached for the phone. The swelling had receded a bit and the blood-stiff hair was gone. Hot showers are mostly forgettable events, but there are times when they're just a notch or two below desperation sex. This morning's shower was the stuff of top ten lists. My long nap had reduced my headache from crashing cymbals to the tinkle of a lone triangle and I no longer smelled like Sunday at Augusta.

"Yeah, what?" My voice was thick with sleep.

Silence.

"Okay," I said, "I don't have time for this bullsh—"

"How is your head?"

The voice was unfamiliar and it took a few seconds for the question to register. I guess there were parts of me other than my voice still thick with sleep. *Who knew about my head?* No one. I hadn't wanted to bother explaining about my getting KO'ed by Bambi, so I'd left that part out of my call in to Carmella and she was the only person I'd spoken ... *Holy shit!*

"The head's better. What should I call you?" I asked.

"Patrick."

"Don't be an asshole, kid."

"No, really, that's my name. It's weird, right?"

"After all this, why are you calling me now? We could have saved ourselves a lot of trouble and me a headache if you'd have just talked to me this morning."

"I'm scared of Ray."

"Ray Martello?"

"Yeah. When I spoke to him he was crazy mad at me for letting you get that close."

I started noticing things about the kid's voice. His accent was mostly flat with a bit of a nasally twang. Half the kids that Sarah went to the University of Michigan with had that same accent. I thought about what approach to take with Patrick, if that was his name. Should I play the understanding, avuncular stranger or the outraged victim? Should I play softball or hardball? I went with hardball.

"Ray's a scary guy," I said. "What do you want from me and why the fuck should I care? Don't forget, kid, you've spent the last few weeks terrorizing my family and committing felonies."

"I didn't know. I swear to God I didn't know." His voice cracked.

"What did you think you were doing?"

"Making a movie."

"Don't bullshit me, kid. I'm from Brooklyn and you're not." I threw a high hard fastball under his chin. "You need cameras to shoot a movie. Seen any of those around lately? Maybe when you got the job you believed that movie crap, but not anymore."

"Okay, you're right. I'm really sorry about what I did to your wife and all, but I was in too deep to ..."

I had him and it was time to start pressing my advantage.

"How did Martello get a recording of Patrick's—?"

"If I come in, can you protect me?" His voice took on a real urgency.

"Sure."

"You don't sound so sure," he said.

"You blame me for not trusting you? Why should I believe a fucking word you say?"

"I swear to God, Mr. Prager, I'll come in. I just want to get away from this guy. He's got a crazy temper. I thought he was going to kill me this morning."

"That's twice you've invoked God in this conversation, kid. Stop swearing to God and start giving me some proof I should trust you. Where did Martello get a tape of Patrick Maloney's voice?"

"I don't know. I swear to—Okay, forget that, but I really don't know. He hasn't let me in on any stuff that doesn't directly involve me. I don't even know why he hates you so much."

"That one I have the answer to. Who's the guy with the eye-patch?" I asked.

"I don't know. I guess he's an old cop friend of Martello's dad. He drives me around some of the time. That's all I know about him. We don't talk much."

"All right, kid, come on in."

"No, you have to come get me." It was his turn to play hardball.

I thought about calling his bluff, but couldn't afford to let him get away again. Besides, if what he was saying about Martello's temper was accurate—I had every reason to believe it was—and he sensed the kid was ready to bolt, he would cut his losses and get rid of the hired help. Bottom line was, I needed the kid alive. Without him there was no case.

"You win. I'll come to you."

Silence. He was having second thoughts. He might be scared but he was also likely sacrificing the most money he'd ever made. I helped his thought process along.

"Listen, Patrick, I'll pay you to come in and I'll do my best to shield you from the cops."

"Twenty grand."

"That means he's paying you ten, some of which you've already received. Five," I said, "and I'll have it with me when I pick you up. If you help me put this cocksucker away, I'll take care of you."

"Okay. Two hours."

"Where?"

"I'm pretty close to you."

"That doesn't help me, kid." I wasn't going to call him Patrick again if I could avoid it.

"Manhattan Court, number sixty-nine, downstairs. It's a garden apartment that he rented for me."

"Manhattan Court over by Coney Island Hospital?"

"That's it."

"You *are* close. Two hours?"

"Bring the money," he said, all the big bad fear gone out of his voice.

I thought about calling Katy and Sarah, but I remembered what her shrink had said. I could serve this kid and Martello up on a silver tray and Katy would still resent me. She had to deal with her issues and I had to deal with mine. That worked for me, for the time being.

Squeezed in between Avenues Y and Z and perpendicular to Ocean Parkway, Manhattan Court was a small, forgettable block of post-Korean War garden apartments with a row of low slung garages behind. The "gardens" out front were actually lawns of weeds cut low to give the illusion of grass. Each unit had a brick and concrete stoop just large enough to hold a few beach chairs and a portable charcoal grill. I suppose Manhattan Court and the surrounding blocks of garden apartments must once have seemed like a little bit of heaven in the concrete and asphalt world of Brooklyn. Now it seemed in need of repair or bulldozing.

I knew Manhattan Court because Crazy Charlie had lived there. Charlie and I went to Cunningham and Lincoln together. We called him Crazy Charlie because he would do shit no person with half a brain would do. You tell him you'd give him twenty bucks to climb the Parachute Jump and he'd say, "Fuck, yeah," and climb it. Most kids, me included, were afraid to climb the fence that surrounded the ride, but there was Crazy Charlie two hundred-fifty feet in the air screaming for his twenty bucks.

He also tended to be loose with his fists. For him, one a day wasn't a vitamin, but a description of how many fights he averaged. Sometimes he took Sundays off. "I'm a good Catholic," he'd say. Crazy Charlie didn't care how big you were, who you were, or who you knew. If you pissed him off—and, trust me, it didn't take much to piss Crazy Charlie off—he was going to smack you. Of course, throwing the first punch didn't always equate to victory. I'd seen Charlie get the shit kicked out of him on more than a few occasions. There's no future for guys like Crazy Charlie. Last few times I saw him was in the mid-70s when I was still on the job. I'm walking by the holding pen at the Six-O and I hear someone calling my name.

"Moe fuckin' Prager, that you?"

"Crazy Charlie, what the fuck you doing in there?"

"I ain't Crazy Charlie no more, Moe. I mean, I'm still crazy, but it ain't dignified for a man, that name, you know what I'm saying?"

"What are you going by these days?"

"Charlie Rolex."

"Selling fake watches, huh?"

"Good fakes. But yeah, a man gotta make a livin', right?"

"Right."

"So you should come by one day and have a beer with me."

"You still on Manhattan Court?"

"Yeah. My dad bit the big one, but Mom's still kickin.'"

"Okay, Charlie Rolex. I'll do that."

And I did.

When I went over to his house that last time, he was shirtless, wearing an army helmet, and drinking beer out of a mixing bowl. Oh yeah, he also had a loaded police special on the table. He let me drink my beer out of the can and we talked about the nutty stuff he used to pull. After a few minutes of reminiscing, he leaned over to me conspiratorially and whispered, "You're a Jew, right?"

"You know I am, Charlie."

He looked around to make sure no one was listening. "You don't see any of your people in jail."

Well, actually I did, but Charlie wasn't up for a debate.

"No, Charlie, you don't."

"See, that's what I'm saying."

Frankly, I had no idea what he was saying and I got out of there a little while later with fake Rolexes for Aaron, Miriam, and me. They all broke the first time we put them on. A few years later I heard Charlie had taken to living on the streets. From there it was only a short drop off the edge of the earth into oblivion. Like I said, there's never any future for guys like Charlie Rolex.

I put Charlie right out of my head the minute I turned left onto Manhattan Court from East 6th Street. Carmella and Brian Doyle were probably already here. I told them to park blocks away and walk into their positions; Carmella across the way on the even side of the street and Brian Doyle atop the garages around back. There was good reason for the precautions. Martello hadn't shown up for his shift that day—neglecting to call in sick—nor, apparently, had he returned to his house in Great River. Missing a shift without calling in meant he was getting sloppy and sloppiness from a guy like Martello was a sure sign of desperation. To me it felt like he was preparing to cover his ass and that meant trouble for the kid.

I scanned the cars parked on both sides of the street. I had already circled the surrounding blocks a few times checking for pewter Yukons. None in sight. It was a good sign, but didn't mean Martello hadn't taken the same precautions as Carmella and Doyle. He was, after all, a cop and knew what we knew. At this juncture, however, I was certain he would be more concerned with being expeditious than judicious. I parked my car directly in front of number sixty-nine, collected the kid's five grand, and got out. Traffic was streaming in both directions along Ocean Parkway as I stepped up onto the stoop. I found comfort in the din of the traffic. I felt for the bulge at the small of my back and found comfort in that too.

The heavier front door pushed right back, exposing the staircase that led up to the second floor apartment and, on my right, the door to the kid's apartment. Ignoring the bell, I rapped my knuckles hard on the kid's door and waited. I could hear the sound of the TV coming through the door, but no footsteps.

"Hey, kid! Patrick, it's me. Open up." I wasn't shouting exactly. I tried the bell and waited a minute. Still no footsteps. I called the kid's cell phone. I heard ringing through the door. The ringing stopped when I hung up. I dialed Carmella.

"What?" she whispered.

"Maybe trouble."

"You want me to come across the—"

"No, stay put and keep your eyes open. I think the kid may have bolted or is ready to bolt. Call Brian and give him the heads up."

"Okay."

I knocked again. Nothing. I tried the doorknob. It turned easily and the door fell back, but stopped after only a few inches. A dim shaft of light filtered through into the dark hallway. I pushed harder without completely shouldering the door and it moved a bit more, but not much. There was definitely something propped against the other side. I peeked through the four inches of space I'd managed to clear and was relieved not to see arms and legs. While I still couldn't look around the door to see what was blocking it, I saw the kid's cell phone on a beat up coffee table. The sound from inside had come from a boombox stereo sitting on the bare wood floor, not from a TV.

"Kid. Patrick. Come on, it's me, Moe," I called, a little more urgency in my voice this time. No response. I hit the door square with my right shoulder and it gave way. I patted the wall for a light switch and found one. An overhead fixture came on and I saw the red plastic milk crate full of dumbells and weights that had held the door shut.

I was standing in the living room. The coffee table and the boombox were the only things in there. This apartment had the same layout I remembered from Crazy Charlie's. There was a dining room ahead and to my right, a galley kitchen off that, a hallway to the left of the dining room with a bathroom on the right, a large bedroom on the left, and a small bedroom at the end of the hall. I slid my arm around my back, under my jacket, and pulled the .38 from its holster. I knelt down and killed the music.

"Kid. Patrick. I've got your five grand in my pocket."

I took the slow, measured steps of a tightrope walker, letting my gun hand lead. The dining room and kitchen were clear. There was no furniture in the dining room and no food in the kitchen. The living room closet set beneath the stairs up to the second floor was empty. When I stepped into the hallway a little gust of wind hit me square in the face. There must have been a window open in one of the bedrooms. A thunderstorm had been brewing all day and I smelled it's inevitability in the air. There was another scent in the breeze that I couldn't quite make out.

The bathroom was the size of a closet and nothing much larger than a waterbug could have hidden in there. The small bedroom was even more empty than the other rooms. It was totally barren except for cob webs and the window was shut tight. No one had set foot in the room for weeks. The uncorrupted layer of dust on the floor told me as much. Stepping back toward the last unexplored room in the house, I caught another rush of air. Now I knew what that other scent was hiding behind the humid must of the storm: blood.

"I'm coming in there, motherfucker!" I screamed like a madman and kicked the door above the knob. The door flew away and I ran in blind, fueled by fear and weeks of frustration. Crazy Charlie would have been proud of me. Not five feet through the door I tripped over something and crashed to the floor. Looking back, I saw what had taken my feet out from under me. This time, it wasn't a fawn.

When I crawled over to the kid, my hand slid in a pool of what I supposed was his blood. It wasn't warm, exactly, but it was fresh. I held my bloody palm up near my face. In the dimness, the blood almost looked like chocolate syrup. I put my other hand over the kid's heart and got nothing. He was still warm, as warm as he would ever again be. I found his neck. There was no pulse to feel. As I stood up, lightning flashed and I caught a glimpse of the kid. I didn't have to see him clearly to know he was dead. I found the light switch.

The kid's shirtless body lay so that his open eyes seemed to be looking straight through the ceiling, through the roof, into infinity. *How's the view, kid?* There wasn't a lot of blood anywhere except around his body, but the only visible wound was a long, diagonal gash across his liver. The blood that had seeped out of it was thick and dark. Yet as grisly as the gash was, I couldn't believe it could account for all the blood puddled on the floor. My bet was the detectives would find some nasty wounds in his back when they rolled him over. I dialed 911 and listened to myself talk to the operator as if from another room.

I didn't quite know what to do with myself. I was frozen, as incapable of movement as the kid. He did indeed resemble Patrick, but from here, in the stark light, it was clear he was no twin. He even looked a little different from that morning. I suppose getting murdered will do that to you. I knew he wasn't Patrick, not *my* Patrick, but his death dredged it all up again and the past twenty-two years—the lies, the secrets, and deceptions—came crashing down around me. Only this time it came down all at once. I tried distracting myself, gazing around the room at anything but the body.

There was an unfurled sleeping bag, a few pairs of jeans, some rock t-shirts from bands I never heard of, and two pair of those stupid Shinjo Olympians. The window was wide open and I thought I could already hear sirens, an army of sirens, coming my way. The wail of the sirens unfroze me and I stepped into the living room to wait. *Living room.* The phrase took on new meaning. Outside rain fell in solid sheets.

I must have been hallucinating about the sirens, because it took ten minutes for the first unit to arrive. The two uniforms were named Kurtz and Fong. Kurtz was nearly as old as me, too old to still be in a uniform without stripes, and Fong was a fresh-faced Asian kid trying hard to act blasé. By the time they came in, I had sufficiently recovered my wits and had since called Carmella and Brian and filled them in. I told them to stay away as the situation was going to get complicated enough without involving them. I did ask Carmella to give one of our lawyer contacts a heads up.

I had my old badge out to show the uniforms. Neither Kurtz nor Fong were much impressed. After they patted me down, removing my .38 from its holster, checking out my wallet and credentials, we got to know each other a little. I didn't bother going into great detail about the reasons for my being at 69 Manhattan Court. *I was a licensed PI working a case. Blah, blah, blah ...* They seemed satisfied I hadn't killed the kid. *Yeah, Prager, whatever ...* Besides, making the case wasn't their headache.

"Hey," I said, "what took you guys so long to get here. I thought I heard sirens almost immediately after I called."

Both uniforms turned to each other and laughed. I must have missed the joke.

"Aren't there any fucking chairs in this place for a man to sit down?" Kurtz whined, rubbing his lower back.

"Nope."

"You did hear sirens," he said, still unhappy about the lack of chairs.

"We were right around the corner. You notice how wet we are?" Fong asked.

"Now that you mention it."

The bottoms of their trousers were dark with rain and beads of water covered the bills of their caps.

Kurtz shook his head. "My partner's not exaggerating. We had a traffic fatality at Avenue Y and Ocean Parkway. A guy ran right out into the traffic and got launched. When he came down he skidded and then got pancaked by like four other vehicles. It was ugly."

"Sounds it."

"Yeah, ugly," Fong agreed with his partner's assessment. "And really too bad. The guy was a cop."

That got my attention. "A cop?"

Kurtz sneered. "Yeah, if you consider them glorified, overpaid motherfuckin' meter maids in Suffolk County cops."

My heart was doing that jumping into my throat thing again. "A Suffolk cop?"

"A sergeant," said Fong.

"Was his name Ray Martello?"

Both Fong and Kurtz looked at me like Jesus walking on water. Lightning flashed again. If thunder followed the lightning, I didn't hear it. I thought I heard the rain falling.

[CHAPTER NINETEEN]

I sat with Paul Dukelsky in an interrogation room at the Six-One precinct on Coney Island Avenue. The Duke, as he was known around the city's courthouses, was one of the best criminal defense attorneys in New York. Dukelsky was a shark with a square jaw, green eyes, and a good heart. For every rich scum bag he defended, there were two or three wrongly convicted men now walking the streets. We had done some work for his firm, but not enough to warrant his driving in from the Hamptons to play my white knight. That was Carmella's doing. Like most straight men with a pulse and a libido, he had a thing for my partner. Good looks and confidence are magnetic qualities in any woman, but when she carries a gun and can probably kick your ass ... Well then, that's something else.

"So, Moe, let's go over this again." The Duke instructed, looking down at his wrist. I wasn't sure if he was checking the time or his tan. I did know he hadn't gotten his watch from Charlie Rolex.

"No."

"No?"

"No. Between you and the cops, I've been over this twenty times. The details aren't going to change. Ray Martello killed the kid, not me. Call Sheriff Vandervoort in Janus. Call my wife's doctors, for chrissakes! They'll tell you what's been going on. I've had it. It's what, like seven in the morn—"

"Eight-ten," Dukelsky corrected me.

"I'm exhausted and hungry and I'm not doing this anymore."

"As your attorney, I must insist you—"

"Go take Carmella out for breakfast or something and leave me the fuck alone."

He flushed red. I'd hit a nerve. "I don't see what that has to do with anything, Moe. I'm not here to discuss Carmella and me."

"I didn't know there *was* a Carmella and you."

He bowed his head, clearly trying to regroup. It never failed. Beauty and desire cut through the bullshit. For all the trappings of success, the Duke was, on the inside, like every other man I knew; an insecure fifteen year old boy who wanted to sleep with the prettiest girl in school.

"Listen, Moe ... I wanted to talk to you about—"

There was a knock on the door. Whoever was on the other side didn't bother waiting for permission before stepping into the room. It was Detective Feeney with Carmella Melendez in tow. Feeney was old school right down to his brush cut gray hair, white shirt, and squeaky black shoes. He smelled of cigarettes and coffee and wore an expression that bespoke a perpetual sour stomach. The detective had his face in a file even as he walked. Carmella's expression was hard to read.

"Looks like you were right about Martello," Feeney said, pitching the file on the desk. "We've tentatively matched a hunting knife we found on his body with the weapon used to kill the kid. And there's a bloody sole print by the bedroom window that's a match for the shoes he was wearing. And I just got off the phone with that Vandervoort guy upstate. He confirmed your story."

"Do you have an identity on the kid?"

"The vic? John James, born August eighteenth, nineteen eighty-one, San Pedro, California. He's got a sheet. Arrested several times by the LAPD for everything from shoplifting to sword swallowing, if you catch my meaning."

"That was his name, John James? Did he have an alias?" I asked.

"If he did," Feeney said, scanning the file, "it's not on his sheet. Why?"

"Nothing. Forget it." It was stupid, I know, but I was pissed off that the kid had lied to me about his name. I think maybe I was madder at myself for believing him. No one likes being played for a fool.

"We found Martello's Yukon parked on Ave Y. The sick bastard had human remains in the vehicle, a bag of bones complete with skull."

"My brother-in-law?"

"Probably. That'll take a few days to confirm. We'll be a week going over the stuff he had inside that SUV. All I know is, this guy musta hated you something wicked to go through this rigamarole. It was me and I wanted revenge, I'da just shot you."

Dukelsky's eyes got big. "I'm certain my client takes great comfort in that knowledge, Detective Feeney."

"Hey, I knew Martello's old man, the captain. He was an asshole too, but this is some crazy shit the son was doing. He made a cottage industry outta revenge."

"Is Mr. Prager free to go now, Detective Feeney?"

Feeney winked at me. "Sure, but don't go to the south seas until this is all buttoned down, okay?"

He shook my hand and Carmella's, wished us both luck. Dukelsky was smart enough not to offer up his hand. Feeney was the type of cop who had no use for lawyers and would have told Dukelsky to shove his hand up his ass.

Outside, the wind in the wake of the thunderstorms was crisp, almost autumnal, but the strength of the sun, even this early in the morning, put the lie to that. The three of us stood there in front of the precinct. I just wanted to get home, take a shower, and get some sleep. I didn't care who drove me back to my car. Dukelsky kept looking at his watch, but didn't seem that anxious to leave. Carmella still had that funky, unreadable expression on her face.

"Would you guys like to go to breakfast? My treat," said the lawyer.

"No thanks. I just need somebody to drive me back to my car before I collapse."

Carmella sighed with relief. "I'll take you. Come on."

"Just as well," Dukelsky said, "I've got to get back to Sag Harbor."
He was lying and rather unskillfully at that.

"Thanks, Paul," I said, shaking his hand. "I can't thank you enough
for helping me out. Send me the bill. I'm sorry about getting cranky in
there. It's been a rough couple of weeks for me."

"Tell me about it. Don't worry about the bill."

"Okay then."

"So long, Carmella," he said.

"Bye, Paul."

Carmella drove me toward my house and not to my car. She said
she would just arrange to have my car driven to my house and that she
didn't trust me to drive in my present state. I didn't argue. I fell asleep
before we made it to Sheepshead Bay Road.

[CHAPTER TWENTY]

The sun wasn't particularly bright nor the sky severely blue. The clouds that drifted overhead weren't shaped like angels' wings nor were they ominous and gray. The wind blew, but only enough to disappoint. It was a plain summer's day that no one would ever sing about or write a poem about or paint a picture of. In this way, it was like most days of most lives; a nearly blank page in a forgotten diary. I think if we could remember our individual days, life wouldn't seem so fleeting. But we aren't built to work that way, are we? We are built to forget.

The Maloney family plot was, as Father Blaney had pointed out on that dreary Sunday in the rain, a pretty place to be laid to rest. And the priest, in spite of himself, presided over the third burial of Patrick Michael Maloney. It was a small gathering: Katy, Sarah, Pete Vandervoort, and me. I had thought to invite Aaron and Miriam and their families, but Sarah confided in me that she had had to lobby her mother just to let me come. Katy was still pretty delicate, her feelings raw, nerves close to the surface. We all had new things to work through.

Wisely, Katy had waited for the press to lose interest before putting her little brother into the ground for a last time. It was a hot story, but only briefly. Most of the reporting focused on the sensational aspects of the kid's homicide and the Martellos', senior and junior, history of misdeeds. There were only a few oblique references to my involvement and nothing about Katy. I'm sure the press would have made more of it if they could have, but no one was talking. A story is like a fire, rob it of oxygen and it dies. Y.W. Fenn taught me that.

No one claimed the kid's body and John James was buried out in a field somewhere with the rest of the unclaimed, unwanted, and anonymous human refuse New York City seemed so proficient at collecting. I think in my younger days I might have made some gesture, maybe to pay for a decent burial or to find the kid's people. Not this time, not anymore. My time for the useless grand gesture had come and gone. I just couldn't muster much sympathy for the kid, even if he had gotten in too deep and hadn't meant to hurt anyone. It was petty, I know, but I was still pissed at his lying to me about his name. I also couldn't ignore the fact that his antics had helped shatter whatever fragile bonds that remained between Katy and me after the divorce. Sure, things might someday have collapsed under their own weight, but I would never know that now. Ray Martello had his revenge.

The day after the murder, I put in a call to Mary White to let her know how things had turned out. The awkwardness between us that began during my visit to Dayton had a long shelf life. I heard the strain in her voice during our conversation. I guess she just wanted to move on after all these years. Who could blame her? I wanted the same thing. There was genuine surprise in her voice when I told her about Martello's revenge.

"Really?" she said. "The police are certain it was him?"

"One hundred percent. His car was full of evidence linking him not only to the murdered boy, but to the plot itself. There were cash receipts, fake IDs, just a ton of stuff."

"If you're sure then ..."

"Well, yeah. Jack's grave will be left alone from now on. I'm sorry for your troubles. Be well, Mary."

Blaney kept it short and managed not to scowl during the graveside service. Maybe the priest did have a heart. Still, he used it sparingly. Fallon hung back, waiting for us to clear out before filling in the earth atop Patrick's newest coffin. The caretaker had already done a masterful job of repairing the damage to the plot. The grass bore none of the scars of the desecrations, the hedges were trim and perfect, but Fallon was no miracle worker. It would be another month before my

father-in-law's new headstone arrived, so Fallon had fashioned a serviceable wooden cross to mark the grave. The simple cross suited him
well. In the end, Mr. Roth was right; kaddish and ashes was the way
to go.

With the last *Amen* of the day, the Prager Family of Sheepshead
Bay, Brooklyn, NY, broke fully and finally apart. I found myself thinking of what Howard Bland nee Judas Wannsee had said a few days back
about the soft tissue of dinosaurs and how it was lost to history. So it
was for us, the bonds that had tied us together as one were gone. In
the grand scheme of things, the dissolution of my family was no more
significant than the death of a may fly. The earth kept turning. There
was now only Katy and Sarah, Sarah and me. I pulled Sarah aside.

"Listen, hon, I'm going to get out of here."

"I think that's best, Dad. Mom will be okay. This is her shit she's
dealing with. Someday she'll be okay and we can be—get together, the
three of us. What are you smiling at?"

"You really are the best of us, kiddo. So what are you going to do?"

"I'm going to stay with Mom until mid-August, then I'll head
back up to school."

"I don't suppose the cute deputy sheriff has anything to do with
your staying up here."

She cat grinned. "Robby? Maybe a little."

"Stay away from cops. They're nothing but trouble."

"Not all of them." Sarah slipped into my arms and kissed me on
the cheek. "Not you, Dad."

"Me most of all."

"I love you."

"Me too. Come down and visit before you go."

I watched Sarah and Katy get into Katy's car and drive off. Sarah
looked back at me. Katy never did.

[CHAPTER TWENTY-ONE]

I had heard that it was possible for a man to float on quicksand, but I didn't know if it was possible for a man to walk across it. I couldn't have anticipated that I was about to find out.

The page was turning on the first week of August when Sarah came down to Brooklyn on the day after her birthday. We went to dinner at a Thai place in Sheepshead Bay, had Carvel for dessert, then we drove into Coney Island to ride the Cyclone and the Wonder Wheel. The Cyclone was great. I must've ridden it a thousand times since I was a kid. On the other hand, I despised the Wonder Wheel. I never met a ferris wheel I liked and the Wonder Wheel was my least favorite. For one thing, it was gigantic and it had big cars that rocked and slid along rails as the huge wheel turned. My daughter always took perverse pleasure in watching me go pale and squirm.

"You crack me up, Dad. You'll ride any rickety, crappy, old rollercoaster, but this thing scares you."

"I just always feel like the bottom's going to drop out."

Sarah clucked at me like a chicken.

"How's your mom?"

"Nice segue," she said.

"Seriously."

"She was doing well for the first week or so after the burial, now ... I don't know. She's been really quiet and to herself for the last couple of days. Kinda nervous and jumpy. I guess she's just got stuff to work through."

"I suppose. You all set to get back to school?"

"Yeah." Sarah frowned.

"Robby can come visit, you know?"

"No fooling you, huh Dad?"

"Nope."

We had Nathan's hot dogs for a nightcap and Sarah dropped me back at my condo. She made some noise about wanting to get back up to Janus to see Robby, which was probably true, but I could tell she was worried about Katy. I hugged her tight, then let her go. I was doing a lot of that lately, letting go.

When I got inside, my answering machine was winking at me. I gave serious consideration to not listening. Aaron was pissed at me because I extended the time I'd taken off to work the case into a vacation. When he started ranting, I reminded him about what he had said about the stores thriving without me for twenty years. He didn't much care for my throwing his own words back at him. It was a big brother vs. little brother thing. Still, I've never been good at avoidance or procrastination. Bad news was better than no news. I pressed PLAY.

First message:

"Hello, Moe, it's me, Connie Geary ... Oh this is terribly awkward, isn't it? I'll just say it then. Truthfully, I got tired of waiting for you to call me, so I decided to call you. I hope you weren't simply humoring me that day when you said we could have dinner together. It was great seeing you and it brought back the happiest times of my life. Let's say you pick me up on Friday at eight. If I don't hear from you between now and then, I'll assume we're on. Okay then, that's Friday the eleventh at eight."

It had been a long time since I had that nervous feeling in my belly. Suddenly, I was back in high school again, staring at the phone, trying to summon up the courage to ask a girl out. Oh, God, the terror of those days. I had the phone in my hand even before listening to the second message. I put it down.

I wasn't going to live out the rest of my life in monk's robes and if I was going to be dating again, Constance Geary was a hell of a start. We had shared history, people in common, things to talk about. There wouldn't be any of those endless, awful silences to be filled in with uncomfortable stares or panicky trips to the rest rooms. And Connie was certainly pleasant enough to look at.

Next message:

"Yo, Five-O, dis Marlon Rhodes, man ... You remember me ... from Cincinnati? We talked once 'bout dat crazy lady, Jack White's sista. I got all up in your face and shit. Dat was a bad day when y'all called me. You still interested, I can be put in a better mood, if y'all hear what I'm sayin'."

End of new messages.

I heard what he was saying, all right, but that ship had sailed. Poor Marlon had missed his big payday. Yet, I couldn't help but wonder why he'd chosen today to call.

I opened my eyes on the Irish Wolf Hound of dog days. It was nearly a hundred degrees by noon and the humidity was beyond ridiculous. You could have baked French bread on the sidewalk and grown orchids in your car. Even the stop signs were wilting. When I was a kid, this weather never bothered me. Back then, summer weather divided up only two ways; it was either raining or it wasn't; you could play ball or you couldn't. It was simple. Life was simple. My biggest concern was how many innings of stickball I could pitch. Nothing was simple now, especially not sleep.

Sleep was heavy on my mind because I woke up in worse shape than when I went to bed. After sending Sarah on her way, I hadn't been able to get to sleep and then, when sleep finally came, it kicked my ass. I tried blaming it on the weather. That was total bullshit. My condo was as cold as a meat locker. No, something was up besides the heat and humidity. It wasn't the stress of the final breakup or Sarah's impending return to school. It wasn't even those damned phone calls, though they were part of it. Connie's call made me happy and nervous. Marlon Rhodes' made me curious. Curious had its dangers.

The truth was that had I never received either call, I still wouldn't have slept well. I hadn't slept well since the day John James was murdered. I knew it was ridiculous, but it still bugged me that the kid lied about his name. I made the mistake of sharing that information with Carmella.

"Are you out of your fucking mind?"

"I told you I knew it was dumb."

"Dumb! This isn't dumb. This is stupid. I would never have closed a case if I looked for every little thing to make me miserable. The stars don't ever align the way you think they should."

"But why would he lie to me? He had nothing to gain from it."

"C'mon, Moe. You're looking for logic where there is none. The kid was a piece of shit. He was in the game. You know what hustlers are like. He lied because that's what skells do. It's a reflex, they don't think it out."

The cop's blanket answer for everything. I had known all of that before she said it. I'd uttered versions of it several times myself. I even agreed with her, yet ...

I was wise enough not to share with Detective Feeney the reason I asked him to lunch. We met at a Chinese restaurant on Avenue U near Ocean Avenue. His choice. He was already seated in a red vinyl booth when I arrived. He was dressed as he was the first time we met: white shirt, same polyester tie. His hair must've been made of real bristles the way that brush cut stood up to the humidity. We shook hands and stared at the menus. I don't understand why people stare at Chinese menus. They always know what they're going to order.

"Food good here?"

"Who cares? The air conditioning's great." Feeney grinned.

Feeney was old school down to what he ordered: egg drop soup, chicken chow mein, and pork fried rice. Christ, it was like eating with my parents. I ordered crispy duck that wasn't especially crispy and was barely duck.

"So," he said, shoveling a fork full of fried rice into his mouth, "does this mean we're goin' steady?"

"I just wanted to say thanks for not making it as hard on me as you could have."

"Don't bullshit me, Prager." Funny, I had said those same words to the kid. "You got a bug up your ass about something. Wait ..." He put down his fork, wiped his mouth with his linen napkin, and then reached under his chair. "You wanna take a look at the file, right?"

"I do."

"Last person who said those words to me had my children."

"From me, you'll have to settle for the chow mein," I said.

He plopped the file on the table, but kept his forearm across it. "Before I let you take a look-see, I just wanna give you a chance to forget it, to finish your meal and walk away."

"And why would I do that?"

He tapped the folder with stubby fingers. "Because you ain't gonna find what you're lookin' for in here. The only thing you're gonna find is unhappiness."

"How do you know what I'm looking for?"

"I know. Believe me, Prager, I know. You think you're the first ex-cop I ever dealt with?" Feeney didn't wait for an answer. "Ask your partner, Melendez, she'll tell you."

"She already did."

"See, this here file contains the answers to questions of what and when, but that ain't what you want. You don't wanna know a what or a when. You wanna know a why. Am I right or am I right?"

"Right. But why agree to have lunch?"

"I was hungry."

"Very funny, but why do this for me?"

"I didn't do it for you. I did it for me, so I can get some peace. If I didn't let you see it, you'd be calling me with all sorts a stupid questions. Eventually, you'd show up with a court order and I don't got time for that shit. I got cases on my desk from the year of the flood. This way, I figured to save me a lot of time and grief."

I didn't argue. Why argue with the truth? When I reached for the file, however, his arm didn't budge.

"Last chance, Prager. Take my advice. There's only more unhappiness waitin' for you in here."

"I'll take my chances."

"First, I wanna know what's eatin' you. Then you can see the file."

I guess I blushed a little bit.

"That stupid, huh?" he said. "Oh, this is gonna be good."

I explained about the kid lying to me about his name. Feeney had enough respect to let me finish before he started laughing. When he got done wiping the tears from his eyes, he slid the file across the table.

We didn't speak again for another quarter hour. During that time, Feeney finished his meal, had a dish of pistachio ice cream, and a plate of pineapple chunks. When I was done, I slid the file back across the table to him.

"You satisfied?" he said, patting his full belly. "What'd I tell you? It's as solid a case as I ever made. We got every kinda evidence against Ray Martello that's ever been invented and then some."

"Yeah, it was like he wrapped himself up in a neat little package for you and then by getting himself squished, saved the mess of a trial. No loose ends. Nice and tidy. Pretty convenient all the way around."

"Perfect."

"Yeah, maybe a little too perfect," I said.

"What's that supposed to mean?"

"Let's take a ride."

Feeney agreed, a look of resignation on his face. My guess was he knew this was coming and he had already cleared a few hours to waste with me.

I parked my car on Avenue Y in approximately the same spot Ray Martello had parked his Yukon on the night he killed the kid. As I slipped into the space, Feeney's resigned expression reshaped itself into a knowing smile. When I unlocked the doors, he didn't move.

He said, "Where're you goin'? We can do this in here in the air conditioning, you know?"

"Do what?"

"Weren't you gonna ask me to explain why Martello would park his SUV on the west side of Ocean Parkway while he committed the homicide on the east side? That's six busy lanes of traffic he had to cross at night to make his escape, right? Why would he do that? Then you were gonna point out to me that most of the witnesses, includin' the drivers that hit him, swear Ray Martello was runnin' not away from the crime scene but towards it when he got smacked. Am I right?"

"You know you are," I said.

"See, Prager, it's all those why questions, they're gonna make you miserable. I don't know why he parked his Yukon here. Maybe he couldn't get a spot on the other side of Ocean Parkway or maybe he didn't want anyone to notice his car. Why was he running the wrong way? Maybe he thought he forgot something at the crime scene. Maybe he got disoriented because he didn't know Brooklyn so good. Maybe because really killing someone ain't as easy as people think and it fucks 'em up a little. Maybe because he had twice the legal limit of alcohol in his bloodstream mixed with Xanax. You see, I don't have to know why he did those things. I only have to know that he did them."

"What about the alcohol and Xanax?"

"What about them?" Feeney asked. "You ever kill anybody?"

"No."

"You think if you were gonna have to kill someone you knew in cold blood, and a kid at that, that you might have to fortify yourself a little? I know I would."

"But he had enough alcohol and drugs in him to make an elephant loopy."

"He was a cop, not a pharmacist, Prager. Besides, maybe that's why he was disoriented and ran in the wrong direction."

What he said was making sense and it made me realize how silly and desperate I must have sounded, but I guess I'd already passed the point of caring just how silly.

"Did he have a prescription for the Xanax?" I asked.

"You're shittin' me, right? We can drive into your old precinct and within twenty minutes I could buy enough Xanax, Valium, Methadone, and Oxycontin to put out a herd of fuckin' elephants. Trust me, Prager, as a brother cop and as a guy who's seen a lot of good men torture themselves over stupid details, leave it be. The answers you're lookin' for, you ain't gonna find here, not on these streets, not in that file. Ray Martello was a sick bastard who was willin' to go a long way to get his revenge. He killed the kid, panicked, and ran into traffic. End of story. You're never gonna know why the kid lied to you about his name. He just did."

I was almost ready to give in, but not yet. "What about this mysterious guy who drove the kid around, Martello's friend with the eyepatch? You haven't been able to find him."

"Frankly, we haven't been lookin' real hard. Maybe he exists, maybe he doesn't. Bottom line, the people who matter in this case are dead." Feeney said, running out of patience.

"And the bloody shoe print ... Why was there only one? Martello had to cross almost the entire length of the room to get out the back window, but he only left one print."

"Cause Martello was part kangaroo and hopped to the window. Remember, I don't have to know why. There was only one print because there was only one print. Drive me back to the Six-One now, okay? You can keep a set of the autopsy photos as a momento of our date, but playtime is officially over."

When I dropped him back at the precinct, he thanked me again for lunch and warned me not to call him about the case. I promised I wouldn't, but I had my fingers crossed.

During my ride into Brooklyn Heights, I went over everything Detective Feeney had said. The thing of it was, he was right. With Ray Martello and the kid dead, I could research the hell out of their histories, interview everyone who ever knew them, put their lives under the world's most powerful microscope, and I would still be asking why. It dawned on me, that the real question of why didn't have to do with the kid lying to me about his name, but about why I cared. I thought about what the late Israel Roth would have said vis-a-vis my state of mind.

"Mr. Moe," he'd say, "you are hanging onto the case because you don't want to let Katy go. Patrick bound the two of you together as powerfully, more powerfully maybe than wedding vows or gold rings. When in the hospital you told her about the fake Patrick and she got so angry, it was the same. It's like this number on my forearm, even if you could scrub it away, I would still be bound, for good or bad, to my past. If you said to me, come Izzy, I could get that thing removed, I'm not sure I would go."

It's funny, even when I imagined the words Mr. Roth might say, I heard his voice in my head. I put my hand to my mouth. I was smiling. By the time I got into the office, the weight of the whys had lifted. I walked directly into Devo's command center and released him from wasting anymore time on my preoccupation.

"Devo, forget working on any of that stuff related to Katy's brother and tackle the backlog. We have to make some money around here with paying customers."

"Are you quite sure, Moe? I have sharpened some of the—"

"Forget it. I'm moving on. Just bag the stuff up and I'll return it."

"Okay."

Carmella was in her office and was standing by a file cabinet when she told me to come in. I couldn't help but stare. She followed my eyes.

"You're showing a little," I said.

"You're grinning like an idiot, Moe."

I didn't say anything, but walked up to her and reached out my hand to feel her little belly. I stopped myself. People often don't realize what an incredibly intimate and loaded gesture it is to place your hand on a pregnant woman's abdomen. It's reaffirming, connective, even sexual. I remembered complete strangers touching Katy without a thought of asking permission when she was pregnant with Sarah. It's almost instinctive, tribal, at least.

"It's okay for you to touch me."

And I did. She placed her hand on top of mine. "You're keeping it," I said.

"I am. It's a pretty amazing thing to have someone growing inside you."

"Now *you're* grinning like an idiot."

"Am I?" She blushed.

"We are going to have to rearrange things around here, if this little girl's go—"

"—boy. Little boy. I know it."

"If this little boy's going to get a healthy start."

She removed her hand from mine. "We'll talk about it when the time comes."

"Fair enough," I said.

Her grin faded as suddenly as it had appeared and her mood darkened. "Moe, I guess I should tell you that the baby is—"

"—Dukelsky's. I know. I knew the minute he showed up at the Six-One. It was a guilty favor he was doing. It all fit together. I think he tried to talk to me about you two, but I stopped him."

"Some of the things I said about him, they were … not fair. He just doesn't want a baby now or to get married. He's been married and divorced and has two kids. I don't want to marry him anyway. This was my fault. I chased him, Moe. I have for years."

"Why?" There was that question again. "You could have any man you want."

She brushed the back of her hand against my cheek. "No, I can't."

"Come on, Carmella, let's not do this again."

"That's right." Her eyes burned. "We can't be together because it makes too much sense. We can't be together because of your rules. Because some man raped me as a little girl, because it was you who saved my life, because my parents changed my name, because I lied to you about who I was, because I got my shield and you didn't, because your wife tossed you to the curb, be—"

"Stop it!"

"Get out of my office!" she hissed. "Get out of here. At least Paul was honest with himself and me. Get out!"

Down on Court Street, the air was thick enough to swim through. Truck fumes coagulated around bits of dust, falling to the asphalt like volcanic ash. People on the sidewalk were defeated. A city bus stopped in front of me. A pair of brown eyes much like Carmella's stared out at me from an ad on the side of the bus. The eyes were set in the face of a watch. The copy read: *Timing isn't everything. It's the only thing. Harmony Watches.*

"Kiss my ass," I heard myself mutter. So too, apparently, did the woman standing next to me. She just shook her head no.

[CHAPTER TWENTY-TWO]

The heat broke while I slept, massive thunderstorms washing away the haze and defeat. I bought a cup of coffee, walked across the street, and watched the fishing boats set out for blues or porgies or whatever else was foolish enough to bite at the thousands of tangled lines dropped into the Atlantic off the coast of New Jersey or Montauk. The decks were packed with beer-for-breakfast buddies full of good cheer and anticipation. A little chop on the water would wipe away those smiles in an instant, but for now the world was perfect. The boats' throaty motors revved up and one by one they headed directly into the rising sun. One hour down, the rest of my life to go.

As tired of the wine business as I was, I didn't do well with spare time. I'd made sure to never really have a lot of it. Between the wine stores and the agency and Katy and Sarah, I managed to keep myself pretty much occupied. But now with Sarah staying in Ann Arbor most of the year and with my more recent exile from Katy-ville, spare time seemed like it was going to be a bigger part of my life. I had at least the next two weeks off and I was bored silly an hour into my day. In the short term, my date with Connie couldn't get here soon enough. In the long term, Carmella getting fat with child would mean more work for me at the agency. *Hallelujah! Praise the Lord!*

I bought every newspaper I could find, another cup of coffee, and headed back upstairs to read myself blind. The phone machine came to my rescue. I was halfway hoping it was Aaron or Klaus needing me to fill in at one of the stores, but it was a confused and impatient

Marlon Rhodes wondering why I hadn't taken him up on his offer. This time I called him back. I got his machine.

"Mr. Rhodes, this is Moe Prager returning your—"

"Yo, yo, yo! Marlon here, man." He referred to himself in the third person.

"Sorry I didn't get back to you sooner."

"So, y'all still interested in Mr. White's crazy-ass sista?"

"Depends."

"Man, don't play me like dat."

"How should I play you?"

"I play for pay, man."

"Yeah, I figured that out already. I got no problem with paying if I get a taste of what it is I'm paying for. But I have to warn you, Marlon, I'm not nearly as interested as I was that first time we spoke."

He thought about that a second. "Fair 'nough."

"I'm listening."

"Mr. White, he was a good man. He really gave a shit 'bout his students and all. Helped me out with money sometimes too. Got me into treatment and everything, f'all the good dat did. When he died, his sista tried to make us into like some fucked up little family, havin' us over for dinners and shit, but she wasn't like Mr. White. She was all spooky Jesus and shit. She be playin' us like old cassette tapes of Mr. White wishing her Happy Birthday or Merry Christmas. It was weird, man, hearin' his voice and all. Then she get judgmental and shit, tryin' to tell us all how to act. Mr. White, he wasn't never dat way."

"These cassette tapes, were they only Jack's voice?"

"Mostly, but sometimes there was this other man on there."

"Patrick?"

"If you say so. He was young. I *can* say dat. Been a long time, man."

My heart was racing and my mind was a blur.

"Yo, Five-O, y'all still there?"

"Sorry, Marlon. I got distracted there a second. What happened with these dinners?

"Without Mr. White, most of us, we went our own ways. Some of us went farther then others, if y'all hear what I'm sayin'.'"

I read between the lines. "How long a stretch did you do?"

"Ten year bid in Kentucky for movin' a little rock."

"That's a long time inside."

"Man, when y'all doin' nigga time in Kentucky, ten minutes a long time inside."

"I can imagine."

"No you can't."

Touche. "So what happened?"

"I don't hear from his sista again until like eight weeks ago. I guess she heard I sometimes still went out to the cemetery. Dat's how she got my number, from one of the others."

"What did she say?"

"She all nice and shit now, sayin' how she appreciates me still visitin' her brother and all."

"But ..."

"But dat she askin' everybody not to go out to the cemetery for a few weeks. She say some shit about them doin' some ground work."

"That's weird."

"I told you, man. She crazy."

"Marlon, I gotta ask. Why didn't you talk to me when I first called you and why'd you wait until now to call back?"

He didn't answer. It was price setting time, but I didn't feel like haggling.

"How much?" I said.

"Five hundred."

"Sold. Now let's hear it."

"Y'all think I'm some kinda fool nigga? Dat was way too easy. My price goin' up."

"Don't mistake my impatience with stupidity, Marlon. I'll throw you another hundred, but then the bank's closing forever. There's a limit to how much I'm willing to spend to satisfy my curiosity."

"Okay, cool. Six hundred."

"Six hundred," I repeated. "So what took you so long to call me back?"

"She call me last Friday, all apologetic and religious and shit. Kept sayin' she was sorry and dat the Lord will be with me. Hell, man, the next time the Lord is with me, dat'll be the first time. But I didn't disrespect her or nothin'. I guess she jus' a crazy old lady after all."

"Maybe," I said. "Maybe. Did she say what she was sorry for?"

"I didn't ask. Jus' wanted to get off the phone."

"Hey, Marlon, how'd you like me to hand deliver that money tomorrow?"

"Tonight would be better, but I s'pose I can wait."

"I suppose you'll have to."

[CHAPTER TWENTY-THREE]

I knew something wasn't right the minute I turned the corner onto Mary White's street. There was a local agent's For Sale sign up at the edge of the meticulous little yard in front of her house. Hung beneath the larger sign was a smaller one. "Priced to Sell," it read. Both signs swung gently in the early afternoon breeze. A blue jay perched on the mailbox, cocked its head at the signs and flew away. He wasn't buying.

Marlon Rhodes had wanted to tag along and though I could've used the company, I decided to part ways with him and my money back in Cincinnati. Showing up on Mary White's doorstep with Marlon in tow would have been tough to explain away. Never mind Marlon, I couldn't think of what the hell I was going to tell her about *my* being there. I guess I needn't have worried.

There was no answer when I knocked or pressed the front door-bell. I called her number on my cell. The phone rang and rang and ... That was funny. I knew she had an answering machine. I'd left messages on it. I could hear her old fashioned phone ringing out in the street. My belly tied itself in knots. I remembered what happened the last time I listened to an unanswered telephone. I walked around the house, cupping my hands against side and back windows. I knocked on the rear door. Mary White was gone. Coming back around the front of the house, a young, chubby-faced woman with dull brown hair and a lazy eye called to me from the adjoining yard.

"She ain't around," Lazy Eye said, a little boy crying from inside her house.

"I can see that."

"You interested in the house?"

"Might be," I lied. "Do you know where the owner is?"

"Traveling."

"Traveling?"

"Yup, that's—" She was interrupted by the boy's crying. "Shut up! I'll be right in. Eat your cereal."

"Do you know where she went?"

"Nah. My neighbor and me, we don't get along so well. But you can try the real estate agent. He's nice. Name's Stan Herbstreet. Sold me and Larry our house. Stan's office number's on the sign. You a family man?" she asked, with a suspicious twist of her mouth.

"Sure am. Got a grown daughter and a little boy about three from my second marriage," I lied some more. "Gonna do some work at the air force base."

She stepped toward me and whispered conspiratorially, "Please take the house. The old lady's a nasty bitch who hates my kid." On cue, the kid wailed. She turned over her shoulder. "Shut up! Mommy's talking to the nice man who's going to buy Mary's house."

"Well," I said, "I guess I'll make that call to the real estate agent. Thanks for—"

"Listen, if you are *really* interested ..." Lazy Eye stepped even closer, looking this way and that. "I know how you can have a peek around inside without bothering Stan. The old biddy keeps a key in the wood planter on the patio. This way when you call Stan, you'll have a better idea of what you should offer."

"Gee, thanks a ton ..." I offered her my hand.

She took it. "Roweena. Roweena with a double-e."

"Thanks, Roweena double-e. I hope I like the house."

"For our sake, I hope so too."

The key was right where she said it would be. I smiled and waved that I had found it. I walked very slowly to the back door, praying Roweena would go attend to her screaming kid. She did, finally. The key slid into the cranky old lock and turned with a little help. Stepping in, I held my breath. Finding the kid dead affected me more than I was willing to let on ... even to myself. When, at last, I inhaled, there was a bit of mustiness in the air, but nothing more.

The museum piece house was as neat and clean as I remembered it. All of it except for Mary's bedroom. Understandably, this room hadn't been part of the original tour. It smelled of camphor, cloves and orange peel, of lilacs and roses, of dried flowers from a dried up life tied in a sack and tucked away in a corner somewhere amongst her unrealized dreams. Mary had packed in a hurry. Her ancient dresser drawers were all open and askew, the closet door ajar. Empty hangers were strewn about the room: on the bed, on the floor, at the foot of the full length mirror. Her jewelry box was empty too, dumped upside down on the bed on a pile of hangers.

I searched the dresser drawers, remembering how my dad had grown odd at the end, obsessed with making lists of the inconsequential aspects of his life. He wrote reams and reams of lists on foolscap. When he died, we knew where his hankies and t-shirts, his pens and broken watches, his rings and school yearbooks could be found, but we could never find where his happiness had got to. We wondered if he had ever truly been happy at all. There are some things it's better for kids not to wonder about their parents.

There wasn't anything to be found in the dresser drawers or in the closet or beneath the bed, but in the nightstand drawer were old letters from Jack, all with New York postmarks. Behind the family Bible and photo albums on the nightstand shelf were twenty neatly stacked cassette boxes. Each box was labelled with Jack's name, an event, and or a corresponding date. *Jack, Christmas 1976*. There were tapes in nineteen of the twenty boxes. It did not take me long to figure out where that missing tape had gone. Questions filled my head. How had Ray Martello gotten to Mary White? What could he have told her? How much could he have paid her? What had Katy or I ever done to her except treat her with respect?

I shook my head, thinking Mary mustn't have understood what was going on. But in my bones I knew that was wrong. Not only had Mary White known, she was an active participant. Now I understood Mary's discomfort around me, her strange affect on the phone, the weirdness in the cemetery. There were never any roses on her brother's grave or, if there had been, Mary White placed them there herself. No one painted on Jack's headstone. Mary simply scrubbed the stone for my benefit, the missing dirt from where she'd washed it had been enough to convince me of the vandalism.

I slid a few of the cassettes into my pocket and headed toward the back door, but decided to take a second, more careful look around. In the kitchen, I found some flight information, two phone numbers, and an address in Kentucky scribbled onto a pad. Next to the address was the notation, #12. I ripped off the sheet and tucked it into my pocket with the cassettes. There was nothing else to see. I tiptoed out the back, replacing the key in the planter. Unfortunately, Roweena— double e, one lazy eye—had been keeping watch.

"Well?"

"Nice," I said, "but a bit claustrophobic."

She didn't look pleased. I fairly ran to my rental car. Her kid was still crying.

Locating the cemetery proved more challenging than expected. With some help from a trucker, I found my way. Once through the gates, I was confident I'd be able to find Jack's resting place. *Wrong.* I thought I retraced the route Mary had taken—around the huge stone crucifix, two lefts, straight ahead twelve rows, a right and a left—but I just couldn't find the small chunk of stone adorning Jack's grave. I tried it three more times with some minor variations before admitting defeat and heading into the administrative offices.

The woman at the desk checked the book.

"You weren't wrong, sir, Mr. White is indeed interred there, but your confusion is understandable." She made a sour face. "The headstone has been recently replaced."

Had it ever. No wonder I hadn't recognized the site. In place of the tasteful block of bevelled granite which had stood vigil at the head of Jack White's grave was a massive black tombstone vaguely reminiscent of the monolith in *2001*. I couldn't quite believe the scale of it; a sequoia among the shrubbery. Carved into the rich black stone were prayerful hands, crosses, scrolls, angels, and a rendering of Jack's face. There was a bible quotation, lines from a favorite poem. With all that, there was still enough empty space on the stone to have added the entire text of *War and Peace* or to list the names of America's war dead. All of them, ever. A mourners bench had been added as well. It was constructed of the same black stone, tasteful only by comparison to the monolith. I suppose Mary could have tried to buy Cleopatra's Needle or Stonehenge, but she'd done okay on her own. Looking past the hideousness of the new monuments, I realized just how much they must have set Mary back. Ray Martello had paid her a pretty penny for her betrayal.

Without his sister around to scowl at me, I considered placing a rock atop Jack's new headstone. Unfortunately, Mary hadn't thought to include an elevator or build steps into the side of the headstone. I placed a pebble at the base of the black giant and walked away. Poor Jack. If anything ever cried out for a sledgehammer, it was that thing in my rearview mirror.

Not unexpectedly, the address in Kentucky was a cheap motel near the airport. One of the phone numbers Mary had scribbled down was traceable back to room twelve at that same motel. The desk clerk, a Pakistani kid, was happy to help. The fifty bucks I slipped him was more of an incentive than the bullshit story I laid on. I described Mary, gave him the date of her flight, and asked him to check on who had been registered in room twelve that day.

"No, I am very very sorry," he said in an Urdu inflected lilt. "We did not have a woman like you describe in the room that day." He read me a list of three names, all men, none of them familiar. I asked if he remembered what any of the men looked like. "One was a nasty older fellow. Big, with an eyepatch."

The desk clerk might have said something else, but I didn't hear him. I think I might have thanked him. So, there was a mystery man, but his existence raised some questions not even Feeney could ignore. Suddenly, I didn't feel quite so stupid or desperate.

Back in my rental, I called the other phone number Mary White had written down. Someone picked up. I could hear breathing on the other end.

"Hello," I said, feeling cocky, overplaying my hand.

He snickered at me and hung up. I got a chill, but not because I knew who had been on the phone. I didn't. I didn't need to know. I could recognize a ghost when I heard one.

[CHAPTER TWENTY-FOUR]

US Air to New York. Aer Lingus to Dublin. Those were Mary White's flight details. I had checked the numbers out at the airport before getting on my plane back to LaGuardia. Problem was, both of her flights were one passenger short. At least that's what Feeney told me. Mary White was somewhere, but it wasn't Dublin, Ireland. Dublin, Ohio was more likely.

Detective Feeney was a stubborn bastard, not a fool, so when I returned from Cincinnati armed with a little bit more than desperate questions, he was, at least, willing to listen. I had to give the man credit. Most detectives with such a neatly closed case would have told me to go fuck myself. On the other hand, he wasn't exactly reopening the investigation. He agreed, if grudgingly so, to keep an eye out for Mary White. He'd also alerted both the Dayton PD and the Ohio State Police that Mary White was a "person of interest" for the NYPD—although she was only of interest to me—and that she might be on the run. But that was as far as it went. Feeney had no intention of looking for the mystery man.

"But why would this guy be meeting with Mary White after Martello was dead?"

"Don't push it, Prager. This mystery man's not my problem. Maybe he was a real loyal friend to Ray Martello and was fulfilling a promise or somethin'. You know, like makin' a last payment. Frankly, I don't know and I don't give a shit. I'll do you the one favor and keep tabs on what the Ohio cops come up with about the old broad, but this mystery guy's your headache."

So it was official, Cyclops was my headache. Now he was Brian Doyle's headache as well. I got Brian to take the few personal days we owed him. He was glad to do it seeing as I was matching his per diem—in cash—plus expenses. Double time and expenses; nice gig if you can get it. I just couldn't bring myself to march back into the office and reinvolve the staff, not officially. I'd already used the agency for my private business for too long. It was bad for business and bad for morale. Until I had something more substantial than a missing cassette tape from Mary White's bedroom and a meeting in an airport motel between an old lady and a one-eyed man, I would play it close to the vest.

The worst part was I hadn't told Carmella about this little arrangement between Doyle and me. I had no intention of telling her, not yet, anyway. She would murder me, and rightfully so, for going behind her back. But so far I wasn't getting much return on my investment. Brian was batting 0 for two days. He hadn't found any of Martello's friends or family or fellow cops who either matched the mystery man's description or knew of someone who did. I thought it was kind of strange that Doyle had gotten nowhere. The one-eyed man, from everything Mira Mira and the desk clerk in Kentucky had said, was a hard man to forget. Let's face it, the eyepatch alone would be pretty memorable.

"Anything?" I asked, squeezing the cell phone between my neck and ear.

"Nada, boss. No one knows this guy and believe me, Moe, I talked to alotta people. I mean, I was going to hell anyways before you had me do this little job for you, but I've lied so much to so many people in the last coupl'a days … I couldn't say enough Our Fathers or Hail Marys or light enough candles to atone for the bullshit I've been spreading. I'm telling the cops I'm Martello's brother. I'm telling his family I'm a Suffolk cop. I'm telling some of his friends that I'm a cop and some that I'm family. I'm lying so much, I can't even keep track. I wouldn't mind so much if it was getting me somewheres."

"Okay, listen, get into Brooklyn and canvass Manhattan Court."

"Where Martello killed the kid?"

"Right. Describe both Martello and our mystery man to the neighbors. Ask if they remember either man being around that day or ever."

"What's the point, boss? I mean, we know Martello murdered the kid."

"Maybe it's time to pretend we don't know anything for sure. Just do it, Doyle. For what I'm paying your lazy ass, you shouldn't be asking why."

"I'll leave in a few minutes. I'll be happy to get outta here. Long Island is creepy. Too quiet for me."

"I know exactly what you mean."

"Where you headed, boss?"

"Long Island." I hung up before he could ask any other questions. The last thing I needed was to try and explain my dating Connie Geary to him. I'd have to explain it to myself first.

At eight in late June or July, the sun would have still been pretty well up. That's how I had seen the Geary manse the first time I came calling. Back then, I'd also gotten to meet Senator Steven Brightman. He was full of promise and full of shit; the perfect con man and consummate politician. I should've known I was being played by how hard everyone was working me. Thomas Geary threatened and bribed. Brightman charmed. In my own defense, I had been bullied into taking the case in the wake of Katy's miscarriage. I was still reeling from the turmoil that followed in its wake. On the heels of losing a baby of my own, how could I not take the case of a missing daughter of an ex-NYPD cop? How could I not save the politician who was going to save us all?

Brightman was the serpent to my Eve and I bit the apple hard. Not unlike Judas Wannsee, Brightman had that magical ability to make you feel like you were the most important person in the room, the only person in the room. He could talk to a crowd, but you felt—no, you knew—he was talking directly to you. And when we met that evening in 1983, he worked his stuff. The myth is that great politicians know when to lie. The opposite is the reality. It's how they parse the truth. The night we met, Brightman answered my questions directly, even admitting that he and Moira Heaton had slept together. He had innoculated himself by telling me a negative truth. It was brilliant, just not brilliant enough.

I'm not necessarily a big believer in the truth. Katy will tell you that about me, but that's not how I mean it. What I mean is that the truth doesn't conform to the rules of Sunday school or sermons, to cliches or adages. The truth doesn't always come out in the wash or in the end and it's frequently not for the best. The truth often makes things worse, much worse. The truth can be as much poison as elixir, cancer as cure. And I knew some ugly truths about Steven Brightman that had put an end to his political career, but that gave no comfort to the dead and grieving.

I put Steven Brightman out of my head. It was an August sun falling down over the brim of the earth. The sky was a heavy shade of dusk, the stars more than vague hints of light. The darkening air was rich with the sweet scent of nicotina and lavender from the gardens. Their sweetness playing nicely against the predominant smell of fresh cut grass drifting over from the golf course next door. I pulled up to the house, my shirt slightly damp from nervous sweat. But I was enjoying the delicate buzz of excitement and anticipation I had going. It had been a very long time.

Connie met me at the door, her blond hair swept back, her white smile and clear blue eyes sparkling. We sort of stared awkwardly across the threshold at each other, not knowing quite what to do. She reached out, taking my hand, and pulled me into the house. When I was inside, she kissed me shyly on the lips. I kissed her back as shyly. No one ran screaming. We had gotten by the first hurdle. Both of us took deep breaths.

"Hi, Moe. God, I've been so nervous all week. I was worried you'd cancel. A scotch?"

"Sure."

"Come on into the den."

I followed. She was dressed in a clingy floral print and open-toed shoes with a low heel. Her muscular calves flexed as she walked to the bar. I noticed not only what she was wearing and how she looked, but the pleasant effect it was having on me.

"I've been looking forward to this as well, I think even more than I knew," I said.

"Really?" She handed me my scotch and we clinked glasses. "What's been going on in your life?"

I thought about not answering or deflecting the question with the usual nonsense, but thought it would be a bad precedent. I told her.

"My lord," she said, refilling my glass. "What madness. Can revenge really be such an obsession?"

"Apparently. It was so important to my father-in—to my late ex-father-in-law, that he wanted it from his grave. Good scotch."

"You sold it to me. Your store did, at least."

"Listen, Connie, can we stay off the subject of graves and revenge for now? I've spent a little too much time in cemeteries lately."

"Absolutely."

Connie put her drink down, pressed herself against me, and kissed me in a way I would not describe as shyly. I returned her kiss and then some. Connie had other talents besides playing the piano. Kissing Connie didn't come with the baggage of kissing Katy nor with the depth of feeling and darkness of kissing Carmella. It was, in any case, an amazing sensation. Other than those two weak moments I shared with Carmella and the spontaneous moment with Tina Martell, Connie was the only woman beside Katy I had kissed in the last twenty years.

"How's your dad doing?" I changed subjects.

"I'm afraid he's taken a bit of a bad turn. He's in the hospital, but should be home next week some time."

"Sorry to hear it."

"What can one do? It's the nature of the disease. Mom will be back by then. At least my son doesn't have to deal with it. He's up at football camp for the next two weeks. Come, let's get out of here and leave these depressing things behind us. In fact," she said, reaching into her clutch and pulling out her cell phone, "can we make a deal? How about we shut out the rest of the world for the evening and focus only on the two of us?"

"Deal," I said, making a show of shutting off my cell phone.

She put hers down on the bar.

"I'll drive," I said.

"Oh, no you won't. The car will be here in a few minutes. We're focusing on each other, no distractions."

My first impulse was to argue. I didn't. It felt good to give in, to turn control of things over to someone else for a change.

"Would you like me to play for you until the driver gets here?"

"Maybe later," I said, pulling her close. "Maybe later."

I hadn't been on a date in about a quarter century, so nearly every inch of the night was a revelation. Around our second bottle of old vine Zinfandel, when it became clear that bed had gone from our possible to our inevitable destination, the rate of revelation picked up speed. The odd thing about marriage is that it lulls you into a comfortable forgetfulness. You forget that the dance you do can be nearly the same and yet be almost completely different. You forget what it's like to discover excitement instead of relying on it. You forget that even awkwardness has its potent charms and that first times do still exist in the universe. You can know in your head that every woman has a different taste, a different scent, a different feel, but to be reawakened to the sense of it was an indescribable and unexpected shock.

Connie Geary was everything I would have wanted for my debut in the world of the recently single. She was good company, familiar enough, but not too familiar. She was comfortable with herself, at ease with me, smart, skeptical, not cynical. She was unembarrassed by her family's wealth, but not blind or unsympathetic to the plight of the rest of the world. In bed, Connie was eager, sharing, unafraid. She was all of those things and yet I knew I would never visit her bed again.

The night had been both wonderful and hollow somehow. For all the laughs and kisses, wanting looks, flirtatious touches, and orgasms, there didn't seem to have been an ounce of spontaneity in the entire evening. I don't want to say it all felt staged—no man wants to think the moans and clenches, the screams and spasms, are the result of careful rehearsal and not passion—but I couldn't escape the sense of things having been story-boarded, that each step had been premeditated. Even when I got up at five to shower, I knew Connie Geary would follow me in a few minutes later and take me in her mouth. Knowing didn't stop me from enjoying.

Perhaps the strangest aspect of the whole experience was the parting. We had, it seemed, used up all our awkwardness in our twelve hours together. Our farewell was almost business-like; pleasant, courteous, distant. There were no hard feelings, no angry words, no accusations. Pulling down the driveway, I could see Connie in my sideview mirror. She stood at the edge of the portico, giving me a goodbye wave so slight it was barely noticeable. The look on her face was unvarnished and predatory.

Is this, I wondered, what being alone did to you? Had Connie played out this scene over and over again with any number of men? Had they all disappointed her? Was she disappointed even before they showed up? Is that why it was, in spite of all the heat, so empty an experience? Christ, it was all so very odd. Heading back to Brooklyn, I didn't find myself missing Katy so much as the marriage itself.

[CHAPTER TWENTY-FIVE]

I knew the second I walked through the condo door that the world had changed when I wasn't looking. My phone machine was flashing without pause. I'd never seen anything like it. Reflexively, I reached for my cell and remembered the deal I'd made with Connie Geary about leaving distractions behind. The second I turned it back on, it buzzed. It was an easy choice for me between answering machine and cell. I preferred hitting one button to cell message retrieval.

First message:

"Dad, it's Sarah, listen ... We've gotta talk. Something's up with Mommy. I ... I think she's losing it. I think she's seeing Uncle Parick again. Please call me back. I'm supposed to leave for Ann Arbor to-morrow, but I don't really want to leave with Mommy like this. Call me back as soon as you get this."

The second and third messages were much the same only more frantic. Sarah was increasingly worried not only about Katy, but by her inability to reach me. The fourth and fifth messages were from Aaron and Carmella, respectively. Both had gotten calls from Sarah concerning my whereabouts and why I wasn't picking up my cell phone.

Next message:

"Yeah, Prager, this is Detective Feeney. We got a location on Mary White. She never made it outta the Ohio-Kentucky area. The airport cops found her in the trunk of her car in the short term lot. The tags had been switched. Preliminary report is the old lady was strangled. Give me a call."

There was another round of calls from Sarah and Aaron, alternating between panic and anger.

Next message:

"Hey, boss, it's Doyle. It's weird, but no one on Manhattan Court can ever remember seeing Martello. I even showed his picture around. Nothing. But the minute I mentioned the guy with the eyepatch, like ten people knew who I was talking about. And here's the really weird thing, two or three of the neighbors remember the guy with the eyepatch being there the night the kid bought it. Gimme a call. Whadaya want me to do from here?"

I picked up the phone and dialed Sarah's cell, half listening as the messages continued playing. *One ring.* The next message was from Sheriff Vandervoort. *Second ring.* Sarah had called the sheriff's station and was panicked. *Third ring.* When Sarah got up and went to check on Katy, she was gone; her bed unslept in. Her car still in the garage. *Fourth ring.*

"Dad, where the hell have you been? Mommy is—"

"I know, kiddo, I'm listening to my messages."

"Where have—"

"It's a long story, Sarah. Tell me what's going on."

She pretty much repeated what Pete Vandervoort had described and then started losing it.

"Shhhh, Sarah, calm down, calm down. It won't help anyone if you lose control. You said you thought Mom was seeing Uncle Patrick again. What makes you say that?"

"She was acting weird, like ... like she was before she tried to—"

"Weird how?"

"She was all nervous, always looking over my shoulder when we were together. She started staying in her bedroom all the time, smoking cigarettes. I could smell them through the door. She tried to get me to stay at Robby's or to come back to your place. Dad, I'm really scared."

"We'll take care of it. Your mom'll be fine," I said, in spite of all the evidence to the contrary. "I'll be up there in a few hours. In the meantime, put in a call to her shrink, okay? I'm on my way."

I stayed and listened to the remainder of the messages. They were from Aaron and Carmella, another one from Pete Vandervoort. All wondered where I was and why I still hadn't picked up my cell. Walking to my bedroom to change, I half-listened to another message, the last message. It was mostly silence, a vague, familiar silence, a chilling silence. Then a snicker.

End of new messages.

I have seldom in my life been thankful for traffic. Being thankful for traffic is akin to joy over an exit wound, but I was thankful for it that day. With the Belt Parkway jammed in both directions, I hadn't even gotten out of Brooklyn. And given all that was going on, I'd've thought my mind would be cluttered by fear over Katy's disappearance, worry for Sarah, the news of Mary White's murder. Then there was the peculiar nature of what Brian Doyle had said about no one having seen Martello on the night of the kid's murder. Never mind the call from the snickering ghost.

Yet, there in the traffic, the radio blasting *Black Coffee in Bed*, my progress measured by inches, not in miles per hour, all I could think about was Connie Geary and the expression on her face as I drove away that morning. I looked at my sideview mirror as I had earlier, trying to recreate her face with the paint of memory. Her expression was predatory, almost feral. Again, I wondered where it had come from. I wondered if she meant for me to see it. It was always the small details: Connie's expression, the kid lying to me about his name, Katy seeing ... Suddenly, I was short of breath and then the world went away.

Things became so clear to me that I hurt, I ached. I wanted to peel my skin away from my muscle, tear my muscle away from my bone, wrench all feelings away from my heart. Horns filled the air, but I could not move, could not blink, could not ... All senses deserted me. I was numb and deaf, dumb and blind. The only thing I tasted was my own bile. I heard the horns again. They were angrier now, even vengeful. Beneath the blare was a distant tapping. Still, I could not move. The tapping grew more insistent.

"Hey, buddy ... pal ..." The tapping had a voice. "Buddy, you okay?"

The world rushed back in as I turned to see a man's face pressed against my window. I looked ahead and the traffic had broken up.

"Yeah, I'm fine. Sorry."

He shrugged his shoulders, hitched up his eyebrows, the corner of his mouth. He tapped the window one more time and said, "Okay, then let's go."

I stepped on the gas and drove blind.

Although in my heart I now knew who had been pulling the strings all along, I wanted some confirmation, something tangible I could show Feeney and Pete Vandervoort. Too many times in my life I had operated on whims and hunches. Not this time, because if what I suspected was true, *was* true, then Katy's life, Sarah's, and mine were in real danger. Everything, even the murders of Mary White, the kid, Martello—yes, Martello— had been the preliminaries, the overture and first two acts. Before I went rushing upstate, I needed to know for sure.

I called ahead to Vandervoort and Sarah and warned them I might be delayed in getting to Janus. Car trouble, I'd said. The sheriff knew I was full of shit and Sarah believed me out of desperation and habit. I considered telling Vandervoort the truth, but changed my mind. There was too much to explain and if I was wrong, I didn't want to risk the sheriff shifting the focus off the search for Katy. If I was right about who had her, she'd be safe for now. The last act required me as audience.

Devo was already in the office waiting for me.

"I have it queued up for you, Moe."

The lights in his office were dimmed and he had me sit in front of one of his computer monitors. He stood behind me to my right.

"The view, I am afraid, is far from sharp, but you can make out a face," Devo said, then began explaining the mechanics of how he had coaxed the image from the gas station's security video.

"Just show it to me."

"What you will see is a continually sharpening image. When the image is at its highest resolution, the frame will freeze." He touched the mouse.

There on the monitor was the image of a slightly tinted driver's side window of a 2000 GMC Yukon. *Click.* I could barely make out the ghostly silhouette of someone in the driver's seat. *Click. Click. Click.* In tiny increments the window tinting seemed to brighten and, as it did, the silhouette became less and less ghostly. *Click.* A human face began to emerge out of the darkness. *Click.* A few seconds later I could make out a black bulge over the left eye of the emerging face. *Click.* Then, just before the frame froze, I recognized the face of the mystery man. In that brief second before the fear and resignation set in, I smiled. For now I knew where a bullet I fired in Miami Beach in 1983 had landed. I'd shot out Ralphy Barto's left eye.

Mira Mira had almost been right. While Ralph Barto wasn't a cop, he had been a US marshal and a PI. Bullet wound or not, this wasn't about revenge for his missing left eye. After all, the prick was trying to kill me when I returned fire. No, Ralph Barto was a professional lackey, not a master of the universe. Dead roses, ghosts, and graves were not his franchise. If Barto had wanted revenge, he'd have sought me out long ago, stuck a gun in my mouth, and made like Jackson Pollack. This wasn't about Ralph Barto, at least not directly, but about his boss, a man who had murdered a little boy and a political intern in coldest blood.

In 1983, Ralph Barto had two bosses: Joe Spivack and Steven Brightman. Spivack, another ex-US marshal, had owned a security firm in the same building where Carmella and I now kept our offices. His firm had done the initial investigation attempting to clear Steven Brightman from any taint in connection to his intern's disappearance. After I got involved and we cleared Brightman, Spivack went to his cabin upstate and blew his brains out. Spivack's suicide, along with some other nagging doubts, led me to question my own conclusions about Brightman's innocence. At Spivack's funeral, Ralph Barto offered his services to me. I had no way of knowing that he was Brightman's boy, a mole meant to keep tabs on me. When I got too close to the truth, he tried to kill me.

I could understand Brightman wanting revenge as much or more as Martello, but why now? Why seventeen years later? Something had had to set him off and I wanted to know what that was before we crossed paths.

"Devo," I said, "do me a favor and get on the internet."

"Sure, Moe, but why?"

"Steven Brightman."

"What about him?

"Everything, but especially about his ex-wife."

[CHAPTER TWENTY-SIX]

Connie Geary had made it happen. I knew that without Devo having to look it up. She was in this. I just didn't know how deeply. She had planted the idea of our date weeks ago. She made the call. She set the time. She made sure we were alone and I was unreachable. She arranged for the car. She picked the restaurant. She gave me the first kiss. Christ, even fucking was her idea. At least she let me choose the wine. Had she known what Brightman really had in mind? I'd like to think not. She had probably financed him. Financing Brightman's campaigns seemed to be a Geary family habit.

For a little while there, I thought about heading to Crocus Valley and grabbing her ass for trade bait. It was a good thing her son wasn't around, because I was in the kind of mood to have used him too. That's how fucked up I was. But even if I had been far gone enough to have used them both, it wouldn't have mattered. Bargaining requires that the parties value what the other party possesses, but Brightman wouldn't care about Connie or her kid. Too bad Connie was blind to that. She wouldn't be for much longer. If she had understood the end game and not involved herself, then maybe Brightman would've been forced to come directly at me instead of my family. That wasn't his way.

I was pretty sure I had some time and that Katy was in no immediate danger. My guess, my *hope* was that Brightman needed my presence to bring down the final curtain. Was I certain? No. I'd been wrong about almost everything else, but I knew Brightman, the way his twisted mind worked. So before heading into town, I stopped at the cemetery to talk with Fallon. I don't know why it had taken me so long to realize what was right in front of me from the first; that a man with a backhoe, a shed full of pick axes, shovels and sledges, a man with unfettered access to the Maloney family gravesite, was a more obvious suspect than neighborhood kids, vandalous ghosts or avenging angels. That the sheriff had also neglected this point was of no comfort.

The crunch of the gravel beneath my tires brought it full circle. I once again thought of that long ago winter's day in the cemetery with Mr. Roth. God, how I missed that man, but the love I felt for him was always tainted with guilt over my father. We're funny creatures, us humans. We live in hope that even the dead will change. I know I did. My dad loved us. We loved him, but he had cut himself off from us. He could never bring himself to meet us halfway. *So far, no further.* He was a failure at business. Even his failures were unspectacular. I don't think Aaron, Miriam or I cared about that, but he did. We saw him as a failure because he saw himself that way, because he failed us that way. Israel Roth came with none of that baggage. That baggage was reserved for his son. He was the father I chose. I was the son he wished he had. It was a cruel bargain for everyone but the both of us.

I parked in front of Fallon's neat little bungalow, but I didn't make it up the front steps. The shed door was open, creaking as it swung lazily in the early evening breeze. I reached around for my .38. Something was wrong. I could feel it in my bones. Besides, cemeteries just tend to throw me off my game. No one likes confronting the inevitable. When your life spreads out before you, there are countless possibilities. Not in the end. In the end, it's all the same. Death is the most egalitarian of things. Cemeteries, like a constant whisper in the ear, had a nasty way of reminding you of that fact.

"Fallon!" I called out. "Mr. Fallon. It's Moe Prager, Katy Maloney's ex."

The only answer was the whine of mosquito wings. They'd come out for a light supper. In the distance I heard a faint *clink, clink, clinking.* When I grabbed hold of the door and peeked around, I saw why it refused to close. Mr. Fallon's workboots were doorstops. The caretaker lay face down, one end of a pick axe stuck so completely through his left shoulder blade that the handle nearly rested on his back. There wasn't much blood, not on his back anyway. His head was pretty well smashed up. The little blood that had pooled around the wound was thick with mosquitos.

I looked up at the door header and ceiling of the shed as I backed out. Fallon hadn't been killed in the shed. No way an assailant could have swung the pick high enough to gather the momentum it would have taken to gouge through the body that way. I took a look around. On the far side of the equipment barn, I found the source of that faint *clink, clink, clinking.* Fallon's abandoned backhoe was still running, the exhaust cap popping up and down in rhythm to the puffing of diesel fumes. The blood missing from the shed was all here, but not pooled all in one place. The caretaker had received quite a beating before dying.

My cell phone buzzed even as I grabbed it to call the sheriff. It was Brian Doyle.

"You were right, boss," he said. "The tattoo babe confirmed it."

"Thanks."

I clicked off and called the sheriff.

"Pete."

"Yeah, what's up?"

"Have you seen my daughter?"

"Sarah? She was just in here with Robby, why?"

I let out a big sigh of relief. "Keep an eye on her."

"Why? What's up?"

I didn't bother explaining. "Listen, Fallon's dead."

"Fallon, the guy from the cemetery?"

"Yeah. I'm at the cemetery now. Fallon's in the tool shed, a pick axe sticking halfway out his back. My guess is—"

I never finished the sentence because a baseball bat had, at that instant, introduced itself to my right kidney. *It's way back. The left-fielder's on the warning track ... at the fence ... looking up. That ball is ... outta here!* I'll be pissing blood for a month, I thought, crumpling to the ground, if I live that long. My cell phone seemed free of the bonds of gravity and flew off somewhere, far far away. The involuntary tears and choking mucus that filled my eyes, throat, and sinuses was the least of it. The nausea, the puking, that was the bad part. It made everything else that much worse, especially the pain. When I was done puking, someone slipped a pillowcase over my head, taped it closed around my neck, and cuffed my hands behind me. Two men—I guessed there were two and that they were men—dragged me by my elbows along the dirt and gravel. I was shoved into the back of a car—my car, by the sound of it—and driven away. Someone spoke. The voice was familiar, but it wasn't Brightman's or Barto's.

"You didn't think you was gonna blow up our kitchen and get away with it, did ya?"

It was Crank.

The ride was a fairly short one. That much I could say, but I was still disoriented from the whack in the kidney and the growing pain in my head. The tape, tight around my neck, wasn't helping my respiration any and the buildup of my own vomit-sour fumes in the pillowcase was hard to take. When we stopped, I was yanked out of the car and dragged along some new dirt and stone. A door opened. I was bent into a sitting position with my legs and ass on a cool, damp floor and my back against a rough wooden wall. Something tore open the linen cocoon around my head. The rush of fresh air made me swoon. If there had been anything left in my guts, I would have puked again. As it was, I dry-retched until my head nearly exploded. Someone kicked me in the ribs and the dry heaves stopped. I wish I had known that trick in college.

"Okay, Prager," Crank said, straddling my legs, twisting my shirt in his hands. "Who are you working with?"

"The KGB."

"Funny man." He backslapped my face, but not as hard as I supposed he could have. There was also something in his eyes that belied his angry demeanor. "We know there's someone working for the Feds inside this organization and you're the outside contact."

I didn't answer right away. Instead, I looked around the room. We were in a cabin not unlike the one Crank and I had been in the last time. For all I knew, it might have been the same cabin. Standing behind Crank were four bikers from central casting. Behind them was a suit. The bikers wore black leather and greasy cut denim, beards, big boots, belt buckles, and bandannas. The suit had cop written all over him, but he wasn't local. No, Suit's brown eyes had the requisite sheen of condescension found primarily in Feds.

"ATF or DEA?" I asked the suit.

He smiled. I didn't. Suit opened his mouth to speak.

"Come on, Prager," Crank interrupted, "talk to me now and we'll skip the blow torch and pliers bullshit. Gimme a name."

"Make some suggestions and I'll give you a name. I'm not joking here. I just don't know what the fuck you're talking about."

"Get the barbed wire," said Suit to the bikers. "We'll rearrange his face a little and when he sees how much blood pours out, then maybe he'll—"

"Wait a second!" Crank barked. "This is my thing. The lab blew on my watch. I'll handle this shit."

"Yeah," Suit said, "like how you let him slip away the same night you let a few million dollars of potential income go up like a roman candle? I don't think so."

Crank jumped up, pulled a hunting knife out of the sheath on his belt, and stuck it right under Suit's chin. For a barrel-bellied guy, Crank moved more like a ballerina.

"Listen, Swanson, you dickless motherfucker, don't start giving me fucking orders. You get your cut from us, not the other way around. Remember that."

"And I fucking protect you guys," said Agent Swanson.

"And we're paying for your retirement, asshole."

"Gee, and I thought cops were the only ones who hated Feds."

Crank back-kicked his leg and hit me square in the belly with his heavy boot. "Who the fuck asked you? Unless you got a name for me, shut the fuck up."

That one hurt, but the damage could have been much worse had he got me in the jaw. Probably would've broken it. As it was, I couldn't catch my breath.

Crank refocused on Swanson. "Back the fuck off, you suited prick. I don't take orders from nobody. Just ask my Desert Storm commander. I broke his arm in three places, one place at a time."

Swanson tried to look cool, but there was real fear in his eyes. "Okay, okay, but we need that name."

Crank pulled the knife away from the agent's neck and put the blade back in its sheath. He turned his attention back my way, lifted me off the ground and shoved me into a chair. He spoke softly to me, almost cooing, trying to cajole an answer out of me.

Wouldn't I feel better getting it off my chest? Wouldn't I rather avoid the torture, which would surely come? Wouldn't I like a chance to live until morning? Wouldn't I ...

I would have been happy to give him an answer had I any notion of what he was going on about. I felt like a character from one novel who had fallen through the looking glass into another book; *Alice in Fatherland,* maybe. My mind drifted, I wondered if this was all part of Brightman's grand scheme. But when I retraced my steps to my original contact with Crank, I rejected the idea. This was wrong place wrong time at its worst. Yet in spite of the threat and bluster, not much was happening. Crank even got me a drink and cloth to clean me up some. More than an hour must have passed since I was first brought into the cabin. I got the sense that he was playing for time.

"This is bullshit!" one of the gang of four bikers growled. "Are we gonna kiss this guy's ass until he gives us a name or what? Deuce and Deadman are gonna be here any minute and they're gonna wanna know what the fuck is what."

Swanson raised his hands like a traffic cop. "Hey, don't look at me. That's one of your boys talking, Crank, not me."

"All right, Max, get the wire," Crank said matter-of-factly. "Prager, gimme a name now, or you're gonna bleed."

Only I could see Crank's face. His back was to the bikers and Swanson. There was something both imploring and reassuring in his expression. It was if he was telling me that things would be okay if I could only give him something to work with. I scoured my memory, trying to recall how things had played out the night the lab exploded. If I wasn't already motivated enough, seeing the razor wire kicked it up a couple of notches.

"Cutter," I said. "It's Cutter."

Crank winked at me in a brief second of calm. Then one of the bikers, a rough looking dude with a long beard, sunglasses and prison tats lunged at me.

"You lyin' motherfuckin' snake."

Well, now I knew who Cutter was. Instinctively, I pushed back and my chair went down and I tried to roll away. Crank threw out his left fist, catching Cutter in the Adam's apple. Cutter, gasping for air, went down on top of me.

"Get ZZ Top off me!"

Agent Swanson actually laughed at that. The other bikers were on Cutter, punching him and kicking him even as they pulled him off. A few minutes of that and he'd look like Fallon sans pick axe.

"Gag the rat and cuff him!" Crank ordered. "We'll let Deuce and Deadman deal with him."

Then, as if on cue, the quiet of the woods was ripped wide open by the distinctive throaty rumble of twin Harleys. The two bikes pulled up almost to the front door. The woods again went silent. The door opened. Two more bikers joined us. They didn't look any more fierce or rough than Crank and the four that were already here, but it was evident from the look in everyone's eyes that these two were players; princes among the common scum. There was a round of ritualized hugs and handshakes between the boys. It had the feel of a meet and greet at a Masonic temple. The bikers kept their distance from Swanson. They seemed to regard him as an infectious disease.

"You got my cut?" Swanson said. "I can't be here for the pleasantries."

"Shut the fuck up, man," said the shorter of the two princes. "Ya'll get your money when I'm ready to give it to ya."

Crank pointed at me. "That's the ex-cop. He fingered Cutter as the rat."

Cutter struggled against his restraints and tried to say something. One of the bikers kicked him in the ribs and told him to shut the fuck up. Apparently, I'd chosen the right fall guy. Neither the original gang nor the two princes acted at all surprised by the news of Cutter's disloyalty. Swanson was fidgeting, clearly worried about witnessing what would surely happen to Cutter and me.

"Deuce, pay the cunt and get him outta here," said Deadman, the short prince.

Deuce reached around his back and pulled out a duct-taped brown paper bag. Swanson's eyes got big, but he didn't reach for the stack. Deuce threw it on the cabin floor like scraps for the dog and Swanson couldn't pick it up fast enough. The second the Fed grabbed the package, the world hit a speed bump. There was a flurry of activity outside; gunshots, shotgun blasts, tires skidding, running feet on gravel, motorcycles' rumbling. The cabin flooded with blinding light from all sides.

"Inside the cabin, this is Special Agent William B. Stroby of the Federal Bureau of Investigation and Combined Meth Task Force. The cabin is completely surrounded. You are all under arrest. Any attempt at escape will be futile and will result in additional charges. Please follow my instructions promptly and to the letter and no one will be injured. A failure to do so will force me to use all necessary means to effect your arrest. Open the cabin door and throw out all weapons. Then, when I give the word, I want you to knee-walk out of the cabin in single file with your hands clasped behind your heads. Any variation in this procedure or attempt at escape will result in your being fired upon. Starting now I want ..."

As Stroby droned on, Deuce looked my way.

"We got us a bargaining chip," he said, reaching for the butt of a handgun tucked into his pants.

"I don't think so," said Crank, pressing the muzzle of a Glock to Deuce's head. "Prager, stand up." With his free hand, Crank reached into his pants pocket and removed a cuff key. He handed it to Deuce. "Uncuff him."

"You fuckin' mother—"

Crank slammed his boot into the side of Deuce's knee. Something snapped and the prince crumbled, yelping in pain. I almost felt sorry for him. Almost. Crank then ordered one of the original bikers to undo my cuffs. He did so.

"Prager, get that hogleg from Deuce and come over here with me."

I followed Crank's instructions. Deuce's gun was a Colt revolver. The barrel on the damned thing was the size of a deer femur.

"Jesus Christ! Will you look at this thing," I said, pulling back the hammer. "Please, somebody move. I'd love to see what a bullet from this thing would do to you."

Crank got a kick out of that, but then his face went all business. "All right, boys, all weapons out on the floor now."

Stroby was still at it when Crank yelled out the door. Some of Shakespeare's plays had less acts than this guy's speech. Until that point I had been successful at focusing on saving my own neck and not letting my mind drift to Katy's plight. If I got myself killed, Katy had no chance. But now that my freedom was at hand, it all came rushing back in.

"Stroby, will you please shut the fuck up!" I thought I heard some of the assault team laughing. "This is Agent Markowitz," Crank yelled. "The code word is pelican and the color is green. I repeat, this is Markowitz. The code word is pelican and the color is green."

Stroby shut up.

No one was stupid enough to make a run for it and within fifteen minutes, the weapons had been collected, the bikers and Swanson arrested, the tension gone. Crank—Markowitz—had an EMT look me over. He gave me something for the pain, but that ache in my kidney was going to require weeks of healing and something stronger than glorified aspirin to take the sting out. The EMT had some stuff with him to help me wash up. He even had some mouthwash. Still, I looked and smelled like last week's garbage.

"You okay?" Markowitz asked, handing me back my cell phone and .38.

"Define okay." I checked my phone for messages. None. "Listen—"

"Yeah, pretty dumb question, huh?"

"I've heard dumber, but not many. Listen, I've gotta get outta here."

"In a minute," he said. "I've got to get clearance for you to leave from my C.O."

"So, you want to tell me what the fuck this was all about? I mean, I can figure out that you're a Fed and that you've been undercover in this meth ring, but why drag me into it?"

"I'm ATF and I didn't drag you into it. You put yourself in it. Who told you to come looking for me? Who told you to show up the night I blew the lab?"

"*You* blew the lab!"

"Sshhhhh! Keep it down, Prager. Technically, I'm not supposed to destroy evidence like that, but the case wasn't ready yet and we were going to ship out a huge volume of product. I couldn't let it hit the streets, not even for the case. This shit's like a plague, a fucking cancer. If you thought crack was bad ... You ever see what a tweaker looks like after a few months on this shit?"

"Okay, I get it, but why reinvolve me?" I asked, looking impatiently at my watch, wondering when his C.O. would clear me to leave.

"I didn't reinvolve you. They've been keeping eyes out for you. They knew someone was leaking info to the cops and Feds. I told you that night the lab blew that your timing sucked. These kinda guys don't believe in coincidence. You show up and their lab goes boom ... When you got away, they started looking at me. I couldn't afford that, so ..."

"So you told them there was someone inside and a contact outside. I was the obvious candidate for the outside contact."

"These guys are cutthroats, not geniuses, and they sample a little too much of the product. Too much and it makes you paranoid as all hell. I just fed their paranoia a bit. Yeah, so someone spotted you on the road leading to the cemetery earlier. Good thing I was around."

"Tell that to my kidney."

"Sorry about that."

"Listen, Markowitz, I'm not joking. I gotta get outta—" My cell phone buzzed. "Excuse me," I said and stepped a few feet away.

"Remember my voice, Moe?" It was Brightman.

"I remember."

"You were pretty smug the last time we spoke. You feeling smug now?"

"Not at all."

"Good, but you're late," he said.

"Late for what?"

He ignored that. "You were doing so well and then you seemed to disappear on us. Where have you been?"

"Before or after I found Fallon?"

"That, oh well … How about after the cemetery?"

"You wouldn't believe me if I told you."

"Try me."

"No."

Brightman moved his mouth away from the phone, but not so far that I couldn't hear him. "Hurt her," he said. There was a second delay and then a woman screamed. He got back on the phone. "Don't do that again, Moe. I want to kill her in front of you, but if you put me in a bad frame of mind, I'll do it and they'll never find her body."

"Okay. What do you want?"

"I can't have what I want, but short of that I want you to go for a ride, alone, and keep your cell phone available. I'll call you when it suits me."

"Where should I—"

"Head toward the County of Kings. Yes, that suits me fine. Take the thruway and remember, Moe, old stick, alone."

"I'll remember."

I clicked the phone shut.

"You don't look so good," Markowitz said. "Who was that?"

"The man who is going to murder my wife."

[CHAPTER TWENTY-SEVEN]

I had just pulled onto the New York State Thruway, heading south toward the city, when Brightman called. He had changed his mind, he said. It seemed I wasn't destined for Brooklyn after all. He had me circle back north and head into the Catskills. Then as he continued reciting the directions, it hit me. I knew where he wanted me to go. I shaped my lips to form the words Old Rotterdam. I wasn't even certain I had spoken them aloud until Brightman answered.

"Yes, Moe, Old Rotterdam, very good. Do you remember the grounds of the Fir Grove Hotel?"

"I do."

"Then I'll see you in an hour or so. Now, without hanging up, toss your cell phone out your car window. I want to hear it hit the pavement. Toss the phone."

"No," I said. "First, I want to talk to Katy. And don't give me that hurt her stuff again. Put her on the phone and then I'll toss it."

Again, he moved his mouth away from the phone, but not far away. "Bring her over here."

I heard some background noise, the shuffling of feet, then, "Moe. Moe, what's going—" It *was* Katy.

Brightman got back on the phone, his voice edgier, the threat closer to the surface. "Don't try anything cute. You're being watched. Now, toss the fucking phone!"

I tossed it. The phone bounced once before being crushed under the wheels of a semi coming up fast on my left. I used the opportunity to check my mirrors to see if Brightman was bluffing about my being followed. It was impossible to tell in the dark in the midst of hundreds of cars. Even when I turned off and circled around, too many other vehicles exited and entered for me to have spotted a tail. It was moot. Destiny lay ahead, not behind me.

The Fir Grove Hotel was gone. It had been gone that first time I drove up its huge semi-circlular driveway in 1981. All the bulldozers and dump trucks that had leveled the compound and carted away the debris were mere formalities in the aftermath of the workers' quarters fire, the broom and dust pan sweeping away the refuse of shattered crystal. No, not crystal. Glass, cheap glass. The Fir Grove, The Concord, all the Catskill hotels that had pretentions were never really anything more than baloney sandwiches. Once people saw what the rest of the world had to offer, the Catskill Mountains became the lunch meat option, a vacation spot for poor schmucks and sentimental fools. In spite of what the locals thought, the Fir Grove fire was nothing more than an exclamation point on the Catskills' death certificate. My eyes adjusting to the darkness, I noticed that now even the grand driveway was gone. I couldn't tell if anything more than memories remained.

I parked down at the bottom of the hill and popped my trunk to get my flashlight. People say the crisp mountain air is good for you, that it smells fresh without the taint of the city. They say a lot of things. All I could smell was smoke from the distant fire that killed Andrea Cotter, the first girl I ever loved. A cop becomes intimately familiar with what fire does to the human body. The image of Andrea's charred body flashed into my head and I shuddered. Although it felt like a million years since I'd last done crowd control at a fire scene, I could taste the acrid stink of burnt hair on my tongue and in my nostrils.

Bang! I stopped in my tracks, trying to remember the date. *August ...* Christ, it was the anniversary of the Fir Grove fire. *Was it the thirty-fourth anniversary? The thirty-fifth?* I couldn't recall. It had been so many lies, so many secrets, so many lifetimes ago. Brightman had done his research. He was going to kill the last woman I loved where the first had been murdered. It was all so symmetrical in a twisted kind of way.

I had to put Andrea Cotter out of my head. Three and a half decades had passed and she was as dead as she was ever going to be. She had met the end of time, the clock had stopped ticking on her nevers and forevers. Katy's clock was still running. She was who I had to think about. I couldn't let Brightman play with my head. He already had too much of an advantage. I slammed my trunk shut.

"Stop!" a voice came out of the darkness.

"Ralphy Barto."

"You remember?"

"I remember. Hitting you in the eye like that, it was a lucky shot."

"Not for me."

"As I recall, you were trying to kill me at the time."

"There was that," he said, a smile in his voice. "You carrying?"

"I got my .38 tucked into the small of my back. You want me to—"

"No thanks," he said, stepping out of the darkness. "I'll handle it."

He was carrying a submachine gun of some kind, a long, thick sound suppressor on the end of its barrel. In spite of the eyepatch and years, Barto actually looked better than he had in 1983 and I told him as much.

"Yeah, I take care of myself these days. Anyone in the car?"

"Brightman told me to come alone."

"That's not what I asked."

Before I could say anything else, Barto sprayed my car with bullets. The rate of fire was amazing, the suppressor—silencer is a misnomer—keeping each shot down to a loud snap and hiss. He paid careful attention to the trunk and backseat.

"No," I said too late. "I'm alone."

"That you are, my friend." He replaced the clip, took my .38, and patted me down. He knew I wouldn't risk Katy's life by trying anything.

"Christ, you smell like puke. You're scared, huh? Somehow, I didn't figure you as a puker."

"Bad shrimp."

"Cute," he said. "Listen, he's gonna kill her one way or the other. There's nothing I can do about that, but if you wanna run, I won't shoot you. I'll lay this thing down and you can split."

"I can't do that."

"I know, but I figured I'd ask. Come on. Up the hill. You try anything now, I'll wound you and it won't change anything."

"Is she okay?" I asked.

"She's a little freaked, I guess."

"Has he hurt her?"

"Not really."

It was a tough climb up the hill. We stopped at the top to rest a minute before heading toward where the guest parking lot had been. The parking field was gone as were the wildly overgrown hedges that had once marked the rear boundry of the lot, but the concrete steps that lead down to where the pool area and ball courts used to be still remained. The same could not be said for the pool and courts themselves. Now nothing but a great flat field with hills in the distance appeared in the beam of my flashlight. We started across the field.

About fifty yards on was where the late Anton Harder had established his angry white boys town; a collection of ratty trailers, abandoned cars, and abandoned souls. The people who lived there were a rag tag collection of losers, misfits, and bigots. Harder had his own reasons for choosing the Fir Grove property as base camp. His mother Missy, a hotel chambermaid, had died in the fire. As the flames had consumed his mother, the hate had consumed him. He had even built a shrine to her not very far away from the foundation of the workers' quarters.

"Come on, let's go." Barto nudged me along with his gun.

We kept on ahead, insects hurtling themselves into my hand as they flew toward the source of the light.

"Did you kill the kid?"

"Yeah," he said, as if he were telling me the time.

I was glad I hadn't run when he gave me the chance. He would have shot me. I could see where this was headed. Brightman would kill Katy and Barto would kill me. It was to be a neat and tidy little package of revenge.

"The other kid, the one really named Patrick, are you going to kill him too?"

"You know, Prager, that's pretty good. How did you know there was two of them?"

"I wasn't sure until earlier today. The tattoo artist confirmed that wasn't her work on the autopsy photos of John James that my man showed her. But I think I had doubts the night I found the kid's body. He just didn't look quite right and I could never figure out why the kid would've lied to me about his name when there was nothing to gain by it. I guess Patrick is the one that looks more like Katy's brother."

"I don't know. They looked the same to me. Maybe it's the one eye thing. You ask me, it was a lot of trouble to go through because of a grudge, but I'm not paying the freight."

"You think Connie Geary knows what she's been paying for?" I asked.

"Moe, you figured a lot of this shit out. I'm impressed. I gotta hand it to you, you're pretty fucking smart."

"Yeah, just not smart enough. I'm the one walking with the gun stuck in his back. So, Ralph, you didn't answer me. Are you going to kill the other kid?"

"Nah."

"No!"

"No. He's already dead. Brightman killed him in front of your wife. Wanted to give her some closure after all we put her through. It was the least we could do." Barto snickered as he had on the phone, his true nature showing itself.

That did it. I lost control and spun around swinging. I caught Barto off guard, but I wasn't quite quick enough. I got in one good punch, but it glanced off his jaw. He simply stepped back, letting my momentum and gravity pull me down.

"Nice try," he said. "I'm gonna enjoy killing you. Let's go!"

I ignored the threat and tried to regain my equilibrium. I couldn't let him get to me anymore. I started talking.

"What about Martello?"

"That asshole, what about him? Truth is, it took you a lot longer to get to him than we figured. We thought you'd interview him right away, but you never was very conventional in the way you did things. I suppose if you were, I'd still have my left eye, you'd have your gold shield, and Brightman'd be president. You shoulda just left things alone back then, Moe. What did finding the truth get you anyway?" Barto coughed and spit. "Fucking bugs keep getting in my throat."

"That's why you picked a pewter Yukon, because Martello drove one!"

"Right. Good thing he liked a roomy ride. It would've been hell for me if he drove a Miata. I'd look pretty stupid driving them kids around behind the wheel of one of those little things. Woulda looked like the clown car at the circus. Let me tell you something about that guy Martello, Moe, he mighta come after you one day on his own. He fucking hated you."

"When you told Ray what you had in mind for him, did he feel any better about you sacrificing his life in a just cause? I mean, you did drug him up, stick the murder weapon in his pocket, and force him to run into the traffic on Ocean Parkway."

Barto snickered again. "You shoulda seen him bounce and skid, man. It was pretty cool."

We had nearly reached the crest of the hill. Just a hundred feet ahead and down the hill, in a small glen was where the workers' quarters had been. I had no doubt that was where Brightman and Katy were waiting. Only a few yards before the crest, Barto ordered me to stop.

"Turn around!"

When I turned, I saw Barto raising his weapon at me. *What the fuck are you doing? This isn't the way it's supposed to happen, asshole.* I opened my mouth to say something, but found I was so angry I couldn't speak. He ordered me to back up to the crest. When I stopped, he put twenty or thirty shots at my feet and above my head. I didn't have time to react. He shook his head at me.

"Nah, you ain't a puker," he said, regarding me with a sick kind of admiration. "You look more pissed off than scared."

"Can I ask you one thing before we go?"

"Sure."

"Do you really think you're going to get away with this?"

"Me, I *am* gonna get away with it. As for Brightman ... I don't think he gives a shit whether he will or not. I think he's sorta beyond that. Now, let's go."

When we came over the crest, I saw the little campsite set up where I remembered the foundation had been. There was a sizeable fire going, a pretty big tent, and not another thing in sight. This was no place for a Brooklyn boy to die. Still, any place was better than a hospital, I thought. As we approached, the tent flap opened and Brightman emerged. Katy was nowhere to be seen. That wasn't good for a lot of reasons. While I was still confident he hadn't killed her, I had no hope of saving her if I didn't know where she was to be saved.

"Hello, Moe. Still not feeling very smug, are you?"

"Where's Katy?"

"She's close enough."

"Where's Katy?"

"Ralph, please teach our guest some manners."

I clenched in anticipation of the blow, but it didn't come.

"Cut the shit, Brightman," Barto said, "and let's get this over with."

"Where's Katy?"

"Goodness, Moe, you sound like a broken record."

"CD."

"What?"

"There are no records anymore, Brightman. It's CDs and soon there won't be any of those. That's your problem, you're living too much in the past."

"Oh, yeah, do you think so? I'll show you what *your* problem is."

He went back into the tent and came out dragging Katy by her hair. She didn't struggle. That scared me. She was trussed up, hands to ankles behind her, a strip of duct tape across her mouth. He pulled her up onto her knees. She wasn't bleeding and there were no obvious cuts or bruises on her, but her eyes were impassive. I hoped it was just shock, but I knew it was more, much more. The last month had plunged her into a deep well with slick and very steep walls. Brightman had an automatic in his waistband, but asked Barto for my .38.

"*This* is your problem, Moe," he said, pulling back the hammer of my .38 and pressing the short barrel to Katy's temple. He didn't pull the trigger. It wasn't time. He hadn't gone through all of this to shoot her within two minutes of my arrival. That was good. The longer he took, the better our chances of getting out of this, if not unscathed, then alive.

"I'm not playing, Brightman."

"Yeah," Barto seconded, "shoot the bitch so I can kill this asshole. Let's get outta here."

"Quiet! I want to savor this. Once she's dead, I don't care what you do to him. That's the deal."

"Whatever," Barto said.

Brightman got on his knees next to Katy and wrapped his free arm around her shoulder. "I just want you to know that this is all your ex-husband's doing. Did he ever tell you about what really happened between us? Shake your head yes or no."

Katy, her eyes still impassive, shook no.

"I didn't think so. Moe does like his secrets, doesn't he?"

Silent tears began rolling down Katy's cheeks and I nearly collapsed. Secrets, the gifts that keep on giving. The pain my silence had caused seemed endless. In a voice barely above a whisper, Brightman explained to Katy how instead of accepting my gold detective's shield and living happily ever after, I had reopened the investigation into Moira Heaton's murder. He told her how I had backtracked and discovered that he, Brightman, not Ivan Alfonseca, had murdered Moira.

"Moira knew too much," he said. "She knew that I had killed a neighborhood boy when I was a kid. I hadn't meant to kill him, not really, but what do intentions ever have to do with anything, especially in the face of murder?"

The flow of tears was much heavier now and Katy's body shook, the tape muffling her sobs.

"But did your husband go to the police with the truth? No, he didn't. Moe, tell Katy what you did."

"I told you, Brightman, I'm not playing."

Barto shoved me in the back. "Do it!"

"No."

"Okay, then *I'll* do it," Barto said. Brightman's eyes got angry, but Barto had the bigger gun. "Moe set Brightman up and goaded him into a confession. Even made him piss his pants. What Brightman didn't know was that his wife and Thomas Geary had watched and listened to the whole thing. There. Now, can we get this over with?"

I could see in his eyes that Brightman was getting ready for the finale.

"How could I go to the police?" I said. "I had no proof and all the witnesses were dead."

"I thought you weren't playing," he said.

"I waited until you started lying."

He shoved the .38 into Katy's ribs so hard she crumpled in pain. He pulled her back up. The passivity was gone from her eyes.

"That's right, instead of being satisfied with ruining my career, he had to hurt my wife. Ruining me professionally didn't really cut it for Moe Prager. No, he wanted to punish me in a personal way, so he used my wife."

"I always regretted doing that. I realized I'd punished her more than you."

"Katerina divorced me in about thirty seconds. She couldn't understand how she could have shared her bed with a murderer and not have known. That question haunted her for the rest of her life. Did you know she—"

"—died last summer. Yeah, I know. I'm sorry. Katerina was really sweet and one of the most stunningly beautiful women I've ever met," I said. "Cancer, right?"

"No, it wasn't cancer, it was the haunting and the guilt."

"Guilt?"

"Oh, so there are things you don't know?" Brightman taunted.

He whispered something into Katy's ear that I couldn't hear. There was immediate and crushing ache in Katy's eyes. I hadn't seen anything like it since the miscarriage, since Connie Geary's wedding day, when Katy sat sobbing in a stall of the women's bathroom at the Lonsesome Piper County Club. She sobbed now so that even the tape couldn't contain the sound of it. She cried so hard that her body seemed to convulse.

"Do you want to know what I told her, Moe?"

No. "Yes."

"I told her that a week after you confronted me on the street and got me to confess my sins, Katerina had an abortion. She was empty after that, empty ever after. That's what killed her, not cancer."

More than anything, I wanted to call him a lying motherfucker. I wanted to accuse him of fabricating that story so he could torture the both of us with it, but I knew he was telling the truth even before the words were fully out of his mouth. And now, finally, I understood why he had gone to such elaborate means.

"Kill me," I said, spreading my arms out. "Just leave her alone. Don't repeat my mistake."

Brightman aimed my .38 as his mouth formed the word no, but I couldn't hear him. I couldn't hear anything above the *thwap thwap*

thwap of the helicopter blades. The downwash kicked up a storm of dirt and rocks. An intense and blinding spotlight encircled us. I shielded my eyes. There was the bark of gun fire. I spun. Barto's head rocked back. Crimson spray danced in the light. A flash. Several flashes. Something bit hard into my ankle and burned its way into the bone. I went down. More shots. I pushed my face out of the dirt. Brightman was no longer standing. He was on his back, arms thrown out, one leg bent completely beneath him. I crawled over to Katy.

The pain in her eyes was gone, with it had gone the light. I pulled the tape off her mouth and put my lips to hers. They were still warm, but the pressure of my weight on her body forced blood out of her mouth and onto my lips. I smeared her blood across my face. I hoped my tears would never wash it away. I was wrong about my destiny. It didn't lay in front, but behind me.

There was a hand on my shoulder. I turned to see Agent Markowitz standing at my back, a mournful, pleading look on his face. He was speaking but it was all just twisted lips and a jumble of noise. He pointed at my wrecked ankle, the blood gushing out of it, mixing with the dirt, mixing with the blood of the dead. Markowitz pulled off his shirt and pressed it hard against my leg, his mouth moving the whole time. I was starting to catch words now, a few at a time. He was shouting the same thing at me over and over again. Finally, I understood.

"How do you feel?"

I didn't answer. Brightman's words were so loud in my head, I didn't think I would ever hear anything else again. *How does it feel? How did I feel? How would I feel?*

Empty.

Empty ever after.

[EPILOGUE]
SPREADING THE ASHES

Sarah received the videotape about a week after we buried Katy. The tape was from Brightman, mailed by proxy—maybe his lawyer, but probably Connie Geary—shortly after his death. On the tape, he confessed to the murders of Carl Stipe, the little boy from his home town, Moira Heaton, and Patrick Farner, the other Patrick Michael Maloney impersonator. Ralph Barto, he said, had murdered John James, Fallon, Martello, and Mary White. He explained to my daughter why he had murdered her mother. It was, he said, my fault for having slowly killed his ex-wife. He took great pains to discuss the details of my involvement.

When Sarah came to me, there was little I could refute. I hadn't left things well enough alone all those years ago. I had indeed rejected the offer of the gold shield I had so desperately wanted in order to dig and dig and dig until I found the truth out about Steven Brightman. When I found the truth, I set Brightman up to confess in front of his wife. I had wanted to punish him by using her. And in the end, I shared the truth with almost no one who was directly involved. Carl Stipe's mother and Moira Heaton's father went to their graves without knowing what had actually happened to their children.

Sarah hasn't spoken to me in nearly a year. She took a leave of absence from the University of Michigan and moved into Francis Maloney's old house on Hanover Street in Janus. To think that I lost Sarah to him not because of anything he did, but because of my own blindness is irony beyond even my ability to comprehend. Sometimes on rainy nights when I can't sleep, I imagine I can hear him laughing at me. On those nights I pour myself a Dewar's, look out my window at the black waters of Sheepshead Bay, and raise my glass to him. "Yes, Francis," I say, "I do believe in ghosts."

Pete Vandervoort keeps me updated about Sarah. She's still dating Robby, the deputy sheriff. Pete tells me they're pretty happy together and that Robby's a good cop. I've got nothing against the kid, but I hope like hell he finds another job or Sarah finds another man. Mostly I hope that Sarah can someday forgive me and try to understand that I meant for none of this to happen and that if I could bargain with God, if there was a god to bargain with, I would gladly sacrifice myself to take back even the least of the damage. But as Brightman remarked that night, "What do intentions ever have to do with anything, especially in the face of murder?"

Brightman gave a lot of other information on the tape, stuff only of interest to me and Feeney and the Ohio and Kentucky cops. He explained how he and Barto had picked Martello as the fall guy—*He hated your father maybe more than I did and he tended to act out*—how they arranged for fake credit cards in Martello's name—*Ralph Barto was well acquainted with a Nigerian gang that specialized in identity theft*—how they induced Mr. Fallon to do the grave desecrations—money, and the phony deed to a nonexistent house on Galway Bay—how they got Mary White to conspire—*We falsified some New York City Department of Public Health forms indicating that Patrick Maloney had been the one to infect her brother with HIV. Of course, Patrick had died years before anyone had ever heard of HIV or AIDS, but our money helped cloud Mary's memory.*

Steven Brightman didn't deem either John James or Patrick Farner worthy of explanation. Why would he? Chess players don't bother explaining the sacrifice of their pawns. There was also one other glaring omission in his taped confession. He hadn't discussed how he managed to finance his revenge. I chose not to discuss it either, at least not on the record.

In October, I was thumbing through the *Daily News* when I saw the obituary for Thomas Geary. He had been buried in a private family ceremony days before the story was released to the press. I waited out the week before driving to Crocus Valley. When Connie saw my face on the security monitor, she said nothing, buzzing me through the front gate even before I pressed the intercom. Riding up to the house, I passed some teenagers tossing a football around on the lawn. I watched for a little while. It was easy to pick out Connie's son, Craig Jr. He had the Geary genes. He was tall and handsome and had perfect form when throwing the football.

"Hello, Moe," she said, relief in her voice and resignation on her face. "I've been expecting you for months."

"I know you have."

"You're limping."

"I'll be limping for a long time," I said. "The cast just recently came off."

"Well, you better come in."

We did what we did. Connie played and I drank scotch. No show tunes today. I didn't question her, but just let her speak when she was ready.

"The first time I slept with Steven, I was sixteen years old. It was magical. He was nothing like the boys I'd been with at camp or at school. He took his time with me, treated me like a woman, always pleasing me first. Of course he would treat me that way. He was a man, not a boy. He taught me how to enjoy my own body. Even now, knowing all that I know about what a horrible man he was, I'm wet thinking about him. I disgust you, Moe, don't I?"

"This is your story to tell, Connie," I said, pouring myself more scotch.

"Of course I think my father knew almost immediately. Sixteen year old girls think they are very good at keeping secrets, but they're almost transparent. You would know that. You have a girl."

I knew more about secrets than sixteen year old girls. Having a child doesn't make you an expert on children; it doesn't even make you an expert on your own child. I didn't say a word. Connie took that as a cue to continue.

"My father gave his tacit, if not spoken, approval to our relationship. It was a useful tool that helped him control us both. Controlling people, that was very important to my dad."

"I know."

"Yes, you would know. My father's approval came to an end when he saw that Steven had an unlimited future as a politician. He made us break it off, but not by confronting me. He went to Steven."

"I bet your dad didn't have to threaten Brightman, did he?"

"I don't actually know, but my father could be incredibly persuasive without ever having to resort to direct threat."

That was another aspect of Thomas Geary's personality I was well familiar with. Connie went on to explain that they hadn't fully broken it off until Brightman got engaged to Katerina.

"Of course he loved Katerina. She was wonderful and god-awfully beautiful. I know women who had crushes on her." Connie Geary blushed. "After their divorce and the resignation, my dad kept Steven afloat. I suppose he felt responsible for him, like Dr. Frankenstein for his monster. It wasn't a week before we were sleeping together again."

She went on explaining about how her own marriage fell apart— *I never really loved Craig. I didn't even love the idea of him*—and how, after her father's illness, she managed the family's funds. Brightman's stipend grew ever larger. But they had never managed to recapture the early magic. *Even when he was fucking me, he was fucking her.*

"You see, Moe, it was easy for me to act the whore for you. I had been acting as a whore for years. And," she said, reaching across the piano placing her hand on mine, "you made it easy on me. You were good and you were present."

I pulled my hand away.

"I didn't know about the murders, I give you my word. I did know about the scheme to frighten and confuse your wife with the actors. I helped him. I financed him, but I was desperate to exorcise Katerina's ghost. After she died, her ghost took up more and more room in our bed."

There was a knock on the front door. I stood up. "That'll be the police," I said, pulling the wire out from under my shirt. "I'm through keeping secrets, Connie. The secrets stop here. Don't worry. I doubt you'll do time."

If I was expecting anger or defiance, I didn't get it. Constance Geary, I think, wanted this over as much as anyone. The wealthy understand the cost of doing business and paying a fair price.

Israel K. Prager was born on March 29th, 2001. He weighed exactly what Sarah had weighed at birth. It was to laugh, no? Who can explain these things? Klaus thinks the K is for him. Kosta thinks it's for him. Carmella and I let people think what they want. When he's old enough to understand, I will explain it to him. The three of us live pretty well and happily in my condo. Although I'm not sure my single neighbors are too thrilled with the arrangement. I guess we'll eventually buy a house somewhere, but not yet.

Before Carmella and I got married, I asked if she wanted to change her name back to Marina. It was, after all, her real name, the name she had when we first met. For me, there never was and never will be any shame associated with it. She said no, that as long as we knew the truth about who and what we were, that was the only important thing. I suppose it was. To say I love my son as if he was my own is cliché. It is nonetheless true. He is magic. Sometimes at night, I hold him in my arms and tell him about his big sister. I tell him that if we could make a family out of broken parts and discards, there's always room for one more.

Not long after Katy's funeral and the fallout from Brightman's tape, I was called to testify in front of a federal grand jury. The government was preparing its case against the bikers and I was a peripheral witness. My testimony, as the US Attorney explained, was the cherry on the whipped cream on top of the cake. Even without me, all of these guys were going away for a very long time. I had been a part of and around law enforcement long enough to know that the Feds believed in piling on. Why charge someone with a hundred counts when you can charge them with a hundred and one. If the government wants you, you're in trouble. Once they've got you, you're fucked.

Outside the grand jury room I walked past a man in a neat blue suit and silk tie.

"Moe!" he called after me. It was Agent Markowitz.

"Crank in a suit. You clean up pretty good," I said. "You've lost weight. I didn't recognize you."

"Crank," he repeated shaking his head. "Great name, huh? I just wanted to apologize again about—"

"Don't apologize. You guys nearly pulled it off. It was my fault, not yours."

"It's just that using the tracking device on your car, we couldn't get men in place in time. We had to use the chopper." He pointed at the cast on my leg. "How's the ankle?"

"Hurts like a sonovabitch."

"The funeral, how did that go?"

"Divorce fucks everything up, including death. It's a long painful story, so let's forget it."

"Okay."

We shook hands and I hobbled out of the courthouse. I didn't look back. It hurt too much to look back.

In December, Steven Roth and I flew to Warsaw, Poland carrying a very special piece of cargo, the urn containing the ashes of Israel Roth. I had held onto his ashes for nearly ten years. For in spite of what Mr. Roth had said to me in my car on that long ago day when I'd taken him to say Kaddish at his wife's grave, I hadn't known where to spread his ashes. I hadn't known until fate and a false ghost interceded.

We took a train from Warsaw to Krakow and hired a car. At six the next morning we met our guide and an official of the Polish government at the hotel. Both the official and tour guide checked our papers and we set off for Oswiecim or, as most of the world knows it, Auschwitz-Birkenau. The ride took a little over an hour, but seemed to have taken much much longer. It might have helped if someone had uttered a single word.

The weather was just as Mr. Roth had described it to me. It was cold and dreary. A mixture of rain and snow fell on us as we walked from the car. The camp, a museum since 1947, opened at 8:00 AM. The government official was keen that we finish our business before the gates opened. He wasn't mean spirited about it, just nervous. I got the sense that what Steven and I were doing wasn't standard operating procedure. Our guide was crestfallen, but he needn't have worried. No matter how many newsreels, movies, or documentaries you've seen, no matter how many books you've read, no matter what you know or what you think you know about the Holocaust, being at Auschwitz, even for a few minutes, changes you. But as hard as it was for me to be there, it was much worse for Steven. For the sins visited upon his father had lived on to be visited upon him. There were victims of the Holocaust yet to be born.

We explained to our guide what we were looking for and he said he knew just such a place. He walked us over to the spot. It's hard to say that one frozen patch of snow covered earth is better than another, but for our purposes this patch of earth seemed well chosen. We asked the guide and the government man to excuse us. After they left us, Steven and I spread handfuls of Israel Roth's ashes onto the slippery ground. When there was nothing left in the urn, I took a card out of my coat pocket and began to recite Kaddish, the mourner's prayer. *"Yis-ga-dal v'yis-ka-dash sh'may ra-bo, B'ol-mo dee-v'ro ..."*

As I read off the card, Steven Roth joined in. He didn't need the card. After finishing the prayer and saying our amens, I held Steven's hands in mine.

"Kaddish and ashes, it's what he wanted," I said. "I guess part of him never left this place."

"Part of us will never leave here either."

Who was I to argue?

BACH'S
ORCHESTRA

A CHOIR GALLERY
1732

BACH'S ORCHESTRA

BY

CHARLES SANFORD
TERRY

LONDON
OXFORD UNIVERSITY PRESS
NEW YORK   TORONTO

Oxford University Press, Amen House, London E.C.4

GLASGOW NEW YORK TORONTO MELBOURNE WELLINGTON
BOMBAY CALCUTTA MADRAS KARACHI KUALA LUMPUR
CAPE TOWN IBADAN NAIROBI ACCRA

ML
410
B1
T4

First edition 1932
Reprinted 1958

PRINTED IN GREAT BRITAIN

CAROLO STRAVBE

MVNERE

QUOD ILLE SEBASTIANVS OLIM EXSEQVEBATVR

NVNC DIGNISSIME FVNGENTI

FOREWORD

BY THURSTON DART

TO the history of musical instruments and their use the scholars of Britain have made a notable contribution. The story begins at least as early as 1695 with a Cambridge enthusiast named James Talbot; his great collection of documents and measurements relating to the instruments of his day remains one of the most important sources of its kind. From the eighteenth century came the treatises, histories, and dictionary articles of such men as North, Grassineau, Hawkins, and Burney; from the nineteenth, the studies of Bunting and Armstrong on the harp and similar instruments, of Rimbault on the organ and pianoforte, of Rockstro on the flute, and many others.

During the last sixty or seventy years the pace has quickened. Ellis, Wood, Jeans, and Lloyd have written on the acoustics of instruments; Hayes, the brothers Hill, and St. George on the viol, the violin, and the bow; Welch, Carse, Blandford, Rendall, Langwill, Halfpenny, and Baines on wind instruments; James, Harding, Sumner, and Boalch on keyboard instruments; Piggott, Moule, Day, Fox Strangways, Robson, Stainer, Farmer, Kirby, Schlesinger, and Picken on non-European instruments. Galpin, Pulver, Donington, and others have prepared textbooks and dictionaries; hundreds of fine craftsmen, working in dozens of workshops, have produced instruments which will endure. To this incomplete review must be added the foundation in England of a flourishing Society, named after Canon Galpin, for the study of the history and use of instruments; and it may be said that the preparation of some of the best exhibitions and catalogues of instruments has taken place under English auspices.

Amongst all this activity Charles Sanford Terry's outstanding book *Bach's Orchestra* has long secured for itself an honoured place. First published in 1932, it is based on a simple and essentially humble point of view which has become increasingly accepted during recent decades. This may be summed up in the phrase 'the composer knew best'. Thousands of professional and amateur musicians from all countries now believe, as Terry did, that Bach was a wise, careful composer with a most discriminating ear; if he chose to write for the bass viol or the harpsichord or the recorder, in preference to the equally available cello or organ or flute, then there is every reason to suppose that his choice was made not capriciously but after deliberate thought. The conclusion seems clear. Bach's music will be best served, first, by discovering his intentions, and then by obeying them as scrupulously as circumstances permit. Terry decided to find out Bach's wishes about instruments by the simple means of examining his scores and the archives of his time. The present book contains the stimulating results of the search.

No one needs to be persuaded that such an approach works well for the music of Mendelssohn or Beethoven or Mozart. We do not find it necessary to touch up the overture to *Ruy Blas*, to re-score for full orchestra Beethoven's septet, or to add parts for trombones, harp, and piccolo to the 'Jupiter' symphony. Yet earlier music is too often regarded as an opponent to be overthrown in a kind of all-in wrestling match, with no holds barred, and the moment we turn to the performance of music composed before 1750 or so our first instinct is usually to behave like Procrustes on a bad day. Handel's delicate web of sound is stretched to cover the Albert Hall; Bach's extraordinarily sensitive pattern of tone-colours is warped and cut away to fit the structure of the modern orchestra. We would do well to remember that few who stayed overnight with Procrustes were able to make a second visit, and that early music is no Theseus.

Terry's book shows clearly that, by comparison with the first half of the eighteenth century, the variety of tone-colours commonly available to a composer has not increased. On the contrary, it is today much smaller. In the orchestra of Bach or Handel a musician could choose, for instance, from two contrasting families of flute-tone (recorders or transverse flutes), two independent families of bowed strings (viols or violins), and three coexisting families of plucked strings (lutes, harps, harpsichords). Of the seven honourable and important families in this list, only three are represented in an orchestra of our own time. Bach composed his sixth Brandenburg concerto as a septet, for a chamber music group drawn from three different instrumental families: two violas, one cello, two fretted bass viols, one violone, and an accompanying harpsichord. It seems to be the unanimous opinion ot most modern conductors that, at the time, Bach cannot really have known what he was doing. They publicly rebuke his implied affront to our more enlightened taste; his chamber septet is played, rather loudly throughout, by an ensemble of twenty or thirty instruments all belonging to a single family (violas, celli, contra-basses); and his expressed desire for the cheerful, necessary jangle of the harpsichord is firmly ignored, since this cannot be anything but another instance of his deplorable insensitivity to nuances of instrumental timbre.

Many feel that such an attitude of mind, to the music of a man respected everywhere as a very great genius, is little better than that of a cannibal. A single reading of Terry's book suggests that conductors may possibly be mistaken in thinking Bach lamentably stupid, inexcusably slipshod, or quite reprehensibly deaf. A second reading of Terry brings reassurance that Bach was a good musician, who meant what he wrote. It also brings high admiration for Terry's exemplary accuracy, as well as for the affectionate respect which permits him to allow Bach to speak for himself. During the last thirty years many scholars have added to our knowledge of Bach and of the instruments he had at his disposal. Yet, so far as I am able to judge, no part of Terry's masterly study needs amending in the light of this more recent work. Most of what he has to say seems even more apt than it can have been twenty-five years ago.

To draw attention to the merits of Terry's book may seem something of an impertinence on the part of a musician two generations his junior. I hope it may not be so considered. To the book and to its author I owe a debt of gratitude for what I have learned over a long period of time about Bach and about the instruments he had in mind for his music. The writing of a foreword can be no more than a token repayment of that debt.

Jesus College,
  Cambridge,
  1958.

NOTE

BACH'S usage and characterization of his instruments is the major theme of these pages. Of all the Masters whose art has continuing and unabated vogue, he especially spoke through voices silent in the modern orchestra. Some cannot certainly be identified. Of others his prescriptions are unprecise or ambiguous. Thus the subject is approached through obscurities. If I have succeeded in clarifying them, I must attribute it largely to experts in their several spheres who have given me their counsel—Mr. F. T. Arnold, Mr. W. F. H. Blandford, Mr. Gerald R. Hayes, and, above all, Canon Galpin, whose patience is as inexhaustible as his knowledge. But I must not be held to commit them collectively to the conclusions here maintained. My second and sixth chapters, in particular, bristle with arguable topics—for instance, the significance of Bach's 'corno' and 'corno da caccia', from my interpretation of which, *inter alia*, Mr. Blandford dissents. But my debt to one and all is considerable and I warmly acknowledge it.

Closely connected with my main thesis is another, whose relationship has been impressed upon me in the course of my research. Students of Bach's genius are tempted to forget that his cantatas and their like are *occasional* music, whose wider publicity was unforeseen, indeed, unimaginable by their composer. While he held office, in Leipzig or elsewhere, he could repeat them at recurring intervals. But thereafter—oblivion! Another would provide his official quota of original music, and eke it out occasionally from the church's library of dusty manuscript. Into that repository no more than a fraction of Bach's vocal scores found its way. His elder sons divided them, and the eldest dissipated his portion. Only the widow's share returned to the shelves of the Thomasschule, relinquished for a few thalers to relieve her poverty. These circumstances—need it be said?—could not dull Bach's lofty purpose. But they necessarily affected his utterance. Composing for the occasion, he was controlled, and not seldom hampered, by local conditions, particularly in his instrumentation. What those conditions were I have endeavoured to reconstruct in my opening chapter, and the local background has been held in view throughout.

The gist of Chapter III appeared in *The Musical Times* for February 1931. I thank Messrs. Novello for permission to reproduce it. Messrs. Kistner & Siegel have kindly allowed me to include Haussmann's portrait of Gottfried Reiche. Canon Galpin and Mr. Arnold have increased my obligation to them by their close reading of these pages in proof.

C. S. T.

July 1932.

CONTENTS

TABLES

ILLUSTRATIONS

TEXT FIGURES

REFERENCES AND ABBREVIATIONS

The works named below are referred to throughout the pages by the indicated abbreviations

Adlung = 'Musica mechanica organoedi.' By Jakob Adlung. 2 vols. Berlin: 1768 (facsimile 1931).

Agricola='Musica instrumentalis deudsch'. By Martin Agricola. Wittenberg: 1529 (new edition 1896).

Altenburg = 'Versuch einer Anleitung zur heroisch-musikalischen Trompeter- und Pauker-Kunst.' By Johann Ernst Altenburg. Halle: 1795 (facsimile 1911).

Archiv f. M. = 'Die Leipziger Ratsmusik von 1650 bis 1775.' By Arnold Schering. In 'Archiv für Musikwissenschaft', 1921, Heft I.

Arnold = 'The art of accompaniment from a thorough-bass as practised in the seventeenth and eighteenth centuries.' By F. T. Arnold. London: 1931.

Bach = 'Versuch über die wahre Art, das Clavier zu spielen.' By Carl Philipp Emanuel Bach. 2 parts, Berlin: 1753–62 (reprint 1925).

B.-G. = 'Johann Sebastian Bach's Werke. Herausgegeben von der Bach-Gesellschaft in Leipzig.' Leipzig: 1850–1900.

B.-J. = 'Bach-Jahrbuch.' Herausgegeben von der Neuen Bachgesellschaft. Leipzig: 1904– .

Baron = 'Historisch-theoretisch und practische Untersuchung des Instruments der Lauten.' By Ernst Gottlieb Baron. Nürnberg: 1727.

Bojanowski = 'Das Weimar Johann Sebastian Bachs.' By Paul von Bojanowski. Weimar: 1903.

Dolmetsch = 'The interpretation of the music of the seventeenth and eighteenth centuries revealed by contemporary evidence.' By Arnold Dolmetsch. London: 1915.

Eichborn = 'Die Trompete in alter und neuer Zeit.' By Hermann Ludwig Eichborn. Leipzig, 1881.

Eichborn (2) = 'Das alte Clarinblasen auf Trompeten.' By Hermann Ludwig Eichborn. Leipzig: 1894.

Fitzgibbon = 'The story of the flute.' By H. Macaulay Fitzgibbon. London: Revised and enlarged edition 1928.

Forkel = 'Johann Sebastian Bach, his life, art, and work.' By Johann Nikolaus Forkel (1802). Ed. Charles Sanford Terry. London: 1920.

Francœur = 'Traité général des voix et des instruments d'orchestre.' By Louis Joseph Francœur. Paris (?) 1772 (new edition 1813).

Galpin = 'Old English instruments of music, their history and character.' By Francis W. Galpin. 3rd edition. London: 1932.

Gerber = 'Historisch-Biographisches Lexicon der Tonkünstler.' By Ernst Ludwig Gerber. 2 vols. Leipzig: 1790–92.

Götz = 'Schule des Blockflötenspiels nach Lehr und Art der mittelalterlichen Pfeifer.' By Robert Götz. Cöln: 1930.

Grove = 'Grove's Dictionary of music and musicians.' 3rd edition. Edited by H. C. Colles. 5 vols. London: 1928.

Hayes = 'Musical instruments and their music, 1500–1750. II. The viols, and other bowed instruments.' By Gerald R. Hayes, London: 1930.

Heckel = 'Der Fagott. Kurzgefasste Abhandlung über seine historische Ent-wicklung, seinen Bau und seine Spielweise.' By William Heckel. 2nd edition. Leipzig: 1931.

Hiller = 'Lebensbeschreibungen berühmter Musikgelehrten und Tonkünstler neuerer Zeit.' By Johann Adam Hiller. Leipzig: 1784.

Jordan = 'Aus der Geschichte der Musik in Mühlhausen.' By Dr. Jordan. Mühlhausen: 1905.

Kinsky = 'Musikhistorisches Museum von Wilhelm Heyer in Cöln. Kleiner Katalog der Sammlung alter Musikinstrumente.' By Georg Kinsky. Cöln: 1913.

Kirby = 'The kettle-drums. A book for composers, conductors, and kettle-drummers.' By Percival R. Kirby. London: 1930.

Kittel = 'Johann Christian Kittel, der letzte Bach-Schüler.' By Albert Dreetz. Leipzig: 1932.

Mahillon = 'Catalogue descriptif et analytique du Musée instrumental du Con-servatoire royal de musique de Bruxelles.' By Victor-Charles Mahillon. Gand: 1893–1922.

Mattheson = 'Das neu-eröffnete Orchestre.' By Johann Mattheson. Ham-burg: 1713.

Mersenne = 'Harmonie universelle, contenant la théorie et la pratique de la musique.' By Marin Mersenne. Paris: 1736.

Mozart = 'Versuch einer gründlichen Violinschule.' By Leopold Mozart. Augsburg: 1756.

North = 'Memoires of Musick.' By Roger North (1653–1734). Ed. F. Rim-bault. London: 1846.

Piersig = 'Die Einführung des Hornes in die Kunstmusik und seine Verwen-dung bis zum Tode Joh. Seb. Bachs.' By Fritz Piersig. Halle: 1927.

Pirro = 'L'esthétique de Jean-Sébastien Bach.' By André Pirro. Paris: 1907.

Pirro (2) = 'Johann Sebastian Bach, the organist, and his works for the organ.' By A. Pirro. With a Preface by Ch.-M. Widor. Translated from the French by Wallace Goodrich. New York: 1902.

Praetorius = 'Syntagmatis musici . . . Tomus secundus. De organographia.' By Michael Praetorius. Wolfenbüttel: 1618 (facsimile 1929).

Quantz = 'Versuch einer Anweisung die Flöte traversière zu spielen.' By Johann Joachim Quantz. Berlin: 1752 (new edition 1906).

Roxas = 'Leben eines herrlichen Bildes . . . Grafen von Sporck.' By Ferdinand van der Roxas. Amsterdam: 1715.

Sachs = 'Real-Lexikon der Musikinstrumente.' By Curt Sachs. Berlin: 1913.

Sachs (2) = 'Sammlung alter Musikinstrumente bei der staatlichen Hochschule für Musik zu Berlin. Beschreibender Katalog.' By Curt Sachs. Berlin: 1922.

Sachs (3) = 'Verzeichnis der Sammlung alter Musikinstrumente im Bachhous zu Eisenach.' By Curt Sachs. 2nd edition. Leipzig: 1918.

Schering = 'Musikgeschichte Leipzigs . . . von 1650 bis 1723.' By Arnold Schering. Leipzig: 1926.

Schubart = 'Ideen zu einer Ästhetik der Tonkunst.' By Christian Friedrich Daniel Schubart. Vienna: 1806.

Schweitzer = 'J. S. Bach.' By Albert Schweitzer. 2 vols. London: 1911.

Spitta = 'Johann Sebastian Bach. His work and influence on the music of Germany, 1685–1750.' By Philipp Spitta. 3 vols. London: 1899.

Tappert = 'Sebastian Bach's Compositionen für die Laute.' By Wilhelm Tappert. Berlin: 1901.

Terry = 'Bach: a biography'. By Charles Sanford Terry. London: 1928.

Terry (2) = 'Bach: the historical approach.' By Charles Sanford Terry. London and New York: 1930.

Terry (3) = 'The origin of the family of Bach musicians.' By Charles Sanford Terry. London: 1929.

Terry (4) = 'Joh. Seb. Bach: Cantata texts, sacred and secular.' By Charles Sanford Terry. London: 1926.

Virdung = 'Musica getutscht und aussgezogen.' By Sebastian Virdung. Basel: 1511 (facsimile 1931).

Wäschke = 'Die Hofkapelle in Cöthen unter Joh. Seb. Bach.' By H. Wäschke. Zerbst: 1907.

Walther = 'Musicalisches Lexicon oder Musicalische Bibliothec.' By Johann Gottfried Walther. Leipzig: 1732.

Weissgerber = 'Johann Sebastian Bach in Arnstadt.' By Diaconus Weissgerber. Arnstadt: 1904.

Woehl = 'Musik für Blocknoten . . . Heft I. Blockflötenschule.' By Waldemar Woehl. 2nd edition, Kassel: 1930.

Wustmann = 'Musikgeschichte Leipzigs . . . bis zur Mitte des 17. Jahrhunderts.' By Rudolf Wustmann. Leipzig and Berlin: 1909.

CHAPTER I

THE LOCAL BACKGROUND

AFTER brief service in a chamber orchestra at Weimar, Bach, a lad of eighteen, found himself in the summer of 1703 his own master at Arnstadt, in an occupation laboriously prepared for since his not-distant schooldays at Ohrdruf. In the interval his genius had been surprisingly nurtured by experience. He had heard music at its most active centres, and in all forms then current. In the Particularschule of Lüneburg he had served a society whose musical apparatus surpassed any he so far had known, whose library revealed to him the classics his own art was destined to enrich and supersede. At Hamburg he had heard Opera under Reinhard Keiser, its most prolific and popular composer. Brought up in the severer ecclesiastical tradition, he had found there an orchestra which spoke with independent eloquence, not merely as an accompanist of the human voice, but as its equal partner in the presentation of Biblical and secular drama. At Hamburg, too, the genius of Reinken had made a deep impression on his greatest disciple. At Celle another idiom was encountered. Here, at the Court of its jovial Duke, the gallant music of France was performed by an orchestra of Frenchmen, with the elegant finish and refined technique characteristic of their nation. So, if untoward bereavement expelled Bach from his native Eisenach, it was the happiest stroke in the moulding of his genius that immediately took him thence to his brother's home at Ohrdruf; for his later educative experiences were consequent upon that initial step.

Arnstadt

As organist of the lately restored Bonifaciuskirche at Arnstadt, Bach filled a subordinate position, whose shortcomings were for the moment outweighed by access to an organ entirely his own. In the civic Gymnasium he held no official position, and drew from it its least competent singers. On the civic instrumentalists his call was precarious. Count Anton Günther, seated in Schloss Neideck on the fringes of the town, maintained a Capelle of some twenty players, occasionally heard in the Augustenburg, modelled on the pleasure house of his wife's Brunswick home. To them were added, when need arose, Michael Bach of Gehren, later Sebastian's father-in-law, the Cantor at Breitenbach, and a bassoon player from Sondershausen.[1] Bach, too, no doubt, was employed.

---

[1] Weissgerber, p. 5.

Following contemporary practice, the Count's musicians also filled domestic or administrative posts in his household. Christoph Herthum, Bach's relative by marriage, combined the posts of Court Organist and Clerk of the Kitchen. The Capellmeister, Paul Gleitsmann, functioned as Groom of the Chamber.[1] The church registers of the period record an inordinate number of Court Trumpeters, who, as elsewhere, were efficient on the other instruments of their craft, 'oboists', and 'lackeys' whose position in the Capelle cannot be determined.[2]

With an orchestra drawn from these sources Bach produced his earliest extant cantata, *Denn du wirst meine Seele nicht in der Hölle lassen* (No. 15), probably on Easter Day (23 March) 1704. But the peremptory orders of the Consistory could not induce him to compose another 'Stück'. For a consuming thirst for instruction drew him in 1705 to distant Lübeck, to hear Dietrich Buxtehude and the famous 'Abendmusiken'. Here he realized fully for the first time the potential contribution of music to the ritual of public worship, and, returning to Arnstadt, awaited with impatience an opportunity to exercise his new convictions elsewhere.

Mühlhausen

The call came in the summer of 1707, when he was elected organist of the noble Blasiuskirche of Mühlhausen. A succession of fires, the most recent of which immediately preceded his arrival, had consumed valuable records of its past history. But one surviving document,[3] dated 6 March 168⅝, discloses a musical organization with which we must associate the only cantata positively composed by Bach for church use in his new sphere. *Gott ist mein König* (No. 71) was performed at the Ratswahl service in the Marienkirche on Septuagesima Sunday (4 February) 1708, closely following the festivals of the Virgin Mary and St. Blaise, to whom Mühlhausen's two principal churches are dedicated. The score is laid out in four 'Choirs': (i) three trumpets and drums; (ii) two flutes and violoncello; (iii) two oboes and bassoon; (iv) two violins, viola, and violone. The voices, too, are grouped in a 'Coro pleno' and a 'Coro in ripieno', the former of which Bach's autograph distinguishes as the 'Capella'. Apparently the ripienists were less expert singers—we may liken them to the Leipzig 'Motettenchor', which provided the 'Coro secondo' of the *Mat-*

---

[1] Weissgerber, *loc. cit.*
[2] It has not been possible to obtain more detailed information regarding the Arnstadt players. I must thank Geheimer Studienrat Dr. Grosse for his assistance in the matter.   [3] Jordan, p. 14.

thäuspassion. In the opening chorus they merely shout intermittently, 'Gott ist mein König'. In the second chorus they are silent, and in the final movement only enter at the *Vivace* section to support the Capella's acclamation of Kaiser Joseph and its fervent wishes for 'Glück, Heil und grosser Sieg!'

The score, therefore, demands exceptional resources, vocal and instrumental, whose source is revealed in the document mentioned above. It discloses the existence, as early as 1617, of a local 'musicalische Societät' or 'musicalisches Kränzchen', whose membership embraced the singers and players of the city and surrounding district. Its nucleus comprised those whom its statutes term 'Schulcollegen' and 'Adjuvanten', i.e. the staff of the town-school, and local amateurs whose services assisted the regular singers and players of the civic church choirs. Another category, described as 'Exteri', was evidently drawn from the country-side. That the villages near-by were actively musical we know from Bach's own statement.[1] The 'Societät' was distinct from the lads of the town-school, the official church choristers, though on the instrumental side it included the civic organists and '6 Musici' (Stadtpfeifer). The abnormal score of Bach's Ratswahl Cantata probably was due to its co-operation. If so, we are probably correct in identifying its members with the 'Coro in ripieno', and the 'Capella' with the 'Coro pleno' of school *alumni*.

Weimar

Before the end of the summer of 1708 Bach was installed in ducal service at Weimar, in touch with an orchestral body whose association with him continued over a considerable period (1708–17). His precise situation at the outset is not definitely ascertained. Certainly he entered the Capelle as 'Cammermusicus' (chamber violinist), and subsequently, perhaps after a short interval, was appointed Court Organist. Neither post required him to compose, and as Cammermusicus he was simply a member of the select string orchestra which performed in the Duke's private apartments in Schloss Wilhelmsburg. In March 1714, however, he was promoted to the position of Concertmeister, with the duty of composing cantatas for the ducal chapel.[2] What were his resources for their performance? The singers numbered six boy sopranos and two singers in each of the under parts, twelve in all, a small body, but experienced and efficient. Of the instrumentalists three lists are extant, from which we can deduce the composition of the ducal orchestra. It included three violinists (of whom one

---

[1] Terry, p. 83.   [2] Cf. Terry, pp. 91–3.

must be supposed a viola player), one violonist, one fagottist, six trumpeters, and one drummer—in all twelve players. Until his death in 1716 (1 December) the director of the musical organization was Capellmeister Johann Samuel Drese, whose son, Johann Wilhelm Drese, acted as his deputy (Vice-Capellmeister), and, to Bach's chagrin, succeeded in 1716 to the higher post. The personnel of the Capelle is recorded in the following Table:[1]

Office	Name	Dates
Capellmeister	Joh. Samuel Drese	d. 1 Dec. 1716.
	Joh. Wilhelm Drese	1716–
Vice-Capellmeister	Georg Christoph Strattner	d. Apr. 1704.
	Joh. Wilhelm Drese	1704–16.
Concertmeister	Joh. Sebastian Bach	2 Mar. 1714–2 Dec. 1717.
Violinists (3)	Joh. Paul von Westhoff	d. 1705.
	Joh. Georg Hoffmann	
	August Gottfried Denstedt ⎱	Entered Capelle before
	Andreas Christoph Ecke ⎰	1714.
Violonist	Joh. Andreas Ehrbach	
Fagottist (1)	Christian Gustav Fischer	d. before 1714.
	Bernhard Georg Ulrich	Entered Capelle before 1714.
Trumpeters (6)	Joh. Georg Beumelburg	
	Joh. Wendelin Eichenberg	
	Joh. Martin Fichtel	
	Joh. Christoph Heininger	
	Joh. Martin Fase	d. before 1714.
	Dietrich Dekker	d. before 1716.
	Joh. Christian Biedermann ⎱	Entered Capelle *circa* 1714.
	Conrad Landgraf ⎰	
Timpanist	Andreas Nicol	

The Duke's conservative disinclination for change, evidenced by his stubborn refusal to release Bach from his service, is illustrated by the composition of the Capelle, whose personnel changed little while Bach was a member of it. The reason was due in part to the fact that, as elsewhere, the Weimar musicians discharged domestic duties in the ducal Court, whose efficient fulfilment probably outweighed deficiencies in their instrumental technique. Westhoff, a violinist of distinction, who had toured widely as a virtuoso, functioned also as 'Cammersecretarius'. Ehrbach was employed as 'Kunstcämmerer' (Superintendent of the Art Museum). Heininger, a trumpeter, was 'Cammerfourier' (Groom-in-waiting). Biedermann, another trumpeter, acted as 'Schloss-Voigt' (Palace Overseer). Denstedt, a violinist, shared the duties of Court Secretary. Of the singers, Andreas Aiblinger, a tenor, held office as 'Secretarius'. Gottfried Ephraim Thiele, a bass, was

[1] Unless the dates indicate the contrary, the persons named were in office during the whole of Bach's service in Weimar.

Court Secretary and Master of the Pages. Christoph Alt, the other bass, was a junior master (Quintus) in the Weimar Gymnasium.

The Court chapel, in which Bach's Weimar cantatas were heard, was ill-adapted for concerted music.[1] The building was lofty and narrow, and the organ[2] was placed aloft in a small roof-gallery, whose accommodation was confined and inconvenient for singers and players. The conditions explain the light instrumentation of the Weimar cantatas.[3] All but five of them (Nos. 59, 70, 147, 162, 185) are scored for strings and wood-wind. Even the Easter Day Cantata *Ich weiss, dass mein Erlöser lebt* (No. 160) is not embellished with trumpets and drums, as was Bach's custom at Leipzig. Brass instruments are rarely prescribed—a single trumpet is scored in Nos. 70, 147, 185, and a corno da tirarsi in No. 162. Drums are scored only in the Whit-Sunday Cantata *Wer mich liebet* (No. 59), in association with two trumpets. Even flutes and oboes are rarely called for, and neither trombones nor horns are required.

Cöthen

A new chapter in Bach's professional experience opened in 1717, on his appointment to the post of Capellmeister at the Court of Prince Leopold of Anhalt-Cöthen. The situation was more dignified than the one he vacated. But Cöthen could not vie with Weimar in the scale of its establishment, and the Prince's Calvinist chapel withheld the opportunities the other capital had afforded Bach as a composer. As Capellmeister, he directed an orchestra, chiefly of strings, which entertained its sovereign in the Ludwigs-bau of the Schloss. Its personnel was grouped in three categories: (1) the 'Cammermusici' (chamber musicians), eight in number; (2) four 'Musici', local players retained for occasional employment at a nominal wage; and (3) a corps of trumpeters and drummer, three in all. A copyist—a rare luxury in Bach's experience—completed the establishment, sixteen in all.[4] Six of them had been drawn from Berlin on the dissolution of its Capelle in 1713, and, alone of the chamber musicians, their instruments can be indicated. The following Table names those who served under Bach, 1717–23:

---

[1] See the picture and description of the building in Terry, p. 96.
[2] For its specification see chap. vii, *infra*.
[3] Neither Nos. 21 nor 31 illustrates the resources of the Weimar Capelle. The former was performed at Halle, the second survives as revised in 1731. The Weimar chapel cantatas are Nos. 18, 59, 61, 70, 106, 132, 147, 150, 152, 155, 158, 160, 161, 162, 163, 182, 185, 189, and *Mein Herze schwimmt im Blut*. In these pages the cantatas are generally referred to by their numbers. For their titles cf. Table XXII.   [4] See Terry, p. 119.

Name	Instrument	Dates
Chamber Musicians.		
Josephus Spiess	Violin	
Joh. Ludwig Rose	Oboe	
Martin Fr. Markus	Violin	Left June 1722.
Joh. Christoph Torlee	Bassoon	
Joh. Heinrich Freytag	..	d. 1721.
Christian Ferdinand Abel	Violin and Gamba	
Joh. Gottfried Würdig		
Christian Bernhard Linigke	Violoncello	
Joh. Valentin Fischer	..	Admitted Aug. 1719.
Christian Rolle	..	Admitted June 1722.
Emanuel Heinrich Gottlieb Freytag	..	Promoted Apr. 1721.
Musicians.		
Joh. Freytag, senior		
Wilhelm Harbordt	..	Left Jan. 1718.
Adam Weber		
Emanuel Heinrich Gottlieb Freytag	..	Promoted 1721 (*supra*).
Trumpeters.		
Joh. Christoph Krahl		
Joh. Ludwig Schreiber		
Timpanist.		
Anton Unger		
Copyist.		
Johann Kräuser	..	Left Dec. 1717.
Joh. Bernhard Göbel	..	Admitted Dec. 1717.
Joh. Bernhard Bach ⎫ Emanuel Leberecht Gottschalk ⎭	..	⎰ Admitted and left ⎱ 1718–19.
Carl Friedrich Vetter	..	Admitted Aug. 1719.

To this point, in so far as his extant work is a guide, Bach, as a composer, had not been drawn to purely instrumental music, except for the organ and clavier. But Cöthen afforded scope for no other. With the available literature he was familiar: at Weimar he had studied French and Italian scores with his accustomed thoroughness. But his genius could not rest content with foreign models. His Cöthen years, therefore, produced, especially in the Brandenburg Concertos, absolute instrumental music surpassing any in existence in the variety of its colouring, the freedom of its technique, and the masterliness of its touch.

It has already been remarked that, excepting the players drawn from Berlin and the trumpeters and drummer, there is no direct indication of the instruments the Capelle provided. Bach's compositions, however, reveal those that were available. The three secular Cöthen cantatas—*Durchlaucht'ster Leopold, Mit Gnaden bekröne*, and *Weichet nur*—are lightly scored for strings and flutes or oboes. His instrumental sonatas were written for violin, violoncello, flute, and viola da gamba. The last-named instrument was Abel's, whose son in later years associated with Bach's youngest son in London. Prince Leopold, too, was a gamba player and may have joined Abel in the sixth Brandenburg Concerto. The frequent violoncello parts indicate that Linigke was a player whom Bach respected, and we can connect Rose with the oboe parts. The Ouvertures in C and B mi., and all but one of the Brandenburg Concertos, were within the competence of the Capelle in respect to the instruments they require. But it supported no horn players, and the well remunerated visit of two guest 'Waldhornisten' on 6 June 1722 undoubtedly indicates a performance of the Branden-burg Concerto in F, probably the first.

But Bach's Cöthen years were an interlude in the ordered scheme of his career. His art was to him, before everything, the servant of religion, and music, in his own words, 'a harmonious euphony to the glory of God'. Every step in his career, from his first employ-ment at Arnstadt, was guided by one compelling purpose, 'the betterment of Church music'. Only the inharmonious conditions of his situation at Weimar, and pique at his exclusion from a post he reasonably held himself to have earned, had taken him to Cöthen in 1717. But the high purpose of his life, though checked, was not stifled. From more than one quarter hands beckoned him to return to the paths whence he had strayed. In 1723 he yielded to the appeal, accepted a call to Leipzig, and there for more than a quarter of a century pursued his life's ideal with unflagging concentration.

Leipzig

Leipzig's municipal orchestra was adequate neither in size nor skill for the uses to which Bach put it. It totalled seven professional players and one apprentice, eight in all. Contrasted with this meagre supply, his requirements, themselves modest, are on record. For the due rendering of Church music, he declared in an illuminating memorandum (August 1730),[1] he needed 'violists', flautists, oboists, and trumpeters. Under the term 'violist' he included all the stringed instruments, and with the trumpeters he associated a drummer. In regard to numbers: he demanded two (preferably three) first violins, a similar number of second violins, two desks of violas (four players), two violoncellists, one violone player, two (or three) oboists, one bassoon player (or two), three trumpeters, and a timpanist—a minimum of eighteen performers.

Bach's statement is instructive. In the first place, though he

[1] Terry, p. 201.

names flutes as necessary, he does not class them as indispensable. He merely states that their inclusion would bring his orchestra to a total of twenty players. In fact, since his appointment to the Cantorship in 1723 they had rarely appeared in his cantata scores. They occur in only eleven (Nos. 8, 46, 65, 67, 81, 119, 145, 157, 164, 181, 195), whereas at Weimar he constantly prescribed them. The explanation is found in the memorandum, whence it appears that he was dependent for flautists on local amateurs—University 'studiosi', or 'alumni' of the Thomasschule. In his first years at Leipzig he was evidently well served from that source, for all the eleven cantatas are referred to the period, in which also fall the *Magnificat* and both Passions.

In the second place, Bach's enumeration apparently excludes both horns and trombones. In fact, they are implicit in his fourth category. For centuries the civic musicians were known as 'the blowers' ('die Bläser'), responsible for 'Blasmusik', whether sounded by trumpets, trombones, or horns. To us, accustomed to the vogue of specialism, the practice appears disadvantageous. But the explanation is simple. Like others of the kind in Germany, Leipzig's municipal orchestra was a guild of professional monopolists, and consequently expert in the technique of all the instruments proper to the discharge of its public duties. The rules of the Saxon 'Instrumental-musicalisches Collegium' (1653) ordain *inter alia*: 'Seeing that an expert musician must profess several instruments, both wind and percussion, and so be well instructed in them, no apprentice shall be released under five years or be held competent to practise his craft' ('Und nachdem ein perfecter Musicant auff vielen Instrumenten, theils *pneumaticis*, theils *pulsatilibus* unterwiesen werden, und darauff auch geübet seyn muss, so soll kein Lehrknabe unter fünff Jahr frey gesprochen, und dass er seiner Kunst erfahren, für tüchtig erkennet werden').[1] The relation of this regulation to Bach's experience at Leipzig will be illustrated later. Here it only needs to be remarked that the performers of his trumpet *obbligati* were the same valiant trio for whom he wrote horn and trombone parts. In the whole range of his music the three instruments are only once so disposed as to require separate players. The single instance to the contrary is in the secular cantata *Der zufriedengestellte Aeolus*, in which three trumpets and two horns are employed in the same movements.[2]

Thus Bach's Leipzig orchestra was a mixed body of professional

---

[1] Spitta (Germ. edn.), i. 145.
[2] The cornett-trombone combination very infrequently employs four players.

and amateur players, varying in size and composition according to the means at his disposal. The relative proportions of the two categories, and their contribution to the orchestra, is revealed in the memorandum. In August 1730 the professionals supplied him with two trumpeters (horn and trombone players), two oboists, one bassoon player (the apprentice), and two violinists, seven in all. Bach styles the latter respectively '1 Violine', '2 Violine', indicating the leaders of the firsts and seconds. Regarding the parts for which he had to look elsewhere, he names two first violins, two second violins, two violas, two violoncellists, one violone player, and two flutes. At the first and second violin desks he therefore had two amateurs and one professional leader, six in all. The number was customary: his predecessor Kuhnau had asked in 1704 to be provided with a box large enough to hold six violins for carriage from church to church.[1] Outside the professional body Bach also needed two viola players, two violoncellists, one violonist, and two flutes. All of these, he explains, were provided occasionally ('zum Theil') by University 'studiosi', but generally ('meistens') by *alumni* of the Thomasschule. From the latter source his second violins generally ('meistens'), and his viola, violoncello, and violone players invariably ('allezeit'), were recruited 'for lack of more expert players' ('in Ermangelung tüchtigerer *subjectorum*'). We can therefore deduce that his amateur first violins and flautists were undergraduates of the University. Most frequently, we may suppose, they had proceeded thither from the Thomasschule.

It must not be inferred that Bach's orchestra regularly and normally numbered twenty, or even eighteen, players. For it associated exclusively with the 'Coro primo' or 'grosse Cantorei' of his singers, which performed the Sunday cantatas and occasional concerted music. In 1730 it numbered seventeen choristers, and as many in 1744. Seventeen may therefore be accepted as its normal strength.[2] Small in number, it was also unevenly balanced. In 1744 it comprised five sopranos, two altos, three tenors, and seven basses. The weakness of the melodic part explains its frequently strong instrumental backing in Bach's scores, especially in the Chorals. The choir was certainly inadequate to associate with an orchestra that outnumbered it. Excepting festal occasions, we can conclude that Bach's instrumentalists rarely exceeded ten or twelve players, besides the organ. If so, his dependence on non-professional aid was not so urgent as must otherwise have been the case. For it is not to be supposed that the professional players were only on duty when the Sunday cantata contained a part for

---

[1] Spitta, iii. 303. [2] Cf. Terry (2), p. 51.

their principal instrument. Indeed, Altenburg[1] advised a trumpeter to make himself efficient on the fiddle. Johann Schneider, Bach's pupil, and organist of the Nikolaikirche, explicitly directed his horn and oboe players in certain movements of a wedding cantata of his composition to put down those instruments and take up their violins. A similar usage obtained in the orchestral concerts which began to be a feature of Leipzig's musical activity in the same period,[2] Bach's players undoubtedly observed the convention.

Thus, on Sunday mornings, at the chief service of the day (Hauptgottesdienst), the choir gallery of St. Thomas's or St. Nicholas's accommodated a body of about thirty performers for the rendering of the cantata. On festal occasions the number would be larger, but not considerably. The choir was not usually augmented, save for occasional 'Adjuvanten' in the under parts. In the orchestra trumpets (or horns) and drums were added to the instruments normally heard. But their presence did not necessarily enlarge the personnel. On special occasions, however, Bach could increase his forces considerably. In the *St. Matthew Passion*, for instance, the inclusion of his 'Coro secondo', or 'kleine Cantorei', of twenty voices brought the tale of his singers to nearly forty; and, since he used two orchestras, each of at least twelve players, singers and instrumentalists together totalled about sixty. Nowhere else does he demand so large a 'Kirchenorchester', though some of his secular cantatas made heavy calls on his resources, and for an obvious reason: they were written for open-air performance.

The arrangement of Bach's singers and players in church is apparently revealed by a closely contemporary (1710) print, which, in some particulars, confirms the speculations of the preceding paragraph.[3] It shows the choir gallery of the Thomaskirche during the performance of a 'Stück' (cantata) in the Cantorship of Johann Kuhnau, Bach's immediate predecessor. The organ is on the west wall, and the performers are grouped on either side of and behind the organist seated at the manuals in the middle of the picture. On his left is the violonist, and next to him a lute player, an instrument the cembalo superseded, and of which Bach made little use in his church music. In front of these players a quartet of strings is observed, two violins and two violas, and on their left, immediately behind the organist, the timpanist faces his kettledrums. In the foreground the Cantor beats time with a roll in his

---

[1] P. 119.   [2] Schering, p. 100.
[3] See the frontispiece to the present writer's *Bach's Cantata Texts* (1926).

hand. On his left is a group of three, two playing natural trumpets,[1] the third, a horn player, with the bell of his instrument held upward, as was customary. In all, the players number ten, and are stationed generally on the Cantor's left, facing the singers, who are ranged on his right in three groups of four, twelve in all. Their costumes show that they are not separated in parts (soprano, alto, tenor, bass), but that each quartet is a complete vocal unit, the bass in each acting as group-conductor, and taking the beat from the Cantor. Including the organist, the performers number twenty-three.

As an indication of Bach's disposition of his forces, and of his place among them, the picture is unreliable. The gallery of St. Thomas's was far smaller than it is to-day, and its front was filled by the imposing case of the Rückpositiv.[2] The singers and players were grouped round the harpsichord, which probably stood midway between the organ and Rückpositiv. As the frontispiece to his *Musicalisches Lexicon*, published in 1732, Joh. G. Walther, Bach's Weimar friend, used a picture of what we may perhaps identify as the organ gallery of the civic church in that town.[3] The conductor stands close to the organist, on the left of the console, and therefore in a position to control the most powerful voice in his orchestra. Immediately behind him are the continuo players and strings, with the brass instruments in the rear. The singers are not visible, but their position is indicated by the attitude of the conductor, who faces them across the intervening harpsichord. He has a roll of music in either hand. Johann Bähr, Bach's contemporary and acquaintance at Weissenfels, remarks that conductors varied in their methods: some stamped with their feet; others, their feet being employed, beat time with their head; some used one hand, some both hands; one waved a roll of paper, another grasped a roll in each hand; and some used a stick.[4] Of Bach as a conductor we have his son Carl Philipp Emanuel and his pupil Agricola's statement that he was precise and particular, and preferred a lively *tempo*.[5] Gesner, under whom as Rector he served for a short time, is more descriptive. He seats Bach at the keyboard, whence 'he controls this one with a nod, another with the rhythm of the measure, a third with a directing finger'.[6]

Since Bach occasionally used the harpsichord and organ, displacing the regular player of the latter, he would adopt a position as conductor which would give him quick access to both keyboards,

---

[1] They are holding their instruments below the boss and so control only one position.   [2] Cf. *infra*, p. 12.   [3] See the frontispiece to this volume.
[4] Spitta, ii. 325.   [5] Terry, p. 267.   [6] *Ibid.*, p. 107.

and at the same time enable him to control his singers and players.
The conductor's position in Walther's frontispiece was admirably
chosen for these purposes, and we may accept it as Bach's habitual
place. The disposition of his choir and orchestra are indicated
on the following plan, which makes their numbers accord with the
facts set forth in an earlier paragraph:

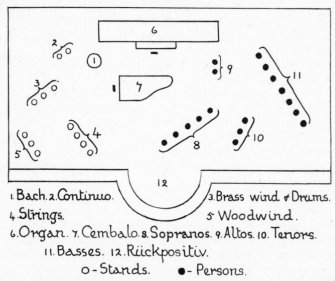

1. Bach. 2. Continuo.   3. Brass wind & Drums.
4. Strings.   5. Woodwind.
6. Organ. 7. Cembalo. 8. Sopranos. 9. Altos. 10. Tenors.
        11. Basses. 12. Rückpositiv.
        o - Stands.   ● - Persons.

It would be agreeable to recover the names of the privileged company who for a quarter of a century introduced Bach's masterpieces
to an indifferent world. We can only guess, though with some
certainty, those of his voluntary helpers. Senior among them
was Joh. Gotthelf Gerlach, who left the Thomasschule in 1723,
became organist of Leipzig's New Church, and eventually succeeded Bach as conductor of the Collegium Musicum (University
Musical Society). His contemporaries Joh. Gabriel Rothe, later
Cantor in Grimma, and Christ. Gottlieb Gerlach, afterwards
Cantor of his native Rochlitz, who left the school respectively in
1723 and 1726, must also have been useful in Bach's early years
at Leipzig.[1] His nephew Joh. Heinrich, son of his Ohrdruf
brother, left the school in 1728 in his twenty-first year. Later he
became Cantor at Oehringen and was competent to requite his
uncle with his service. Towards the middle of Bach's Cantorship,
his favourite, Johann Ludwig Krebs, left the school (1735) and

---

[1] They both proceeded to the University, Gerlach in 1727, Rothe in 1725.

proceeded to the University. The part he played in Bach's un-happy quarrel with the prefects in 1736[1] proves that he continued to assist his former master. In 1737 he became organist at Zwickau. Gottlob Heinrich Neicke and Joh. Ludwig Dietel are also associated with this period of Bach's Cantorship. They left the school in 1733 and 1735 respectively, proceeded to the University, and were Cantors in after-life. Christoph Nichelmann left the school in 1733. His association with Bach's family was close: Bach's eldest son Wilhelm Friedemann was his master for the clavier,[2] and Philipp Emanuel helped to secure his appointment as second cembalist to Frederick the Great. Another alumnus of this middle period was Christ. Friedrich Schemelli, with whose father Bach collaborated as musical editor of the so-called 'Schemelli Hymn-book' (1736). The younger Schemelli left the school in 1734, matriculated at the University in 1735, and eventually succeeded his father as Cantor at Zeitz. We may not include in this proble-matical list of auxiliaries Joh. Gottfried Böhme, afterwards Cantor at Tragheim (?), whose stay in the Thomasschule was brief. He entered it in 1732 and left it 'privily' ('clanculum') in 1733, com-plaining that the tasks of the ordinary curriculum impeded his progress in music![3] Joh. Gottfried Kade, who entered the school in his fourteenth year, and left it (1745) when he was twenty-three, had the greater opportunity to be of service, seeing that he found employment in St. Nicholas's School as Tertius[4] and Cantor. Joh. Wilhelm Cunis, who left the school in 1747 and proceeded to the University, afterwards Cantor in his native Cölleda, was another probable helper. Bach's talented sons undoubtedly aided him, and in the closing years of his Cantorship two others of his name may be recorded in this company: Joh. Ernst Bach, an Eisenach cousin, who came to Leipzig in 1737 and was eventually expelled for taking French leave of absence,[5] and a more reliable relative, Joh. Elias Bach, who entered Bach's household in 1738, served him affectionately till 1742, and left to become Cantor of Schweinfurt. That, regularly or on occasion, some or all of these deciphered Bach's bold manuscript on their playing-desks we can be sure.

No dubiety exists as to Bach's professional players: their names are tabulated on p. 14.

With the addition of the anonymous apprentice-bassoonist, the first seven names on the Table are those of the professional players Bach took over from his predecessor. They represented two

---

[1] Cf. Terry, chap. viii, *passim.*   [2] Gerber, ii. 26.
[3] B.-J. 1907, p. 71.   [4] i.e. third master.   [5] B.-J. 1907, p. 73.

Name	Kunst-geiger	Stadt-pfeifer	Died[1]	Principal Instrument
Gottfried Reiche	1700–6	1706–34	9 Oct. 1734	1st trumpet.[2]
Heinrich Christian Beyer	1706–48	..	21 Sept. 1748	2nd violin.[2]
Christian Rother	1707–8	1708–37	25 Oct. 1737	1st violin.[2]
Christian Ernst Meyer	1707–30	..	Apparently left Leipzig	? 3rd trumpet or 3rd oboe.[4]
Joh. Cornelius Gentzmer	1708–12	1712–51	25 Oct. 1751	2nd trumpet.[2]
Joh. Caspar Gleditsch	1712–19	1719–47	22 May 1747	1st oboe.[2]
Joh. Gottfried Kornagel	1719–53	..	14 Sept. 1753	2nd oboe.[2]
Joh. Friedrich Caroli	1730–38	..	1 March 1738	? 3rd trumpet or 3rd oboe.[4]
Ulrich Heinrich Ruhe	..	1734–87	11 June 1787	1st trumpet or 1st violin.[3]
Joh. Friedrich Kirchhof	..	1737–69	20 May 1769	oboe or flute.[3]
Joh. Christian Oschatz	1738–47	1747–62	13 Jan. 1762	oboe or flute or 2nd trumpet.[3]
Carl Friedrich Pfaffe	1748–53	1753–73	3 Mar. 1773	trumpet.[5]
Andreas Christoph Jonne	1749–62	1762–84	28 June 1784	? violin.[6]

separate, and not invariably harmonious, corporations. The civic office of Stadtpfeifer (town-piper, town-musician) in Leipzig dated from 1479, when the municipality instituted Master Hans Nagel and his two 'sons' (probably apprentices: 'Gesellen', 'Lehr-linge') at a yearly wage of forty gulden and their uniform. They functioned on occasions of public ceremony, but derived their chief emolument from weddings, at which they alone were privileged to perform, receiving fees according to the station of the spouses. A silver-gilt shield denoted their office.[7] Their instruments were the trumpet, Zink (cornett), and trombone.[8] But their monopoly did not remain unchallenged. In the course of the sixteenth century competitors invited public patronage and threatened their pecuniary interests. The challengers were known as 'Feldtpfeifer und Trommelschläger' (drum- and fifers), who so far had served other uses, acting as town-criers, and summoning the citizens to military duty. But in 1550 a civic ordinance permitted 'a drummer and his fifer' to perform at weddings. Conflict between the rival bodies consequently threatened, and was averted by an amicable

[1] The dates are those of burial. I am obliged to Dr. Reinhard Fink for extracting them from the church registers.
[2] Named in Bach's memorandum of August 1730.
[3] So described in the 'Tabula musicorum der Löbl. Grossen Konzert-gesellschaft, 1746–48'. Cf. Archiv f. M., p. 50.
[4] Meyer held one of the posts named by Bach as vacant in August 1730. His successor Caroli, no doubt, received it. Probability indicates the trumpet or oboe as their principal instrument.
[5] Succeeded Gentzmer as Stadtpfeifer. Gentzmer probably had succeeded Reiche as principal trumpeter in 1734.
[6] Perhaps took Beyer's place.   [7] Wustmann, p. 31.   [8] Ibid., p. 33.

agreement concluded in 1587.[1] By then the number of Stadtpfeifer stood fixed at four, and that of their competitors at two pairs of drums and two fifers. The eight now (1587) arranged themselves in four groups to serve in alternation at ceremonies for which their instruments were required, leaving to the Stadtpfeifer exclusively the duty of assisting the music in the churches.

Thus was constituted an orchestra whose activities persisted till Bach's period, and beyond. But whereas the Stadtpfeifer continued to profess the instruments proper to 'Blasmusik', the Feldtpfeifer and Trommelschläger succumbed to the vagaries of public taste. In 1595, responding to the citizens' preference for the newer 'Hausmusik', the Council licensed two fiddlers to perform at weddings.[2] In 1603 we hear of 'public fiddlers', and by 1607 they are definitely 'town fiddlers' ('Stadtgeiger'), with their number fixed at three,[3] as in Bach's period. The Stadtpfeifer, however, retained their traditional privileges. They enjoyed the monopoly of all weddings celebrated 'in der Stadt', and surrendered to their rivals only the meaner sort ('die schlechten Hochzeiten vor den Thoren'), along with the less distinguished, and therefore less profitable, of two weddings fixed for the same day and hour 'in der Stadt'.[4] Again, in 1607, when the Kunstgeiger[5] were at length permitted to participate in the music of the two principal churches, the concession was restricted to association with the 'Coro secondo' or 'kleine Cantorei', reserving to the Stadtpfeifer their traditional right to accompany the 'Coro primo' or 'grosse Cantorei'.[6] But their separation could persist no longer than the character of 'die Musik' permitted. During the Cantorship of Johann Kuhnau (1701–22), Bach's immediate predecessor, the newer cantata style decisively prevailed. It demanded for its due performance a mixed orchestra of wind and strings. 'Stadtpfeifer' and 'Kunstgeiger' accordingly coalesced to assist the 'Coro primo' in the performance of the weekly 'Musik' in that one of the two churches privileged to hear it, leaving the 'Coro secondo', Bach's 'Motet Choir', to sing the old-style music a cappella or accompanied by the organ in the other.[7] At the same time, and for the same reason, the

---

[1] *Archiv f. M.*, p. 19.   [2] Wustmann, p. 155.
[3] B.-J. 1907, p. 34; Wustmann, p. 156.
[4] *Archiv f. M.*, p. 20. Weddings served by the Stadtpfeifer and Kunstgeiger were known respectively as 'grosse oder blasende Hochzeiten' and 'geigende Hochzeiten'. (Cf. *ibid.*, p. 26.) For the practice in Bach's time see *infra*, p. 21.
[5] The term was first used officially in 1626 (B.-J. 1907, p. 34).
[6] Wustmann, p. 156.
[7] In several motet-like choruses Bach reverts to the older tradition, and reinforces the voices with cornett and trombones.

restriction of the two professional bodies to a particular category of instruments, wind or strings, fell into desuetude. Evidence is lacking to determine when the change was accomplished. But in Bach's time, as the Table on page 14 reveals, the Stadtpfeifer were recruited from the Kunstgeiger. Indeed, for half his period of service at Leipzig, his leader of the first violins was a Stadtpfeifer.

The Kunstgeiger, however, remained inferior in status and income, and, though privileged and official, lived in surroundings of discomfort and penury. Bach's appointment in 1723 was almost coincident with an ordinance which, to some degree, bettered their lot. In 1721, towards the close of Kuhnau's Cantorship, they had approached the civic Council with a statement of their grievances. They complained that, unlike themselves, the Stadtpfeifer lived rent free in official lodgings, received a weekly wage of eighteen groschen, were exclusively engaged at University graduations of doctors and masters, received gratuities from well-to-do citizens to whom they offered New Year serenades, were employed at the theatre ('haben sie die Comödie zu blasen') during the three annual fairs, attended public banquets and the Whitsuntide shooting matches, and were preferentially employed at weddings.[1] The facts were correctly stated. Since 1599 the most regular duty of the Stadtpfeifer was to sound fanfares from the Rathaus tower twice daily.[2] Their weekly wage consequently had been increased from fifteen to eighteen groschen, with an allowance for clothing. Till 1717 they paid no local taxes. They lived in a common lodging in the Stadtpfeifergässlein—to-day the Magazingasse—and for their participation in church music received, since 1633, ten thalers. Their 'Neujahrsgeld' brought them two florins six groschen. Moreover, a Stadtpfeifer's widow was privileged to remain a half-year in the house after her husband's death, enjoying his official income and half the fees ('accidentia') his successor might earn in that period.[3] In their effort to share these privileges the Kunstgeiger were only partially successful. Their exclusion from all but the meaner weddings continued. On the other hand, they were granted an official lodging, which, after 1725, they shared with the Stadtpfeifer in the Stadtpfeifergässlein. In 1740 they again petitioned for a closer approximation of their status to that of their house-neighbours. But in vain; the time was not ripe for such a break with tradition.[4]

[1] B.-J. 1907, p. 35.
[2] Specimens of these 'Abblasen' are given by Schering, p. 276.
[3] Archiv f. M., p. 21. Since 1665 a Kunstgeiger's widow had the same privilege as to income. [4] Ibid., p. 23.

Such was the situation when Bach came to Leipzig in 1723. The Stadtpfeifer provided him with four players, the Kunstgeiger with three, and the 'Geselle' added an eighth. The smaller body still viewed the other with envy, and regularly ascended to its ranks. Of the thirteen musicians who served under Bach only two reached Stadtpfeifer rank direct. For, notwithstanding their designation, the Kunstgeiger were not competent on stringed instruments only. Kuhnau, in 1709, reported that 'the Stadtpfeifer, Kunstgeiger, and apprentices, eight in all' ('die aus 8 Personen zusammen bestehenden Stadt Pfeiffer, Kunst Geiger und Gesellen') supplied him with two trumpeters, two oboists or cornettists, three trombonists, and one bassoonist.[1] It must not be concluded that none of the eight was a string player, though Kuhnau complained that such were hard to find. In 1730, as has already been shown, the two bodies gave Bach only two violinists. For the rest of the strings, he, like Kuhnau, depended on 'studiosi' and 'alumni'.[2] The easy transformation of a Kunstgeiger into a Stadtpfeifer, and his general competence to handle the so-called 'Stadtpfeiferinstrumente'—the trumpet, Zink (cornett), horn, trombone, bombard, dulcian, with some facility on the flute, oboe, and strings—is illustrated by the fact that in Bach's time a Kunstgeiger was not subjected to an examination before promotion to the higher post.[3] Two illustrative cases occurred during his Cantorate. In 1745 the Council directed him to settle the conflicting claims of two players to fill the next vacancy among the Stadtpfeifer—Johann Christian Oschatz, already a Kunstgeiger, who alleged that the Council had promised him promotion, and Carl Friedrich Pfaffe, trumpeter Gentzmer's apprentice 'cum spe succedendi' (with the prospect of succession). Oschatz was excused examination on the ground that his competence had been already established in 1738, when he was admitted a Kunstgeiger. Pfaffe submitted himself to trial, and on 24 July 1745 received from Bach a testimonial to his competence 'on the various instruments a Stadtpfeifer must profess, namely, the violin, oboe, traverso [flute], trumpet, horn, and other [wind] instruments' ('auf jedem Instrumente, so von denen Stadt Pfeifern pfleget gebrauchet zu werden, als Violine, Hautbois, Flute Travers., Trompette, Waldhorn und übrigen [Blas] Instrumenten').[4] Five years later a candidate failed to pass the test 'on the three principal instruments, namely, (1) the trumpet, (2) the horn, and (3) the oboe' ('auf den drey Haupt Instrumenten, als 1. Trompete, 2.

[1] Spitta (Germ. edn.), ii. 859.　　　[2] *Supra*, p. 9.
[3] *Archiv f. M.*, p. 37.　　　[4] *Ibid.*, p. 44.

Waldhorn, und 3. Hautbois'), without practical knowledge of
which, his examiners added, no one, 'however many extra instruments he may study, can pass muster as a Stadtpfeifer' ('ob er
gleich noch so viel neben Instrumente verstünde, ohnmöglich
vor einem Stadt-Pfeiffer passiren kan').[1] A third case is recorded
in 1769, when Johann Friedrich Doles examined two candidates
for a vacant post as Stadtpfeifer. Both were required to play the
violone part of a concerted Choral, a simple Choral on all four
trombones, a violin trio, a concerted Choral on the Zugtrompete
(tromba da tirarsi), and either a horn or an oboe and flute concerto![2]

These examples sufficiently indicate the all-round proficiency a
Stadtpfeifer was expected to display. On the other hand, they
provoke doubts as to his competence in the technique of them all.
In his report on the less worthy of the candidates in 1769—Joh.
Gottl. Herzog, a Kunstgeiger since 1763 and for twenty years
(1773-93) a Stadtpfeifer—Doles commented on his bad oboe tone,
inability on the Zugtrompete, inaccurate reading, lack of technique
as a trombonist, and uselessness as a violonist! None the less, a
Stadtpfeifer laid down his office only at his death. None ceased
to function until he was physically incapable, when he supplied a
deputy, who established a sort of claim to succeed him. Of those
in office when Bach came to Leipzig in 1723 one already had
served under two Cantors, and the experience of all went back to a
period when the 'status musices', as Bach called it, was far different
from that of his own generation. Kuhnau wrote contemptuously
in 1709 of his 'couple of Stadtpfeifer apprentices' ('etwa ein Paar
Stadt Pfeiffer Gesellen').[3] 'Discretion', Bach remarked of his
professional players in 1730, 'forbids me to offer an opinion on
their competence and musicianship. I merely observe that some
of them are *emeriti*, and others not in such good *exercitium* as
formerly.'[4] Even a non-professional critic in 1748 suggested that
'more accuracy' ('grössere Accuratesse') in their playing would be
agreeable.[5] It may be doubted whether Bach ever heard his scores
interpreted with even approximate excellence. How much more
fortunate was Handel in London!

It would appear that their instruments were generally as anti-
quated as the players. Kuhnau, soon after his appointment,
invited (1704) the Council's attention to the fact that the church's
trombones were battered and useless from long service. He asked
for a new 'choir' of four—discant, alto, tenor, bass—and also for a

[1] *Archiv f. M.*, p. 45.   [2] *Ibid.*, p. 45.
[3] Spitta (Germ. edn.), ii. 859.   [4] Terry, p. 202.   [5] *Archiv f. M.*, p. 44.

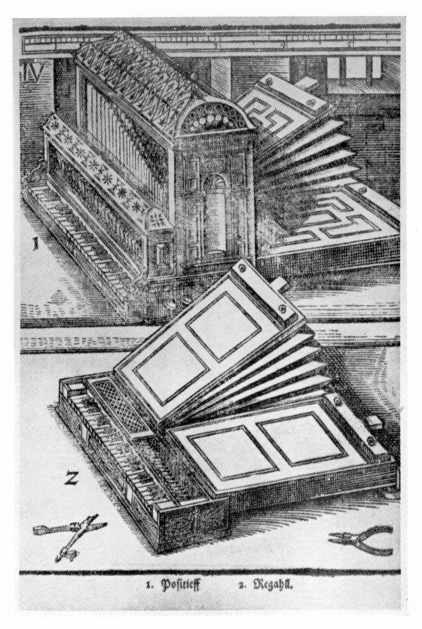

1. Positieff   2. Regahl.

POSITIVE AND REGAL
(*Praetorius*)

colascione,[1] which, though indispensable, he was forced to borrow. He failed to obtain it. Five years later he again begged for one, and also reported that the School violin was damaged beyond the means of the School funds to repair it. As a case for the church violins[2] had not been provided, he asked that nails might be driven into a board in the choir gallery, in order that there might be no excuse for leaving the instruments in jeopardy on the floor. He added that the harpsichords in both churches were in such disrepair that they needed to be patched every time they were used.[3] In 1747 the pipes of St. Thomas's organ were so full of dust and rubbish that many of them would not speak![4]

Both churches possessed their own instruments. When Schelle entered on his Cantorship in 1678, St. Thomas's owned a spinet, violone, octave bombard, bass bombard, fagotto, timpani, two *viole da braccio*,[5] and two violins.[6] The accounts show that there were also available: a flute, a 'choir' of trombones, and two trumpets. The drums, though ten years old in 1678, were not renewed till 1686![7] When Kuhnau took office in 1701, he found in St. Thomas's a violone, fagotto, spinet, five bombards, six trumpets, three trombones, and two recently acquired violins. St. Nicholas's owned a violone, fagotto, bombard, three trombones, two old violins, two violas, and two new violins. An official violoncello was not at Bach's disposal till 1729.[8] The preponderance of wind instruments is evident. An inventory for 1723 has not survived. But it is not doubtful that Bach inherited a collection of instruments which already had done honourable service. For instance, the cembalo in St. Thomas's had been in use since 1672 and was in a ruinous condition. It was not replaced till 1756, six years after his death![9] The School was not equipped with a cembalo, but a Positiv had been installed in 1685. In 1739 Bach begged for a new instrument, and was refused. It was erected and tuned to Cammerton during the Cantorship of his second successor (1756).[10] In St. Nicholas's a cembalo was not available in 1693, when the church's accounts show that it shared St. Thomas's instrument. But Kuhnau's reference in 1709 to 'the large *clavicembali* in both churches' ('in beyden Kirchen befindlichen grossen Clavi-

---

[1] A species of lute. Mattheson (p. 279) calls it 'ein kleines Lauten-mässiges mit 5. einfachen Sayten bezogenes und fast wie die Viola di Gamba gestimmtes Instrument (D. G. c. f. a. d.).' Having regard to its exotic character, Kuhnau's demand is strange.   [2] *Supra*, p. 9.
[3] Spitta (Germ. edn.), ii. 853 f.   [4] *Ibid.*, ii. 870.
[5] In Bach's time the name indicated the ordinary viola.
[6] B.-J. 1907, p. 38.
[7] *Archiv f. M.*, p. 34. They belonged to the two churches in common.
[8] Schering, p. 114.   [9] Schering, p. 112.   [10] B.-J. 1907, p. 41.

cimbeln')[1] shows that the defect had by then been made good, apparently by the generosity of a private donor.[2]

The accounts of the School and the two churches for the period of Bach's Cantorship frequently record the repair of the instruments. But there is the barest indication that any new ones were acquired while he was in office. Zacharias Hildebrand received payment for repairing St. Nicholas's clavicembalo in 1732–3, and for restringing and tuning it in the following years till 1740. Otherwise the accounts reveal no expenditure upon musical instruments. Similar items appear in St. Thomas's accounts, which incidentally reveal that Carl Philipp Emanuel Bach was employed to tune its clavicembalo in 1731–2 and 1732–3. In the year 1729–30 two violins, one viola, and one violoncello were purchased, with their appropriate bows, and in 1739–40 a new 'Pedal-Clavier' was acquired from Johann Scheibe. For school practice a 'large' violone[3] was bought at an auction in 1735–6.[4] But otherwise the instruments that served Kuhnau did duty for Bach without replacement or augmentation—their inventory is repeated with monotonous reiteration annually to 1750:[5]

'*An Musicalischen Instrumenten*

1 *Regal*, so alt und ganz eingegangen.
1 *dito* aõ 1696 angeschaffet.
1 *Violon* aõ 1711.
1 *Violon* aõ 1735, in der *Auction* erstanden [omitted 1723–34].
2 *Violons de Braz*. 2 *Violinen* aõ 1706 repariret.
1 *Positiv* in die Höhe stehend von 4 Registern und Tremulanten, gelb mit Golde angestrichen aõ 1685 angeschafft.
1 *Positiv* in *Form* eines Thresores mit 4 Handhaben, welches ein gedacktes von 8 Fuss Thon hat.
1 Dergleichen von 4 Fuss.
1 *Principal* von 2 Fuss, ist aõ 1720 angeschaffet worden, um bey denen Hauss Trauungen zu gebrauchen.'

It is therefore evident that Bach was dependent on private owners for many of the instruments he employed. The necessity probably accounts for his own large and varied collection. Besides claviers, it included three lutes, a small spinet, two violins, a violino piccolo, three *viole da braccio*, one viola da gamba, two violoncellos, and one violoncello piccolo. That Bach was extraordinarily selective in his search for orchestral colour is admitted. But it is evident that his scoring was restricted by the accessibility

---

[1] See Praetorius, Plate VI, at p. 160.   [2] Schering, p. 112.
[3] Mr. Hayes conjectures that the adjective indicates a double-bass violin.
[4] I am obliged to Dr. Reinhard Fink, who searched the records on my behalf.
[5] Spitta (Germ. edn.), ii. 774.

of particular instruments at the moment he required them. The difficulty did not present itself in regard to wind instruments, for the Stadtpfeifer and Kunstgeiger had their own, or were provided with them to fulfil their civic duties. Reiche, for instance, Bach's chief trumpeter, also possessed a Zugtrompete and Waldhorn. His colleague Gleditsch, Bach's principal oboist, owned a Zink or cornett.[1]

In Leipzig, as in other German towns of the period, the principal and regular duty of the Stadtpfeifer was to blow the 'Abblasen' or 'Turmblasen' daily at 10 a.m. and 6 p.m. from the balcony of the Rathaus tower in the Marktplatz. At festival seasons, and on occasions of civic and academic solemnity, Chorals also were sounded by trombones or cornetts from the church towers.[2] But, for the necessary augmentation of their income, the town's musicians relied particularly on the *accidentia* derived from weddings. These were held in church with or without a Wedding Mass ('Brautmesse'); it might be either 'a whole Mass' (ganze Brautmesse) or 'a half Mass' (halbe Brautmesse).[3] The former took place at four o'clock in the afternoon, the latter at ten o'clock in the morning. At a full Mass both Stadtpfeifer and Kunstgeiger performed; at the morning function only the latter were employed. The poorer citizens, and such as desired to evade the expense of a musical ceremony, were married at eight o'clock in the morning. Some, who misliked the hour and implication of so early a ceremony, held their weddings elsewhere, and roused the ire of the local musicians thereby cheated of their fees.[4] The fee for a full Mass varied according as the bridal pair were received with music on entering church, or processed in silence ('in der Stille'). If music was provided at the wedding banquet which followed, the musicians received an additional fee. At half Masses the Kunstgeiger monopolized the wedding and the breakfast after it. The Cantor only attended a full Mass and received a fee of two thalers and a measure of wine. Their scoring indicates that all Bach's extant Leipzig wedding cantatas were performed at a full Mass. At the wedding banquet that followed, the Cantor with his 'Coro primo' was not infrequently invited to provide a cantata. Bach's 'Coffee Cantata', *O holder Tag*, *Vergnügte Pleissen-Stadt*, and *Weichet nur, betrübte Schatten* were composed for the purpose. His daughter Lieschen was married in St. Thomas's at a half Mass on 20 January 1749,[5] and it is probable that the 'Three Wedding

---

[1] *Archiv f. M.*, p. 34.   [2] Schering, pp. 271, 278, 285.
[3] Cf. *Archiv f. M.*, p. 31. Schering, p. 91.
[4] Cf. Terry, p. 180.   [5] *Ibid.*, p. 257.

Chorals', from the score of which drums and trumpets are absent,
were sung on the occasion.

Funerals, which chiefly augmented the Cantor's salary—Bach
estimated their annual contribution to his income as considerable[1]
—brought no grist to his instrumentalists. For funerals were no
longer conducted with the musical pomp still permitted to decorate
weddings. Instead, memorial services were held at a short interval
after the funeral, when a sermon was preached and music might
be sung. Five of Bach's motets were composed for such occasions.
But they were sung *a cappella*, and only one of them received
orchestral accompaniment. It was performed in memory of an
academic dignitary in the University chapel (Paulinerkirche), a
building not subject to the civic rule which forbade instruments to
be heard in the churches on such occasions. Another composition
of this character is the *Trauer-Ode*, also composed for the University Chapel, and, like the Motet, provided with orchestral accompaniment. Both ceremonies were controlled by the University,
and to the score of neither work were the distinctive 'Stadtpfeiferinstrumente' admitted. On the other hand, Bach's motet *O Jesu
Christ, mein's Lebens Licht* is scored for them, for what occasion
is not known. Certainly it was not performed in a Leipzig church,
but probably at the grave-side.

[1] Terry, p. 205.

CHAPTER II

TRUMPET, HORN, CORNETT, TROMBONE

The Tromba

BACH'S younger contemporary, Johann Ernst Altenburg, son and pupil of a famous trumpeter, concisely particularizes his instrument. 'Our ordinary trumpet,' he writes,[1] 'known by the Romans as *Tuba*, by the French as *Trompette*, and by the Italians as *Tromba* or *Clarino*, is familiar as a musical and military, in particular a cavalry, instrument. Its tone is mettlesome, penetrating, clear, somewhat shrill in the high notes, but strident in its lower register. It rings out above all others, and justifies its title— "Queen of instruments". Mattheson characterized it as "resonant and heroic", and Schmidt as "exultant". It is usually made of hammered silver or brass, in six sections forming three tubular lengths, expanding funnel-wise towards the bell-end, and fitted with a mouthpiece proportionate with its narrow tubing.'

With rare exceptions Bach gives the trumpet its Italian name— *Tromba*. Only in the Arnstadt (No. 15) and the three Leipzig cantatas (Nos. 24, 48, 167) does he particularize the *Clarino*, and the *Principale* only in No. 15. The distinction is one of compass, to which players formerly rigidly adhered. Francœur, in his treatise published in 1772,[2] gives the compass of the clarino ('le premier Dessus') as from *g'* to *c'''* inclusive, and that of the principale ('second Dessus') as from *c* to *d''*. But these limitations ceased to be regarded, and by Bach were not observed. For that reason the terms 'Clarino' and 'Principale' occur so seldom in his scores, though, when both instruments are prescribed, as in cantata No. 15, the limitations of their registers are considered. For the same reason he disregards the convention which required the principale's part to be in the alto C clef. His trumpet parts are normally written in the treble G clef: the only exceptions are in cantata No. 15, where he uses the soprano C clef for the third trumpet; in cantata No. 63, where the third and fourth trumpets respectively are in the soprano and alto C clefs; and in cantata No. 119, where the fourth trumpet is scored in the soprano C clef. In all four cases the instrument accepts the register of the principale.[3]

What were the appearance and mechanism of Bach's 'Tromba'? The popular notion is confused by the so-called 'Bach Trumpet', invented by Julius Kosleck and used at Joachim's performance of the

---

[1] P. 9.   [2] P. 66.   [3] See Table I.

B minor Mass (*Hohe Messe*) in Eisenach, at the unveiling of the Bach
Statue, in September 1884. Improved by Walter Morrow, it was
formerly used for the trumpet parts in Bach and Handel scores. A
smaller instrument in D, first made by Mahillon, is now employed.
Bach's 'Tromba' was not a straight instrument with pistons, of the
coach-horn or 'Aida' type, but an eight-foot tube bent in three
parallel branches, uniform in bore throughout, but expanding in

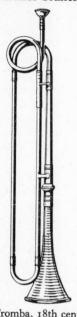

Tromba, 18th cent.,
length 65 cm.

the last of its windings to a bell-shaped aperture. As Bach and Handel used it, it differed
in appearance and technique hardly at all from
the trumpets of the fifteenth century. Many
examples of it survive. Canon Galpin's collection
includes a specimen by Johann Wilhelm Haas,
of Nürnberg, dating from *circa* 1690, apparently
pitched about E flat in the then normal tuning.
Excluding the mouthpiece, its length is 67½ cm.
(roughly 2 ft. 3 in.). The full length of tubing
is 205 cm. (roughly 6 ft. 8½ in.). The diameter
of its bore internally at the mouthpiece end is
0·9 cm. and the bell is 11 cm. across (roughly 4
in.). The original mouthpiece is lost. But,
using a shallow one, Walter Morrow was able
to play the highest harmonics upon it with the
utmost fluency.[1] The instrument hardly survived
the Master in whose art it exhibited its most brilliant qualities. From Mozart's scores it was
already excluded, though his father wrote a concerto for it (1762).

Bach's normal trumpet was a 'natural' instrument, equipped neither with slides, valves, nor
pistons: Its fundamental note varied according to the length of
tubing; the Berlin collection contains examples in C, D flat, D,
E flat, F, F sharp (probably for a flat pitch G). Another in high
A flat is in the Heyer Collection at Leipzig. But the trumpet
in D was most generally used.[2] Its natural scale, i.e. the notes
it normally produced, was as follows in terms of the key of C:

---

[1] I owe the information to Canon Galpin. In 1895 Morrow demonstrated
'Clarinblasen' before the Musical Association on instruments lent and exhibited
by Mr. W. F. H. Blandford. See the *Musical Times* for July 1895.

[2] The Heyer Collection exhibits an example (No. 1824) by Joseph Schmied,
of Pfaffendorf, 1772. It is pitched to the E flat of its period (not F, as in Kinsky,
p. 195). On doubtful authority it is said to have been used for the trumpet part
in the second Brandenburg Concerto. See Richard Hofmann's article in
B.-J. 1916.

The open tube gives the fundamental (1) and its octave (2), notes of poor quality infrequently prescribed: within the lowest two octaves c–c' the third harmonic is the only note of practicable utility. In the third octave c'–c'' the series gives a pure fourth (4), major third (5), minor third (6), minor third (7), and major second (8). In the fourth octave c''–c''', by increased lip-tension

Mouthpieces (from left to right): Clarino, Tromba, Principale, Waldhorn.

and wind-pressure, the player sounds the harmonic scale. There is no reason to suppose these high harmonics, which modern technique deems unduly exacting, to have presented abnormal difficulty to Bach's players. His trumpet parts frequently soar to the eighteenth harmonic (d'''), and, in a single case (cantata No. 31), to the twentieth (e''') on the trumpet in C. Altenburg[1] actually takes the harmonic scale up to g''' and beyond!

So extended a compass could not be conveniently covered by a single instrument of uniform capacity. Hence the player was assisted by appropriate mouthpieces; that of the clarino was shallow and saucer-shaped; the principale's was larger, deeper, more cup-shaped. By this means it was practicable and convenient, when a 'choir' of trumpets was employed, to allot to each a particular section of the harmonic scale. Clarino I took charge of the

[1] P. 69.

harmonics from g' and upwards.[1] Clarino II slightly overlapped it over the octave $g'-g''$. The principale covered the lower section from c to d''. Bach, however, was at no pains to observe this convention. His first trumpet frequently descends to c', sometimes falls below the second trumpet,[2] and even touches g.[3] The average compass of his second trumpet is $c'-a''$, but on occasion it rises to $c\sharp'''$ and d'''. His principale's normal range is $c'-g''$, and its extreme compass (in the *Magnificat* and *Aeolus*) $a-b''$. In the two scores in which he uses a fourth trumpet he employs a true principale: its compass is $g-g'$ in the first (cantata No. 63) and $g-c''$ in the second (cantata No. 119). In both cases it sounds only the third, fourth, fifth, sixth, and eighth harmonics[4] and generally supports the rhythm of the drums.

The wide range of Bach's trumpet parts may invite the suggestion that, at least for the high clarino, two players were employed, a concertist and ripienist, of whom the former reserved himself for the upper harmonics. No practical difficulty opposed the accommodation. But its assumed necessity is founded on a misapprehension of the circumstances. In Bach's experience the compromise was neither feasible nor necessary. His resources were too limited to permit the allocation of two players to a part within the competence of one, and the difficulties the modern player encounters were not apparent to musicians schooled by long tradition in the technique his scores demanded.

It has already been stated that trumpets were available in every key. But Altenburg[5] remarks that a 'Concerttrompeter' required only three, or at most four, in G, F, D, and B flat. For movements in A major, the G or 'English' trumpet, raised to the higher key by means of a 'Sordun',[6] was available; for G major, the same without the mute; for F major, the F or 'Field' or 'French' trumpet; for E major, the same lowered a semitone by a shank ('Setzstück');

---

[1] Altenburg writes (p. 95): 'Wir verstehn unter Clarin oder unter einer Clarinstimme ungefähr das, was unter den Singstimmen der Discant ist, nemlich eine gewisse Melodie, welche grösstentheils in der zweygestrichenen Oktave [$c''-c'''$], mithin hoch und hell geblasen wird.'

[2] Cantatas 74, 197, *Christmas Oratorio*, Pt. VI, Sinfonia in D.

[3] Cantatas 20 and 31.

[4] Excepting four notes in bars 33–34 of cantata No. 119 (No. 7: Coro).

[5] P. 85.

[6] Altenburg (p. 86) defines the 'Sordun' (Surdun: Sordin): 'Das Surdun oder der Sordin, hat seinen Namen von Surdus, das ist: schwach oder gedämpft. Eigentlich ist es ein von hartem und festem Holze rund ausgedrehetes Instrument, das zwar an sich selbst keinen Klang von sich giebt; wenn es aber unten in die Trompete gesteckt wird, so giebt es ihr nicht nur einen ganz andern, fast einer Oboe ähnlichen Klang, sondern erhöhet ihn, wenn er gut gedrechselt ist, auch um einen ganzen Ton.' To play in A, he therefore directs the player to use a G trumpet 'und stoffe den Sordun hinein'.

for E flat major, the same crooked down a tone; for D major, 'the German Cammerton D trumpet'; for C major, the same crooked down a tone.[1] Altenburg remarks on the non-existence of a 'short' B flat trumpet for music in that key, and recommends the performer to play an octave lower, on the 'long' instrument. Bach approved Altenburg's suggestion. In cantatas Nos. 5, 46, and 90 he prescribes a trumpet in B flat, but its notes lie between $b\flat-b\flat''$ in each of the three scores. After his appointment to the Leipzig Cantorate in 1723 his usage preferred the trumpet in D. Prior to that date he had exclusively employed the tromba in C.[2]

The addition of three, sometimes four, trumpets and drums constituted Bach's festival orchestra. They are rarely lacking in his Christmas, Easter, Whit-Sunday, and festival church music, and are invariably heard in his secular cantatas of public and gratulatory character. To all of them the trumpet communicates stately exhilaration, invariably in the choruses, occasionally in the arias and recitatives.[3] Yet, when Bach came to Leipzig in 1723, the trumpet had been for less than twenty years a licensed intruder in church music; his predecessors, Knüpfer and Kuhnau, rarely used it.[4] Into his normal orchestra of strings and wood-wind it seldom intrudes. It is obbligato in so few as sixteen arias. It adds a note of triumph to the concluding Choral of the Easter cantata No. 31. Infrequently it is woven into the orchestral texture of a chorus; jubilantly, as in the first movement of the Easter cantata No. 66:

> Rejoice now, ye faithful!
> Be mirthful and joyful!

On the eve of Advent, in the first chorus of No. 70, it sounds the watchman's call:

> Watch ye! pray ye!
> Ready be, night and day!
> Soon upon the clouds ye'll see
> God to judge all mortals coming.

---

[1] Altenburg (p. 12) distinguishes as German the 'chortönige C-Trompete' and 'kammertönige D-Trompete'; as French, the 'kammertönige F-Trompete'; and as English, the 'kammertönige G-Trompete'. For the Italian 'gewundene' trumpet, or tromba da caccia, see *infra*, p. 48.

[2] The second Brandenburg Concerto is the only exception to the statement. The trumpet there is in F, consistently with Bach's habit of putting the instrument in the key of the movement. This was in accordance with custom. Altenburg (p. 83) writes: 'Da ich nun bereits erwähnt habe, dass die Trompete . . . nur diatonisch modulirt, und höchstens in G dur, wegen des hohen fis cadenziren kann, so muss daher der Blasende, wenn er mit andern Instrumenten zugleich einstimmen will, seine Trompete darnach einrichten, dass sie zu der Tonart, woraus das Stück geht, genau harmonire.'

[3] See Table I.

[4] Cf. Schering, p. 151. Its use was licensed by a 'Trompetermandat' of 1706 (*ibid.*, p. 297).

In cantata No. 76 the Psalmist's paean constrains Bach to add a seraphic trumpet to the chorus of exultation. In the opening chorus of cantata No. 126 it rallies the Church against her pressing foes:

> Hurl them down headlong, foeman so haughty!
> Confound their scheming, bring them to naught!
> May hell's abysses yawning devour them!
> Make their plots wither, sternly o'erpower them!

So sings a bass voice in the aria. Bach reacts to this belligerent command, and the trumpet in the first chorus sounds its challenge to the enemies of the Word. In the second movement (coro) of the Easter cantata No. 145 jubilant trumpet figures acknowledge the festival's promise of salvation. Again, in the opening chorus of No. 147 the trumpet brilliantly acclaims the Saviour. In No. 148, for the Seventeenth Sunday after Trinity, it obeys the injunction of the opening chorus to praise and worship God. In this category, cantata No. 181 must also be mentioned. Like No. 126, it is an anthem for Sexagesima and illustrates the prescribed topic—God's Word. As always when that thought is present, Bach's perceptive mind pictures a citadel beleaguered, but impregnable. So, in the final chorus he sounds a flourish of victory, to which the trumpet adds triumphant music over a continuo that marches with inexorable rhythm and confidence.

With similar discrimination and restraint Bach associates the trumpet with a solo voice, usually a bass. In cantata No. 70, for the Twenty-Sixth Sunday after Trinity, the theme of the Second Advent informs the text, especially in the bass recit. and aria of Part II. In the first, the trumpet sounds the appropriate Advent melody, 'Es ist gewisslich an der Zeit'. In the aria

> Welcome Resurrection morn!
> Peal out, ring out, Judgement call!

the trumpet peals a sternly urgent summons above the agitated strings and continuo—

> Heaven and earth in wrack are falling!

With similar significance it is heard in the alto aria of No. 20, and in the bass aria of No. 127, for Quinquagesima—

> When loud and clear the trumpet calleth,
> And when the frame of earth to atoms falleth.

Bach here writes agitated descending passages for the strings, above which sound the clamorous trumpets of the Judgement. In cantata No. 128 the bass aria acclaims the risen Christ:

> Up, up, ye trumpets, call!
> Tell forth to one and all,
> Jesus on high is throned!

As a vehicle of praise the trumpet is also much used by Bach, as though he borrowed from the angels the inspired instrument of their adoration. In the familiar bass aria in Part I of the *Christmas Oratorio*:

> Mighty Lord and King supernal!

how brilliantly the trumpet acclaims the Eternal Majesty! Two soprano arias of cantata No. 51 are accorded a trumpet obbligato:

> Praise ye God, all men, adore Him!
> Heaven and earth, His praises sing!

and particularly the brilliant 'Alleluia' of the second aria. Similarly, in the bass aria of the Christmas cantata No. 110:

> Ye strings, well tuned to sing devotion,
> Your praise up-roll ye as an ocean
> To God enthroned in pomp on high!

Bach adds oboes to his choir and the trumpet peals above them all. It sounds, again, in the bass aria of cantata No. 147:

> Of Jesu's wounds my soul is singing
> A song of praise and loud thanksgiving.

Easter joy pervades the bass aria in cantata No. 145 and explains the trumpet's intrusion, though the actual words do not directly invite it. Nor do those of the bass aria of No. 75:

> My doubting heart is stilled;
> For Jesu's self doth love me,
> And with his flame surrounds me.

Here the trumpet proclaims the victory of faith over doubt. It utters a militant call in the bass aria of cantata No. 5:

> Disperse, ye lords of hell!
> I mock your proudest might!

Also in the bass aria of No. 76:

> Avaunt, ye godless crew!

And again in the bass aria of cantata No. 90:

> In anger and fury the Judge will avenge Him,

where the trumpet is the flashing sword of the Avenger. In the alto aria of No. 77 it voices the authority of the Law.

An obvious conclusion is invited. Bach's trumpet is never irrelevant, never purely orchestral, but the expression of a definite mood, a detail in a picture keenly visualized.[1]

[1] Bach's employment of a 'choir' of trumpets is considered in Chapter III.

The Tromba da tirarsi (Zugtrompete)

Bach's tromba parts do not rigidly exclude certain notes normally alien to the instrument's natural scale. For the eleventh harmonic he writes *f♮"* and *f♯"* indifferently, as was usual before the adoption of hand-stopping or a similar device. Infrequently he slips in *b'* as a passing note in rapid passages, or in positions where it is unstressed. He also occasionally writes the following notes:

But these ultra-harmonic notes are used so rarely, and with such careful avoidance of stress, that their presence does not necessarily indicate another instrument than the natural trumpet. On the other hand, the diagram on page 25 shows three notes in the octave *c'–c"* to have been absolutely outside its scale:

Since these notes are definitely ultra-harmonic, their presence in a part bearing the indication 'Tromba' is reliable proof that it was not written for the natural trumpet. Whether they could be produced on it by 'faking' need not be discussed. Bach deemed them beyond its ability, and excluded them from parts undoubtedly written for it.[1] They must therefore be associated with another instrument. In cantatas Nos. 5, 20, 77, Bach names it 'Tromba da tirarsi', a term apparently not found outside his scores.[2] In cantata No. 46 he offers the alternative 'Tromba o Corno da tirarsi', and in cantatas Nos. 67 and 162 prescribes a 'Corno da tirarsi'. These definite indications are found in fourteen movements, in eight of which the instrument reinforces the melody of a Choral 'col Soprano', and in one other plays the Choral melody obbligato. Its compass in these Choral movements falls mainly in the octave *e'–e"*. But its full range is in no way behind the natural trumpet's, since, in three of the fourteen movements, it functions in an obbligato with the freedom and fluency of that instrument.

What kind of instrument was this trumpet, which could accomplish all and more than the natural tromba? In what respect, if at all, did it differ from the corno da tirarsi? As its name (Tr. da

---

[1] Whenever the tromba is associated with the drums the natural instrument was certainly used.

[2] The instrument was in use in Leipzig in 1769. See *supra*, p 18.

tirarsi) indicates, it was equipped with a slide. Editing cantata
No. 5 for the Bachgesellschaft in 1851, Moritz Hauptmann supposed
it to have been the discant (alto) trombone. Some fifty years
earlier (1795) Altenburg[1] had already remarked its constructional
resemblance to that instrument: 'The Zug-
trompete, generally used for playing the Chorals
from church towers'—a significant detail—'re-
sembles the alto trombone, since, during the act
of blowing, its slide-action conveniently produces the lacking harmonics.'[2] Mahillon, writing
in 1880,[3] inclined to Altenburg's opinion. There
exists, however, in the Berlin Hochschule für
Musik, the unique example of an instrument
which exactly fits Bach's definition and is capable of fulfilling the purposes to which he put
the tromba da tirarsi.

The Berlin Zugtrompete (slide trumpet) has
the appearance of an ordinary natural trumpet.
But, unlike the latter, its mouthpiece is pro-
longated by an inner tube, which, at the player's
will, slides out and in within the topmost of the
instrument's parallel branches. The length of
its slide is 56 cm. (22·050 in.). The tubing,
apart from the slide, is 143 cm. (roughly 56 in.
=4 ft. 8 in.) long, and the conical length of the
instrument is 57 cm. (roughly 1 ft. 10½ in.).
Thus, with the slide drawn to its fullest extent,
the trumpet measures roughly 112 cm. (3 ft.
8 in.) from mouthpiece to bell. Its internal
diameter at 25 cm. of length is 12·8 mm. (under
half an inch), and at the bell-end 98 mm.
(roughly 4 in.).[4] The instrument is in D[5] of its

Zugtrompete, 1651,
fully extended,
length 112 cm.

period, was made by Hans Veit of Naumburg, and bears the date
1651 engraved on the bell.

The possibility must not be overlooked, that in the Berlin
Zugtrompete we have a simple device for tuning the tromba down
from D to C without crooking. On the other hand, the Berlin
example is generally competent in the uses to which Bach puts his

[1] P. 12.
[2] Mr. W. F. H. Blandford is of opinion that Altenburg had in mind some
model with a double 'trombone' slide.   [3] Vol. i. 281.
[4] I am indebted to Dr. Curt Sachs for these measurements.
[5] On its measurements, Mr. Blandford makes it intermediate between E
natural and E flat diapason normal.

tromba da tirarsi. When the slide is pushed home it becomes a
natural tromba, indeed is more easily played, owing to the narrower
bore of the tube receiving the slide. No doubt it was difficult for
the player to hold the mouthpiece to his lips with his left hand,
while his right moved the instrument up or down the slide. But
rapid movements were not necessary. Experimenting with a slide
on his Haas trumpet, Canon Galpin found that it has three positions: (1) When 5 inches of the slide are withdrawn, the pitch is
lowered from d' to $c\sharp'$, with a corresponding fall throughout the
scale. (2) When $10\frac{1}{2}$ inches of the slide are exposed, the pitch falls
two semitones, from d' to c', and by an equal interval all over.
(3) When the slide is at 17 inches, the fall of yet another semitone
follows, and d' becomes b natural. These positions indicate
considerable movements of or along the slide, first of 5 inches,
then of $5\frac{1}{2}$ inches, and again of $6\frac{1}{2}$ inches, owing to the slide operating in a single, and not, as with the trombone, a double tube.[1]
For that reason the instrument may have been held sloping
downwards with greater convenience, a position which might
account for Altenburg likening it to the alto trombone.

Canon Galpin's experiment permits us to apply the technique
of the Berlin Zugtrompete to Bach's tromba da tirarsi parts. As
the Table on page 191 reveals, he uses the latter chiefly to sound
the melody of a Choral, in movements whose *tempo* is moderate
and their notes sustained. Slide movements consequently would
be deliberate. For instance, the concluding Choral of cantata
No. 5, in which, along with the first violins and two oboes, the
tromba da tirarsi is 'col Soprano',[2] could be played thus on Veit's
trumpet in D:

---

[1] At the concerts of the Paris Société de Musique d'autrefois a Zugtrompete
is in use, a slide being adapted to the tromba, as in the Berlin example. While
agreeing that Veit's trumpet proves that a distinct form of Zugtrompete existed,
Mr. Blandford is of opinion that the collection of parts attributed to it in Table II,
infra, is too complex for a single instrument of Veit's pattern, even aided by
extra mouthpieces. Certainly deeper instruments similarly constructed would
be handled with difficulty.

[2] The figures 0, 1, 2 indicate respectively the open notes with closed slide
and its first and second shifts. The $b\flat'$ throughout must be slightly sharpened.

Or take the concluding Choral of cantata No. 20, where also the tromba da tirarsi, with other instruments, is 'col Soprano' in C:

These examples demonstrate the ease with which a player using the Zugtrompete could produce the ultra-harmonic notes of Bach's tromba da tirarsi Chorals. And its obbligato parts are both few in number and present no greater difficulties. In the bass aria of cantata No. 46 only a single note, though persistent and emphatic, lies outside the normal harmonic series of the instrument. In cantata No. 103 (tenor aria), again, the slide is called into action only in bars 19–22. In cantata No. 24 (coro) the part is dotted with extra-harmonic notes, and, at bars 27 and 35, repeated a'''s and f'''s, but they occur in the least florid passages and do not require rapid movements of the slide. The concluding Choral of cantata No. 24 is peculiar in its use of the alto clef for repeated low f's and a's.

As has already been remarked, the tromba da tirarsi is generally associated by Bach with Chorals, either as a support to the voices in the melody,[1] or (as in cantatas Nos. 12 and 24) to supply an obbligato above it, or (as in cantatas Nos. 10, 12, 48, 75, 77, 137, and 185) to sound the Choral melody itself as an obbligato in a chorus, or duet, or instrumental movement. But in three move-

---

[1] All of the Choral melodies in which the instrument is simply indicated as 'col Soprano' could be played on an instrument in C. But to obtain the best notes, and to obviate considerable shifting of the slide, instruments in B♭, A, and high D may also have been used. In the above example a' must be slightly sharpened throughout.

ments—two arias and one coro—his slide trumpet serves the purposes to which Bach elsewhere puts the natural instrument.

In the bass aria of cantata No. 46 the trumpet adds a detail of terror to the storm which overthrows Jerusalem—

> Long since a tempest hath been brewing,
> At last the storm in fury breaks,
> And havoc dire and awful makes.
> Thy sin and pride commingled
> God's angry fires have kindled,
> And doomed thee evermore to ruin.

In the tenor aria of cantata No. 103 the trumpet contributes a note of exhilaration to a movement of utter gaiety:

> Away with care, O troubled mortal!
> Ne'er give thyself to sighs and woe!
> No more to sorrow ope the portal,
> Nor let hot tears of anguish flow!
> Lord Jesu, Thou wilt come to save me;
> O rapture sweet beyond compare!
> Thy promise doth with longing fill me;
> Come, take my all into Thy care.

An apparent incongruity presents itself in the third movement (Coro) of cantata No. 24. The words, 'Whatsoever ye would that men should do unto you, even so do unto them' (St. Matthew vii. 12), hardly invite a trumpet to the score. But the German text begins with the word 'Alles', a word to which Bach invariably accords spacious treatment: 'Alles nun, das ihr wollet, das euch die Leute thun sollen, das thut ihr ihnen.'[1] In the present case he actually repeats the word six times before proceeding with the text, and the whole movement is pervaded by a spirit of vivacious animation, which tells us he was thinking less of the duty of neighbourliness than of the initial suggestion of multitude.

The Corno da Tirarsi

Bach's scores prescribe not only a 'slide trumpet' but also a 'slide horn'. In cantata No. 46 they are alternative, though the prescription 'Tromba o Corno' might indicate variant names of the same instrument, did not cantatas Nos. 67 and 162 mention the corno da tirarsi alone. What, then, was the 'Corno' da tirarsi?

Unlike the slide-trumpet, of which an example is extant, there is no other evidence than Bach's nomenclature that a slide-horn

---

[1] See, for example, the opening chorus of *Alles nur nach Gottes Willen* (No. 72); the soprano-bass duet 'Alles was von Gott geboren' of No. 80; and the 'Alles was Odem hat' section of the motet *Singet dem Herrn*.

was known to his generation. Praetorius gives no indication of such an instrument, and Bach's predecessors in the Leipzig Cantorate did not use one. But Tables II, V, VI show that in his church cantatas the 'slide horn' occurs as frequently as the ordinary instrument. In the majority of cases it sustains the melody of a Choral. Otherwise, but rarely, it furnishes an independent obbligato. Its parts differ neither in compass nor character from those of the slide-trumpet; indeed, without Bach's indication it would be difficult to decide which he intended.[1] The facts suggest that his prescription 'Corno da tirarsi' does not indicate an actual instrument, but some device or adjustment for producing horn tone.[2]

Consider, for example, the 'Choral Cantatas' written *circa* 1740–4, thirteen of which are included in Table II. They are built on a uniform plan: their opening chorus elaborately treats a Choral, whose melody is generally sustained by the sopranos in unison with a trumpet (cantatas Nos. 10 and 48) or a horn (cantatas Nos. 26, 62, 78, 96, 114, 115, 116, 124, 125). They all conclude with a Choral, in which the melody is similarly supported, in three cases by a trumpet (cantatas Nos. 10, 48, 126), in ten by a horn (cantatas Nos. 3, 26, 62, 78, 96, 114, 115, 116, 124, 125). We infer from these figures that Bach preferred horn tone to trumpet tone for this particular purpose, owing, no doubt, to its closer blending with the human voice. But what instrument did he use? Not one of the parts indicated above was playable on the natural horn. But all of them were practicable on the Zug-trompete, which, by substituting the appropriate mouthpiece, could produce horn tone as well. Thus, in cantatas Nos. 24 and 167, a very shallow-cupped mouthpiece would give the sharp, penetrating clarino tone the score prescribes. In cantatas Nos. 14, 16, 89, 107, and 109, where Bach indicates the corno da caccia, a short conical cup-like mouthpiece would communicate to the Zug-trompete its peculiar mellow tone. A tromba mouthpiece, having a slightly deeper cup than the clarino's, would produce a more ringing tone than the latter, while the long conical cup of the Waldhorn would impart the characteristic cooing tone of that

---

[1] Cf. B.-J. 1908, p. 141, where Dr. Curt Sachs identifies Bach's 'Corno da tirarsi' with the Zugtrompete discussed in the preceding section, an opinion he has since rejected.

[2] I owe the suggestion to Canon Galpin. Admittedly, no historical evidence supports it. On the other hand, none refutes it, nor, so far, has one more plausible been advanced. Mr. Blandford doubts the skill of players exposed to this test; but the trumpeters also played the horn and trombone (*supra,* p. 8).

instrument. Thus, at pleasure, the Zugtrompete could become a corno da tirarsi, or a corno da caccia da tirarsi, by the device which enabled it as easily to act as a tromba da tirarsi or a clarino da tirarsi.[1]

The addition 'da tirarsi' completes the direction 'Tromba', 'Corno', 'Corno da caccia' only in six cantatas (Nos. 5, 20, 46, 67, 77, 162). Elsewhere the music itself is the only guide to Bach's selection. And here an interesting point presents itself. In 1769, nineteen years after Bach's death, Johann Friedrich Doles, his second successor in the Leipzig Cantorate, examined two candidates for a vacancy in the ranks of the Stadtpfeifer. Of one he wrote: 'He cannot manage the concerted Choral on the Zugtrompete, and has to do the best he can on an alto trombone' ('Mit dem concer-tirenden Choral konnte er auf der Zugtrompette gar nicht fort-kommen und musste er es auf der Altposaune versuchen, so gut es gehen wollte'). On the other he reported: 'He played the simple Choral well on the discant, alto, tenor, and bass trombones' ('Den simplen Choral auf der Discant- Alt- Tenor- und Bass-Posaune . . . hat er gut geblasen').[2] The inference is clear: in simple four-part Chorals the trombone was customarily used; the Zugtrompete in the elaborate choruses with which the Choral Cantatas begin. If, as is probable, this was the practice in Bach's time, we are confirmed in the conclusion that the tromba da tirarsi (as in the first chorus of cantata No. 5), the corno (as in the first chorus of cantata No. 8), and the corno da caccia (as in the first chorus of cantata No. 16), were all represented by the Zug-trompete equipped with appropriate mouthpieces. As regards the simple Chorals, we must either conclude that Doles had ceased to follow his great predecessor's example, or, as is more probable, that the trombone was occasionally used instead of the Zug-trompete. One thing is evident: the Zugtrompete was *not* identical with the alto trombone.

The Cornett

For sustaining Choral melodies Bach was not restricted to the tromba and corno da tirarsi. In eleven cantatas[3] he prescribes a cornett, and employs it in every case but two to sound the Choral

---

[1] Canon Galpin points out that, provided the mouthpieces were practically of the same diameter internally, the inside shape of the cup would make no difference to the player, though it affected his tone. Altenburg, chap. ix, enlarges on the mouthpiece technique. The interchange of mouthpieces was facilitated, it must be recognized, by the fact that every player professed all the 'Stadtpfeiferinstrumente'.

[2] *Archiv f. M.*, p. 45. On Bach's neglect of the discant (alto) trombone see *infra*, p. 40.　　　　　　　　　　　　　　　　　　　[3] See Table III.

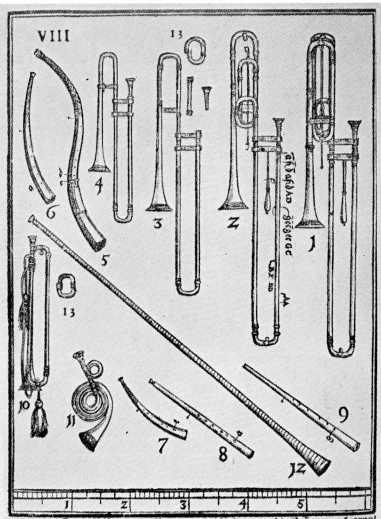

TRUMPET, CORNETT, TROMBONE, JÄGER-TROMPETE
(*Praetorius*)

cantus.[1] The instrument, one of the oldest, was already obsolescent. Known in England as the Cornett, in Italy as the Cornetto, in France as the Cornet à bouquin, and in Germany as the Zink, it was used in two forms, the straight and the curved. The former (cornetto diritto, c. muto, gerader Zink, stiller Z.) was in one piece, mouthpiece and tube. The curved variety (c. curvo, krummer Zink) was made of two pieces of wood, planed to an octagonal shape, slightly curved, bound together in black leather with metal clasps, and fitted with a shallow mouthpiece (its only resemblance to the modern cornet) of horn, hard wood, or ivory.[2] Straight or curved, the instrument was pierced with six holes on the upper surface for the fingers, and one underneath for the thumb. Made in different sizes, the cornett, according to Praetorius,[3] sounded the chromatic scale over a normal compass of two octaves $a–a''$, and, like the trombones, formed a complete 'choir' of instruments, the lowest[4] of which (cornetto torto, cornon, great Zink) sounded from d upwards. Bach made no use of these various forms. The compass of his cornett parts—from d' to a''[5]—shows that he wrote for the ordinary Zink—the 'recht Chor Zink' of Praetorius—whose compass ranged from a to a''.

The cornett had a brilliant tone. In his *Harmonie universelle* (1636) Marin Mersenne likened it to 'a ray of sunshine piercing the gloom and darkness, when heard among the voices in some cathedral or chapel' ('un rayon de Soleil, qui paroist dans l'ombre ou dans les tenebres, lors qu'on l'entend parmy les voix dans les Églises Cathedrales, ou dans les Chapelles').[6] Roger North, a hundred years later, declared in Bach's lifetime: 'To say the truth, nothing comes so near, or rather imitates so much, an excellent voice, as a cornet-pipe,'[7] a eulogy which explains its vogue with Bach and other composers. Mattheson, North's contemporary, lamented its decreasing use, remarking its value in church music.[8] Its decline was in some measure due to the onerous tax it laid on the lungs of the player. North observed that 'the labour of the lips is too great, and it is seldom well sounded'. It survived in Germany after it had passed from use elsewhere, but barely survived the dawn of the nineteenth century. Writing in 1806, Schubart[9]

---

[1] It is perhaps open to question whether Bach desired clearly to distinguish between 'corno' and 'cornetto' in these movements.
[2] See Praetorius, Plate VIII, at p. 36.　　　　　　　　[3] P. 36.
[4] Excluding the Serpent.
[5] In cantata No. 118 he carries it exceptionally to d''' on the 'little Zink'.
[6] Bk. V, p. 274.　　　　　[7] P. 79.　　　　　[8] P. 269.
[9] 'Es ist aber so schwer für die Brust zu blasen, weil der Hauch nur durch eine ganz kleine Oeffnung hinein gebracht wird, dass sich schon mehr als ein Zinkenist, Schwindsucht und Tod damit zugezogen hat. Schwerlich gibt es

surmised that German lung-power had deteriorated, since so few Zink players were to be found.

The cornett, being a Stadtpfeifer instrument, has no place in Bach's scores before 1723, and is associated chiefly with the cantatas of his latest period. Almost invariably it supports the sopranos in a Choral melody, associated always, excepting cantatas Nos. 133 and 135, with trombones.[1] It is never obbligato in Bach's usage, though the opening chorus of No. 133 suggests that he shared Mersenne's admiration of its quality. The cornett there is 'col Soprano'. The accompanying instruments are the strings and two *oboi d'amore*, the second of them in unison with the viola. The words—the first stanza of Caspar Ziegler's 'Ich freue mich in dir'—dwell on the thought of Jesus as the Brother of man:

> How sweet the word doth sound!
> (*Ach, wie ein süsser Ton!*)

sing the voices. Bach pointedly prolongs the word 'Ton' over three bars and a half. The cornett and sopranos sustain it on $c\sharp''$, the oboe d'amore and viola on $c\sharp'$, while the under voices thrice ejaculate 'Ach, wie ein süsser Ton!' 'One need but read the words', remarks Pirro,[2] 'to realize that Bach contrives a rare and charming effect, intending that the voices shall not idly sing the words "Ah! quel doux ton!" ' In cantata No. 135 the cornett is restricted to the concluding Choral, the *canto fermo* being in the bass of the opening chorus. In the remaining nine cantatas the instrument acts as the discant of a choir of trombones.

The Trombone

Praetorius[3] names four instruments of the trombone family:

(1) The *Alto* or *Discant-Posaun* (*Trombino: Trombetta picciola*), in D.

(2) The *Gemeine rechte Posaun* (*Tuba minor: Trombetta: Trombone piccolo*), in A.

(3) The *Quart-Posaun* (*Tuba major: Trombone grando: Trombone majore*), sounding a fourth or fifth (*Quint-Posaun*) below the preceding.

(4) The *Octav-Posaun* (*Tuba maxima: Trombone doppio: Trombone all'ottava basso*), in A, sounding an octave below the second of the series.

---

ein die Gesundheit so angreifendes Instrument wie dieses. Das mag wohl Ursache seyn, warum sich so wenige Menschen bis zur Meisterschaft darauf legen' (p. 317).

[1] The cornett displaced the discant trombone owing to its more brilliant and effective tone.

[2] Pirro, p. 242.   [3] P. 31. See his Plates VI and VIII at pp. 36 and 160.

The Octav-Posaun was rarely used, Praetorius adds. It was made in two forms; either its length was twice that of the Gemeine rechte Posaun, or (the recent invention of Kunstpfeifer Hans Schreiber) the fitting of an extra bend between the bell and the slide enabled the dimensions of the instrument to be conveniently shortened. Of the discant (an octave above his No. 3) Praetorius remarks,[1] that, though agreeable for playing a melody ('mit welcher ein Discant gar wol und natürlich geblasen werden kan'), it was too insignificant in tone for concerted music ('wiewol die *Harmony* in solchem kleinen *Corpore* nicht so gut').[2] No. 2 of Praetorius's series can be identified with the tenor B flat trombone in modern use,

for he gives as its lowest note. So, accepting his

indications of their pitch relatively to the Gemeine rechte Posaun, we deduce that his

Quart-Posaun, being a fourth lower, was in F;

Quint-Posaun, being a fifth lower, was in E flat;

Octav-Posaun, being an octave lower, was in B flat;

Alto-Posaun, being an octave higher than the Quart- or Quint-Posaun, was in F or E flat.

We may reasonably put the working compass of the four trombones in Bach's period as follows, in actual sounds:

1. Discant in B flat . . . . . . $e\flat$–$b\flat''$
   (The notes below c' are very poor and a'' and $b\flat''$ are difficult.)
2. Alto in F . . . . $b\flat,$–f''
   (The notes below f are poor; $e\flat''$ and f'' are difficult. Alto in E flat a tone lower.)
3. Tenor in B flat . . . . . . $e\flat,$–$b\flat'$
   (The low notes are fairly good; a' and $b\flat'$ are difficult.)
4. Bass in F . . . . $b,,$–f'
   (The low notes are fairly good; e' and f' are difficult. Bass in E flat a tone lower.)

Bach's scores reveal his preference for a 'choir' of three or four trombones. The prescription of a single instrument is very exceptional. In cantata No. 3 a bass trombone strengthens the Choral melody voiced by the basses. In the duet of cantata No. 4 both voices are supported in a free treatment of the Choral melody, the soprano by a cornett, the alto by an alto trombone. In cantata

[1] The reason for its supersession by the cornett has been stated on p. 38 *supra*.
[2] Mr. Blandford observes that Breughel's picture 'Hearing', in the Prado, painted before 1625, shows a trombone with two crooks or 'tortils' between the bell and the slide. We may have here a picture of Schreiber's invention.

No. 96, in whose opening chorus the altos sing the Choral *cantus*, they are reinforced by an alto trombone and a horn. In the opening chorus of cantata No. 135 the Choral *cantus* is given to the continuo, and a bass trombone helps to sustain it. Elsewhere Bach scores for either a quartet of trombones or for a cornett and three trombones.

The discant trombone is not among the instruments mentioned in the preceding paragraph. Nor does Bach often prescribe it, even in the concluding simple Chorals, where, according to the usage of 1769,[1] it was customarily employed. Evidently Bach shared the opinion of Praetorius regarding its quality, which has been quoted on an earlier page. Taking

as its effective compass, we can deduce its employment only in cantatas Nos. 2, 21, and 38, where it is associated in every case with an alto, tenor, and bass trombone. Elsewhere and invariably Bach prefers the cornett to complete his quartet.[2] It follows that, in the majority of cases, his prescription 'Trombone I' indicates the alto trombone in F, e.g. in cantatas Nos. 4, 23, 25, 28, 64, 68, 96, 101, 118, and 121. The tenor B flat must be inferred as 'Trombone III' in cantatas Nos. 2, 21, and 38, in which the discant instrument has the soprano part, but as 'Trombone II' in cantatas Nos. 4, 23, 25, 28, 64, 68, 101, 118, 121, where a cornett has the discant. The bass trombone in E flat or F is the 'Trombone IV' of cantatas Nos. 2, 21, 38, and the 'Trombone III', generally in F, of cantatas Nos. 4, 23, 25, 28, 64, 68, 101, 118, and 121. Its usage in cantatas Nos. 3 and 135 has been recorded in the preceding paragraph.

Unlike the horn, proper to the pageantry of Courts, the trombone was a Stadtpfeifer instrument, adapted for civic ceremonial. Bach's employment of it was timid and consistent. As an independent obbligato instrument it has no place in his scores. Even if his text invites him to display it—e.g. in the bass recit. of cantata No. 70, where the voice sings of the 'Posaunen Schall' at the Second Advent—he prefers the trumpet, having in mind the mundane associations of the other instrument.[3] And he employs it infrequently. It is prescribed in so few as fifteen cantatas, and nowhere else in his music.[4] With one exception, the fifteen belong to the Leipzig period. For neither the Weimar nor Cöthen Capelle was

---

[1] *Supra*, p. 36.   [2] See Table IV.
[3] The obbligato in Handel's 'The trumpet shall sound' is said to have been formerly played on the alto trombone. Either the story is untrue, or the experiment was an exhibition of misdirected skill.   [4] See Table IV.

equipped with an instrument alien to Court ritual. Cantata No. 21,
the single pre-Leipzig score which includes a trombone, was
composed for Halle, where, as later at Leipzig, 'Stadtpfeiferinstrumente' were accessible. Even at Leipzig Bach rarely prescribed
it. Of the fourteen cantatas of that period, ten
belong to the last decade of his activity as a composer
(1734-44), and in the preceding decade (1723-33)
trombones are found in only four.[1] The fact may
indicate that the instruments themselves were un-
serviceable: Kuhnau, in 1704, described the church's
set as battered and useless.[2]

But a more probable reason can be offered for
Bach's infrequent use of the trombone. In every
score in which it is found it is used in association
with a Choral or a chorus of the older motet form.
Excepting three cases, it never sounds independently
of the voices, but simply reinforces the vocal parts.
In the first of these, cantata No. 25, a quartet of
three trombones and cornett adds a harmonized
Choral to the orchestral scheme. In the second,
cantata No. 118, a similar quartet provides the
instrumental accompaniment. In the third, cantata
No. 135, a single trombone strengthens the continuo
in the *cantus* of the Choral on which the chorus is
founded. Saving these exceptions, Bach's trombones
merely reinforce the vocal parts. Moreover, seven
of the fourteen Leipzig scores in which they are
found belong to his last series of Choral Cantatas,
and their usage in that period seems to indicate   Trombone,
the deficiencies of his choristers, for which, it must   17th cent.,
be admitted, he was himself in some measure   length 108 cm.
responsible. At least, it is clear that Bach connected the trombone,
like the cornett, with the older 'Status musices' rather than the
new. Of its orchestral capabilities, which Mozart and Beethoven
were soon to reveal, there is in his scores no glimmer of
recognition.

The Horn (*Corno: corno da caccia*)

Bach's 'Corno', like his 'Tromba', is a problem the lexicons
confuse and do not resolve. Riemann (*s.v.* Horn) groups as exchangeable the 'Naturhorn, Waldhorn, Corno di caccia, Cor de
chasse, French horn'. 'Grove's' list of alternatives is as generous.

---

[1] Nos. 4, 23, 25, and 64.   [2] *Supra*, p. 18.

Miss Kathleen Schlesinger, whose erudite articles distinguished the classic Eleventh, but are characteristically excised from the latest, self-styled 'humanized', *Encyclopaedia Britannica*, places in a single category 'The French horn (*Fr. cor de chasse* or *trompe de chasse, cor à pistons*; Ger. *Waldhorn, Ventilhorn*; Ital. *corno* or *corno di caccia*)'. Adopting, as almost invariably, their Italian style, Bach names either a 'Corno' or a 'Corno da caccia', and once, in cantata No. 14, a 'Corno par force'. All three indicate a 'natural' horn, a simple coiled tube operated without keys, valves, or slides. Whether his varying nomenclature indicates two types of horn is a preliminary problem to be faced.

The earliest form of the corno da caccia was the 'Jagdhorn' or 'Jägerhorn' figured by Praetorius (Plate XXII), elementary specimens of which, known as 'Hiefhörner' or 'Hifthörner', were only capable of sounding rhythmic signals to the huntsmen. This early type was never wound in circles large enough to surround the body, was less slenderly tubed than its improved successor, and terminated in a bell not exceeding seven inches in diameter. As an orchestral instrument it was of no value, and was not so employed. It underwent considerable improvement in the seventeenth century, however, and, at about the period of Bach's birth (1685), a new type, recently invented in France, and distinguished as the 'French horn', so interested the Bohemian dilettante Franz Anton Count von Sporck (1662–1738)[1] that he caused his musicians to learn the instrument and introduced it, certainly before 1715,[2] into Germany, where it was generally known as the 'Waldhorn' or, much enlarged, as the 'Parforcehorn' (*corno par force*).[3]

Thus the Waldhorn was a novelty when Bach's career as a composer was about to begin. Handel used it in his 'Watermusic' (? 1717) in honour of George I, at the period when Bach was entering on his service at Cöthen. But Germany was not behindhand in appreciating its qualities for other uses than the characteristic fanfares of operatic hunting scenes or calls to arms in dramatic situations. Reinhard Keiser particularly was adventurous in experiments at Hamburg, where Mattheson penned a eulogy which proves that, in that active centre, if not elsewhere, the Wald-

---

[1] Shortly before his death Sporck received from Bach the parts of the B minor 'Sanctus'.

[2] Gerber is usually quoted for the statement. Mr. Blandford, however, finds contemporary evidence in Sporck's *Life* by Ferdinand van der Roxas (Friedrich Rothscholz) published in 1715.

[3] See Plate XXI in Sachs (2).

horn was in service before 1713. 'The stately mellow-sounding Waldhorn', he wrote,[1] 'has come a good deal into vogue of late . . . partly because it is less raucous than the trumpet, partly because it is more easily handled. . . . It produces a rounder tone and fills out the score better than the shrill and deafening *clarini*.' It generally superseded the *Jagdhörner* (few specimens of which have survived) in the ceremonious uses associated with the latter, and at the same time commended itself to composers, who, from the first

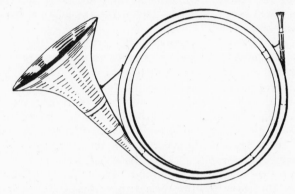

Waldhorn, 18th cent., length 58 cm.

decade of the eighteenth century, if not earlier, added it appreciatively to their orchestra.

In the first decade of the eighteenth century Hamburg was the musical capital of Germany, and we should err in supposing its musical apparatus to have been completely available elsewhere. Its adoption of the Waldhorn, consequently, cannot certainly indicate contemporary use of the instrument by the smaller communities to which Bach devoted his earliest service. Till his arrival in Leipzig the horn is named only twice in his scores. He prescribed one in his Weimar secular cantata *Was mir behagt* (1716), and again, five years later at Cöthen, in the first Brandenburg Concerto, in F (1721). In both he named it 'Corno da caccia', and in both prescribed it for performance by other players than his own—the earlier for the Weissenfels Capelle, the later for that of Brandenburg. Consequently, even if his 'Corno da caccia' was a Waldhorn, its prescription in those two works does not prove that it was at his disposal at Weimar and Cöthen.

[1] P. 267.

After his arrival at Leipzig, Bach's indications are no longer uniform. Twice in 1724 (cantatas Nos. 16 and 65), once in 1729 (No. 174), twice in 1733 (*Hohe Messe* and *Hercules*), thrice in or about 1735 (Nos. 14, 128, 143), and thereafter not at all, he prescribes, as at Weimar and Cöthen, a 'Cors de chasse,' a 'Corno da caccia', a 'Corne da caccia'. But in one of his earliest Leipzig cantatas, No. 40, performed on 26 December 1723, he for the first time writes 'Corno' *tout court*. In 1724, 1725, 1726 it appears again in his scores, and, after an interval, in 1730?–31–32–34. Finally, eight more examples fall in the last years of his activity as a composer.[1]

Was the 'Corno' a different instrument from the 'Corno da caccia'? Its parts in Bach's scores afford no assistance to an answer. His 'Corno' is crooked to seven keys—D, F, G, A, B flat, D (high), F (high), sounding a minor seventh, perfect fifth, perfect fourth, minor third, and major second below their parts in C, and a major second and perfect fourth above it. He uses his 'Corno da caccia' in similar keys—C (sounding an octave below), D, F, G, and B flat. Nor is there appreciable difference in the compass of the parts allotted to the two, nor do they exhibit differences of technique by which they can be distinguished. One or the other term, however, certainly indicates the Waldhorn, or French horn, first heard by Count von Sporck at Paris in 1680,[2] known also as the 'Corno par force', a term Bach uses, on a single occasion, in 1735 (cantata No. 14). The fact that the 'Corno' first appears in his Leipzig scores favours the opinion that the word was his equivalent for the Waldhorn. On the other hand, since the variety of Waldhorn used in the chase bore indifferently in France the names 'cor de chasse' and 'Trompe de chasse', the former of which Bach himself uses both in its French form and Italian equivalent (*corno da caccia*), it is maintainable that by that term, and not the more concise 'Corno', the Waldhorn is indicated. In that case, Bach's nomenclature must distinguish not the older Jagdhorn and more recent Waldhorn, but the Waldhorn in its original form as an instrument of the chase, and the Waldhorn modified in tone and structure for other purposes. Such modifications, however, were improbably within Bach's experience. Mr. Blandford remarks that even the French were not equipped with the orchestral horn until the decade following Bach's death, and that the change of tone was associated with the adoption of an embouchure different from that used by horn players in the time of Bach and Handel, who placed the mouthpiece on the lower lip; while, in the horn

[1] See Tables V and VI.   [2] Gerber, ii 547.

embouchure, two-thirds of the mouthpiece lies on the upper lip, and the rim, narrower than that of a trumpet mouthpiece, is sunk in the red part of the under lip.

Such, in concise outline, is the problem, a positive solution of which may not be attainable. A decided judgement, however, can be expressed on one or two very relative points. In the first place, the nature of Bach's horn parts forbids one to suppose that he ever used the obsolete Jagdhorn of Praetorius' time. In the second place, Mattheson's eulogy of the 'lieblich' Waldhorn certainly indicates an agreeably mellow tone which distinguished it from the hunting horn it immediately superseded. In the third place, the view that 'Corno' and 'Corno da caccia' indicate the same instrument is contradicted by Bach's practice. If there is one thing clearly revealed in his scores, it is his meticulous indication of instrumental *tone*. Hence we have sound reason for supposing that the terms 'Corno' and 'Corno da caccia' distinguish the mellow tone Mattheson associated with the Waldhorn, and the more strident tone of the traditional Jagdhorn, which the newer instrument had not yet supplanted at those princely Courts, e.g. Weimar and Cöthen, where the horn was still an instrument of the palace. It is certainly significant that Bach's use of the 'Corno' exactly coincides with the cessation of his courtly service, and with the beginning of his career in a community in which the ceremonial hunting horn had not a similar vogue. That he was ever familiar with the refinements of the orchestral horn is not suggested. But that he could have had at his disposal not only the 'lieblich' Waldhorn, but also the large coiled Jagdhorn, is evident from the existence of such a horn in the Heyer Collection, dated 1740 and specifically associated with church usage.[1] Its tone differed from the Waldhorn's, and since in outward form the two instruments were indistinguishable, the difference, no doubt, arose from their mouthpieces, the Waldhorn's deeply conical, the Jagdhorn's shallow and conical, and its tube cylindrical throughout its whole extent, to the point where it widens to form the bell.

To the hypothesis that Bach's 'Corno' was the Waldhorn and his 'Corno da caccia' the Jagdhorn further support is afforded by his evident characterization of the latter. In his use of it his reaction to the feudal conventions of his generation is evident. The author of a recent disquisition[2] has advanced the wayward

---

[1] The instrument (No. 1664 of the Heyer Collection), in D or E flat, by Johann Werner, is inscribed 'in die Kirche zu Priesnitz gehörig' (Kinsky, p. 185).

[2] Rutland Boughton, *John Sebastian Bach* (London, 1930).

thesis that Bach's music breathes a spirit of revolt against his social environment. In fact, he was as stout a conservative as his contemporary, Samuel Johnson. However stubborn he could show himself on occasion, when confronted by authority menacing his freedom as an artist, he accepted the ritual of Germany's petty Courts as readily as the Lutheran *Formula Concordiae*. Hence his use of the corno da caccia was governed by approving experience of its ceremonial associations. On such domestic occasions as those for which the 'Peasant Cantata' (*Mer hahn en neue Oberkeet*) or *Aeolus* were composed, the 'Corno' satisfied him. But for Duke Christian's 'Tafelmusik' (*Was mir behagt*), or for the *Hercules* music in honour of Saxony's Crown Prince, the corno da caccia was imperative; its notes by long tradition were the salute of princes.

Nor does Bach restrict this deference to his secular scores. The naïve literalness so prominent in his character invited him to salute the Lord of lords with the same instrumental voice. The familiar bass aria of the *Hohe Messe*, 'Quoniam tu solus Dominus', is an instance. The words acknowledge the sovereignty of Christ, throned with the Father in Heaven; the horn obbligato is an obeisance to his Kingship. In cantata No. 16 it sounds again; for the theme is the same—a free version of the *Te Deum laudamus*. And again in No. 65, an Epiphany anthem:

> Three kings from the East, as long foretold,
> Did come with myrrh, with incense, with gold,
> Alleluia! Alleluia!

Bach remembered the Introit proper to the festival: 'Ecce advenit dominator Dominus, et regnum in manu ejus, et potestas et imperium'—God's majesty implicit in the Child's infant frame. So the horn again pays conventional homage. With similar purpose the instrument is scored in No. 128, for Ascension Day:

> I see Christ through the starlight
> In brightness passing sunlight
> Enthroned as God's dear Son.

The same theme—the majesty of God—inspires cantata No. 143, an anthem for the New Year, to whose orchestral accompaniment, and here only, Bach adds three *corni da caccia* and drums. Its bass aria, 'The Lord is Sovereign everywhere', exceeds the 'Quoniam tu solus' in the elaborateness of its ceremonial courtesy. The horns echo and re-echo their familiar 'call':

Cantata No. 174 affords another example. Two *corni da caccia* are prescribed in the opening Sinfonia, a movement borrowed from the third Brandenburg Concerto written eight years earlier. But, to pay homage to 'the Highest', the horns are an addition to the original score.

Bach's 'Corno' was not identified in his mind with similar associations. He uses it purely for its orchestral value, and rarely outside his choruses and Chorals. On the infrequent occasions when it has pictorial significance, it decorates a pastoral and not a ceremonious scene. For instance, in the opening chorus of cantata No. 112:

> The Lord my Shepherd deigns to be.

Again, in the opening chorus of No. 1:

> How brightly shines yon Morning Star,
> Whose beams shed blessing near and far!

Again, in the tenor aria of No. 40, composed for the second day of the Christmas festival, whose Gospel (St. Luke ii. 15–20) relates the visit of the shepherds to the Manger. And again in the bass aria that opens cantata No. 88. The text is from Jeremiah xvi. 16: 'And after will I send for many hunters, and they shall hunt them from every mountain.' The horns sound a sonorous summons to the mountain-side.

Cantata No. 118 requires particular consideration. It is a motet for S.A.T.B. with wind accompaniment—a cornett, three trombones, and two instruments Bach names 'Lituus'. The music was composed for an open-air funerary ceremony, perhaps at the graveside. But what was the 'Lituus'? Praetorius[1] defines it as the 'Krummhorn',[2] an instrument with a long English tradition.[3] Bach's Weimar friend, Johann G. Walther, describes it as a Zink, but remarks that formerly the name denoted the 'tuba curva' or 'Heerhorn'.[4] Dr. Max Schneider, editing the motet for the Neue Bachgesellschaft, supposed it to be a 'Flügelhorn' (or 'Bügelhorn'). But the problem is solved by the more recent publication[5] of a catalogue of musical instruments preserved at Ossegg (Bohemia) in 1706. It mentions two 'litui, vulgo Waldhörner'. Bach's instruments are in high B flat, sounding bb–a'', a rare instance of his employment of horns in that key. And nowhere else does he

---

[1] P. 40.
[2] The range of the parts in cantata No. 118 is the best evidence that the instrument was not a Krummhorn.
[3] Cf. Galpin, p. 164.   [4] B.-G. xxiv, p. xxiii.   [5] B.-J. 1921, p. 96.

use the term 'Lituus'. His use of it clearly is related to the fact
that the cantata is the only one he scored exclusively for 'Stadtpfeiferinstrumente'.

It has already been remarked that Bach did not use the corno da
caccia at a higher pitch than B flat. But the trumpet part in the
second Brandenburg Concerto suggests that he may have scored
that work for the high Jagdtrompete, a trumpet coiled like the
horn. Eichborn[1] quotes a late seventeenth- or early eighteenth-
century writer who distinguished the trumpets of his period in
four classes: (1) the German or 'ordinar-Trommete'; (2) the
French, higher than the German; (3) the English, higher than the
French; and (4) the Italian or 'gewundene' (circular) trumpet.
Altenburg also places the 'gewundene' trumpet in a 'Zweyte Klasse',
distinct from the German, French, and English trumpets. 'In this
connexion', he writes,[2] 'the so-called "Invention" or Italian
trumpet merits the highest consideration; for, owing to the
frequent windings of its tube, its form is particularly convenient.
It is much used in Italy and has the same trumpet *timbre* as those
of the other class.' ('Hier verdient die sogenannte Inventions- oder
italienische Trompete den ersten Rang, weil sie, wegen der
öftern Windung, auf eine bequeme Art invertirt ist. Sie sind
vorzüglich in Italien gebräuchlich, haben den nemlichen Trom-
petenklang, wie die vorigen [i.e. the *trombe* of the "Erste Klasse"],
und sind von verschiedener Grösse.') So these Italian trumpets
were coiled horn-wise, not folded like the tromba. An example
can be seen in E. G. Haussmann's portrait of Gottfried Reiche,[3]
Bach's most accomplished Stadtpfeifer. It represents him holding
one in his right hand, with four coils of tubing. After taking
exact measurements Mr. Blandford concludes that it was in D,
at a pitch rather below diapason normal, with a C crook. In his left
hand Reiche holds the manuscript of one of his 'Abblasen'. Its
compass is from bb to bb'':

---

[1] Eichborn (2), p. 22.   [2] P. 12.
[3] See the illustration at p. 48, and Praetorius, Plate VIII, at p. 36.

GOTTFRIED REICHE
(*From the portrait by E. G. Haussmann*)

Few specimens of this high tromba da caccia survive. The Heyer Collection, now in the University of Leipzig, exhibits one 'in Des' (= D in the pitch of its period), described in the Catalogue (No. 1819) as less blaring than the D-tromba, with a compass to a''''. It is a Leipzig instrument, made by Heinrich Pfeifer, and dated 1697.[1] Another example, apparently in D, was loaned to the exhibition of musical instruments at South Kensington in 1872; it bears the date 1688 and was made by Wilhelm Haas of Nürnberg.[2] The Brussels Conservatoire has one in E, by the Vienna maker Michael Leichamschneider, dated 1713. Mahillon[3] conjectures that it was pitched to the F of its period.

[1] Pfeifer was distinguished as a trombone maker. He was appointed 'Thomastürmer' in 1680 and died in 1718, aged 66. Cf. Schering, p. 295.
[2] It is now in the Hohenzollern Museum at Sigmaringen. Mr. Blandford is not disposed to group it with the Pfeifer and Reiche specimens.
[3] Vol. ii. 381.

CHAPTER III

THE TIMPANI

PRAETORIUS[1] names three varieties of drum—(1) the 'grosse Heerpaucken', kettle-shaped, copper-framed, proper to the ceremonial of Courts and the discipline of war; (2) 'Soldaten Trummel', or side-drum, associated with the transverse or Swiss pipe; and (3) the 'klein Paucklin', or little drum, used by the French and Dutch, which a man could beat with his right hand while supporting a three-holed pipe at his mouth with the left—the pipe and tabor of the Morris Dance.[2]

The timpani or 'Heerpaucken', originally military (cavalry) drums, were admitted to the concert orchestra before Bach's birth (1685), and from an earlier period were fitted with a tuning mechanism. In Sebastian Virdung's[3] illustration the parchment is held taut by a surrounding circlet of metal, and its tension is regulated by ten screw-joints operated by a detachable key. Praetorius,[4] in the following century, illustrates them with six screws. But rapid changes of tuning were impossible, and by Bach and his contemporaries were not attempted.

Bach usually indicates the instrument under the name 'Tamburi', a word which strictly connotes the big drum or 'Trommel'. The rare exceptions are cantata No. 100, where he writes 'Tympalles'; the revised (D major) *Magnificat*, in which he uses the form 'Tympali'; and cantata No. 191, where he writes the contraction 'Tymp.'. Only in the memorandum addressed to the Leipzig Council in August 1730[5] he employs the German 'Pauken', probably reflecting that those he addressed would find another word unintelligible!

Bach's use of the timpani was governed by a convention scrupulously observed. They sounded, according to his contemporary Altenburg,[6] 'the fundament or bass of the trumpet's heroic music'. The two instruments even shared their technical terms, e.g. 'einfache Zungen' (single tonguing), 'doppel Zungen' (double tonguing). Hence, in Bach's tradition, the timpani were an ingredient of 'Blasmusik' (music for wind instruments) and, apart from it, claimed no place in his scores. In his orchestral music they are found only in the Violin Sinfonia in D[7] and the two *Ouvertures* in that key.[8] They are scored in both the Oratorios, but neither of the *Passions*; in the *Hohe Messe*, but not in the four shorter

[1] P. 77.
[2] See Praetorius, Plates IX and XXIII, at pp. 54 and 64.
[3] P. 25.
[4] See his Plate XXIII, at p. 54.
[5] Terry, p. 201.
[6] P. 25.
[7] B.-G. xxi (1)
[8] B.-G. xxxi (1).

Masses; in the *Magnificat, Sanctus* in C,[1] thirty-four church cantatas, and seven secular works—in all, forty-nine separate compositions.[2] They are associated invariably with seasons of festal mood or public ceremony. Only four of the church cantatas in which they occur are not definitely of that character (Nos. 21, 69, 100, 137). No. 21, however, was performed under exceptional conditions at Halle in 1713,[3] and the festal scores of the other three (for the Twelfth and Fifteenth Sundays after Trinity) are probably accounted for by the nearness of those Sundays to the Ratswahl (Inauguration of the Council) service, for which they probably served again. At Leipzig the instruments were shared by the two principal churches, being transported from one to the other as occasion required.

The drums are never found in Bach's orchestra except in association with (*a*) three (rarely four) natural trumpets;[4] or (*b*) two natural horns (Waldhorn); or (*c*) three natural *corni da caccia* (Jagdhorn). The first category far outnumbers the others: the *Corni-Timpani* combination is found in only four scores (cantatas Nos. 79, 91, 100, 195); the *Corni da caccia-Timpani* group in one (cantata No. 143). Being inconsistent with the Motet form, drums have no part in Bach's *Cornett-Trombone* category.

The larger and lower of the two orchestral drums was styled the 'G drum', though, as in Bach's usage, its pitch might be raised to *a,* or lowered to *f,*. The smaller and higher instrument was distinguished as the 'C drum', though, as in Bach's scores, it frequently sounded *d* and occasionally *bb,*. The larger instrument was placed at the player's right hand, and the smaller on his left. A black cloth ('ein schwarzes Tuch'), spread over the parchment, muted the tone when occasion required.[5]

Owing to their close association with a 'choir' of trumpets, the drums were normally tuned in fourths in the eighteenth century. They were thereby enabled, in Altenburg's words, 'to sound the Fundament or Bass' ('das Fundament oder den Bass machen'). In old trumpet marches the fourth trumpet part was often written in fourths to allow it to be played on the drums if necessary.[6] Bach, however, does not always adopt the conventional tuning. Invariably his drums are transposing instruments, scored in C in the bass clef. But their tuning varies with the instruments with which he associates them. When scored with trumpets he tunes

them in fourths: and generally puts the movement

---

[1] B.-G. xi (1).   [2] See Table VII.   [3] Terry, p. 101.
[4] The Weimar cantata No. 59 is the sole exception. Only two trumpets are in the score.   [5] Cf. Altenburg, p. 127.   [6] Kirby, p. 12.

into the key of D major.[1] In but thirteen cases C major is the tonic
key. The only other exception to D major normality is the
Magnificat in its first form. Bach wrote it originally in E flat,
tuning his drums in fourths, tonic, and (lower) dominant. Why he
chose this exceptional key is not clear. It was unsuited to the
conditions at Leipzig, for whose churches a revised version in D
was subsequently prepared. As festival music the E flat score is
unique in its tonality.

The association of drums and horns is found in four scores—
cantatas Nos. 79, 91, 100, 195. Here the three trumpets of the *Trombe-
Timpani* category are replaced by two natural horns (Waldhorn:
Corno) in G (the key of the movement), and the drums are tuned

in fifths (dominant and tonic):   The absence of a

third horn is observable. Bach never admits more than two natural
horns to his scores. His tuning of their associated drums in fifths
instead of fourths must be attributed to the fact that the tonic G
could not be sounded on the smaller C drum.[2] Also, by putting it
on the larger and lower 'G drum', the upper in some degree
supplied the third trumpet (principale) of the *Trombe-Timpani*
category. The *Corni da caccia-Timpani* group occurs in a single
cantata (No. 143). The three horns here are in B flat (the key of
the movement), and the drums are tuned in fourths, sounding

the tonic and (lower) dominant: A tuning in

fifths (dominant and tonic), though practicable, was obviously
not preferable, since it diminished the resonance.

In all three categories Bach's treatment of the drums is uniform.
Their pitch remains unchanged throughout the entire work. If a
movement modulates into a key incongruous with their original
tuning, they and their associated 'choir' are silent till the initial
key returns. The drummer had merely to count his bars, un-
hampered by the need to adjust his instruments to changing
tonality. An example may be taken from the early cantata No. 15.
The terzetto which opens Part II begins in F major and ends in
E minor, with two intervening sections in C major (the key of the
cantata). In the C major sections alone the drums and trumpets
are sounded.

With the rarest exceptions[3] Bach never assigns an obbligato or

---

[1] See Table VII.
[2] The limitations of tuning in the eighteenth century were respectively *bb,*–
and *f,*–*c* for the smaller and larger drum.   [3] See *infra*, p. 54.

solo part to the drums, but restricts them to those passages in which their associated trumpets or horns are also sounding. Instances to the contrary are so infrequent, that one might declare it his rule for the drums not to sound unless all the voices of the 'choir' above them are simultaneously speaking. Like Altenburg, he viewed them as the peculiar fundament, or Toccato, of 'Blasmusik', and allowed them to speak only as members of that body.

Bach's reticent use of the drums was largely due to fear lest they should seem over boisterous on an ecclesiastical platform. This is evidenced not only by his disinclination to give them a solo part—a point discussed later—but also by deliberate neglect of their more elaborate and noisy 'beatings'. Altenburg[1] indicates the 'Schlag-Manieren' (beatings) in use in 1768, less than twenty years after Bach's death. They number twelve:

1. Viertel (Crotchets).   2. Halbe Takte (Half-bars).   3. Ganze Takte oder Schläge (Whole bars or beats).

4. Achtel oder einfache Schläge (Quavers or single beats).

5. Einfache Zungen (Single tonguing).   6. Doppel- oder gerissene Zungen (Double or rapid tonguing).

7. Tragende Zungen.   8. Ganze Doppel-Zungen.

9. Doppel-Kreuzschläge (Double cross beats).   10. Triolen (Triplets).

11. Wirbel (Roll).   12. Doppel-Wirbel (Double roll).

[1] P. 129.

Bach's scores only afford examples of the first five. Demisemi-quaver beats occur infrequently—for instance, in the final movement of cantata No. 71. Professor Kirby states that the roll (Wirbel) was not much used in the period. Bach frequently indicates it (e.g. the opening chorus of the *Christmas Oratorio*). More generally he uses the measured *tremolo*, as throughout cantata No. 80. Whether he desired semibreves and minims to be rolled when the *tr.* above them was omitted, it is not possible to say. Almost surely a drummer would roll a long closing note. But the scores of the two *Ouvertures* in D seem to indicate that Bach required the notes to be struck and sustained unless the roll was indicated. Indeed, since he used the instrument with fairly slack parchments, a held note without rolling would have ample resonance.

Such being Bach's standpoint, it is not surprising that the infrequent examples of a drum obbligato are, with one exception, found in his secular music. The first occurs in the opening chorus of *Vereinigte Zwietracht der wechselnden Saiten*, composed in 1726. The text invites it:

> Sweet voices harmonious of strings softly playing,
> Ye thundering drum-rolls exultant and clear,
> Hither draw listeners, coaxed by the sound!

The drums (bar 30), in an otherwise silent orchestra, acknowledge the reference in a simple rhythmic figure:

Timpani in D.

It is worth observing that, while Bach's drums here perform a rhythmic beating where an actual *roll* is invited, the voices and continuo, with exaggerated energy, picture an object gyrating in curves!

The second example of a drum obbligato occurs in the opening chorus of *Tönet, ihr Pauken*.

Here the drums actually open the movement, more familiar as the first chorus of the *Christmas Oratorio*. The writer has expressed the opinion[1] that the music was originally written to the Oratorio text, a conclusion Bach's treatment of the drums appears to

[1] See the *Musical Times*, Oct.–Dec. 1930, Jan.–Mar. 1931.

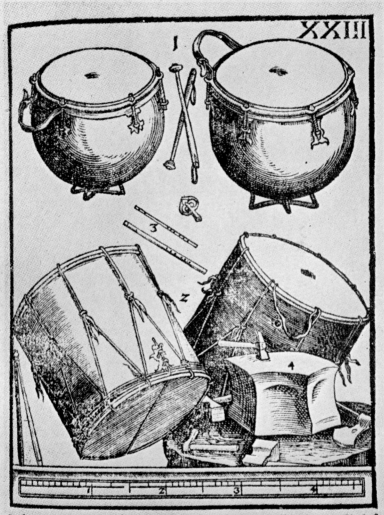

XXIII

1. Heerpaufen. 2. Soldaten Trummeln. 3. Schweiter Pfeifflin 4. Amboß
C iij

DRUMS
(*Praetorius*)

challenge. Certainly the opening drum-solo and following trumpet-calls are more obviously appropriate to the command 'Tönet, ihr Pauken! erschallet, Trompeten!' than to the Oratorio text, which mentions neither drums nor trumpets. But the words 'Christians, be joyful!' to which the Oratorio chorus is generally sung in English, do not correctly translate the original 'Jauchzet, frohlocket!' 'Jauchzet' invites a mood of unrestrained exhilaration, to which, in Bach's view, the drums seemed peculiarly appropriate. For, in the second movement of cantata No. 120, the repeated and imperative injunction 'Jauchzet!' moves him there also to insert an obbligato for the drums (see p. 56).

It has already been observed that the conventional tuning of the drums in fourths was due to their association with the trumpet

'Chor', in that it enabled them to double or replace the fourth trumpet in a part sounding the tonic and (lower) dominant. We detect this convention in cantatas Nos. 63 and 119, in which the drums are associated with four trumpets. Here are the two related parts in the first chorus of the Christmas cantata No. 63, composed in 1723:

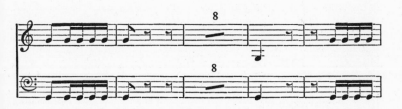

Da Capo.

In cantata No. 119, also composed in 1723, the correspondence is less close, but conspicuous. Here are the two parts in the opening chorus:

CORO.
Tromba IV in C.

Naturally Bach introduces the drums chiefly in choruses, where they complete his festival orchestra. But, associated always with a 'choir' of trumpets or horns, they are occasionally heard in other movements, to whose texts he held them appropriate. In the church cantatas they are present in six arias. In the alto aria of No. 71 they appropriately proclaim the 'mächtige Kraft' of the Mühlhausen Council, in whose honour the cantata was composed. In the Michaelmas cantata No. 130 they accompany the bass aria:

> With writhing fury Satan stands,
> Fresh mischief patiently he plans.

Satan's name always summoned to Bach's vision one of two pictures. Either he saw, and delineated, a sinuously beguiling serpent, or the fallen archangel in arms against the faithful legions. In this aria he paints a stirring battle-piece. The blare of trumpets, the tuck of drums, ring out from the first bar to the last. In the New Year cantata, No. 143, he scores the bass aria 'Der Herr ist König ewiglich' with three *corni da caccia* and drums. As in the 'Quoniam tu solus sanctus' of the *Hohe Messe*, he here naïvely indicates the Saviour's royal dignity by introducing the hunting horn, typical of the pastime of the Courts with which he was familiar. Here its proud flourishes are enhanced by the insistently beating drums. In the Whit-Sunday cantata, No. 172, the invocation to the Trinity in the bass aria

> Blessed Holy Trinity,
> God of might and glory!

invites a display of pomp which Bach's trumpets and drums heartily afford. In the early Easter cantata, No. 15, they are consonant with the season rather than with the words of the two arias into which they are introduced. The comment applies equally to the two duets (cantata No. 59 and the *Easter Oratorio*) in which drums and trumpets are found. To the truculent trio of No. 15 they are wholly appropriate.

The drums add their voice to a single recitative. It occurs in the Ratswahl cantata, No. 119, in a movement for bass heavily scored. The text is a patriotic invocation of Leipzig:

> How bravely stand'st thou, city blest!

Bach gives the sentiment the proudest decoration, befitting the presence of the civic Council on the day which inaugurated its year of office.

In the secular cantatas, Bach normally reserves the drums for the spirited choruses which flowed so easily from his fluent pen. But they accompany the vigorous bass aria 'Zurücke, zurücke' in

Aeolus, and the bass recit. 'Ja! ja! die Stunden' in the same cantata. In the latter, Aeolus summons the Winds in one of the most vivid storm-pieces in musical literature. The trumpets shriek, the drums rattle their thunder, the strings and flutes discharge lightning! A less tempestuous commotion occurs in *Preise dein' Glücke*, in the bass recit. 'Lass doch, o theurer Landesvater', where a reference to the menace of French hostility, when 'alles um uns blitzt und kracht', rouses the drums to another coruscation of fury.

Though the German drummers of Bach's generation were reputed particularly expert, his scores made no unusual demands upon their skill. As with Handel, the instrument was chiefly rhythmical in his usage. He prescribed only two drums, whose tuning, as already shown, remained unaltered throughout an entire work, however lengthy, and they remained silent when its tonality deserted the original key. His 'beatings' are straightforward and without complications, and the parts are rarely annotated with dynamic or other markings. Very occasionally he indicates *forte*, *piano*, *staccato* (e.g. in the better known Ouverture in D). And he rarely phrases.[1] But his orchestra was a permanent body, schooled by frequent oral instruction in his requirements.

[1] See the 'Gloria' of the *Hohe Messe* and the opening choruses of cantata No. 130, *Phoebus und Pan*, and *Schleicht, spielende Wellen*.

CHAPTER IV
THE FLUTES

The Blockflöte, Flûte à bec, Flûte douce

THE monopoly it enjoyed till the middle of the eighteenth century permitted the Blockflöte, disdaining its rival, to be known
without qualification as 'the flute' (Flöte; flûte; flauto). Bach invariably names it so (Flauto; Fiauto), adding the classifying 'à bec' in
only one of his scores.[1] The term is derived from the feature which
distinguished the instrument from the modern variety—the whistle
or fipple (whence 'fipple flute') mouthpiece, that allowed the player
to hold the instrument vertically, as the clarinet and oboe in
present usage. Praetorius names it 'Blockflöte' or 'Plockflöte',
because its upper aperture was partially obstructed, leaving a
narrow channel through which the wind passed from the player's
lungs. Comparison with its noisier fellow gave it the name
'flûte douce', and to its weaker volume of tone it owed the definition 'flauto d'èco', a term Bach uses in the fourth Brandenburg
Concerto in G, where two flutes discourse with a solo violin.
As the 'Recorder' it had a long English tradition.[2]

The size of the instrument varied according to pitch. But
generally it formed a cylindrical, or cylindrical and partly sphero-
conical, tube, originally in one piece, latterly jointed, most frequently made of wood, pierced with seven lateral holes in front,
and having one for the thumbs behind. Its *timbre* was softer than
the transverse flute, and the lack of overtones gave it a tenuous
quality which commended it to Bach for the uses to which he
put it. It needed delicate manipulation, for some of its notes,
naturally impure, required correction by breath pressure or
fingering. But it blended equally well with the voice and strings,
and Bach employed it, though sparingly, throughout his active
career; it is first found in his scores in 1708 and appears in his
latest cantatas *c.* 1740. Owing to the fact that the transverse
variety superseded it in the period when modern instrumental
technique was beginning, it underwent little modification or improvement during its currency, and passed out of use in the form
in which it had been known since the sixteenth century. It
survives in its main feature only in the English and French

[1] Clavier Concerto in F.   See Table VIII.
[2] Cf. Galpin, chap. viii.

flageolets, the so-called 'penny-whistle', and the flutework of the organ.[1]

The *Blockflöten* formed a considerable family of one-key instruments. Praetorius[2] cites eight varieties, twenty-one of which were needed to complete the band of flutes so popular in the sixteenth and seventeenth centuries.[3] He enumerates the following:

1. Klein Flöttlin in g''
2. Discant   ,, d''
3. Discant   ,, c''
4. Alto   ,, g'
5. Tenor   ,, c'
6. Basset   ,, f
7. Bass   ,, bb'
8. Gross Bass   ,, f'

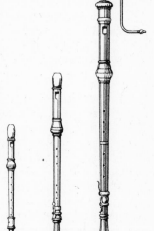

With an effective compass of two octaves and one note, which an expert player could extend some four or five notes upwards, the Blockflöte of Bach's generation was available in various keys, discant, alto, tenor, and bass. Those in general use were the

1. Discant sounding $a'-a'''$
2. Discant   ,, $g'-g'''$
3. Discant   ,, $f'-f'''$
4. Alto   ,, $eb'-eb'''$
5. Alto   ,, $d'-d'''$
6. Alto (Tenor) ,, $c'-c'''$
7. Tenor   ,, $bb-bb''$
8. Bass   ,, $f-f''$

Discant, Tenor, and
Bass Blockflöte,
18th cent.

To these must be added high discants (*flauto piccolo*) in f'', d'', c'', bb', the first and second of which Bach employs in cantatas No. 96 and No. 103 respectively. But the compass-chart in Table VIII shows that he made little use of any but discants Nos. 1–3. Only in one score (cantata No. 13) the instrument descends to c'. In two others (cantatas No. 39 and No. 152) it touches d'. Its lowest note averages f'. As a general statement it may be said that an alto flute served when the compass fell below that note to e', d', c', and a discant for parts whose lowest note was a', g', and even f', except when that note occurred frequently or was stressed,

---

[1] Cf. Dolmetsch, p. 457.   [2] Pp. 21, 33; see his Plate IX at p. 64.
[3] Cf. Praetorius, p. 13.

conditions which demanded an alto instrument. Table VIII does not indicate such differences of compass as permits a definitive allocation. But, in those infrequent cantatas in which three flutes are prescribed,[1] it may be safely concluded that the third is an alto. The 'Bass' and 'Gross-Bass' mentioned by Praetorius had already passed out of use, being found too soft in tone. Bach employed neither of them. Nor can we anywhere detect his usage of the bass f–f''. The tenor bb–bb'' may have been used in cantata No. 25, but not elsewhere. Thus, in Bach's scores the Blockflöte is essentially a soprano instrument.

Observing a convention whose practical utility is not apparent in his own case, Bach wrote for the Blockflöte in the French violin G clef set on the bottom line 𝄞 Players accustomed to the normal G clef for the transverse flute must have been confused by the practice. Certainly Bach's Blockflöte tends to soar higher than the other variety. But the difference is not considerable, nor is it adequate to explain his use of the two clefs. At an earlier period, however, the French clef had an obvious advantage; for, as Praetorius shows, the Blockflöte discants were then keyed to higher pitches. Bach evidently preserved a convention for which his own music made no urgent call.

The Blockflöte, being a one-key instrument, normally sounded the notes as written in its peculiar clef. The player selected the one most conveniently keyed for the music before him. But in Bach's scores are six cases in which the flute part is transposed:

1. Cantata No. 18. Excepting a few bars, in which they are silent, the flutes throughout are in octaves with the first and second violas. The latter are scored in the alto C clef in the key of the work (G minor). The former are keyed in A minor in the French violin G clef, transposing down a whole tone. Consequently on the stave the notes are identical (see p. 65).

The significant point here is, that Bach does not, as we should expect, score the flutes for the alto C in the key of the movement, but transposes their part for the tenor B flat. It is improbable that the former instrument was not available. Hence we must conclude that Bach deliberately chose the tenor in order to secure the uniform notation already remarked.[2] For, as it stands, the flute part sounds right, whether in the French G clef, as written, or (an

---

[1] Nos. 25, 122, 175.
[2] The argument is not affected by the possibility that the high discant in B flat rather than the tenor B flat was used here. The former would relieve the sombre colour of the score.

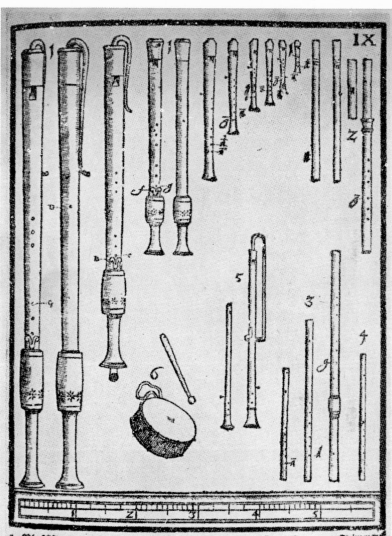

IX

FLUTES
(*Praetorius*)

octave lower) in the alto C clef, which an inexperienced player could readily visualize or substitute. It has been shown in an earlier chapter that Bach was dependent on unprofessional players for his flute parts. His practice here is therefore readily explained. It emphasizes the fact, often overlooked, that his scores do not always reveal his preferences, but rather the inadequate material at his disposal.

2. Cantata No. 103. The opening chorus is in B minor (S.A.T.B., continuo, strings, oboe d'amore I and II). The Block-flöte piccolo is scored in D minor and transposes down a minor third. Since the pitch of the Leipzig organ does not account for the interval of transposition, we must suppose that Bach's player was accustomed to the discant in f'. Fingering f'' on the piccolo, he here sounds d'', the lowest note on the smaller instrument.

3. Cantata No. 106. The work is in E flat major (S.A.T.B., continuo, viola da gamba I and II). The flutes are in F, sounding a major tone below the part as written. The occasion for which the work was composed is not certainly determined. Probably it was composed for a service in commemoration of the Weimar Rector, Philipp Grossgebauer, in 1711. In that event it was per-formed in the Stadtkirche. That it was not intended for the ducal chapel is proved by the fact that a tone, and not a minor third, separates the pitches of the flutes and organ.[1]

4. Cantata No. 152. The short work is in E minor (S.B., con-tinuo, viola da gamba, viola d'amore, oboe). The flute is in G minor, transposing down a minor third, to suit the high pitch (Cornett-Ton) of the Weimar organ.

---

[1] Cf. *infra*, chap. vii.

5. Cantata No. 161. All the movements in which the flutes participate are in C major (continuo, organ, strings, S.A.T.B.). The flutes are in E flat, transposing down a minor third.

6. Cantata No. 182. The movements in which the flute is employed are in G major and E minor (S.A.T.B., strings, continuo). The flutes are in B flat, transposing down a minor third.

It is noteworthy that, excepting No. 103, all the cantatas named above belong to Bach's Weimar period. The ducal Capelle was not equipped with flautists,[1] and Bach had to look elsewhere for players. Consequently he rarely used the instrument. Indeed, beyond the five instances already given there is no certain evidence of his use of either flute there. For both cantatas No. 142 and No. 189, attributed to those years, are of doubtful authenticity, which the present argument further undermines. Bach's transposition of the flute parts was due to the high pitch of the organ in the ducal chapel, and the fact that the parts stand a minor third higher than the ordinary Cammerton indicates that it was tuned to Cornett-Ton.[2]

The high discant (*flauto piccolo*), in d'' and f'', is found in only two scores, and those among the latest—cantatas No. 103 and No. 96. In both it occurs in a single movement (Coro), and in both reinforces, or is reinforced by, another instrument at the octave: in No. 96 it is 'col Violino piccolo', in No. 103 'col Violino concertante o Flauto traverso'. In both we discern Bach's intention to mitigate the shrillness of the little instrument, and in both its employment is evidently related to the words. In No. 103 it is appropriate to Luther's text of St. John xvi. 20, on which the chorus is built. In No. 96 the lines

> He is the Star of Morning,
> Whose beams declare the dawning,
> When other stars do pale.

prompt Bach, invariably moved to make a picture, to suggest the distant spaces of the sky. Yet these were not his first opportunities to use the little discants, whose belated employment indicates how alertly experimental his genius·remained to the end.

The earliest example of Bach's usage of the Blockflöte merits attention, since it adds a detail to our knowledge of the conditions attending the first performance of the cantata in which it occurs. The cantata, No. 71, is scored for trumpets, drums, flutes, violoncello, oboes, bassoon, strings, and organ, arranged in four 'Cori', of which two—(1) trombe–timpani and (2) strings, as well as the

---

[1] *Supra*, p. 3.
[2] The subject of pitch and tuning is dealt with in Chapter VII.

voices and organ—are scored in C, while the other two—(3) flutes-violoncello and (4) oboes-bassoon—are in D, in the autograph score and printed parts. The inference from this strange dissimilarity is clear: the organ of the Mühlhausen Marienkirche, in which the cantata was performed on 4 February 1708, was tuned to high (Chorton) pitch. The young composer consequently put the low-pitched Cammerton flutes, oboes, and bassoon up to D, and transposed the violoncello also to the higher key to keep it uniform with its associated flutes in the second 'Coro'.[1]

Of no other instrument is Bach's characterization so clear and consistent as the Blockflöte. His comparatively infrequent employment of it indicates that he associated with it peculiar qualities to be reserved for particular uses. To him, as to Mersenne,[2] it expressed 'le charme et la douceur des voix', tender, plaintive, eloquent of the pious emotions of the soul, appropriate to voice the quiet agony of death, or mental sorrow, and by its purity to carry the soul's devotion to the throne of God. No other instrument identifies itself so closely with the simple piety of Bach. It voices his tenderness for his Saviour, his serene contemplation of death as the portal to bliss eternal. Only rarely, in cantatas No. 71 and No. 119, it intrudes into a score of pomp and circumstance. Elsewhere, as in No. 65, it is the vehicle of the mysticism so deep-rooted in Bach's nature.

Guided by this key to Bach's treatment of the Blockflöte, we approach the scores in which it occurs. As Table VIII discloses, he employed it chiefly in the cantatas, where we most readily apprehend his meaning. Cantata No. 13 is inspired by the Saviour's words, 'Mine hour is not yet come' (St. John ii. 4). Its two arias consequently are in a mood of sorrow, to which the flutes communicate their poignant note. In cantata No. 18, however, they seem to owe their presence less to congruity with the text than to the orchestral limitations of the Lenten season. Bach's stalwart Protestantism never failed to build an impregnable musical foundation when his topic, as here, is the 'Word of God'. To the solid structure of the opening Sinfonia and the soprano aria

The Word of God my treasure is

with its confidently moving continuo, the flutes make a contribution incongruous with their normal utterance. In the aria they weave an arabesque of almost purring contentment.[3]

[1] The violoncello and bassoon parts are not identical. Had they been so, another reason for the former's transposed part could be proposed.
[2] Bk. V, p. 237.
[3] Schweitzer, ii. 145, supposes that the flutes here represent waves, a figure incongruous with the text.

In cantata No. 25 the word 'Jesu' evokes from Bach a spasm of tenderness which the flutes interpret. In the same soft murmurous tones in which they sound the melody of the penitential hymn 'Ach Herr, mich armen Sünder', in the opening chorus, they echo the melodious petition of the soprano aria:

> Hearken to my halting praises,
> Jesu, with a gracious ear!

In a similar mood of prayerful approach they weave an embroidery of tender feeling round the soprano aria of cantata No. 39:

> Father, all I bring Thee
> Thou Thyself hast given me.

In cantata No. 46 (*Schauet doch und sehet*) the flutes express another mood. The chorus 'Behold and see if there be any sorrow like unto my sorrow' is a persisting wail of lamentation, in which they raise their tempered voices, one answering the other, as if in rivalry to express their grief. Their threnody continues in the following tenor recitative, 'Lament, lament God's city now in dust!' In contrast with these gloomy numbers is the alto aria:

> But Jesus still His faithful shieldeth,
> A present help in danger's hour.
> His sheep He loves, their love beseecheth,
> And folds them safe when storm-clouds pour.

Here, as always, the thought of Jesus as the Good Shepherd moves Bach to fashion a pastoral scene, to which the flutes contribute their decorous piping.

The practice of his generation, and his own strong inclination, always moved Bach to give nature's moods pictorial illustration. So, in cantata No. 81, which treats of Christ's stilling of the tempest, the flutes and strings in the opening chorus undulate in gentle wavelets on the lake's surface. But, significantly, the strings alone portray their furious motion in the tenor aria:

> The waters of Belial
> Their storm-crests are tossing
> And raging like hell!

Here the flutes are silent in a scene incongruous with their gentle nature. They are scored, in fact, only in the first chorus and do not reappear even in the concluding Choral.

In the next two[1] cantatas in the Table the flutes, as in No. 46, are the vehicle of lamentation. In No. 103 the unusual intrusion of the piccolo into the opening chorus undoubtedly indicates Bach's desire to emphasize the word 'heulen' (howl, yell). Soaring

---

[1] For cantatas Nos. 71 and 96 see *supra*, p. 66.

to its highest register it sounds a piercing cry. Again in No. 106,
a funeral anthem, the flutes assist its sombre mood. Associated
with two *viole da gamba*, in Schweitzer's[1] vivid words, 'their
veiled *timbre* belongs to the very essence of the music. We seem
to see an autumn landscape with blue mists floating across it.'

In cantata No. 122 the flutes have another meaning. They sound
only in the soprano recit., and with evident significance. The
text pictures the angelic host filling the sky with the incense of their
praise. Bach puts a song into their mouths, the Christmas hymn
'Das neugebor'ne Kindelein', and gives the melody to the flute
high above the stave; for the text speaks of the angelic singers
'in lofty choir'. A similar impression of sound from ethereal spaces
is conveyed by the flutes in cantata No. 127, in the soprano aria:

> In Jesu's arms my spirit resteth
> While earth-bound still my body lies.
> So, call me hence, sad bells of mourning!
> Death, sound thy summons! Fear I'm scorning!
> For Jesus beckons from the skies.

Here, in Bach's customary device, the pizzicato continuo tolls the
'sad bells of mourning', and the flutes' persistent quavers measure
the endless seconds of a timeless sphere. For their note is not
funereal; rather they express the soul's quiet contentment, at rest
in the Saviour's arms. As Pirro writes,[2] 'elles chuchotent, pour ne
point troubler ce grand sommeil, mais elles ne gémissent pas'.

Cantata No. 152[3] provides another example of Bach's disposition
to address the Saviour directly through the flûte douce, as here in
the soprano aria, where he is apostrophized as 'the Corner Stone':

> Rock, beyond all else my treasure,
> Aid me ever all my days
> Faith to show Thee without measure,
> Build on Thee my hope always,
> Soon in heaven to do Thy pleasure!

The continuo moves with the always confident pulse of Bach's
music when the thought of man's reliance on God is uppermost,
while the flute and viola d'amore, in happy mood, illustrate the
word 'Seligkeit'.

The thought of death ever excited ardent longing in Bach.
The flutes give it expression in cantata No. 161. In the opening
alto aria they stress the recurring word 'süss':

> Kindly [süsser] Death, come, quickly call me!
> .   .   .   .
> Grant me, Lord, a gentle [süsse] passing!

[1] Vol. ii. 126.
[2] P. 228. 'They speak in whispers, unwilling to disturb this everlasting sleep;
but with no note of lamentation.'   [3] See *supra*, p. 66, for No. 142.

Again in the final chorus they illustrate the word:

> Heaven's joy, so calm [süsse] and blissful.

In the intervening alto recit.:

> Then, hasten, Death! O make no long delay!
> Come, toll thy knell and let me hence away!

we hear the tolling bells and the flutes' echo of them in the high ether.

Bach's association of the flute with a pastoral scene was natural, and has already been remarked in cantata No. 46. In No. 175 the opening tenor recit. and following alto aria provide another instance:

> (R.) 'He calleth his own sheep by name, and leadeth them out' (St. John x. 3).
> (A.) Come, lead me hence!
> My spirit yearns to walk in heaven's pasture.
> With eager eyes and longing sighs
> I wait Thee, Shepherd, Master.

Both movements are scored for continuo and three flutes, which in the aria pipe a deliciously care-free measure as they lead the flock to the green pastures of Paradise.

That Bach selected the flûte douce to voice his most sacred emotion is particularly evident in cantata No. 180, one of five scores in which the traverso appears as well. The latter is obbligato in the tenor aria.

> Arouse thyself, the Bridegroom knocks!
> Throw open wide the gates before Him!

The music is animated, eager, joyous; yet its vivacity is physical rather than emotional. But in the opening chorus, alto recit., and soprano aria, where the gentler instrument is prescribed, Bach prostrates himself before the Great Mystery:

> He, our God, so gracious minded,
> Hath for us a feast provided.
> He Who in the heavens reigneth
> Here to feed His children deigneth.

In cantata No. 182 (*Himmelskönig, sei willkommen*), Bach's only extant anthem for Palm Sunday, the flute apparently owes its presence to the conditions of the Lenten season. Normally Bach would have put other colours on his canvas.

Besides the church cantatas, the flûte à bec is scored in the *Easter Oratorio, St. Matthew Passion,* the secular *Was mir behagt,* and three orchestral Concertos. Bach presents both varieties of the instrument in the first two, and in each employs the flûte à bec in but one movement. To the tenor aria of the Oratorio:

> Death's a sleep! I fear no longer.
> 'Tis a slumber.
> Jesus risen hath made it so.

it lends its murmurous tone. But the joy of Easter is voiced by the traverso. In the *St. Matthew Passion*, too, its note is pathetic (tenor recit., No. 25):

> O grief! How throbs His woe-beladen heart!

In *Was mir behagt*, as in cantata No. 175, its piping is pastoral (aria of Pales, No. 9):

> Happy flocks in surety wander
> While the shepherd watch doth keep.

These examples completely reveal Bach's usage of the flûte à bec. That the traverso was of more general utility is evident from Tables VIII and IX. But the flûte à bec had his deeper regard. For in its clear tones he could utter the ponderings of his devout mind. But its delicate *timbre* put it at a disadvantage in the orchestral era that followed the death of Handel. The very qualities that commended it to Bach prejudiced its competition with the rougher and louder rival. So, it passed from the orchestra to the museum,[1] superseded, but not excelled, by its competitor.

The Transverse Flute

Germany's particular association with the transverse or orchestral flute is implicit in the fact that both France and England, throughout the eighteenth century, distinguished it from the other variety as 'the German flute' (*flûte d'Allemagne*; *flûte allemande*). The crosswise manner of holding it gave it the appellations *flauto traverso, traversa, flûte traversière, Traversflöte, Querflöte*. The same characteristic caused Sebastian Virdung,[2] writing in 1511, to name it *Zwerchpfeiff*. The tradition that it piped the Swiss to battle at Marignano in 1515 impelled Agricola a few years later (1528) to call it the *Schweizerpfeiff*. Bach generally adopted the Italian styles *flauto traverso, traversa*, but occasionally uses the French indication *traversière*.

---

[1] There has been, of late years, a revival of interest in the *Blockflöten*. Instrument-makers are again building them, and manuals of instruction are published, e.g. Robert Götz's *Schule des Blockflötenspiels* (Verlag P. J. Tonger: Cöln) and Waldemar Woehl's *Blockflötenschule*. The latter is published by the firm of Bärenreiter at Cassel, from whom can also be obtained a set of instruments. Those made by Mr. Arnold Dolmetsch are of particular excellence, and a full consort is to be heard at the Haslemere festivals.   [2] P. 14.

From Agricola's period onwards the transverse flute formed a family of three instruments,[1] (1) Discant, (2) Alto-Tenor, (3) Bass, at the respective pitches:

Praetorius,[2] ninety years later, puts them a fifth higher:

with a compass of two-and-a-half octaves in each case. He adds that the middle instrument was used as a discant, and so carries forward the tradition of the orchestral D flute from the age of Virdung and Agricola to that of Bach and Handel.

To this point the mechanism of the instrument was of the simplest. It formed a one-piece wooden tube, cylindrically bored, and pierced laterally with six finger-holes, sounding the chromatic scale over a compass of fifteen tones (two-and-a-half octaves). But, unlike the Blockflöte, it was improved in the seventeenth and early eighteenth centuries by various devices. Lully's introduction of it to the French Opera *circa* 1677 roughly dates the beginning of these changes, for which French makers are credited. They consisted, first, in the substitution of a conoidal for a cylindrical bore, its taper widening from the lower end towards the head of the instrument. At about the same time the one-piece tube was divided into three sections, respectively distinguished as the *tête*, *corps*, *pied*. Subsequently the *corps* itself was divided, so that inserted pieces of suitable length could adjust the instrument to the conflicting pitches then in vogue. These changes left the scale still controlled exclusively by the six lateral finger-holes. Towards the close of the seventeenth century, however, a metal key (*Klappe*; *clef*), pressed by the little finger of the right hand,[3] was added to

the tail section (*pied*), enabling the player to sound

and its octaves.

[1] Cf. Mahillon, i. 249 f.; *Encyc. Britannica*, 11th edn., x. 579 f.; Fitzgibbon, chap. 3.   [2] P. 22. See his Plate IX at p. 64.

[3] As may be seen in the picture of Lully and his flautists in the National Gallery, London, the key moved on an axle and was kept closed by a spring. Its mechanism was fitted into a wooden ring or rib encircling the tail section at the proper position. The picture is figured in Fitzgibbon.

Thus, on the threshold of the eighteenth century, the transverse flute in D sounded the scale in the fundamental octave by successively opening the finger-holes from the bottom upwards, interposing the key before opening the first:

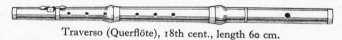

By increasing the breath-pressure, and allowing it to impinge less acutely on the outer edge of the embouchure, the upper octave

Traverso (Querflöte), 18th cent., length 60 cm.

was obtained. Semitones foreign to the scale—*d♯'*, *d♯''*, *d♯'''* excepted—were got by 'forking' or 'cross-fingering' (*doigté fourchu*; *Gabelgriffe*). Thus, by closing the *e'* and *g'* and opening the *f♯'* holes the note *f♮'* was obtained:

Similarly *bb'* was got by 'forking' the *a'* and *c♯''* holes:

And *c♮'* thus:

But the notes obtained by 'forking' were impure and needed manipulation for their satisfactory production. Flute makers consequently planned to extend the key system already in operation for *d♯'*. During his stay in Paris in 1726, Johann Joachim Quantz, subsequently flute-master of Frederick the Great, added a key for *eb'*, flatter than the *d♯'* which so far served for it. Though Germany approved the device, the innovation was elsewhere ignored. Four years earlier (1722) two supplementary keys had

been added to the lengthened tail-joint for

Unlike the *d#'* key, they sounded only their fundamental notes,
adversely affected the tone of the instrument, and temporarily
were abandoned.

Meanwhile a contrivance had been adopted to mitigate the
inconvenience caused by the variety of pitches then in vogue,
which necessitated the appropriate lengthening or shortening of
the middle joint (*corps*). For the purpose a player needed to carry
as many as seven pieces of varying length. This rough and ready
adjustment, however, affected the relations of the other sections
of the instrument, and therefore, in order to establish a just proportion, the tail-joint (*pied*) was now divided below the key, its two
pieces being brought by a tenon-adjustment into accurate relationship with the middle-joint (*corps*). Instruments so constructed
were known as *flûtes à registre*. Still more accurate tuning was
aided by a device whose invention followed closely upon Bach's
appointment to the Leipzig Cantorate. Quantz, about 1726,
added a nut-screw regulating the cork-stopper in the upper joint
(*tête*) of the instrument, on whose correct adjustment its accurate
pitch in great measure depended.

The innovations described in the preceding paragraphs have been
stated in reference to the discant or orchestral flute in *d'*. They
were equally applicable to the other members of the family, which,
when Quantz published his *Method of playing the transverse flute*
in 1752, were four in number, pitched respectively, (1) a fourth
below, (2) a third below, (3) a fourth above, and (4) an octave
above the discant in *d'*. Nos. 1, 3, 4 were known respectively as
the 'low fourth', 'little fourth', and 'octave' or 'piccolo'. No. 2,
distinguished for its soft and mellow tone, was for that reason
termed the *flûte d'amour*. Taking the ordinary discant or concert
flute as a flute in C, these four instruments would be pitched as
follows:

But, as the low C key was not in use, the lowest sounding notes
on Nos. 1–3 were

Such was the equipment of the instrument as it reached Bach.

Excepting cantata No. 189, whose authenticity is challenged, there is no extant instance of his use of it until his prescription of 'due Traversieri' in the secular cantata *Durchlaucht'ster Leopold* at Cöthen in or about 1718. He employed it again in the fifth Brandenburg Concerto and other instrumental scores of that period.[1] But it was not until his appointment to the Leipzig Thomasschule in 1723 that the transverse flute regularly contributed to his concerted music. The compass chart in Table IX shows that, with the rarest exceptions, he preferred and used the discant in *d'*, introducing it most often into sharp keys, of which those of G and D major far outnumber the rest. Out of seventy-eight scores in which it is found, only fourteen have a flat signature.[2] A collation of his scores shows that at all periods his players—who in this case provided their instruments—were equipped with the *d#'* key. The note was not obtainable by 'forking', and its almost constant presence in his flute parts—whether as *d#'* or *eb'* or their octaves—supports the deduction. The key was in use before 1707, when Bach took office in the Blasiuskirche at Mühlhausen.

Whether Bach's players were also provided with the long keys extending the compass downward to *c'* and *c#'* is a point which repays investigation. They were added about 1722, and therefore were available when he went to Leipzig. On the other hand, they were generally condemned as blemishing the tone of the instrument, and on that account Bach might be expected to frown upon them. In fact he seldom carries his flute parts below

The following are the rare exceptions to this restriction of compass. They not only settle his usage of the long keys, but also indicate definitely the members of the traverso family he preferred and employed.

1. Cantata No. 26. At bar 42 of the opening chorus the flute has this descending passage:

The *c'* is not repeated elsewhere, and, as the flute is in unison with the first oboe, it is not improbable that Bach momentarily

---

[1] See Table IX.

[2] Cantatas Nos. 55, 78, 101, 102, 114, 146, 164, 180, 189 (? authentic), *Ich bin in mir vergnügt*, the two *Passions*, Flute Sonata No. II, and the trio and canon in the *Musicalisches Opfer*.

overlooked its limitations of compass. It would be rash, in such conditions, to accept the single note as proof of a long key.

2. The second flute has a similar lapse in cantata No. 79 (1. Coro).

3. Cantata No. 45. At bar 79 of the opening chorus the second flute has this passage in unison with the second oboe:

The third bar, however, is a copyist's error. For elsewhere the *c♯′* is avoided, and at bar 15 the same passage is correctly marked:

4. Cantata No. 164. In the soprano-bass duet the two flutes in unison touch *c′* in the following bars:

Being in unison with the oboes and violins, their common part is printed on a single stave. But the repetition of the note puts the case in another category from that of No. 1, and a collation of the flute part at Berlin confirms the correctness of the Bachgesellschaft score. The player, however, may have used a B flute and transposed.

5. Cantata No. 192. In 'Verse 3' (chorus) the following passages occur:

Flute I.
Bar 16 and 31.

Flute II.
Bar 19 and 66.

Bar 58.

As in the examples already given, the flutes share the stave with other instruments: the first is in unison with the first oboe and first violins, the second with the second oboe and second violins. In the original parts at Berlin there is no indication that they took the low notes at an upper octave, and we must therefore conclude that the second flute, at any rate, was the 'low fourth' in A.

6. The *Hohe Messe* in B minor. At bar 21 of the final movement the second flute plays

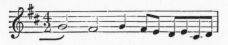

Here there is no room for doubt. The *c♯′* is definite in the autograph score. A long key can therefore be presumed to have been used if that note actually was played. But it must certainly be regarded as an oversight on Bach's part. For it is patent from the opening bars of the 'Kyrie' that the flute was not fitted with a long key. There the second flute is generally in unison with the second oboe. But on every occasion when the oboe touches *c♯′* the flute is provided with an alternative note within its normal register.

7. A similar intention can be inferred in *Angenehmes Wiederau*.

8. *St. Matthew Passion*. In the opening movement of the second Part (bar 69) the first flutes of both 'Cori' have the passage:

Here, again, the autograph score is definite: 'Trav. e Hautb. d'amour 1° concordant'. As in cantata No. 192 a 'low fourth' flute must have been used here, and in this movement only. Throughout the rest of the work the traverso in *d′*, with the *d♯′* key, was adequate.

9. *St. John Passion*. At bar 62 of the opening chorus the first flute plays:

The flute here is in unison with the first oboe, and the single *c′* can hardly establish the use of a long key. On the contrary, at bar 7 of a later chorus ('Sei gegrüsset'), where the second oboe descends to *c′*, Bach substitutes for the flute a note within its compass:

He does so again at bar 7 of the chorus 'Schreibe nicht'. The flutes
here and throughout the *Passion* are the *d♯'*-keyed discant in *d'*.
Alternatively, here, as in cantata No. 164, the player may have used
a B flute.

    10. *Vereinigte Zwietracht.* In the opening chorus the flutes are
in unison respectively with the first and second *oboi d'amore*, and
repeatedly sound the notes

They are therefore of the 'low fourth' variety. Elsewhere in the
cantata Bach employs the normal discant in *d'*.

    These conclusions emerge from the foregoing analysis:

    1. Excepting four scores, Bach generally used the discant
traverso in *d'*, but nowhere the high discant in *d''*.[1]

    2. There is no satisfactory evidence that his instruments were
fitted with a *c'* key, the general objection to which he must be held
to have shared.

    3. There is no convincing instance of his use of a *c♯'* key.

    4. Other than the discant in *d'*, and perhaps a B flute, the
only instrument of the traverso family for which he scored was the
'low fourth'. It is found only in cantata No. 192, the *St. Matthew
Passion*, and *Vereinigte Zwietracht*. If, however, the authenticity
of cantata No. 189 is conceded, the compass of its flute part
(*b♭'–d'''*) indicates the same instrument.

    To an extent a modern composer of reputation would not tolerate,
Bach's orchestras included amateurs. His flute players were
generally drawn from the University Collegium Musicum, and
there must have been periods when they were not forthcoming.
For that reason, we may conclude, only forty-one of his Leipzig
cantatas are scored for the traverso. They are scattered over the
whole span of his Cantorship, but with intervals in their occur-
rence most apparent in its last active decade. We certainly
should not be justified in measuring the ability of his amateur
flute players by the parts he wrote for it. For there are many which

---

[1] The compass of the instrument in cantata No. 78 suggests the so-called
'military flute' in E flat. But the compass was easily obtained on the *d'* discant.

demand high executive skill. Moreover, contrary to Handel's general practice,[1] they most often cover the entire compass of the instrument. On that account we may suppose that, from time to time, Bach's professional oboists were also competent on the flute, though frequent instances of his employment of both instruments in the same score prove that he was not independent of amateur assistance. Still, it frequently happens that the oboist could, if required, play the obbligato parts in arias in which his own instrument was silent.

To the immaturity of his players we must attribute the fact that Bach's flute parts are so frequently written in unison with other supporting instruments. With comparative rarity he entrusts an aria solo obbligato to it, and the movements in which they occur belong chiefly to the last period of his fertility. When, as in cantata No. 102, he prescribes a violino piccolo, or, as in the *Easter Oratorio*, a violin, as an alternative to the traverso, we must not infer that he was indifferent as to which instrument was played, but that he was doubtful of the availability of a competent flautist.

Bach's treatment of the traverso has peculiar interest. His immediate predecessors, Knüpfer and Kuhnau, employed it occasionally and tentatively[2] during the supremacy of its rival. But, when Bach succeeded Kuhnau in 1723, the sovereignty of the Blockflöte was no longer conceded, and his scores reveal the fact. Mr. Fitzgibbon[3] advances the curious proposition that, 'living under Frederick the Great', Bach 'naturally paid considerable attention to the favourite instrument of that monarch'. As a Saxon subject, Bach owed no allegiance to Prussia, and his usage of the traverso goes back a quarter of a century before his famous visit to Quantz's pupil. Certainly Frederick's notorious preference may have accentuated the declining vogue of the Blockflöte. But, in matters affecting his art Bach was not swayed by the vagaries of fashion. In the traverso he recognized a useful orchestral voice, and his scores reveal his experimental usage of it.

We remark, in the first place, his disinclination to employ it in purely instrumental movements. There are many in the cantatas, sacred and secular. But the traverso is scored in only one of them (*Non sa che sia dolore*). The so-called 'pastoral' Sinfonia in Part II of the *Christmas Oratorio* is the only piece of sacred instrumental music to which he admitted the traverso, and there with obvious intention. Elsewhere he preferred the gentler Blockflöte. His secular instrumental scores declare the same preference. For, though the Flute Sonatas were written for the traverso, and also

[1] Fitzgibbon, p. 118.   [2] Cf. Schering, p. 151.   [3] P. 118.

the Trio in G for flute, violin, and bass, as well as the one in C minor offered to Frederick the Great, the instrument is found in his larger orchestral works only in the Brandenburg D major, the Clavier Concerto in A minor, and Ouverture in B minor. All of them have a characteristic in common with the Sinfonia of the *Christmas Oratorio* which explains Bach's preference of the traverso in them —in none are horns or trumpets prescribed. He was therefore not deterred from employing the coarser of the two flutes, whose tone, augmenting the brass, would have unbalanced his orchestral scheme. His concerted vocal music suggests a similar deduction. We should expect to find the traverso in choruses where his festival orchestra is employed, when trumpets and drums, or horns and drums, augment the normal body. In fact, it is more often absent than present. In the Leipzig cantatas it is omitted from twenty movements of this character.[1]

The cantatas and larger concerted vocal works exhibit Bach's employment of the traverso in every form then customary—chorus, aria, recitative, Choral. In the choruses, notwithstanding considerable variety of usage, one practically invariable rule is observed. So close seemed the instrument's affinity with the oboe, that in only two Leipzig flute cantatas—Nos. 173 and 184—are they not together. That these exceptions were due to abnormal conditions is evident from the fact that the two cantatas were performed on consecutive days, 14 and 15 May 1731. The rougher tone of the traverso clearly invited a closer association with the oboe than Bach was willing to sanction in the case of the Blockflöte. There is, in fact, only one instance of the latter being in unison with the oboe. It occurs in cantata No. 152, in the concluding soprano-bass duet. But the direction there is 'Gli Stromenti all'unisono' and includes other instruments than the two in question. It therefore does not challenge the general statement, that Bach nowhere links the Blockflöte with the coarse-toned oboe. On the other hand, it was his frequent practice with the traverso, whose tone was more congruous with the other instrument. Instances occur in cantatas Nos. 26, 45, 67, 78, 79, 110, 117, 191, 195, the *Hohe Messe, St. John Passion*, and *St. Matthew Passion*, but rarely in an aria.

In Bach's choruses the traverso serves one of two purposes, and occasionally a third. Either it adds an independent strand to the woven web of polyphony, or it merely strengthens the texture of one otherwise provided. Occasionally it is both independent and pictorial. It would be convenient to detect consistent develop-

---

[1] Nos. 19, 29, 41, 43, 50, 63, 69, 74, 80, 91, 120, 137, 143, 149, 171, 172, 190, 197, *Herr Gott, Beherrscher*, and *Christmas Oratorio*, Part VI.

ment in Bach's practice. In fact, examples of the three categories can be drawn from his earliest as from his latest Leipzig music. Excluding the suspect cantata No. 189, and the secular *Durchlaucht'ster Leopold*, composed at Cöthen, Bach's earliest use of the traverso in a concerted chorus is observed in the two major works whose performance distinguished his first year at Leipzig—the *St. John Passion* and the Latin *Magnificat*. In the former, performed on 26 March 1723, his use of the traverso is curious and was not repeated. It plays an independent part only in two soprano arias, the short chorus 'Wir haben keinen König', and the tenor arioso 'Mein Herz'. Elsewhere the two flutes either double the oboe parts, or (in unison) are concordant with the first violins or sopranos, or (in unison) play an octave above the violas or vocal tenors. There is no patent reason why Bach should have used the flutes in so many movements to sound the octave of the instrumental and vocal tenors. Either the reason was particular, or he disliked the effect: the experiment was not repeated.

The composition of the *Magnificat* must have been begun at no considerable interval after the performance of the *St. John Passion*. But it indicates a decided change in Bach's usage of the traverso. In the earlier work the instrument is an auxiliary, in the latter a principal. It contributes nothing original to the structure of the *Passion*. In the *Magnificat* it raises an individual voice, excepting the chorus 'Omnes generationes', where the accompaniment conforms to a fugal plan. Nor, excepting the alto-tenor duet 'Et misericordiam', where the flutes and violins are in unison, is it bracketed with another part. So, an instrument admitted on probation in March 1723 has the freedom of the orchestra in the following December.

But it must not be supposed that Bach thereafter consistently followed the method employed in the *Magnificat*. Certainly he did so in his other major church compositions—the *Trauer-Ode*, *St. Matthew Passion*, *Christmas Oratorio* (for the most part), and the latter part ('Credo' and 'Osanna') of the *Hohe Messe*. In all the Leipzig secular choruses, also, the traverso has an individual voice, excepting, to some extent, *Schleicht, spielende Wellen*. We can place in the same category cantatas Nos. 8, 9, 11, 107, 115, 123, 125, 173, 180, 184, 191 (in part), and 192. But they are matched by almost as many in which the instrument is for the most part auxiliary. Excepting the 'Qui tollis' and a few bars of the 'Cum sancto spiritu', the 'Kyrie' and 'Gloria' of the *Hohe Messe* are in this category. So are cantatas Nos. 45, 67, 78, 79, 110, 117, 191 (in part), and 195, already mentioned, to which we may add Nos. 101, 129, and 181. Among these only three obbligato solos are found (Nos. 45, 78, 79), and his treatment of the traverso in them generally supports the deduction already drawn—that it depended not infrequently on the competence of the players at his disposal.

In the arias Bach's experimental treatment of the traverso is apparent and in contrast with his usage of the Blockflöte in similar movements. The differing *timbre* of the two flutes explains the fact that he infrequently duplicates the traverso, but, excepting the two Weimar cantatas Nos. 152 and 182, never uses only one Blockflöte in an aria accompaniment. It is rare, again, for the Blockflöte to be supported by the continuo alone in movements of that nature: the only instances to the contrary are in cantatas Nos. 39, 119, 142, 175, 182, and *Was mir behagt*. On the other hand, the traverso is so treated in arias more frequently than any other combination, most often with an alto or tenor voice. These arias occur in cantatas Nos. 45, 55, 78, 79, 94, 96, 99, 102, 103, 113, 114, 123, 130, 164, 180, *Easter Oratorio*, *Phoebus und Pan*; *Ich bin in mir vergnügt*; *Schleicht, spielende Wellen*; *O holder Tag*; *Schweigt stille*; *Tönet, ihr Pauken*; and *Die Freude reget sich*. The presence of two *traversi* is unusual: they are found only in cantata No. 164 (which has already been discussed), the Mass in A, *Phoebus und Pan*, and *Tönet, ihr Pauken*, in which they have independent parts; and *Preise dein' Glücke*, where they are in unison, for the same reason, apparently, as in No. 164. In *Schleicht, spielende Wellen*, however, Bach's literalness compels him to use three flutes in one aria which sings of 'the choir of flutes' ('der Flöten Chor').[1] In cantatas Nos. 79 and 103 the traverso is alternative, in No. 79 to an oboe, in No. 103 to a violin. In the first Bach may have had the same player in mind for both instruments. In the second he proposed to fall back on his leader should a flautist not be available on the more or less distant date of performance.

In the traverso-continuo category must also be placed a few arias in which an organ accompaniment is definitely prescribed. The most familiar are the plaintive alto aria 'Buss und Reu' ('Grief for sin') in the *St. Matthew Passion*, and the tenor pastoral aria 'Frohe Hirten' ('Happy shepherds') in Part II of the *Christmas Oratorio*. Other instances are the soprano aria of cantata No. 100, the tenor aria (No. 6) of No. 107, the tenor aria of No. 110, the alto aria 'Esurientes' of the *Magnificat*, and the soprano aria 'Ich folge dir' in the *St. John Passion*. Excepting Nos. 107, 110, the *Passions*, and the *Magnificat*, these *obbligati* are for a single flute. In the soprano

---

[1] Notwithstanding his text, 'Schweigt, ihr Flöten', in the soprano aria in *O holder Tag*, however, Bach had to be content with one flute.

aria of the *Easter Oratorio* the continuo is augmented by a bassoon. As in the case of No. 103, the obbligato is alternatively for a traverso or violin, and for the same reason.

In general the traverso solo *obbligati* are such as Bach could not willingly have entrusted to an inexpert player. Nor are they merely decorative; on occasion they contribute to a pictorial design. In the tenor aria of No. 55:

> Have mercy, Lord!
> Look with pity on my crying,
> Let Thy heart regard my sighing,
> And for Jesu's sake, Who loved me,
> Turn Thy heavy anger from me!

the flute weaves an embroidery of lamentation reminiscent of the earlier 'Erbarme dich' ('Have mercy, Lord') of the *St. Matthew Passion*. In the alto aria of No. 94:

> O foolish world, O foolish world!
> Vain your power, pomp and gold!

the flute obbligato, flickering hither and thither, typifies the world's 'falscher Schein'. In the tenor aria of No. 99:

> Let nothing thee dismay, O fainting spirit!

Bach is at pains to paint the initial word 'Erschüttre'—shake, convulse, stagger—in agitated demisemiquavers and leaping intervals. A similar interpretation fits the flute obbligato to the tenor aria of No. 102:

> Affrighted, pause,
> O vain presumptuous spirit.

in which the traverso (or violino piccolo) discharges cascades of agitated notes. But this congruity between text and obbligato is not always observed. An instance occurs in cantata No. 130, where Bach adapts the words of the tenor aria:

> Thou of angel hosts the leader,
> Prince of God's heroic band!

to a tuneful gavotte introduced by the traverso:

No historical incident supports such treatment of St. Michael![1]
We must conclude that Bach was either indifferent to the incongruity or anxious to use and hear an attractive tune. Did he write
it with one by François Couperin in his mind?

We frequently observe Bach's liking for a pizzicato or staccato
continuo in arias in which a traverso is employed. The acoustic
qualities of the Leipzig churches may account for a direction not
otherwise explicable. Examples are found in cantatas Nos. 78, 102,
123, *Tönet, ihr Pauken*, and also in No. 107, the *St. Matthew Passion*,
the *Magnificat*, and *Easter Oratorio*.

It cannot be altogether fortuitous that these traverso-continuo
obbligati fall chiefly in the last years of Bach's fertility, that is, in
the period 1735–44. It would appear that he could in those years
rely on professional players whose executive skill exceeded that of
the amateur *studiosi* on whom formerly he was dependent. The
inference is buttressed by the significant fact that in that period
two of his players, Johann Friedrich Kirchhof and Johann Christian
Oschatz, were engaged as flautists by the Leipzig Concertgesell-
schaft. Both were skilled oboists, whose membership of the Kunstgeiger and Stadtpfeifer corporations dated respectively from 1737
and 1738. Their talents, however, must have been recognized and
employed before their formal admission to that body.[2] With
some confidence we may associate one or both of them with these
traverso solos.

Next to its employment with the continuo only, Bach's most
frequent usage of the traverso in the arias adds to it both strings and
continuo. The examples are found in cantatas Nos. 8, 26, 30, 34,
115, 117, 129, 157, 173, *Ehre sei Gott*, Mass in A major, *St.
Matthew Passion*, *Vereinigte Zwietracht*, *Preise dein' Glücke*, *Non
sa che sia dolore*, *Durchlaucht'ster Leopold*, *Die Freude reget sich*,
and *Mer hahn en neue Oberkeet*. Bach achieves in these examples a
variety of combinations, sometimes obeying the prompting of his
text, often impelled by an imperative inclination to experiment
with his palette. Most frequently the flutes are set against a background of tone produced by the full orchestra of strings—violin,
viola, and continuo. A familiar example is the soprano aria
('Blute nur') in the *St. Matthew Passion*, where the two flutes
independently stress the poignant lamentation of the text. In a

---

[1] It has been suggested that for St. Michael, 'a parfit gentil knight', the courtly
Gavotte was not inappropriate!   [2] *Supra*, p. 14.

similar setting, but in another mood, the traverso embroiders the
bass aria in cantata No. 8 with florid, care-free trills of melody
befitting the words:

> A truce to my sorrow, so noisily storming!
> My Jesus doth call me and who would not go?

Again, in the alto aria of No. 30 the flute lilts a glad greeting above
the strings:

> Come, ye sinners, wayworn, tearful!
> Come rejoicing, be not fearful!
> 'Tis your Saviour, hear His cry!

Here the first violins throughout are 'col sordino', now 'alcuni',
now 'tutti', tempered for the flute with which they are largely
concordant. The other parts are marked 'pizzicato', the organ
'staccato'. The alto aria of cantata No. 34 is similarly planned.
The two *traversi* are generally at the octave with the first and second
violins, which are muted, as also are the violas. The melody bears
evident relationship to that of the alto aria of No. 30 and exhales
the same ecstasy of spiritual happiness:

> Rejoice, ye souls, God's vessels chosen,
> Whom He His dwelling deigns to make.

The mood is present again in the alto aria of No. 117:

> So, all my mortal life along,
> O God, I'll sing Thy praises.
> All men shall hear the happy song
> My glad heart to Thee raises.

where a single traverso flutes to the accompaniment of the strings.
In the secular cantatas named above Bach invariably employs this
combination, in the soprano arias of *Non sa che sia dolore*:

> Away, then, with dismal repining!

and

> Go thy way and grieving, leave us!

in the dance-like soprano aria of *Mer hahn en neue Oberkeet*:

> Klein-Zschocher must be
> E'er blithe and bonny!

in the alto aria of *Die Freude reget sich*:

> The good things that God showers on thee,
> The praise that greeteth thee to-day,
> To us as e'en our own are dear.

and in the two soprano arias of *Durchlaucht'ster Leopold*, in both
of which the two flutes in unison are in unison with the first
violins. The three instruments are similarly associated in the tenor

aria of cantata No. 173, save in the third bar from the end, where
the violins descend below the compass of the traverso in d'.

Instead of setting the traverso against an accompaniment of
string tone, Bach sometimes associates with it a particular instrument of that family in a duet over a continuo accompaniment. The
examples occur in cantatas Nos. 26, 115, 129, 157, and *Ehre sei
Gott*. In three of them a violin is paired with the traverso. The two
instruments contribute to Bach's realistic picture of 'ein rauschend
Wasser' in the tenor aria of No. 26:

> As swift in channels waters whirl,
> So quickly days and hours are flying.

In the soprano aria of No. 129 they perform a duet of formal
character—the text invites no other—an ascription of praise to the
Third Person of the Trinity. The violin part is marked 'Solo'.
We cannot decide whether the omission of that direction from the
flute part indicates Bach's desire for it to be played *tutti*. In the
violin part the restriction is intelligible, for two or three players
normally occupied the desks of both firsts and seconds. But Bach
was precariously supplied with flautists. Here its absence from
the flute part may imply no more than that the direction was superfluous. Yet there are six cases in which the instruction 'Solo' is
attached to the traverso part: in cantatas Nos. 26, 96, 100, 102, 114,
and 123. All belong to the period in which, as has already been
suggested, Bach could rely on professional players. In these
instances, therefore, the direction 'Solo' may instruct his *studiosi*
to be silent. Still, we may not conclude that, when the direction is
absent, more than one player was available.

In the bass aria of No. 157 the traverso is again paired with a
violin. The movement breathes the yearning happiness which
Bach always found in the contemplation of death:

> Ah yes! I hold to Jesus firmly
> While faring on my homeward way.
> For at the Lamb's high feast awaits me
> A glorious crown of purest ray.

The rhythmic continuo speaks the word 'feste' (firmly) in every
bar, and above it, in one of Bach's characteristic 'joy' rhythms,
the flute and violin voice the happy assurance of the text.

The remaining instances in this category—cantata No. 115 and
Ehre sei Gott—substitute a violoncello for the violin as the traverso's
associate. In the opening alto aria of the Christmas *Ehre sei Gott*,
in which two flutes discourse, the violoncello has an independent
and significant part. The words address the cradled Jesus:

> Precious gift beyond compare,
> Come forth from Thy cradle lowly,
> Take my heart and make it holy,
> Meet for Thee, a dwelling fair!

To the movement, a tender lullaby, the violoncello contributes a persistently rocking figure of patent meaning. In the soprano aria of No. 115 the traverso is paired with a violoncello piccolo over a staccato continuo. The movement bears one of Bach's infrequent markings, 'Molto Adagio':

> Ever trustful raise your prayer
> In the night's long vigil!

Flute and violoncello converse in a duet of intimate emotion, to which the latter instrument adds, in M. Pirro's words,[1] the 'verdeur suave d'une voix jeune'.

A curious device is used in the soprano arias of the Mass in A and *Preise dein' Glücke*, of which the Ascension Oratorio (cantata No. 11) affords a third example. Bach dispenses in all three with the normal continuo and substitutes the violins and violas in unison. In the aria of the Mass the two flutes discourse above the 'Violini

e Viola all'unisono', whose part, however, falls to and

whose staccato crotchets, rising in steady and recurring progressions, contribute a detail to a picture vivid in Bach's mind. The words are the 'Qui tollis' of the *Gloria in excelsis*, the Church's petition to Christ the Mediator 'seated at the right hand of God'. By withdrawing the normal continuo and building on a higher foundation Bach reaches up to the supreme altitude where 'the one, full, perfect and sufficient sacrifice, oblation and satisfaction for the sins of the whole world' is offered and renewed. That this is the meaning of the device is evident from the Ascension Oratorio aria.[2] But the interpretation is not applicable to the third example —the soprano aria 'Durch die von Eifer entflammeten Waffen' in *Preise dein' Glücke*. Here also the *traversi* are accompanied by the 'Violini e Violetta' in unison. But the mundane words merely offer fulsome adulation to Augustus III. The incongruity is explicable. The music is borrowed from the *Christmas Oratorio*, where the aria is set in F sharp minor for a bass voice. In the secular cantata a soprano sings it in B minor, to an accompaniment pitched a fourth higher. It was not practicable to transpose the normal continuo to the higher key, and therefore Bach substituted

---

[1] P. 223. 'The fragrance and freshness of a youthful voice.'
[2] See *infra*, p. 90.

the 'Violini e Violetta'. It is worth observing that all three examples of this device fall round the year 1734.

The remaining example in the traverso—strings—continuo category occurs in the alto aria of *Vereinigte Zwietracht*. Here the two *traversi* have independent parts above a freely moving continuo, between which and themselves the first and second violins and violas, in unison and 'piano sempre', execute a persistent rhythmic figure:

It is not melodic, but alters its pitch to accord with the other parts. Its significance is revealed in the text:

> Should not this august occasion
> Into marble form be hewn?

Bach's inveterate disposition to make a picture employs the rhythmic figure to suggest the sculptor's mallet and chisel!

Having regard to the close association of the two instruments in the concerted choruses, it is curious to remark the comparative infrequency of arias in which the traverso and oboe are brought together. They are so associated in only sixteen scores—cantatas Nos. 11, 55, 125, 145, 146, 151, 181, 189, in both of the *Passions*, *Christmas Oratorio* (Part II), *Trauer-Ode*, and in the secular cantatas: *Phoebus und Pan*, *Ich bin in mir vergnügt*, *Angenehmes Wiederau*, and *O holder Tag*. They cover the whole span of Bàch's Leipzig Cantorate, but occur comparatively infrequently in the regular cantatas of the normal ecclesiastical year. These facts point, as before, to the occasional lack of competent players, though at special seasons Bach was not similarly impeded; for instance, in the second Part of the *Christmas Oratorio* he could muster four oboists and two flute players, and in the *St. Matthew Passion* could employ, or at least score for, four flutes and as many oboes.

Bach shows marked preference for the oboe d'amore in the arias associated with a traverso, and the combination serves voices of all registers, especially the soprano. It assumes various forms, and exhibits his inexhaustible curiosity in experiment. In the soprano aria of No. 146:

> Now see my teardrops falling
> From eyes with weeping sore!

the plaintive flute obbligato is accompanied by two *oboi d'amore*[1]

---

[1] Cf. the soprano aria 'Zerfliesse, mein Herze', in the *St. John Passion*, where *oboi da caccia* are associated with the *traversi* in a similar text.

and continuo. In the soprano aria of the Christmas anthem (No. 151), accompanied by strings and continuo, an oboe d'amore is in unison with the first violin, whose soothing tones complete the lullaby for the infant Jesus:

> Comfort sweet! Lord Jesus comes
> In our flesh to dwell among us.

The traverso here pours forth a flood of loving emotion which the picture of the Manger at Bethlehem always evoked from Bach. The work belongs evidently to the period (1735–40) in which he could rely on a competent flautist. In the tenor aria of the *Trauer-Ode* the traverso is scored with an oboe d'amore, violins, two gambas, two lutes, and continuo. The *Ode* was composed for the service held in the Paulinerkirche in memory of the Electress-Queen, and Bach's choice of instruments was guided by his desire to make the most decorous and restrained gesture of homage to a personality deeply loved.[1] Here the traverso, standing out over a sedate accompaniment, sheds the kindly glance an earlier movement had invited:

> Turn, Princess, turn an earthward glance
> From Salem's star-bespangled haven,
> To see our scalding tears fast falling
> Amid thy funeral circumstance!

Again, in the soprano aria of *Ich bin in mir vergnügt*:

> Heavenly gift, O sweet content!

the traverso is obbligato in an accompaniment of strings and oboes, the latter in unison with the violins. The first violins and first oboe not infrequently reinforce its theme, but the traverso is the principal, and 'Himmlische Vergnügsamkeit' the evident key to its song. In the soprano aria of Part II of the *St. Matthew Passion* its obbligato exhales the very essence of hopeless despair:

> For love of me my Saviour's dying

and its poignancy is increased by the accompaniment of two *oboi da caccia* without continuo.

The familiar alto aria that opens Part II of the *St. Matthew Passion* exhibits the traverso in an unusually intimate association with an oboe d'amore. The two are in unison in the expressive obbligato which so graphically pictures Zion's eager and baffled search for the Saviour. They are associated also in the bass aria of *Phoebus und Pan*, where, against a background of muted strings,

---

[1] As the ceremony was a University function, however, Bach may have been restricted to instruments available among the *studiosi*.

their melodious obbligato expresses the word 'Verlangen' in every bar:

> With fond *longing*, see, I kiss thy cheek so tender.

In the concluding soprano aria of *O holder Tag* the two instruments, largely in unison, deliciously supplement each other in a *vivace* movement very apt to the mood of this wedding cantata:

> Joy be yours, happy lovers!
> Happy lovers, joy to you!

In four arias the traverso shares the obbligato with another instrument in a quasi duet in which it generally has the upper part. In No. 11 (*Ascension Oratorio*; soprano aria) two flutes (in unison) are paired with the first oboe over a continuo provided only by the violins and viola in unison. The movement has already been referred to.[1] The high-pitched continuo was certainly suggested by the text, which pictures the Saviour, heavenward rising, bestowing a last look of love on his faithful below. The tender, melodious obbligato-duet seems to float on the upper air, as though it were indeed the 'Gnaden-Blicke' (loving glance) of which the text speaks:

> Jesu, Thy last glance, so loving,
> Can I still in fancy see.

In the opening tenor aria of No. 55 the traverso is paired with an oboe d'amore over a string accompaniment, from which the viola is omitted. Here the obbligato-duet is flagrantly incongruous with the words:

> Poor wretched man, a slave of sin,
> Before God's judgement-seat appearing,
> With dreadful awe and fearful trembling;
> Unjust, how can I justice win?

To a lilting gavotte, and not 'mit Furcht und Zittern' (with awe and trembling), the traverso and its partner conduct the sin-stricken soul on its fearful journey. In the alto aria of No. 125 the same instruments provide an obbligato over an irregular *basso ostinato* marked 'tutto ligato'; they express the wistful longing of the text:

> Toward Thee, my Saviour, am I gazing
> With eyes that see the coming gloom.

In another mood is the bass aria of No. 145. Generously scored for the Easter festival—tromba, traverso, two *oboi d'amore*, two violins (but again no violas), and continuo—the instruments are grouped in pairs, the two oboes together, the two violins together,

---

[1] *Supra*, p. 87.

and the traverso with the tromba, with which it asserts an equality, soaring above it in its highest compass. In the vigorous bass aria 'Mighty Lord and King supernal' in Part I of the *Christmas Oratorio* they are again in comradeship.

The other examples in this category show the traverso less prominent in the aria score. In the bass aria of No. 181 it merely adds its note to a recurring and significant theme which it shares with an oboe and the first violins. The text was suggested by the Gospel for Sexagesima:

> Shallow natures, flighty creatures,
> Rob the soil of seeds that fall.

Bach marks the movement 'Vivace', the continuo 'staccato', above which the flute, oboe, and first violin announce vigorously a theme repeatedly stated but never developed, to which the first line of the aria is set—'Leichtgesinnte Flattergeister'. Schweitzer's[1] interpretation is not extravagant: 'We instinctively see a swarm of crows descending upon a field with beating wings and wide-stretched feet', an etching made more vivid by the downward flights of the continuo. In the two tenor arias of the doubtfully authentic No. 189 the flute is merely the discant in a quartet (flute, oboe, violin, continuo) accompanying the voice. In the exquisite alto aria 'Slumber, my dear one' of the *Christmas Oratorio*, Part II, however, it has a part effective, though auxiliary. The score also includes strings, two *oboi d'amore*, two *oboi da caccia*, and continuo. Excepting a few bars in the second part of the aria, the *oboi d'amore* and first violin have the melody of the accompaniment in unison. The second violin, viola, and *oboi da caccia* fill in the harmony above the continuo. The flute doubles the voice part at the octave. The effect of this crooning lullaby is inexpressibly tender.

The duets in which the traverso is scored do not indicate new varieties of treatment. Sometimes it is paired with an oboe d'amore in a duet-obbligato over a continuo, as in cantatas No. 9 and No. 99; or with an oboe da caccia to similar accompaniment, as in No. 101. With an oboe, violin, and continuo it supports the voices in No. 157, or supplements the strings in the melodious minuet-duets of No. 173 and *Durchlaucht'ster Leopold*, and in No. 184. In No. 164 a paucity of dependable players must explain the overloaded obbligato of the soprano-bass duet, in which the flutes, oboes, and violins are in unison over a continuo. Again in the soprano-bass duet of No. 192 and the 'Et misericordia' of the *Magnificat* (alto-tenor) the traverso is in unison with an oboe and

[1] Vol. ii, p. 199.

violin, or with violins alone. Concisely, it is only independent and individual in the soprano-tenor duet of No. 191, the 'Domine Deus' (soprano-tenor) of the *Hohe Messe*, and the alto-tenor duet of *Aeolus*.

In his recitatives Bach's infrequent use of the traverso is adventurous, sometimes surprising. In a few cases a couple of flutes play over a continuo sustained or detached notes, such as elsewhere he writes for strings in similar movements: for instance, in the brief bass and alto recits. of the *Ascension Oratorio* (cantata No. 11); in the bass and alto recits. of Part III of the *Christmas Oratorio*; in the soprano-bass recit. (No. 10) of *Aeolus*; in the bass recit. (No. 8) of *Tönet, ihr Pauken*, in which two oboes also are employed; and in the bass recit. of the *Trauer-Ode*, which is similarly scored. A less normal example of this type is afforded in the bass recit. (No. 65) of the *St. Matthew Passion*. Here the two *traversi* and continuo sound short staccato notes to the sustained chords of the gamba.

Bach occasionally embellishes his recitatives with a flute duet over a continuo, and makes it interpretative of the text. (Those it thus embellishes are lyrical, never Biblical.) The most familiar example is the alto recit. (No. 9) 'Du liebster Heiland' of the *St. Matthew Passion*, in which the flutes' obbligato expresses the most poignant melancholy. Another example is in cantata No. 184. Its text being based on the Gospel of Christ the Good Shepherd, the opening tenor recit. apostrophizes the 'longed-for, joyous Light' vouchsafed to man 'through Christ our Lord and Shepherd'. Schweitzer[1] interprets the phrases uttered by the two flutes in thirds as 'the flute-call of the shepherd . . . sounded brokenly, as if [he] were walking on distant heights, and his melody floated down only in fragments'. One supposes them rather inspired by the word 'Freuden*licht*', and that, appropriately in this Whitsuntide anthem, they represent the Pentecostal tongues of flickering flame. A third example of similar usage is provided by the soprano recit. 'Ja, ja! Gott ist uns noch' in *Preise dein' Glücke*. 'Doth not the Baltic', the singer challenges, 'where Vistula her waters pours, own Augustus' sway?' The two flutes speak for the river—'der Weichsel Mund'—in detached and rippling wavelets of homage. In the soprano recit. of the wedding cantata *Dem Gerechten muss das Licht* (No. 195) the flute part again has pictorial significance. 'The nuptial knot is tied,' declares the singer. Thereon the flutes, over *oboi d'amore*, in a series of scales, ascending and descending, weave the word 'knüpfet', and almost boisterously 'tie' or 'bind'

[1] Vol. ii, p. 163.

the contract. No particular significance attaches to the smoothly flowing duet-obbligato which the traverso and oboe d'amore contribute to the soprano recit. (No. 9) of *O holder Tag*.

In two cases the flutes take part in a recitative elaborately scored. In the alto recit. of the *Trauer-Ode* their repeated high-pitched semiquavers sound the harmonics of the tolling bells—'The bells' repeated thrilling sound the anguish of all hearts recordeth, and in our mourning souls vibrateth'. In the bass recit. (No. 2) of *Aeolus* they augment the colossal clash of elements the angry potentate commands.

Bach's earliest associations were with the flûte douce, and to the end he used it to express his most intimate moods. But, from his usage of it, he evidently admired the qualities of the traverso, and, on the ground of general utility, even preferred it. As he himself wrote in 1730,[1] 'The present *status musices* is quite different from what it was'. The sweeter, less noisy flute was no longer fitted to the uses the newer technique required it to fulfil. For, in the eighteenth century, music enlarged its platform from the chamber to the concert-room and opera-house. The gentle-toned instruments of an earlier age ceased to be heard, and the traverso came at length into its kingdom. Leipzig, perhaps more than any other community in that period, was soundly educated by Bach to appraise its qualities.

[1] Terry, p. 203.

CHAPTER V

THE OBOES AND BASSOON

EXCEPTING the flutes, the wood-wind instruments of Bach's orchestra trace their ancestry to the 'Bombart' or 'Pommer' family, known to the French, writes Praetorius,[1] as the 'Houtbois', to the English as 'Hoboy', and their discants as 'Schalmei' (*anglice* Shawm). He names six members:

(1) Klein Schalmei,   (4) Tenor Pommer, or Basset,
(2) Discant Schalmei, (5) Bass Pommer,
(3) Alt Pommer,   (6) Gross Doppel Quint-Pommer.[2]

They differed in size, from the smallest, some eighteen inches long, to the largest, a monster nearly ten feet in length. But uniformly they were blown through a double reed, and, pierced with six finger holes, sounded respectively as their lowest notes:

Keys permitted all but Nos. 1 and 2, lengthened, to extend their compass downwards, No. 6 (4 keys) to 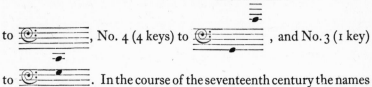, No. 5 (4 keys) to ＿＿, No. 4 (4 keys) to ＿＿ , and No. 3 (1 key) to ＿＿. In the course of the seventeenth century the names

'Pommer' and 'Schalmei' were superseded by the one the instrument has since retained. In France, where they were extensively used, Nos. 1–4 were distinguished as 'haulx bois' or 'hautbois', and their larger relatives (Nos. 5 and 6) as 'gros bois'. The distinction achieved general currency, and thus the 'hautbois' of France became the 'oboe' of Germany, the 'hautboy' or 'hoboy' of England, and the 'oboè' of Italy. In the same period, moreover, two of the hautbois (Nos. 1 and 4) fell into disuse, leaving the discant (No. 2) and alto (No. 3) to become the ordinary oboe and oboe

---

[1] Chap. X.
[2] Nos. 1–5 are illustrated on his Plate XI at p. 96; No. 6 on his Plate VI at p. 160.

d'amore of Bach's orchestra, retaining their traditional pitches of *d'* and *a*. The alto instrument also survived as the oboe da caccia, while the two 'gros bois' became the fagotto and contra-fagotto of modern usage.

The Oboe

In the form in which Bach used it, the oboe made its début at the production of Robert Cambert's *Pomone* in the Paris Salle du Jeu de Paume de la Bouteille on 19 March 1671. Sounding *d'* when its six finger-holes were closed, it was equipped[1] with two keys for *c'* and *d♯'*. Its tube being conical, from the reed downwards, the player could overblow the octave in a compass of fifteen notes (*c'–d'''*), and, excepting *d♯'*, whose small key was sometimes duplicated to suit right and left-handed players, could obtain the chromatic scale by fork-fingering and lipping the reed for the octave. The production of semitones was eased by the duplication of the lowest of the upper set of three finger-holes, two small ones side by side displacing the single larger one. By closing one of them *g♯'* was obtained, by closing both, *g♮'*. But the *g♯'* thus produced was not in perfect intonation, and *a♯'*, got by fork-fingering, was as unsatisfactory. Hence, in 1727, four years after Bach's appointment to the Leipzig Thomasschule, Gerhard Hoffmann,[2] later Bürgermeister of Rastenberg, added keys for those two notes. Bach must have been acquainted with the innovation; for Hoffmann entered ducal service at Weimar a few months after he abandoned it, and left in 1728 on his appointment as 'Cämmerer' at Rastenberg, a town not far from Cöthen. Hoffmann's keys, however, were not approved by makers till after Bach's death: it is reasonably certain that his players were at no time provided with them.

Somewhat earlier than Hoffmann's innovation, the flautist Quantz is credited with the addition of a long key for *c♯'*. But contemporary opinion regarded it with little favour, and, since fork-fingering was impracticable in that position, players were restricted to the only method by which the note could be sounded. By partially depressing the *c♮'* key the *d'* hole was 'shaded' sufficiently to flatten it. Got by this method, however, the note was risky and impracticable save as a passing-note. Bach's scores abundantly disclose his disinclination to use it. It occurs in only thirty-four cantatas—Nos. 2, 17, 24, 25, 28, 29, 30, 31, 34, 35, 43, 44, 45, 50, 57, 68, 70, 86, 94, 104, 110, 113, 128, 129, 136, 148, 149, 152, 157, 169, 171,

---

[1] Certainly before 1688, when an English drawing of a 'French Hoboy' reveals them. Cf. *Encyc. Brit.* (11th edn.), xix. 951.

[2] Gerber, i. 654, gives a considerable account of Hoffmann.

174, 185, and 193. Most often the note is a rapid quaver or semi-quaver, generally occurs in the second oboe part, and only twice (cantatas Nos. 24 (Coro, No. 3), and 157 (Duetto, No. 1)) is a semibreve. In the larger concerted works it occurs with equal rarity—in Parts I and VI of the *Christmas Oratorio*, three movements of the *St. Matthew Passion*, two choruses of the *St. John Passion*, the 'Credo' and final chorus of the *Hohe Messe*, the *Magnificat*, the Masses in G major and G minor, four secular Cantatas (*Aeolus, Hercules*; *Tönet, ihr Pauken*; *Preise dein' Glücke*), and the first Ouverture in D. But this analysis does not fully reveal Bach's aversion. Unsatisfactory and difficult on the ordinary instrument, the note could be got with ease and accuracy as the *e'* and *d♯'* of the low A and B flat oboes. In twenty-three of the 34 cantatas[1] one or other of them was used. There remain only eleven in which Bach adventured the note on the ordinary oboe, never frequently, never emphatically, and sometimes, one supposes, absent-mindedly.

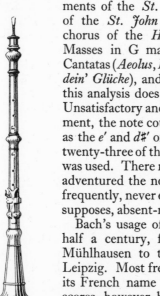

Oboe, 18th cent., length 57 cm.

Bach's usage of the oboe extended over nearly half a century, from the cantatas composed at Mühlhausen to those of his ripest maturity at Leipzig. Most frequently he gives the instrument its French name 'hautbois'. In his Mühlhausen scores, however, he prescribes '2 Obboe' (No. 71), and 'una Oboe' (No. 131). At Weimar and Cöthen he usually adopted the French form, and at Leipzig employed it with rare exceptions, as in cantata No. 95 ('Oboe ordinaria'), the *Hohe Messe* ('3 Oboi'), and *St. John Passion* ('2 Oboe'). Table X establishes his preferential use of the ordinary C oboe: the number of scores in which the compass falls below *c'* is small. In these exceptional cases he either used a B flat oboe, a whole tone below the ordinary instrument, of which specimens are extant, or an alto A oboe, of the same pitch and compass as the oboe d'amore, but with an open bell instead of the closed 'Liebesfuss' of that instrument. At Mühlhausen he seems to have used the C instrument exclusively, and at Weimar generally the oboe in B flat. At Cöthen and thenceforward his use of the C oboe is almost regular. He regarded *c'–d'''*—two octaves and a note—as its normal compass, agreeing therein with J. G. Walther (1732) and Diderot and d'Alembert (1751). In three cases, however,

---

[1] See Table X.

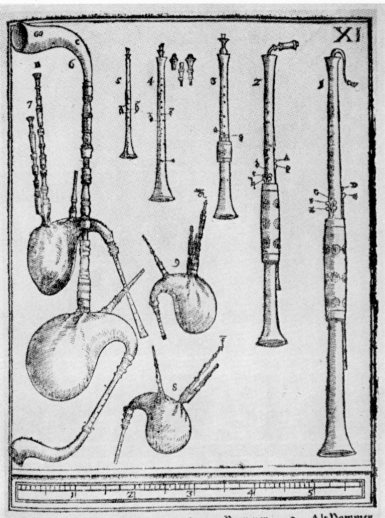

OBOES AND BASSOONS
(*Praetorius*)

he carries it actually to *e'''* (cantatas Nos. 43, 128, 192)! They are all dated *c.* 1735 and probably indicate the services of a particularly expert performer. With the other two instruments he was less exacting, though he carries the B flat oboe to *d'''* in the opening choruses of cantatas Nos. 10 and 35, and the A oboe to *c♯'''* in the first chorus of No. 17.

Normally Bach sets the oboe in the treble G clef. In cantata No. 132, however, written for the Weimar ducal chapel, he adopts an unusual device. The work is in A major, and the oboe part is thus written:

Using the second signature, the player put his oboe at high Cammerton in accord with the organ at Cornett-Ton, a minor third higher. Ordinary transpositions of the oboe part, for the same purpose, occur in cantatas Nos. 31 and 152, both of which were written for the Weimar chapel. At Leipzig, during the Cantorate of Bach's predecessor Kuhnau, the flutes and oboes were at low Cammerton pitch, a semitone below high Cammerton. In his early Leipzig cantata No. 194 Bach was similarly served;[1] otherwise his wood-wind instruments there were at high Cammerton.

Table X appears to indicate an abnormal compass in a number of scores in which the oboe part falls below the range even of the alto instrument. But the table records the extreme range of the instrument in the entire work, and not necessarily its compass in a particular movement. In cantata No. 21, for instance, the compass is given as *bb–d'''*. But the player did not accomplish this upon one instrument exclusively; for the single movement in which his part soared to *d'''* he used the ordinary oboe, and for the rest the oboe in B flat. Bach, however, generally avoided a duplication of instruments. He was careful to write in keys which offered no complications. The three sharps' signature in cantatas Nos. 17, 86, 132, 136, 185, *Aeolus*, and *Preise dein' Glücke* is quite abnormal. A four sharps' signature appears only in cantata No. 45. Three flats are rare (cantatas Nos. 12, 47, 48, 102, 105, 140, 159, *Mein Herze schwimmt im Blut*, and the Mass in G minor).[2] As a general rule, Bach writes for the oboe in C, G, D, F, and B flat, the signature of two flats far outnumbering all others. Moreover, though not only on this account, he avoids changes of tonality in the course of the work, particularly those of a nature to complicate

[1] Cf. Spitta, ii. 324, 677.   [2] Also in the last chorus of both *Passions*.

the task of his players. When they do occur, the modulation is of the simplest. Thus, in general, an initial flat signature indicated a B flat oboe for the entire work, and one in sharps invited the ordinary instrument in C. The players' preferences would guide their selection, but cases in which a single instrument would not suffice for the entire work are few in number, namely:

Work	Oboe in		
	C	B	A
Cantata No. 21	Movement No. 11	Movements Nos. 1–3, 6, 9	..
,, 94	,, 1	.. ..	Movement No. 3
,, 192	,, 1, 2	.. ..	,, 3
,, 193	Movement Nos. 1, 3, 7	.. ..	,, 5
Christmas Oratorio, Pt. I	Movement No. 1	.. ..	,, 7
Hohe Messe	Generally	.. ..	,, 13
Aeolus	Movements Nos. 1, 2, 15	.. ..	,, 3

From its introduction into the Opera orchestra, onwards to the period when it asserted an individuality of its own in the classical Symphony, the oboe, like the violin, was used in pairs, and generally as a ripieno instrument in unison with the violins. Bach observed both conventions. His fidelity to the latter explains the fact that in ten scores the oboe, and especially the second oboe, is invited to descend to g, the lowest note of the violin register:

Cantata	Movement	Instrument	Compass
No. 2	5. Aria	Ob. I, II	g–d'''; g–d'''
,, 16	1. Coro	,, II	g–d''
,, 29	1. Sinfonia	,, I, II	g–c'''; g–a''
,, 43	1. Coro	,, I, II	g–e'''; g–d'''
,, 44	6. Aria	,, II	g–a''
,, 70	8. Aria	,, I	g–b''
,, 76	1. Coro	,, II	g–b''
,, 105	1. Coro	,, II	g–f''
,, 169	1. Coro	,, II	$g\sharp$–a''
Ich bin in mir vergnügt	8. Aria	,, I, II	g–d'''; g–$b\flat''$

These instances cover the whole period of Bach's activity. But his players were certainly never provided with an instrument capable of sounding g, except the taille, whose use here is not in question. The note's presence in these scores is due to the fact that always when it occurs the oboes are in unison with the violins. Writing out their respective parts, Bach, or his copyist, failed to remark that the strings were carrying the oboes out of their depth, till the work was rehearsed and the error was corrected verbally. Cantata No. 169, however, affords an instance of miscorrection. Bach lets the second oboe descend to *g♯* in a passage otherwise unisonous with the second violins. Remarking the oboe's inability, he inadvertently takes the second violins up to *e'*, leaving the oboe part uncorrected:

We might conclude that the Bachgesellschaft edition is in error, did not the original score and parts confirm its accuracy.

Though eighteenth-century custom favoured the use of the oboe in pairs, Praetorius[1] had remarked its agreeableness when three were employed ('drey und drey zusammen'). Bach, but infrequently, endorsed the opinion. His memorandum to the Leipzig Council in August 1730[2] complains that no player was available for the '3 Hautbois oder Taille'. And though the vacancy caused by Meyer's departure[3] was soon filled, Bach must often have been similarly handicapped; for more than two oboes are prescribed only in thirty-two cantata scores, the 'Sanctus' of the *Hohe Messe*, one secular cantata, and three orchestral pieces.[4] We might suppose that he deemed a trio or quartet of oboes inappropriate in any but festal scores but for the fact that over half the cantatas in which they appear are of a ferial character. Certainly the only one (No. 31) in which he employs four oboes is for a festal season, and three are in the scores of all those for Michaelmas. But, in general, the chief consideration that weighed with him was the availability of competent players. For his third oboe he uses, in place of the taille, an oboe da caccia in six cantatas (Nos. 6, 74, 87, 110, 128, 176), the two instruments being identical in pitch (*f–g"*). The taille, however, was a straight-tubed tenor with an open bell, while the oboe da caccia was curved, and, at a later period, had a closed bell similar to that of the cor anglais. Its employment in the six cantatas was evidently due to circumstances of the moment, for four of them (Nos. 74, 87, 128, 176) were performed consecutively (May 15, 19, 29, and June 5) in 1735.[5]

The association of oboes and taille accorded with Praetorius's

---

[1] P. 37.   [2] Cf. Terry, p. 202.   [3] *Supra*, p. 14.   [4] See Table X.
[5] Abnormal low notes in cantatas Nos. 19, 31, 35, 56, 122, 186, are in association with the viola. A Basset oboe is hardly to be inferred there.

'ander [Art] zum Tenor und Alt'. His 'Art zum Bass' is less frequently illustrated in Bach's association of oboes and bassoon. The partnership of the latter exclusively with the ordinary oboe is found in only twelve scores.[1] They exhibit Bach's practice at Mühlhausen, Weimar, and Cöthen. In the later of his Leipzig periods he seems to have been less inclined to treat the oboe-bassoon combination as an integral and separate section of the orchestral body.

The oboe had served a military apprenticeship before its admission to churches and concert-rooms. Military bandsmen in Germany were known as 'Oboisten'; for instance, Bach's younger brother Johann Jakob, whom he designates by this title in the *Ursprung*.[2] In the English Guards the oboe displaced the fife early in the eighteenth century, and its participation in church music apparently dates from the same terminus. For, of Bach's immediate predecessors, only Kuhnau, the most recent, employed it.[3] It is therefore curious that Bach should have seldom put it to orchestral use. It is found in the first and second Brandenburg Concertos, the Violin Concerto (Sinfonia) in D major, and three *Ouvertures*. In the first Brandenburg Concerto a quartet of oboes and bassoon performs in jovial antiphony with the strings. In the second Brandenburg Concerto the single oboe is for the most part ripieno in the first movement, but in the *Andante* and *Allegro assai* plays on equal terms with the other obbligato instruments —flute, violin, and tromba. In the Concerto (or Sinfonia) in D major the two oboes link the strings and 'choir' of drums and trumpets, now supporting the violin concertante, now adding individual touches to the string accompaniment, now swelling the volume of the *tutti* passages. In the Ouverture in C they are treated in another manner. Associated with the bassoon, they form a body to which obbligato passages marked 'Trio' are frequently assigned in the opening movement. As a trio they are scored in the second Gavotte, second Bourrée, second Passepied, and (except-ing the second Bourrée) always to the accompaniment of the strings. Otherwise the two oboes and bassoon double the first violin and continuo. In the more familiar Ouverture in D Bach's subservi-ence to tradition is equally apparent. Except in the middle (fugal) section of the opening movement (in which the two oboes are in unison generally with the two violins), in the *tutti* passages, in those marked *piano* to which they make independent contribution, and in the second Gavotte, where also they unite with the two violins, the oboes throughout are in unison with the

[1] See Table X.   [2] Cf. Terry (3).   [3] Schering, p. 151.

first violin, whose melody they uphold against the voluble 'choir' of drums and trumpets. In the second Ouverture in D, as in the Sinfonia in D, Bach scores for a quartet of oboes and bassoon, and, as in the Sinfonia, gives it considerable individuality and independence, though, for a considerable part of every movement, the four instruments merely double the strings and continuo. But, beyond any other of the *Ouvertures*, Bach here frees himself from the restricting traditions which tied the oboe to the violin, making his quartet of *haut-* and *gros-bois* an equal partner of the 'choirs' of trumpets and strings above and below it. It is probable that the two Ouvertures in D are separated from the one in C by a considerable interval of years. The more modest score of the latter refers it to the Cöthen period. Dörffel associates the two in D with Bach's conductorship of his Leipzig Collegium Musicum. As probably they were written for the Dresden Hofcapelle, to which Bach was admitted as 'Compositeur' in 1736. (He had particularly offered his talents in orchestral music.[1]) Perhaps he may also have written for Dresden the Oboe Concerto attributed to him in Breitkopf's New Year Catalogue for 1764.[2] Since the work is there advertised as 'I', he would seem to have composed others. Handel expressed himself in that form in six still extant. Bach's Concertos have not survived.

No other wind instrument had such constant and varied usage by Bach as the oboe. It is absent from only sixty-two of the extant 198 church cantatas. Of those composed at Leipzig only forty-nine are without it. But as thirty-seven of the number are scored for oboe d'amore or oboe da caccia, the number of oboe-less Leipzig cantatas is actually twelve—Nos. 4, 51, 53, 54, 90, 143, 153, 165, 172, 173, 175, 184. Bach's Leipzig audience was consistently educated to regard the oboe as a natural participant in church music and to appreciate his use of it. It is found almost invariably in the choruses of the cantatas in which it is scored, sustains the *cantus* in their concluding Chorals, and generally accompanies at least one aria, but is rarely found in recitatives or duets. Bach, in fact, esteemed it chiefly as a ripieno instrument. This is particularly evident in his larger scores. Out of twenty-one movements in which it participates in the three Oratorios, only two are arias, and in only one of the two it is 'Solo'. In the two *Passions* it is freely used in the choruses and Chorals, but in only one aria and one recitative. In the *Hohe Messe* and *Magnificat* it is heard only in the choruses.

Bach's restricted usage is explained by the quality of the

[1] Cf. Terry, p. 216. [2] Spitta, iii. 143 n.

instrument, of which Mersenne[1] had written in the previous century: 'It is suited to large functions . . . because it makes a big noise and fine harmony. Indeed, excepting the trumpet, its tone is louder and more violent than that of any other instrument.' Its quality is revealed in the four scores in which Bach prescribes all three varieties of oboe. In cantata No. 80 it is used in the opening chorus and soprano-bass duet only to make prominent the obbligato Choral melody. In No. 110, excepting the opening and closing chorus, it is admitted only to the bass aria, where it strengthens the strings to support the trumpet obbligato. In No. 128 it is excluded from all but the opening chorus and concluding Choral. In No. 147, as in No. 110, it occurs only in those movements in which the tromba is scored, and for the same purpose. Cantata No. 95 affords another illustration. The music, inspired by the thought of death, is of the tenderest texture. Bach therefore prescribes the oboe d'amore. But, at the point where the melody ' Mit Fried' und Freud' ich fahr' dahin ' is introduced into the opening chorus, he marks the oboe parts 'Oboe ordinaria'. It is the only instance of his substitution of one kind of oboe for another in the same movement, and its significance is clear.

The rude sonority of the instrument is exemplified also in a number of arias which Bach scores for three oboes and continuo. They are found in cantatas Nos. 20, 26, 41, 52, 68, 91, 101, 148, and *Was mir behagt*. Their text (exc. No. 148) indicates an assertive, militant, sometimes truculent, mood, which a trio of oboes was qualified to interpret. In No. 20 (bass aria, No. 5) it maintains God's righteousness, and in No. 26 (bass aria, No. 4) expresses contempt of the world's treasure. In No. 41 (soprano aria, No. 2) it hails the New Year. In No. 52 (soprano aria, No. 5) and No. 68 (bass aria, No. 4) it is again defiant. In No. 91 (tenor aria, No. 3) it salutes the majesty of the infant Jesus. In No. 101 (bass aria, No. 4) it utters the harsh sentence of Divine wrath, and in *Was mir behagt* offers to the lord of Weissenfels a ceremonious flourish.

One cannot in the same manner interpret the few arias in which the oboe part is marked 'Solo'. The most familiar is the soprano 'Flösst, mein Heiland' in Part IV of the *Christmas Oratorio*:

> Tell me, Saviour, I entreat Thee,
> Need my soul show dread to meet Thee?
> Must it one day reckoning pay?
> 'Nay,' Thou answ'rest gently, 'Nay!'

Here Bach uses the oboe to produce the answering echo with which text and music make such play. In the alto aria of No. 22,

[1] Vol. v, p. 303.

again, his phrasing of its obbligato clearly illustrates the words '*ziehe* mich nach dir':

Lord Jesus, *draw* me near to Thee!

But generally the texts of the arias in which the oboe has a solo obbligato do not invite pictorial treatment, and to that circumstance the oboe generally owed its selection.[1] In brief, Bach's oboe was not the plaintive, nervous voice of the modern orchestra, but an adaptable ripienist, convenient for yoking with instruments of every *timbre*, and even as a competitor with the trumpets and horns not despicable.

The Oboe da Caccia

More deliberately than the ordinary oboe, the alto Pommer developed into the oboe da caccia of Bach's usage. Longer than its fellow, it assumed, some time in the eighteenth century, a curved form for the player's convenience in handling, an innovation attributed to the brothers Giovanni and Giuseppe Ferlendis, Italian oboists in service at Salzburg.[2] The attribution, if correct, would imply that Bach was only familiar with the instrument in its earlier form, for Giuseppe Ferlendis was not born till five years after his death. In fact, the attribution is problematical. Moreover, the innovation was not found satisfactory; for, since it was impracticable to bore a curved tube, the latter needed to be made in two pieces, of maple or boxwood, glued and bound with leather. But, as the inside of the tube remained rough, preventing good tone, makers speedily reverted to the vertical Pommer form. Meanwhile, the curved instrument's supposed resemblance to an English hunting-horn is alleged to have given it the name 'cor anglais' (*corno inglese*, English horn) it has since retained. There is no record of such an instrument in English usage, and, more probably, 'cor anglais' is a corruption of 'cor anglé', a term appropriate to the early bent specimen. Bach never gives it that designation, though it was so called by Gluck for the performance of his *Alceste* at Vienna on 26 December 1767. It was unknown, however, or at least not in use, when Gluck's opera was repeated in Paris on 23 January 1776; oboes consequently were used. But it was merely a difference of nomenclature: for the Paris substitute was the alto Pommer or 'haute-contre de hautbois'.

Whether curved or straight, the oboe da caccia at Bach's disposal was uniform in compass and mechanism. Its practicable register (with the 'C' key) was f–g'', though he never takes it above $f\sharp''$,

---

[1] The respective movements are indicated in Table X.
[2] *Encyc. Brit.* (11th edn.), xix. 952. Mahillon, i. 231, places them at Strasbourg.

and most often is satisfied with *d"* or *e"*.[1] He uses it generally to the lowest extremity of its (keyed) compass, and in the tenor aria of cantata No. 186 twice takes it down to *d*, each time on an emphatic note. But this was beyond its ability.[2] As with the ordinary oboe, Bach uses the simpler keys: sharp signatures are rare, those of two and three flats the most numerous. The chromatic scale was obtained as on the ordinary oboe, and the key system was similar. By means of 'C' and 'D♯' keys—the latter generally doubled, as on the other instrument—*f* and *g♯* were got. As or the ordinary oboe, too, the bottommost of the three top finger-holes—'G' (*c'*)—was generally duplicated; and, for the same reason, the topmost of the lower three—'F♯' (*b*)—was frequently doubled also. The note *f♯* was as difficult to get as its counterpart *c♯'* on the ordinary instrument. Bach avoids it: it occurs only five times (cantatas No. 65, coro; No. 80, duetto (twice); No. 176, coro; and No. 186, aria), either as a quaver, semiquaver, or demisemiquaver. The bell, as yet, was open, the tone penetrating, mellower and more plaintive than the ordinary oboe's.

The instrument is scored exclusively in Bach's Leipzig music. For, though found in cantata No. 147, performed at Weimar on the Fourth Sunday in Advent (20 December) 1716, the movement in which it occurs (the alto recitative in Part II) is a Leipzig addition to Salomo Franck's original text. It is scored for two *oboi da caccia* and continuo, but the parts exist on paper bearing the watermark of the period 1723–7, while the relative pages of the score indicate the year more precisely as 1727. The cantata thus revised can be attributed to the Feast of the Visitation (2 July 1727).

So, the *St. John Passion* exhibits Bach's earliest usage of this instrument. The work was performed on 26 March 1723, some weeks before his formal induction into the Cantorship, and in the main was composed at Cöthen in circumstances of unsettlement and anxiety. It is strange that he should have introduced himself in a score containing an instrument which till then he does not appear to have used. Nor did he employ it frequently thereafter. It is scored in the *St. Matthew Passion*, the second Part of the *Christmas Oratorio*, in twenty-two church cantatas, but nowhere in his secular music, vocal or instrumental. In his sacred music he introduces it into every variety of movement, and in the arias associates it with all four voices. He uses it infrequently in choruses, in which he often sets one or two ordinary oboes above it. He treats it as non-transposing, puts it in the alto clef in the key of the movement, and leaves the performer to find his notes in the scale of the instru-

---

[1] See Table XI.   [2] The Basset oboe descended to *c*.

ment (f–f''). This satisfied an experienced player. Another might prefer his part to indicate C-scale fingering, leaving the instrument automatically to make the transposition. In that event—since f was equivalent to c'—the part needed to be written a fifth higher than the required notes, and so under a signature of one sharp more or one flat less than the key of the movement. In a single movement (the alto-tenor duet of cantata No. 80) Bach adopts the latter method. Evidently he desired to give the player the utmost assistance, for the oboe part there not only transposes down a fifth, but is also in the soprano G clef. It is the only exception to his normal practice.

The texts with which Bach associates the oboe da caccia reveal its qualities. Vibrant and somewhat metallic, it was appropriate to express grief and tragedy. Its notes breathe the quintessence of anguish in the *St. Matthew Passion*, in which it has no voice until the dark agony of Gethsemane is unfolded (No. 25). It speaks again (Nos. 57 and 58) when Christ stands condemned before Pilate, again at the supreme moment on Calvary (Nos. 69 and 70), and for the last time at the Tomb (No. 75). In the earlier *St. John Passion* its use is more restricted, but its voice is the same. Bach withholds it almost till the end, when the Victim hangs lifeless on the Cross (Nos. 62 and 63). The instrument can also express the emotion of adoration, as in the *Christmas Oratorio*. How tender and serene is the pastoral scene it helps to sketch in the opening Sinfonia of Part II! And what deep emotion underlies the alto's cradle-song (No. 10)!

> Slumber, my dear one, and take Thy repose!
> Soon Thou'lt awaken, new joy to earth bringing.
> Lulled on my breast
> Find comfort and rest
> While to Thee our hearts are singing.

It is significant, too, that the aria texts with which Bach associates it seem, with the rarest exceptions, to come direct from his own devout lips, expressing his unswerving faith and spiritual exaltation. For example, in cantata No. 1:

> With longing and rapture my spirit is yearning,
> With fervour is burning
> To taste here, a mortal, love's heavenly feast.

And in cantata No. 13 (with the addition of two flutes):

> Lord, my weeping, tears, and sighing
> Melt my heart with aching care.
> Ah, dear God, in pity spare!
> Save me, hopeless, doomed, and dying!

Or in cantata No. 16:

> O blessèd Jesu, Thou alone
> My heart's fond treasure art, mine own!

In cantata No. 74:

> Come, come, my heart is open to Thee,
> Thy dwelling-place, Lord, of it make!

And in cantata No. 87:

> Forgive, O Father, our offence!
> Have patience still, nor drive us hence,
> As for Thy grace we pray Thee.

Again, in cantata No. 177:

> I pray Thee, from my deepest heart,
> My foes be all forgiven!
> Lord, bid, this hour, my sins depart,
> And grant me rest in heaven!

In cantata No. 179:

> Sin afflicts me grievously,
> Poison rankles in my being.
> Help me, Jesus, God's dear Lamb,
> Lest in shame to death I come!

And, once more, in cantata No. 186:

> My Saviour worketh only
> In deeds of love and mercy.

Even in arias in which the instrument is set in a larger score it appears to owe its inclusion to the same characteristic in the text. For instance, in cantata No. 65:

> Take me, Saviour, for Thine own!
> See, my heart is laid before Thee!
> All I have is Thine alone,
> Every thought and deed adore Thee.

Again, in cantata No. 74:

> From hell's dreadful slavery
> There's naught can protect me
> But Jesu's dear care.
> His Anguish and Passion
> Have won me salvation:
> Hell's fury I dare!

In cantata No. 180:

> Sun of heaven, shine upon me,
> Thou Who all my being art!

And in cantata No. 183:

> Blessèd Spirit, Comfort rare,
> Guide me ever, lest I err
> And mar my wandering way!

The infrequent Chorals in which the instrument is scored have the same note of personal feeling. Its dark tone explains its use

in cantata No. 6, whose Easter text is based on the evening walk
to Emmaus, and in cantata No. 87, where its colour appropriately
suggests the 'gloom' of which the alto aria (No. 3) sings. In cantata
No. 46 Bach secures an appropriate pastoral atmosphere for the
alto aria, in which the thought of Christ as the Good Shepherd is
uppermost, by giving the accompaniment to two flutes and two *oboi
da caccia*; the latter are in unison and serve as a continuo. They
are used in the same manner, but with different purpose and effect,
in the poignant soprano aria (No. 58) of the *St. Matthew Passion*:

> For love of man the Saviour dieth,
> Who knoweth naught of shame and sin.

In cantata No. 65 they seem intentionally to add a bizarre decoration to the Wise Men:

> Three kings from the east, as long foretold,
> Did come with myrrh and incense and gold.

But these are the instrument's abnormal tones. Bach used it
primarily for a more intimate purpose, and among the instruments
of his orchestra it can be linked with the Blockflöte as the object of
his regard.

The Oboe d'Amore

The opinion may be hazarded that the oboe d'amore (*hautbois
d'amour; Liebesoboe*) owed its construction to the vogue of the
viola d'amore in the earlier half of the eighteenth century. The
traditional association of the violin and oboe families invited it;
for the ordinary viola was already matched with the alto 'A' oboe.
It is at least noteworthy that the appearance of the oboe d'amore
was coincident with the introduction of the viola d'amore to public
notice. Attilio Ariosti was demonstrating the latter's qualities to
London audiences while Bach was in service at Weimar, and published his *Lezioni per Viola d'amore* five years (1728) after Bach's
migration to Leipzig. Between those dates the oboe d'amore also
made its début. The name and locality of its inventor are unknown.
Two examples of it were in the Prince's collection at Cöthen,[1]
and Bach used it uninterruptedly from 1723 onwards, more consistently and adventurously than any of his contemporaries. After
his death it fell into desuetude till Richard Strauss revived it for
his *Sinfonia domestica* in 1904.

In appearance and mechanism the oboe d'amore was the counterpart of the ordinary instrument, excepting the bell, which, being
pear-shaped, with a contracted outlet, produced the veiled tone
that gave the instrument its name. In pitch it stood between the

---

[1] B.-J. 1905, p. 43.

ordinary oboe and oboe da caccia. It sounded the scale *b–b'* and its octave, the chromatic intervals being assisted by duplicated 'F♯' and 'G' finger-holes. The addition of a 'C' key extended its compass downwards and gave it an effective range of *a–b''*. Bach actually takes it down to *g♯* or *g* in six scores—cantatas Nos. 80, 103, 104, 195, the *Christmas Oratorio* (Part I), and the *St. John Passion*. Certainly, there was in use in that period an alto oboe d'amore in G, having an open bell, and Mahillon[1] describes two instruments in the Brussels collection which, though giving the scale *a–a'*, were in the one case almost, and in the other fully, a tone below the normal. Such an instrument would be convenient for use with a high-pitched organ. In that case, however, the part would need transposition, which it does not receive in any of the six scores. The problem would be solved if we could suppose that the natural scale of the oboe d'amore was *a–a'*, and that the 'C' key lowered it to *g*. But that conjecture is refuted by the notation of cantatas Nos. 75 and 76.[2] So, either these abnormal notes were an oversight, or Bach must have prescribed them for an alto 'G' oboe. The former alternative is the more probable. For the oboe is always in unison with a violin, and in the alto aria (No. 4) of the *Christmas Oratorio* (Part I), where *g* is sounded twice, receives a significant quaver rest for the first, but is uncorrected for the second.

With few exceptions,[3] Bach uses the French designation, 'haut-bois d'amour', but in cantata No. 157 names the 'Grand-Oboe', a title English rather than French. He treats *b''* as the upper limit of the instrument's compass, but occasionally takes it up to *c♯'''*—as in cantatas Nos. 49, 145, *O holder Tag*, and *Phoebus und Pan*, and even to *d'''*—as in cantatas Nos. 103, 120, 195, and the *St. Matthew Passion*. But these abnormal notes are generally supported by the violin in unison. Only in the *St. Matthew Passion* and *Phoebus und Pan* is this not the case. The instrument is scored almost universally in sharp keys; those of D and A major are the most frequent; E major is very rare. Only in cantata No. 55 the oboe is used in a flat key (G minor).

Bach's early scores indicate indecision as to the notation of the instrument. The earliest in which it is found are the *St. John Passion* and cantatas Nos. 75 and 76, all three of which were composed at Cöthen in the months immediately preceding his call to Leipzig. In the first the oboe simply doubles another part. But in both cantatas, in which it is obbligato, Bach adopts a com-

---

[1] Vol. ii. 251.   [2] *Infra*, p. 109.
[3] Cantata No. 30, '2 Oboi'; cantata No. 100, '1 Oboe d'Amore'; *St. John Passion*, '2 Oboe'; *Hohe Messe*, '2 Oboi'; *O holder Tag*, '1 Oboe d'Amore'.

plicated notation, which reveals uncertainty as to the experience
of his Leipzig players in handling the new instrument:

Bach here offers alternative clefs and alternative fingering. Since
the instrument sounded a minor third below the ordinary oboe,
the signatures A minor—C minor, E minor—G minor, were
exchangeable. Thus the performer could either play the notes in
the C clef in the scale of the movement, or treat them as transposing down a minor third in the G clef. The alternative notation
had the practical advantage of assisting a player familiar only
with the fingering of the ordinary instrument. This is the only
instance of the kind. But in one of his latest scores (cantata No. 138)
Bach uses the two G clefs in the same way (see p. 110) and for the
same reason. In cantata No. 24 he uses the soprano C clef alone, and
in three scores (cantatas Nos. 95, 145, and 157[1]) the French
violin G clef on the first line; only in the last two the instrument
is transposing. These instances, no doubt, are accounted for by

---

[1] In the parts, but not the score, of No. 157.

particular circumstances. For it was his otherwise almost invariable rule to score the instrument in the ordinary G clef and key of the movement and treat it as non-transposing. To this there are few exceptions—cantatas Nos. 60, 69, 100, 136, 147, the *Magnificat*, and *Schleicht, spielende Wellen*, in which the part is scored in that clef a minor third above the notes as sounded.

Bach's earliest use of the oboe d'amore, as of the oboe da caccia, is discovered in the *St. John Passion*. To establish the statement it is necessary to disqualify the competing claims of two Weimar scores—cantatas Nos. 147 and 163—which, if allowed, would also indicate an earlier year for the instrument's invention than has so far been accepted. The earlier of the two, No. 163, was performed at Weimar on 24 November 1715. But the extant score and parts leave no doubt at all that in its existing state the work belongs to the Leipzig period, when Bach revised its instrumentation.[1] The second cantata, No. 147, has already been examined.[2] Produced at Weimar on 20 December 1716, it was revised at Leipzig eleven years later, and in its existing form was performed there on 2 July 1727. Bach's usage of the oboe d'amore, as of the oboe da caccia, was therefore restricted to his Leipzig period, so far, at least, as his extant music is an indicator.

It is a misfortune that Bach's oboe music is so seldom rendered by the instruments for which he wrote it. The modern oboe accurately replaces neither his ordinary instrument nor the oboe d'amore, for which it is generally made to deputize. The cor anglais, too, is not an entirely satisfactory substitute for the oboe da caccia. And, at the best, we hear only two contrasted oboe voices, whereas Bach coloured his scores with three. He nowhere brings them together in a single movement, but prescribes them all in four cantatas (Nos. 80, 110, 128, 147), in which his apprecia-

---

[1] Cf. Spitta, i. 640.   [2] *Supra*, p. 104.

tion of their contrasted voices is apparent. In these works, as elsewhere, his chief use of the oboe d'amore is as an obbligato instrument in arias. He seldom scores it in simple Chorals, preferring the coarser-toned ordinary oboe to lead the congregational voice. In those of the two *Passions*, in which they are numerous and congregational, the oboe d'amore has no part. In those of the cantatas in which it is found it owes its place to his preference—evident in all six Parts of the *Christmas Oratorio*—to end a work in the same colour-mood as that in which it opens. Only in cantatas Nos. 81 and 168 is this rule broken, and both are peculiar in not having an initial chorus. In choruses, too, the instrument is infrequently used: it is present only in those lightly scored, in which its peculiar *timbre* would not be smothered. The strings, flutes, and occasionally horns, are its associates in them. Only in four movements is it scored with trumpets or trombones, but without an individual voice. In cantatas Nos. 120 and 121 it merely doubles the violins. In No. 195 and *Vereinigte Zwietracht* it is in unison with the flutes.

In the arias, especially those in which it is 'Solo', the individuality of the instrument expresses itself. A collation of them does not permit us to associate it in Bach's mind with a particular mood or pictorial colour. We may suspect that his sensitiveness to verbal suggestion prescribed it in certain arias in which he scores it; for instance, in the bass aria (No. 5) of the *Christmas Oratorio* (Part V):

> Erleucht' auch meine *finstre* (dark) Sinnen.

Or in the soprano aria of No. 94:

> Es halt' es mit der *blinden* (blind) Welt.

Even in the soprano aria (No. 3) of the *Magnificat*:

> Quia respexit *humilitatem* (lowliness) ancillae suae.

But in general Bach used it for its own sake, and, perhaps, because it seemed more decorous in church than its noisier relations. Thus, in his arias, he associates it over a continuo with the flute (cantatas Nos. 9, 99, 125, 195), violoncello piccolo (cantata No. 49), viola da gamba (cantata No. 76), violins and viola in unison (cantatas Nos. 151 and 154), *oboi da caccia* (cantata No. 183 and *Christmas Oratorio*, Part II, No. 10). And often he puts it in unison with the violin (cantatas Nos. 3, 7, 49, 88, 103, 104, 151, 154, 170, *Christmas Oratorio*, Part I, No. 4, *O holder Tag*, and *Preise dein' Glücke*. Still more frequently its peculiarly sensitive *timbre* is sounded by one or two of its kind over a continuo. In an instrumental score Bach evidently regarded it as unsatisfactory. In such a context, with the single exception of the short Ritornello in *Vereinigte Zwietracht*, he uses it not at all in his secular music. Its most familiar employment in an instrumental movement is in the Sinfonia of the *Christmas Oratorio*. He employs it also in those of cantatas Nos. 49 and 76. All three are lightly scored, and the last is an arrangement (for oboe, viola da gamba, and continuo) of the E minor Sonata for two manuals and pedal. Clearly Bach recognized the deficiencies which after his death doomed the instrument to neglect. It perished indeed, with the Church Cantata, which it was admirably fitted to embellish, but whose vogue hardly survived the Master whose genius had exalted them both.

The Bassoon

The Bassoon (*Fagotto, Basson, Fagott*), as has already been stated, was a development of the Bass Pommer, which it superseded because of its more easy handling. Praetorius, in his eleventh chapter, mentions four varieties: the

1. Discant Fagott,
2. Fagott piccolo,
3. Chorist Fagott,
4. Doppel Fagott.

The compasses of Nos. 3 and 4, according to his 'Tabella Universalis',[1] corresponded in their lowest register with those of the Bass Pommer and Gross Bass Pommer, the former sounding ⸬, the latter ⸬. The precise year and locality in which the Chorist Fagott assumed its modern shape and characteristics are not known. In its earlier form it was cut from a single block of wood. But, at some time before Bach's birth (1685), it took the form of two separate parallel tubes conically bored, having a continuous, but bent, air column. Thus, while the compass of the Bass Pommer was retained, the bending of the air column reduced its unwieldy length to a manageable four feet or so. As early as 1532 such an instrument had suggested the jocular name 'Fagott', which the Italians gave it. The French and English preferred the word 'bassoon' to indicate its function as the bass of the wood-wind. Sounded through a double reed, and pierced with eleven finger-holes, three of them controlled by

[1] P. 23. See his Plates VI and XI at pp. 96 and 160.

finger-keys,[1] it made its public début, with the oboe, at the performance of Robert Cambert's *Pomone* at Paris on 19 March 1671,
fourteen years before Bach's birth. Its compass was from

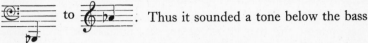 to [music notation]. Thus it sounded a tone below the bass

Pommer, its lowest note *bb,,* being obtained by the action of a key.
Two other keys gave the third and fifth above it, the keyed system

consequently controlling the notes [music notation].

Such was the instrument at Bach's disposal when, in 1708, he
first introduced it into a score (cantata No. 71). Till the last
decade of his career it underwent no important change, and then

acquired a fourth key sounding [music notation] or [music notation].[2] Whether

the new key was at Bach's disposal cannot be determined with
certainty. The note is absent from less than one-quarter of his
scores—cantatas Nos. 63, 75, 147, 155, 160, the *Sanctus* in
D, the Mass in F, and the two secular cantatas *Was mir behagt*
and *Durchlaucht'ster Leopold*. More than half the number belong
to his Weimar and Cöthen periods, and two others (cantatas
Nos. 63 and 75) were not improbably composed before he was
inducted into the Leipzig Cantorate. On the other hand, the note is
found in over twice as many pre-Leipzig scores as those from which
it is omitted (cantatas Nos. 18, 21, 31, 61, 70, 71, 131, 150, 162, 185,
186, the first Brandenburg Concerto, Ouverture in C, and *Mein
Herze schwimmt*). The presence of the note in a score is therefore not
a safe indicator of a finger-key. Greater significance attaches to the
fact that Bach avoids signatures which made its use natural and
frequent. A three sharps signature occurs only in cantatas Nos. 42,
185, and *Durchlaucht'ster Leopold*, and a three flats signature only
in cantatas Nos. 12, 21, 159, and *Mein Herze schwimmt*. Moreover,
his use of the note is always economical. In several scores it is
not sounded more than once or twice, and with the utmost rarity
is sustained for more than a beat or a fraction of a beat. Hence,
even if the *g#,* key was in use earlier than 1751, in which year
Diderot and d'Alembert's *Encyclopédie* specifically mentions it,
Bach's scores cannot safely be adduced in evidence.

[1] Cf. Heckel, p. 13.
[2] The key is on an English bassoon dated 1747, owned by Canon Galpin,
and on another at Brussels (No. 997), dated 1730. Cf. *Encyc. Brit.* (11th edn.),
xix. 952.

Table XIII reveals the fact that Bach rarely takes the bassoon to the limit of its lowest register. In only five scores—cantatas Nos. 31, 42, 69, 71, 155—he carries it below ♪. In the last four of the five he writes an occasional *b,,* or *bb,,,*. But in the first (No. 31) the part frequently descends to ♪, and the instrument used was not the 'Chorist' or ordinary bass bassoon, but the 'Doppel Fagott' described by Praetorius, with a compass descending to ♪. Bach appears to have had little liking for that instrument, whose faulty construction and rattling tone[1] caused its disuse until the late Dr. W. H. Stone revived it. Bach prescribed it also in one of the versions of the *St. John Passion*,[2] but otherwise neglected it.

Bach accepts ♪ as the normal limit of the bassoon's upper compass. Praetorius put it at ♪, and in a few scores —cantatas Nos. 97, 149, and 177—Bach touches that note. In the bass aria (continuo) of cantata No. 42 and the obbligato to the 'Quoniam' (No. 10) of the *Hohe Messe* the bassoon actually reaches ♪, a peak to which Haydn also took it in his 'Military' Symphony in G, sixty-one years later (1794). Bach's notation is practically invariable: with two exceptions he puts the bassoon in the bass clef and treats it as non-transposing. The exceptions are cantatas Nos. 131 and 150. The latter belongs to his Mühlhausen period, but, unlike cantata No. 71, does not appear to have been composed for the Mühlhausen churches. It is apparently a funeral anthem, whose simple score (two violins, bassoon, and continuo) indicates that the musical resources of its locality were slender. No. 131, scored for a violin, two violas, oboe, bassoon, and continuo, supports the same inference. In both the bassoon part transposes, sounding in No. 131 a tone, and in No. 150

[1] Cf. *Encyc. Brit.* (11th edn.), vii. 41.
[2] A 'Continuo pro Bassono grosso' part is mentioned.

a minor third, below the notes as written. The transposition adjusted the instrument's scale to an organ tuned respectively to Chorton (No. 131) and Cornett-Ton (No. 150).

The infrequent use of it in his church music indicates that Bach did not employ the bassoon as a regular continuo instrument. At the same time, its most frequent function in his usage was as a ripienist to support the continuo, in other words, the violone and violoncello. Even so, the occasions on which the instrument was heard at Leipzig were relatively few. Of the thirty-six church cantatas in which it is scored nearly half were composed at Mühlhausen and Weimar. Of Mühlhausen's town musicians we have no information. Weimar's Capelle supported only a single 'Fagottist', and at Cöthen Bach could occasionally command the services of one. At Leipzig ability to play it was not one of the tests to which an aspiring 'Stadt Musicus' was subjected, and, as we learn from Bach himself,[1] the general apprentice of that body was entrusted with it. His experience cannot have been considerable, and his skill was certainly immature. It is not surprising, therefore, that Bach gave him infrequent opportunities, and that, of the scores in which it is obbligato, those of the Leipzig period—cantatas Nos. 42, 66, 143, 149, 177, 197, the *Easter Oratorio*, and *Hohe Messe*—are localized in two cycles of years, 1731–3, 1735–7. Evidently it was only in those restricted periods of his Cantorship that a player competent to undertake an independent obbligato was at his disposal.

It is observable also that Bach makes no use of the bassoon in the secular cantatas composed at Leipzig, and employs it hardly at all in his purely orchestral music. He scores it only in the first Brandenburg Concerto in F[2] and the Ouverture in C, both of which were composed at Cöthen. In both he treats it conventionally. While it reinforces the general continuo, it serves as a particular bass for the wood-wind—three oboes in the Concerto, two oboes in the Ouverture. In the former it belongs so intimately to that section of the orchestral body, that it is silent when only the strings are in action, leaving them to the support of the violone and violoncello. A similar purpose is apparent in the Trios which precede the final and general Menuetto. Each section of the orchestra advances in turn, performs a pirouette, as it were, and retires—first the oboes and bassoon, next the strings (Polacca), and finally the horns with oboes in unison. In the Ouverture, too, Bach's use of the instrument is conventional. In general, the oboes and first

---

[1] *Supra*, p. 9.
[2] The Sinfonia in F is the same music (omitting the Polacca and second *Allegro*), prepared, as is probable, for use in a church cantata.

violins are in unison; consequently, in these passages their continuos are consonant. But in the opening movement the strings are frequently silent while the oboes and bassoon perform an independent trio. In the second Bourrée also the latter play a similar part.

Thus Bach's usage shows no originality in these early works. He treats the instrument as custom prescribed, denying it the individuality with which Handel endowed it in *Saul* (1738) some eighteen years later. There is evidence, however, of experimental development in the instrumental movements of the church cantatas in which the bassoon is scored. The Cöthen standard is apparent in those of the Weimar period—Nos. 12, 18, 21, 31, 150. The Sinfonia or Sonata which opens all of them generally exhibits the bassoon in strict unison with the continuo, or tied to the oboes when they are present. Though composed *c.* 1730, cantata No. 52 shows no advance; its Sinfonia is simply the first movement of the first Brandenburg Concerto in F. Similarly, the Sinfonia of cantata No. 174, a work composed in 1729, exhibits the older pattern; it is the first movement of the third Brandenburg Concerto, to the original continuo of which a bassoon is added to balance the three oboes which augment the original strings. But the Symphonies of cantata No. 42 and the *Easter Oratorio* reveal an advance on the original plan, and both fall within the cycle in which, as has already been suggested, circumstances allowed Bach to be adventurous. In the former the oboes and bassoon do not, as in the earlier scores, merely interpose an occasional trio. They function as a separate body throughout, independent of the strings, and make their own contribution to the thematic texture of the work. The bassoon consequently only seldom reinforces the continuo. In the *Easter Oratorio* it plays an individual part in florid passages distinguished as 'Solo'.

In concerted movements for voices and orchestra Bach's bassoon is usually a continuo instrument. Very infrequently it supports the vocal basses in the concluding Chorals, and the Mass in F affords the only example of its association with them in a general chorus. It is in the arias in which it is obbligato that Bach gives it an individual voice, showing himself as sensitive to its merits as his young contemporary, Haydn. To the duet (No. 4) of cantata No. 42 (1731) it contributes an obbligato in unison with a violoncello, a partnership customary in the Hamburg operas of the period,[1] with which Bach would be familiar. He had in fact employed the device some years before at Cöthen, in the bass aria of *Durchlaucht'ster Leopold*. It does not appear to have pleased him;

[1] Cf. Pirro, p. 237.

at least, these are the only examples of it in his scores. But the obbligato of cantata No. 42 is peculiar on other grounds. It was evidently written to accompany a melody *never actually sounded*, such as Gounod audaciously added to the C major Prelude (No. I) of the *Wohltemperirte Clavier*. The indication 'Choral' which heads the Aria affords the clue. The text is the first stanza of Joh. Michael Altenburg's hymn, and, since it was Bach's custom always to associate a hymn with its melody, we can feel reasonably sure that it was in his mind in the present case. The sympathetic relationship of the obbligato and continuo with the concealed melody is revealed in the bars associated with the first line of the hymn-stanza:

The violoncello-bassoon obbligato in *Durchlaucht'ster Leopold* does not call for particular notice. In cantata No. 66, though Bach's own hand has written 'Bassono oblig.', the instrument merely adds some exuberant ornamentation to the continuo. Its part is written under the oboes in the aria, and Bach styles it 'obbligato' in order to enforce the necessity of its association with them to complete the wood-wind 'choir'.

Cantata No. 143 reveals a definite characterization of the instrument. Composed for the Feast of the Circumcision, it has a festival score—three *corni da caccia*, drums, strings, and continuo. Bach, however, adds a bassoon, not to augment the normal continuo, but to sustain the corno-timpani body, under whose parts its own is written in the score, and with which it is consistently associated. The work is a jubilant setting of Psalm cxlvi, *Lobe den Herrn, meine Seele*, in which the bass aria in particular (with a free bassoon obbligato) affirms God's sovereign majesty—'Der Herr ist *König* ewiglich'. That Bach framed his score in order to offer the salute the word 'König' demanded is evident when we discover a similar combination of instruments in the bass aria 'Quoniam tu solus *Dominus*' of the *Hohe Messe*. In the latter case he employs two bassoons and a single horn. But, as in cantata No. 143, the combination produces the ceremonious atmosphere he thought appropriate. Clearly he endorsed Mattheson's[1] appreciation of the bassoon's 'stately' deportment. M. Pirro[2] interprets its obbligato to the alto-tenor duet in the Michaelmas cantata No. 149:

> Watch o'er me, ye heavenly guardians!
> The shades of night are near.

as a 'voile d'ombre' appropriate to the second line of the text. He is surely in error. The obbligato is by no means sombre in colour, and seems rather a courtly salute to the captains of the angelic band. In the trio (A.T.B.) of cantata No. 150 the obbligato again has pictorial significance. Its stolid rhythm is in contrast with the agitated continuo, an antithesis invited by the text:

> Cedars tall, their branches tossing,
> Rent by tempests fiercely blowing,
> Oft are levelled to the ground.
> Comfort take! For God has spoken.
> Have no fear of hell and Satan;
> On God's Word thy going found!

A more exaggerated pictorial design is assisted by the obbligato to the alto-tenor duet of cantata No. 155:

> Be of courage, hope on ever,
> Let thine own God's will obey!
> When 'tis meet He'll comfort give thee,
> Filling all thy heart with joy.

Here the bassoon wreathes an embroidery of almost delirious

---

[1] 'Der stoltze Basson', he calls it (p. 269).   [2] P. 237.

ecstasy and confident faith, expressed in a formula expressive of both emotions:

The instrument skips with agile fluency, in a manner to astonish the bassoon player quoted by M. Pirro,[1] who in 1708 protested that he had never been asked to play a demisemiquaver! Writing the above passage eight years later, Bach made heavier demands on his Weimar 'Fagottist', Bernhard Georg Ulrich. Indeed, in the literature of the instrument this obbligato is a landmark, alike in Bach's adventurous experimentalism and in the general recognition of its qualities as an orchestral voice.

To the Leipzig period in which Bach was served by an exceptionally competent performer belongs cantata No. 177, in the tenor aria of which the bassoon is paired with a violin concertante over a continuo. To that epoch, too, we refer the exquisitely tender bass aria of No. 197, a wedding cantata. The young couple would not be aware that it was borrowed from the incomplete Christmas cantata *Ehre sei Gott in der Höhe*, where, appropriately, it is a cradle song. In the wedding cantata it is scored for an oboe, two violins (muted), 'Fagotto obbligato', and continuo. The bassoon gives out a rhythmically rocking figure, without meaning in association with the wedding text, but of obvious import in its original context.

The conclusion of this survey is patent and need not be stressed. Bach's scores show increasing independence in handling the bassoon. Accepting at first the conventions of his period, he was not backward in estimating the qualities in it which invited more intimate treatment. Not even his great successors surpassed him in the boldness of his usage of it and the fertility of his experiments. Had he been born into a later generation we cannot doubt that he would have anticipated Mozart's Concerto for the instrument and Beethoven's symphonic treatment of it. But, as in other instances, it was his lot to employ the instrument in forms of expression which from the outset the modern orchestra discarded.

[1] P. 236.

CHAPTER VI

THE STRINGS

FOR his stringed instruments Bach drew from two sources closed to the modern composer. Necessity, or inclination, caused him occasionally, but not frequently, to employ instruments then obsolescent or of lesser vogue. Thus he supplemented the violin with the violino piccolo, the viola with the viola d'amore and violetta, the violoncello with the viola da gamba, the cembalo with the lute. In the second place, the imperfect technique of his players, inadequate to extract full orchestral value from certain instruments then in use, impelled him to invent new ones. Thus he experimented with the violoncello piccolo and Lautenclavicymbel, which have vanished, as the curios of earlier generations. To the instruments of these two categories this chapter is mainly devoted.

The Normal Strings

It may be stated broadly that the louder-voiced violin family began to oust the gentler viols when music sought a public platform in churches and concert-rooms. Their supersession was not completely accomplished in Bach's period, though their supremacy had been threatened since the early seventeenth century. Praetorius[1] devotes but thirteen lines to the 'Violin de Bracio', excusing himself from a fuller exposition on the ground that the subject was familiar ('jedermänniglichen bekandt ist'). Mersenne, eighteen years later, wrote ecstatically of 'le Violon . . . le Roy des instrumens',[2] of which Jacques Cordier, Queen Henrietta Maria's dancing-master, was already a famous exponent. In Italy, Giovanni Legrenzi was writing sonatas for it some twenty years before Bach was born. Tommaso Albinoni was eloquent in the same art in the same period, and Arcangelo Corelli published his first set of sonatas for two violins two years (1683) before Bach came into the world. In Germany the instrument was also in vogue. Johann Jakob Walther, formerly of the Dresden Capelle, published his *Scherzi di violino solo* in 1676, and twelve years later (1688) his *Hortulus chelicus, uni violino, duabus, tribus et quatuor subinde chordis simul sonantibus*. England was in no wise behind her contemporaries. William Young published his 'Sonatas' at Innsbruck in 1653. Orlando Gibbons, John Jenkins, William Lawes, and, later, Purcell were pioneers in the same field. These names are signifi-

[1] Chap. 22.   [2] Bk. III. 177.

cant; they indicate the growing literature of the instrument when
Bach was first attracted to it at Celle and Weimar. With the works
of Legrenzi and Albinoni he was early familiar, and of those of
Antonio Vivaldi, a younger pen, he made extensive use.

Praetorius names the following members of the violin family in
his 'Tabella Universalis':[1]

1. Klein Discant-Geig:

2. Discant-Geig Violino:

3. Tenor-Geig:

4. Bass-Geig de Braccio:

5. Gross Quint-Bass:

No. 1 is Bach's violino piccolo, tuned a tone higher. No. 2 is
the present-day violin. No. 3 is the viola of Bach's scores and
modern usage. No. 4 (2) is the violoncello as he employed it,
tuned then as it is to-day. No. 4 (1), the true tenor of the family,
has unfortunately, and somewhat unaccountably, passed out of
general use. Tuned originally a fifth below the alto (No. 3), and with
a length of string some twenty inches from nut to bridge, it filled a
distinctive place in the gamut of the violin family. Mr. Hayes[2]
justifiably deplores its loss, as having robbed both the chamber
quartet and the larger orchestra of a distinctive voice. The two
viole da braccio Bach uses in the sixth Brandenburg Concerto
appear, from their compass, to have been the alto (No. 3) rather
than the true tenor (No. 4). For his continuo bass he generally
used the six-stringed violone, a late survivor of the ancient viols,

tuned thus ⎯⎯⎯ and having a fretted finger-board.[3] There is

no positive evidence that he employed the contrabass (No. 5). But
the score of *Was mir behagt* prescribes a 'Violone grosso'.[4]

[1] P. 26. See his Plate XXI, at p. 124.   [2] P. 204.
[3] See Praetorius, Plate VI, at p. 160.   [4] Cf. *supra*, p. 20.

The violin family provided the nucleus of Bach's orchestra. And yet, as has been made clear in an earlier chapter,[1] its players were generally casual amateurs or elder *alumni* of the Thomas-schule. From only nine church cantatas[2] and a single secular cantata[3] is the full quartet of strings absent.[4] All of them, except *Ehre sei Gott*, are of the pre-Leipzig period. There are relatively few of his concerted scores in which the violin does not also receive an obbligato or solo part. But the frequency with which he sets the violins in unison over the continuo also carries the suspicion that he often lacked a player of adequate ability as an obbligatist. Yet the inference is not invariably well founded. Bach, no doubt, had good reasons for assigning the obbligato of the alto aria in the *St. Matthew Passion*, 'Können Thränen meiner Wangen' (No. 61), to the whole body of violins in unison, whereas in two other movements a first violin is solo. In the *Hohe Messe*, again, the player to whom he entrusted the *obbligati* of the 'Laudamus te' and 'Benedictus' could, no doubt, have undertaken that of the 'Agnus Dei', had Bach desired. On the other hand, the obbligato of the 'Benedictus' is only by assumption given to the violin. Professor Tovey expresses 'grave suspicions of violin music that never goes below the compass of the flute', and fails to detect any unmistakable violin figure in it, observing that 'any of Bach's flute solos in minor keys will present constant resemblance to its turns of phrase'.

The weakness of Bach's violins in numbers and technique is indicated occasionally by his direction to the violas to unite with the violins in an obbligato.[5] A similar deficiency in the violas is in three cases[6] suggested by the unison of violins and violas in a part written in the alto C clef. But here again the deduction is qualified by the fact that the violin obbligato to the bass aria of cantata No. 178 is in the alto clef. In the bass aria of cantata No. 62 the violins and viola are directed to play 'sempre col Continuo': their part, in the score, stands actually in the bass clef!

A collation of Bach's violin *obbligati*[7] reveals his disinclination to use the instrument in its highest register. In this he obeyed the conventions of his period. Writing in 1756, the sixth year after

---

[1] *Supra*, p. 9.
[2] Nos. 18, 106, 118, 150, 152, 158, 160, 189, and *Ehre sei Gott* (incomplete).
[3] *Amore traditore.*   [4] The score of No. 118 puts it in a class apart.
[5] Cantatas Nos. 61, 80, 83, 85, 156, 166, 172, 174, and *Vereinigte Zwietracht.*
[6] Cantatas Nos. 24, 140, Mass in A.
[7] In cantatas Nos. 2, 13, 26, 29, 30, 32, 36, 39, 51, 57, 58, 60, 66, 74, 76, 83, 84, 86, 97, 101, 103, 108, 117, 120, 129, 132, 137, 139, 147, 148, 157, 158, 160, 171, 177, 182, 184, 197, the *Christmas Oratorio, Easter Oratorio, Hohe Messe*, Mass in F, Mass in A, *St. Matthew Passion, Weichet nur, betrübte Schatten, Ich bin in mir vergnügt, Aeolus, Schleicht, spielende Wellen, Was mir behagt.*

Bach's death, and the year of Wolfgang's birth, Leopold Mozart[1] states that there were in use two ways of holding the violin, 'sideways against the breast' ('an der Höhe der Brust seitwärts'), or under the chin and on the shoulder. In the former position only four notes above the open string would be within the easy compass of the player, since the left hand needed to maintain a firm un-shifting grip. So held, the effective range of the instrument would be *g–b''*. Even expert professional players who adopted the other position apparently used its opportunities with conservative caution. The 'half-shift', or second position, is said, probably inaccurately, to have been the belated invention of Nicola Matteis, a London player at the period of Bach's birth; it advanced the compass of the violin to *c'''*. The ascription is contested, but the material point is that Bach learnt the instrument at Eisenach when its compass was thus restricted. In the *obbligati* already mentioned, and also in the Sonatas, he takes the instrument comparatively rarely beyond the 'little finger' note *d'''*. Only in eleven scores[2] it soars above *e'''*, and the seventh position (to *a'''*) is required only in the *Hohe Messe* and Violin Concerto (Sinfonia) in D major. But, if their compass is generally moderate, Bach's violin parts demand advanced technique; his double-stopping is frequently of the most intricate complexity, requiring from the executant powers of the highest order. If, as is probable, Bach wrote no violin music he could not play himself, we can judge his ability to have been exceptional. Probably he disliked the modern Italian inward-curving bow, and preferred the older arched bow, which facilitated the player's execution, since it permitted him to vary tension by the pressure of the thumb on the hairs.[3]

Bach's particular affection for the viola is stated by Forkel.[4] Of his orchestra it was a normal member, and from the scores of only six cantatas[5] is it omitted. His memorandum to the Leipzig Council in 1730[6] demanded four viola players for the proper accompaniment of church music. Since he drew them from amateur sources, he cannot regularly have had that number at his disposal. Indeed, he rarely scores more than one viola part. There are two in cantatas Nos. 4, 12, 31, 54, 61, 131, 172, 182, *Hercules*, and the sixth

[1] P. 53.

[2] To *f'''* in the Concerto I in A minor, Fugue in G minor, and Solo Sonata in G minor; to *f♯'''* in the *Hohe Messe* ('Benedictus') and Cantata No. 171 (soprano aria); to *g'''* in *Aeolus* (soprano aria), Solo Sonata in C major, Partita in D minor, Cantatas Nos. 101 (tenor aria) and 158 (soprano-bass duet); and *a'''* in the *Hohe Messe* ('Laudamus te') and Sinfonia in D major for violin and orchestra (B.-G. XXI (1)).

[3] Cf. B.-J. 1904, p. 113; Hayes, pp. 202–4.   [4] P. 108.

[5] Nos. 118, 150, 158, 160, 189, and *Ehre sei Gott*.   [6] Terry, p. 201.

Brandenburg Concerto; three in cantata No. 174 and the third
Brandenburg Concerto; and four in cantata No. 18 only. As an
obbligato instrument he seldom employed it by itself: its part is
'solo' only in the tenor aria of cantata No. 5, where it gives the
murmurous effect of deep waters.[1] Bach's inclination to put the
violins and violas in unison has been referred to above, and to
the examples given there may be added the alto aria of cantata
No. 132, where the instrument is in unison with a 'solo' violin.
Another curious example is in the alto aria of cantata No. 170,
where the violas serve as the bass for an organ obbligato.

Bach's violoncello was normally a continuo instrument.[2] For
obbligato purposes he preferred the violoncello piccolo, whose
usage is explored in a later section of this chapter. Infrequently,
however, he employed the ordinary violoncello in that manner.
The instances occur in only seven scores and fall into two groups:

(a) Pre-Leipzig

Work.	Movement.	Date.	Occasion.	Compass.
Cantata No. 163	3. Aria (B.)	24 Nov. 1715	Trinity XXIII	$e,-g'$
Cantata No. 70	3. Aria (A.)	6 Dec. 1716	Advent II	$c,-a'$
Durchlaucht'ster Leopold	7. Aria (B.)	29 Nov. 1718?	Prince Leopold's birthday	$d\sharp,-f\sharp'$

(b) Leipzig

Work.	Movement.	Date.	Occasion.	Compass.
Cantata No. 42	4. Duet (S.T.)	1 Apr. 1731	Easter I	$b\sharp,,-g'$
Cantata No. 172	5. Duet (S.A.)	13 May 1731	Whit-Sunday	$c,-f'$
Cantata No. 56	2. Recit. (B.)	30 Sept. 1731	Trinity XIX	$d,-d\flat'$
Cantata No. 188	3. Aria (A.)	14 Oct. 1731	Trinity XXI	$c,-e'$

The *obbligati* call for little comment. They are generally *cantabile*,
without chording or double stopping, and their compass in the
higher register falls short of that of the violoncello piccolo by
about a fifth, i.e. of a fifth string. Only in cantata No. 56 the
violoncello reveals a pictorial design. 'Our journey through the
world', the voice declaims, 'is as one fares at sea. Affliction, stress
and woe, like billows our destruction threaten, and day by day to
shipwreck beckon.' The obbligato's curving periods outline a
heaving surface, too regular, however, to menace shipwreck. For
Bach had in mind the stanza's concluding promise of safe harbour-
age in the heavenly haven-home. In cantata No. 188 the obbligato
merely reinforces the organ continuo.[3]

---

[1] Bach appropriately repeated the subject in the opening chorus of cantata
No. 7.

[2] C. P. E. Bach remarks (*Versuch*, Pt. II, p. 3): 'The most perfect accompaniment for a solo . . . is afforded by a keyed instrument along with a violoncello.'

[3] The incomplete cantata *Ehre sei Gott* contains the fragment of an aria having
a violoncello obbligato.

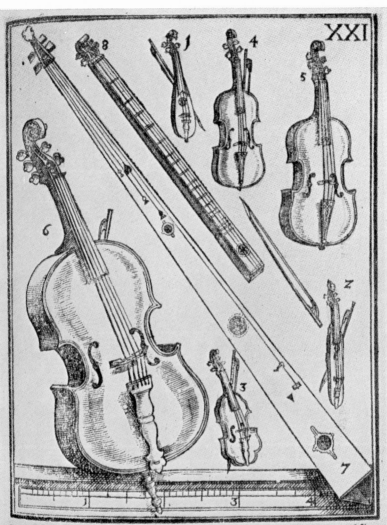

XXI

VIOLINO PICCOLO AND OTHER STRINGS
(*Praetorius*)

The chief interest of the Table is in the third column, which indicates that, after an interval of fifteen years, Bach wrote a violoncello obbligato for his Easter cantata in 1731; that in the course of the following six months he employed the instrument three times for that purpose; and, after 14 October 1731, ceased altogether to use it in that way. He had, in fact, on the previous Sunday (7 October) performed his first obbligato for the violoncello piccolo, which thenceforward he used exclusively for the purpose.

The Violino Piccolo

It is evident that in 1731 Bach was in a highly experimental mood. The alleviation of his circumstances since the arrival of Johann Matthias Gesner as Rector in September 1730,[1] and some abatement of his pedagogic duties, may partially account for it. But, whatever the cause, we find him at that period decisively turning his back on obsolescent instruments—the viola d'amore, viola da gamba, and lute—which till then he had been willing to employ, and bringing forward others long neglected or of recent invention. The series of organ *obbligati* which decorate his church cantatas in that year[2] also seem to indicate an experimental mood which bore fruit in the trial of more than one new instrument.

Another indication of Bach's peculiar alertness at that period is furnished by his introduction of the violino piccolo into a cantata score. Leipzig heard it, apparently for the first time during his Cantorship, on the Tenth Sunday after Trinity (29 July) 1731, again on the Twenty-seventh Sunday after Trinity (25 November) 1731, and thereafter, for the last time, some nine years later.[3]

The violino piccolo, as has already been stated, was the Klein Discant-Geig, described by Praetorius as the smallest member of the violin family. Though of lesser size, it exhibited the parts and proportions of the ordinary violin, in which respect it differed

from the 'pochette' or 'kit'. Praetorius gives its tuning as ,

a fourth above the ordinary violin, an octave above the viola. This appears to be generally accepted.[4] Mr. E. J. Payne, however, in the second edition of 'Grove'[5] gives its stringing as 'a minor third higher than the ordinary violin, its highest string having the same pitch as the highest string of the Quinton'.

On the evidence of Bach's manuscripts Mr. Payne is correct.

[1] Cf. Terry, p. 207.   [2] *Infra*, p. 171.   [3] See Table XIV.
[4] For instance, in Hayes, p. 211; Grove (3rd edn.), v. 525; and Dolmetsch, p. 455.   [5] Vol. iv, 813.

For in the first Brandenburg Concerto and in the soprano-bass duet of cantata No. 140, the two scores in which it has an independent part, it sounds a minor third higher than the written notes, evidently for the convenience of a player accustomed to the fingering of the ordinary violin; its bottom note consequently

sounded 🎼 though written 🎼 .[1] The compass

column of Table XIV indicates that Bach did not use its upper register conspicuously beyond that of the ordinary violin, and the closer approximation of their tunings partially explains the fact.

Violino piccolo, 18th cent., extreme length 55 cm.

Bach's use of the violino piccolo was infrequent and intermittent. It is found in only four scores, and in but two of them has a distinctly independent part. In the opening chorus of cantata No. 96 it is in unison with the flauto piccolo, for a reason suggested in the section on that instrument.[2] In the tenor aria of cantata No. 102 it is prescribed as alternative to the traverso. But it is obbligato in the soprano-bass duet of cantata No. 140, one of Bach's most dramatic scores. The duet is a dialogue between Christ and the Soul:

Soul. When com'st Thou, my Lord?
Christ. Behold Me, thine own!
Soul. Come, Jesu!
Christ. I seek thee, for thee am I yearning.

Round these tender words the obbligato wreathes an embroidery of spiritual exaltation which such a text always inspired in Bach. In the Brandenburg Concerto No. I, in F, the violino piccolo is definitely obbligato only in the *Adagio* and following *Allegro*, and is silent in the two Trios and Polacca. It is improbable that Bach scored the Concerto to suit the equipment of the. Cöthen Capelle, which did not possess a violino piccolo during his period of office. He had left it at least three years before it acquired an instrument, dated 1726, from Gottlieb Hoffmann.[3]

Bach's restricted usage of the violino piccolo indicates its

[1] In the opening chorus of cantata No. 140, in which it is col violino I, the part once touches *a*; an oversight.
[2] *Supra*, p. 66.   [3] B.-J. 1905, p. 38.

declining vogue: in fact, it hardly survived his own career. Writing in 1756,[1] Leopold Mozart gives the reason. 'Whereas', he remarks, 'concertos were once written for the instrument, nowadays it can be dispensed with, since parts that formerly required it can now be played in the higher positions on the ordinary violin' ('Man spielet alles auf der gewöhnlichen Violin in der Höhe').[2]

The Violetta

In 1724, again in 1727, and for the last time in 1734, Bach employed an instrument called by him 'Violetta'. It is neither prominent nor indispensable in the three scores in which it is prescribed. In cantata No. 16 it is alternative to an oboe da caccia in the obbligato accompanying the tenor aria. In cantata No. 157 it takes the part of, and is indistinguishable from, the viola in the string accompaniment to the tenor recitative, and in the concluding Choral is in unison with the vocal tenors. Along with the violins, it provides a quasi-bass foundation for the soprano aria in *Preise dein' Glücke*. That is the extent of Bach's employment of it.

What was the instrument thus designated? Its name, the alto clef associated with it, the situation of its part in the score of cantata No. 157, and the general character of the music allotted to it, all indicate a stringed instrument of viola range. In the eighteenth century 'violetta' could denote the ordinary viola (Bratsche).[3] But it cannot have that meaning in Bach's scores, since he prescribes them both together in cantata No. 16 and *Preise dein' Glücke*. The viola d'amore also was occasionally indicated by the name. But it, too, must be ruled out; Bach would hardly call the same instrument 'viola d'amore' on 26 March 1723 (*St. John Passion*) and 'violetta' on 1 January 1724 (cantata No. 16). Again, in the sixteenth and seventeenth centuries the treble viol was sometimes styled 'violetta'. But its tuning gave it approximately the compass of the violin, a fact which, along with the disuse of the smaller viols in Bach's period, puts it out of consideration in the present case. Canon Galpin has suggested tentatively[4] that Bach's 'violetta' was identical with the viola pomposa, whose invention is incorrectly attributed to him. But, since the viola pomposa was known to and used by his contemporaries under that name, he is not likely to have given it another. Nor do the diminutive 'violetta' and the adjective 'pomposa' seem appropriate to the same instrument. On the other hand, Herr Carl Engel draws attention to a Concerto by Joh.

---

[1] P. 2.   [2] But the tone-colour would differ.
[3] Mr. F. T. Arnold instances Porpora's MS. violoncello concerto with quartet accompaniment. Mr. Hayes (p. 182) gives others.
[4] *Music and Letters*, Oct. 1931.

Gottlieb Graun scored for 'Violino pomposo o Violetta concertata',
or, as in a duplicate MS., for 'Violino o Viola Pomposa concertata'. The compass of the part for the instrument bearing the
alternative names Violino pomposo and Viola pomposa is g–$c\sharp'''$,
which indicates a violin tuning incongruous with Bach's violetta
parts. At the same time, the Concerto proves that the violetta, of
one kind, was interchangeable with the viola pomposa.[1]

The correct interpretation is perhaps afforded by Walther,[2]
who describes the violetta as 'a medium violin' ('eine Geige zu
Mittel-Partei'). He adds that the alto viola da gamba also bore
the name. Either would fit Bach's violetta parts, whose character
indicates that the unfamiliar instrument was employed as a convenience, not as an embellishment. In all three works in which it is
employed it raises merely an alternative voice. Certainly its
obbligato to the tenor aria of cantata No. 16 is written on a
separate sheet inscribed 'Violetta'; but the oboe part also has it.
Its inclusion in the score of cantata No. 157 was an afterthought:
its part is on a separate sheet in the alto clef, but the score indicates
only traverso, oboe, violin, and continuo. In *Preise dein' Glücke*,
though the score prescribes 'Violini e Violetta' in the soprano aria,
the ordinary viola part contains its notes, without any indication
corresponding to that direction. Since Bach was able to prescribe
it over the decade 1724–34, it was evidently permanently accessible,
probably among the instruments of the two churches. It may have
conveniently supplied one of Bach's amateurs whose 'Bratsche'
was temporarily out of commission.

The Viola d'Amore

Having regard to the regularity of his routine, Bach's employment of certain stringed instruments then in declining vogue was
infrequent and irregular. After scoring the violino piccolo in 1721
he made no further use of it till 1731, and allowed nearly as long an
interval to elapse before he employed it again. Of the viola da gamba
his use was as economical: at Leipzig he scored it every second
year, and after 1729 not at all. The viola d'amore he used once at
Weimar, apparently not at all at Cöthen, at Leipzig in 1723 for the
St. John Passion, again in 1725 for *Aeolus*, once more for *Schwingt
freudig euch empor* some five years later, and thereafter not at all.
We cannot suppose these infrequent scores to have been the only
ones Bach deemed appropriate to the instruments he so sparingly
used. Rather, we must infer, they indicate the intermittent periods
when competent players were available. For all of them he was

[1] *Zeitschrift f. Musikwissenschaft*, Oct. 1931, p. 58.   [2] P. 637.

dependent at Leipzig upon persons outside his professional body;
the only stringed instruments in which candidates for admission
to it were tested were the violin and 'der grosse Violon', by which
the contrabass is probably indicated.[1]

The viola d'amore appears to have been originally a smaller
form of the viola bastarda.[2] Though he
does not mention the viola d'amore by
name, Praetorius[3] speaks of the vibratory
strings, which were its characteristic, as
being a contemporary English invention.[4]
The instrument so named, strung with wire,
but without sympathetic strings, was a
novelty in 1679, however, and also, as recorded by Burney, nearly forty years later
(1716).[5] Its vogue, more established in
Germany than elsewhere, was advanced by
Attilio Ariosti, who published his *Lezioni
per Viola d'amore* in 1728, having introduced
the instrument to a London audience sixteen
years earlier. Vivaldi wrote a concerto for
viola d'amore and lute towards the end of
his life (*ob.* 1743). Bach's use of it falls
between those two boundaries.

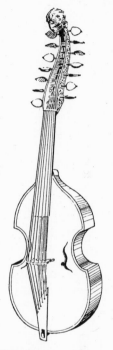

The viola d'amore exhibited the qualities
both of the viols and violin. It was akin to
the former in its possession of more than
four strings, in its non-uniform tuning, in
the structure of its body, and in the 'flame'
type of its sound-holes. On the other hand,
it was bowed and held like a violin, and its
finger-board was not fretted. But, unlike
both, it was fitted with sympathetic strings

Viola d'amore, 18th cent.,
extreme length 82 cm.

of fine brass or steel, which passed from the tail-piece through small
holes drilled in the lower part of the bridge, and thence under the
finger-board to pegs or wrest-pins in the peg-box, which the head
of a blindfold Cupid usually surmounted. The sympathetic strings,
responding to the vibration of the ordinary strings, produced an
ethereal silvery ring which won it the sentimental name it bears.
The suggestion that its name is a corruption of 'viol de Moor',

---

[1] Cf. *Archiv f. M.*, pp. 44, 45; Quantz, p. 219.
[2] The viola bastarda is figured in Praetorius's Plate XX at p. 132.
[3] p. 47.
[4] John Playford (1661) attributes it to Daniel Farrant.
[5] Cf. Dolmetsch, p. 452; Hayes, p. 215; Mahillon, i. 321; Grove, v. 515.

indicating an Eastern origin, seems fantastic. The Arab 'Kamanga rûmî', however, was fitted with similar sympathetic strings.[1]

The gut strings on the finger-board were uniform neither in number nor tuning. Extant examples at Eisenach, Brussels, Berlin, and elsewhere, suggest that six strings were most common, tuned as follows:

 (d-d″)

A seven-stringed specimen (No. 36) in the Bach Museum at Eisenach carries the compass down a fourth:

 (a,-d″)

Though the finger-board, relatively to the strings upon it, was not so long as the ordinary viola's, it is probable that upon instruments thus tuned the player could touch the octave of the top string,

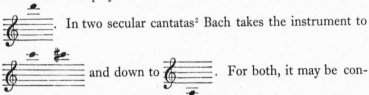. In two secular cantatas[2] Bach takes the instrument to

and down to . For both, it may be con-

cluded, a six-stringed instrument, tuned as above, was employed. Cantata No. 152, composed at Weimar, was served by an instrument tuned a tone higher than the seven-string viola at Eisenach:

This is inferred from the chords of the opening Concerto:

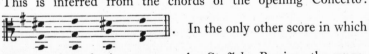. In the only other score in which

Bach employs the instrument—the *St. John Passion*—the movements in which it participates are in a flat key, and the compass extends *f–c‴*. This would be playable on a normally strung instrument, or upon one strung a tone higher than the seven-stringed specimen at Eisenach, raising the top string (*chanterelle*) to *e″*, a tuning that possibly required the player in that work to use the first position in only three bars in one movement.

[1] Cf. Mahillon, i. 188.   [2] See Table XVI.

The infrequent examples of his use of the viola d'amore in-adequately buttress Dr. Curt Sach's assumption[1] of Bach's 'love' for the instrument, and Schweitzer's opinion,[2] that only in the *St. John Passion* need its loss be deplored, cannot be confidently contested. In cantata No. 152, the only church cantata in which it is scored, it sustains the tenor part in an instrumental quartet (flute, oboe, viola d'amore, viola da gamba) in the opening Concerto, is in unison with the other instruments in the soprano-bass duet, and is obbligato in the soprano aria, a lullaby over the infant Jesus of the utmost beauty and tenderness, to which the 'tender and languishing' quality Mattheson found in the instrument is peculiarly appropriate.[3] In *Aeolus* again it is scored along with a viola da gamba in the tenor aria, where its part is in the soprano G clef. Bach evidently desired to suggest the languorous atmo-sphere of the 'frische Schatten' invoked by Zephyrus:

> Shady hollows, ye're my pleasure!
> Can I see you droop and wither?
> Come, reject the cruel smart!
> Stir your leaves to life, dear branches!
> Throw sad glances
> On my sorrow-laden heart!

The soprano aria of the secular cantata *Schwingt freudig* (viola d'amore and continuo) was used by Bach on at least four occasions, for three of which he retained the original line of the text:

> Auch mit gedämpften schwachen Stimmen
> (With notes all hushed and distant sounding).

The score of one of the three is lost, but in it, as in the other two, no doubt, he painted literally the word 'gedämpften'. In cantata No. 36 he gives the obbligato to a *muted* violin, and in the secular cantata similarly entitled employs a viola d'amore in the treble clef. His purpose is obvious when it is observed that in the secular cantata *Die Freude reget sich*, in which he used the movement a fourth time, he changed the words and substituted the traverso for the viola d'amore.

Of the two movements in the *St. John Passion* in which the viola d'amore is prescribed, only the tenor aria (No. 32) was not in the original version performed in 1723. The bass arioso that precedes it also was added for a later occasion.[4] In both Bach employs two *viole d'amore* and puts their parts in the treble clef. The two movements follow the narrative of the scourging of Jesus, and the

---

[1] Sachs (3), p. 11.   [2] Vol. ii. 431.
[3] 'Die verliebte Viola d'Amore . . . führet den lieben Nahmen mit der That und will viel *languissantes* und *tendres* ausdrücken' (p. 282).   [4] *Infra*, p. 143.

instrument contributes its plaintive tone to the poignant situation. In the tenor aria, accompanying the rhythmic figure of scourging, its melodic lines seem to sketch the rainbow of forgiveness of which the text speaks:[1]

> God's rainbow light of grace is glowing,
> To show thee pardoned in His sight.

The silvery violas increase the ethereal beauty of both movements so charged with emotion.

The term 'obsolescent' applied to the viola d'amore needs qualification, perhaps withdrawal: it survived Bach's usage of it and is still occasionally scored by composers. Carl Stamitz (1746–1801), one of the famous Mannheim orchestra, was a noted performer on it. Meyerbeer introduced it into *Les Huguenots* (1836). Karl Zoeller (1840–89), bandmaster of the Second English Life-guards, was the author of an authoritative treatise on it. Louis van Waefelghem (1840–1908), also well known in London, devoted himself to its study and revival. Richard Strauss employed it in his *Sinfonia domestica* (1904), and Paul Hindemith wrote a concerto for it in 1928. In America Charles Martin Loeffler used it in his symphonic poem *The Death of Tintagiles* (1897).

The Viola da Gamba

The ancient family of the consort viols, or *viole da gamba*,[2] had five members: the

1. High discant (Pardessus de viole),
2. Discant (Dessus de viole),
3. Alto (Haute-contre),
4. Tenor (Taille), and
5. Bass.

Of these No. 5 was the viola da gamba *par excellence*. Until the period of Bach's birth (1685), it was a six-stringed instrument, tuned, after the manner of the lute, in fourths, with a midway interval of a third:

Marin Marais and Sainte-Colombe are stated to have added a seventh string and to have increased the sonority of the

---

[1] Cf. Schweitzer, ii. 181.   [2] See Praetorius, Plate XX, at p. 132.

VIOLA DA GAMBA, VIOLA BASTARDA, AND LYRA DA BRACCIO
(*Praetorius*)

three lower ones of the six by strengthening their texture.[1] Thus equipped, the instrument, though about the size of the violoncello, exceeded it in compass. Its top string was tuned a fourth higher, and, owing to its greater length and more delicate texture, was more extended in its upper register. It lacked the volume of the violoncello, but its tone was more delicate, its chords richer and more varied, and its fretted finger-board more assistant to the player's accuracy. France preferred the seven-stringed tuning. England and Germany were more conservative in their liking for the

six-stringed variety, tuning down the lowest string to ,

however, when the key of the composition required the change. Bach's scoring demands a seven-stringed gamba only in the *St. Matthew Passion* and the Gamba Sonata in D. Elsewhere he was content with the six-stringed instrument at its normal tuning, though in cantata No. 76, the *St. John Passion*, and *Aeolus*, he

takes down the lowest string to .

The classic period of the viola da gamba was in the seventeenth and early eighteenth centuries, when it attracted players whose technique excelled that of the performers on the violin: in England, Alphonso Ferrabosco (*ob*. 1628), John Cooper (*ob*. 1627), Tobias Hume (*ob*. 1645), William Brade (*ob*. 1630), John Jenkins (*ob*. 1678), and especially Christopher Simpson (*ob*. 1669); in France, Marin Marais (1656–1728), Antoine Forqueray (1671–1745) and his son, Jean Rousseau (fl. 1678–87), Louis de Caix d'Hervelois (*ob*. 1760); in Germany, August Kühnel (b. 1645), Johann Schenk, and Ernst Christian Hesse (*ob*.1762). Excepting de Caix d'Hervelois and Hesse, all were of an earlier generation than Bach, who handled the instrument in a period in which its vogue was no longer general.

The viola da gamba was the last of its family to disappear. Early in the seventeenth century the discant viol was challenged by the violin, and *c*. 1650 the alto-tenor had to meet the competition of the viola. But the viola da gamba maintained its monopoly. It was everywhere the popular instrument of accompaniment, the foundation of instrumental *ensemble*. It held the violoncello at bay, relegating its rival to the continuo, as Bach generally used it. So it lived to decorate music more lofty than ever before had used it. But, from the advent of Haydn, Mozart, Beethoven, and the string quartet, it associated unequally with the violins and viola, and at

[1] Cf. Hayes, p. 8.

length gave place to the violoncello. Bach's son's friend and London partner, Carl Friedrich Abel, was the last of its *virtuosi*. Gerber wrote truly in his revised *Lexicon* that Abel's instrument passed in 1787 with Abel himself into the oblivion of the grave.

Viewing the circumstances set forth in the preceding paragraph,

Bach's infrequent use of the viola da gamba is not surprising. At Weimar he found it useful in two cantatas, Nos. 106 and 152. At Leipzig he introduced it into five scores, sparingly in the two *Passions* and *Aeolus*, more lavishly in the *Trauer-Ode* and cantata No. 76. After 1729, apparently, he made no use of it, a significant fact in view of his subsequent employment of the violoncello piccolo. Of chamber music for the instrument he wrote little, and exclusively at Cöthen, where Prince Leopold was a player of it, and Christian Ferdinand Abel, the father of the above-named Carl Friedrich, was a member of the Capelle. The three Sonatas for cembalo and viola da gamba, in G ma., D ma., and G mi., may well have been written for the former; the cembalo, as providing two out of the three obbligato parts, dominates; and the gamba has comparatively little opportunity to display its technique; indeed, the first Sonata is an adaptation of one for two *traversi* and continuo, in which the viola da gamba receives the part of the second traverso. Forkel[1] observes that 'they are admirably written and pleasant to listen to, even to-day (1802)'. But their interest is in the music rather than their instrumental technique. In the sixth Brandenburg Concerto the two *viole da gamba* generally complete the harmonic accompaniment.

Viola da gamba, seven strings, 1725; extreme length 121 cm.

In his concerted music, also, Bach's viola da gamba parts do not generally permit the instrument to display its traditional technique. In cantata No. 76, excepting the Sinfonia and alto aria of Part II —where it forms a trio with an oboe d'amore and bass—it strengthens the continuo. In cantata No. 106 ('Actus tragicus'), as in the *Trauer-Ode*, the two *viole da gamba* contribute an elegiac colour to the funeral music. In cantata No. 152, where the instru-

[1] p. 130.

ment is confined to the opening concerto, it is again closely associated with the continuo. In the tenor aria of *Aeolus* it plays a second to the viola d'amore over a bass. But in the two *Passions* it stresses the emotion the unfolding drama evoked from Bach's pondering soul. What depth of feeling is expressed in its solo obbligato to the alto aria 'Es ist vollbracht' ('It is finished') of the *St. John Passion*! In the bass aria, 'Komm, süsses Kreuz', of the *St. Matthew Passion* Bach writes his only typical viola da gamba part. It yields a colour the violoncello cannot impart, is eloquent over a compass that instrument could not equal, and reaches to depths it could not plumb.[1] How Bach met the exceptional orchestral demand the *St. Matthew Passion* made on his slender and irregular resources is a matter for wonder. That he had the services of a finished viola da gamba player is evident, for the obbligato needs one. Is it improbable that Christian Ferdinand Abel from Cöthen was a guest for the occasion?

The Violoncello Piccolo

Bach certainly regretted the absence of an instrument of bass quality adequate for solo *obbligati*. The violoncellist had not developed the necessary technique. The viola da gamba was deficient in tone on the public platform it had exchanged for the intimate atmosphere of its classic period. As far as we know, Bach never introduced it into a score after his composition of the *St. Matthew Passion* in 1729. Two years later, at Easter 1731, he for the first time used the violoncello at Leipzig as an obbligato instrument. He repeated the experiment thrice in the course of the following six months, and for the last time on 14 October 1731,[2] having on the previous Sunday (7 October 1731) made his first trial of a new instrument, invariably called 'violoncello piccolo' in his scores. Four years elapsed before he used it again, in 1735, on four occasions between 24 April and 31 May. In 1736 he scored it twice, and that his interest in it was prolonged to a later date is evident in cantatas Nos. 115 and 180.

It is not without significance that the inventory of instruments belonging to the Cöthen Capelle discloses a five-stringed violoncello piccolo by J. C. Hoffmann, of Leipzig, bearing the date 1731, the year in which Bach first employed it. That it was the product of their joint planning and experiment can be supposed. But, as Dr. Kinsky[3] observes, Bach's association with the instrument is

---

[1] In an alternative version of the tenor recitative (No. 40), 'Mein Jesus schweigt' (B.-G. iv. 290), a viola da gamba supplements the two oboes of the original score. The addition is of doubtful authority.
[2] Nos. 42, 172, 56, 188.   [3] *Zeitschrift f. Musik.*, March 1931, pp. 325 f.

mentioned by no writer during his lifetime. Moreover, its identi-
fication and quality are confused by nearly contemporary writers,
who, as is probable, miscall it 'viola pomposa'. Johann Nikolaus
Forkel, the earliest to give particulars of it, so names it in his
Musicalisches Almanach für Deutschland (1782). Johann Adam
Hiller mentions it in his *Lebensbeschreibungen berühmter Musikgelehrten* (1784), and Gerber records precisely in the 'Instrumenten-
Register' at the end of his second volume (1792): 'Viola pomposa:
Erfand Joh. Seb. Bach zu Leipzig, ums Jahr 1724.' Bach, he states
in a short biography, was led to experiment with it owing to 'the
stiff manner in which the violoncello was played at that period'.
He remarks that it rendered 'very high and rapid passages' easier
of performance; that it was somewhat longer than a viola, was tuned
like the violoncello, but with a fifth string a fifth higher; and that
in use it was laid on the arm ('an den Arm gesetzt wurde'). Forkel,
who gives the same particulars, adds that it was fitted with a strap
or ribbon ('mit einem Bande befestigt') for the easier holding of
it 'vor der Brust und auf dem Arme'.

Thus—the deduction is material—Bach's so-called 'viola
pomposa' was designed to make good the deficiencies of a *bass*
instrument, particularly in rapid and high-pitched passages. To
that end it had the violoncello stringing, with an additional fifth
string sounding e':

Is there corroborative evidence of an instrument so named and
strung? We learn from Hiller[1] that, shortly before Lent 1738, the
violin virtuoso Franz Benda visited Dresden at the invitation of
Concertmeister Pisendel, and on one occasion was accompanied
by him on a 'viola pomposa'. He does not describe it as a new
instrument, neither does he associate Bach with it. Nor, in fact,
does Bach himself use the term 'viola pomposa' in his scores.
Moreover, a 'viola pomposa' was in contemporary use elsewhere
than Dresden. Mr. F. T. Arnold[2] has brought to light a 'Sonata
à solo per la Pomposa col Basso' by C. G. Lidarti, written apparently about 1760. Canon Galpin[3] has revealed two duets for viola
pomposa (or violin) and flute by G. P. Telemann, published at
Hamburg in 1728. It would be easy, of course, for an instrument
invented by Bach about 1724 to make its way to Hamburg by

---

[1] p. 45. [2] *Zeitschrift f. Musik.*, Dec. 1930.
[3] *Music and Letters*, Oct. 1931, p. 354 and *Zeitschrift f. Musik*, Oct. 1931.

1728, and to Pisa or Vienna about 1760. But Canon Galpin has recently argued that the viola pomposa used by Lidarti and Telemann and, no doubt, Pisendel, was another instrument altogether, not of bass, but of viola quality, probably tuned d, g, d', g', c'', and therefore in compass distinct from the violoncello-strung viola described by Forkel and Gerber, whose lowest strings carried down the compass of the instrument two whole fifths below that of the authentic pomposa. The latter, indeed, with a compass extending from d to c''', was almost mezzo-soprano in pitch, and by Telemann, at least, was grouped with the violin. That Forkel, and Gerber, who copied his statement, associated its name with Bach's instrument must be attributed to misinformation: after all, Bach's scores were not accessible to them.

Of the Telemann-Pisendel-Lidarti pomposa at least five examples are extant. The Bach Museum at Eisenach exhibits one (No. 56), made 'Mitte 18. Jahr.', with the following dimensions: total length about 30 inches (75 cm.), length of body about 18 inches (45·5 cm.), upper breadth about $8\frac{1}{4}$ inches (21·5 cm.), lower breadth about $10\frac{1}{4}$ inches (26 cm.), and the depth of ribs about 3 inches (8 cm.).

Another example is in the Brussels collection (Allemagne, 1445). It was made by Hoffmann himself. Its dimensions accord

Viola pomposa,
c. 1750,
extreme length 75 cm.

closely with those of the Eisenach specimen: total length $31\frac{1}{2}$ inches (80 cm.), maximum width about $10\frac{1}{2}$ inches (27 cm.), depth of ribs about 3 inches (75 mm.). Two examples, also by Hoffmann, are in the Heyer Collection at Leipzig. One is dated '1732': total length about $30\frac{1}{2}$ inches, body length about 18 inches, and depth of ribs about $3\frac{1}{2}$ inches.[1] The other is dated '1741'. Dr. Kinsky[2] instances another example, also by Hoffmann, dated 1732, and at present in the possession of Herr Albin Wilfer, violin-maker, Leipzig, who claims that it can bear the $c_{,}$, $g_{,}$, d, a, e' tuning alleged by Gerber and Forkel.

Thus, as Canon Galpin concludes, the authentic viola pomposa varied in total length from about $29\frac{1}{2}$ inches to $31\frac{1}{2}$ inches, with a

[1] Figured in *Grove*, v. 524.   [2] *Zeitschrift f. Musik.*, Dec. 1931, p. 178.

vibrating length of string from nut to bridge of 16¾ to 17¾ inches, and a rib-depth of 3 inches to 3½ inches. It was, in fact, a large-sized viola, midway between the ordinary viola and the violoncello piccolo. Conceivably, it might have been played 'on the arm', certainly not under the chin, and could not effectually have borne the stringing Forkel and Gerber attribute to Bach's 'invention'.

The rejection of the Telemann-Lidarti pomposa as the instrument attributed to Bach by Forkel and Gerber establishes the violoncello piccolo as the one to which they confusedly refer. It was some 10 inches longer than the smaller instrument, some 7 inches longer from nut to bridge, and about 1 inch thicker in rib-depth.[1] Manifestly such an instrument could only have been played between the knees. Equally certainly, its lower strings can have had little sonority. It is, therefore, not surprising that in the nine movements Bach wrote for the violoncello piccolo the lowest string

is needed in only four (cantatas Nos. 41, 68, 115, 175). In no case is it employed for sustained notes or passages. In the florid obbligato of cantata No. 41 this string is touched for only thirteen notes, all but three of which are detached quavers or semiquavers, the bow merely flicked. In the still more lengthy obbligato of cantata No. 68 only sixteen notes are written for it, all of which are short and detached except the final minim. In cantata No. 115 fifteen notes only are sounded on it, all of them unstressed. In cantata No. 175 the string is touched lightly for no more than three notes in a movement of 130 bars.

Of the fourth string

Bach's use is hardly less economical. In cantata No. 85 it sounds less than thirty notes in a movement of 61 bars, and none of them are sustained. In cantata No. 180 the string is touched for four semiquavers only, in rapid arpeggios. In cantata No. 183, in an obbligato of similar character, it sounds eighteen notes, short and detached, in a movement of 46 bars. For sustained legato playing the fourth string is not used at all. As an obbligato instrument, consequently, Bach's use of the violoncello piccolo was

---

[1] An example is in the Kunsthistorisches Museum, Vienna.

almost restricted to its three upper strings, the topmost of which

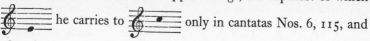 he carries to only in cantatas Nos. 6, 115, and

183; for the violoncello piccolo player was as diffident as the violinist in adventuring upon the highest register.

Bach employs a notation for the instrument neither uniform nor invariably simple. Its part falls within the compass of a single

(From left to right) Viola, extreme length c. 66 cm.; Violoncello piccolo, extreme length 99–105 cm.; Viola pomposa, extreme length 75–80 cm.

clef only in five scores (cantatas Nos. 6, 49, 85, 180, and 183). He uses the alto C clef in Nos. 6 and 180, the treble G clef in Nos. 49 and 85, and the tenor C clef in No. 183. Otherwise its part is written under the bass F and treble G clefs, as in No. 41; or in the bass F and alto C clef, as in No. 115; or in the bass F and tenor C clef, as in Nos. 68 and 175. These present no peculiarities. But others, written in whole or part in the treble G clef, exhibit a feature unusual, and at first sight confusing. For example, the following passages occur in No. 41:

Evidently the treble notes are intended to sound an octave below their written position, and the reason for the apparent complexity is revealed when we discover the obbligato, in Bach's autograph, written in a first violin part. For the four upper strings of the violoncello piccolo were tuned to the same intervals as those of the violin, but an octave lower. Consequently, the fingering being so similar, it can be concluded that in cantatas Nos. 41, 49, 85, where the violoncello piccolo part is wholly or partly in the treble G clef, it was played by a violinist rather than a violoncellist, a supposition supported by the duplicate copy for the instrument already noticed. Otherwise, it seems probable, the part was entrusted to a viola player, who would be equally at home on the four lower strings, and for the same reason. Both players, however, would be more inconvenienced than a violoncellist by the 'à gamba' position.

As we should infer from the reasons for its invention, the chief characteristic exhibited by the violoncello piccolo in Bach's scores is agility in its upper and middle compass. Otherwise it displays no qualities which can have invited him to employ it; it has no consistent characterization in his usage, and is associated with arias of diverse sentiment—with a picture of the Good Shepherd (Nos. 85 and 175), an evening scene (No. 6), a eucharistic hymn (No. 180), prayer (No. 115), a eulogy of peace (No. 41), a challenge to death (No. 183). Or it simply expresses care-free gaiety, as in No. 49, or light-hearted joy, as in the soprano aria, 'My heart ever faithful', of No. 68. Generally Bach associates it with a soprano voice, but with a bass not at all. Its lack of tone probably explains his disinclination to associate another obbligato instrument with it—in six of its nine movements the continuo alone supports it, and in the others a traverso or an oboe (with violin) are its partners.

Excepting the Sonatas for the viola da gamba, Bach wrote no music with clavier accompaniment for any instrument of violoncello quality. The six Suites for violoncello solo composed at Cöthen are the only chamber music for the instrument, a fact which may indicate the high talents of Christian Bernhard Linigke, a former member of the Berlin Hofcapelle, whom Prince Leopold secured as violoncellist during Bach's period of office as Capell-meister. Both Schweitzer[1] and Spitta[2] suppose that the sixth Suite was written for viola pomposa—that is, for Bach's violon-cello piccolo. Their assumption is based on the fact that the original MS. has the heading:

Suitte 6ᵐᵉ a cing acordes

The tuning is that of the five-stringed violoncello piccolo. A good deal of use is made of the top string, but otherwise there is little to distinguish the Suite from the other five. Nor is there evidence, or indeed in the circumstances, likelihood, that the instrument existed at the period (*c.* 1720) when the Suite was composed. The Cöthen specimen of Hoffmann's handiwork was dated 1731. But the Prince also owned two ordinary violoncellos by Hoffmann, dated 1715 and 1720 respectively, and also one by Jakob Steiner,[3] one or more of which may have been five-stringed.[4] On the other hand, the possibility cannot be excluded that the sixth Suite was a Leipzig addition to the other five. Bach's original autograph of the set is lost. But a copy is extant in the hand of his wife, Anna Magdalena, the title-page of which indicates that it was written at Leipzig:

Pars 2
Violoncello Solo senza Basso
composée par Sr. J. S. Bach. Maitre
de la Chapelle et Directeur de la Musique a Leipsic.
ecrite par Madame Bachen. Son Epouse.

The paper bears the watermark 'MA', which Spitta[5] shows Bach to have been using about 1730, when the problem of the violon-cello piccolo was engaging him. The sixth Suite probably was written for it at that period.[6]

The Lute

The lute (*Laute, luth, liuto*), the favourite instrument of the sixteenth and seventeenth centuries, declined in vogue in the earlier half of the eighteenth, and passed from use in the half-century following Bach's death (1750). For domestic music it was superseded by the clavichord and guitar, and on the public

---

[1] Vol. i. 393.   [2] Vol. ii. 100.   [3] B.-J. 1905, p. 38.
[4] Five-stringed violoncellos are rare.   [5] Vol. ii, p. 690.
[6] Canon Galpin remarks that a five-stringed violoncello existed with a vibrating string an inch or so less than the ordinary violoncello. He conjectures that the sixth Suite was written for this instrument.

platform was excluded from the new orchestra: its latest appearance
in such company is said to have been at the production of Handel's
opera *Deidamia* in 1740. Bach therefore employed it almost at
the moment of its disappearance.

Yet, at Leipzig more than elsewhere, its tradition was cherished,
its disuse regretted.[1] Cultural relations with Silesia, Poland, and
Bohemia had always been close, and those countries produced the
best lute players. From Breslau came Johann Kropfgans (b. 1668)
and his son of the same name, who visited Bach in 1739. Silvius
Leopold Weiss (1686–1750), for whom, it is probable, Bach composed or arranged lute music, was another Bohemian. Adam
Falkenhagen was teaching the lute in Leipzig shortly before Bach
came to the city, and Johann Caspar Gleditsch (d. 1747), his principal oboist, composed for the instrument. Of Bach's own pupils
two were distinguished lute players—Rudolph Straube, an *alumnus*
of the Thomasschule 1733–40, who published two lute sonatas in
1746,[2] and eventually settled in London, a contemporary there of
Johann Christian Bach; and Johann Ludwig Krebs, an older
alumnus (1726–35), for whom his master had particular affection;
the Berlin Staatsbibliothek owns the autograph of two lute concertos by him.[3] Kuhnau, Bach's immediate predecessor, set great
store by the instrument: his request to be supplied with a bass lute
has been mentioned elsewhere.[4] A print of St. Thomas's organ-
loft during his Cantorship shows a lutenist among the players.[5]
Moreover, in Johann Christian Hoffmann Leipzig boasted a lute-
maker of European reputation.[6] It is therefore not surprising
that among the instruments that crowded Bach's lodging in the
Thomasschule were three of lute character, and that his lute
music must be referred to the Leipzig period.

A D minor 'eleven course' lute was tuned thus, all but the top
two strings being duplicated, in octaves or unison:

Such a compass was not always adequate: the lute part in the

Trauer-Ode, for instance, touches ⊙ , and in two scores[7]

---

[1] Cf. Schering, pp. 413–23.
[2] The British Museum has a copy of the work.   [3] B.-J. 1931, p. 77 note.
[4] *Supra*, p. 19.   [5] See the frontispiece in Terry (4).
[6] Baron, chap. vii, particularly praises Hoffmann's lutes for their proportions
and tone.   [7] See Table XIX.

descends to . For these Bach may have used a 'twelve course' lute, of which an example is exhibited in the Bach Museum at Eisenach, tuned thus:

Excepting the top two 'melody strings', the catgut and silver-spun strings are duplicated. All are carried to a pegboard set at right angles to the finger-board, which is fretted to measure the semitones, eight or more frets to each pair of strings. The low $ab_{''}$ would be got by the normal method of adjusting the octave strings to the tonality of the movement.

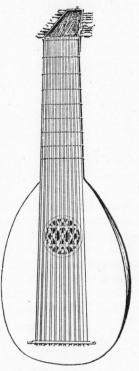

As has been already observed, Bach's practical interest in the lute was first displayed at Leipzig, where he employed it in two concerted vocal works and a few instrumental compositions. The fact that both vocal works are associated with the year 1727 indicates that a lute player was then at his disposal. The earlier of them, a revised version of the *St. John Passion*, was performed in St. Thomas's on Good Friday (April 11) in that year. Bach wrote for it the bass arioso (No. 31) 'Betrachte, meine Seele', whose score indicates an accompaniment by two *viole d'amore*, lute, organ, and continuo. The lute part is missing, and an alternative one, marked 'Organo ò Cembalo (obbligato)' in Bach's autograph, was used at some other performance when a lute player was not available. He was not under that disability in October 1727 when he produced the

Lute, 17th cent., extreme length 105 cm.

Trauer-Ode in St. Paul's, the University Church. The occasion was of official significance and Bach was not restricted to the sources from which his players were normally drawn. The work, accordingly, is scored for two lutes, which, excepting the remarkable alto recitative (No. 4), where they echo the 'bebendes Getön' of the

funeral bells, merely strengthen the continuo. This accorded with
the practice of Court orchestras in that period;[1] Bach's exceptional
conformity with it suggests that members of the Dresden Capelle
assisted him at this ceremonial performance. There are no other
extant examples of his employment of the lute in circumstances
which invited his predecessor's frequent use of it. His neglect
therefore cannot have been exclusively due to the lack of competent
players. For strengthening his continuo, one supposes, he preferred instruments of more masculine tone.

In his instrumental music, also, evidences of Bach's interest in
the lute are infrequent. 'III. Partite à Liuto Solo' by him were
offered for sale in manuscript by Breitkopf in 1761.[2] They have
disappeared. Others are extant, however, which were written
for the instrument or adapted to it. In particular, the Suites in
E major, E minor, and C minor, printed as clavier music in the
Bachgesellschaft edition. The E major Suite:[3]

is also extant as the third Partita for violin,[4] in which the solo part
is set an octave higher. The autograph does not indicate the
instrument for which the work was composed. But Herr Hans
Neemann, instructed by long and practical acquaintance with lute
music, finds the Prelude unplayable on the normally strung instrument in D minor, and suggests that the work was composed
neither for lute, clavier, nor violin, but for the harp![5]

The Suite in E minor:[6]

is among the manuscripts of Bach's pupil, Johann Ludwig Krebs,
inscribed: 'Praeludio con la Svite da Gio: Bast: Bach aufs Lauten

[1] B.-J. 1931, p. 76.   [2] Spitta, iii. 166.   [3] B.-G. xlii. 16.
[4] Ibid. xxvii (1), 48.   [5] B.-J. 1931, p. 85.   [6] B.-G. xlv (1), 149.

Werck.' Its association with a 'Lauten Werck' is interesting. Among the instruments owned by Bach and valued in the inventory of his belongings were:[1]

1 Lauten Werck	. . . .	30 Reichsthaler	
1 „ „	. . . .	30 „	
1 Laute	. . . . .	21 „	

Clearly Bach's 'Lauten Werck' was not the ordinary lute (Laute), and its greater costliness supports the conclusion that it was the lute-harpsichord or 'Lautenclavicymbel' built to his specification by the organ-builder Zacharias Hildebrand. Adlung[2] describes it as being shorter than the clavier, with two unisons of gut strings and an octave register of brass wire. The combination of tone, smothered by a cloth damper, produced sounds so like those of an ordinary lute that even a professional lutenist could not distinguish them. According to Adlung, Hildebrand made an instrument of this kind for Bach in or about 1740. But a more precise date can be suggested. In July 1739 Friedemann Bach came home from Dresden for a month's holiday, bringing with him the master-lutenists, Silvius Leopold Weiss and Johann Kropfgans.[3] A particular purpose must have invited the concurrent arrival of these *virtuosi*, and they produced 'something extra good in the way of music', reported Johann Elias Bach, then resident in the Cantor's house. Probably Bach's 'Lauten Werck' had been recently constructed, and Weiss and his colleague were invited to test its quality.[4] The Suite in E minor may have been composed for the occasion.

[1] Terry (Germ. edn.), p. 329.
[2] *Musica mechanica organoedi* (1768), ii. 139: 'Der Verfasser dieser Anmerkungen erinnert sich, ungefähr im Jahre 1740 in Leipzig ein von dem Hrn. Johann Sebastian Bach angegebenes, und vom Hrn. Zacharias Hildebrand ausgearbeitetes Lautenclavicymbel gesehen und gehöret zu haben, welches zwar eine kürzere Mensur als die ordentlichen Clavicymbel hatte, in allem übrigen aber wie ein ander Clavicymbel beschaffen war. Es hatte zwey Chore Darmseyten, und ein sogenanntes Octävchen von messingenen Seyten. Es ist wahr, in seiner eigentlichen Einrichtung klang es, (wenn nämlich nur ein Zug gezogen war,) mehr der Theorbe, als der Laute ähnlich. Aber, wenn der sogenannte, und auch hier § 561 angeführte Lautenzug, (der eben so wie auf den beyden Clavicymbeln war,) mit dem Cornetzuge gezogen wurde, so konnte man auch bey nahe Lautenisten von Profession damit betrügen. Herr Friderici hat auch dergleichen gemacht, doch mit einiger Veränderung' (vol. ii. 139).
[3] Terry, p. 247.
[4] Dr. Curt Sachs, *Real-Lexikon der Musikinstrumente* (*s.v.* Lauten-Clavier), describes a similar instrument made by Joh. Christoph Fleischer of Hamburg in 1718. Adlung (*op. cit.* ii. 135) also mentions one made by Joh. Nikolaus Bach (1669–1753) of Jena. Herr Neemann is not convinced that 'Lauten Werck' and 'Lautenclavicymbel' are exchangeable terms, and judges the E mi. Suite to be normal lute music.

The Suite (*Fantasia, Sarabande, Giga*) in C minor:[1]

exists in the Leipzig Stadtbibliothek as a 'Partita al Liuto. Composta dal Sigre Bach', a MS. in the collection of Carl Ferdinand Becker, sometime organist of St. Nicholas's Church. Internal evidence indicates that the Suite, adapted subsequently for the clavier, was originally composed for the lute.[2]

In the same collection of 'Pieces pour le lut par Sre J. S. Bach' is the MS. of a Suite in G minor, the autograph of which, preserved in the Fétis Library at Brussels, bears the title: 'Suite pour la Luth à Monsieur Schouster par J. S. Bach.' Mons. Schuster was probably a member of the Dresden Capelle so named, who functioned as Chamber musician and bass singer, and was the father of Joseph Schuster, subsequently Capellmeister there. If so, the autograph can be associated with Bach's middle Leipzig period. The Suite, however, is not an original composition for the lute, but an arrangement, by Bach himself, of the violoncello 'Suite discordable' in C minor.

In addition to these elaborate works, a few short pieces are claimed for the lute. The third of the 'Zwölf kleine Praeludien', in C minor:[3]

is a simple two-part exercise. A copy of it by Johann Peter Kellner, a pupil of Bach's contemporary, Johann Schmidt, bears the inscription 'Praelude in C mol pour la Lute di Johann Sebastian Bach'. Dörffel[4] questions the ascription 'pour la Lute'. Herr Neemann finds the piece eminently 'lautenmässig'.[5]

---

[1] B.-G. xlv (1), 156.
[2] Cf. Dörffel's note in B.-G. xxvii (1), p. xviii, and B.-J. 1931, p. 79.
[3] B.-G. xxxvi. 119.   [4] B.-G. xlv (1), p. li.   [5] B.-J. 1931, p. 83.

No doubt exists in the case of the Prelude in E flat:[1]

Bach's autograph[2] indicates it as a 'Prélude pour la Luth ò Cembal'. It includes three movements—*Prelude, Fugue, Allegro.*

Finally in this enumeration must be recorded a 'Fuga del Signore Bach', the MS. of which in lute tablature is in the Leipzig Stadtbibliothek. Its authenticity is attested by the fact that it appears elsewhere as the fugue of the Violin Sonata in G minor[3] and of the Organ Prelude and Fugue in D minor.[4]

All three versions are so appropriate to their respective instruments that it is impossible to declare positively for which of them the music was originally designed.

But sufficient evidence has been adduced to establish Bach's intimate acquaintance with the technique of the lute, both as composer and player, though, so far as the material affords a clue, his interest in the instrument was confined to his Leipzig period, and to a restricted portion of it. In those years—the seventeen-thirties—the construction of the lute-harpsichord (Lautenclavicymbel) engaged him, and Spitta[5] supposes that the lute partitas were written for it. Pirro[6] expresses the same opinion. Herr Neemann[7] scouts the proposition. But the circumstances support the conjecture.[8]

[1] B.-G. xlv (1), 141.
[2] Formerly in the possession of Mr. Henry Huth, the autograph is now in the collection of Dr. Karl. Frh. von Vietinghoff-Scheel, Kaiserin-Augusta Strasse 75–76, Berlin, N.W.
[3] B.-G. xxvii (1), p. 4.   [4] B.-G. xv. 149.   [5] Sp. iii. 167.
[6] German edition, p. 178. The statement does not appear in the original French edition.   [7] B.-J. 1931, p. 87.
[8] Bach's lute music (ed. E. D. Bruger) is published by Zwissler, Wolfenbüttel (1925). See also Wilhelm Tappert's *Seb. Bachs Kompositionen für die Laute* (Berlin, 1901).

CHAPTER VII

THE CONTINUO

THE preceding chapters have reviewed the instruments of Bach's orchestra which appear in his scores under their individual names. There remain for consideration others which function anonymously, in a part generally distinguished by him as 'Continuo', and once (cantata No. 112) as 'Basso per Fundamento'. Considering its general currency after Viadana's *Cento concerti* (1602) brought it into use, early in the seventeenth century,[1] Bach's avoidance of the complete term 'Basso continuo' is noticeable. But, like it, his 'Continuo' provided a continuous or 'thorough' bass accompaniment supporting the musical structure. Whether it was unfigured, or figured with numerals indicating the composer's intended harmonies, was irrelevant to its function as the unbroken foundation of the vocal or instrumental parts above it. In Bach's usage, accordingly, the word 'Continuo' denotes two distinct orchestral voices: (1) the unfigured part for the bass instruments, strings and wind, supporting the keyboard bass ('Basso per l'Organo', 'Basso per il Cembalo'); and (2) the figured part, from which the organist or cembalist supplied the harmonic accompaniment the numerals indicated.

Thus the continuo was essentially 'the accompaniment', to which keyed, string, and wind instruments made their contribution in accordance with certain recognized conventions. The clearest and most definite exposition of the practice of Bach's generation is afforded by his son Carl Philipp Emanuel,[2] who introduces the second Part of *The correct art of clavier-playing*, which deals particularly with the art of accompaniment, with the following paragraphs:

'1. The keyed instruments most generally used for accompanying are the organ, harpsichord, fortepiano, and clavichord.

'3. For church-music, with its fugues, powerful choruses, and syncopations, the organ is indispensable.[3] It enhances the effect and keeps everything together. ("Sie befördert die Pracht und erhält die Ordnung.")

'4. But, for arias and recitatives sung in church, the harpsichord must be employed, particularly when the middle [instrumental] parts are of such simplicity as to leave the voice practically free and independent

---

[1] Arnold, p. 6.   [2] Bach, Pt. II, p. 1.
[3] A 'Bindung' was more than a syncopation. It implied a discord. Cf. Arnold, p. 127.

("alle Freyheit zum Verändern lassen"). Without it, as we are able to judge much too frequently, how bald the music sounds! . . .

'7. So, no piece is satisfactorily rendered except to the accompaniment of a keyed instrument. Even in music on the largest scale ("bey den stärksten Musiken"), in opera, even at open-air performances, where we might suppose a harpsichord unable to make itself heard, one misses it if it is absent. Listening from above, its every note comes through distinctly. I speak from experience, and any one can make the test.

'8. In their solos some people are content to be accompanied only by a viola, or even a violin, unsupported by a keyed instrument. If they do so for lack of competent harpsichord players they may be excused. But a performance of that kind is necessarily quite unbalanced ("sonst aber gehen bey dieser Art von Ausführung viele Ungleichheiten vor"). If there is a good bass part, the solo becomes a duet; if it is bad, how thin the piece sounds, lacking the harmony! . . . And how bare is the chording sometimes found in the instrumental part without a foundation-bass to support it! The beauties the harmony brings out are quite lost, especially in pieces of an expressive character ("bey affectuösen Stücken").

'9. The most complete and unexceptionable accompaniment to a solo is provided by a keyed instrument associated with a violoncello.'

If Carl Philipp Emanuel's prescriptions represented his own custom at Hamburg, they are no less appropriate to his father's circumstances at Leipzig. There, on every Sunday morning outside Lent and Advent, and also on certain saints' days and public festivals, Bach's office required him to compose or provide an anthem (cantata) for chorus, *soli*, and orchestra, of from twenty to thirty minutes' duration. Their scheme was uniform—an elaborate opening chorus, a couple of arias, as many recitatives, and a concluding Choral. Exceptionally the cantata was prolonged into a second Part, performed after the sermon. Sometimes, too, the arias and recitatives exceeded the normal number, or Bach inserted another of his 'starke Chöre', or an extra Choral, or an instrumental movement to serve as an introduction. But the ingredients remained constant—choruses, arias, recitatives, and Chorals. The singers, soloists and ripienists alike, were the *alumni* of the Thomasschule. The orchestra was formed by the Stadtpfeifer, Kunstgeiger, and amateurs drawn from the School and the University. The performances were given on alternate Sundays in the western gallery of the two principal churches, St. Thomas's and St. Nicholas's. Both were equipped with organs and maintained their own organist. Bach's peculiar duty was to conduct the performance. Whether he also took part in the accompaniments at the organ or harpsichord is a point for later discussion. Here it need be remarked only that, at least for a large proportion of the arias and recitatives, the accompaniment of a keyed instrument was imperatively required. An analysis of no more than those of the first twenty cantatas suffices to establish the statement:

	ARIAS.			RECITATIVES.		
CANTATA.	Fully scored.	Continuo only.	Continuo & obbligati.	Fully scored.	Continuo only.	Continuo & obbligati.
No. 1	1	..	1	..	2	..
,, 2	1	..	1	1	1	..
,, 3	..	1	1	..	2	..
,, 4	1	2	1	..	..	..
,, 5	1	..	1	..	2	1
,, 6	1	..	2	..	1	..
,, 7	1	1	1	1	1	..
,, 8	1	..	1	1	1	..
,, 9	..	..	2	..	3	..
,, 10	1	1	1	1	1	..
,, 11	..	..	2	..	4	2
,, 12	..	..	3	1	..	..
,, 13	2	..	1	..	2	..
,, 14	1	..	1	..	1	..
,, 15	1	..	5	..	2	..
,, 16	..	..	1	..	2	..
,, 17	1	..	1	..	3	..
,, 18	..	..	1	..	1	..
,, 19	1	..	1	1	2	..
,, 20	4	1	..	..	3	..
TOTAL	18	6	28	6	34	3

The Table reveals that, out of 95 movements, only 24—little more than one-quarter—are sufficiently scored to make a filling-in accompaniment by a keyed instrument, organ or harpsichord, dispensable. Of 52 arias only 18 are in a condition of completeness, of 43 recitatives no more than 6. How shall we explain this? Certainly the practice of Bach's period favoured figured basses in lieu of fully written-out accompaniments: they saved time and labour, particularly when instruments of another order shared the accompaniment with the harpsichord. But the explanation does not meet the fact that Bach allowed his players to sit inactive during so large a part of the performance in which they were engaged. Nor does the music itself afford a clue to his meagre treatment of one aria and elaborate decoration of another. The probable solution is that he shrank from overtaxing his ripieno players. It will be observed in the Table that arias accompanied by the continuo with obbligato instruments are the most numerous. They employed the professional players, who, relatively to the less expert amateurs, did not need similar consideration. The latter, we can suppose, would be sufficiently occupied in mastering their parts in the concerted movements. We can imagine, too, that even Bach's unflagging vigour could be daunted by the unbroken

monthly calls upon his genius. But, whatever the explanation of his
practice, it is as certain that a keyed instrument was essential for
the accompaniment of his arias and recitatives, as that the organ
was a regular member of his church orchestra.

It is evident, therefore, that Bach shared his son's views regarding the accompaniment of church music. But, as has already been
remarked, his continuo instruments function for the most part
anonymously. They are rarely prescribed by name in his scores,
and for their identity and service we need to turn to his orchestral
parts.

Having in view their recurring performances, it was Bach's
habit to file the parts of his church cantatas in a wrapper on which
he recorded its contents: e.g. cantata No. 78:

> *Dominica 14 post Trinit.*
> *Jesu der du meine Seele.*
> *â 4 Voci, 1 Traversa, 2 Hautbois, 2 Violini, Viola, e Continuo di Sig.*
> *J. S. Bach.*

The top line indicates the Sunday to which the cantata was
appropriate; the second records its title; the third shows its instrumentation, information assisting the Cantor-composer, looking
ahead, to select his anthem for a future occasion. The wrapper
normally contained a single part for each instrument engaged, but
duplicates were occasionally provided for the violins and, necessarily, for the continuo. The Table on p. 152, based on the
editorial notes in Jahrgang XXIV and XXVI of the Bachgesellschaft edition, gives representative examples.

We observe that a single copy sufficed for each of the four
parts (S.A.T.B.) of Bach's choir, a circumstance which is at
variance with the picture representing the organ-gallery of St.
Thomas's Church,[1] which displays the singers in separate quartets.
We notice also that the soloists were not provided with separate
parts: in fact, they were members of the chorus body. It is
evident, too, that a single desk for each part usually accommodated Bach's first and second violins and violas, and that in
numbers the instrumentalists almost equalled his singers. We
must conclude also that, if one of the two continuo parts was the
organist's, a single part usually accommodated Bach's continuo
basses. With the single exception of No. 119,[2] however, the instruments so employed are not specifically named in any of the twenty
cantatas included in the Table. They are rarely indicated on the

---

[1] *Supra*, p. 11.
[2] In the score the opening chorus is annotated: 'Violoncelli, Bassoni è Violoni
all'unisono col'Organo.'

CANTATA	Voices	Violin I, II.	Viola	Flutes	Oboes	Horns	Tromba or Cornetto	Trombones or Timpani	Continuo	Total Parts	Total Players
No. 111	4	4	1	·	2	·	·	·	2	13	15
,, 112	4	4	1	·	2	2	·	·	3	16	17
,, 113	·	·	·	·	·	·	·	·	·	·	·
,, 114	4	2	1	1	2	1	·	·	2	13	13
,, 115	·	·	·	·	·	·	·	·	·	·	·
,, 116	4	2	1	·	2	1	·	·	2	12	12
,, 117	·	·	·	·	·	·	·	·	·	·	·
,, 118	·	·	·	·	·	·	·	·	·	·	·
,, 119	·	·	·	·	·	·	·	·	·	·	·
,, 120	·	·	·	·	·	·	·	·	·	·	·
,, 121	4	2	1	·	1	·	1	3	2	14	14
,, 122	4	2	1	·	3	·	·	·	2	12	12
,, 123	4	2	1	2	2	·	·	·	2	13	13
,, 124	4	2	1	·	1	1	·	·	2	11	11
,, 125	4	2	1	1	1	1	·	·	3	13	12
,, 126	4	2	1	·	2	·	1	·	2	12	12
,, 127	4	2	1	2	2	·	·	·	2	13	13
,, 128	4	2	1	·	3	2	·	·	2	14	14
,, 129	4	2	1	1	2	·	3	1	3	17	16
,, 130	·	·	·	·	·	·	·	·	·	·	·

The parts of Nos. 113, 115, 117–20, and 130 are not extant. In calculating the number of players, it is assumed that each violin and viola part served two, and, of the continuo parts, that one was the organist's, and that the other, or others, accommodated two players.

wrapper, on the continuo parts themselves, or in the score, the bottom line of which Bach generally simply labels 'Continuo'. For this indefiniteness a practical reason can be advanced. In an earlier chapter it has been shown that, before admission, a Stadt-pfeifer was tested in his competence on the violone.[1] That one or more played it when their principal instrument was not in use may be supposed. But we have Bach's statement that he depended on a more precarious source. In his report to the Leipzig Council in August 1730[2] he complained: 'Owing to the lack of more expert *subjecta*,I have had to take my viola, violoncello, and violone players from the *alumni* of the School.' These juvenile amateurs are not likely to have given him regular or expert assistance. And for the bassoon, the normal continuo wind-instrument, he was as in-adequately served. He depended for it, as we read in his report to the Council, on the inexperienced assistant-apprentice of the Stadtpfeifer body. To the precarious service of his continuo instruments, accordingly, his omission to particularize them must in part be attributed. Normally two players were at his service, who shared the single part he wrote for them. But, composing his score some weeks ahead of the performance, he could not foresee which instruments—violoncello, violone, bassoon—would be at his disposal, and therefore refrained from specifying them in particular. On such parts as are marked the violoncello and bassoon are most frequently indicated. The violone is definitely mentioned in less than twenty scores. In two cases (cantatas Nos. 76 and 152) a viola da gamba is specified, and in two others (Nos. 64 and 135) Bach was constrained to employ a trombone. That a contrabass was occasionally at his disposal is suggested by the apparent exis-tence of a part in the *St. John Passion* and *Was mir behagt*.

Bach normally prepared two continuo parts, an unfigured one for the string (violone and violoncello) or wind (bassoon) basses, a figured one for the organ. But in relatively few instances[3] the number of extant parts is greater, owing, probably, either to the replacement of lost copies subsequently recovered, or to a revision

---

[1] For an instance of this test see *supra*, p. 18. Agostino Agazzarı, writing in 1607, prefers the violone to 'proceed gravely, sustaining with its mellow resonance the harmony of the other parts, keeping as much as possible to the thick strings, and often touching the octave below the bass', i.e. playing an octave lower than the notes written. Quoted in Arnold, p. 72.

[2] Terry, p. 203.

[3] Cantatas Nos. 5, 6, 13, 21, 24, 28, 30, 31, 33, 36, 40, 42, 43, 47, 48, 51, 55, 57, 58, 62, 63, 67, 70, 71, 81, 82, 93, 94, 96, 97, 98, 100, 108, 109, 112, 125, 129, 133, 134, 136, 172, 178, 182, 185, 187, 192, 194, 195, *Herr Gott, Beherrscher, Christmas Oratorio, St. Matthew Passion, St. John Passion, Sanctus* in C, *Sanctus* in G, *Hohe Messe* ('Sanctus'). See Table XX.

of the parts for a repeated performance. Moreover, a strengthened continuo would be required on festal occasions. Thus all six Parts of the *Christmas Oratorio* except the fourth have duplicate unfigured continuo parts. So have both *Passions*, the 'Sanctus' of the *Hohe Messe*, and about one-quarter of the cantatas.[1] Occasionally[2] we find the unfigured parts, two or more, in different keys, one in that of the movement, the other a tone lower. A figured organ part is lacking in all the cantatas specified except Nos. 5, 63, 185, and 194, and in all but Nos. 63 and 185 the score is wholly or partially unfigured. Since Bach occasionally completed his scores on the very eve of performance,[3] and as the figured continuo was the last part he prepared, the transposed unfigured copy in the sixteen instances mentioned in note 2 below may be an uncompleted organ part. In such circumstances, it is probable that Bach himself was at the organ.

In the irksome and continuous labour of preparing the orchestral parts Bach was assisted by his wife, sons, and pupils. Of a large number of cantatas the parts no longer survive. But such as are extant show that he usually made, or closely revised, the figured continuo himself. The figuring, in particular, is generally wholly or partly in his autograph. After collating the parts with the score, and adding infrequent dynamic markings, his practice was to indicate on the organ part the harmonic accompaniment he desired. That the process marked the final stage of his work is evident in the figured continuo parts of cantatas Nos. 124 and 126. Following the last bar of the latter he writes 'Fine S[oli] D[eo] G[loria]', to indicate the completion of his labour. In the case of No. 124, the unfigured continuo part concludes with 'Fine' in his autograph, but the figured part again is marked 'Fine S D G'. In general, it must be observed, dynamic expression, ornament, and figuring are found on Bach's parts rather than his scores. He rarely figured the latter;[4] cantata No. 186 is an unusual instance to the contrary.[5] In the Bachgesellschaft edition the figuring has generally been added from the organ part. An unfigured score indicates that that important manuscript is lost, or that it was not available to the editor.[6]

Bach's particular concern with the organ part was due to another cause. The circumstances under which church music was per-

---

[1] See Table XX.
[2] Cantatas Nos. 5, 25, 28, 48, 52, 55, 56, 63, 64, 85, 88, 116, 183, 184, 185, 194.
[3] e.g. *Tönet, ihr Pauken*, the *Trauer-Ode*, and cantata No. 174. The last, for Whit-Monday 1729, was finished on the previous day.
[4] Cf. B.-G. ii, p. iii.   [5] *Ibid.*, xxxvii, p. xxix.   [6] See Table XX.

formed at Weimar and Leipzig compelled him to transpose it at an interval determined by the organ pitch in use. Seeing that in the score the organ part is normally written in the key of the movement, the preparation of a transposed part required more skill than the simple task of copying. In most cases Bach reserved it for himself. During his career he was served by organs tuned to two pitches—Cornett-Ton and Chorton. The former stood a minor third, the latter a major tone above the high chamber pitch (hoher Cammerton) in general use for concerted music. To accommodate the organ to the latter it was necessary to transpose its part down a minor third or whole tone, according as the instrument was at Cornett-Ton or Chorton. At Weimar the former was in use.[1] This is evident in the scores of several cantatas composed for the ducal chapel. For instance: No. 31 is in C major, but the oboes and bassoon are in E flat.[2] In No. 132 the continuo and strings are in A major, but the oboe obbligato is in C. In No. 150 the strings and continuo are in B minor, the bassoon in D minor. In No. 152 the continuo and viola da gamba are in E minor, the flute, oboe, and viola d'amore in G minor.[3] In the alto-tenor duet of No. 155 the bassoon obbligato is in C minor in the original score, but the voices and continuo are in A minor. A trumpet part exists for the first and last movements of No. 185. The score is in F sharp minor, but the trumpet is in G minor. As trumpet pitch was a tone higher than Cammerton, the G minor part indicates, like the other examples, that the organ was at Cornett-Ton.

The following is the specification of the 2-manual Weimar organ as it existed in Bach's period of office:[4]

Upper Manual (Great Organ)

1. Principal	8′	5. Quintatön	4′
2. Quintatön	16′	6. Octave	4′
3. Gemshorn	8′	7. Mixtur, 6 ranks	
4. Gedackt	8′	8. Cymbel, 3 ranks	

Lower Manual (Choir Organ)

1. Principal	8′	5. Kleingedackt	4′
2. Viola da gamba	8′	6. Octave	4′
3. Gedackt	8′	7. Waldflöte	2′
4. Trompete	8′	8. Sesquialtera, 4 ranks	

[1] Cf. Spitta, i. 381.

[2] The existence of a fully figured organ part in B flat shows that this work was also performed at Leipzig.

[3] They are printed in E minor in the B.-G. score.

[4] The specification is given by Gottfried Albin Wette, *Historische Nachrichten von ... Weimar* (1737), p. 174. See also Pirro (2), p. 84; Adlung, i. 282.

Pedal Organ

1. Gross-Untersatz	32'	5. Principal-Bass	8'
2. Sub-Bass	16'	6. Trompete-Bass	8'
3. Posaun-Bass	16'	7. Cornett-Bass	4'
4. Violon-Bass	16'		

Unlike the Weimar organ, those of the Leipzig churches, St. Thomas's and St. Nicholas's, in which Bach functioned as Cantor, and in which his cantatas, *Passions*, and oratorios were performed, were tuned to Chorton. Observing that Bach's figured continuo is generally duplicated,[1] one part standing in the key of the work, the other a tone lower, Moritz Hauptmann concluded[2] that the organs of those churches were at different pitches, St. Thomas's at Chorton, St. Nicholas's at Cammerton. He supposed the transposed part to have been prepared for St. Thomas's, and the other to have served St. Nicholas's, an error probably due to the fact that the organ of the latter church, with which he was familiar, stood at Cammerton. But it was not the instrument Bach used; it dated only from 1793, when it was erected at a cost of 7,000 thalers. Bach's organ was a veteran nearly a century old when he was born—it dated from 1597–8. Praetorius[3] gives its disposition at that period (1618), when it had twelve stops on the Great, four on the Brustwerk, ten on the Choir, and three on the Pedals. More than half of them (sixteen) were still in use in Bach's period.[4] Considerable repairs upon it were carried out by the Merseburg organ-builder, Zacharias Thayssner, in 1693, thirty years before Bach's arrival in Leipzig. It was again renovated in 1724–5, when 600 thalers were expended on it, and so remained throughout his Cantorate. In 1750–1 it again needed repair, and a generation later was replaced by a Cammerton organ, which was in use when the early volumes of the Bachgesellschaft edition were in course of publication, and survived until 1862.[5] Chorton being the normal organ pitch at Leipzig, the conversion of St. Nicholas's instrument to Cammerton during its renovation in 1724–5 would have been recorded had it been made. Moreover, it would have been foolishly unpractical to alter its pitch from that of St. Thomas's, seeing that both churches were platforms for the same music. It must, therefore, be concluded that the pitch of both organs was at Chorton, and that the transposed organ parts served them both.

---

[1] See Table XX.   [2] B.-G. i, Preface.   [3] P. 179.
[4] They are marked with an asterisk in the Table on p. 157.
[5] Cf. Schering, p. 110; Spitta, ii. 286, 676.

The 3-manual organ in St. Nicholas's in Bach's time was thus equipped:[1]

Oberwerk (Great Organ)

*1.	Principal	8'	*8.	Grobgedackt	8'
2.	Sesquialtera	1⅓'	*9.	Quintatön	16'
*3.	Mixtur, 6 ranks		*10.	Nasat	3'
*4.	Super Octave	2'	11.	Waldflöte	2'
*5.	Quinte	3'	12.	Fagott	16'
*6.	Octave	4'	13.	Trompete	8'
*7.	Gemshorn	8'			

Brustwerk[2]

1.	Schalmei	4'	5.	Octave	2'
*2.	Principal	4'	6.	Sesquialtera	1⅓'
3.	Mixtur, 3 ranks		7.	Quintatön	8'
4.	Quinte	3'			

Rückpositiv (Choir Organ)

*1.	Principal	4'	*6.	Quintatön	4'
*2.	Gedackt	8'	7.	Octave	2'
3.	Viola da gamba	4'	8.	Sesquialtera	1⅓'
4.	Gemshorn	4'	9.	Mixtur, 4 ranks	
5.	Quinte	3'	*10.	Bombard	8'

Pedal Organ

1.	Cornett-Bass	2'	4.	Octave-Bass	4'
*2.	Schalmei-Bass	4'	5.	Gedackter Sub-Bass	16'
3.	Trompete-Bass	8'	*6.	Posaun-Bass	16'

A smaller organ, which stood beside the larger one in St. Nicholas's west gallery, was broken up in 1693; its materials assisted the repair of the larger instrument.[3] It was not replaced.

St. Thomas's principal organ was of greater antiquity than the instrument in St. Nicholas's. After serving the Marienkirche at Eiche, not far distant, it was set up in St. Thomas's in 1525 and led the congregation in 1539, when Luther preached in the church. Its disposition at that period probably did not differ from that recorded by Praetorius[4] in 1618. It then had twenty-five stops— nine on the Great, two on the Brustwerk, twelve on the Choir, and two on the Pedals. Seventeen survived the many renovations of the organ, and were still in position in Bach's time.[5]   In 1721, shortly before his appointment, the organ was thoroughly

---

[1] Schering, p. 111; Spitta, ii. 286. For the significance of the asterisks see *supra*, p. 156, note.
[2] The Brustwerk was not enclosed in a shuttered swell-case in Bach's time.
[3] Schering, p. 111.   [4] P. 180.
[5] They are distinguished by an asterisk in the Table on p. 159.

overhauled, yet needed attention in 1730 and renovation in 1747, when its condition rendered it almost useless.

A problem presents itself here. Bach's employment of the organ as a solo instrument in 1731[1] suggested to Rust[2] that St. Thomas's Rückpositiv had recently been made independent of the main organ by the provision of a separate keyboard coupled to the old action. The contrivance would enable the instrument to be used simultaneously on the two keyboards, one providing the accompaniment, its normal function, the other performing an obbligato part, rarely entrusted to it. Accepting Rust's hypothesis. Spitta[3] found supporting evidence in the accounts of St. Thomas's for 1730–1, which record the payment of fifty thalers to the organ-builder Johann Scheibe 'for the repair of the organ' ('vor die beschehene Reparatur an der Orgel'). With less than his customary care, Spitta supposed that the 'reparation' involved the building of a separate keyboard for the Rückpositiv, and found confirmation of his conjecture in the judgement of an organ-builder of his acquaintance, who assured him that fifty thalers would have sufficed in 1730 to carry out the work. Bach's relation to the performance of his church music would be clearer to us if Spitta's hypothesis could be accepted. In fact, it is untenable: in a letter dated 27 February 1730[4] Scheibe precisely specifies the work for which he was paid—the removal of dust and dirt from the pipes, their re-tuning, and the strengthening of the sixteen-foot Posaun-Bass on the Pedal organ. The Rückpositiv, no doubt, benefited by Scheibe's tedious labour ('eine langweilige und mühsame Arbeit'), but it was not the special object of his attention; still less did it receive a new and independent keyboard. Hence, throughout Bach's period of office the Rückpositiv was playable only on the lowest of the three manuals at the main console, and could not be simultaneously sounded by a second player. The Rückpositiv in St. Nicholas's was similarly conditioned.[5]

Apart from its alleged additional keyboard, the precise situation of the Rückpositiv bears on the conditions under which Bach performed his cantatas. Adlung[6] declares that it was no longer customary to set up the Rückpositiv in a separate case behind the organist, but rather to enclose its pipes with those of the Oberwerk, Brustwerk, and Pedal Organ, in the main frame. It was, however, still customary, he continues, to apply the term Rückpositiv to the lowest manual. The Leipzig organs were erected at a period when the Rückpositiv occupied the detached and rear position indicated

[1] *Infra*, p. 171.　　　　[2] B.-G. xxii, p. xvi.　　　　[3] Spitta, ii. 675.
[4] B.-J. 1908, p. 52.　　　[5] Spitta, ii. 676.　　　　 [6] Vol. i, p. 20.

by its name, a situation in which it assisted the performance of the double-choir motet. No authentic picture of St. Thomas's organ gallery in Bach's period survives, but Rust states that its Rück-positiv was an 'imposing' structure, projecting like an oriel window over the front of the choir-gallery ('das Erker-ähnlich über die Brüstung des Chores in die Kirche hineinragte'). The late Professor Bernhard Fr. Richter, himself the son of one of Bach's successors in the Cantorship, states with equal definiteness, that in both of the principal churches, St. Thomas's and St. Nicholas's alike, their Rückpositiv occupied this prominent and detached position.[1] In St. Nicholas's, Bach and his performers were probably less inconvenienced by the obstruction.[2] But in St. Thomas's, its bulky and decorated frame must have intervened, a deadening curtain, between him and his audience.

The specification of St. Thomas's organ, after its enlargement in 1721, was as follows:[3]

Oberwerk (Great Organ)

*1.	Principal	16'	*6. Super Octave	2'
*2.	Principal	8'	7. Spiel-Pfeife	8'
3.	Quintatön	16'	8. Sesquialtera, doubled	
*4.	Octave	4'	9. Mixtur, *6, 8, 10 ranks	
*5.	Quinte	3'		

Brustwerk

1.	Grobgedackt	8'	6. Cymbel, 2 ranks	
2.	Principal	4'	7. Sesquialtera	
3.	Nachthorn	4'	*8. Regal	8'
4.	Nasat	3'	*9. Geigenregal (Violin	4'
5.	Gemshorn	2'	Regal)	

Rückpositiv (Choir Organ)

*1.	Principal	8'	8. Mixtur, 4 ranks	
*2.	Quintatön	8'	9. Sesquialtera	
*3.	Lieblich Gedackt	8'	*10. Spitzflöte	4'
4.	Klein Gedackt	4'	11. Schallflöte	1'
*5.	Traversa (Querflöte)	4'	12. Krummhorn	16'
*6.	Violine	2'	*13. Trompete	8'
7.	Rauschquinte, doubled			

Pedal Organ

1.	Sub-Bass (of metal)	16'	*4. Schalmei-Bass	4'
*2.	Posaun-Bass	16'	5. Cornett-Bass	3'
3.	Trompete-Bass	8'		

[1] B.-J. 1908, p. 49.
[2] See the illustration of its organ-gallery in Terry (Germ. edn., No. 43).
[3] Cf. Schering, p. 108; Spitta, ii. 282; Pirro (2), p. 87. For the explanation of the asterisks see *supra*, p. 157.

St. Thomas's owned a smaller, and even older, organ. Built in 1489, it remained in its original position in the western gallery after the larger instrument was introduced there in 1525. The two stood in close juxtaposition till 1639, when the smaller was transferred to a chamber on the opposite (eastern) wall of the nave. Here it remained for just a century, used at high festivals and on exceptional occasions, but otherwise neglected. It was in a state of semi-dilapidation in 1727, when Zacharias Hildebrand was commissioned to recondition it. Thirteen years later (1740) it was dismantled, and such of its parts as were serviceable were put into the new organ of the Johanniskirche. Bach's use of it must have been restricted to the years 1728–40; indeed, we might suppose that Hildebrand's renovation was undertaken at his request, in anticipation of the production of the *St. Matthew Passion* in 1729. But Johann Christoph Rost[1] makes no mention of it in that year, though in his unpublished note-book he particularly records that the *Passion* music was sung at St. Thomas's in 1736 (when the *St. Matthew Passion* was certainly repeated) 'with both organs'. The smaller was a 3-manual instrument with twenty-one stops:[2]

Oberwerk (Great Organ)

1. Principal	8′	5. Rauschquinte		3′ and 2′
2. Gedackt	8′	6. Mixtur, 4, 5, 6, 8, 10 ranks		
3. Quintatön	8′	7. Cymbel, 2 ranks		
4. Octave	4′			

Brustwerk

1. Trichter-Regal	8′[3]	3. Spitzflöte	2′
2. Sifflöte	1′		

Rückpositiv (Choir Organ)

1. Principal	4′	5. Octave	2′
2. Lieblich Gedackt	8′	6. Sesquialtera, doubled	
3. Hohlflöte	4′	7. Dulcian	8′
4. Nasat	3′	8. Trompete	8′

Pedal Organ

1. Sub-Bass (wood)	16′	3. Trompete-Bass	8′
2. Fagott-Bass	16′		

As Cantor, Bach's duties associated him only with the two principal churches ('Hauptkirchen'), St. Thomas's and St. Nicholas's. But on at least two occasions he directed his own music in St.

[1] Cf. Terry (4), p. ix.   [2] Cf. Schering, p. 109; Spitta, ii. 284.
[3] 'a sort of *Vox humana*' (Pirro (2), p. 87).   Cf. Adlung, i. 150.

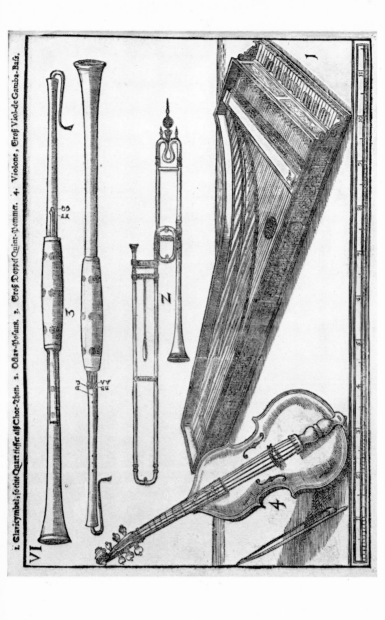

CLAVICEMBALO, OCTAVE TROMBONE, DOUBLE QUINT BASSOON, VIOLONE

(*Praetorius*)

Paul's, the University church. Thirteen years before his appointment, the Faculty of Theology had instituted Sunday services in
it (1710), and after much delay an organ was erected in the west
gallery. Bach knew it from the moment of its completion. At the
University's request he came over from Cöthen in 1717 to inspect
and report on it.[1] Ten years later, in 1727, his *Trauer-Ode* was
performed in the church, and at another memorial service, in
1729, his motet *Der Geist hilft unsrer Schwachheit auf* was sung.
Spitta[2] supposes that an instrument so superior to those of St.
Thomas's and St. Nicholas's—it was, in fact, one of the finest in
Germany[3]—was generally used by Bach for the exhibition of his
powers as an organist. But the jealousy with which he was regarded
by the University's official musicians makes it doubtful whether
St. Paul's organ-gallery was open to him, except at the academic
laureations in which the Cantor of St. Thomas's had an established
right to take part. Its specification was as follows:[4]

Hauptwerk (*Great Organ*)

1. Gross Principal	16′	8. Quinte	3′
2. Gross Quintatön	16′	9. Quint-Nasat	3′
3. Klein Principal	8′	10. *Octavina*	2′
4. Schalmei	8′	11. Waldflöte	2′
5. *Flûte allemande*	8′	12. Grosse Mixtur, 5 and 6 ranks	
6. Gemshorn	8′	13. *Cornetti*, 3 ranks	
7. Octave	4′	14. Zink, 2 ranks	

Brustwerk

1. Principal	8′	7. Nasat	3′
2. Viola da gamba	?	8. *Sedecima*	1′
3. Grobgedackt	8′	9. Schweizer Pfeife	1′
4. Octave	4′	10. Largo	?
5. Rohrflöte	4′	11. Mixtur, 3 ranks	
6. Octave	2′	12. Cymbel, 2 ranks	

Unter-Clavier (*Choir Organ*)

1. Lieblich Gedackt	8′	7. Viola	2′
2. Quintatön	8′	8. *Vigesima nona*	1½′
3. *Flûte douce*	4′	9. Weitpfeife	1′
4. *Quinta decima*	4′	10. Mixtur, 3 ranks	
5. *Decima nona*	3′	11. Cymbel, 2 ranks	
6. Hohlflöte	2′	12. Sertin(?)	8′

Pedal Organ

1. Gross Principal	16′	3. Octave	8′
2. Gross Quintatön	16′	4. Octave	4′

[1] Cf. Terry, p. 124.   [2] Vol. ii. 287.   [3] Schering, p. 319
[4] Spitta, ii. 287.

5. Quinte	3'	11. Gross Principal	16'
6. Mixtur, 5 and 6 ranks		12. Sub-Bass	16'
7. Grosser Quinten-Bass	6'	13. Posaune	16'
8. Jubal	8'	14. Trompete	8'
9. Nachthorn	4'	15. Hohlflöte	1'
10. Octave	2'	16. Mixtur, 4 ranks	

For these Leipzig organs (St. Paul's exceptionally) Bach prepared his figured continuo parts, transposing the bass down a tone in order to adapt their Chorton to the Cammerton of the other instruments and voices. The purpose they served, and Bach's general supervision of them, make the transposed usually more reliable than the untransposed continuo parts, and from the surviving cantatas of his Leipzig period they are rarely absent. From those whose parts are extant a figured organ part is lacking in only twenty-five: Nos. 11, 12, 17, 25,* 28,* 32, 34, 35, 45, 48,* 49, 52,* 55,* 56,* 64,* 69, 79, 85,* 88,* 103, 116,* 156, 169, 183,* 184.* Their loss is regrettable, but not surprising. But Table XX reveals that, for nearly half of them (marked with an asterisk), transposed, but unfigured, organ parts were prepared, in addition to the ordinary Cammerton continuo. In almost every case they are marked and revised by Bach; indeed, two of the three sheets of the unfigured transposed continuo part of No. 116 are in his autograph. Its incorrect deviations from the score, no less than the script itself, indicate that the task was undertaken in haste and left incomplete, a circumstance which invites a deduction applicable to all the cantatas in this category. We must suppose that Bach, in these comparatively rare cases, lacking leisure or inclination to revise and figure the parts, adopted the alternative of taking the organ himself and playing from his score or an unfigured continuo. That this was not his normal practice is self-evident: he would have figured the score rather than a separate and bare bass part had the accompaniment been regularly in his own hands. In fact, as has been shown, his score is rarely figured and a figured organ part is seldom missing.

Another problem is stated by the existence of non-transposed parts figured in whole or part. The supposition that they were prepared for St. Nicholas's lower-pitched organ has been considered and rejected.[1] If further disproof is needed, the rarity of these figured Cammerton parts provides it. Only twenty-seven survive over the whole range of Bach's Leipzig career—cantatas Nos. 3, 4, 6, 7, 10, 33, 38, 40, 42, 44, 46, 67, 81, 93, 96, 102, 109, 114, 136, 147, 166, 169, 176, 195, *Christmas Oratorio* Part IV, *Hohe Messe*

---

[1] *Supra*, p. 156.

('Missa'), and the *Sanctus* in G. Seeing that St. Nicholas's shared equally with St. Thomas's the privilege of hearing Bach's music, indeed enjoyed superior opportunities as the senior church, it is inconceivable that so few figured Cammerton basses should be found, if their purpose was as Moritz Hauptmann supposed.

Spitta[1] advances another untenable explanation. He concludes that when a figured Cammerton and a figured Chorton bass are found together, the latter was used in church, and the former at rehearsals elsewhere. If so, we should find at least as many of one part as of the other, for they were equally indispensable. But the suggestion can be challenged on other grounds. Rehearsals were held in the School-building, in the practice-room on the second floor, whose windows looked out on the Pleisse and its clattering mill.[2] But no harpsichord was available there, nor did the School possess one during Bach's period of office.[3] Pupils practised on his private instruments in his own apartments.[4] The School's only effective keyed instruments during the years 1723–50 were two Positiv organs.[5] One of them, acquired in the year of Bach's birth (1685), stood in the room on the first floor allotted to the Second Class. It was tuned to Chorton—so it cannot have required a Cammerton continuo part—and was only replaced by one at Cammerton pitch in 1756. A second Positiv, which Kuhnau induced the Council to purchase in 1720, stood, presumably, in the practice-room. It had two Gedackt stops of 8' and 4', a Principal of 2', and required four lads for its transportation when it accompanied the choir to private houses. Its pitch is not stated, but is not likely to have differed from its fellow. As it was in use until 1771, it is obvious that the figured transposed continuo parts served as well for rehearsals with the School Positiv as for performances with the church organ.

What, then, was the purpose of the figured untransposed basses? There is no question that they were written for a keyed instrument, and, since their pitch was not adapted to the church organs, they must have been prepared for a harpsichord. That they were not required for the general School-rehearsals has been demonstrated. There remain, therefore, two alternatives: either they served for private and individual practices in Bach's own apartments, or for the harpsichord which stood in the choir-galleries of both churches. In the former case we should expect them to be more numerous, for Bach must regularly have rehearsed his singers, and especially his soloists, under those conditions. Indeed, Johann Christian

---

[1] Vol. ii. 656. [2] Cf. Terry, p. 166. [3] *Supra*, p. 19.
[4] Schering, p. 63. [5] See Praetorius, Plate IV, at p. 18.

Kittel, one of his best pupils, recalled that, when his master 'performed' church-music, one of the most capable students accompanied 'auf dem Fluegel' ('on the harpsichord'), and that if he did his task badly he would find Bach's hands and fingers displacing his own on the keyboard, 'adorning the accompaniment with masses of harmony more impressive even than the unsuspected proximity of his strict preceptor'.[1] Kittel distinctly writes 'performed' ('wenn Seb. Bach eine Kirchenmusik auffuehrte'), but he was nearly eighty when he published the statement, and it is obvious that such incidents as he records occurred at general rehearsals in the gallery of one or other of the churches, and not at a public performance. A harpsichord was installed in both, and for what purpose if not for use? Yet, in a lengthy note,[2] Spitta concludes positively against Bach's employment of it. He instances the *Trauer-Ode* as the 'one single instance known to us' to the contrary, and insists that Bach was as much opposed to the harpsichord's regular use in church ('von einem ständigen Cembalo bei der Kirchenmusik') as to theatrical music there. Spitta, however, misstates the premisses on which he founds his positive conclusion. The *Trauer-Ode* is *not* the only instance of Bach's use of a harpsichord in church. In 1724 he was ready to deprive St. Nicholas's of its turn to hear the Good Friday Passion music, because, for one reason, its harpsichord was not serviceable.[3] A figured harpsichord (*cembalo*) part exists for cantata No. 8. Originally the accompaniment of the alto aria in No. 27 was for oboe da caccia 'e cembalo obligato'.[4] Among the parts of No. 109 is one definitely 'Continuo pro Cembalo' (Coro II) and figured. In No. 154 the tenor aria, in which the united violins and viola displace the continuo, is accompanied by a figured cembalo. In the *St. Matthew Passion* both organ parts and a 'Continuo pro Cembalo' are in Bach's autograph and figured. In his preface to the Bachgesellschaft edition[5] Julius Rietz remarks that the *secco* recitatives of the *Passion* were probably accompanied by the continuo basses and the cembalo,[6] an instrument, he adds, which Bach had always in readiness ('immer bei der Hand hatte'). Again, at one of the performances of the *St. John Passion* Bach substituted a harpsichord for the lute in the bass arioso 'Betrachte, meine Seele' (No. 31). These instances, though not numerous, suffice to indicate that Bach's attitude towards the harpsichord was not antagonistic, as

---

[1] Kittel, p. 10. Cf. Arnold, p. 34.
[2] Vol. ii, p. 655. The problem of Bach's use of the cembalo is also discussed in Schweitzer, ii. 447; B.-J. 1904, p. 64; B.-J. 1906, p. 11; B.-J. 1908, p. 64.
[3] Terry, p. 179.   [4] Spitta, ii. 451 n.   [5] B.-G. iv, p. xxii.
[6] The organ parts do not confirm this opinion.

Spitta supposes. It is therefore a feasible proposition that the figured Cammerton basses are other examples of its usage. In only a few cases the parts are not completely figured, and it is clear that they had a function distinct from and independent of the organ continuo. That they were used simultaneously is an improbable explanation, though both instruments may have been used when both chorus and orchestra were simultaneously in action. That the parts were employed alternatively is a more reasonable explanation, if we remember that Bach's cantatas received repeated performances, and that his organs, as has been shown, were not seldom undergoing repair. In such circumstances, to fall back on the church's harpsichord was natural, though the effect could not be completely satisfactory. The supposition, at least, is not contradicted by circumstances, as are the views of Hauptmann and Spitta. In regard to the parts partially figured there is less room for doubt; it is a fair inference that the cembalo was only active in those movements for which figured harmonies were provided. Instances have already been given, and another is found in cantata No. 114, where the transposed organ part is figured throughout, while the Cammerton continuo is marked only for the opening chorus and alto aria.

Of the Leipzig cantatas, three—Nos. 23, 97, 194—possess abnormal continuo parts, two of which indicate the participation of an organ at Cornett-Ton. In Leipzig, as at Weimar, that pitch was formerly in use. Writing to Mattheson on 8 December 1717,[1] Kuhnau, Bach's predecessor in the Cantorship, remarks: 'From the first moment of my appointment as director of church music here[2] I abolished Cornett-Ton, and substituted Cammerton, a tone or minor third, whichever you please, below it, though the consequent necessity of transposing the continuo parts is not always agreeable.' The change is explicable; for Kuhnau's period of office saw the decisive establishment of the new style cantata as the musical 'Hauptstück' of public worship, superseding the old style motet, with which the Stadtpfeifer had been traditionally associated. Cornett-Ton being the normal pitch to which that body conformed,[3] and as the organs were tuned to it, the necessity for a transposed continuo did not arise. Balancing the interests of music against his own convenience, Kuhnau decided for the former. The complications of transposition which he had consequently

[1] The letter is printed in Mattheson's *Critica musica* (1725), ii. 235. Cf. Schering, p. 244.

[2] Kuhnau became Cantor in 1701, having been organist of St. Thomas's since 1684.

[3] Riemann, ii. 856, defines it as 'die Stimmung der Stadtpfeifer'.

to face are illustrated by a note appended to the score of his Whit-Sunday cantata *Daran erkennen wir, dass wir in ihm verbleiben*: '1. This piece is set in B flat Chorton [C Cammerton] for viols,[1] voices, and thorough bass. 2. The trumpets [normally in D] are written in C natural; so they must be crooked a tone down to Cammerton. In like manner the drums must be tuned a tone lower to that pitch. The oboes and bassoons being in Cammerton, their parts must be written out a tone higher than those of the viols. In this way all will be consonant.'[2]

So, Cammerton was the performing pitch at Leipzig for nearly a quarter of a century before Bach succeeded Kuhnau. It is therefore, at first sight, strange to detect an apparent indication of Cornett-Ton in Cantata No. 23, composed in 1723 and almost certainly performed in 1724. The explanation, however, is not far to seek. Bach wrote the music at Cöthen, intending to perform it as his trial piece ('Probestück') for the Leipzig Cantorship.[3] Excepting the figured continuo, the parts are in his autograph, as also is the score, written with particular care. The figured continuo is neither in his script nor adapted to the conditions for which the cantata was composed: it is transposed a minor third down to A minor. The absence of a figured Chorton bass may be explained by Bach's desire to take the organ himself at the cantata's first performance. But the figured continuo in A minor must indicate a performance outside Leipzig, in a church whose organ was tuned to the older Cornett-Ton. Probably it was given under the direction of the writer of the transposed part. For, occasionally, Bach permitted others to use his scores, though with unwillingness always. A request for the loan of one received the following reply from his secretary-cousin, Johann Elias Bach, in 1741:[4] 'My cousin regrets he cannot send it; he has lent the parts to the bass singer Büchner, who has not returned them. As to the score, he won't allow it out of his hands; he has lost several through lending them to other people.'

Cantata No. 97 belongs to the year 1734. The score is in B flat and the normal continuo parts, both Cammerton and Chorton, are extant. In addition, there survives an incompletely figured organ part in G, written with extreme care by Bach himself, and interesting apart from its tonality. In his original scheme Bach marked the organ part 'tacet' in three movements—the tenor recitative (No. 3) and aria (No. 4), and the soprano-bass duet (No. 7)—and left them unfigured. For a later performance he figured the tenor recitative

---

[1] i.e. all the strings.   [2] Cf. Spitta, ii. 677.
[3] Cf. Rust's remarks in B.-G. v (1), p. ix, and Spitta, ii. 679.
[4] Terry, p. 249.

and aria, leaving the organ silent in the soprano-bass duet as before. Finally he re-wrote the whole part in G, and partially figured the duet. The fact that he left unfigured the last forty bars of it suggests that he took the organ himself on the occasion, and the tonality of the part indicates its use at a performance elsewhere than in Leipzig, perhaps in Weimar, with whose court he was on cordial terms since the death of the martinet Duke Wilhelm Ernst in 1728. Certainly, at some time subsequent to that event, he visited Weimar for a performance of *Was mir behagt* in the reigning duke's honour. It is not improbable that the score and parts of cantata No. 97 accompanied him for a Sunday service in the ducal chapel.

Cantata No. 194 was composed for the opening of a new organ at Störmthal on 2 November 1723. The work is in B flat, for strings, oboes, bassoons, and continuo. Among the parts are four for the continuo, two in B flat unfigured, another in A flat unfigured. There is also extant the fragment of a figured continuo in G. On the analogy of other similarly transposed organ parts, we should suppose the one in G to have been prepared for Störmthal's presumably Cornett-Ton organ, and the other parts for use at Leipzig on a repetition of the cantata. The reverse is the case. The Continuo in G is marked 'sub Communione' at the beginning of the second Part, indicating its use during that portion of the Leipzig office; while the score and all other parts are inscribed 'post Concionem' ('after the address') at that point.[1] The explanation is found in the fact that all the B flat instrumental parts are marked 'tief Cammerton' ('low chamber pitch'), from which we learn that the oboes at Bach's disposal at Leipzig at the beginning of his career there were at that pitch, their B flat sounding A Cammerton. This necessitated tuning down the strings by a similar interval, and the transposition of the part for St. Nicholas's[2] Chorton organ down to G, which, at its high tuning, was the equivalent of A Cammerton.

So many of Bach's cantata scores having passed under his editorial eye, Rust[3] gave his emphatic opinion that, invariably in that period, 'Church music scored for an orchestra was accompanied by the organ'. Bach's pupil, Kirnberger,[4] was no less positive to the same effect than Bach's son in a passage quoted on an earlier page.[5] We might therefore expect Bach's manuscript to yield abundant confirmation. In fact, in less than forty cantata

---

[1] B.-G. xxix, p. xx.

[2] As the senior church, St. Nicholas's presumably heard the cantata on Trinity Sunday, when it was repeated at Leipzig. If so, Hauptmann's opinion regarding its pitch (*supra*, p. 156) is conclusively inaccurate.

[3] B.-G. ix, p. xvi.   [4] Cf. Spitta, ii. 659.   [5] *Supra*, p. 148.

scores the organ is linked by name with the continuo.[1] In so few was Bach at pains to prefix 'Organo è' to the 'Continuo' which distinguished his bottom stave. Nor do his continuo parts add more than a few instances.[2] The reason is patent: the convention alleged by C. P. E. Bach and Kirnberger was so much Bach's normal habit that he deemed it superfluous invariably to specify the organ by name as a member of the continuo.

The organ (transposed) continuo parts rarely indicate Bach's intentions; he would convey them by word of mouth at rehearsals, or in private. Still, there is patent evidence that the organ accompaniment was discontinued in particular movements, or sections of movements. Certain numbers, for instance, were obviously planned to be independent of the organ, since they lack an actual bass: e.g. in the soprano aria 'Jesu, deine Gnaden-Blicke', of No. 11, the violins and viola in unison displace the normal continuo. Two *oboi da caccia* are similarly used in the alto aria 'Doch Jesus will' of No. 46. The violas provide the foundation in the soprano aria 'Wie zittern und wanken' of No. 105. In the alto aria 'Jesu, lass dich finden', of No. 154, the violins and viola are in unison at the octave of a figured cembalo bass. Evidently Bach desired to add clearness and distinctness to the latter. A similar intention is observed in the bass aria 'Streite, siege, starker Held!' of No. 62. Other movements lacking an actual bass are: the alto aria 'Wie jammern mich', of No. 170, in which the organ 'a 2 Clav.' is obbligato above the violins and viola in unison; the soprano aria 'Aus Liebe will mein Heiland sterben', of the *St. Matthew Passion*, which has an oboe da caccia foundation; the soprano aria 'Qui tollis peccata', of the Mass in A, in which the violins and viola in unison function as in No. 170; and the soprano aria 'Durch die von Eifer', of *Preise dein' Glücke*, where the violins and violetta play a similar part.[3]

Bach's scores and parts afford other indications of the organ's occasional inactivity. The second movement (tenor aria) of cantata No. 26 is pointedly unfigured, the only movement of the cantata so treated. In No. 94 the bass, alto, and soprano arias, marked 'tacet', stand unfigured in the organ part. In No. 95 the tenor aria is both unfigured and marked 'senza l'organo'. The original organ part of No. 97 is frequently labelled 'tacet' after the opening chorus. Similar directions exclude the organ from verses 2, 3, 5 of cantata

---

[1] Nos. 21, 26, 29, 30, 33, 36, 41, 42, 50, 52, 57, 61, 63, 64, 67, 71, 78, 80, 82, 94, 97, 100, 107, 110, 139, 161, 196, and the six parts of the *Christmas Oratorio*.

[2] e.g. Nos. 8, 13, 23, 111, 124, 125, 129, 162, 174, 177, 187.

[3] Cantata No. 118 is wholly without a continuo.

No. 100, and from verses 2, 3, 4 of No. 177. In No. 125, though the organ part was figured by Bach himself, the alto aria is without figures, and in No. 139 the organ is silent between the opening chorus and final Choral.

It is incontestable, therefore, that some other instrument than the main organ, and some other manuscript than the transposed organ part, provided the accompaniment in the above instances. That Bach himself undertook the task is a natural inference, and the absence of supplementary figured parts indicates that he used his score. In cases where the organ part is wholly unfigured he must have played the main organ and placed his first prefect to beat time in the choruses. But the instances before us are in another category, since they indicate the substitution of another keyed instrument, specifically the harpsichord, in movements which, on the ground of their difficulty, or of his liking for them, or of his want of confidence in the singer or organist, he preferred to accompany himself.

That Bach himself should have accompanied particular movements is not improbable, though each church had its own organist —St. Nicholas's, Johann Gottlieb Görner (till 1730) and Bach's pupil Johann Schneider; St. Thomas's, Christian Gräbner (till 1729) and Johann Gottlieb Görner.[1] Of the three men, Schneider alone seems to have had Bach's full confidence, while Görner, his associate throughout his Cantorship, was a player of moderate ability and unbounded self-esteem. But even if their technique had been extraordinary, Bach could not expect from them a completely accurate interpretation of his music. For, unlike the modern organist, they could neither study their score beforehand, nor play from one at the performance. Only a bare bass part faced them above the manuals, figured in a script not always easily deciphered. And, however legible, it left much to the skill and imagination of the player, as is known to all who have endeavoured to build up an accompaniment from Bach's figured indications. Certainly, he rarely lays the exclusive burden of accompaniment on the continuo, a responsibility which required the player at the keyboard to invent melodic interludes before and between the vocal passages. It is further evident, in the Table on page 150, that his continuo is 'solo' chiefly in recitatives. But even in those arias— and they are the most numerous—in which a further exposition of his scheme is revealed in fully written-out instrumental *obbligati*, the responsibility of the player of the keyed instrument remained onerous. That Bach on occasion instructed performers of his figured basses has an interesting proof. The bass aria 'Empfind'

[1] Terry, pp. 156, 159.

ich Höllenangst und Pein', of cantata No. 3, stands in his score with no other accompaniment than an unfigured continuo. There is extant, however, in his autograph,[1] a fully written-out accompaniment of the first fifteen bars over the bass, interesting in itself, and particularly when placed alongside the effort of a modern editor. Here are the first half-dozen bars of Bach's autograph:

And here are the first four bars in the Breitkopf edition!

When we contemplate the enormous gap that generally separated Bach's conception from his accompanist's pedestrian performance,

[1] The autograph is facsimiled in Liepmannsohn's auction catalogue, 21 and 22 Nov. 1930.

we must picture him constantly exasperated by, or despondently acquiescent in, the imperfect accompaniments to which he was forced to listen. Michel de Saint-Lambert, in his *Nouveau traité de l'accompagnement du clavecin*, published in Bach's lifetime, is illuminating:

'When the *tempo* is so rapid that the accompanist cannot conveniently play all the notes, it will suffice if he play and accompany only the first notes of each bar, leaving to the [string] basses the task of playing them all, which they can do much more easily, having no accompaniment to attend to in addition. Very rapid *tempi* are not suited to the accompanying instruments. If very quick passages are encountered, even in a slow movement, the accompanist may leave them to the other [continuo] instruments. Or, if he plays them himself, he may so modify them as to play only the principal notes, i.e. the notes which fall on the strong beats of the bar.'[1]

We must attribute Bach's abnormal use of a solo organ in 1731 to exceptional circumstances. Only two examples occur before that year, only two after it. Cantata No. 47, which contains the earliest, was composed at Cöthen in 1720. Its soprano aria 'Wer ein wahrer Christ will heissen' is scored for continuo (figured) and 'Organo obligato'. The obbligato is simple, a solo such as might be allotted to a flute or oboe. In the second of the pre-1731 examples, No. 73, one of the earliest Leipzig cantatas, the 'Organo obligato', restricted to the opening chorus, merely deputizes for a 'Corno' generally sounding the Choral melody. We infer that Bach's horn player failed him, that he consequently prepared an organ part, placed on its lower stave the normal figured bass, and on the upper the horn part (Rückpositiv), with brief phrases for the Brustpositiv, on which, while his right hand was engaged with the Rückpositiv, the organist supplied the harmony with his left hand.

These simple devices are the only examples of Bach's use of a solo organ prior to 1731, when we come upon eight cantatas in which the organ is again obbligato. The following, in chronological order, are their titles:

No.	Title.	Occasion.	Date, 1731.
172	*Erschallet, ihr Lieder*	Whit-Sunday	May 13
170	*Vergnügte Ruh'*	Trinity VI	July 1
35	*Geist und Seele wird verwirret*	Trinity XII	Aug. 12
29	*Wir danken dir, Gott*	Council Election	,, 27
27	*Wer weiss, wie nahe*	Trinity XVI	Sept. 9
169	*Gott soll allein*	Trinity XVIII	,, 23
49	*Ich geh' und suche*	Trinity XX	Oct. 7
188	*Ich habe meine Zuversicht*	Trinity XXI	,, 14

[1] Quoted in Pirro (2), p. 80. Cf. Arnold, p. 196.

Rust's supposition, that Bach's obbligato use of the organ in 1731 was made possible by the recent addition of a separate keyboard to St. Thomas's Rückpositiv, has been shown to be groundless.[1] Another suggestion came, in 1887, from Franz Wüllner,[2] who hazarded the opinion that the second keyboard was provided by the School Positiv.[3] Professor B. Fr. Richter found confirmatory evidence in the School records,[4] which reveal its removal to St. Thomas's during the enlargement of the School buildings, an operation which compelled occupants and contents to find lodging elsewhere. This evacuation took place in the spring of 1731, and the reconstruction was not completed till the summer of 1732.[5] Thus, on the testimony of the School records, the School Positiv was available in the very period to which Bach's obbligato organ parts belong. Professor Richter computes that six, if not all, of the eight cantatas in which they occur were performed in St. Nicholas's, whereas the Positiv appears to have been housed in St. Thomas's. He is of opinion, too, that Bach wrote the obbligato organ parts as a compliment to, and for the use of, his pupil, Johann Schneider, organist of that church. In the latter conjecture Richter is probably incorrect; more practical reasons can be advanced for the production of these unique cantatas at this particular juncture.[6] And, as to the location of the Positiv, having once been loosed from its moorings in the School, it could be navigated as easily from one church to the other as from the School to St. Thomas's. The material point is that, when these eight cantatas were composed, Bach had at his disposal a keyed instrument not normally a member of his orchestra, which permitted him, if he desired, to employ the permanent organ of the church for other than its accustomed function.

The earliest of the 'Organ Cantatas', No. 172, was called for by circumstances already deduced in regard to No. 73.[7] In both, the organ obbligato is confined to a single movement, in No. 73 as a substitute for, in No. 172 to support, another instrument. The soprano-alto duet of the latter was scored originally for violoncello and violin *obbligati*, the violin sounding the Choral melody 'Komm, heiliger Geist, Herre Gott'. As Bach entrusts the obbligato of the preceding aria to all the violins and viola in unison, we judge that his players were not reliable. For that reason, it is probable, he altered his original scheme for the duet, and put both *obbligati* on the organ. It is the only unfigured movement in the cantata, and he probably took the organ himself.

---

[1] *Supra*, p. 158.   [2] B.-G. xxxiii, p. xxxi.   [3] *Supra*, p. 19.   [4] B.-J. 1908, p. 54.
[5] Cf. Terry, pp. 208, 212.   [6] Cf. *infra*, p. 175.   [7] *Supra*, p. 171.

In cantata No. 170, the second of the series, the organ is obbligato in the second and third of the three arias. In the second ('Wie jammern mich') its part is set out on two manuals and transposed down a tone. The movement is as original in its instrumentation as it is emotional in mood, and lacks an actual bass. In the third aria ('Mir ekelt mehr zu leben') the existence of an autograph traverso part seems to indicate a subsequent performance of the cantata.[1] The Positiv may have been used for the obbligato, for the part stands in the key of the aria.

So far Bach's experiments with an organ obbligato were tentative and simple: the organ functioned like any other wind instrument, contributing a single melodic line to the polyphonic structure. But in the third cantata of the series, No. 35, performed on the Twelfth Sunday after Trinity (12 August), the organ sounds in its full majesty. The cantata is in two parts, each prefaced by a movement of a Clavier Concerto in D minor, transformed into a Concerto for organ and orchestra.[2] That Leipzig had ever heard the organ in such conditions is improbable. To Bach himself the occasion must have been of exceptional interest, and the fact that no separate organ-part survives strengthens the agreeable belief that he played it himself. The organ is obbligato throughout, excepting the recitatives, and the form of the alto aria 'Geist und Seele wird verwirret' suggests that it is the middle movement of the original concerto.

Little more than a fortnight later (27 August), Bach gave St. Nicholas's another feast of concerted organ music. The occasion was of particular solemnity and pomp; for the burgomaster and councillors were present to inaugurate their year of office. Bach's normal orchestra, accordingly, was augmented by the trumpeter Reiche, his colleagues, and the drums. The cantata (No. 29) opened with the first movement of the Violin Concerto in E, adapted for organ and orchestra, an exhilarating sinfonia which, on its repetition eight years later, Their Magnificences applauded as 'clever and agreeable music' ('eine so künstlich als angenehme Music')![3] It is noteworthy that the organ is obbligato only in the opening sinfonia and last aria, and that the continuo is figured with particular care in the intervening movements. We infer that Bach was too concerned with the direction of his composition to displace Schneider altogether at the organ.

A fortnight later (9 September) the fifth of the organ cantatas (No. 27) was produced. Here the obbligato is confined to the alto aria 'Willkommen! will ich sagen'. The subject of the upper stave

[1] Cf. Spitta, ii. 453.　　[2] Cf. B.–G. xvii, p. xx.　　[3] Terry (4), p. 528.

is independent, on the lower the organ reinforces the continuo, a circumstance which, along with the fact that only the arias are unfigured, suggests that Bach himself took the organ for their performance. The score prescribes a harpsichord, though the organ part and the cover of the parts are marked 'organo obligato'.[1]

Again a fortnight intervened before Bach, in the same church, performed (23 September) the sixth of the organ cantatas (No. 169). He now borrowed and adapted the Clavier Concerto in E for the opening sinfonia and second aria. The organ is obbligato throughout, excepting the recitatives, alto arioso, and final Choral. Its part is so far unique, in that it contains both the obbligato and also the figured continuo, as is evident not only in the indication 'Organ obligato e Continuo', but also in the fact that the part is transposed down a tone in the score in every movement in which the organ is engaged.

On 7 October 1731, after another fortnight's interval, Bach produced the last but one (No. 49) of the eight. Its relationship to its predecessor is of the closest: the introductory sinfonia is the last movement of the same E major Clavier Concerto. Moreover, the organ obbligato and continuo are conjoined in the sinfonia, bass aria, and concluding duet. As in No. 169, also, the organ part is transposed down a tone in the score.

A week later (14 October), Bach conducted the last of the eight organ cantatas (No. 188). The date indicates that it was not performed in the same church as its immediate predecessors, and it is planned upon a smaller scale. The organ is obbligato only in the alto aria 'Unerforschlich ist die Weise'. But a note in the score (copy) directs that the first movement of the Clavier Concerto in D minor be played as an introductory sinfonia. The series ended, therefore, with music in which the organ displayed its full majesty.[2]

It has already been proposed that Bach's employment of an obbligato organ in 1731 was made possible by the transference of the School's Positiv to the churches during the building operations. Bach himself must have been seriously incommoded by them, since he was compelled to remove his family, furniture, and instruments while they were in progress. His unsettled conditions are evident in his choice of a libretto for the *Passion* music in 1731, and probably in his performance of the *St. Luke Passion*, an inferior work by another hand, in 1732. For similar reasons, while the school was excluded from its accustomed quarters, he appears to

---

[1] Cf. Spitta, ii. 451.
[2] Apart from the sinfonia, the authenticity of the cantata has been questioned. The hand of Friedemann Bach is suggested. Cf. Terry (4), p. 476.

have made large use of old material in his cantatas, or performed
solo anthems in which the choir's participation was confined to
the concluding Choral. Thus all three cantatas for the Whitsun
Festival 1731 are revisions of earlier material, as also is the Michaelmas cantata for that year. Those performed on the Nineteenth
and following three Sundays after Trinity are for a solo voice.[1]
It is a tenable proposition, therefore, that Bach's abnormal usage
of the organ in 1731 was invited by the disturbing conditions in
which he was placed. Nor can it be fortuitous that, with one exception in No. 49, all the arias having an organ obbligato are for an
alto voice. Did Bach draw upon arias already sung in the domestic
music-making he so much loved?

Only twice again, and in his latest years, Bach repeated the
experiments of 1731. For the wedding cantata *Herr Gott, Beherrscher aller Dinge* he adapted the first movement of the third Violin
Partita in E as a sinfonia for organ and orchestra. In cantata
No. 146 the opening sinfonia is an adaptation of the first movement
of the Clavier Concerto in D minor, which had done the same service
for No. 188 in 1731. The chorus that follows is an adaptation of
the slow movement of the concerto, and in both the organ is
obbligato. The authenticity of the rest of the cantata is suspect.
Carl Philipp Emanuel's hand is suggested, as is Friedemann's in
No. 188.[2] Is it only a coincidence that their father threw the same
ballast into both?

Not only in church did the conventions of Bach's period
require a keyboard accompaniment. In chamber and orchestral
music the organ's part was taken by the harpsichord. This is
self-evident in Bach's domestic vocal music: e.g. the secular
cantata *Amore traditore* has only a cembalo accompaniment; for
the 'Coffee cantata' (*Schweigt stille*) he wrote a cembalo part in
addition to the quartet of strings; for *O holder Tag* a part exists
inscribed 'La voce e Basso per il Cembalo', and another for violone,
the former figured. Even his elaborate cantatas written for open-
air performance require the harpsichord. Of the two continuo
parts of *Schleicht, spielende Wellen*, performed in Leipzig's market-
place on 7 October 1734, one is figured in his own hand.

In pure orchestral music the harpsichord was no less essential,
though the number of Bach's figured continuo parts that survive
is small.[3] Of the Brandenburg Concertos, he prescribes for the
second a 'Violone in Ripieno col Violoncello e Basso per il Cembalo'; for the third, 'tre Violoncelli col Basso per il Cembalo'; for
the fifth, 'Violoncello, Violone e Cembalo concertato'; and for the

[1] Cf. Terry, p. 209.   [2] Cf. Terry (4), p. 250.   [3] See Table XX.

sixth, 'due Viole da Gamba . . . e Cembalo'. The parts of all but
the fifth have not survived, and, alone of the six, its continuo is
figured. But the figuring is confined to the bars above which stands
the instruction 'accompagnamento', that is, in which the cembalo
is not 'concertato'. The score does not reveal whether the figured
passages were played by a second cembalo.

Of the four Ouvertures, again, a part for 'Fagotto con Cembalo'
was provided for the first, and the continuo of the first and second
is figured throughout.

Turning to the concertos for harpsichord and orchestra: in the
seven for a single clavier ('cembalo certato') Bach simply indicates 'continuo'. But for No. 4, in A, in addition to one for the
violone, a second continuo part, completely figured, exists in his
autograph, and an additional, accompanying, cembalo was certainly
employed in them all. On the other hand, another cembalo was
superfluous in the concertos for two, three, and four claviers with
orchestra. Its addition, as Rust[1] remarks, would create 'a musical
pleonasm of the most confusing character'. The concertos for
violin and orchestra, however, needed a harpsichord accompaniment, and for two of them—No. II in E and No. III (double)
in D minor—figured continuo parts exist. The Concerto in A
minor for clavier, flute, violin, and orchestra reveals the same
treatment of the cembalo as in the fifth Brandenburg: the part is
figured only in those bars in which the upper manual is not
engaged, i.e. in which the instrument is not 'concertato', but
merely accompanying. As with the fifth Brandenburg, a second
cembalo perhaps was employed.

In regard to Bach's music for a solo instrument and clavier, it
must be borne in mind[2] that a 'Sonata for violin and clavier' was
not the same as a 'Sonata for clavier and violin'. A 'Sonata for
violin and clavier' represented solo music for the violin accompanied by a figured bass on the cembalo, while a 'Sonata for
clavier and violin' treated the two instruments on a platform of
equality. In our phraseology such a movement would be called a
'duet'. But Bach's epoch reckoned the obbligato parts, not the
number of instruments engaged. Hence, if the cembalo part was
written in two parts, as with Bach's sonatas is generally the case,[3]
the piece was deemed a 'trio'. Thus the Sonatas (or Suites) for
clavier and flute, for clavier and violin, for clavier and viola da
gamba are in the category of trios. On the other hand, in a sonata
for an instrument, or instruments, 'and continuo', the cembalo is
an accompanying member, and its part is figured, as we find it in

[1] B.-G. xxi (2), p. vii.   [2] Cf. Schweitzer, i. 394.   [3] See Table XX.

Bach's Sonatas for flute, violin, and continuo; two violins and continuo; two flutes and clavier; flute and continuo; and violin and continuo.

The significance of Bach's continuo parts, and the need to use them as he intended, is expressed by Wilhelm Rust[1] in sentences with which this chapter can appropriately be brought to an end:

'Just as in pictures of historical scenes we need a background, however slight, on which to display the characters, so do Bach's polyphonic parts move freely, like persons passing on their lawful occasions, across a harmonic background. And as figures, lacking this pictorial background, lose their relationship to the whole design, even though their outline, colour, and character remain, so with Bach's music,[2] its full impression is not conveyed unless we hear it in its harmonic setting.'

[1] B.-G. xxii, p. xiv.   [2] 'Kirchenwerken.'

INDEX INSTRUMENTORUM

(The principal reference is indicated in figures of heavier type.)

INDEX NOMINUM

INDEX OPERUM

INDEX RERUM

THE TABLES

$c_{,,}$ $c_{,}$ c c' c'' c'''

TABLE I. THE TROMBA

NOTE. *The Instrument is in C unless the contrary is stated*

(A) CHURCH MUSIC

Cantata.	Date.	Movement.	Score.	Sounding Compass.
No. 5	1735	5. Aria (B.)	In Bb	$bb–bb''$
11	c. 1736	1. Coro 11. Choral	In D. 3 Tr.+Timp. ,, ,, ,,	I $f\sharp'–e'''$ II $d'–d'''$ III $a–f\sharp''$
15	1704	1. 4. Aria (B.) (T.) 6. Terzetto 9. Coro and Choral	3 Tr.+Timp.[1] ,, ,, ,, ,,	I $g'–b''$ II $e'–b''$ III $c'–c''$
19	1726	1. Coro 7. Choral 5. Aria (T.)	3 Tr.+Timp. ,, ,, Choral melody; obbl.	I $e'–c'''$ II $c'–b''$ III $c'–a''$
20	c. 1725	8. Aria (B.)	...	$g–c'''$
21	1714	11. Coro	3 Tr.+Timp.	I $e'–c'''$ II $c'–a''$ III $g–e''$
29	1731	1. Sinfonia 2. Coro 8. Choral	In D. 3 Tr.+Timp. ,, ,, ,, ,, ,, ,,	I $d'–d'''$ II $d'–b''$ III $a–c\sharp''$
30	1738	1. Coro 12. Coro	In D. 3 Tr.+Timp. ,, ,, ,,	I $d'–d'''$ II $d'–b''$ III $d'–f\sharp''$
31	1715	1. Sonata 2. Coro 9. Choral	3 Tr.+Timp. ,, ,, Obbligato	I $g–e'''$ II $g–bb''$ III $g–a''$
34	1740–1	1. Coro 5. Coro	In D. 3 Tr.+Timp. ,, ,, ,,	I $a'–e'''$ II $a'–c\sharp'''$ III $d'–g\sharp''$
41	1736	1. Coro 6. Choral	3 Tr.+Timp. ,, ,,	I $g'–d'''$ II $e'–b''$ III $c'–g''$
43	c. 1735	1. Coro 7. Aria (B.)	3 Tr.+Timp. Solo	I $c'–c'''$ II $g'–bb''$ III $c'–f''$
50	c. 1740	Coro	In D. 3 Tr.+Timp.	I $f\sharp'–e'''$ II $d'–b''$ III $a–g''$

[1] 2 Clarini and Principale.

Cantata.	Date.	Movement.	Score.	Sounding Compass.
No. 51	1731–2	1. Aria (S.) 5. Aria (S.)	...	$c'-d'''$
59	1716	1. Duetto (S.B.)	2 Tr.+Timp.	I $c''-c'''$ II $c'-a''$
63	1723	1. Coro 7. Coro	4 Tr.+Timp. ,, ,,	I $g'-d'''$ II $e'-b''$ III $g-g''$ IV $g-g'$
66	1731	1. Coro	In D	$d'-e'''$
69	1724	1. Coro 6. Choral	In D. 3 Tr.+Timp. ,, ,, ,,	I $d'-d'''$ II $d'-a''$ III $d'-a''$
70	1716	1. Coro 2. Recit. (B.) 9. Recit. (B.) 10. Aria (B.)	... Choral melody. Obbl.	$c'-c'''$
71	1708	1. Coro 5. Aria (A.) 7. Coro	3 Tr.+Timp. ,, ,, ,, ,,	I $c'-bb''$ II $c'-g''$ III $g-c''$
74	1735	1. Coro	3 Tr.+Timp.	I $e'-c'''$ II $g'-b''$ III $c'-e''$
75	1723	12. Aria (B.)	...	$c'-c'''$
76	1723	1. Coro 5. Aria (B.)	...	$e'-c'''$
77	c. 1725	5. Aria (A.)	Solo	$g'-c'''$
80	1730	1. Coro 5. Choral	In D. 3 Tr.+Timp. ,, ,, ,,	I $d'-e'''$ II $d'-c\sharp'''$ III $d'-a''$
90	c. 1740	3. Aria (B.)	In Bb	$bb-bb''$
110	post 1734	1. Coro 6. Aria (B.) 7. Choral	In D. 3 Tr.+Timp. ,, Choral melody; Tr. I. col. S.	I $d'-e'''$ II $d'-c\sharp'''$ III $d'-a''$ $b'-f\sharp''$
119	1723	1. Coro 4. Recit. (B.) 7. Coro	4 Tr.+Timp. ,, ,, ,, ,,	I $c'-d'''$ II $c'-c'''$ III $c'-g''$ IV $g-c''$
120	1730	2. Coro	In D. 3 Tr.+Timp.	I $d'-d'''$ II $d'-b''$ III $d'-e''$
126	c. 1740	1. Coro	In D	$a'-d'''$
127	c. 1740	4. Recit. and Aria (B.)	...	$c'-c'''$
128	1735	3. Aria (B.)	In D	$a'-d'''$
129	1732	1. Coro 5. Choral	In D. 3 Tr.+Timp. ,, ,, ,,	I $f\sharp'-d'''$ II $f\sharp'-c\sharp'''$ III $d'-a''$
130	c. 1740	1. Coro 3. Aria (B.) 6. Choral	3 Tr.+Timp. ,, ,, ,, ,,	I $c'-d'''$ II $c'-c'''$ III $g-a''$
137	1732	1. Coro 5. Choral	3 Tr.+Timp. ,, ,,	I $c''-d'''$ II $g'-g''$ III $c'-e''$

TABLE I. THE TROMBA   189

Work. Cantata.	Date.	Movement.	Score.	Sounding Compass.
No. 145	1729–30	2. Coro 5. Aria (B.)	In D ,,	$d'-d'''$
147	1716	1. Coro 9. Aria (B.)	...	$c'-c'''$
148	c. 1725	1. Coro	In D	$f\sharp'-d'''$
149	1731	1. Coro 7. Choral	In D. 3 Tr.+Timp. ,, C. ,, ,,	I $d'-d'''$ II $d'-a''$ III $d'-f\sharp''$
171	c. 1730	1. Coro 6. Choral	In D. 3 Tr.+Timp. ,, ,, ,,	I $d'-e'''$ II $d'-b''$ III $d'-d''$
172	1731	1. Coro 3. Aria (B.)	3 Tr.+Timp. ,, ,,	I $c'-c'''$ II $c'-b\flat''$ III $g-g''$
175	1735	6. Aria (B.)	In D. 2 Tr.	I $d''-e'''$ II $d'-a''$
181	c. 1725	5. Coro	In D	$a'-d'''$
190	1725	1. Coro 2. Choral 7. Choral	In D. 1 3 Tr.+Timp. ,, 2 Parts missing ,, 3 Tr.+Timp.	I $d''-c'''$ II $d''-c'''$ III $d'-d''$
191	1733	1. Coro 3. Coro	In D. 3 Tr.+Timp. ,, ,, ,,	I $f\sharp'-e'''$ II $d'-d'''$ III $d'-b''$
195	c. 1726	1. Coro 5. Coro	In D. 3 Tr.+Timp. ,, ,, ,,	I $a'-e'''$ II $d'-c\sharp'''$ III $d'-a''$
197	1737	1. Coro	In D. 3 Tr.+Timp.	I $d'-d'''$ II $f\sharp'-a''$ III $d'-f\sharp''$
Christmas Oratorio, Pt. I	1734	1. Coro 8. Aria (B.) 9. Choral	In D. 3 Tr.+Timp. ,, ,, 3 Tr.+Timp.	I $a-d'''$ II $d'-b''$ III $d'-a''$
Christmas Oratorio, Pt. III	1734	1. Coro	In D. 3 Tr.+Timp.	I $d''-d'''$ II $f\sharp'-a''$ III $d'-e''$
Christmas Oratorio, Pt. VI	1734	1. Coro 11. Choral	In D. 3 Tr.+Timp. ,, ,, ,,	I $d'-d'''$ II $f\sharp'-b''$ III $d'-b''$
Easter Oratorio	1736	1. Sinfonia 2 {Duetto (T.B.) {Coro 10. Coro	In D. 3 Tr.+Timp. ,, ,, ,, ,, ,, ,, ,, ,, ,,	I $d'-d'''$ II $d'-d'''$ III $a-g''$
Magnificat	1723	1. Coro 6. Coro 11. Coro	In D. 3 Tr.+Timp. ,, ,, ,, ,, ,, ,,	I $f\sharp'-e'''$ II $d'-d'''$ III $a-b''$
Hohe Messe	1733	4. Coro 6. Coro 11. Coro 13. Coro 17. Coro 19. Coro 20. Coro 21. Coro 24. Coro.	In D. 3 Tr.+Timp. ,,	I $d'-e'''$ II $d'-d'''$ III $d'-c\sharp'''$
Sanctus in C.	...	...	3 Tr.+Timp.	I $c'-c'''$ II $c'-g''$ III $c'-e''$

(B) SECULAR CANTATAS

Work. Cantata.	Date.	Movement.	Score.	Sounding Compass.
Aeolus	1725	1. Coro 2. Recit. (B.) 11. Aria (B.) 15. Coro	In D. 3 Tr.+Timp. ,, ,, ,, ,, ,, ,, ,, ,, ,,	I d′–e‴ II d′–c♯‴ III a–b″
Phoebus und Pan	1731	1. Coro 15. Coro	In D. 3 Tr.+Timp. ,, ,, ,,	I d′–d‴ II d′–a″ III d′–f♯″
Angenehmes Wiederau	1737	1. Coro 13. Coro	In D. 3 Tr.+Timp. ,, ,, ,,	I d′–d‴ II d′–b″ III d′–f♯″
Schleicht, spielende Wellen	1734	1. Coro 11. Coro	In D. 3 Tr.+Timp. ,, ,, ,,	I d′–d‴ II d′–c♯‴ III d′–d‴
Preise dein' Glücke	1734	1. Coro 8. Recit. (S.T.B.) 9. Coro	In D. 3 Tr.+Timp. ,, ,, ,, ,, ,, ,,	I d′–e‴ II d′–c♯‴ III d′–g″
Tönet, ihr Pauken	1733	1. Coro 7. Aria (B.) 9. Coro	In D. 3 Tr.+Timp. ,, ,, 3 Tr.+Timp.	I a–d‴ II d′–b″ III d′–a″
Vereinigte Zwietracht	1726 ⎫	1. Marcia 2. Coro	In D. 3 Tr.+Timp. ,, ,, ,,	I f♯′–d‴ II d′–a″
Auf, schmetternde Töne (omitting Nos. 1 and 7)	1734 ⎭	7. Ritornello 11. Coro	,, 2 Tr. ,, 3 Tr.+Timp.	III a–g″

(C) INSTRUMENTAL MUSIC

Sinfonia	...	...	In D. 3 Tr.+Timp.	I a–e‴ II d′–d‴ III a–a″
Ouverture in D (1)	...	...	In D. 3 Tr.+Timp.	I d′–d‴ II d′–b″ III a–a″
Ouverture in D (2)	...	...	In D. 3 Tr.+Timp.	I d′–e‴ II d′–c♯‴ III d′–a″
Brandenburg Concerto, No. 2	1721	...	In F	f–g″ or f′–g‴[1]

[1] See B.–J., 1916, pp. 1–7.

TABLE II.   THE ZUGTROMPETE (TROMBA DA TIRARSI)[1]

Cantata. No.	Date.	Movement.	Score.	Sounding Compass.
3	c. 1740	6. Choral	'Corno' col S. (in C or A). Choral melody	$e'-d''$
5	1735	1. Coro	'Tromba da tirarsi' col S. (in C or B♭). Choral melody	$g'-f''$
		7. Choral	'Tromba da tirarsi' col S. (in C or B♭). Choral melody	$g'-f''$
8	c. 1725	1. Coro	'Corno' col S. (in C or A). Choral melody	$d\sharp'-e''$
		6. Choral	'Corno' col S. (in C or A). Choral melody	$d\sharp'-e''$
10	c. 1740	1. Coro	'Tromba' col S. and A. Choral melody	$c'-f''$
		5. Duetto (A.T.)	'Tromba' col Ob. I, II (in C or B♭). Choral melody, obbl.	$d'-c''$
		7. Choral	'Tromba' col. S. (in C or B♭). Choral melody	$g'-f''$
12	1724–5	6. Aria (T.)	'Tromba.' Choral melody, obbl.	$g'-b\flat''$
		7. Choral	'Oboe o Tromba.' Obbligato	$a'-c'''$
14	1735	1. Coro	'Corno di caccia.' Choral melody, obbl.	$f'-d''$
		5. Choral	'Corno di caccia' col S. (in C or B♭). Choral melody	$f'-d''$
16	1724	1. Coro	'Corno di caccia' col S. (in C). Choral melody	$e'-c''$
		6. Choral	'Corno di caccia' col S. (in C). Choral melody	$a'-e''$
20	c. 1725	1. Coro	'Tromba da tirarsi' col S. (in C). Choral melody	$f'-f''$
		7 & 11. Choral	'Tromba da tirarsi' col S. (in C). Choral melody	$f'-f''$
24	1723	3. Coro	'Clarino'	$d'-b\flat''$
		6. Choral	'Clarino.' Obbligato	$f-e\flat''$
26	c. 1740	1. Coro	'Corno' col S. (in C). Choral melody	$a'-f''$
		6. Choral	'Corno' col S. (in C). Choral melody	$a'-f''$
27	1731	1. Coro	'Corno' col S. (in C or B♭). Choral melody	$g'-a\flat''$
		6. Choral	'Corno' col S. (in C or B♭). Choral melody	$g'-f''$
40	1723	3. Choral	'Corno I' col S. (in C or B♭). Choral melody	$g'-d''$
		6. Choral	'Corno I' col S. (in C or B♭). Choral melody	$g'-f''$
		8. Choral	'Corno I' col S. (in C or B♭). Choral melody	$f'-f''$
43	c. 1735	11. Choral	'Tromba I, II' col S. (in C). Choral melody / 'Tromba III' col A. (in C). Choral melody	{ I, II $g'-g''$ / III $b-b'$
46	c. 1725	1. Coro	'Tromba o Corno da tirarsi' col S. (in D)	$e'-a''$
		3. Aria (B.)	'Tromba o Corno da tirarsi.' Obbligato	$b\flat-b\flat''$

[1] Since the positions of the slide would have to be altered, at any rate slightly, for each key, when crooks were used, it is pertinent to remark that trombone players of the period had no difficulty in adjusting their slide-positions to an altered pitch.

Cantata.	Date.	Movement.	Score.	Sounding Compass.
No. 46	c. 1735	6. Choral	'Tromba o Corno da tirarsi' col S. (in C). Choral melody	$e'-d''$
48	c. 1740	1. Coro	'Tromba.'[1] Choral melody, obbl.	$g'-g''$
		3. Choral	'Tromba' col S. (in C or B♭). Choral melody	$f'-d''$
		7. Choral	'Tromba' col S. (in C or B♭). Choral melody	$d'-d''$
60	1732	1. Duetto (A.T.)	'Corno.' Choral melody, obbl.	$d'-d''$
		5. Choral	'Corno' col S. (in D or C). Choral melody	$a'-e''$
62	c. 1740	1. Coro	'Corno' col S. (in D or C). Choral melody	$a'-f\sharp''$
		6. Choral	'Corno' col S. (in D or C). Choral melody	$a'-f\sharp''$
67	c. 1725	1. Coro	'Corno da tirarsi'	$a-b''$
		4. Choral	'Corno da tirarsi' col S. (in D). Choral melody	$f\sharp'-f\sharp''$
		7. Choral	'Corno da tirarsi' col S. (in D). Choral melody	$g\sharp'-e''$
68	1735	1. Coro	'Corno' col S. (in C). Choral melody	$d'-g''$
70	1716	7. Choral	'Tromba' col S. (in C). Choral melody	$d'-e''$
		11. Choral	'Tromba' col S. (in C). Choral melody	$c'-d''$
73	c. 1725	1. Coro	'Corno, ossia Organo obligato.' Mainly Choral melody	$f'-e♭''$
		5. Choral	'Corno' col S. (in C or B♭). Choral melody	$g'-g''$
74	1735	8. Choral	'Tromba I' col S. (in C). Choral melody	$g'-e''$
75	1723	8. Sinfonia	'Tromba' (in high G). Choral melody, obbl.	$d''-e'''$
76	1723	7 & 14. Choral	'Tromba.' Choral melody	$c'-e''$
77	c. 1725	1. Coro	'Tromba da tirarsi.' Choral melody, obbl.	$c'-c'''$
78	c. 1740	1. Coro	'Corno' col S. (in C or B♭). Choral melody	$f'-e♭''$
		7. Choral	'Corno' col S. (in C or B♭). Choral melody	$f'-e♭''$
83	1724	5. Choral	'Corno I' col S. (in C). Choral melody	$c'-d''$
89	c. 1730	1. Aria (B.)	'Corno' [da caccia]. Obbligato	$c'-f''$
		6. Choral	'Corno' [da caccia] col S. (in C or B♭). Choral melody	$g'-f''$
95	1732	1. Coro	'Corno.' Choral melody col S. (in C) and obbligato	$c'-a''$
		6. Choral	'Corno' col S. (in C). Choral melody	$d'-d''$
96	c. 1740	1. Coro	'Corno e Trombone coll' Alto' (in C). Choral melody	$d'-c''$
		6. Choral	'Corno' col S. (in C or D). Choral melody	$d'-c''$
99	c. 1733	1. Coro	'Corno' col S. (in C). Choral melody	$d'-e''$
		6. Choral	'Corno' col S. (in C). Choral melody	$d'-e''$
103	1735	5. Aria (T.)	'Tromba'	$d'-d'''$
		6. Choral	'Tromba' col S. (in D or C). Choral melody	$f\sharp'-e''$

[1] Marked 'Clarino' on the parts.

TABLE II. THE ZUGTROMPETE (TROMBA DA TIRARSI) 193

Cantata. No.	Date.	Movement.	Score.	Sounding Compass.
105	c. 1725	1. Coro 5. Aria (T.)	'Corno ed Oboe I', 'Corno'	d'–d''' f'–bb''
107	c. 1735	1. Coro 7. Choral	'Corno da caccia' col S. (in D or C). Choral melody 'Corno da caccia' col S. (in D or C). Choral melody	f♯'–g'' f♯'–f♯''
109	c. 1731	1. Coro 6. Choral	'Corno da caccia' 'Corno da caccia' col S. (in C or D). Choral melody	c'–c''' d'–e''
114	c. 1740	1. Coro 7. Choral	'Corno' col S. (in C or Bb). Choral melody 'Corno' col S. (in C or Bb). Choral melody	f'–d'' f'–d''
115	c. 1740	1. Coro 6. Choral	'Corno' col S. (in C). Choral melody 'Corno' col S. (in C). Choral melody	g'–g'' g'–g''
116	1744	1. Coro 6. Choral	'Corno' col S. (in A or C). Choral melody 'Corno' col S. (in A or C). Choral melody	g♯'–e'' g♯'–e''
124	c. 1740	1. Coro 6. Choral	'Corno' col S. (in A or C). Choral melody 'Corno' col S. (in A or C). Choral melody	e'–f♯'' e'–f♯''
125	c. 1740	1. Coro 6. Choral	'Corno' col S. (in C). Choral melody 'Corno' col S. (in C). Choral melody	d'–e'' d'–e''
126	c. 1740	6. Choral	'Tromba' col S. (in C). Choral melody	g'–g''
137	1732	4. Aria (T.)	'Tromba.' Choral melody, obbl.	g'–g''
140	1731–42	1. Coro 7. Choral	'Corno' col S. (in C or Bb). Choral melody 'Corno' col S. (in C or Bb). Choral melody	eb'–g'' eb'–g''
147	1716	6 & 10. Choral	'Tromba' col S. (in C). Choral melody	g'–f''
162	1715	1. Aria (B.) 6. Choral	'Corno da tirarsi' 'Corno da tirarsi' col S. (in C). Choral melody	c'–c♯'' e'–e''
167	c. 1725	5. Choral	'Clarino' col S. (in C). Choral melody	d'–d''
185	1715	1. Duetto (S.T.) 6. Choral	'Oboe (Tromba).' Choral melody, obbl. 'Tromba' col S. (? in D or A). Choral melody	e'–f♯'' e'–f♯''

TABLE III. THE CORNETT

Cantata.	Date.	Movement.	Score.	Sounding Compass.
No. 4	1724	2. Coro	Choral melody col S.[1]	$e'-g''$
		3. Duetto (S.A.)	,, ,, col S.	$d\sharp'-f\sharp''$
		8. Choral	,, ,, col S.[1]	$e'-f\sharp''$
23	1724	4. Choral	Choral melody col S.[1]	$bb'-f''$
25	c. 1731	1. Coro	Choral melody[1]	$d'-d''$
		6. Choral	,, ,, col S.[1]	$g'-a''$
28	c. 1736	2. Coro	Choral melody col S.[1]	$g'-g''$
		6. Choral	,, ,, ,,	$a'-e''$
64	1723	1. Coro	Col S.[1]	$d\sharp'-a''$
		2. Choral	Choral melody col S.[1]	$d'-e''$
		4. Choral	,, ,, ,, [1]	$d'-e''$
		8. Choral	,, ,, ,,	$e'-g''$
68	1735	5. Coro	Col S.[1]	$d'-a''$
101	c. 1740	1. Coro	Choral melody col S.[1]	$d'-f''$
		7. Choral	,, ,, ,,	$d'-f''$
118	c. 1737	Coro	Mainly Choral melody[1]	$f'-d'''$
121	c. 1740	1. Coro	Choral melody col S.[1]	$e'-d''$
		6. Choral	,, ,, ,,	$e'-d''$
133	1735-7	1. Coro	Choral melody col S.	$f\sharp'-e''$
		6. Choral	,, ,, ,,	$f\sharp'-e'$
135	c. 1740	6. Choral	Choral melody col S.	$d'-d''$
Sanctus in D		...	Col S.	$d'-a''$

[1] Associated with Trombones.

TABLE IV.   THE TROMBONE   195

TABLE IV.   THE TROMBONE

				Sounding Compass.			
Cantata.	Date.	Movement.	Score.	Soprano.	Alto.	Tenor.	Bass.
				I	I, II	II, III	III, IV
No. 2	c. 1740	1. Coro	Tromb. I-IV col S.A.T.B. Choral Motet. No free instrumental parts except Continuo	f♯'–a''	d'–d''	f–a'	g–e♭'
3	c. 1740	6. Choral	Tromb. I-IV col S.A.T.B.	…	…	…	…
			Tromb. col B. Choral melody	…	…	…	e–d''
4	1724	2. Coro	Tromb. I-III col A.T.B. Cornett col S. (Choral melody)	…	g–c♯''	c–f♯'	e,–d'
21	1714	3. Duetto	Tromb. I col A. Free Choral. Cornett col S.	…	…	…	…
		8. Choral	Tromb. I-III col A.T.B. Cornett col S.	…	a–c♯''	…	…
		9. Coro	Tromb. I-IV col S.A.T.B. Choral. No free instrumental parts	d'–d''	a–d''	d–g'	f,–e♭'
23	1724	4. Choral	Tromb. I-III col A.T.B. Cornett col S.	…	c'–d''	d–a♭'	f,–e♭'
25	c. 1731	1. Coro	Tromb. I-III + Cornett. Choral in four instrumental parts. Voices independent	…	g♯–b'	e–f'	e,–a
28	c. 1736	6. Choral	Tromb. I-III col A.T.B. Cornett col S.	…	a–d''	d–g'	d,–d'
		2. Coro	Tromb. I-III col A.T.B. Cornett col S. Choral Motet	…	…	…	…
38	c. 1740	6. Choral	Tromb. I-III col A.T.B. Cornett col S.	…	a–d''	e–a'	g,–e'
		1. Coro	Tromb. I-IV col S.A.T.B. No free instrumental parts except Continuo. Choral Motet	e'–d''	…	…	…
64	1723	6. Choral	Tromb. I-III col A.T.B. Cornett col S.	…	b–d''	d–a'	a,–f♯'
		1. Coro	Tromb. I-IV col S.A.T.B. No free instrumental parts except Continuo	…	…	…	…
68	1735	2.} 4.} 8.} Choral	Tromb. I-III col A.T.B. Cornett col S.	…	a–e'	d–a'	g,–e'
		5. Coro	Tromb. I-III col A.T.B. Cornett col S. No free instrumental parts except Continuo	…	…	…	…
96	c. 1740	1. Coro	Corno e Trombone col A. Choral melody	…	d'–c''	d–a'	f♯,–d'
101	c. 1740	1. Coro	Tromb. I-III col A.T.B. Cornett col S. Choral Melody	…	a–c''	d–a'	…
118	1737	7. Choral	Tromb. I-III col A.T.B. Cornett col S.	…	f–c''	d–g'	d,–c'
121	c. 1740	1. Coro	Tromb. I-III + Cornett. Choral Motet	…	b–e''	e–a'	g,–e'
135	c. 1740	6. Choral	Tromb. I-III col A.T.B. Cornett col S. No free instrumental parts except Continuo. Choral Motet	…	…	…	…
		1. Coro	Trombone col Continuo. Choral Melody	…	…	…	d–d'

TABLE V. THE WALDHORN (CORNO)

(A) CHURCH MUSIC

Work. Cantata.	Date.	Movement.	Key.	Sounding Compass.
No. 1	c. 1740	1. Coro	F	$\begin{cases} a-g'' \\ f-e'' \end{cases}$
		6. Choral	F	$\begin{cases} f'-f'' \\ f-c'' \end{cases}$
14	1735	1. Coro	F	$f'-d''$
		2. Aria (S.)	B♭	$b♭-c'''$
40	1723	1. Coro	F	$\begin{cases} f-f'' \\ f-d'' \end{cases}$
		7. Aria (T.)	F	$\begin{cases} f-f'' \\ f-c'' \end{cases}$
52	c. 1730	1. Sinfonia	F	$\begin{cases} \text{I } c-f'' \\ \text{II } f-d'' \end{cases}$
		6. Choral		$\begin{cases} \text{I } f'-d'' \\ \text{II } f-a' \end{cases}$
79	1735	1. Coro	G	$\begin{cases} \text{I } g'-g'' \\ \text{II } g-d'' \end{cases}$
		3. Choral	G	$\begin{cases} \text{I } d'-g'' \\ \text{II } g-e'' \end{cases}$
		6. Choral	G	$\begin{cases} \text{I } a'-g'' \\ \text{II } d'-d'' \end{cases}$
83	1724	1. Coro	F	$\begin{cases} \text{I } a-f'' \\ \text{II } f-d'' \end{cases}$
88	1732	1. Aria (B.)	G	$\begin{cases} \text{I } d'-a'' \\ \text{II } g-d' \end{cases}$
91	c. 1740	1. Coro	G	$\begin{cases} \text{I } g'-a'' \\ \text{II } b-f\sharp'' \end{cases}$
		6. Choral	G	$\begin{cases} \text{I } g'-g'' \\ \text{II } g-c'' \end{cases}$
100	c. 1735	1. Coro	G	$\begin{cases} \text{I } g-g'' \\ \text{II } g-f\sharp'' \end{cases}$
		6. Choral	G	$\begin{cases} \text{I } d'-g'' \\ \text{II } g-g'' \end{cases}$
112	1731	1. Coro	G	$\begin{cases} \text{I } g'-g'' \\ \text{II } g-e'' \end{cases}$
		5. Choral	G	$\begin{cases} \text{I } g'-d'' \\ \text{II } g-b' \end{cases}$
118	c. 1737	Coro	B♭ ('Lituus')	$\begin{cases} \text{I } f'-a'' \\ \text{II } b♭-ab'' \end{cases}$
136	c. 1725	1. Coro 6. Choral	A col S.	$a-a''$ ...
195	c. 1726	6. Choral	G	$\begin{cases} \text{I } g'-e'' \\ \text{II } g'-c'' \end{cases}$
Mass in F	c. 1736	Kyrie	F	$f'-d''$
Christmas Oratorio, Pt. IV	1734	1. Coro	F	$\begin{cases} \text{I } f-g'' \\ \text{II } f-e'' \end{cases}$
		7. Choral	F	$\begin{cases} \text{I } f-f'' \\ \text{II } f-c'' \end{cases}$
Three Wedding Chorals	(?) 1749	...	G	$\begin{cases} \text{I } d'-g'' \\ \text{II } g-e'' \end{cases}$

TABLE V.   THE WALDHORN (CORNO)   197

(B) SECULAR CANTATAS

Cantata.	Date.	Movement.	Key.	Sounding Compass.
Mer hahn en neue Oberkeet	1742	16. Aria (B.) 18. Aria (S.)	G D[1]	g–e'' d–a'
Aeolus	1725	1. Coro	D	I d–d'' II d–b'
		2. Recit. (B.)	D	I d–c♯' II d–a'
		11. Aria (B.)	D	I f♯–d'' II d–c♯''
		15. Coro	D	I d–d'' II d–a'

[1] The compass of the Horns in D is given in terms of the lower instrument.

TABLE VI.   THE JAGDHORN (CORNO DA CACCIA)

(A) CHURCH MUSIC

Work. Cantata.	Date.	Movement.	Key.	Sounding Compass.
No. 14	1735	2. Aria (S.)	B♭	b♭–c''
16	1724	3. Coro & Aria (B.)	C	c–c''
65	1724	1. Coro	C	I e–a' II c–g'
		6. Aria (T.)	C	I c–c'' II c–b♭'
128	1735	1. Coro	G	I g–a'' II g–g''
		5. Choral	G	I g'–g'' II g–c''
143	1735	1. Coro	B♭	I f'–b♭'' II f'–g'' III b♭–c''
		5. Aria (B.)	B♭	I b♭–b♭'' II b♭–b♭'' III b♭–b♭'
		7. Choral	B♭	I f'–a♭'' II d'–g'' III f–b♭'
174	1729	1. Sinfonia	G	I g–a'' II g–g''
Hohe Messe	1733	10. Aria (B.)	D	d–d''

(B) SECULAR CANTATAS

Work. Cantata.	Date.	Movement.	Key.	Sounding Compass.
Was mir behagt	1716	2. Aria (S.)	F	I f–c'' II f–c''
		11. Coro	F	I f–d'' II f–b♭'
		15. Coro	F	I f–d'' II f–b♭'
Hercules	1733	1. Coro	F	I f–g'' II f–e''
		13. Coro	F	I f'–g'' II f–a'

(C) INSTRUMENTAL MUSIC

Work.	Date.	Movement.	Key.	Sounding Compass.
Brandenburg Concerto, No. 1 in F	1721[1]	...	F[3]	{I f–f'' {II c–d''
Sinfonia, in F	1721[2]	...	F[3]	{I c–f'' {II f–d''

[1] The first movement serves as the Introduction to Cantata No. 52. But the horns used there are not indicated as Corni da caccia.
[2] Another score of the Brandenburg Concerto, No. 1 in F. In B.–G. xxxi (1).
[3] Perhaps a Jagdtrompete an octave higher.

TABLE VII. THE TIMPANI
(A) CHURCH MUSIC

Cantata.	Date.	Movement.	Key.	Score.	Tuning.
No. 11	c. 1736	1. Coro 11. Choral	D	3 Tr.+Timp. ,, ,,	d–a,
15	1704	1. Aria (B.) 4. Aria (T.) 6. Terzetto (A.T.B.) 8. Sonata 9. Quartetto and Choral	C	3 Tr.+Timp. ,, ,, :, ,, ,, ,, ,, ,,	c–g,
19	1726	1. Coro 7. Choral	C	3 Tr.+Timp. ,, ,,	c–g,
21	1714	11. Coro	C	3 Tr.+Timp.	no part
29	1731	1. Sinfonia 2. Coro 8. Choral	D	3 Tr.+Timp. ,, ,, ,, ,,	d–a,
30	1738	1. Coro 12. Coro	D	3 Tr.+Timp. ,, ,,	d–a,
31	1715	1. Sonata 2. Coro 9. Choral	C	3 Tr.+Timp. ,, ,, ,, ,,	c–g,
34	1740–1	1. Coro 5. Coro	D	3 Tr.+Timp. ,, ,,	d–a,
41	1736	1. Coro 6. Choral	C	3 Tr.+Timp. ,, ,,	c–g,
43	c. 1735	1. Coro	C	3 Tr.+Timp.	c–g,
50	c. 1740	Coro	D	3 Tr.+Timp.	d–a,
59	1716	1. Duetto (S.B.)	C	2 Tr.+Timp.	c–g,
63	1723	1. Coro 7. Coro	C	4 Tr.+Timp. ,, ,,	c–g,
69	1724	1. Coro 6. Choral	D	3 Tr.+Timp. ,, ,,	d–a,
71	1708	1. Coro 5. Aria (A.) 7. Coro	C	3 Tr.+Timp. ,, ,, ,, ,,	c–g,
74	1735	1. Coro	C	3 Tr.+Timp.	c–g,
79	1735	1. Coro 3 & 6. Choral	G	2 Cor.+Timp. ,, ,,	d–g,

TABLE VII. THE TIMPANI 199

Work. Cantata.	Date.	Movement.	Key.	Score.	Tuning.
No. 80	1730	1. Coro 5. Choral	D	3 Tr.+Timp. ,,　,,	d–a,
91	c. 1740	1. Coro 6. Choral	G	2 Cor.+Timp. ,,　,,	d–g,
100	c. 1735	1. Coro 6. Choral	G	2 Cor.+Timp. ,,　,,	d–g,
110	post 1734	1. Coro	D	3 Tr.+Timp.	d–a,
119	1723	1. Coro 4. Recit. (B.) 7. Coro	C	4 Tr.+Timp. ,,　,, ,,　,,	c–g,
120	1730	2. Coro	D	3 Tr.+Timp.	d–a,
129	1732	1. Coro 5. Choral	D	3 Tr.+Timp. ,,　,,	d–a,
130	c. 1740	1. Coro 3. Aria (B.) 6. Choral	C	3 Tr.+Timp. ,,　,, ,,　,,	c–g,
137	1732	1. Coro 5. Choral	C	3 Tr.+Timp. ,,　,,	c–g,
143	1735	1. Coro 5. Aria (B.) 7. Choral	B♭	3 Cor. da caccia +Timp.	b♭,–f,
149	1731	1. Coro 7. Choral	D	3 Tr.+Timp. ,,　,,	d–a,
171	c. 1730	1. Coro 6. Choral	D	3 Tr.+Timp. ,,　,,	d–a,
172	1731	1. Coro 3. Aria (B.)	C	3 Tr.+Timp. ,,　,,	c–g,
190	1725	1. Coro 2. Choral 7. Choral	D	3 Tr.+Timp. ,,　,, ,,　,,	d–a,
191	1733	1. Coro 3. Coro	D	3 Tr.+Timp. ,,　,,	d–a,
195	c. 1726	1. Coro 5. Coro 6. Choral	D G	3 Tr.+Timp. ,,　,, 2 Cor.+Timp.	d–a, d–g,
197	1737	1. Coro	D	3 Tr.+Timp.	d–a,
Christmas Oratorio, Pt. I III VI	1734	1. Coro 9. Choral 24. Coro 54. Coro 64. Choral	D	3 Tr.+Timp. ,,　,, ,,　,, ,,　,, ,,　,,	d–a,
Hohe Messe	1733	4. Coro 6. Coro 11. Coro 13. Coro 17. Coro 19. Coro 20. Coro 21. Coro 24. Coro	D	3 Tr.+Timp. ,,　,, ,,　,, ,,　,, ,,　,, ,,　,, ,,　,, ,,　,, ,,　,,	d–a,
Magnificat	1723	1. Coro 6. Coro 11. Coro	D	3 Tr.+Timp. ,,　,, ,,　,,	d–a,
Easter Oratorio	1736	1. Sinfonia 2. Duetto and Coro 10. Coro	D	3 Tr.+Timp. ,,　,, ,,　,,	d–a,
Sanctus in C	...	Coro	C	3 Tr.+Timp.	c–g,

TABLE VII. THE TIMPANI

(B) SECULAR CANTATAS

Work. Cantata.	Date.	Movement.	Key.	Score.	Tuning.
Aeolus	1725	1. Coro 2. Recit. (B.) 11. Aria (B.) 15. Coro	D	3 Tr.+Timp. ,, ,, ,, ,, ,, ,,	d–a,
Angenehmes Wiederau	1737	1. Coro 13. Coro	D	3 Tr.+Timp. ,, ,,	d–a,
Phoebus und Pan	1731	1. Coro 15. Coro	D	3 Tr.+Timp. ,, ,,	d–a,
Preise dein' Glücke	1734	1. Coro 8. Recit. (S.T.B.) 9. Coro	D	3 Tr.+Timp. ,, ,, ,, ,,	d–a,
Schleicht, spielende Wellen	1734	1. Coro 11. Coro	D	3 Tr.+Timp. ,, ,,	d–a,
Tönet, ihr Pauken	1733	1. Coro 9. Coro	D	3 Tr.+Timp. ,, ,,	d–a,
Vereinigte Zwietracht	1726	1. Marcia 2. Coro 11. Coro	D	3 Tr.+Timp. ,, ,, ,, ,,	d–a,

(C) INSTRUMENTAL MUSIC

Sinfonia in D	...	...	D	3 Tr.+Timp.	d–a,
Ouverture in D (1)	...	...	D	3 Tr.+Timp.	d–a,
Ouverture in D (2)	...	...	D	3 Tr.+Timp.	d–a,

TABLE VIII
THE FLÛTE À BEC (BLOCKFLÖTE: FLÛTE DOUCE)
(A) CHURCH MUSIC

Cantata.	Date.	Movement.	Score.	Sounding Compass.
No. 13	c. 1740	1. Aria (T.) 3. Choral (A.) 5. Aria (B.) 6. Choral	3. Unison col A. 5. Unison col Vn. obbl.	{I c'–e''' {II c'–e♭'''
18	1714	1. Sinfonia 3. Recit. (T.B.) and Coro 4. Aria (S.) 5. Choral	4. Unison 5. Col S.	{I e'–a''' {II e'–g'''
25	c. 1731	1. Coro 5. Aria (S.) 6. Choral	1. Unison 6. Col S.	1. d''–d''' 5.{I g'–g''' {II g'–e''' 6.{III f'–b♭''
39	1732	1. Coro 5. Aria (S.) 6. Choral	5. Unison 6. Col S. in 8va	{I d'–f''' {II d'–f'''
46	c. 1725	1. Coro 2. Recit. (T.) 5. Aria (A.) 6. Choral	...	{I a'–g''' {II f'–g'''
65	1724	1. Coro 2. Choral 6. Aria (T.)	2. Unison col S. in 8va	{I f'–g''' {II f'–g'''

TABLE VIII. THE FLÛTE À BEC (BLOCKFLÖTE: FLÛTE DOUCE) 201

Work. Cantata.	Date.	Movement.	Score.	Sounding Compass.
No. 71	1708	1. Coro	...	1. {I g′–g″ / II g–g″
		4. Arioso (B.)	...	4. {I g′–c‴ / II e′–g″
		6. Coro	...	6. {I eb′–ab″ / II eb′–ab″
		7. Coro	...	7. {I g′–a″ / II e′–b″
81	1724	1. Aria (A.)	...	{I g′–f‴ / II g–c‴
96	c. 1740	1. Coro (Flauto piccolo)	Col Violino piccolo	f″–f‴
103	1735	1. Coro (Fiauto piccolo)	Col Violino concertante or Fl. traverso	e″–f♯‴
106	(?) 1711	Sonatina, &c.	...	{I eb′–d‴ / II eb′–d‴
119	1723	1. Coro / 4. Recit. (B.) / 5. Aria (A.) / 7. Coro	5. Unison	{I f′–g‴ / II f′–g‴
122	c. 1742	3. Recit. (S.)	...	{I g″–g‴ / II c″–bb″ / III g′–g″
127	c. 1740	1. Coro / 3. Aria (S.) / 5. Choral	5. Col S. in 8va	{I a′–g‴ / II f′–g‴
142	1712 or 1713	1. Concerto / 2. Coro / 7. Aria (A.) / 8. Choral	... / (?) authentic / 7. Col Violini	{I e′–e‴ / II e′–c‴
152	1715	1. Concerto / 4. Aria (S.) / 6. Duet (S.B.)	6. Gli Stromenti all'unisono	d′–e‴
161	1715	1. Aria (A.) / 4. Recit. (A.) / 5. Coro / 6. Choral	...	{I ab′–g‴ / II f′–g‴
175	1735	1. Recit. (T.) / 2. Aria (A.) / 7. Choral	...	{I a′–g‴ / II a′–e‴ / III g′–c♯‴
180	c. 1740	1. Coro / 4. Recit. (A.) / 5. Aria (S.)	...	{I f′–g‴ / II f′–g‴
182	1714 or 1715	1. Sonata / 2. Coro / 5. Aria (A.) / 7. Choral / 8. Coro	...	e′–f♯‴
Easter Oratorio	1736	6. Aria (T.)	...	{I g′–e‴ / II g′–d‴
St. Matthew Passion	1729	25. Recit. (T.) and Coro[1]	...	{I g′–eb‴ / II f′–c‴
Was mir behagt	1716	9. Aria (S.)	...	{I a′–g‴ / II f′–eb‴

[1] Wrongly indicated as Flauto transverso in the B.–G. Score. See B.–G. x, p. xxii.

(C) INSTRUMENTAL MUSIC

Work.	Date.	Movement.	Score.	Sounding Compass.
Clavier Concerto, No. 6 in F	...	...	...	{I $f'-f'''$ {II $f'-f'''$
Brandenburg Concerto, No. 2 in F	1721	...	...	$f'-g'''$
Brandenburg Concerto, No. 4 in G	1721	...	...	{I $g'-g'''$ {II $f'-g'''$

TABLE IX
THE TRANSVERSE (GERMAN) FLUTE (QUERFLÖTE)
(A) CHURCH MUSIC

Cantata.	Date.	Movement.	Score.	Sounding Compass.
No. 8	c. 1725	1. Coro 4. Aria (B.) 6. Choral	6. Col S.	$e'-a'''$
9	(?) 1731	1. Coro 5. Duetto (S.A.) 7. Choral	7. Col S.	$e'-f'''$
11	c. 1736	1. Coro 3. Recit. (B.) 6. Choral 8. Recit. (A.) 10. Aria (S.) 11. Choral	6. Col S. 10. Unis.	{I $d'-e'''$ {II $d'-e'''$
26	c. 1740	1. Coro 2. Aria (T.) 6. Choral	1. Col Ob. 1. 2. 'Solo' 6. Col S.	$c'-d'''$ [1]
30	1738	1. Coro 5. Aria (A.) 6. Choral 12. Coro	6. Col S.	{I $d'-e'''$ {II $d'-e'''$
34	1740 or 1741	3. Aria (A.)	...	{I $g\#'-f\#'''$ {II $e'-d'''$
45	c. 1740	1. Coro 5. Aria (A.) 7. Choral	1. Col Ob. 5. Solo	{I $d'-e'''$ [2] {II $b-c\#'''$
55	1731 or 1732	1. Aria (T.) 3. Aria (T.) 5. Choral	3. Solo 5. Col S.	$e'-eb'''$
67	c. 1725	1. Coro 4. Choral 6. Aria (B.) and Coro 7. Choral	4. Col S. 7. Col S.	$d'-f\#'''$
78	c. 1740	1. Coro 4. Aria (T.) 7. Choral	4. Solo 7. Col S. in 8va	$f'-g'''$

[1] See *supra*, p. 75.   [2] See *supra*, p. 76.

TABLE IX. THE TRANSVERSE (GERMAN) FLUTE (QUERFLÖTE) 203

Cantata.	Date.	Movement.	Score.	Sounding Compass.
No. 79	1735	1. Coro 2. Aria (A.) 3. Choral 6. Choral	1. Col Ob. 2. Or Oboe. Solo. 3. Col S.	{I d'–c''' {II c'–c'''
94	1735	1. Coro 4. Aria (A.) 8. Choral	4. Solo 8. Col S. in 8va	d'–g'''
96	c. 1740	3. Aria (T.)	'Solo'	d'–e'''
99	c. 1733	1. Coro 3. Aria (T.) 5. Duetto (S.A.) 6. Choral	3. Solo 6. Col S. in 8va	d'–g'''
100	c. 1735	1. Coro 3. Aria (S.) 6. Choral	3. 'Solo'	d'–g'''
101	c. 1740	1. Coro 6. Duetto (S.A.) 7. Choral	7. Col S. in 8va	e'–f'''
102	1731	5. Aria (T.) 7. Choral	5. 'Solo.' Or Vn. piccolo. 7. Col S. in 8va	d'–e'''
103	1735	3. Aria (T.) 6. Choral	3. Or Violin. Solo. 6. Col S.	e'–d'''
107	c. 1735	1. Coro 6. Aria (T.) 7. Choral	6. Unison. Obbl.	{I d'–e''' {II d'–e'''
110	post 1734	1. Coro 2. Aria (T.) 7. Choral	1. Col Ob. 1. 2. Soli. 7. Col S.	{I d'–e''' {II d'–d'''
113	c. 1740	5. Aria (T.)	5. Solo	d'–f#'''
114	c. 1740	2. Aria (T.)	2. Obbl. 'Solo'	d'–e'''
115	c. 1740	1. Coro 4. Aria (S.) 6. Choral	6. Col S.	d'–f#'''
117	c. 1733	1. Coro 7. Aria (A.)	...	{I d'–e''' {II d'–c'''
123	c. 1740	1. Coro 5. Aria (B.) 6. Choral	5. 'Solo' 6. Col S. in 8va	{I d'–e''' {II f#'–e'''
125	c. 1740	1. Coro 2. Aria (A.) 6. Choral	6. Col S. in 8va	e'–e'''
129	1732	1. Coro 3. Aria (S.) 5. Choral	5. Col S. in 8va	d'–e'''
130	c. 1740	5. Aria (T.)	Solo	d'–e'''
145	1729 or 1730	5. Aria (B.)	...	d'–a'''
146	c. 1740	5. Aria (S.)	(?) authentic	d'–e'''
151	c. 1735–40	1. Aria (S.) 5. Choral	5. Col S.	e'–e'''

Work. Cantata.	Date.	Movement.	Score.	Sounding Compass.
157	1727	1. Duetto (T.B.) 4. Aria (B.) 5. Choral	5. Col S. in 8va	$d'-e'''$
164	1723 or 1724	3. Aria (A.) 5. Duetto (S.B.)	3. Soli	I $c'-e'''$ ¹ II $c'-e'''$
173	1731	2. Aria (T.) 4. Duetto (S.B.) 6. Coro	2. Col Violini	I $d'-d'''$ II $d'-c'''$
180	c. 1740	2. Aria (T.)	2. Solo	$d'-e'''$
181	c. 1725	1. Aria (B.) 5. Coro	...	$d'-c''$ ²
184	1731	1. Recit. (T.) 2. Duetto (S.A.) 5. Choral 6. Coro	1. Soli 5. Col S.	I $d'-d'''$ II $d'-c'''$
189	c. 1707–10	1. Aria (T.) 5. Aria (T.)	(?) authentic	$bb'-d'''$
191	1733	1. Coro 2. Duetto (S.T.) 3. Coro	1. Col Ob.	I $d'-e'''$ II $d'-e'''$
192	c. 1732	1. Coro 2. Duetto (S.B.) 3. Choral	...	I $c'-e'''$ ¹ II $a-d'''$
195	c. 1726	1. Coro 4. Recit. (S.) 5. Coro 6. Choral	1. Col Ob. 5. ,, ,, 6. Col S. in 8va	I $d'-e'''$ II $d'-e'''$
Ehre sei Gott	1728	4. Aria (A.)	4. Soli	I $g'-e'''$ II $g'-d'''$
Christmas Oratorio, Pt. I	1734	1. Coro 5. Choral 8. Aria (B.) 9. Choral	5. Col S. in 8va 9. ,, ,, ,,	I $d'-e'''$ II $d'-e'''$
Christmas Oratorio, Pt. II	1734	1. Sinfonia 3. Choral 6. Aria (T.) 8. Choral 10. Aria (A.) 12. Coro 14. Choral	3. Col S. in 8va 6. Solo 8. Col S. in 8va	I $d'-e'''$ II $d'-e'''$
Christmas Oratorio, Pt. III	1734	1. Coro 3. Coro 4. Recit. (B.) 5. Choral 9. Recit. (A.) 10. Choral 12. Choral	5. Col S. in 8va 10. ,, ,, 12. ,, ,,	I $d'-e'''$ II $d'-d\sharp'''$
Easter Oratorio	1736	4. Aria (S.)	4. Or Vn. Solo.	$d\sharp'-d'''$
Magnificat	1723	1. Coro 3a. Coro 5. Duetto (A.T.) 6. Coro 8. Aria (A.) 11. Coro	5. Col Violini 8. Soli	I $d'-f\sharp'''$ II $d'-e'''$

¹ See *supra*, p. 76.

TABLE IX. THE TRANSVERSE (GERMAN) FLUTE (QUERFLÖTE) 205

Work.	Date.	Movement.	Score.	Sounding Compass.
Trauer-Ode	1727	1. Coro 4. Recit. (A.) 7. Coro 8. Aria (T.) 9. Recit. (B.) 10. Coro	...	{I *d'–f♯'''* {II *d'–d'''*
Mass in A	*c.* 1737	1. Coro 2. Coro 4. Aria (S.) 6. Coro	4. Soli	{I *e'–f♯'''* {II *d'–f♯'''*
Hohe Messe	1733	7. Duetto (S.T.) and choruses	24. Col Ob.	{I *d'–g'''*1 {II *c♯'–g'''*

St. John Passion	1723	13. Aria (S.)
		62. Arioso (T.)
		63. Aria (S.)
		    and Choruses
		    and Chorals
			1. &c. Col Ob.
			13. Solo
				{I *c'–f♯''''*1
				{II *d'–f♯'''*

St. Matthew Passion	1729	9. Recit. (A.)
		10. Aria (A.)
		12. Aria (S.)
		26. Aria (T.) and
		    Coro
		33. Duetto (S.A.)
		    and Coro
		36. Aria (A.) and
		    Coro
		58. Aria (S.)
		65. Recit. (B.)
		    and Choruses and
		    Chorals
			9. Soli
			10. ,,
			36. Col Ob.
				I{I *a–g'''*2
				 {II *d'–g'''*
				II{I *a–e'''*
				  {II *d'–e'''*

(B) SECULAR CANTATAS

Work.	Date.	Movement.	Score.	Sounding Compass.
Aeolus	1725	1. Coro 2. Recit. (B.) 10. Recit. (S.B.) 13. Duetto (A.T.) 15. Coro	10. Soli 13. Obbl.	{I *d'–g'''* {II *d'–g'''*
Angenehmes Wiederau	1737	11. Aria (T.)	A version of Cantata No. 30. Excepting the Tenor Aria flutes do not appear to be in the score	*c♯'–g''*2
Die Freude reget sich	*c.* 1733	1. Coro 5. Aria (A.) 7. Aria (S.)	7. Solo	*d'–e'''*
Durchlaucht'ster Leopold	?1718	2. Aria (S.) 4. Duetto (S.B.) 6. Aria (S.) 8. Coro	2. Col Vn. I.	{I *d'–e'''* {II *d'–e'''*
Ich bin in mir vergnügt	*c.* 1730	6. Aria (S.) 8. Aria (S.)	6. Solo	*d'–e'''*
Mer hahn en neue Oberkeet	1742	14. Aria (S.)	...	*e'–d'''*

1 See *supra*, p. 77.   2 See *supra*, p. 78.

Work. Cantata.	Date.	Movement.	Score.	Sounding Compass.
Non sa che sia dolore	...	1. Sinfonia 3. Aria (S.) 5. Aria (S.)	...	$d'-e'''$
O holder Tag (O angenehme Melodei)	1746	6. Aria (S.) 9. Recit. (S.) 10. Aria (S.)	6. Solo	$d'-f\sharp'''$
Phoebus und Pan	1731	1. Coro 5. Aria (B.) 13. Aria (A.) 15. Coro	13. Soli	$\begin{cases}\text{I } d'-f\sharp'''\\ \text{II } d'-f\sharp'''\end{cases}$
Preise dein' Glücke	1734	1. Coro 6. Recit. (S.) 7. Aria (S.) 8. Recit. (S.T.B.) 9. Coro	6. Soli 7. Solo	$\begin{cases}\text{I } d'-e'''\\ \text{II } d'-e'''\end{cases}$
Schleicht, spielende Wellen	1734	1. Coro 9. Aria (S.) 11. Coro	9. Soli	$\begin{cases}\text{I } d'-e'''\\ \text{II } d'-d'''\\ \text{III } d'-a''\end{cases}$
Schweigt stille	1732	4. Aria (S.) 10. Coro	4. Solo	$d'-e'''$
Tönet, ihr Pauken	1733	1. Coro 3. Aria (S.) 8. Recit. (B.) 9. Coro	3. Soli	$\begin{cases}\text{I } d'-f\sharp'''\\ \text{II } d'-f\sharp'''\end{cases}$
Vereinigte Zwietracht (Auf, schmetternde Töne)	1726	2. Coro 9. Aria (A.) 11. Coro	... ...	$2\begin{cases}\text{I } a-g\sharp''\\ \text{II } a-e''\end{cases}$ $9\begin{cases}\text{I } d'-e'''\\ 11\text{II } d'-d'''\end{cases}$

(C) INSTRUMENTAL MUSIC

Work.	Date.	Movement.	Score.	Sounding Compass.
Sonata I, in B mi., for Clavier and Flute[1]	...	...	...	$e'-g'''$
Sonata II, in E♭ ma.	...	...	...	$d'-d'''$
Sonata III, in A ma.	...	...	...	$d'-e'''$
Sonata IV (Trio), in G ma.	...	...	...	$d'-e'''$
Sonata for 2 Flutes and Clavier, in G ma.	...	...	...	$\begin{cases}\text{I } d'-d'''\\ \text{II } d'-d'''\end{cases}$
Clavier Concerto VIII in A mi.[2]	...	...	...	$d'-e'''$
Brandenburg Concerto, No. 5, in D ma.	1721	...	...	$d'-d'''$
Ouverture in B mi.[3]	...	...	...	$d'-f\sharp'''$
Sonata I for flute and Clavier, in C ma.[4]	...	...	...	$d'-e'''$
Sonata II, in E mi.[4]	...	...	...	$d'-g'''$
Sonata III, in E ma.[4]	...	...	...	$e'-e'''$
Trio, and Canon, in C mi.[5]	1747	...	...	$d'-e\flat'''$

[1] The five Sonatas are in B.-G. ix.
[2] In B.-G. xvii.　　　[3] In B.-G. xxxi (1).　　　[4] In B.-G. xliii (1).
[5] In B.-G. xxxi (2): 'Musicalisches Opfer'.

TABLE X. THE OBOE (HAUTBOIS)
(A) CHURCH MUSIC

Cantata.	Date.	Movement.	Score.	Sounding Compass.
No. 2	c. 1740	1. Coro 5. Aria (T.) 6. Choral	5. Col Vn. I	$\{$ I g–d'''' [1] $\{$ II g–d'''
5	1735	1. Coro 4. Recit. (A.) 5. Aria (B.) 7. Choral	4. Choral obbligato 5. Col Vn. I	$\{$ I c'–d''' $\{$ II c'–$b\flat''$
6	1736	1. Coro 6. Choral	1. Ob. da caccia as Taille	$\{$ I d'–$b\flat''$ $\{$ II c'–$b\flat''$
10	c. 1740	1. Coro 2. Aria (S.) 5. Duetto (A.T.) 7. Choral	5. Col Tromba. Choral obbligato	$\{$ I c'–d''' $\{$ II $b\flat$–d'''
11	c. 1736	1. Coro 6. Choral 10. Aria (S.) 11. Choral	...	$\{$ I d'–d''' $\{$ II d'–$c\sharp'''$
12	1724–5	1. Sinfonia 2. Coro 4. Aria (A.) 7. Choral	4. Obbligato 7. Or Tromba; obbligato	c'–c'''
14	1735	1. Coro 4. Aria (B.) 5. Choral	4. 2 Ob.+Cont.	$\{$ I c'–c''' $\{$ II c'–$b\flat''$
16	1724	1. Coro 3. Coro and Aria(B.) 6. Choral	1. Col Violini 3. ,, ,,	$\{$ I a–c''' $\{$ II g–a''
17	c. 1737	1. Coro 7. Choral	...	$\{$ I $c\sharp'$–b'' $\{$ II a–$c\sharp'''$
19	1726	1. Coro 7. Choral	1. Col Violini 7. ,, ,,	$\{$ I d'–b' $\{$ II b–a'' $\{$ III c–d'' [2]
20	c. 1725	1. Coro 5. Aria (B.) 7. Choral 8. Aria (B.) 11. Choral	5. 3 Ob.+Cont. 8. Col Violini and Viola	$\{$ I c'–d''' $\{$ II c'–a'' $\{$ III c'–f''
21	1714	1. Sinfonia 2. Coro 3. Aria (S.) 6. Coro 9. Coro 11. Coro	3. Obbligato	$b\flat$–d'''
22	1723	1. Coro 2. Aria (A.) 5. Choral	2. 'Solo'	c'–c'''
23	1724	1. Duetto (S.A.) 2. Recit. (T.) 3. Coro 4. Choral	1. 2 Ob.+Cont. 2. 2 Ob. col Vn. I	$\{$ I c'–c''' $\{$ II c'–c'''
24	1723	3. Coro 6. Choral	3. Col Violini 6. ,, ,,	$\{$ I c'–d''' $\{$ II $b\flat$–$b\flat''$

[1] For this and other examples of an abnormal Oboe compass see *supra*, p. 98.
[2] Cf. Nos. 31, 35, 36, 122, 186, and p. 99, note 5, *supra*.

Cantata.	Date.	Movement.	Score.	Sounding Compass.
No. 25	c. 1731	1. Coro 5. Aria (S.) 6. Choral	1. Col Violini 5. ,, ,,	I $c'-d'''$ II $a-a''$
26	c. 1740	1. Coro 4. Aria (B.) 6. Choral	4. 3 Ob.+Org. and Cont.	I $c'-d'''$ II $c'-c'''$ III $c'-c'''$
27	1731	1. Coro 6. Choral	...	I $c'-c'''$ II $c'-a''$
28	c. 1736	1. Aria (S.) 2. Coro 6. Choral	...	I $e'-b''$ II $c'-g''$ III $f-d''$
29	1731	1. Sinfonia 2. Coro 5. Aria (S.) 8. Choral	1. Col Violini 2. ,, ,, 8. ,, ,,	I $g-c'''$ II $g-a''$
30	1738	1. Coro 6. Choral 7. Recit. (B.) 12. Coro	7. 2 Ob.+Org. and Cont. 12. Ob. I col Fl. I	I $d'-d'''$ II $c\sharp'-d'''$
31	1715	1. Sonata 2. Coro 8. Aria (S.) 9. Choral	8. Oboes with Fagotto foundation	I $b-b\flat''$ II $b-g''$ III $a-d''$ IV $d-c''$
32	c. 1740	1. Aria (S.) 5. Duetto (S.B.) 6. Choral	...	$d'-d'''$
33	c. 1740	1. Coro 5. Duetto (T.B.) 6. Choral	5. 2 Ob.+Org. and Cont.	I $c'-d'''$ II $c'-c'''$
34	1740–1	1. Coro 5. Coro	...	I $d'-d'''$ II $c\sharp'-b''$
35	1731	1. Sinfonia 2. Aria (A.) 5. Sinfonia 7. Aria (A.)	...	I $b\flat-d'''$ II $b-d'''$ III $e-e''$
38	c. 1740	1. Coro 3. Aria (T.) 6. Choral	3. 2 Ob.+Cont.	I $c'-c'''$ II $c'-g''$
39	1732	1. Coro 3. Aria (A.) 7. Choral	3. Ob.+Vn. Solo+ Cont.	I $c'-c'''$ II $c'-a''$
40	1723	1. Coro 3. Choral 4. Aria (B.) 6. Choral 7. Aria (T.) 8. Choral	7. 2 Ob.+2 Cor.+ Cont.	I $c'-d'''$ II $c'-c'''$
41	1736	1. Coro 2. Aria (S.) 6. Choral	2. 3 Ob.+Org. e Cont.	I $d\sharp'-d'''$ II $c'-a''$ III $c'-a''$
42	1731	1. Sinfonia 3. Aria (A.) 7. Choral	...	I $d'-c\sharp'''$ II $c'-a''$
43	c. 1735	1. Coro 5. Aria (S.) 9. Aria (A.) 11. Choral	1. Col Violini 5. ,, ,, 9. 2 Ob.+Cont.	I $g-e'''$ II $g-d'''$

TABLE X. THE OBOE (HAUTBOIS)   209

Cantata.	Date.	Movement.	Score.	Sounding Compass.
No. 44	*c.* 1725	1. Coro (T.B.) 2. Coro 3. Aria (A.) 6. Aria (S.) 7. Choral	2. Col Violini 3. Ob.+Fag. e Cont. 6. Col Violini	{I *c'–d'''* {II *g–bb''*
45	*c.* 1740	1. Coro 7. Choral	1. Col Flauti	{I *d'–c♯'''* {II *a–c♯'''*
47	1720	1. Coro 4. Aria (B.) 5. Choral	4. Ob.+Vn.+Cont.	{I *c'–d'''* {II *c'–c'''*
48	*c.* 1740	1. Coro 3. Choral 4. Aria (A.) 6. Aria (T.) 7. Choral	4. 'Solo'+Cont. 6. Col Vn. I	{I *c'–c'''* {II *d'–bb''*
50	*c.* 1740	Coro	...	{I *e'–d'''* {II *e'–b''* {III *a–g♯''*
52	*c.* 1730	1. Sinfonia 5. Aria (S.) 6. Choral	1. Oboes with Fagotto foundation 5. 3 Ob.+Cont.	{I *c'–d'''* {II *c'–a''* {III *c'–f''*
55	1731–2	5. Choral	5. Col Sop.	...
56	1731	1. Aria (B.) 3. Aria (B.) 5. Choral	1. Col Violini and Viola 3. 'Solo'	{I *c'–d'''* {II *bb–ab''* {III *d–e''*
57	*c.* 1740	1. Aria (B.) 8. Choral	1. Col Violini and Viola	{I *d'–c'''* {II *c'–g''* {Taille *f–eb'*
58	1733	1. Duetto (S.B.) 5. Duetto (S.B.)	1. Col Violini and Viola 5. ,, ,,	{I *c'–d'''* {II *c'–g''* {III *g–f''*
62	*c.* 1740	1. Coro 2. Aria (T.) 6. Choral	2. Col Violini	{I *d'–c'''* {II *d'–a''*
63	1723	1. Coro 3. Duetto (S.B.) 6. Recit. (B.) 7. Coro	1. Oboes with Fagotto foundation 3. 'Solo'	{I *e'–c'''* {II *c'–a''* {III *c'–f♯''*
66	1731	1. Coro 3. Aria (B.)	3. Oboes with Fagotto foundation	{I *d'–d'''* {II *d'–d'''*
68	1735	1. Coro 2. Aria (S.) 4. Aria (B.) 5. Coro	1. Col Violini and Viola 4. 3 Ob.+Cont. 5. Col Violini and Viola	{I *c'–d'''* {II *c'–g♯''* {III *f–d''*
69	1724–30	1. Coro 3. Aria (A.) 6. Choral	1. Oboes with Fagotto foundation 3. Oboe+Vn.+Cont.	{I *d'–d'''* {II *d'–a''* {III *d'–b''*
70	1716	1. Coro 2. Recit. (B.) 7. Choral 8. Aria (T.) 11. Choral	8. Col Vn. I	*g–c'''*
71	1708	1. Coro 4. Arioso (B.) 6. Coro 7. Coro	1–7. Oboes have Fa- gotto foundation	{I *c'–c'''* {II *c'–g''*

Cantata.	Date.	Movement.	Score.	Sounding Compass.
No. 72	c. 1726	1. Coro 4. Aria (S.) 5. Choral	...	{I $c'-d'''$ {II $c'-c'''$
73	c. 1725	1. Coro 2. Aria (T.) 5. Choral	2. Ob.+Cont.	{I $c'-c'''$ {II $c'-b\flat''$
74	1735	1. Coro 6. Recit. (B.) 7. Aria (A.) 8. Choral	1–7. Ob. da caccia as Taille	{I $c'-d'''$ {II $c'-b''$
75	1723	1. Coro 3. Aria (T.) 7. Choral 14. Choral	7. Col Violini 14. ,, ,,	{I $d'-d'''$ {II $c'-c'''$
76	1723	1. Coro	1. Col Violini	{I $c'-d'''$ {II $g-b''$
77	c. 1725	3. Aria (S.)		{I $e'-c'''$ {II $c'-b''$
78	c. 1740	1. Coro 6. Aria (B.) 7. Choral	6. Obbligato	{I $c'-d'''$ {II $c'-d'''$
79	1735	1. Coro 2. Aria (A.) 3. Choral 6. Choral	1. Col Flauti 2. 'Solo'; or Fl.	{I $d'-c'''$ {II $c'-c'''$
80	1730	1. Coro 2. Duetto (S.B.) 5. Choral (?)	...	{I $d'-f\sharp''$ {II $d'-f\sharp''$ {III $g-d''$
82	c. 1731	1. Aria (B.) 5. Aria (B.)	...	$c'-d\flat'''$
83	1724	1. Aria (A.) 5. Choral	...	{I $d'-c'''$ {II $c'-a''$
84	1731–2	1. Aria (S.) 3. Aria (S.) 5. Choral	3. Ob.+Vn. Solo+ Cont.	$d'-d'''$
85	1735	1. Aria (B.) 3. Choral (S.) 6. Choral	3. 2 Ob.+Cont.	{I $c'-c'''$ {II $c'-c'''$
86	c. 1725	3. Choral (S.)	3. 2 Ob.+Cont.	{I $b-a''$ {II $b-a''$
87	1735	1. Aria (B.) 7. Choral	1. Col Violini and Viola. Ob. da caccia as Taille	{I $d'-c'''$ {II $b\flat-b\flat''$
88	1732	1. Aria (B.)	1. Taille. Col Viola	$c-e''$
89	c. 1730	1. Aria (B.) 5. Aria (S.) 6. Choral	5. Ob.+Cont.	{I $c'-d'''$ {II $c'-d'''$
91	c. 1740	1. Coro 3. Aria (T.) 6. Choral	3. 3 Ob.+Cont.	{I $d'-d'''$ {II $c'-c'''$ {III $c'-g''$
93	1728	1. Coro 6. Aria (S.) 7. Choral	6. Ob.+Cont.	{I $c'-d'''$ {II $c'-c'''$

TABLE X. THE OBOE (HAUTBOIS) 211

Cantata.	Date.	Movement.	Score.	Sounding Compass.

No. 94	1735	1. Coro
		3. Recit. and
		   Choral (T.)
		8. Choral
			1. Col Violini
			3. 2 Ob.+Cont.
				{ I a–d'''
				  II b–a''

95	See	Table XII		
96	c. 1740	1. Coro 5. Aria (B.) 6. Choral	...	{ I d'–d''' II c'–c'''

97	1734	1. Coro
		8. Aria (S.)
		9. Choral
			1. Oboes have Fagotto
			   foundation
			8. 2 Ob.+Cont.
				{ I c'–c'''
				  II c'–d'''

98	c. 1732	1. Coro
		3. Aria (S.)
			3. 'Solo'+Cont.	{ I c'–bb''
				  II Col A.
				  III Col T.

101	c. 1740	1. Coro
		4. Aria (B.)
		7. Choral
			4. 3 Ob.+Cont.	{ I d'–d'''
				  II c'–b''
				  III f–d''

102	1731	1. Coro 3. Aria (A.) 7. Choral	3. Ob.+Cont.	{ I c'–d''' II c'–bb''

104	c. 1725	1. Coro	...	{ I d'–c'''
				  II c'–a''
				  III g–e''

105	c. 1725	1. Coro 3. Aria (S.)	1. Col Violini	{ I c'–d''' II g–f''
109	c. 1731	1. Coro 5. Aria (A.) 6. Choral	5. 2 Ob.+Cont.	{ I c'–c''' II c'–c'''

110	post 1734	1. Coro
		6. Aria (B.)
		7. Choral
			1. Oboes have Fagotto
			   foundation
			6. Col Violini and
			   Viola. Ob. da
			   caccia as Taille
				{ I c#'–d'''
				  II d'–b''
				  III c'–g''

111	c. 1740	1. Coro 5. Recit. (S.) 6. Choral	5. 2 Ob.+Cont.	{ I e'–d''' II c'–c'''
113	c. 1740	1. Coro	...	{ I e'–b'' II c#'–g''
114	c. 1740	1. Coro 5. Aria (A.) 7. Choral	...	{ I c'–c''' II d'–c'''
117	c. 1733	1. Coro	...	{ I d'–d''' II d'–c'''

119[1]	1723	1. Coro
		7. Coro
			...	{ I d'–c'''
				  II c'–a''
				  III c'–a''

122	c. 1742	1. Coro
		6. Choral
			1. Col Violini and
			   Viola
				{ I d'–c'''
				  II c'–a''
				  III d–eb''

125	c. 1740	1. Coro 6. Choral	...	c'–c'''
126	c. 1740	1. Coro 2. Aria (T.) 6. Choral	2. 2 Ob.+Cont.	{ I c'–d''' II c'–d'''

[1] An alternative score of No. 118 introduces an oboe.

Cantata.	Date.	Movement.	Score.	Sounding Compass.
No. 127	c. 1740	1. Coro 3. Aria (S.) 5. Choral	...	{I $c'-d'''$ {II $c'-c'''$
128	1735	1. Coro 5. Choral	1. Col Violini. Ob. da caccia col Viola	{I $d'-e'''$ {II $b-g''$
129	1732	1. Coro 5. Choral	...	{I $d'-d'''$ {II $c\#'-a''$
130	c. 1740	1. Coro 6. Choral	...	{I $g'-d'''$ {II $d'-b''$ {III $c'-a''$
131	1707-8	1. Coro 2. Duetto (S.B.) 3. Coro 5. Coro	2. Ob.+Cont.	$c'-d'''$
132	1715	1. Aria (S.)	...	$b-b''$
134	1731	2. Aria (T.) 6. Coro	...	{I $c'-c'''$ {II $c'-c'''$
135	c. 1740	1. Coro 3. Aria (T.) 6. Choral	3. 2 Ob.+Cont.	{I $e'-c'''$ {II $c'-b''$
136	c. 1725	1. Coro 6. Choral	1. Ob. II is a d'amore 6. Ob. II col S.	I $c\#'-d'''$
137	1732	1. Coro 3. Duetto (S.B.) 5. Choral	3. 2 Ob.+Cont.	{I $e'-c\#'''$ {II $c'-a''$
140	1731-42	1. Coro 6. Duetto (S.B.) 7. Choral	6. 'Solo'+Cont.	{I $c'-bb''$ {II $c'-g''$ {III $f-eb''$
141	1721-2	1. Coro 2. Aria (T.)	? Authentic	{I $d'-b''$ {II $c'-b''$
142	1712-13	1. Concerto 2. Coro 5. Aria (T.) 8. Choral	? Authentic 5. 2 Ob.+Cont. 8. Col Violini	{I $e'-c'''$ {II $d'-c'''$
146	c. 1740	1. Sinfonia 7. Duetto (T.B.)	? Authentic (exc. Sinfonia)	{I $c'-d'''$ {II $c'-d'''$ {III $f-e''$
147	1716	1. Coro 6. Choral 9. Aria (B.) 10. Choral	1. Col Vn. I 6. " " 9. Col Violini 10. Col Vn. I	{I $c'-c'''$ {II $a-c'''$
148	c. 1725	4. Aria (A.)	4. 3 Ob.+Cont.	{I $b-a''$ {II $b-f\#''$ {III $g-d''$
149	1731	1. Coro 7. Choral	1. Oboes have Fagotto foundation	{I $d'-d'''$ {II $c\#'-a''$ {III $d'-f\#''$
152	1715	1. Concerto 2. Aria (B.) 6. Duetto (S.B.)	2. Ob.+Cont. 6. Col Fl. and Viole	$a-a''$
154	1724	3. Choral 8. Choral	Col Soprano	...
156	1729-30	1. Sinfonia 4. Aria (A.) 6. Choral	4. Ob.+Vn.+Cont.	$c'-d'''$

TABLE X. THE OBOE (HAUTBOIS) 213

Cantata.	Date.	Movement.	Score.	Sounding Compass.
No. 157	1727	1. Duetto (T.B.) 5. Choral	...	b–a''
158	1708–17	2. Duetto (S.B.)	2. Col S.	...
159	1729	2. Duetto (S.A.) 4. Aria (B.) 5. Choral	2. Col S.	c'–c'''
164	1723–4	5. Duetto (S.B.) 6. Choral	5. Col Violini and Flauti	{I c'–c''' {II c'–c'''
166	c. 1725	1. Aria (B.) 2. Aria (T.) 5. Aria (A.)	2. Ob.+Cont.	c'–c'''
167	c. 1725	5. Choral	...	c'–d'''
169	1731	1. Sinfonia 7. Choral	1. Col Violini	{I a–b'' {II $g\sharp$–a'' {III f–d''
171	c. 1730	1. Coro 5. Recit. (B.) 6. Choral	5. 2 Ob.+Cont.	{I d'–d''' {II $c\sharp'$–g''
174	1729	1. Sinfonia 2. Aria (A.) 5. Choral	2. 2 Ob.+Cont.	{I d'–d''' {II c'–a'' {III g–$d\sharp''$
176	1735	1. Coro 5. Aria (A.) 6. Choral	5. 2 Ob.+Ob. da caccia (all unison)+ Cont.	{I c'–a'' {II c'–f''
177	1732	1. Coro 5. Choral	...	{I d'–$b\flat''$ {II c'–c'''
178	c. 1740	1. Coro 7. Choral	...	{I d'–d''' {II c'–d'''
179	1724	3. Aria (T.) 6. Choral	3. Col Vn, I	{I c'–d''' {II c'–d'''
180	c. 1740	1. Coro 5. Aria (S.)	Ob. II da caccia	I d'–d'''
181	c. 1725	1. Aria (B.) 5. Coro	...	d'–c'''
185	1715	1. Duetto (S.T.) 3. Aria (A.) 6. Choral	1. Ob. (or Tromba)+ Cont.	b–b''
186	1723	1. Coro 6. Choral 10. Duetto (S.A.)	1. Col Violini	{I c'–d''' {II c'–$b\flat''$ {III c–$e\flat''$
187	1732	1. Coro 3. Aria (A.) 5. Aria (S.) 7. Choral	3. Ob. I col Vn. I 5. 'Solo'+Cont.	{I c'–d''' {II d'–$b\flat''$
188	1731	1. Aria (T.)	...	c'–d'''
189	1707–10	1. Aria (T.) 5. Aria (T.)	...	f'–$b\flat''$
190	1725	1. Coro 2. Choral 7. Choral	...	No parts exc. for No. 7
191	1733	1. Coro 3. Coro	1. Col Flauti	{I d'–d''' {II d'–$c\sharp'''$

Work. Cantata.	Date.	Movement.	Score.	Sounding Compass.
No. 192	c. 1732	1. Coro 2. Duetto (S.B.) 3. Choral	2. Ob. I col Vn. I and Fl. I 3. Col Violini and Flauti	I c′–e‴ II a–d‴
193	c. 1740	1. Coro 3. Aria (S.) 5. Aria (A.) 7. Coro	5. Ob.+Cont.	I a–d‴ II d′–d‴
194	1723	1. Coro 3. Aria (B.) 6. Choral 10. Duetto (S.B.) 12. Choral	1. Oboes have Fagotto foundation 10. 2 Ob.+Cont.	I c′–c‴ II c′–bb″ III c′–bb″
195	c. 1726	1. Coro 5. Coro 6. Choral	1. and 5. Col. Flauti 5. Ob. II d'amore	I d′–b″ II d′–a″
197	1737	1. Coro 6. Aria (B.) 9. Recit. (B.)	...	I d′–d‴ II d′–a″
Mein Herze schwimmt	1714	2. Aria (S.) 8. Aria (S.)	2. Ob.+Cont.	bb–ab″
Easter Oratorio	1736	1. Sinfonia 2. Duetto (T.B.) and Coro 10. Coro	...	I d′–d‴ II d′–d‴
Christmas Oratorio, Pt. I	1734	1. Coro 5. Choral 7. Duetto S.B. 9. Choral	7. Ob.+Ob. d'amore +Cont.	I b–c♯‴ II b–b″
Christmas Oratorio, Pt. III	1734	1. Coro 5. Choral 10. Choral 12. Choral	...	I f♯′–d‴ II d′–b″
Christmas Oratorio, Pt. IV.	1734	1. Coro 4. Aria (S.) 7. Choral	4. 'Solo'+Cont.	I c′–d‴ II c′–a″
Christmas Oratorio, Pt. VI	1734	1. Coro 6. Choral 11. Choral	...	I d′–d‴ II c♯′–d‴
St. Matthew Passion	1729	Excepting No. 40 (Recit. Tenor) the Oboe is scored only in the Choruses and simple Chorals	Coro I 40. 2 Ob.+Cont. Coro II	I c′–d‴ II c′–c‴ I c′–c♯‴ II c′–c‴
St. John Passion	1723	Excepting No. 11 (Aria, Alto) the Oboe is scored only in the Choruses and simple Chorals	11. 2 Ob.+Cont.	I c′–c‴ II c′–c‴
Hohe Messe	1733–	The Oboe is scored only in the Choruses	3rd Oboe only in the 'Sanctus'	I d′–d‴ II a–c♯‴ III d′–g♯″
Mass in F	c. 1736	4. Aria (S.) and 3 Choruses	4. 'Solo'+Cont.	I c′–d‴ II c′–g″
Mass in G mi.	c. 1737	4. Aria (A.) 5. Aria (T.) and 3 Choruses	5. Ob.+Cont.	I c′–d‴ II c′–d‴

TABLE X.   THE OBOE (HAUTBOIS)   215

Work.	Date.	Movement.	Score.	Sounding Compass.
Mass in G ma.	c. 1738	5. Aria (T.) and 3 Choruses	5. 'Solo'+Cont.	{I c'–c''' {II c'–c'''
Magnificat	1723	The Oboe is scored only in the Choruses	...	{I d'–d''' {II c♯'–a''
Sanctus in C	...	...	...	{I c'–c''' {II c'–a''
Sanctus in G ma.	...	...	...	{I d'–d''' {II d'–c'''

(B) SECULAR CANTATAS

Work.	Date.	Movement.	Score.	Sounding Compass.
Aeolus	1725	1. Coro 2. Recit. (B.) 3. Aria (B.) 15. Coro	3. Col Vn. I	{I b–d''' {II c♯'–d''
Angenehmes Wiederau	1737	See Cantata, No. 30		
Hercules	1733	1. Coro 7. Aria (T.) 13. Coro	7. Ob.+Vn.+Cont.	{I c'–d''' {II c'–a''
Ich bin in mir vergnügt	c. 1730	2. Aria (S.) 8. Aria (S.)	2. 2 Ob.+Cont. 8. Col Violini	{I g–d''' {II g–b♭''
Mit Gnaden bekröne	? 1722	1. Aria (T.) 7. Coro	...	{I c'–c''' {II c'–c'''
Phoebus und Pan	1731	1. Coro 15. Coro	...	{I d'–d''' {II d'–b''
Preise dein' Glücke	1734	1. Coro 2. Recit. (T.) 5. Aria (B.) 8. Recit. (S.T.B.) 9. Coro	2. 2 Ob.+Cont.	{I c♯'–d''' {II c♯'–b''
Schleicht, spielende Wellen	1734	1. Coro 11. Coro	11. Col Flauti	{I d'–d''' {II d'–a''
Tönet, ihr Pauken	1733	1. Coro 5. Aria (A.) 8. Recit. (B.) 9. Coro	5..2 Ob. (unison)+ Cont. 8. Fl. unis.+2 Ob.+ Cont.	{I a–d''' {II a–b''
Trauer-Ode	1727	4. Recit. (A.) 9. Recit. (B.)	...	{I f♯'–e'' {II c'–c♯''
Vereinigte Zwietracht	1726	2. Coro 7. Ritornello 10. Recit. (S.A.T.B.) 11. Coro	3rd Oboe	g♯–d''
Was mir behagt	1716	7. Aria (B.) 11. Coro 15. Coro	7. 3 Ob.+Cont. 11. Col Violini and Viola 15. Oboes have Fagotto foundation	{I c'–c''' {II b–a'' {Taille f–d''
Weichet nur	1717–22	1. Aria (S.) 7. Aria (S.) 9. Aria (S.)	7. Ob.+Cont.	d'–b''

(C) INSTRUMENTAL MUSIC

Work.	Date.	Movement.	Score.	Sounding Compass.
Brandenburg Concerto, No. 1, in F ma.	1721	...	'ē Bassono'	I $c'-d'''$ II $c'-b''$ III $c'-g''$
Brandenburg Concerto, No. 2, in F ma.	1721	...	...	$c'-d'''$
Sinfonia in D ma.[1]	...	...	...	I $d'-d'''$ II $d'-a''$
Ouverture in C ma.	...	...	...	I $d'-d'''$ II $c'-d'''$
Ouverture in D ma.	...	...	...	I $d'-d'''$ II $c\sharp'-d'''$
Ouverture in D ma.	...	...	...	I $d'-d'''$ II $d'-b''$ III $c'-g''$
Sinfonia in F ma.[2]	...	...	...	I $c'-d'''$ II $c'-bb''$ III $c'-f''$
Trio (Violin, Oboe, Continuo) in F ma.[3]	...	...	Fragment	$c'-b''$

[1] B.-G. xxi (1), p. 65.
[2] Brandenburg Concerto, No. I.   [3] B.-G. xxix, p. 250.

TABLE XI.   THE OBOE DA CACCIA
(ENGLISH HORN: HAUTBOIS DE CHASSE)
(A) CHURCH MUSIC

Cantata.	Date.	Movement.	Score.	Sounding Compass.
No. 1	c. 1740	1. Coro 3. Aria (S.) 6. Choral	3. Ob.+Cont.	I $f-f''$ II $f-f''$
6	1736	1. Coro 2. Aria (A.) 6. Choral	1. As Taille 2. Ob.+Cont.	$f-f''$
13	c. 1740	1. Aria (T.) 3. Choral (A.)	3. Col A.	$f-eb''$
16	1724	5. Aria (T.)	5. Or Violetta+Cont.	$f-d''$
27	1731	3. Aria (A.)	3. Ob.+Org. obbl.+ Cont.	$f-eb''$
46	c. 1725	1. Coro 5. Aria (A.)	5. 2 Fl.+2 Ob. in unison	I $f-eb''$ II $f-eb''$
65	1724	1. Coro 2. Choral 4. Aria (B.) 6. Aria (T.)	4. 2 Ob.+Cont.	I $g-e''$ II $f-e''$

TABLE XI.   THE OBOE DA CACCIA   217

Work. Cantata.	Date.	Movement.	Score.	Sounding Compass.
No. 74	1735	1. Coro 2. Aria (S.) 6. Recit. (B.) 7. Aria (A.) 8. Choral	1. As Taille 2. Ob.+Cont. 6. As Taille 7. ,, ,,	$g\text{–}f''$
80	1730	7. Duetto (A.T.)	7. Ob.+Vn.+Cont. Transposed	$f\sharp\text{–}f\sharp''$
87	1735	1. Aria (B.) 3. Aria (A.) 7. Choral	1. As Taille col Viola 3. 2 Ob.+Cont.	$\{$I $f\text{–}e\flat''$ $\{$II $f\text{–}b''$
101	c. 1740	6. Duetto (S.A.)	6. Fl.+Ob.+Cont.	$f\text{–}e''$
110	post 1734	6. Aria (B.) 7. Choral	6. Col Viola 7. Col T and Viola	$e'\text{–}d''$
119	1723	3. Aria (T.) 4. Recit. (B.)	3. 2 Ob.+Cont.	$\{$I $g\text{–}d''$ $\{$II $g\text{–}d''$
128	1735	1. Coro 5. Choral	1. As Taille	$f\sharp\text{–}e''$
147	1716} 1727}	8. Recit. (A.)	8. 2 Ob.+Cont.	$\{$I $a\text{–}e''$ $\{$II $f\text{–}d''$
167	c. 1725	3. Duetto (S.A.)	3. Ob.+Cont.	$g\text{–}f''$
176	1735	1. Coro 5. Aria (A.) 6. Choral	1. As Taille 5. 2 Ob. and Ob. da caccia in unison+ Cont.	$f\text{–}f''$
177	1732	3. Aria (S.)	3. 'Solo'+Cont.	$f\text{–}f''$
179	1724	5. Aria (S.)	5. 2 Ob.+Cont.	$\{$I $f\text{–}d''$ $\{$II $f\text{–}d''$
180	c. 1740	1. Coro 5. Aria (S.)	1. As 2nd Oboe 5. ,, ,,	$g\text{–}f''$
183	1735	1. Recit. (B.) 3. Recit. (A.) 4. Aria (S.) 5. Choral	1. With 2 Ob. d'amore and Cont. 3. As No. 1 with strings 4. Unison	$\{$I $g\text{–}f''$ $\{$II $g\text{–}f''$
186	1723	5. Aria (T.)	5. Ob.+Cont.	$d\text{–}e''$[1]
Christmas Oratorio, Pt. II	1734	1. Sinfonia 3. Choral 5. Recit. (B.) 8. Choral 9. Recit. (B.) 10. Aria (A.) 12. Coro 14. Choral	5. With 2 Ob. d'amore +Cont. 9. As No. 5 10. Col Vn. II and Viola	$\{$I $g\text{–}e''$ $\{$II $g\text{–}c\sharp''$
St. Matthew Passion	1729	25. Recit. (T.) and Coro 57. Recit. (S.) 58. Aria (S.) 69. Recit. (A.) 70. Aria (A.) and Coro 75. Aria (B.)	57. 2 Ob.+Cont. 58. Fl.+2 Ob. 69. As No. 57 75. Col Violini	$\{$I $g\text{–}f''$ $\{$II $f\text{–}f''$
St. John Passion	1723	62. Arioso (T.) 63. Aria (S.)	63. 2 Fl.+2 Ob. unison +Cont.	$\{$I $f\text{–}d\flat''$ $\{$II $f\text{–}d\flat''$

[1] For this abnormal compass see *supra*, p. 104.

(B) INSTRUMENTAL MUSIC
See *Christmas Oratorio* (supra), No. 1.

TABLE XII. THE OBOE D'AMORE
(HAUTBOIS D'AMOUR: LIEBESOBOE)

(A) CHURCH MUSIC

Cantata.	Date.	Movement.	Score.	Sounding Compass.
No. 3	c. 1740	1. Coro 5. Duetto (S.A.) 6. Choral	5. Col Violini	{I a–b'' {II b–b''
7	c. 1740	1. Coro 6. Aria (A.) 7. Choral	6. Col Vn. I	{I b–c''' {II b–c'''
8	c. 1725	1. Coro 2. Aria (T.) 6. Choral	2. Ob.+Cont.	{I a–b'' {II a–b''
9	?1731	1. Coro 5. Duetto (S.A.) 7. Choral	5. Fl.+Ob.+Cont.	a–b''
19	1726	3. Aria (S.)	3. 2 Ob.+Cont.	{I b–b'' {II a–b''
24	1723	5. Aria (T.)	5. 2 Ob.+Cont. Soprano C Clef	{I a–a'' {II a–f''
30	1738	8. Aria (B.)	...	d'–b''
36	c. 1730	1. Coro 2. Choral (S.A.) 3. Aria (T.) 4. Choral 6. Choral (T.) 8. Choral	2. Col S.A. 3. 'Solo'+Cont. 6. 2 Ob.+Cont.	{I a–b'' {II a–b''
37	c. 1727	1. Coro 5. Aria (B.) 6. Choral	...	{I c#'–b'' {II b–b''
49	1731	1. Sinfonia 4. Aria (S.) 6. Duetto (S.B.)	1. Col Violino I 4. Ob.+Vcello piccolo +Cont. 6. Col Violino I	a–c#'''
55	1731–2	1. Aria (T.)	...	d'–c'''
60	1732	1. Duetto (A.T.) 3. Duetto (A.T.) 5. Choral	Transposed	{I a–b'' {II a–b''
64	1723	7. Aria (A.)	7. Ob.+Cont.	a–a''
67	c. 1725	1. Coro 2. Aria (T.) 4. Choral 6. Aria (B.) and Coro 7. Choral	...	{I c#'–b'' {II a–b''
69	c. 1730	5. Aria (B.)	Transposed	b–a''
75	1723	5. Aria (S.)	5. Ob.+Cont.	c'–a''
76	1723	8. Sinfonia 12. Aria (A.)	12. Ob.+Va. da gamba +Cont.	a–a''
80	1730	5. Choral	5. With Taille	{I g#–b''[1] {II a–b''
81	1724	5. Aria (B.) 7. Choral	...	{I c'–a'' {II a–a''

[1] See p. 108, *supra*.

TABLE XII.   THE OBOE D'AMORE   219

Cantata.	Date.	Movement.	Score.	Sounding Compass.
No. 88	1732	1. Aria (B.) 3. Aria (T.) 5. Duetto (S.A.) 7. Choral	1. Col Violini and Viola 5. Col Violini	{I a–b'' {II a–b''
92	c. 1740	1. Coro 4. Choral (A.) 8. Aria (S.) 9. Choral	4. 2 Ob.+Cont.	{I a–b'' {II a–b''
94	1735	7. Aria (S.)	7. 'Solo'+Cont.	b–b''
95	1732	1. Coro 2. Recit. (S.) 4. Aria (T.) 6. Choral	1. Ord. Oboes for last 53 bars 2. Ob. (unis.)+Cont.	{I a–b'' {II a–a''
99	c. 1733	1. Coro 5. Duetto (S.A.) 6. Choral	5. Fl.+Ob.+Cont.	a–b''
100	c. 1735	1. Coro 5. Aria (A.) 6. Choral	5. Ob.+Cont. Transposed throughout	a–b''
103	1735	1. Coro 5. Aria (T.) 6. Choral	5. Col Vn. I	{I g–d''' {II g–d'''
104	c. 1725	3. Aria (T.) 5. Aria (B.)	3. 2 Ob.+Cont. 5. Col Vn. I	{I g–b'' {II a–f#''
107	c. 1735	1. Coro 2. Recit. (B.) 5. Aria (S.) 7. Choral	2. 2 Ob.+Cont. 5. 2 Ob.+Cont. 7. Col Violini	{I c#'–b'' {II b–b''
108	1735	1. Aria (B.) 4. Coro 6. Choral	4. Col Violini	{I a–b'' {II b–e''
110	post 1734	4. Aria (A.)	4. 'Solo'+Cont.	a–a''
112	1731	1. Coro 2. Aria (A.) 5. Choral	2. 'Solo'+Cont.	{I a–b'' {II c'–a''
113	c. 1740	3. Aria (B.)	3. 2 Ob.+Cont.	{I a–b'' {II a–g''
115	c. 1740	1. Coro 2. Aria (A.) 6. Choral	...	a–c'''
116	1744	1. Coro 2. Aria (A.) 6. Choral	2. 'Solo'+Cont.	{I a–b' {II a–b''
117	c. 1733	3. Aria (T.)	3. 2 Ob.+Cont.	{I b–a'' {II a–f#''
120	1730	1. Aria (A.) 2. Coro	2. Col Violini	{I a–d''' {II a–a''
121	c. 1740	1. Coro 2. Aria (T.) 6. Choral	1. Col S. 2. 'Solo'+Cont.	a–a''
123	c. 1740	1. Coro 3. Aria (T.) 6. Choral	3. 2 Ob.+Cont.	{I b–b'' {II a–b''
124	c. 1740	1. Coro 3. Aria (T.) 6. Choral	1. Ob. concertante	a–b''

Cantata.	Date.	Movement.	Score.	Sounding Compass.
No. 125	c. 1740	2. Aria (A.)	2. Fl.+Ob.+Cont.	a–b″
128	1735	4. Duetto (A.T.)	4. Ob.+Cont.	a–a″
129	1732	4. Aria (A.)	4. Ob.+Cont.	a–b″
133	1735–7	1. Coro 2. Aria (A.) 6. Choral	1. Col Vn. II and Va. 2. 2 Ob.+Cont.	{I b–b″ {II a–f♯″
136	c. 1725	1. Coro 3. Aria (A.)	1. Ob. I is not d'amore 3. Ob.+Cont. Transposed	{I a–g♯″ {II a–a″
138	c. 1740	1. Coro 3. Choral and Recit. (S.A.T.B.) 7. Choral	...	{I e′–a″ {II a–f♯″
139	c. 1740	1. Coro 4. Aria (B.) 6. Choral	...	{I a–b″ {II a–b″
144	c. 1725	5. Aria (S.)	5. Ob.+Cont.	a–a″
145	1729–30	5. Aria (B.)	5. Generally col Violini Transposed	{I d′–c♯‴ {II d′–c♯‴
146	c. 1740	5. Aria (S.)	? Authentic	{I b–b″ {II a–f″
147	1716} 1727}	3. Aria (A.)	3. Ob.+Cont. Transposed	a–g″
151	1735–40	1. Aria (S.) 3. Aria (A.) 5. Choral	1. Col Vn. I 3. Ob.+Violini and Viola (unis.)+Cont.	a–b″
154	1724	4. Aria (A.) 7. Duetto (A.T.)	4. Ob.+Violini and Viola (unis.)+Cont. 7. Col Violini	{I a–a″ {II a–g♯″
157	1727	2. Aria (T.)	2. Ob.+Cont.	a–a″
163[1]	1715	1. Aria (T.)	...	a–c‴
168	c. 1725	2. Recit. (T.) 3. Aria (T.) 6. Choral	2. 2 Ob.+Cont. 3. 2 Ob.+Cont.	{I a–a″ {II a–a″
170	1731	1. Aria (A.) 5. Aria (A.)	1. Col Vn. I 5. ,, ,,	a–b″
178	c. 1740	4. Choral (T.)	4. 2 Ob.+Cont.	{I b–b″ {II a–f♯″
183	1735	1. Recit. (B.) 3. Recit. (A.) 5. Choral	1. 2 Ob.+2 Ob. da caccia+Cont. 3. ,, ,, +Strings	{I a′–a″ {II c♯′–e″
190	1725	5. Duetto (T.B.)	5. Ob.+Cont.	a–g♯″
195	c. 1726	3. Aria (B.) 4. Recit. (S.) 5. Coro	3. Col Violini 4. 2 Fl.+2 Ob.+Cont. 5. Ob. II only is d'amore	{I b–b‴ {II g–d‴
197	1737	3. Aria (A.) 8. Aria (S.)	8. Vn. Solo+2 Ob.+Cont.	{I a–a″ {II a–e″
Ehre sei Gott	1728	6. Aria (B.)	6. 'Solo'+Cont.	a–a″

[1] In its extant state the Cantata belongs to the Leipzig period.

TABLE XII. THE OBOE D'AMORE   221

Work.	Date.	Movement.	Score.	Sounding Compass.
Sanctus in D ma.[1]	...	...	...	{I $d'-f\sharp''$ {II $d'-f\sharp''$
Easter Oratorio	1736	8. Aria (A.)	...	$a-b''$
Christmas Oratorio, Pt. I	1734	3. Recit. (A.) 4. Aria (A.) 7. Choral (S.B.)	3. 2 Ob.+Cont. 4. Col Vn. I+Cont. 7. Ob.+Ob. d'amore+Cont.	{I $g-a''$ {II $a-a''$
Christmas Oratorio, Pt. II	1734	1. Sinfonia 3. Choral 5. Recit. (B.) 8. Choral 9. Recit. (B.) 10. Aria (A.) 12. Coro 14. Choral	1. With 2 Ob. da caccia 5. +2 Ob. da caccia and Cont. 9. As No. 5 10. With 2 Ob. da caccia 12. ,, ,, 14. ,, ,,	{I $a-b''$ {II $a-a''$
Christmas Oratorio, Pt. III	1734	3. Coro 6. Duetto (S.B.)	3. Col S.A. 6. 2 Ob.+Cont.	{I $c\sharp'-a''$. {II $a-a''$
Christmas Oratorio, Pt. V	1734	1. Coro 3. Coro 4. Choral 5. Aria (B.) 10. Recit. (A.) 11. Choral	3. Col Violini 5. 'Solo'+Cont. 10. 2 Ob.+Cont.	{I $a-b''$ {II $a-a''$
Christmas Oratorio, Pt. VI	1734	4. Aria (S.) 8. Recit. (T.) 9. Aria (T.)	8. 2 Ob.+Cont. 9. ,, ,,	{I $a-b''$ {II $a-b''$
St. Matthew Passion	1729	18. Recit. (S.) 19. Aria (S.) 35. Choral 36. Coro 47. Coro	18. 2 Ob.+Cont. 19. ,, ,, 36. Col Fl. I	{I $a-d'''$ {II $a-b''$
St. John Passion	1723	42. Coro 44. Coro 46. Coro 54. Coro	42. 2nd Oboe is d'amore col A. 44. ,, ,, 46. 2 Ob. is d'amore col Vn. II 54. ,, ,,	$g\sharp-f\sharp''$
Hohe Messe	1733–	1. Coro 3. Coro 9. Aria (A.) 14. Duetto (S.A.) 18. Aria (B.)	3. Col Violini 18. 2 Ob.+Cont.	{I $b-c'''$ {II $a-b''$
Magnificat	1723	3. Aria (S.) 3a. Coro	3. 'Solo'+Cont. Transposed	{I $a-a''$ {II $b-g\sharp''$

(B) SECULAR CANTATAS

Work.	Date.	Movement.	Score.	Sounding Compass.
Aeolus	1725	7. Aria (A.)	7. Ob.+Cont.	$a-a''$
Angenehmes Wiederau	1737	7. Aria (B.) 11. Aria (T.)	...	$a-b''$
Hercules	1733	5. Aria (A.)	5. Ob.+Cont.	$a-a''$
O holder Tag (O angenehme Melodei)	1746	2. Aria (S.) 4. Aria (S.) 8. Aria (S.) 9. Recit. (S.) 10. Aria (S.)	2. Col Violino I 4. Ob.+Vn.+Cont.	$a-c\sharp'''$

[1] B.–G. xli. 177.

Cantata.	Date.	Movement.	Score.	Sounding Compass.
Phoebus und Pan	1731	5. Aria (B.) 9. Aria (T.)	9. 'Solo'+Cont.	a–c♯'''
Preise dein' Glücke	1734	3. Aria (T.)	3. Unison. Col Vn. I	a–a''
Schleicht, spielende Wellen	1734	7. Aria (A.)	7. 2 Ob.+Cont. Transposed	I a–a'' II a–a''
Schwingt freudig	1730–4	1. Coro 3. Aria (T.) 9. Coro	3. Ob.+Cont.	a–b''
Trauer-Ode	1727	1. Coro 6. Recit. (T.) 7. Coro 8. Aria (T.) 10. Coro	6. 2 Ob.+Cont.	I b–b'' II a–b''
Vereinigte Zwietracht	1726	2. Coro 4. Aria (T.) 7. Ritornello 10. Recit. (S.A.T.B.) 11. Coro	2. Col Flauti 7. Col Taille 10. Col Violini	I a–b'' II a–g''

(C) INSTRUMENTAL MUSIC

See *Vereinigte Zwietracht* (supra), No. 7; *Christmas Oratorio*, Pt. II, No. 1; Cantata No. 49, No. 1, and Cantata No. 76, No. 8.

TABLE XIII. THE BASSOON (FAGOTTO)
(A) CHURCH MUSIC

Cantata.	Date.	Movement.	Score.	Sounding Compass.
No. 12	1724–5 (? Weimar)	1. Sinfonia 2. Coro 3. Recit. (A.) 7. Choral	...	c,–b♭
18	1714	1. Sinfonia 2. Recit. (B.) 3. Recit. (T.B.) and Coro 5. Choral	5. Col Bassi	c,–e♭'
21	1714	1. Sinfonia 2. Coro 4. Recit. (T.) 5. Aria (T.) 6. Coro 7. Recit. (S.B.) 9. Coro 11. Coro	...	c,–e♭'
31	1715	1. Sonata 2. Coro 9. Choral	1. With four Oboes	g,–d'

TABLE XIII. THE BASSOON (FAGOTTO) 223

Cantata.	Date.	Movement.	Score.	Sounding Compass.
No. 42	1731	1. Sinfonia 2. Recit. (T.) and all other movements	1. With two Oboes 4. 'Fagotto e Violoncello' obbligato	b♯,,–a'
44	c. 1725	1. Coro and all movements	...	c,–f'
52	c. 1730	1. Sinfonia and all movements	1. With three Oboes	c,–e'
61	1714	1. Coro 6. Choral	6. Col Bassi	c,–e'
63	1723	1. Coro 6. Recit. (B.) 7. Coro	With three Oboes	c,–e'
66	1731	1. Coro 3. Aria (B.)	'Bassono oblig.'	c♯,–f♯'
69	c. 1730	1. Coro 2. Recit. (S.) and every movement	1. With three Oboes	b,,–f♯'
70	1716	1. Coro and every movement	...	c,–e'
71	1708	1. Coro 4. Arioso (B.) 6. Coro 7. Coro	With two Oboes	b♭,,–c'
75	1723	1. Coro	Fagotti	d,–f♯'
97	1734	1. Coro	Fagotti	c,–g'
110[1]	post 1734	1. Coro 2. Aria (T.)	...	c,–f♯'
131	1707–8	1. Coro 3. Coro 5. Coro	Transposed	c,–e♭'
143	1735	1. Coro 4. Aria (T.) 5. Aria (B.) 6. Aria (T.) 7. Choral	6. Obbligato	c,–f'
147	1716} 1727}	1. Coro	...	d,–e'
149	1731	1. Coro 6. Duetto (A.T.) 7. Choral	6. Obbligato 7. Col Bassi	d,–g'
150	c. 1712	1. Sinfonia 2. Coro 4. Coro 5. Terzetto (A.T.B.) 6. Coro 7. Coro	5. Obbligato 6. „	c,–f'
155	1716	2. Duetto (A.T.)	Obbligato	b,,–d'
159	1729	2. Duetto (S.A.)	Fagotti	d,–e♭'
160	1714	1. Aria (T.) 3. Aria (T.) 5. Aria (T.)	...	d,–d'
162	1715	1. Aria (B.) 6. Choral	6. Col Bassi	c,–d'

[1] Apparently bassoons supported the continuo in No. 119.

Work. Cantata.	Date.	Movement.	Score.	Sounding Compass.
No. 165	1724	1. Aria (S.) 4. Recit. (B.) 6. Choral	6. Col Bassi	$c_{,}-c'$
172	1731	1. Coro 3. Aria (B.) 6. Choral	...	$c_{,}-d'$
174	1729	1. Sinfonia	...	$c_{,}-e'$
177	1732	4. Aria (T.) 5. Choral	4. Obbligato	$eb_{,}-g'$
185	1715	2. Recit. (A.) 3. Aria (A.) 4. Recit. (B.) 5. Aria (B.) 6. Choral	6. Col Bassi	$c\sharp_{,}-d'$
186	1716} 1723}	1. Coro	...	$c_{,}-f'$
194	1723	1. Coro	1. With three oboes. Fagotti	$c_{,}-f'$
197	1737	6. Aria (B.)	Obbligato	$d_{,}-e'$
Mein Herze schwimmt	1714	1. Recit. (S.) 3. Recit. (S.) 4. Aria (S.) 7. Recit. (S.) 8. Aria (S.)	...	$c_{,}-f'$
Sanctus in D[1]	...	...	...	$d_{,}-f\sharp'$
Easter Oratorio	1736	1. Sinfonia 2. Duetto (T.B.) and Coro and every movement	1. 'Solo'	$c\sharp_{,}-f\sharp'$
Christmas Oratorio, Pt. I	1734	1. Coro and every movement	...	$c_{,}-c'$
St. John Passion	1723	1. Coro	'Continuo pro Bassono grosso'	$c_{,}-f$
Mass in F	c. 1736	1. Kyrie	Fagotti. Col Bassi	$f_{,}-c'$
Magnificat	1723	...	No parts	...
Hohe Messe	1733–	10. Aria (B.) and Choruses of 'Kyrie' and 'Gloria'	Fagotti 10. 2 Fagotti obbl.	{ I $c\sharp_{,}-a'$ { II $c\sharp_{,}-f\sharp'$

(B) SECULAR CANTATAS

Work. Cantata.	Date.	Movement.	Score.	Sounding Compass.
Durchlaucht'ster Leopold	?1718	7. Aria (B.)	Obbligato col 'Cello	$d\sharp_{,}-f\sharp'$
Was mir behagt	1716	11. Coro 15. Coro	Fagotti. Generally col Violoncello	$c_{,}-e'$

(C) INSTRUMENTAL MUSIC

Work. Cantata.	Date.	Movement.	Score.	Sounding Compass.
Brandenburg Concerto, No. 1 in F	1721	...	...	$c_{,}-eb'$
Ouverture in C	...	...	...	$c_{,}-f'$
Sinfonia in F	...	...	In the first Trio, two Oboes and Fagotti	$c_{,}-eb'$

[1] B.–G. xli. 177.

TABLE XIV. THE VIOLINO PICCOLO

Work. Cantata.	Date.	Movement.	Score.	Sounding Compass.
No. 96	c. 1740	1. Coro	Col Flauto piccolo	$f'-f'''$
102	1731	5. Aria (T.)	Or Flauto traverso	$d'-e''$
140	1731	1. Coro 3. Duetto (S.B.) 5. Recit. (B.) 7. Choral	1 & 5. Col Violino I 3. Obbligato. Solo 7. Col S. in 8va	1 & 5. $a-d'''$ 3. $b\flat-e\flat'''$
Brandenburg Concerto, No. 1	1721	...	...	$b\flat-e\flat'''$

TABLE XV. THE VIOLETTA

Work. Cantata.	Date.	Movement.	Score.	Sounding Compass.
No. 16	1724	5. Aria (T.)	Or Oboe da caccia	$f-d''$
157	1727	3. Recit. (T.) 5. Choral	5. Col T.	$e-b'$
Preise dein' Glücke	1734	7. Aria (S.)	Col Violini	$g-e''$

TABLE XVI. THE VIOLA D'AMORE

Work. Cantata.	Date.	Movement.	Sounding Compass.
No. 152	1715	1. Concerto 4. Aria (S.) 6. Duetto (S.B.)	$b,-f\sharp''$
St. John Passion	1723	31. Arioso (B.) 32. Aria (T.)	{I $g-b\flat''$ {II $f-c'''$
Aeolus	1725	5. Aria (T.)	$c\sharp'-c\natural'''$
Schwingt freudig	1730–4	7. Aria (S.)	$a-c\sharp'''$

TABLE XVII. THE VIOLA DA GAMBA

Work. Cantata.	Date.	Movement.	Sounding Compass.
No. 76	1723	8. Sinfonia 9. Recit. (B.) 10. Aria (T.) 11. Recit. (A.) 12. Aria (A.)	8 & 12. $b_,-c''$ 9–11. $c_,-g'$
106	1707–11	1. Sonatina 2. Coro 3. Duetto (A.B.) 4. Choral	$\{$ I $c-c''$ $\{$ II $d_,-bb'$
152	1715	1. Concerto	$d_,-g'$
St. Matthew Passion	1729	65. Recit. (B.) 66. Aria (B.)	$a_{,,}-c''$
St. John Passion	1723	58. Aria (A.)	$c\sharp_,-c''$
Aeolus	1725	5. Aria (T.)	$c\sharp-b'$
Trauer-Ode	1727	1. Coro 4. Recit. (A.) 5. Aria (A.) 7. Coro 8. Aria (T.) 10. Coro	$\{$ I $f\sharp_,-e''$ $\{$ II $f\sharp_,-b'$
Sonata I[1] in G ma.	c. 1720	...	$b_,-d''$
Sonata II in D ma.	c. 1720	...	$b_{,,}-c\sharp''$
Sonata III in G mi.	c. 1720	...	$f\sharp_,-d''$
Brandenburg Concerto, No. 6	1721	...	$\{$ I $a_,-c''$ $\{$ II $bb_,-bb'$

[1] Sonatas I–III are in B.–G. ix.

TABLE XVIII. THE VIOLONCELLO PICCOLO

Cantata.	Date.	Movement.	Sounding Compass.
No. 6	1736	3. Choral (S.)	$g_,-c''$
41	1736	4. Aria (T.)	$c_,-b'$
49	1731	4. Aria (S.)	$d-b'$
68	1735	2. Aria (S.)	$c_,-bb'$
85	1735	2. Aria (A.)	$g_,-bb'$
115	c. 1740	4. Aria (S.)	$c\sharp_,-c''$
175	1735	4. Aria (T.)	$f\sharp_,-a'$
180	c. 1740	3. Recit. (S.) and Arioso	$c-b'$
183	1735	2. Aria (T.)	$g_,-c''$

TABLE XIX. THE LUTE

Work.	Date.	Movement.	Sounding Compass.
St. John Passion	1727	31. Arioso (B.)	$c_,-bb'$
Trauer-Ode	1727	1. Coro 4. Recit. (A.) 5. Aria (A.) 7. Coro 8. Aria (T.) 10. Coro	$\{$I $b_,,-b'$ $\{$II $b_,,-f\sharp'$
Suite in E ma.[1]	...	...	$a_,,-e''$
Suite in E mi.[2]	...	...	$c_,-c''$
Suite in C mi.[3]	...	...	$ab_,,-f''$
Prelude in C mi.[4]	...	...	$d_,-c''$
Prelude and Fugue in E flat ma.[5]	...	...	$ab_,,-eb''$
Fugue in G mi.[6]	...	...	$g_,-f''$
Suite in G mi.[7]	...	...	$g-d''$

[1] For Clavier, B.-G. xlii. 16; for Violin, B.-G. xxvii (1) 48.
[2] For Clavier, B.-G. xlv (1) 149.
[3] For Clavier, B.-G. xlv (1) 156.
[4] For Clavier, B.-G. xxxvi. 119.
[5] For Clavier, B.-G. xlv (1) 141.
[6] For Violin, B.-G. xxvii (1) 4; for Organ, in D minor, B.-G. xv. 149.
[7] For Violoncello, in C minor, B.-G. xxvii (1) 81.

TABLE XX. THE CONTINUO

(The Score column indicates the completeness, or reverse, of the Continuo figuring)

(A) CHURCH MUSIC

Cantata. No.	Date.	Key.	Continuo Unfigured.	Continuo Figured.	Continuo Unfigured.	Score Figured.	Score Unfigured.	Organ Obbligato.	Cembalo.
1	c. 1740	F	F	E♭	...	only first Coro			
2	c. 1740	G mi.	G	F	...	almost complete			
3	c. 1740	A	A	A	unfigured				
4	1724	E mi.	G·F?	E D	...				
5	1735	G mi.		F	...	Tenor Aria unfigured			
6	1736	C mi.	C	C B♭	...	complete			
7	c. 1740	E mi.		E	...	„			
8	c. 1725	E and D¹	D	C	...	Duet unfigured		...	figured
9	? 1731	E.	E	D	...	complete			
10	c. 1740	G mi.		G F	unfigured				
11	c. 1736	D	D		...	only Sinfonia			
12	1724–5	F mi.	F	C	...	complete			
13	c. 1740	D mi.	D D	F	...	„			
14	1735	G mi.	G	C B	...	very incomplete			
15	1704	C		G	...	T. Aria unfigured			
16	1724	A mi.	A		unfigured	only Sinfonia and first Recit.			
17	c. 1737	A		G	...	complete			
18	1714	G mi.		G		„			
19	1726	C	no indication			„			
20	c. 1725	F	F	E♭		complete			
21	1714	C mi.	C C	C	unfigured	very incomplete			
22	1723	G mi.	no parts		...	T. Aria unfigured			
23	1724	C mi.	F F	A					
24	1723	F	A G	E♭					
25	c. 1731	A mi.	A	...					
26	c. 1740	A mi.		G					

¹ The version in D is a later text.

TABLE XX. THE CONTINUO   229

No.	Date	C mi.	C	Bb			Alto Aria	Alto Aria I (orig. version)
27	1731	C mi.	C	Bb	...	both Arias unfigured	Alto Aria	
28	c. 1736	A mi.	A A G	C	...	very incomplete	Alto Aria	
29	1731	D	D	C	...	complete		
30	1738	D	D D	C Bb	...	„		
31	1715}1731}	C	C		...	„		
32	c. 1740	E mi.	D D		...	only Recits.		
33	c. 1740	A mi.		A G	...	complete		
34	1740–1	D mi.	D		unfigured	Alto Recit.		
35	1731	D mi.	D		...	complete	throughout (no part)	
36	c. 1730	D	D D	C	...	complete		
37	c. 1727	A	A	G	...	„		
38	c. 1740	E mi.		E D	...	Pt. II, unfigured		
39	1732	G mi.	F F	F	...	complete		
40	1723	F	C	F Eb	...	Recits. only		
41	1736	C	D	Bb	...	complete		
42	1731	D	C C	D C C	...	except two Recits.		
43	c. 1735	C		Bb	...	only first two movts.		
44	c. 1725	G mi.	D	F G	...	except Alto Aria, and final Choral		
45	c. 1740	E			unfigured	except S. Aria		
46	c. 1725	D mi.		D C	...	very incomplete	S. Aria (autograph)	
47	1720	G mi.	G G	F	...	...		
48	c. 1740	G mi.	G G F		...		Coro, Bass Aria, Duet	
49	1731	E	E E2		unfigured			
50	c. 1740	D	C C	no parts Bb	„	complete		
51	1731–2	C	F Eb		unfigured			
52	c. 1730	F		no parts	„	complete (copy score)		
53	c. 1723–34	E	G G F	no parts	unfigured			
54	c. 1723–34	Eb	G F	no parts	„	complete		
55	1731–2	G mi.	G G		...	except last two movts.		
56	1731	G mi.	G G					
57	c. 1740	G mi.	C C	F				
58	1733	C		Bb	...			
59	1716}1735}	C	C ?	Bb?	unfigured			

1 Cf. Spitta, ii. 451, note.   2 The continuo and organ parts in the score are in D.

Cantata	Date	Key	Continuo Unfigured	Continuo Figured	Score Unfigured	Score Figured	Organ Obbligato	Cembalo
60	1732	D	D	C	…	incomplete		
61	1714	A mi.	B B	no parts A	unfigured	complete		
62	c. 1740	B mi.	C B♭	B♭	…	complete		
63	1723	C	E D	…	unfigured	"		
64	1724	E mi.	no parts	…	"			
65	1731	D	no parts	…	"			
66	c. 1725	A	A	A G	…	complete		
67	1735	D mi.	D	C	unfigured	"		
68	1724 }	D	D	…	…			
69	1730 }		D	…	unfigured			
70	1716	C	C C	B♭	…	complete		
71	1708	C	D D	C	…	"		
72	c. 1726	A mi.	A	G	…	"		
73	c. 1725	G mi.	G	F	…	"	first Coro (or Horn)	
74	1735	C	C	B♭	unfigured			
75	1723	E mi.	no part	no part	"	only a few bars		
76	c. 1725	C	no parts	no parts F	…	complete		
77	c. 1740	G mi.	G	…	unfigured	very incomplete (copy score)		
78	1735	G	G G	…	…	complete		
79	1730	D	no parts	…	…			
80	1730							
81	1724	E mi.	E	D E	…	complete		
82	c. 1731	C mi.	C C	B♭	…	"		
83	1724	F	F	E♭	…			
84	1731–2	E mi.	E	D	unfigured	only Recits.		
85	1735	C mi.	C B♭	…	…			
86	c. 1725	E	D	C	unfigured	only Recits.		
87	1735	D mi.	D C	…	…			
88	1732	D	C	B♭	unfigured	except Recits.		
89	c. 1730	C mi.	no parts	…	unfigured			
90	c. 1740	D mi.	G	F	…	complete		
91	c. 1740	G	B	A	…	except both Arias		
92	c. 1740	B mi.	C	C B♭	…	complete		
93	1728	C mi.						

TABLE XX.   THE CONTINUO   231

'Cont. pro Cembalo' in D. figd.

...

No.	Date	Key			Figured	Remarks
94	1735	D	D D	C	...	except three Arias
95	1732	G	G	F	...	except T., Aria ('senza l'Organo')
96	c. 1740	F	F	F	...	complete
97	1734	Bb	Bb Bb	Ab G	...	only first Coro
98	c. 1732	Bb	Bb Bb	Ab	...	,,
99	c. 1733	G	G	F	...	complete
100	c. 1735	G	G	F F F	...	except the Arias
101	c. 1740	D mi.	D	C	unfigured	complete
102	1731	G mi.		G F F	...	
103	1735	B mi.	B B	F	...	complete
104	c. 1725	G	G		...	except S. Aria
105	c. 1725	G mi.	no part	no part		a few bars
106	c. 1707 / 1711	Eb	no parts	no parts		
107	c. 1735	B mi.	B	A	...	only three movements (partial)
108	1735	A mi.	A A	G	...	complete
109	c. 1731	D mi.	D	C D	...	,,
110	p. 1734	D	D	C	...	only first Coro (partial) and B. Recit.
111	c. 1740	A mi.	A	G	unfigured	except B. Aria
112	1731	G.	G G	F	...	complete
113	c. 1740	B mi.		G F	...	
114	c. 1740	G mi.			practically unfigured	complete
115	c. 1740	G	A G		practically unfigured	complete (copy score)
116	1744	A	A G		...	
117	c. 1733	G		no parts	,, unfigured	complete
118	c. 1737	Bb		no parts	practically unfigured	only Recits.
119	1723	C		no parts	unfigured	first Coro and Recits.
120	1730	A	no parts		...	complete
121	c. 1740	E mi.	E	D	...	except A. Aria
122	c. 1742	G mi.	G	F	...	complete
123	c. 1740	B mi.	B	A	...	
124	c. 1740	E	E	D	...	
125	c. 1740	E mi.	E E	D	...	
126	c. 1740	A mi.	A	G	...	

Cantata	Date	Key	Continuo		Score		Organ Obbligato.	Cembalo.
			Unfigured.	Figured.	Unfigured.	Figured.		
127	c. 1740	F	F	Eb	...	only Recits.		
128	1735	G	G	F	...	complete		
129	1732	D	DD	C	practically unfigured	,,		
130	c. 1740	C	no part	no part	...			
131	1707–8	G mi.		no parts	...	complete (score)		
132	1715	A	A	C	...	a few bars		
133	1735–7	D	DD	Ab Ab	...	complete		
134	1731	Bb	Bb Bb	no parts	...	only Recits.		
135	c. 1740	A mi.	A	A G	...	complete (copy score)		
136	c. 1725	A		Bb	...	complete		
137	1732	C	C	no parts	...	,,		
138	c. 1740	B mi.		D	unfigured	exc. first Recit. and Arias		
139	c. 1740	E	E	Db	...	complete		
140	1731	Eb	Eb	no parts	...			
141	1721–2	G		no parts	unfigured			
142	1712–13	A mi.		no parts	,,	incomplete (copy score)		
143	1735	Bb		no parts	...			
144	c. 1725	B mi.		no parts	unfigured	incomplete (copy score)		
145	1729–30	D		no parts	...			
146	c. 1740	D mi.		no parts	unfigured	...	Sinfonia and first Coro	
147	1716 } c. 1727	C		C Bb	...	except Chorals		
148	c. 1725	D	D	no parts	unfigured	incomplete		
149	1731	D		C	...	except Terzet		
150	c. 1712	B mi.		no parts	...	only Recits.		
151	1735–40	G		F	...	,, (score)		
152	1715	E mi.	E	no parts	...	complete		
153	1727	E mi.		D	...	,,		
154	1724	B mi.	B	A	...		...	
155	1716	D mi.		no parts	unfigured	only first Recit. (score)		
156	1729–30	F	F F	...	...	complete		A. Aria 'Jesu, lass dich'
157	1727	B mi.	B	A	...	,,		
158	{1708–17 {Leipzig	D	D	C	...			

TABLE XX. THE CONTINUO   233

No.	Date	Key	Pitch	Figured	Completeness	Remarks
159	1729	C mi.	C	...	"	
160	1714	C	no parts — B♭	...	complete (copy score)	
161	1715	A mi.	A — B♭ A[1]	...	complete	
162	1715	B mi.	no parts — A[1]	...	"	
163	1715			practically unfigured		
164	{1723–4 / ? 1715}	G mi.	G — F	...	only Recits.	
165	1724	G	no parts	...	except Arias (copy score)	
166	c. 1725	B♭	A♭ — B♭	...	only first two movts.	
167	c. 1725	G	G — F	...	complete	
168	c. 1725	B mi.	B — A	...	"	
169	1731	D	D — D	...	"	Sinfonia and A. Arias
170	1731	D	D — C	...	a few bars	A. Arias
171	c. 1730	D	no parts — B♭	...	except S. A. Duet	
172	{1724–5 / 1731}	C	C C	...		S. A. Duet (or Violin and Violoncello)
173	1731	D	no parts	unfigured	complete	
174	1729	G	G — F	...	only Recits.	
175	1735	C mi.	G — F	...	complete	
176	1735	G mi.	A A — C B♭	...	"	
177	1732	A mi.	no part — F	...	incomplete	
178	c. 1740	G	no parts — G	unfigured		
179	1724	F	E — no part	"	complete	
180	c. 1740	E mi.	G G G — D	...	very incomplete (score)	
181	c. 1725	G	A G	...	only first movement	
182	1714–15	A mi.	G F	unfigured	(copy score)	
183	1735	G	A G F	...		
184	1731	F♯ mi.	F♯ F F[2]	...	complete (orig. score)	
185	1715	G mi.	G G G	unfigured	complete	
186	1723 (1716)	G mi.	no parts — F	...	only B. Recit.	
187	1732	F	no parts	...	complete	
188	1731	B♭	no part	...	only Nos. 2–4	
189	1707–10	D		unfigured		A. Aria
190	1725	D	no part	"		
191	1733		no parts			

[1] The cantata appears to have been given at Leipzig by raising the other instruments to the pitch of the organ.

[2] Later orchestral parts in G mi. exist.

Work	Date	Key	Continuo — Unfigured.	Continuo — Figured.	Continuo — Unfigured.	Score — Figured.	Score — Unfigured.	Organ Obbligato	Cembalo
192	c. 1732	G	G G	F	...	complete	...		
193	c. 1740	D	no part	no part	unfigured	incomplete	...		
194	1723	B♭	A♭ B♭ B♭	G	...	only first Coro and S. Recit.	...		
195	c. 1726	D	D	D D	...	very incomplete	...		
196	1708	C		no parts	unfigured		...		
197	1737	D		no parts	unfigured	complete	...		
198 '(Trauer-Ode)'	1727	B mi.		no parts	...		...		
'Mein Herze schwimmt'	1714	C mi.	D	C	...	complete	...		
'Ehre sei Gott'	1728	G	D D	no parts	unfigured		...		
'O ewiges Feuer'	p. 1734	D	D D	C	...	complete	...		
'Herr Gott, Beherrscher'	p. 1734	D	G G	F	...	,,	...	Sinfonia	
Christmas Oratorio, Pt. I	1734	D	D D	C	...	incomplete	...		
,, ,, II	1734	G	F	F E♭	...	complete	...		
,, ,, III	1734	D	A A	G	...	,,	...		
,, ,, IV	1734	F	D D	C C	...	,,	...		
,, ,, V	1734	A		C	...	,,	...		
,, ,, VI	1734	D	{E E / E E	{D / D	...	,,	...		
Easter Oratorio	1736	E mi.	G G	F	unfigured	incomplete	...		
St. Matthew Passion	1729		C C	no parts	...	complete	...	...	
St. John Passion	1723	G mi.	D D	B♭	unfigured	,,	...		
Magnificat	1723	D	D	C	...	complete	...		
Sanctus in D¹	...	D		G F	...	complete	...		
,, C	...	C		B	...	complete (copy score)	...		
,, D	...	D		? G	...	complete	...		
,, D mi.	...	D mi.			unfigured	only 'Kyrie' and 'Gloria'	...		
,, G	...	G	G		...	complete	unfigured		'Continuo pro Cembalo' figd. and unfigd.
Hohe Messe	1733	B mi.	'Missa' B / 'Sanctus' D D C			complete	...		
Mass in F	c. 1736	F	no part	no parts	unfigured	complete (other scores)	...		
,, A	c. 1737	A		no parts					
,, G mi.	c. 1737	G mi.			...				
,, G	c. 1738	G		no parts	unfigured				

¹ B.-G. xli. 177.

TABLE XX.   THE CONTINUO   235

(B) SECULAR CANTATA

			Cembalo	no/parts accomp.	unfigured		...	'Cembalo obbligato'
Aeolus	1725	D					...	
Amore traditore	...	A mi.						
Angenehmes Wiederau	1737	D						
Die Freude reget sich	c. 1733	D	D	no parts	,,	some Recits. only		
Durchlaucht'ster Leopold	1718	D						
Hercules	1733	F	F	no parts	unfigured			
Ich bin in mir vergnügt	c. 1730	Bb		no parts	,,			
Mer hahn en neue Oberkeet	1742	A		no parts	,,			
Mit Gnaden bekröne	? 1722	D mi.		no parts	,,			
Non sa che sia dolore		B mi.		no parts	,,			
O angenehme Melodei	c. 1749} 1746}	A	A	A	,,	very incomplete	...	Cembalo
O holder Tag	1731	D	D	D D	...			
Phoebus und Pan	1734	D	D D	D D	unfigured	complete		
Preise dein' Glücke	1734	D		...	...			
Schleicht, spielende Wellen	1732	G	... G	G	...	complete	...	Cembalo obbl.
Schweigt stille	c. 1730-4	D				except four Recits.		
Schwingt freudig	1733}	D	D	no parts	unfigured			
Tönet, ihr Pauken	1726}	D	D D D D	...	,,			
Vereingte Zwietracht	1734}	D			,,			
Auf, schmetternde Töne	1728	C		no parts				
Vergnügte Pleissenstadt	1716	F		no parts	unfigured			
Was mir behagt	1717-22	G		no parts	...	very incomplete		
Weichet nur								

(C) ORCHESTRAL MUSIC

Work.	Date.	Key.	Continuo.	
			Unfigured.	*Figured.*
Concertos for Clavier and Orchestra I	…	D mi.	unfigured	
„ „ II	…	E	„	
„ „ III	…	D	„	
„ „ IV	…	A	unfigured	
„ „ V	…	F mi.	…	complete
„ „ VI	…	F	unfigured	
„ „ VII	…	G mi.	„	
Concerto for Clavier, Flute, Violin, and Orchestra	…	A mi.	„	complete[1]
Brandenburg Concerto I	1721	F	unfigured	
„ „ II	1721	F	practically unfigured	
„ „ III	1721	G	unfigured	
„ „ IV	1721	G	unfigured	
„ „ V	1721	D	…	complete[1]
„ „ VI	1721	Bb	unfigured	
Sinfonia in D (Violin and Orchestra)	…	D	unfigured	
Concertos for Violin and Orchestra I	…	A mi.	„	complete
„ „ II	…	E	„	
„ „ III	…	D mi.	„	„
„ „ IV	…	D	unfigured	
Concertos for two Claviers and Orchestra I	…	C mi.	„	
„ „ II	…	C	„	
„ „ III	…	C mi.	„	
Ouverture I	…	B mi.	…	complete
„ II	…	D	unfigured	
„ III	…	D	„	„
„ IV[2]	…	F	„	
Sinfonia in F	…	D mi.	„	
Concerto for three Claviers and Orchestra I	…	C	„	
„ „ II	…	C	„	
Concerto for four Claviers and Orchestra	…		„	

[1] The concerted Cembalo part alone is figured.
[2] B.–G. xlv (1), p. 190, prints an unauthenticated Ouverture for strings and cembals in G mi.

TABLE XX. THE CONTINUO   237

(D) CHAMBER MUSIC

Work.	Key.	State of Cembalo part.
Sonatas for Cembalo and Flute I . . .	B mi.	Generally two-part. Unfigured. Autograph score.
,, ,, II . .	E♭	Two-part. Unfigured. Copy score.
,, ,, III . .	A	Two-part. Unfigured. Autograph score.
Suite for Cembalo and Violin . .	A	Generally two-part. Unfigured. Autograph parts.
Sonatas for Cembalo and Violin I .	B mi.	Generally two-part. Figured where upper part is silent.
,, ,, II .	A	,, ,, ,, ,,
,, ,, III .	E	,, ,, ,, No figuring.
,, ,, IV .	C mi.	Two part. No figuring.
,, ,, V .	F mi.	Generally two-part. Figuring as in No. I.
,, ,, VI .	G	,, ,, ,,
Sonatas for Cembalo and Viola da gamba I	G	Two part. Unfigured. Autograph parts.
,, ,, ,, II	D	Generally two-part. Figuring where upper part is silent. Copy score.
,, ,, ,, III	G mi.	Two-part. Figuring where upper part is silent. Autograph parts.
Sonata for Flute, Violin, and Continuo .	G	Figured continuo. Autograph parts (?).
Trio ,, ,, ,, .	C mi.	Figured continuo (in the *Musicalisches Opfer*).
Canon ,, ,, ,, .	C mi.	,, ,, "Copies."
Sonata for two Violins and Continuo	C	Figured continuo. "Copies."
Sonata for two Flutes and Cembalo	G	Figured continuo. Cembalo part autograph.
Sonata for Cembalo and Violin	G mi.	Cembalo two-part. Figured where upper part is silent. Copy score.
Sonatas for Flute and Continuo I .	C	Figured continuo. Cembalo three-part in Menuetto I. Copies.
,, ,, II	E mi.	,, ,, Copies.
,, ,, III	E	,, ,, Copies.
Sonata for Violin and ,, .	E mi.	,, ,, Copy score.
,, ,, ,, .	G	,, ,, Autograph.
Fuga for Violin and Continuo .	G mi.	,, ,, Copy.
Sonata for two Cembali . .	F	Each generally in two parts. Unfigured. Copy parts.

Copy score. Partly autograph parts. (bracketing the six Sonatas for Cembalo and Violin)

TABLE XXI

THE CANTATAS IN ALPHABETICAL ORDER

(with a précis of their scores)

The sign + indicates that the instruments following it are in addition to the normal strings and continuo. When no instruments are named, strings are to be inferred. Obsolete instruments are invariably mentioned, excepting the violone, which must normally be associated with the continuo. Wind instruments named in italic type are merely auxiliary and dispensable. Though more than one species of oboe is frequently prescribed in a score, the number of instruments indicated almost invariably exaggerates the number of players required.

Bach's instrumentation should be observed, if possible, for it brings us closer to his mind and meaning. Unfortunately many of his instruments are obsolete, and others are not easily obtainable. The following substitutions are recommended by Professor Whittaker[1] out of his unique experience:

For	*Substitute*
Violino piccolo	Violin
Violetta	Viola
Viola d'amore	Viola or muted violin
Viola da gamba	Violoncello
Violoncello piccolo	Violoncello or viola, or both
Violone	Contrabass
Flute à bec	Flute
Oboe d'amore	Oboe
Oboe da caccia	Cor anglais
Corno da caccia	Horn or Trumpet
Corno da tirarsi	Horn or Trumpet
Cornetto	Trumpet
Tromba da tirarsi	Trumpet
Tromba, Clarino, Principale . .	Trumpet

	NO.	SCORE
Ach Gott, vom Himmel sieh' darein .	2	+2 Ob., 4 *Trombones*
Ach Gott, wie manches Herzeleid . .	3	+*Cor.*, *Trombone*, 2 Ob. d'am.
Ach Gott, wie manches Herzeleid . .	58	+3 Ob.
Ach Herr, mich armen Sünder . .	135	+*Cornett*, *Trombone*, 2 Ob.
Ach, ich sehe	162	+Cor. da tirarsi, Fag.
Ach, lieben Christen, seid getrost . .	114	+*Cor.*, Fl., 2 Ob.
Ach wie flüchtig	26	+*Cor.*, Fl., 3 Ob.
Aergre dich, o Seele, nicht . . .	186	+3 Ob., Ob. da cacc., Fag.
Allein zu dir, Herr Jesu Christ . .	33	+2 Ob.
Alles nur nach Gottes Willen . .	72	+2 Ob.
Also hat Gott die Welt geliebt . .	68	+*Cor.*, *Cornett*, 3 *Trombones*, 3 Ob., Vcello piccolo
Am Abend aber desselbigen Sabbaths .	42	+2 Ob., Fag., Vcello
Amore traditore	—	Cembalo
Angenehmes Wiederau	—	+3 Tr., Timp., 2 Fl., 2 Ob., Ob. d'am.
Auf Christi Himmelfahrt allein . .	128	+Tr., 2 Cor. da caccia, 2 Ob., Ob. d'am., Ob. da caccia
Auf, schmetternde Töne	—	+3 Tr., Timp., 2 Fl., 2 Ob. d'am., Ob.
Aus der Tiefe rufe ich, Herr . . .	131	+Ob., Fag.
Aus tiefer Noth schrei' ich zu dir . .	38	+2 Ob., 4 *Trombones*
Barmherziges Herze	185	+[Tr.], Ob., Fag.
Bereitet die Wege	132	+Ob., Fag.
Bisher habt ihr nichts gebeten . .	87	+2 Ob., 2 Ob. da cacc.
Bleib' bei uns, denn es will Abend werden	6	+2 Ob., Ob. da cacc., Vcello piccolo
Brich dem Hungrigen dein Brod . .	39	+2 Fl., 2 Ob.
Bringet dem Herrn Ehre . . .	148	+Tr., 3 Ob.

[1] *Fugitive Notes on Bach's Cantatas* (1924), p. 254.

TABLE XXI. THE CANTATAS IN ALPHABETICAL ORDER   239

	NO.	SCORE
Christ lag in Todesbanden . . .	4	+*Cornett*, 3 *Trombones*
Christ unser Herr zum Jordan kam .	7	+2 Ob. d'am.
Christen, ätzet diesen Tag . . .	63	+4 Tr., Timp., 3 Ob., Fag.
Christum wir sollen loben schon . .	121	+*Cornett*, 3 *Trombones*, Ob. d'am.
Christus, der ist mein Leben . . .	95	+Cor., 2 Ob., 2 Ob. d'am.
Das ist je gewisslich wahr . . .	141	+2 Ob.
Das neugebor'ne Kindelein . . .	122	+3 Fl., 3 Ob.
Dazu ist erschienen der Sohn Gottes .	40	+2 Cor., 2 Ob.
Dem Gerechten muss das Licht . .	195	+3 Tr., Timp., 2 Cor., 2 Fl., 2 Ob., 2 Ob. d'am.
Denn du wirst meine Seele nicht in der Hölle lassen	15	+3 Tr., Timp.
Der Friede sei mit dir	158	Vn., Ob., Cont.
Der Herr denket an uns . . .	196	
Der Herr ist mein getreuer Hirt . .	112	+2 Cor., 2 Ob. d'am.
Der Himmel lacht, die Erde jubiliret .	31	+3 Tr., Timp., 4 Ob., Fag.
Der Streit zwischen Phoebus und Pan .	—	+3 Tr., Timp., 2 Fl., 2 Ob., Ob. d'am.
Der zufriedengestellte Aeolus . .	—	+3 Tr., Timp., 2 Cor., 2 Fl., 2 Ob., Ob. d'am., Va. d'am., Va. da gamba
Die Elenden sollen essen . . .	75	+Tr., 2 Ob., Ob. d'am., Fagotti
Die Freude reget sich	—	+Fl.
Die Himmel erzählen die Ehre Gottes .	76	+Tr., 2 Ob., Ob. d'am., Va. da gamba
Die Wahl des Herkules	—	+2 Cor. da caccia, 2 Ob., Ob. d'am.
Du Friedefürst, Herr Jesu Christ . .	116	+*Cor.*, 2 Ob. d'am.
Du Hirte Israel, höre	104	+3 Ob., 2 Ob. d'am.
Du sollst Gott, deinen Herren, lieben .	77	+Tr. da tirarsi, 2 Ob.
Du wahrer Gott und Davids Sohn . .	23	+*Cornett*, 3 *Trombones*, 2 Ob.
Durchlaucht'ster Leopold . . .	—	+2 Fl., Fag., Vcello, Cembalo
Ehre sei dir, Gott, gesungen (Part V. Christmas Oratorio)	—	+2 Ob. d'am.
Ehre sei Gott in der Höhe (incomplete) .	—	2 Fl., Ob. d'am., Vcello, Cont.
Ein Herz, das seinen Jesum lebend weiss .	134	+2 Ob.
Ein ungefärbt Gemüthe	24	+Tr., 2 Ob., 2 Ob. d'am.
Ein' feste Burg ist unser Gott . .	80	+3 Tr., Timp., 3 Ob., 2 Ob. d'am., Ob. da cacc.
Er rufet seinen Schafen . . .	175	+2 Tr., 3 Fl., Vcello piccolo
Erforsche mich, Gott	136	+Cor., 2 Ob., 2 Ob. d'am.
Erfreut euch, ihr Herzen . . .	66	+Tr., 2 Ob., Fag.
Erfreute Zeit im neuen Bunde . .	83	+2 Cor., 2 Ob.
Erhalt' uns, Herr, bei deinem Wort .	126	+Tr., 2 Ob.
Erhöhtes Fleisch und Blut . . .	173	+2 Fl.
Erschallet, ihr Lieder . . .	172	+3 Tr., Timp., Fag., Org. (or Vn. and Vcello)
Erwünschtes Freudenlicht . . .	184	+2 Fl.
Es erhub sich ein Streit . . .	19	+3 Tr., Timp., 3 Ob., 2 Ob. d'am.
Es ist das Heil uns kommen her . .	9	+Fl., Ob. d'am.
Es ist dir gesagt, Mensch . . .	45	+2 Fl., 2 Ob.
Es ist ein trotzig	176	+2 Ob., Ob. da cacc.
Es ist euch gut, dass ich hingehe . .	108	+2 Ob. d'am.
Es ist nichts Gesundes an meinem Leibe .	25	+Cornett, 3 Trombones, 3 Fl., 2 Ob.
Es reifet euch ein schrecklich Ende .	90	+Tr.
Es wartet Alles auf dich . . .	187	+2 Ob.
Fallt mit Danken '(Part IV. Christmas Oratorio)	—	+2 Cor., 2 Ob.
Falsche Welt, dir trau' ich nicht . .	52	+2 Cor., 3 Ob., Fag.
Freue dich, erlöste Schaar . . .	30	+3 Tr., Timp., 2 Fl., 2 Ob., Ob. d'am.

	NO.	SCORE
Geist und Seele wird verwirret	35	+3 Ob., Org.
Gelobet sei der Herr, mein Gott	129	+3 Tr., Timp., Fl., 2 Ob., Ob.d'am.
Gelobet seist du, Jesu Christ	91	+2 Cor., Timp., 3 Ob.
Gleich wie der Regen und Schnee	18	4 Ve., Vcello, 2 Fl., Fag., Cont.
Gloria in excelsis Deo	191	+3 Tr., Timp., 2 Fl., 2 Ob.
Gott, der Herr, ist Sonn' und Schild	79	+2 Cor., Timp., 2 Fl., 2 Ob.
Gott fähret auf mit Jauchzen	43	+3 Tr., Timp., 2 Ob.
Gott ist mein König	71	+3 Tr., Timp., 2 Fl., 2 Ob., Fag.
Gott ist unsre Zuversicht	197	+3 Tr., Timp., 2 Ob., 2 Ob. d'am., Fag.
Gott, man lobet dich in der Stille	120	+3 Tr., Timp., 2 Ob. d'am.
Gott soll allein	169	+3 Ob., Org.
Gott, wie dein Name	171	+3 Tr., Timp., 2 Ob.
Gottes Zeit ist die allerbeste Zeit	106	2 Fl., 2 Va. da gamba, Cont.
Gottlob! nun geht das Jahr zu Ende	28	+Cornett, 3 Trombones, 3 Ob.
Halt' im Gedächtniss Jesum Christ	67	+Cor. da tirarsi, Fl., 2 Ob. d'am.
Herr Christ, der ein'ge Gottes-Sohn	96	+Cor., Trombone, Vn. piccolo, Fl., Fl. piccolo, 2 Ob.
Herr, deine Augen sehen	102	+Fl. (or Vn. piccolo), 2 Ob.
Herr, gehe nicht in's Gericht	105	+Cor., 2 Ob.
Herr Gott, Beherrscher (incomplete)	—	+3 Tr., Timp., 2 Ob., 2 Ob. d'am., Org.
Herr Gott, dich loben alle wir	130	+3 Tr., Timp., Fl., 3 Ob.
Herr Gott, dich loben wir	16	+Cor. da cacc., 2 Ob., Ob. da cacc. or Violetta
Herr Jesu Christ, du höchstes Gut	113	+Fl., 2 Ob., 2 Ob. d'am.
Herr Jesu Christ, wahr'r Mensch und Gott	127	+2 Fl., 2 Ob.
Herr, wenn die stolzen Feinde (Part VI. Christmas Oratorio)	—	+3 Tr., Timp., 2 Ob., 2 Ob. d'am.
Herr, wie du willst	73	+Cor. (or Org. obblig.), 2 Ob.
Herrscher des Himmels (Part III. Christmas Oratorio)	—	+3 Tr., Timp., 2 Fl., 2 Ob., 2 Ob. d'am.
Herz und Mund und That	147	+Tr., 2 Ob., Ob. d'am., 2 Ob. da cacc., Fag.
Himmelskönig, sei willkommen	182	+Fl.
Höchsterwünschtes Freudenfest	194	+3 Ob., Fagotti
Ich armer Mensch	55	+Fl., Ob., Ob. d'am.
Ich bin ein guter Hirt	85	+2 Ob., Vcello piccolo
Ich bin in mir vergnügt	—	+Fl., 2 Ob.
Ich bin vergnügt mit meinem Glücke	84	+Ob.
Ich elender Mensch	48	+Tr., 2 Ob.
Ich freue mich in dir	133	+Cornett, 2 Ob. d'am.
Ich geh' und suche mit Verlangen	49	+Ob. d'am., Org., Vcello piccolo
Ich glaube, lieber Herre	109	+Cor. da caccia, 2 Ob., Cembalo
Ich habe genug	82	+Ob.
Ich hab' in Gottes Herz und Sinn	92	+2 Ob. d'am.
Ich habe meine Zuversicht	188	+Ob., Org., Vcello
Ich hatte viel Bekümmerniss	21	+3 Tr., 4 Trombones, Timp., Ob., Fag.
Ich lasse dich nicht	157	+Fl., Ob., Ob. d'am., Violetta
Ich liebe den Höchsten	174	+2 Cor. da caccia, 3 Ob., Fag.
Ich ruf' zu dir	177	+2 Ob., Ob. da caccia, Fag.
Ich steh' mit einem Fuss im Grabe	156	+Ob.
Ich weiss, dass mein Erlöser lebt	160	Vn., Fag., Cont.
Ich will den Kreuzstab gerne tragen	56	+3 Ob. (or Str.), Vcello
Ihr, die ihr euch	164	+2 Fl., 2 Ob.
Ihr Menschen, rühmet Gottes Liebe	167	+Tr., Ob., Ob. da cacc.
Ihr Pforten zu Zion (incomplete)	193	+2 Ob.
Ihr werdet weinen und heulen	103	+Tr., Fl. (or Vn.), Fl. piccolo, 2 Ob. d'am.
In allen meinen Thaten	97	+2 Ob., Fagotti
Jauchzet, frohlocket (Part I. Christmas Oratorio).	—	+3 Tr., Timp., 2 Fl., 2 Ob., 2 Ob. d'am., Fag.

TABLE XXI. THE CANTATAS IN ALPHABETICAL ORDER 241

	NO.	SCORE
Jauchzet Gott in allen Landen . .	51	+Tr.
Jesu, der du meine Seele . . .	78	+Cor., Fl., 2 Ob.
Jesu, nun sei gepreiset	41	+3 Tr., Timp., 3 Ob., Vcello piccolo
Jesus nahm zu sich die Zwölfe . . .	22	+Ob.
Jesus schläft, was soll ich hoffen . .	81	+2 Fl., 2 Ob. d'am.
Komm, du süsse Todesstunde . .	161	+2 Fl.
Kommt, eilet und laufet (Easter Oratorio) .	—	+3 Tr., Timp., 2 Fl., 2 Ob., Ob. d'am., Fag.
Lass, Fürstin, lass noch einen Strahl (Trauer-Ode)	198	+2 Fl., 2 Ob.,2 Ob. d'am.,2 Lutes, 2 Va. da gamba
Leichtgesinnte Flattergeister . . .	181	+Tr., Fl., Ob.
Liebster Gott, wann werd' ich sterben .	8	+Cor., Fl., 2 Ob. d'am., Cembalo
Liebster Immanuel, Herzog der Frommen.	123	+2 Fl., 2 Ob. d'am.
Liebster Jesu, mein Verlangen . .	32	+Ob.
Lobe den Herrn, den mächtigen König .	137	+3 Tr., Timp., 2 Ob.
Lobe den Herrn, meine Seele . . .	69	+3 Tr., Timp., 3 Ob., Ob. d'am., Fag.
Lobe den Herrn, meine Seele . . .	143	+3 Cor. da caccia, Timp., Fag.
Lobet Gott in seinen Reichen . . .	11	+3 Tr., Timp., 2 Fl., 2 Ob.
Mache dich, mein Geist, bereit . .	115	+Cor., Fl., Ob. d'am., Vcello piccolo
Man singet mit Freuden vom Sieg . .	149	+3 Tr., Timp., 3 Ob., Fag.
Mein Gott, wie lang', ach lange . .	155	+Fag.
Mein Herze schwimmt im Blut . .	—	+Ob., Fag.
Mein liebster Jesus ist verloren . .	154	+2 Ob., 2 Ob. d'am, Cembalo
Meine Seel' erhebt den Herren . .	10	+Tr., 2 Ob.
Meine Seele rühmt und preist . . .	189	Fl., Ob., Vn., Cont.
Meine Seufzer, meine Thränen . .	13	+2 Fl., Ob. da cacc.
Meinen Jesum lass' ich nicht . . .	124	+Cor., Ob. d'am.
Mer hahn en neue Oberkeet . . .	—	+Cor., Fl.
Mit Fried' und Freud' ich fahr' dahin .	125	+Cor., Fl., Ob., Ob. d'am.
Mit Gnaden bekröne der Himmel die Zeiten	—	+2 Ob.
Nach dir, Herr, verlanget mich . .	150	+2 Vn., Fag., Cont.
Nimm von uns, Herr	101	+Cornett, 3 Trombones, Fl., 3 Ob., Ob. da cacc.
Nimm, was dein ist	144	+Ob. d'am.
Non sa che sia dolore	—	+Fl.
Nun danket Alle Gott (incomplete) . .	192	+2 Fl., 2 Ob.
Nun ist das Heil und die Kraft . .	50	+3 Tr., Timp., 3 Ob.
Nun komm, der Heiden Heiland . .	61	+Fag.
Nun komm, der Heiden Heiland . .	62	+Cor., 2 Ob.
Nur Jedem das Seine	163	+Ob. d'am., Vcello
O angenehme Melodei	—	+Fl., Ob. d'am., Cembalo
O ewiges Feuer, o Ursprung der Liebe .	34	+3 Tr., Timp., 2 Fl., 2 Ob.
O ewiges Feuer (incomplete) . . .	—	+3 Tr., Timp., 2 Fl., 2 Ob.
O Ewigkeit, du Donnerwort . . .	20	+Tr. da tirarsi, 3 Ob.
O Ewigkeit, du Donnerwort . . .	60	+Cor., 2 Ob. d'am.
O heil'ges Geist und Wasserbad . .	165	+Fag.
O holder Tag	—	+Fl., Ob. d'am., Cembalo
O Jesu Christ, mein's Lebens Licht .	118	2 Litui, Cornett, 3 Trombones (or +2 Litui, Ob., Fag.)
Preise dein' Glücke	—	+3 Tr., Timp., 2 Fl., 2 Ob., 2 Ob. d'am., Violetta
Preise, Jerusalem, den Herrn . .	119	+4 Tr., Timp., 2 Fl., 3 Ob., 2 Ob. da caccia

	NO.	SCORE
Schau', lieber Gott.	153	
Schauet doch und sehet	46	+Tr. (or Cor.) da tirarsi, 2 Fl., 2 Ob. da cacc.
Schlage doch, gewünschte Stunde . .	53	+Campanella
Schleicht, spielende Wellen . . .	—	+3 Tr., Timp., 2 Fl., 2 Ob., 2 Ob. d'am.
Schmücke dich, o liebe Seele . . .	180	+2Fl.,Ob.,Ob. da caccia,Vcello picc.
Schweigt stille, plaudert nicht . . .	—	+Fl., Cembalo
Schwingt freudig euch empor . . .	36	+2 Ob. d'am.
Schwingt freudig euch empor . . .	—	+Ob. d'am., Va. d'amore
Sehet, welch' eine Liebe . . .	64	+Cornett, 3 Trombones, Ob. d'am.
Sehet, wir geh'n hinauf	159	+Ob., Fagotti
Sei Lob und Ehr' dem höchsten Gut	117	+2 Fl., 2 Ob., 2 Ob. d'am.
Selig ist der Mann	57	+3 Ob.
Sie werden aus Saba Alle kommen .	65	+2 Cor. da caccia, 2 Fl., 2 Ob. da cacc.
Sie werden euch in den Bann thun .	44	+2 Ob., Fag.
Sie werden euch in den Bann thun .	183	+2 Ob. d'am., 2 Ob. da caccia, Vcello piccolo
Siehe, ich will viel Fischer aussenden .	88	+2 Cor., 2 Ob. d'am., Ob.
Siehe zu, dass deine Gottesfurcht .	179	+2 Ob., 2 Ob. da caccia
Singet dem Herrn	190	+3 Tr., Timp., 3 Ob., Ob. d'am.
So du mit deinem Munde . . .	145	+Tr., Fl., 2 Ob. d'am.
Süsser Trost, mein Jesus kommt .	151	+Fl., Ob. d'am.
Thue Rechnung! Donnerwort . .	168	+2 Ob. d'am.
Tönet, ihr Pauken!	—	+3 Tr., Timp., 2 Fl., 2 Ob.
Trauer-Ode. See 'Lass, Fürstin'.		
Tritt auf die Glaubensbahn . .	152	Fl., Ob., Va. d'am., Va. da gamba, Cont.
Und es waren Hirten (Part II. Christmas Oratorio)	—	+2 Fl., 2 Ob. d'am., 2 Ob. da caccia
Uns ist ein Kind geboren . .	142	+2 Fl., 2 Ob.
Unser Mund sei voll Lachens . .	110	+3 Tr., Timp., 2 Fl., 3 Ob., Ob. d'am., Ob. da caccia., Fag.
Vereinigte Zwietracht	—	+3 Tr., Timp., 2 Fl., 2 Ob. d'am., Ob.
Vergnügte Pleissen-Stadt . . .	—	[2 Fl., Ob., Vcello, Cembalo]
Vergnügte Ruh'	170	+Ob. d'am., Org.
Wachet auf, ruft uns die Stimme .	140	+Cor., 3 Ob., Vn. piccolo
Wachet, betet, seid bereit . .	70	+Tr., Ob., Fag., Vcello
Wär' Gott nicht mit uns diese Zeit .	14	+Cor. da cacc., 2 Ob.
Wahrlich, ich sage euch . . .	86	+2 Ob.
Warum betrübst du dich . .	138	+2 Ob. d'am.
Was frag' ich nach der Welt . .	94	+Fl., 2 Ob., Ob. d'am.
Was Gott thut, das ist wohlgethan .	98	+3 Ob.
Was Gott thut, das ist wohlgethan .	99	+Cor., Fl., Ob. d'am.
Was Gott thut, das ist wohlgethan .	100	+2 Cor., Timp., Fl., Ob. d'am.
Was mein Gott will	111	+2 Ob.
Was mir behagt	—	+2 Cor., 2 Cor. da caccia, 2 Fl., 3 Ob., Fagotti, Violone grosso
Was soll ich aus dir machen, Ephraim?	89	+2 Ob. da caccia, 2 Ob.
Was willst du dich betrüben . .	107	+Cor. da cacc., 2 Fl., 2 Ob. d'am.
Weichet nur, betrübte Schatten .	—	+Ob.
Weinen, Klagen, Sorgen, Zagen .	12	+Tr., Ob., Fag.
Wer da glaubet und getauft wird .	37	+2 Ob. d'am.
Wer Dank opfert, der preiset mich .	17	+2 Ob.
Wer mich liebet	59	+2 Tr., Timp.
Wer mich liebet	74	+3 Tr., Timp., 2 Ob., Ob. da cacc.
Wer nur den lieben Gott lässt walten	93	+2 Ob.
Wer sich selbst erhöhet . . .	47	+2 Ob., Org.
Wer weiss, wie nahe mir mein Ende	27	+Cor., 2 Ob., Ob. da cacc., Org.

TABLE XXI. THE CANTATAS IN ALPHABETICAL ORDER 243

	NO.	SCORE
Widerstehe doch der Sünde . . .	54	
Wie schön leuchtet der Morgenstern . .	1	+2 Cor., 2 Ob. da cacc.
Wir danken dir, Gott	29	+3 Tr., Timp., 2 Ob., Org.
Wir müssen durch viel Trübsal . .	146	+Fl., 3 Ob., 2 Ob. d'am., Org.
Wo gehest du hin?	166	+Ob.
Wo Gott der Herr	178	+Cor., 2 Ob., 2 Ob. d'am.
Wo soll ich fliehen hin	5	+Tr., Tr. da tirarsi, 2 Ob.
Wohl dem, der sich auf seinen Gott .	139	+2 Ob. d'am.

TABLE XXII

THE CANTATAS IN THE NUMERICAL ORDER OF THEIR PUBLICATION BY THE BACHGESELLSCHAFT

The dates indicate the year to which each volume belongs. Figures in brackets date the Preface when publication was delayed. Page references to the text of the present volume follow the titles

I. CHURCH CANTATAS

JAHRGANG I

1851. ED. MORITZ HAUPTMANN

NO.
1. Wie schön leuchtet der Morgenstern . 47, 105, 150.
2. Ach Gott, vom Himmel sieh' darein . 40, 95, 98, 122, 150.
3. Ach Gott, wie manches Herzeleid . 35, 39, 40, 111, 150, 162, 170.
4. Christ lag in Todesbanden . . 39, 40, 101, 123, 150, 162.
5. Wo soll ich fliehen hin . . . 27, 29, 30, 31, 32, 36, 124, 150, 153, 154.
6. Bleib' bei uns, denn es will Abend 99, 107, 139, 140, 150, 153, 162.
   werden
7. Christ unser Herr zum Jordan kam . 111, 150, 153, 162.
8. Liebster Gott, wann werd' ich sterben 8, 36, 81, 84, 85, 150, 164, 168.
9. Es ist das Heil uns kommen her . 81, 91, 111, 150.
10. Meine Seel' erhebt den Herren . 33, 35, 97, 150, 162.

JAHRGANG II

1852. ED. MORITZ HAUPTMANN

NO.
11. Lobet Gott in seinen Reichen . 81, 87, 88, 90, 92, 150, 162, 168.
12. Weinen, Klagen, Sorgen, Zagen . 33, 97, 113, 116, 123, 150, 162.
13. Meine Seufzer, meine Thränen . 63, 67, 105, 122, 150, 153, 168.
14. Wär' Gott nicht mit uns diese Zeit . 35, 42, 44, 150.
15. Denn du wirst meine Seele nicht in der 2, 23, 52, 60, 150.
    Hölle lassen
16. Herr Gott, dich loben wir . 35, 36, 44, 46, 98, 105, 127, 128, 150.
17. Wer Dank opfert, der preiset mich . 95, 97, 150, 162.
18. Gleich wie der Regen und Schnee vom 5, 64, 67, 113, 116, 122, 124, 150.
    Himmel fällt
19. Es erhub sich ein Streit . . 80, 99, 150.
20. O Ewigkeit, du Donnerwort . 26, 30, 33, 36, 102, 150.

JAHRGANG V (1)

1855. ED. WILHELM RUST

NO.
21. Ich hatte viel Bekümmerniss . 5, 40, 41, 51, 97, 98, 113, 116, 153, 168.
22. Jesus nahm zu sich die Zwölfe . 102.
23. Du wahrer Gott und Davids Sohn . 40, 165, 166, 168.
24. Ein ungefärbt Gemüthe . . 23, 33, 34, 35, 95, 96, 109, 122, 153.
25. Es ist nichts Gesundes an meinem 40, 41, 64, 68, 95, 154, 162.
    Leibe
26. Ach wie flüchtig, ach wie nichtig . 35, 75, 80, 84, 86, 102, 122, 168.
27. Wer weiss, wie nahe mir mein Ende . 164, 171, 173.
28. Gottlob! nun geht das Jahr zu Ende . 40, 95, 153, 154, 162.
29. Wir danken dir, Gott, wir danken dir 88, 95, 98, 122, 168, 171, 173.
30. Freue dich, erlöste Schaar . . 84, 85, 95, 108, 122, 153, 168.

TABLE XXII. THE CANTATAS IN NUMERICAL ORDER 245

JAHRGANG VII
1857. Ed. Wilhelm Rust

NO.
31. Der Himmel lacht, die Erde jubiliret   5, 26, 27, 95, 97, 99, 113, 114, 116, 123, 153, 155.
32. Liebster Jesu, mein Verlangen .   .   122, 162.
33. Allein zu dir, Herr Jesu Christ   162, 168.
34. O ewiges Feuer, o Ursprung der Liebe   84, 85, 95, 162.
35. Geist und Seele wird verwirret.   .   95, 97, 99, 162, 171, 173.
36. Schwingt freudig euch empor   .   .   122, 131, 153, 168.
37. Wer da glaubet und getauft wird   .   —
38. Aus tiefer Noth schrei' ich zu dir   .   40, 162.
39. Brich dem Hungrigen dein Brod   .   63, 68, 82, 122.
40. Dazu ist erschienen der Sohn Gottes   44, 47, 153, 162.

JAHRGANG X
1860. Ed. Wilhelm Rust

NO.
41. Jesu, nun sei gepreiset   .   .   .   80, 102, 138, 139, 140, 168.
42. Am Abend aber desselbigen Sabbaths   113, 114, 115, 117, 124, 135, 153, 162, 168.
43. Gott fähret auf mit Jauchzen   .   80, 95, 97, 98, 153.
44. Sie werden euch in den Bann thun .   95, 98, 162.
45. Es ist dir gesagt, Mensch, was gut ist   76, 80, 81, 82, 95, 97, 162.
46. Schauet doch und sehet, ob irgend ein   8, 27, 30, 33, 34, 36, 68, 70, 107, 162, Schmerz sei   168.
47. Wer sich selbst erhöhet, der soll ernie-   97, 153, 171. driget werden
48. Ich elender Mensch, wer wird mich   23, 33, 35, 97, 153, 154, 162. erlösen?
49. Ich geh' und suche mit Verlangen   .   108, 111, 112, 139, 140, 162, 171, 174, 175.
50. Nun ist das Heil und die Kraft   .   80, 95, 168.

JAHRGANG XII (2)
1862 [1863]. Ed. Wilhelm Rust

NO.
51. Jauchzet Gott in allen Landen .   .   29, 101, 122, 153.
52. Falsche Welt, dir trau' ich nicht   .   102, 116, 154, 162, 168.
53. Schlage doch, gewünschte Stunde   .   101
54. Widerstehe doch der Sünde   .   .   101, 123.
55. Ich armer Mensch, ich Sündenknecht   75, 82, 83, 88, 90, 108, 153, 154, 162.
56. Ich will den Kreuzstab gerne tragen .   99, 124, 135, 154, 162.
57. Selig ist der Mann .   .   .   .   95, 122, 153, 168.
58. Ach Gott, wie manches Herzeleid   .   122, 153.
59. Wer mich liebet, der wird mein Wort   5, 51, 60. halten
60. O Ewigkeit, du Donnerwort   .   .   110, 122.

JAHRGANG XVI
1866 [1868]. Ed. Wilhelm Rust

NO.
61. Nun komm, der Heiden Heiland   .   5, 113, 122, 123, 168.
62. Nun komm, der Heiden Heiland   .   35, 122, 153, 168.
63. Christen, ätzet diesen Tag   .   23, 26, 56, 80, 113, 153, 154, 168.
64. Sehet, welch' eine Liebe hat uns der   40, 153, 154, 162, 168. Vater erzeiget
65. Sie werden aus Saba Alle kommen   .   8, 44, 46, 67, 104, 106, 107.
66. Erfreut euch, ihr Herzen .   .   27, 115, 117, 122.
67. Halt' im Gedächtniss Jesum Christ .   8, 30, 34, 36, 80, 81, 153, 162, 168.
68. Also hat Gott die Welt geliebt .   .   40, 95, 102, 138, 139, 140.
69. Lobe den Herrn, meine Seele .   .   51, 80, 110, 114, 162.
70. Wachet, betet, seid bereit allezeit   .   5, 27, 28, 40, 95, 98, 113, 124, 153.

JAHRGANG XVIII
1868 [1870]. ED. WILHELM RUST
NO.

71. Gott ist mein König . . . 2, 54, 60, 66, 67, 96, 113, 114, 153, 168.
72. Alles nur nach Gottes Willen . . 34.
73. Herr, wie du willst, so schick's mit 171, 172.
mir
74. Wer mich liebet, der wird mein Wort 26, 80, 99, 106, 122.
halten
75. Die Elenden sollen essen . . . 29, 33, 108, 109, 113.
76. Die Himmel erzählen die Ehre Gottes 28, 29, 98, 108, 109, 111, 112, 122, 133,
134, 153.
77. Du sollst Gott, deinen Herren, lieben . 29, 30, 33, 36.
78. Jesu, der du meine Seele . . . 35, 75, 80, 81, 82, 84, 151, 168.
79. Gott, der Herr, ist Sonn' und Schild . 51, 52, 76, 80, 81, 82, 162.
80. Ein' feste Burg ist unser Gott . . 34, 54, 80, 102, 104, 105, 108, 110, 122,
168.

JAHRGANG XX (1)
1870 [1872]. ED. WILHELM RUST
NO.

81. Jesus schläft, was soll ich hoffen? . 8, 68, 111, 153, 162.
82. Ich habe genug . . . . 153, 168.
83. Erfreute Zeit im neuen Bunde . . 122.
84. Ich bin vergnügt mit meinem Glücke 122.
85. Ich bin ein guter Hirt . . . 122, 138, 139, 140, 154, 162.
86. Wahrlich, ich sage euch . . . 95, 97, 122.
87. Bisher habt ihr nichts gebeten in mei- 99, 106, 107.
nem Namen
88. Siehe, ich will viel Fischer aussenden 47, 111, 154, 162.
89. Was soll ich aus dir machen, Ephraim? 35.
90. Es reifet euch ein schrecklich Ende . 27, 29, 101.

JAHRGANG XXII
1872 [1875]. ED. WILHELM RUST
NO.

91. Gelobet seist du, Jesu Christ . . 51, 52, 80, 91, 102.
92. Ich hab' in Gottes Herz und Sinn . —
93. Wer nur den lieben Gott lässt walten 153, 162.
94. Was frag' ich nach der Welt . . 82, 83, 95, 98, 111, 153, 168.
95. Christus, der ist mein Leben . . 96, 102, 109, 168.
96. Herr Christ, der ein'ge Gottes Sohn . 35, 40, 63, 66, 82, 86, 126, 153, 162.
97. In allen meinen Thaten . . . 114, 122, 153, 165, 166, 168.
98. Was Gott thut, das ist wohlgethan . 153.
99. Was Gott thut, das ist wohlgethan . 82, 83, 91, 111.
100. Was Gott thut, das ist wohlgethan . 50, 51, 52, 82, 86, 108, 110, 153, 168,
169.

JAHRGANG XXIII
1873 [1876]. ED. WILHELM RUST
NO.

101. Nimm von uns, Herr, du treuer Gott 40, 75, 81, 91, 102, 122, 123.
102. Herr, deine Augen sehen nach dem 75, 79, 82, 83, 84, 86, 97, 126, 162.
Glauben
103. Ihr werdet weinen und heulen . . 33, 34, 63, 65, 66, 68, 82, 83, 108, 111,
122, 162.
104. Du Hirte Israel, höre . . . 95, 108, 111.
105. Herr, gehe nicht in's Gericht . . 97, 98, 168.
106. Gottes Zeit ist die allerbeste Zeit . 5, 65, 69, 122, 134.
107. Was willst du dich betrüben . . 35, 81, 82, 84, 168.
108. Es ist euch gut, dass ich hingehe . 122, 153.
109. Ich glaube, lieber Herre . . . 35, 153, 162, 164.
110. Unser Mund sei voll Lachens . . 29, 80, 81, 82, 95, 99, 102, 110, 168.

TABLE XXII. THE CANTATAS IN NUMERICAL ORDER 247

JAHRGANG XXIV
1874 [1876]. ED. ALFRED DÖRFFEL

NO.
111.	Was mein Gott will, das g'scheh' allzeit	152, 168.
112.	Der Herr ist mein getreuer Hirt .	47, 148, 152, 153.
113.	Herr Jesu Christ, du höchstes Gut .	82, 95.
114.	Ach, lieben Christen, seid getrost .	35, 75, 82, 86, 152, 162.
115.	Mache dich, mein Geist, bereit . .	35, 81, 84, 86, 87, 135, 138, 139, 140.
116.	Du Friedefürst, Herr Jesu Christ .	35, 152, 154, 162.
117.	Sei Lob und Ehr' dem höchsten Gut	80, 81, 84, 85, 122.
118.	O Jesu Christ, mein's Lebens Licht .	22, 37, 40, 41, 47, 122, 123, 168.
119.	Preise, Jerusalem, den Herrn . .	8, 23, 26, 56, 58, 60, 67, 82, 151.
120.	Gott, man lobet dich in der Stille .	55, 80, 108, 111, 122.

JAHRGANG XXVI
1876 [1878]. ED. ALFRED DÖRFFEL

NO.
121.	Christum wir sollen loben schon .	40, 111, 152.
122.	Das neugebor'ne Kindelein . .	64, 69, 99, 152.
123.	Liebster Immanuel, Herzog der Frommen	81, 82, 84, 86, 152.
124.	Meinen Jesum lass' ich nicht . .	35, 152, 154, 168.
125.	Mit Fried' und Freud' ich fahr' dahin	35, 81, 88, 90, 111, 152, 153, 168, 169.
126.	Erhalt' uns, Herr, bei deinem Wort .	28, 35, 152, 154.
127.	Herr Jesu Christ, wahr'r Mensch und Gott	28, 69, 152.
128.	Auf Christi Himmelfahrt allein .	28, 44, 46, 95, 97, 99, 102, 110, 152.
129.	Gelobet sei der Herr, mein Gott .	81, 84, 86, 95, 122, 152, 153, 168.
130.	Herr Gott, dich loben alle wir .	60, 61, 82, 83.

JAHRGANG XXVIII
1878 [1881]. ED. WILHELM RUST

NO.
131.	Aus der Tiefe rufe ich, Herr, zu dir .	96, 113, 114, 123.
132.	Bereitet die Wege, bereitet die Bahn .	5, 97, 122, 124, 155.
133.	Ich freue mich in dir . . .	38, 153.
134.	Ein Herz, das seinen Jesum lebend weiss	153, 154.
135.	Ach Herr, mich armen Sünder .	38, 40, 41, 153.
136.	Erforsche mich, Gott, und erfahre mein Herz	95, 97, 110, 153, 162.
137.	Lobe den Herren, den mächtigen König der Ehren	33, 51, 80, 122.
138.	Warum betrübst du dich, mein Herz?	109, 110.
139.	Wohl dem, der sich auf seinen Gott .	122, 168, 169.
140.	Wachet auf, ruft uns die Stimme .	97, 122, 126.

JAHRGANG XXX
1880 [1884]. ED. PAUL COUNT WALDERSEE

NO.
141.	Das ist je gewisslich wahr . .	—
142.	Uns ist ein Kind geboren . .	66, 82.
143.	Lobe den Herrn, meine Seele .	44, 46, 51, 52, 60, 80, 101, 115, 118.
144.	Nimm, was dein ist, und gehe hin .	—
145.	So du mit deinem Munde bekennest Jesum	8, 28, 88, 90, 108, 109.
146.	Wir müssen durch viel Trübsal in das Reich Gottes eingehen	75, 88, 175.
147.	Herz und Mund und That und Leben	5, 28, 29, 102, 104, 110, 113, 122, 162.
148.	Bringet dem Herrn Ehre seines Namens	28, 95, 102, 122.
149.	Man singet mit Freuden vom Sieg .	80, 95, 114, 115, 118.
150.	Nach dir, Herr, verlanget mich .	5, 113, 114, 116, 118, 122, 123, 155.

JAHRGANG XXXII
1882 [1886]. Ed. Ernst Naumann

NO.
151. Süsser Trost, mein Jesus kommt   .   88, 89, 111.
152. Tritt auf die Glaubensbahn   .   5, 63, 65, 69, 80, 82, 95, 97, 122, 130, 131, 134, 153, 155.
153. Schau', lieber Gott, wie meine Feind'   101.
154. Mein liebster Jesus ist verloren   .   111, 164, 168.
155. Mein Gott, wie lang', ach lange   .   5, 113, 114, 118, 155.
156. Ich steh' mit einem Fuss im Grabe   .   122, 162.
157. Ich lasse dich nicht, du segnest mich denn   8, 84, 86, 91, 95, 96, 108, 109, 122, 127, 128.
158. Der Friede sei mit dir   .   .   .   5, 122, 123.
159. Sehet, wir geh'n hinauf gen Jerusalem   97, 113.
160. Ich weiss, dass mein Erlöser lebt   .   5, 113, 122, 123.

JAHRGANG XXXIII
1883 [1887]. Ed. Franz Wüllner

NO.
161. Komm, du süsse Todesstunde   .   .   5, 66, 69, 168.
162. Ach, ich sehe, jetzt da ich zur Hochzeit gehe   5, 30, 34, 36, 113, 168.
163. Nur Jedem das Seine   .   .   .   5, 110, 124.
164. Ihr, die ihr euch von Christo nennet   .   8, 75, 76, 82, 91.
165. O heil'ges Geist und Wasserbad   .   101.
166. Wo gehest du hin?   .   .   .   .   122, 162.
167. Ihr Menschen, rühmet Gottes Liebe   .   23, 35.
168. Thue Rechnung! Donnerwort   .   .   111.
169. Gott soll allein mein Herze haben   .   95, 98, 99, 162, 171, 174.
170. Vergnügte Ruh', beliebte Seelenlust   .   111, 124, 168, 171, 173.

JAHRGANG XXXV
1885 [1888]. Ed. Alfred Dörffel

NO.
171. Gott, wie dein Name, so ist auch dein Ruhm   80, 95, 122, 123.
172. Erschallet, ihr Lieder   .   .   .   60, 80, 101, 122, 123, 124, 135, 153, 171, 172.
173. Erhöhtes Fleisch und Blut   .   .   80, 81, 84, 86, 91, 101.
174. Ich liebe den Höchsten von ganzem Gemüthe   44, 47, 96, 116, 122, 124, 154, 168.
175. Er rufet seinen Schafen mit Namen   .   64, 70, 71, 82, 101, 138, 139, 140.
176. Es ist ein trotzig und verzagt Ding   .   99, 104, 162.
177. Ich ruf' zu dir, Herr Jesu Christ   .   106, 114, 115, 119, 122, 168, 169.
178. Wo Gott der Herr nicht bei uns hält   122, 153.
179. Siehe zu, dass deine Gottesfurcht nicht Heuchelei sei   106.
180. Schmücke dich, o liebe Seele   .   .   70, 75, 81, 82, 106, 135, 138, 139, 140.

JAHRGANG XXXVII
1887 [1891]. Ed. Alfred Dörffel

NO.
181. Leichtgesinnte Flattergeister   .   8, 28, 82, 88, 91.
182. Himmelskönig, sei willkommen   .   5, 66, 70, 82, 122, 123, 153.
183. Sie werden euch in den Bann thun   .   106, 111, 138, 139, 140, 154, 162.
184. Erwünschtes Freudenlicht   .   .   80, 81, 91, 92, 101, 122, 154, 162.
185. Barmherziges Herze der ewigen Liebe   5, 33, 96, 97, 113, 153, 154, 155.
186. Aergre dich, o Seele, nicht   .   .   99, 104, 106, 113, 154.
187. Es wartet Alles auf dich   .   .   .   153, 168.
188. Ich habe meine Zuversicht   .   .   124, 135, 171, 174, 175.
189. Meine Seele rühmt und preist   .   .   5, 66, 75, 78, 81, 88, 91, 122, 123.
190. Singet dem Herrn ein neues Lied   .   80.

TABLE XXII. THE CANTATAS IN NUMERICAL ORDER 249

JAHRGANG XLI
1891 [1894]. ED. ALFRED DÖRFFEL

NO.
191. Gloria in excelsis . . . . 50, 80, 81, 92.
192. Nun danket Alle Gott . . . 76, 78, 81, 91, 97, 98, 153.
193. Ihr Pforten zu Zion . . . 96, 98.
Ehre sei Gott in der Höhe . . 84, 86, 119, 122, 123.
O ewiges Feuer, o Ursprung der —
Liebe
Herr Gott, Beherrscher aller Dinge . 80, 153, 175.

JAHRGANG XXIX
1879 [1881]. ED. PAUL COUNT WALDERSEE

NO.
194. Höchsterwünschtes Freudenfest . 97, 153, 154, 165, 166, 167.
Mit Gnaden bekröne der Himmel die 6.
Zeiten —
O angenehme Melodei

JAHRGANG XIII (1)
1863 [1864]. ED. WILHELM RUST

NO.
195. Dem Gerechten muss das Licht . 8, 51, 52, 80, 81, 92, 108, 111, 153, 162.
196. Der Herr denket an uns . . . 66, 168.
197. Gott ist unsre Zuversicht . . 26, 80, 115, 119, 122.
Three Wedding Chorals . . . . 21.

JAHRGANG V (2)
1855 [1856] ED. WILHELM RUST

Weihnachts-Oratorium (Christmas Oratorio):
Part I. . . . . . . 29, 54, 55, 91, 96, 98, 108, 111, 153, 154, 168.
II. . . . . . . 79, 80, 82, 88, 91, 104, 105, 111, 112, 133, 154.
III. . . . . . . 92, 111, 153, 154, 168.
IV. . . . . . . 102, 111, 153, 154, 162, 168.
V. . . . . . . 111, 153, 154, 168.
VI. . . . . . . 26, 80, 96, 102, 111, 153, 154, 168.

JAHRGANG XXI (3)
1871 [1874]. ED. WILHELM RUST

Kommt, eilet und laufet (Easter Oratorio) . 60, 70, 79, 83, 84, 115, 116, 122.

JAHRGANG XIII (3)
1863 [1865]. ED. WILHELM RUST

NO.
198. Trauer-Ode . . . . . 22, 81, 88, 89, 92, 93, 134, 142, 143, 154, 161, 164.

II. SECULAR CANTATAS
JAHRGANG XI (2)
1861 [1862]. ED. WILHELM RUST

Der Streit zwischen Phoebus und Pan . 61, 82, 88, 89, 108.
Weichet nur, betrübte Schatten . . 6, 21, 122.
Amore traditore . . . . 122, 175.
Ich bin in mir vergnügt . . . 75, 82, 88, 89, 98, 122.
Der zufriedengestellte Aeolus . . . 8, 26, 46, 61, 92, 93, 96, 97, 98, 122, 123, 128, 131, 133, 134, 135.

JAHRGANG XX (2)
1870 [1873]. Ed. Wilhelm Rust

Schleicht, spielende Wellen . . .	61, 81, 82, 110, 122, 175.
Auf, schmetternde Töne	—
Vereinigte Zwietracht der wechselnden Saiten	54, 78, 84, 88, 111, 112, 122.

JAHRGANG XXIX
1879 [1881]. Ed. Paul Count Waldersee

Was mir behagt	43, 46, 70, 71, 102, 113, 121, 122, 153, 167.
Non sa che sia dolore . . .	79, 84, 85.
O holder Tag	21, 82, 88, 90, 93, 108, 111, 175.
Schweigt stille, plaudert nicht . .	21, 82, 175.
Mer hahn en neue Oberkeet . .	46, 84, 85.

JAHRGANG XXXIV
1884 [1887]. Ed. Paul Count Waldersee

Die Wahl des Herkules . . .	44, 46, 96, 123.
Durchlaucht'ster Leopold . .	6, 75, 81, 84, 85, 91, 113, 116, 117, 124.
Schwingt freudig euch empor . .	128, 131.
Die Freude reget sich . .	82, 84, 85, 131.
Tönet, ihr Pauken! . . .	54, 55, 82, 84, 92, 96, 154.
Preise dein' Glücke, gesegnetes Sachsen .	61, 82, 84, 87, 92, 96, 97, 111, 127, 128, 168.
Angenehmes Wiederau . . .	77, 88.
Auf, schmetternde Töne der muntern Trompeten	—

CANTATAS PUBLISHED SUBSEQUENT TO 1900

Mein Herze schwimmt im Blut (Neue Bach-gesellschaft)	5, 97, 113.
Vergnügte Pleissen-Stadt (Schlesinger) .	21.
Was sind das für grosse Schlösser (Neue Bachgesellschaft)	—

REPRINTED LITHOGRAPHICALLY BY
JARROLD AND SONS LIMITED
NORWICH